Presented By
**Roger A. van Oosten**
Library Director
Crown College 1986–94
Moody Bible Inst. 1994–

TREASURES OF

2

THE CARIBBEAN

# Passages

# *of Gold*

# JIM & TERRI KRAUS

Tyndale House Publishers, Inc. WHEATON, ILLINOIS

Visit Tyndale's exciting Web site at www.tyndale.com

Scripture quotations are taken from the *Holy Bible,* King James Version.

**Library of Congress Cataloging-in-Publication Data**

Kraus, Jim.
  Passages of gold  /  Jim and Terri Kraus.
    p.   cm.— (Treasures of the Caribbean  ;  2)
  ISBN 0-8423-0382-0 (sc)
  1.  Pirates—Caribbean Area—History—17th century—Fiction   I. Kraus, Terri, date.
II. Title.   III. Series: Kraus, Jim. Treasures of the Caribbean  ;  2.
PS3561.R2876P37   1997
813'.54—dc21                                                                    96-46848

Printed in the United States of America

04   03   02   01   00   99   98   97
 8    7    6    5    4    3    2    1

# PROLOGUE

*December 1641
Unnamed Island,
Caribbean Sea*

The island was no more than a speck in the vast Caribbean Sea; an able man with stout legs could walk the circumference within an hour. The shore was a thin band of white and pink sand, the interior of the island filled with tall palms, shorter palmettos, and the nests of hundreds of oceangoing birds. On the beach lazed dozens of great sea turtles, the sun glinting off their deep green shells.

The shore at the south edge of the island reflected evidence of man's encroachment onto this pristine expanse. The fine smooth sand was littered with the debris of a recent battle at sea. Flotsam had washed ashore in abundance. Wood planking, ropes, tackle, an entire seaworthy longboat with oars strapped inside, a cask of ale, and a stuffed leather ship's trunk, still locked shut, followed the gentle currents to this uncharted islet and bobbed slowly in the languid waters. The wreckage and remnants slid softly into the sand, borne by gentle waves, and then grounded there as the tide receded.

The warm waters, with a soft hiss, flowed over and around a prone human form, sluicing about him with a salty caress. The prostrate man, breathing heavily and gasping, lay facedown in the sand, clutching a large fragment of a splintered ship's rail. His clothes were in tatters, he was barefoot, his hair was plastered to his face, and his neck was burnt red by the sun.

He coughed several times, then weakly scrabbled to his knees and turned to face the sea. His legs wobbled, nearly lacking the strength to hold him vertical. Muttering a vile curse, he breathed in deeply, and with a force of granite will, pulled himself upright and straight. After a few moments' rest, he set about to retrieve the flotsam from the shore, pulling the heavy longboat inland and placing in it what supplies he could salvage.

Lastly he pulled the great ship's trunk from the surf. Taking a heavy piece of tackle, he smashed at the brass lock, and after a half-dozen blows the metal cracked open.

He flipped open the lid, pushed his hands into the trunk's interior, and pulled out a handful of dresses, slightly soggy, yet done in stylish fabrics, colors, and trims.

Radcliffe Spenser bowed his head, shaking it, an angry, sardonic smile twisting on his cracked and burnt lips.

He lifted his head, held a single, scarlet dress toward the sea and, in a thick, wormy voice, swore a vile oath at the heavens.

"Rest easy tonight, Kathryne, you lecherous creation. But rest easy for only a short time. For I, Radcliffe Spenser, will see justice done and you and your horrid father buried. On this island I vow my revenge!"

And with that he threw the dress into the ocean as a seal of that vow. The waves accepted it and began to pull it into the deep.

*Passages of Gold*

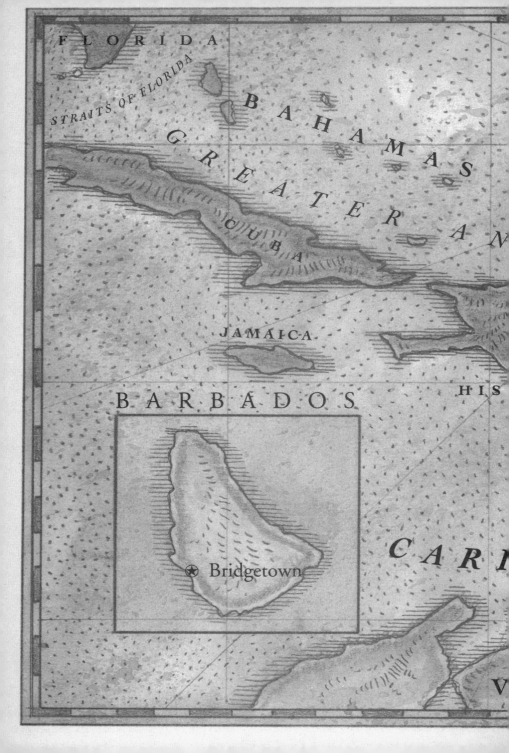

# CHAPTER

I

*December 1641*
*Barbados*

William Hawkes shook his head vigorously, trying to clear the wild thoughts and images racing through his mind. Tears in his eyes, he knelt in the dusty street by a ragged piece of canvas, his right arm bandaged and nestled in a white linen sling tied at his neck. He knelt in front of a thin, wiry-haired black man, with his odd assortment of merchandise spread out by the street. Will felt the locket he now held in his hand, warmed by the early sun and passing its warmth to William. It seemed to have found his heart quickly, and a small cold corner of it opened up in response to this new and welcome heat.

Against all odds, here was that one small locket that had been his mother's, given to him at her graveside in Hadenthorne, England, and stolen by Spanish pirates when they attacked his ship and kidnapped his childhood guardian and mentor, Vicar Thomas Mayhew.

When the pirate attack occurred, William and his ship had been at sea one hundred leagues from the Antilles, voyaging with supplies for the English settlers on Barbados. The Spanish cutthroats had taken all that was valuable from the ship, including William's locket. At the last moment, they had also seized the vicar and had called upon Will to secure a ransom from the Church of England for the captured clergyman. Will was unable to raise any ransom from church officials, but he had set aside money from his own purse. His ship had sailed to the appointed rendezvous place twice, a deserted narrow island passage, and had waited, but no Spanish pirate ship had come to call at the arranged spot. With a heavy heart Will had left those lonely coordinates, fearing that his faithful friend, Vicar Mayhew, was dead.

That disappointment, the culmination perhaps of a lifetime of disappointments, stirred within him the angry catalysts, creating a volatile, explosive mix in William's soul. He turned from the God of his mother and father, and the morals they taught, and became a privateer, legally taking ships and cargo from enemy navies and other countries' merchant fleets. Then Will soon descended into outright piracy and kidnapping as well.

Now as he stared at the delicate miniature of his mother inside the locket, painted on the gold, his tears could not be contained. They splashed against the nicked surface of Will's priceless treasure and washed the dust from it. William read again the inscribed Bible verse that had served his mother so well during her all-too-brief life: *Be still and know that I am God. Psalm 46:10.*

William turned the locket over and gazed at the new inscription: *PSALM 61, T. MAYHEW.*

He may still be . . . he is still alive! William rejoiced. *For if he had this locket, he must be safe. But where?*

Will looked around for a moment, trying to get his bearings again in a world so suddenly turned upside down. He and the old black man sat near the center of Bridgetown, the lively axis for all of the island's activity. To the north of the harbor sat the seaside home of Governor Spenser, where the beautiful and gentle Lady Kathryne, who had stolen his heart by showing him God's love, slept. Across the shallow river at the east side of the harbor grew the skeletal frame of St. Michael's Church. A rickety bridge wobbled its way across the waters. The town was a confusing mix of ramshackle huts, storefronts, warehouses, public houses, brothels, and piers canting into the deep harbor water. Some structures were built of solid English oak or imported hardwoods, some built of native timber and palm. In a single step, one could move from a dwelling as solid as the island to one as solid as the wind. The protected harbor was wide and spacious, able to hold a small armada if need be. A dozen merchant ships bobbed in its crystal-clear waters, and the *Serendipity* lay peacefully at anchor. The harbor curved around a narrow thumb of land that angled westward, south of the town, into the sea. At the far point of that land was the foundation of the fort, overlooking all of the anchorage. To the south of the town were rolling hills, most covered now in tobacco and sugarcane.

Finally William refocused his attention on the man in front of him. "Where was this locket found?" he asked as he held the small gold circle up to the peddler's face on his open palm. "Was it given to you? Did you find it on a beach? Did you buy it? Have you seen Vicar Mayhew? Do you know where he might be found?"

"Many questions dis mornin'. What question be answered fust?"

William inhaled deeply and lowered his hand, closing his fingers tightly about the locket.

*There is no need for haste,* Will told himself. *A few more minutes shall not make a difference after all this time.*

"Yes," Will said with firmness. "Let us start with important matters first." He looked directly into the black man's face, deeply lined and furrowed from the years and the hard labor beneath a harsh sun, and recognized a sense of placidity, of peace about him. "What shall I call you?"

The black man smiled broadly. "Most calls me Calvin."

"Are you a slave, Calvin?"

"Been a slave. Slave on dis boat from a place by de name 'o France. Dey de ones who call me Calvin."

"Did you escape?"

"De boat sank, and I be brung to dis island. De owners gone, so Calvin a free man."

William's knees were beginning to cramp, and he stood up, his bones and muscles popping in reaction. Will leaned back, his spine loudly popping as well.

"Calvin, if you are indeed a free man, can we talk further at a place that provides a bit more comfort?"

Calvin ran his hand over his stubbly white hair while looking up at William. "You be buyin' Calvin a meal?"

William smiled, his heart strangely calm. "If that be reason enough to close up your shop, then I'll be buying you a meal."

With that, Calvin nodded and grabbed at the four edges of his canvas, pulling them to the center, and with a rattle and clank lifted the contents and tied the bundle tight.

"Well den, suh," Calvin said with a smile, "I suspects it be time to eat."

■ ■ ■ ■

Kathryne had slept fitfully, though her body cried out for rest. William Hawkes had escorted her to the front gate of her new island home, and she had left him there, with his promise of returning. He had left her with a smile upon her lips. But by the time she had walked up the long staircase to the first floor of the house, her eyes had nearly dropped shut from exhaustion. She had been escorted to her bedchamber by the cook, Mrs. Potter, with the light of a single candle casting flickering shadows throughout the manse that was to be Kathryne's new home.

Kathryne had tossed on her borrowed sleeping gown and collapsed, like a child's doll, limp onto the bed, her room lit by the glow of the tropical moon.

The air was warm—much warmer than she had anticipated—and more humid than the royal greenhouses in London following a dense summer thunderstorm. Strange calls emanated from the jungle encircling the governor's mansion called Shelworthy. Several times a loud hoot, or a screech, sounding like a shriek of terror, called her back to consciousness after but a short period of sleep. Her bed was soft and the linens crisply pressed and white—foreign after her many weeks on the pirates' secret island where she had been held for ransom. She felt a stranger in civilized surroundings. Kathryne had begun to be comforted by her simple canvas and palm leaf bed in her tiny hut by the beach and the firm, solid feeling it offered.

She closed her eyes and tried to stop her thoughts from swimming before her. As the cloak of sleep covered her and began to knit up her raveled emotions, a face floated before her eyes. . . .

. . . the smiling face of William Hawkes, his lips open and calling to her. . . . As she reached out to him, another face, of a taller man with chestnut-colored hair, a sharp yet pleasing nose, and blue eyes slipped up behind the image of William and, like an eclipse, began to grow larger as William receded into the darkness. Off in the distance, the high, shrill call of a church bell, insistent and piercing . . .

Kathryne turned abruptly in her sleep, the linens wrapping themselves about her legs and pinning her arms to the thick, deeply cushioned featherbed. Her mouth, framed by her full lips, formed the words No . . . no as she called out in the silence of her dream.

■  ▪  ▪  ▪

Governor Aidan Spenser had yet to retire, having spent the entire evening celebrating with other island planters his safe escape from his brother Radcliffe's evil plot. Radcliffe had come within a whisker of putting both Lord Aidan and his only daughter, Kathryne, to the sword until the strange privateer-turned-pirate-turned-savior William Hawkes risked his own life to save the governor and Kathryne.

An insistent voice echoed in Lord Aidan's mind, a shrill voice warning him of more than Kathryne's passing interest in this crude, heathen pirate. He saw, with his own eyes, the tenderness on his daughter's face as she cared for Hawkes' wounds on their brief voyage back to Barbados. It was not unlike Kathryne to be kind to a commoner, but this familiarity beyond simple kindness with a pirate was troubling indeed. The image of her cradling Hawkes' bloodied head in her lap swam before him, and Aidan pushed it from his thoughts.

*I am sure it was a figment of my imagination,* he thought through the haze. *And even if it were more than mere kindness, I would need to nip that in the bud before it sets more island tongues to wagging. But tomorrow is soon enough to deal with such matters.*

There were still a dozen planters, merchants, and shipowners remaining in the drawing room of the Carruthers plantation, toasting their marvelous good fortune at Lord Aidan's safe return to the island. The room was large, hot, and filled with the dizzying smoke of a dozen pipes and thick cigars. The environs were also cluttered by scores of tankards filled with brandy and rum.

The clatter from the assembled noblemen, all near to being lost in their cups, swelled the room as the night grew darker. Candles and lanterns flickered, and laughs and boasts echoed about the mahogany-paneled room.

"Spenser—he's been the best governor we could have hoped for."

"Would have been ruination for all of us if Radcliffe's evil plan had worked. He would have bled the island dry."

"First time we have an honorable governor, and the fates sought to remove him. That blackguard Radcliffe—thank heavens his scheme did not come to fruition."

"'Tis a bloody shame that it be your brother and all, Lord Aidan, but the man had a flaw in his soul. One could tell that by a single look."

"The world seems gone mad indeed, what with the turmoil back in London and all. Imagine trying to dethrone a monarch! Why, that is simply unthinkable."

Several casks of brandy and several more of island rum had been consumed by this small, elite group. As they drank through the evening, plans were being laid for a more formal celebration, with speeches, banquets, and dancing. Everyone on the island wanted to hear the full details of how Radcliffe was outsmarted and defeated by this most unusual man, William Hawkes. Such a story would be the stuff of legend, Governor Aidan realized. He knew no man could stem the tide of the population's desire to participate in such a dramatic and defining moment in the island's young history.

As the new day dawned, Lord Aidan slipped out of the stuffy room and into the relative coolness of Carruthers' parlor and slumped onto a thickly padded bench. He said a silent prayer for the safety of his daughter, now sleeping in her bedchamber in the governor's new home. Reluctantly, he thanked the Almighty for the intervention of William

Hawkes, without whose actions and sacrifice, both he and Kathryne would most surely have met their death. His prayer stopped, and he bowed his head. He thought of his young brother Radcliffe, who had turned base and depraved. He, as his older and supposedly wiser brother, had scarce recognized his sibling's ghastly descent. Aidan recalled the last few chaotic minutes on the deck of the ship, watching William and Radcliffe slash at each other with long swords. And in his mind, as he saw Radcliffe being swept from the deck by the ship's rigging into the sea, salty tears formed at the edge of his eyes.

*Radcliffe, I pray that the Almighty will have mercy on the blackness of your heart,* Lord Aidan prayed, *and that the Lord will send a balm for the rent that has been torn in my heart by what you have brought upon the noble name of Spenser.*

His prayer finished, the governor felt the room and the darkness close in about him.

*It will not harm anyone if I lie back for just a moment, for my eyes have grown so weary,* he thought.

Within moments, his breath slowed to a soft rhythmic count, undisturbed by the laughter, hoots, and calls from a room away.

■ □ ■ □ ■

Vicar Giles Petley woke in a sweat, his bedclothes and linens trapping him in a white sea. He bolted upright from the bed, his eyes open wide in terror. He reached up and felt the side of his head and winced mightily, almost crying out in pain.

*This is where that brigand struck me as I was hauled from the longboat with Kathryne,* he thought, the images coming in a furious spiral. *I remember waking up on ship amidst noise and smoke and trying to escape, then being struck again.*

He touched the left side of his head, finding a second, even more sensitive bruise. *I vaguely remember a day or two of sailing . . . then landing here. But where is here?*

He stood up and made his way, taking very small steps, to the window. He looked out on a small harbor to the right, and to the left, a building under construction, with a steeple nearly completed.

*This must be Barbados,* Giles realized. *But in whose home am I? Is this the parsonage?*

He stumbled back to bed and recalled, almost as a vague dream, a short little bald man in poorly tailored vestments jumping about him in an excited frenzy as Giles staggered from the ship.

The bedchamber door swung open, and there stood the little bald man, still wearing the same poorly tailored and shabby vestments.

"Vicar Petley, so good to see you finally awake and back with the living," he brayed, his tone causing Giles to wince and shrink beneath the sheets.

"I would believe that you have passed the danger point and are well on your way to recovery," the little man brayed again.

Giles looked at him through tiny squints. "Who are you?" he croaked, having the most difficulty finding his voice. "And where am I?"

The little man looked shocked, then tender, as he pulled up a rickety stool to the bedside.

"Why, I am Vicar Alfred Coates. I came to fetch you from the ship last night—the ship that was beset by pirates with cannon fire and sword. All so blessedly exciting, I must say. It appeared that your injuries were suffered at the hands of your captors, Captain Blake and the evil Radcliffe Spenser. But the noble pirate, William Hawkes, rescued you, the honorable Governor Spenser, and his most lovely and beautiful daughter, Kathryne. 'Twas my obligation to bring you back here and all."

"But," Giles whispered, trying to make sounds come from his parched throat, "where in blazes is *here!*"

The good Vicar Coates sat back surprised, his hand over his heart. "Why, this is your new home, the parsonage of St. Michael's Church, your new posting."

Vicar Coates stood to leave, stunned at Giles's anger and confusion. He thought that Vicar Petley must still be suffering from delirium, for no man of God used such words so freely. He vowed that he would be most circumspect for the moment and allow the wounded vicar full time to recover from the brutalities placed upon his person by the evil brigands and heathen pirates.

Vicar Coates was set to withdraw, then hesitated a moment. "And by the way, Vicar Petley, you have received a message," he added. "I took the liberty of reading it, thinking it must be important. It merely reads," he said, holding a small card at arm's length, "'I hope you are well.' It is signed 'K.' Does that make sense to you? Is this 'K' the Lady Kathryne Spenser?"

And as Vicar Coates prattled on, Giles fell back to the bed, his head throbbing, his throat dry, but reassured that Kathryne indeed was still as enamored with him as ever.

CHAPTER

2

From the window in his bedchamber, Geoffrey Foxton could see to the edge of the turquoise sea as it washed against the western coast of the island of Barbados. His land, two hundred acres given to his father by royal land grant, lay at the first gentle rise from the sea, only a short mile's walk inland. Not the most fertile land on the island, Geoffrey agreed, but due to its closeness to the coast, his home would be wonderfully located near to the government buildings, alehouses, and shops of Bridgetown.

*A single man needs to have quick access to pleasant diversions,* Geoffrey often told himself.

And his prime location provided ready access to the main port and other safe harbors for shipping the crop of sugarcane that grew on his earth, now greening and waving in the morning sun.

*When that ripens and the sugar is squeezed from the cane, I shall be a wealthy man,* he thought, nearly tempted to rub his palms together in gleeful greed, as he had once seen an actor do in a play entitled *The Merchant of Venice.*

He smiled again, then reached into the china washbasin and cupped handfuls of tepid water to his face and chest, the water splashing about the room. In moments the basin was empty, and Geoffrey and the floor were sopping wet. Grabbing a linen cloth, he quickly dried himself and tossed on his clothing for the day—tan breeches, the color of a new fawn, a crisp white linen shirt, and a scarlet sleeveless weskit, its edges finished with gold braided trim. He often left the weskit near unbuttoned—almost as often as he left his shirt also undone. Geoffrey fully realized such manner of dress would be regarded as most scandalous at home in England, but Barbados was indeed "beyond the line"—across the vast oceans and beyond the cultural inhibitions of England and the Continent. The new settlers on Barbados felt free to reinvent their island society as they pleased. Geoffrey knew that his dress, so often unfettered, proved most scandalous to even the most liberated ladies of Barbados society. Yet he so enjoyed their polite gasps as he walked into formal rooms, reveling in his own tweaks at the constraining customs of the past.

*It is only harmless fun,* he would tell himself, most often when catching a blushing matron staring at his muscled form from across a parlor or when watching a young maiden giggle and flush red when he strolled into a hushed and proper drawing room.

Foxton's home, called Ridge House, was a modest estate in comparison to the homes of many planters on the island. Geoffrey had it built of native woods. Stone would have been more appropriate in such a moist, tropical situation, but would have been twice as dear. Timber construction would stand only a decade or two, until the rot born of jungle humidity, salt-tainted air, and burrowing insects might return the wood to sawdust. But by then Geoffrey planned on having made his fortune and returning to London to live the life of a rich nobleman.

The house was patterned after the grand homes back in England, but done on a smaller scale. A large entrance dominated the center of the front facade, and a series of tall windows filled the ground-floor walls. The windows were repeated, smaller and shorter, on the second floor. Once inside, there was a large drawing room to one side, and a dining chamber to the other. At the top of the staircase were three bedchambers, the largest used by Geoffrey, the other two remaining sparsely furnished and with simple draperies. The walls were all of a dark ocher color. The men who painted the rooms claimed that the ocher tone better resisted the mold and fungus that other colors seemed to attract and feed. The kitchen and all the servants' quarters were behind and below the main house. Geoffrey seldom visited those rooms and would be hard pressed to offer even a rudimentary description of any of them.

*Why spend my resources on a large estate when it is I who most often eats in town or am invited to others' homes to socialize?* he calculated.

On this morning, Geoffrey looked at his image in the upstairs hall looking glass and approved of what he saw. A tall man, with long, deep-chestnut-colored hair, slim at the waist and broad at the shoulders, he stood before his reflection. He turned both left and right, looking mostly at his nose and eyes. He had imagined his nose too large and too angled for his face, but as he matured, his face gained flesh and some softness, and his chiseled nose seemed to soften as well. He was no longer described as hawklike.

*But after all,* he mused, *this nose has not yet prevented me from sampling the pleasures of the world. And I have been told it looks noble.*

Breakfast, a prodigious meal of eggs, bacon, fish, cold roast pork, fresh fruits, ale, biscuits, tarts, and brandy, was set before the single chair in the dining chamber at the front of the house, facing east. Shafts of brilliant sunshine filled the room, at first warming then quickly heating the air to an unpleasant degree. Geoffrey felt, as did most proper Englishmen, that the air outside should remain on the outside.

When at home, Geoffrey most often dined alone, for there was no general foreman on the premises that might be considered socially acceptable company at the table. Servants and help were never invited guests for dining, no matter how far beyond the line one happened to be.

Geoffrey ate slowly and deliberately, savoring each bite of food. He would never consume all that had been prepared, but he knew such a grand meal was required for a man of his social station and responsibility.

He cut through a thick slab of limp bacon, lifted a large fist-sized portion into his mouth, and began to chew noisily, a few drops of grease slipping down on his chin. As he chewed, he thought back to the evening prior, to his first meeting with Lady Kathryne Spenser.

The news of Governor Aidan's safe return, accompanied by his ransomed daughter Kathryne, had first touched shore at Bridgetown and then swept through the island like a brushfire pushed along by a stiff autumn breeze. Geoffrey had been readying for a dinner at the plantation home of Peter Carruthers, son of the earl of Cheswick, when he had heard the news, and he had dashed to his horse, galloping to town with great dispatch and eagerness.

Tied to a narrow pier was a small ship, the *Serendipity,* filled with citizens eager to hear the tale of how Radcliffe Spenser's evil plans had been thwarted only at the last moment by a remarkable pirate named William Hawkes, a brave and daring Englishman.

Geoffrey had boarded the vessel, greeted the governor warmly, and accepted the extended hand of Kathryne for a gentleman's kiss. He had leaned close to her face, trying to ignore the bedlam on the ship, and had whispered that he was so greatly relieved that she was safe and he was now content, finally having seen her lovely face after imagining it in his mind for so many months.

"You are so much lovelier than I could have imagined," he had told her. "My impoverished imagination was no match for your great beauty."

Kathryne had smiled in response, remaining silent.

"And where is this pirate that saved you, Lady Spenser? I would most like to offer my congratulations and thanks to him as well."

Kathryne, whose hand was still held by Mr. Foxton, had extracted it gracefully and then pointed to the prone figure of William Hawkes, lying on a pallet at the bow of the *Serendipity*.

Geoffrey had boldly walked to William and had knelt at his side, taking Will's hand in his larger fingers, shaking it firmly.

"Mr. Hawkes, I am Geoffrey Foxton. Am I to understand correctly that Lady Spenser and her father owe their lives to your bravery?"

William had been surprised and struggled to answer. "I . . . I simply did what . . . I did what any man in my position would have done. There was a wrong that needed to be righted."

"Nonsense, Mr. Hawkes. You are a hero, and the entire island owes you a huge debt of gratitude," Geoffrey had remarked in a loud voice so that all could listen to his promises. "And I owe you even more. For saving Lady Spenser's life, I will be eternally in your debt. If you require anything while you remain on Barbados, I want you to call on me for assistance. Do you understand, Mr. Hawkes? Anything at all."

"Why . . . yes, I suppose I do . . . but . . . but . . ."

"There will be no buts about my offer." He had stood, turned abruptly, and said, "We must celebrate this monumental occasion. I invite you all within the sound of my voice to Ridge House this very afternoon. Glasses must be raised in celebration."

William had struggled to gain purchase for his feet, but Luke had come from nowhere and pulled him back to his bed.

"Massa Will not leave bed. Not today. Stay!"

Geoffrey Foxton had looked over at the black man restraining Will. "A darkie talks to you that way, Mr. Hawkes?"

Will had glared at him. "Luke is a free man, Mr. Foxton. And he is the ship's doctor."

Geoffrey had arched his eyebrows and shrugged. "Well, then, again, if there be anything you need, Mr. Hawkes, do not feel awkward in asking for my assistance. I will do what I can for you. And now, I must take my leave—for I believe I have guests soon to arrive! 'Tis a pity you will miss such a celebration."

He then had cut through the crowd without looking back.

*Such an odd thing,* Geoffrey had thought as he took his leave of

Kathryne and her father and rode back to his estate to prepare for the evening's festivities. *First, that a pirate is allowed to remain free—regardless of his noble actions. A cutthroat like that should be in irons! Second, that a darkie is allowed free rein on a sailing ship. That sets a poor example for other slaves. And third, that heathen pirate believed he might actually be invited to my home. Did he not have any sense? Did he truly think that a common criminal such as he would actually be allowed inside a gentleman's house? Good heavens, what is the world coming to? Something will have to be done to prevent this island's slide into total incivility.*

By the time Geoffrey had neared the first rise on the island, and home, his thoughts had roamed to more pleasant areas. *No doubt Kathryne was tattered and distracted by her ordeal, but, ye gads! She does possess such a pleasing form and countenance. And those eyes— such deep and sultry green eyes.*

Geoffrey began to whistle a ditty he had heard a balladeer sing at the alehouse by the harbor a fortnight prior. The song recalled the charms of a former lover. The lyrics, near the knuckle, veered toward the bawdy as they described a woman's outstanding physical charms.

Smiling as he whistled, he thought to himself, *A more beautiful form and face I could not have chosen for myself. Governor Spenser was most ungenerous in his descriptions of his charming daughter. How thoughtful that the Almighty has provided me with such an alluring wife. And how tested I will be to wait to sample her charms, as I am sure she will be as well, for I did notice a certain openness in her eyes as she first viewed my form as well.*

CHAPTER

Her face was covered with a thin sheen of perspiration when she awoke near midmorning. Kathryne rose in bed with a start, staring about, eyes frantic, not sure where she was. Her head snapped from left to right.

The room was bare, save the large four-poster bed in which she lay. The walls were whitewashed, and the windows were covered with a plain linen sheet. The floors were a darkly polished wood, dark as jungle soil. The room was quite spacious, more so than her bedchamber back home at Broadwinds in Dorset, England. Perhaps it seemed large due to the near total lack of furnishings. Other than the bed and a series of pegs along one wall, the room was stark and sterile.

As these images swirled into Kathryne's eyes, her heart slowed its frantic beating, for she calmed herself and realized that she had awakened in her bedchamber at Shelworthy, apparently still unfinished.

On a peg near the door hung her delicate gown from the evening before—well suited for evening wear, but certainly not designed for daylight hours in the tropics, Kathryne realized.

*What am I to put on?* she puzzled, recalling that all of her belongings were in her trunks, lost in the sea battle between William Hawkes and Uncle Radcliffe.

*They were only material possessions,* she thought, and as she did a pain welled up in her heart. *How could my uncle have become so evil? Not to show a breath of concern that his brother and myself were to be executed like common criminals!*

Kathryne pondered, her mind a jumble over the most recent events. *How could a man be so deceitful? To think that if it were not for William's bravery both Papa and I would now be gone from this world!*

Kathryne shook her head softly, trying to clear the horrible images of blood and death swirling around her as she was in chains on that ship. She sat quiet for several long moments, her head bowed.

Speaking out loud to the empty room, she said, with as much cheer as she could muster, "Today is the new day the Lord has made. And I will make it a blessing to all I can."

She gathered the linen sheets around herself and shuffled to the window. Standing to one side, she lifted the fabric covering the panes and blinked at the strong sunshine pouring in.

From this window she could see the turquoise expanse of sea that crashed against the cliffs on Shelworthy's eastern border. In front of her the mansion's drive ran straight through the barren front meadow to the gatehouse. A whitewashed fence edged the rough road leading to the harbor and Bridgetown. Outlining the property of the house and its grounds, perhaps two dozen acres in all, were thick stands of palms and palmetto trees. It was apparent that this land had only recently been liberated from a dense and tangled jungle. Downed palm trunks were stacked about the edges of the clearing. A group of black men were digging a shallow trench along the drive, methodically planting an ornamental border of short shrubs, looking much like native English boxwood. Formal plantings were sparse about the perimeter of the residence.

At the end of the drive, Kathryne noticed a cloud of dust rumbling toward the estate from the south. In a moment the breeze picked up and drew away the dust, revealing a single horse and open carriage. The carriage slowed, then turned toward the house. Kathryne could see at the reins a white woman, thin and darkened from the sun, perhaps of her father's age. The driver was wearing a white dress, and perched atop her head was a huge, broad-brimmed straw hat, tied under her chin with a white scarf.

Kathryne's eyes followed the horse and carriage as it made its way to the house. The woman handled the carriage well, holding the reins with a practiced grip.

When she arrived at the front door, the woman driver handed the reins to the doorman and began gesturing with her hands, first pointing to three large leather trunks in the rear of the carriage, then to the house, then back again to the trunks. Kathryne leaned toward the window, trying to hear a bit of what she was saying.

"Lady Kat'ryne?"

Kathryne nearly leapt out the window, and she spun about, the sheet flying about her legs and slipping from her shoulder.

Just inside her doorway was a large black girl no more than twenty years old, her eyes wide and her mouth open in fear.

"Who are you?" Kathryne called out, too loudly for the size of the room, her voice a trembling echo.

As she cried out, the dark girl stepped backward and ran square into the edge of the door, causing her to spin about, frantic that someone had skulked up behind her. Both she and Kathryne shrieked at the same time.

The black girl turned back toward Kathryne, bowing slightly, one hand to her throat, the other held palm facing the ground, as if trying to calm an excited watchdog. "I be Hattie, Lady Kat'ryne, and Miz Potter send me up to see if you be awake."

Kathryne spoke, her voice at the edge of faltering. "Well, I am awake. What is it that you want?"

Despite the fact that Kathryne had spent a month with William and his crew at his hidden cove with a village full of black people—all former slaves—the reality of the presence of a black woman in a white man's house, or more specifically in a white woman's bedchamber, was so new as to be alarming.

Hattie stared at Kathryne, unabashed. "Lady Kat'ryne, I supposes to be your maid, I do believe. But I not be sure yet what you want a maid to do."

Hattie looked like a frightened puppy, not knowing what to do or where to go.

Kathryne took a deep breath and said a short prayer under her breath. *Dearest God, grant me the wisdom and the grace to deal with today. . . .*

She took a step from the window toward Hattie. Kathryne smiled as pleasantly and as naturally as she could.

"Hattie, perhaps our first order of business today is to find me some clothing. I have but one dress to wear, and I do not wish to go about the day dressed in an elegant evening gown."

"Dat be for certain, Lady Kat'ryne." Hattie kept staring. "And you be needin' a hat, my lady."

Kathryne tilted her head, a quizzical look on her face.

"You gots to stay out of de sun. You be de whitest lady I ever done laid eyes on."

Kathryne stood up straighter, at first thinking that she was being criticized or maligned. But then Hattie grinned, and as her wide smile spread, Kathryne smiled and began to giggle, one hand slipping to her mouth, the other clutching tighter at her bedsheet gown.

From behind Kathryne's new maid, a voice called lightly up from the floor below.

"Hattie? Hattie? Are you up there, Hattie?"

Hattie looked first at Kathryne, who was as confused as she. Kathryne merely shrugged her shoulders.

Hattie turned and leaned backward, almost out the door.

"Yes, Miz Potter? You be callin' me?" she whispered loudly.

"Do you know if Miss Kathryne is awake? It appears that she has a visitor."

Hattie took another step backward and craned her neck higher, trying to get a glimpse of who this visitor might be. She then turned back to Kathryne with a still-puzzled look.

"It be all right to say you be awake now, Lady Kat'ryne?"

Kathryne responded by arching her eyebrows and shrugging.

"Dat means it be fine to say you be awake?" Hattie asked again.

Kathryne sighed, resigned to her muddle. "Hattie, I am most awake. I am on a new island, in a new house, in a new room, with a new maid. I am wrapped in a bedsheet. I have one dress to wear, which is designed only for an evening ball. I do not know where my father is, nor where the kitchen is, nor where this house is, for that matter. I do not know when I will have clothes to wear. I do not know who could possibly be calling on me. I am not sure of what I am doing here. . . ."

Kathryne stopped her gentle scolding and almost dropped her hands to her sides in exasperation, but realized that had she done so, the sheet would have dropped as well, and she clutched it closer to her chest.

Hattie stood, polite and quiet, as Kathryne spoke. From the blank look on her face, it was most obvious that the girl comprehended very little of Kathryne's precise English. She turned her head slightly, off to the side.

"Den all dat mean you be awake, Lady Kat'ryne? It appears you gots visitors."

Kathryne closed her eyes and let her head slump forward with a loud sigh.

Hattie turned to the door, ready to call down to announce Kathryne's obvious state of awareness, when from behind her bustled in the small woman Kathryne had observed driving the carriage up the drive of the house a few moments before.

"Stand aside, Hattie, if you please!" the woman called out, in a most pleasant, lilting voice.

Hattie slipped off to the side, and into the bedchamber bustled a small, gray-haired woman, perhaps forty-five years of age, carrying an armful of dresses and undergarments.

"If one was to wait for the proper and civilized manner of doing things on this island, why then not much would ever get accomplished!" she exclaimed with a quick nod of her head.

Kathryne stood there for the longest moment, formulating first a response, then a welcome, then a handful of questions—but in the end, she merely stood there, her mouth almost open and a near-panicked look in her eyes.

"Well, now," the woman said, "there I go taking things a bit too quickly and overwhelming everyone."

She turned to Hattie, handed her the bundle of clothing she carried, and turned back to Kathryne.

"My dear," she said in a more motherly and calming voice, "I am Lady Jenny Pickering. My husband is Lord Pickering of Southampton, but on this island I do not make a stand on the practices of the nobility. You will call me Jenny, for Lady Jenny sounds too much like a garden flower to suit my aging face."

Kathryne continued to stare, unsure of what to do next, almost thinking she should curtsy in response.

"Hattie, place these clothes on pegs if you will . . . if there are pegs in this room."

She turned back to Kathryne.

"Child, I can see you are in a state of befuddlement. Most understandable after all you've been through the last few months. The clothes were my daughter's. She passed on last spring."

Lady Pickering paused for only a heartbeat, holding her eyes closed tight for the briefest of moments.

"No need for condolences, child, for I have set my mind at peace about it. Life indeed does go on. I know for a fact that you're needing a new wardrobe, so pick out something that you might fancy for today. There are three trunks full of her things at the bottom of the stairs, but no sense giving you too many choices all at once. Now get yourself dressed, child. I'll be waiting to have a lemonade with you out on the porch."

Lady Pickering peered closer at Kathryne. "Lemonade would fit your tastes?"

Kathryne nodded, puzzled at the question.

"You're not a drinker of much spirits, are you?" Lady Pickering asked.

Kathryne, still in a puzzle, shook her head and softly said, "No."

"Good," Lady Pickering said with conviction. "Must admit, you don't look the type."

She nodded once again, as if closing the conversation.

"Do come down when you're decent," Lady Pickering added. She turned and left the room, with Hattie close behind. She pulled up quickly.

"Hattie."

"Yes ma'am?" she asked innocently.

"Haven't you been assigned to be Lady Kathryne's maid?"

"Yes ma'am, dat de truth."

Lady Pickering stood at the top of the steps, her arms crossed. "Well then, Hattie, if you are to be Lady Kathryne's maid, it would do you well to help the poor child get dressed, don't you think?"

Hattie turned back to the bedchamber and saw Kathryne still standing near the window, still huddled in the wrapped bedsheets, still confused.

"Well, dat be a good idea, Lady Pickering. I can do dat."

And with that, Hattie turned, walked into the room, closed the door, and said loudly, "Now let's see what sort of dress Lady Kat'ryne might likes to be wearing dis fine mornin'."

## 4

William began to walk to the entrance of the Pelican, the alehouse where he had eaten no more than an hour prior. This time, though, he had Calvin, the ex-slave from France, in tow. There were only two alehouses open for the morning meal in the harbor area, the Goose and the Pelican, and the latter appeared to be newer, more substantial. Will also gave it a slight edge in matters of cleanliness. But Calvin reached out gently and tugged at Will's sleeve, stopping him.

"Not dat place, suh. Dey not happy to have darkies inside der," Calvin said softly. "Dat place der by de water be better."

Will stopped and stared at the alehouse door, only a dozen steps away.

*Would they not allow me to enter with this man?* Will thought. *If they were to voice an objection, I could insist that they need answer to me for an explanation.*

Calvin stood quiet, waiting for Will to turn away.

*But perhaps today is not the day for such confrontation,* Will thought.

"Calvin," Will said, "the food is not that tasty. You are missing no special treat," and steered him along the street toward a rickety alehouse slouched down at the edge of the piers.

Calvin smiled and brightened. "Dat's what I had done heard."

The front door of the Goose squealed its welcome as the two entered the darkened establishment. Will picked a table and benches by an open window that faced the ocean. A woman with flawless ivory skin and deep blue eyes came up to them and smiled, wide and inviting.

*I would not have thought such a pleasant woman would be in such a place,* Will thought.

"Mornin', Calvin," she said, her voice almost a laugh. "I suspect you've done well in your sales, seeing as how you're here and bringing a guest with you." Her voice was low and melodic.

Calvin laughed heartily in return. "He be buyin' de breakfast, Miss Eileen, so you forget 'bout lookin' in me pockets."

The woman eyed Will intently.

"You are the pirate who brought back the governor's daughter?" she asked.

*How fast does news travel here?* Will wondered. *Does this entire island know of my exploits?*

"Yes, Miss . . . ?" Will replied, his answer rounding to a question.

"You can simply call me Miss Eileen, good sir, and I am at your service, anytime you choose," she replied, in a more friendly tone than Will expected.

"Well, Miss Eileen, all that we need this morning is a full breakfast for Calvin, and if you have some coffee I would like a steaming tankard of that for myself."

She smiled broadly at Will and slowly turned away toward the kitchen.

*Was that a wink?* Will wondered. *How much more at sixes and sevens can this day become?*

In a few brief moments several plates of food appeared—a heaping portion of fried eggs, thick slices of roasted wild hog, a mound of fried fish and rice, and a trio of thick biscuits, plus two tankards—one with warm ale and the other with thick and pungent coffee.

As Eileen placed the plates on the table, she stared openly at Will.

"If you need anything further, Mr. Hawkes, you just call out, and I'll be there to serve you," she smoldered in a most languid voice. "Anything at all."

Will fought the urge to blush from her suggestions. Both Will and Calvin watched as she sauntered across the room to serve up ale to a pair of fishermen just back from their night at sea.

"Good-lookin' one," Calvin admitted. "This island don' have dat many pretty ladies just now."

Will nodded in agreement, his thoughts distracted for a time from his questions about the locket.

Calvin began to eat, shoveling great forkfuls of food into his mouth with great enthusiasm. Will watched as he ate, sipping at his coffee, staring off for a moment at the harbor before him and the vast ocean beyond.

In a few minutes, Calvin had cleaned his plates, wiping off the crumbs from his face with a backward pull of his sleeve. He leaned back and patted at his stomach.

"Dat be one powerful good meal, Mr. Hawkes. I do thanks ye most kindly."

He leaned forward, placing elbows on the table, and rested his chin in his hands. "Now ye kin be askin' me most any question ye gots. Calvin feels most like talkin' now."

With the locket resting securely in his hand, almost warming his soul through his palm, Will took another sip of his coffee.

Deep in his heart Will knew that Calvin would have no news of the vicar—either of his life or death—but for the last hour Will had fanned the flickering flame of hope that burned in his heart. Perhaps, just perhaps, the good vicar might still draw breath, somewhere, someplace, and Calvin might direct him there. The warmth of that hope felt too good to abandon and run to the coolness of the truth. Knowing Calvin's answer would be no, he was delaying hearing that hateful word for as long as he could on this beautiful, sunny morning.

"Calvin," Will asked calmly, "where did you get this locket?"

"I done got it from a slave from Antigua. Dat's where he say he from."

Will's heart slumped in his chest. Calvin had not seen or known the vicar, as Will had surmised.

"Where did he get the locket from?" Will asked calmly, fearful of betraying his true emotions with a sudden sob.

"He tole me he got it from a slave on Hispaniola. And dat de slave got it from anodder darkie, who got it from some preacher man who done gave him de locket for a Bible book. I don' know how dat darkie got a Bible book, but dat is what he done tole me, and I don' dink he be havin' no reason to be lyin' to old Calvin."

Calvin stopped and smiled at Will's curiously blank expression. "Why you ask dese questions, Mr. Hawkes? Who you be lookin' for?"

Will looked away, his eyes focused on the sea. Without turning back, Will said flatly, "The man who had this locket, the preacher man, was a most dear friend of mine. I had hoped he was still alive, but I can see that you do not know his state."

Calvin nodded. "Dat be true, Mr. Hawkes, but I don' be knowin' dat de preacher man be dead neither. Maybe he still be on dat island."

Will turned back. "Do you know what island that was?"

Calvin shook his head. "It be someplace nort' of here, but most places nort' of here be islands, plain and simple. Dat darkie did not have de name. And he be long gone from here."

Will nodded, holding his emotions in a tight grip. He looked closely at the small gold locket in his hand.

*Just perhaps,* Will thought, *just perhaps the vicar is indeed alive. The odds of finding this locket again were incalculable—just as finding the vicar alive and well might be.*

"Do you believe in the Christian God, Calvin? Do you believe in God and Jesus?" Will asked in a whisper, placing his white hand over the top of Calvin's black one.

"Calvin sure believes, Mr. Hawkes. I heard about dis God a handful of years before, and I be waitin' for de Promised Land. I do believes."

William looked over at Eileen, who was sitting on a stool at the bar, eyeing him intently.

He quickly turned away. "Calvin, would you pray with me?"

Calvin nodded. "I be proud to do dat, Mr. Hawkes."

"Dear God," William prayed, "I thank thee for returning my mother's locket to me. I had given up hope, yet thou didst not overlook my prayers. I thank thee for Calvin. I ask that if thy will allows, help me to find my friend Thomas Mayhew. Amen."

Will looked up, and Calvin's eyes were filled with tears just starting to slide down his dark cheeks.

"Thank you, Mr. Hawkes, thank God for ye, suh," Calvin called softly from behind his tears. "Dis be de firs' time a white man done prayed wit me."

━━━━━

Geoffrey Foxton finished as much of the breakfast as he could consume without the fear of being accused of the sin of gluttony. He pushed back from the table, wiped his face with an elegant lace napkin, dropping it casually. It fluttered down, landing atop a thick slab of mutton, the grease quickly soaking through the thin, delicate fabric.

His boots echoed on the wooden floor as he walked from the dining chamber through the entry hall by the front staircase, arriving in the sparsely furnished drawing room of his estate. He stopped to retrieve a riding crop that had been left leaning in the corner. He turned about once and noticed the room's bareness.

*I must order some furnishings for this house,* he thought. *Perhaps I can persuade Lady Kathryne to offer me advice on the subject. 'Tis true I know little about such amenities, and I am sure the request would play well to her feminine abilities and begin the process of entwining her to this place.*

Geoffrey stepped out into the rising warmth of the day. *What to do first?* he thought, squinting into the bright shafts of daylight streaming over the line of palms at the end of his drive. *I could ride to the sugar mill to assure that its construction is progressing on schedule. But I am sure my Dutch friends will see to it that all is in working order. After all, they will not receive final payment until the mill is in operation.*

Geoffrey gently slapped the riding crop against his leg absentmindedly as he turned to face south.

*Or I might ride to the far fifty acres that are being cleared by Mr. Sheedy and the darkies. But what will be there to supervise? Mr. Sheedy is an adept taskmaster, and the darkies seem to be in good spirits. I am sure he will provide a report to me on their progress with the clearing and planting. And to be truthful, I do not care to come that close to those savages. Their primitive behaviors are troubling.*

Once again the riding crop slapped his leg. He turned to the north.

*Perhaps I might call on Lady Kathryne this morning? She retired from last eve's impromptu affair so early that I scarce had a chance to visit. But again, it has been a vexing time for her, and it will be a day or two until she locates the proper attire and all the necessary amenities needed to ready herself to accept a gentleman visitor. I trust that our island seamstresses will fit her form with greater care, and perhaps a little more daring, than the gown of last eve.*

Once more the riding crop swished against his leg.

*No, instead I shall send a note to her this afternoon, but will withhold my first official visit until she has had time to make herself ready for my call.*

And now he held the crop up to his chin, pondering his possibilities.

*I might call on Lord Aidan to inquire once again about his concerns over shipping my sugar back to England. I have no desire to pay the government's usurious taxes and would much rather ship with my new Dutch advisors. Perhaps he will see my position more sympathetically now that his daughter is finally here—and now that our families are to be irrevocably bound. After all, business is indeed business. But then again, he has been through much. No, my meeting with the governor can wait a day or two hence.*

Geoffrey looked out at the clouds drifting past. *How I will miss dear Radcliffe. Though we shared not the same proclivities and pleasures, he was always a sure and willing partner in any after-dark affairs. And he was a man who knew the value of silence.*

Geoffrey, near motionless for minutes on the front steps of his estate, finally moved forward and began a slow walk to the stables, a few hundred yards east of the main house.

*Perhaps I shall go for a little ride and drop in at the Goose for my midday meal. Perhaps I will have a game of darts with Miss Eileen. This time, if I best her, I will insist on prompt payment.*

And with that pleasant thought nestled firmly in his mind, he saddled up a spirited mare and began the short ride to the harbor.

# CHAPTER

# 5

With Hattie's help, hesitant as it was, Kathryne selected a modest dress for her first morning in her new home on the island of Barbados. The remaining dresses and gowns were placed on the wall pegs.

Her dress for the day was of a creamy color and made from thin linen material. The skirt was simple, not full, with sleeves only to the elbow, but loose and cooling. Lady Pickering's choice of attire fitted reasonably well, with the only snugness noted in the bodice.

As Hattie buttoned up the tiny ivory buttons at the back of the gown, she remarked, "You be a sight more womanly than Lady Pickering's daughter passed. She was a slight little one. Looked more like a little girl than a woman ready for lookin' at husbands. Didn't surprise me none that the fever took her so soon."

She pulled the fabric to the button, slightly gapped from the difference in sizes. "You be fine, Lady Kat'ryne. Just don' go to breathin' real heavy or some of de buttons will bust loose."

Kathryne turned to Hattie. "Hattie, did you know Lady Pickering's daughter well? What was the affliction that caused her fever?" Kathryne asked, concerned.

"I know her some. I used work in dat house till your father buy me and brung me to dis house."

Kathryne nearly winced when she heard the word *buy* in relationship to another human being. She had always thought that her father would be beyond such practices as buying and selling humans, but perhaps it was that this island dictated special circumstances. He did actually foreshadow such practices in one of his letters, Kathryne recalled.

"Dat girl just caught de fever and den in a wink, she gone. Don' know what fever be called, but it be de fever with chills and sweatin'. Lots of people get fever here—some be dead, some not."

Kathryne shivered at the thought of such a death.

Hattie stared at her. "You not be catchin' fever, Lady Kat'ryne?" she asked, alarmed.

Kathryne placed her hand on Hattie's arm. "No, Hattie, I truly feel most fit and well. I do. The warmth of this place seems to agree with me. But perhaps I should now thank Lady Pickering for the gift of these gowns."

The two made their way to the landing, Kathryne walking slowly, absorbing all the details of the house, the wide trim, the polished floors, the bright colors—all made more dazzling and intense by the tropical sun. Her first viewing was the evening prior, when all was dark. Halfway down the steps, Kathryne's stomach rumbled mightily. Hattie turned, almost alarmed.

Kathryne blushed slightly. "I also think breakfast might be in order as well, Hattie. Do you think that you might fetch me some food?"

Hattie smiled. "Gettin' foodstuffs be one job I be most good at doin', Lady Kat'ryne. I be gettin' ye a good island breakfast," she said, then scampered as fast as she could down the steps, hurrying straight for the back of the house, each step from her bare feet slapping loudly on the bare wood floor.

Kathryne found herself alone in the front hall. Three trunks had been left near the door; one was open, displaying a full interior of dresses and hats.

"Lady Pickering?" she called out in a small voice. "Lady Pickering?"

"Out here on the front porch, child," Lady Pickering called back. "And the name is Jenny."

Kathryne stepped out into the bright warmth of the morning.

"Well now," Lady Pickering said. "That dress quite suits you. Turn about—let me see how it fits."

Kathryne spun.

"Lift your arms," Lady Pickering said.

Kathryne obeyed, as a child obeys a mother who is purchasing one's new wardrobe.

"Well, it fits, but barely," Lady Pickering said as she tugged at the material on the bodice. "I can see that my seamstress will need to let each of these dresses out for you to be most comfortable. My daughter was not nearly as voluptuous as yourself."

Kathryne felt like blushing again.

"And some of the gowns—those with more revealing necklines—

why, I am sure your father would prohibit your wearing them as they are, especially with such a scarcity of eligible ladies on this island. No need in stirring the gentlemen up any more than need be."

Kathryne stood there for another moment, then slumped to a bench, shaded by the long porch roof. She stared down at her shoes, the same ones that she had been wearing on the ship as Will rescued her. All that seemed like a dream now that she was safe on dry land. On the tip of the shoe were a few tiny spots of red. The spots were most certainly blood, and Kathryne could not determine if they were from the wounds on her wrists where the chains had dug into the flesh, or from Will's blood as she cradled his head in her lap following the battle.

Unexpectedly, tears began to form in her eyes.

Lady Pickering sat next to her and draped a motherly arm about her shoulder. "It shall be all right, child. I know that it all seems like such a whirl. Perhaps it might be best if we take your introduction to Barbados at a slower pace."

Through her sobs, Kathryne sniffled, "Lady Pickering—Jenny, nothing here seems normal nor secure. My uncle tried to cruelly dispatch my father and myself, as well as the man who saved me, Mr. William. . . ."

She stopped short of naming her rescuer, unsure of the true reason she could not continue. But in this more civilized setting, that hidden island of the pirates, the waterfall, the North Star, all that seemed so separate and far removed from where Kathryne now sat.

"I am in my father's home, yet I do not know where the kitchen is. I have been given a maid—a slave—who is very black and scarce understands correct English. She knows little about the ways of a proper chambermaid. And her being a slave is a most troubling situation as well. I know few people on this island, and I am most perplexed and unsure of what I should say and when. And I am clothed in the gown of your daughter, so recently deceased. Do you not see why this all seems unreal and most like an apparition?"

Tears began to again form at the corners of Kathryne's deep green eyes, now tinted with a hint of pain and confusion.

Lady Pickering wrapped both arms about her and hugged as tightly as she could and allowed her to sob quietly. After the passage of a quarter hour, Kathryne's cries had grown soft, and she grew limp in Lady Pickering's arms.

"Child," Lady Pickering whispered, "let us move slowly. I see Hattie hovering in the front hall trying her best to determine if we wish to be disturbed. She is a dear girl, and I am sure our English ways are as strange to her as this island is to you right now. I believe I heard you ask for breakfast. Perhaps after you've drawn your strength, we will tour your new home together. Do you think you might manage such an activity? We will go no further than the gentle confines of this house and grounds today."

Kathryne looked up, her eyes red and puffy from her tears. She saw a mother's face in Lady Pickering, and she nodded, sniffed twice, and nodded again.

"Indeed, I am most peckish," Kathryne admitted in a small voice. "It seems like years since I have had a proper meal."

After a leisurely and most delicious breakfast, Kathryne turned to her guest.

"Well, Jenny, shall we explore this fine house that is to be my new home? Perhaps Hattie will join us to help introduce whatever staff my father has enjoined."

"I did assume that your father would be here, this being your first day back," Lady Pickering said, cautious that she open no wounds. "Has he stated when he may return?" she asked as the trio entered once again the main hall of the mansion.

Kathryne looked about again, taking in her new surroundings. "No. Perhaps he stayed over at the Carruthers plantation, for there did seem to be a great many toasts offered. The planters were most joyous at his safe return. And I saw my father consume more of those libations than I have in the past. I am sure that he will return when he awakes."

Shelworthy was no more than half, perhaps a third, as grand as Broadwinds. The structure seemed roomy enough to Kathryne. A grand dining chamber was included, plus a great chamber on the ground floor that would be well suited for balls and parties. The kitchen, unlike that in their home in England, was located in one of the separate back service buildings. Despite the heat of the ovens, it actually proved to be the coolest room in the house, for much of it was below ground level and shaded from the sun by a jungle of palms behind the home.

"I used to go to the kitchen in Broadwinds to escape the chill and sit by the fire," Kathryne said as they walked through. "I can see I will come to Shelworthy's kitchen to escape the heat and sit in the cool shade."

Kathryne met Mrs. Potter, the official cook of the house, who was busy preparing meals for the callers she knew would be arriving this evening to offer their congratulations for Lord Aidan's rescue.

The sun was high in the sky as Lady Pickering and Kathryne found their way back to the entry hall. Hattie had stayed in the kitchen, with Kathryne's approval, to help Mrs. Potter in her preparations. The trunks had been taken to Kathryne's room by two slaves who were in charge of the grounds about the house.

Lady Pickering took Kathryne's hand. "Child, I know there must be hundreds of unanswered questions you have, but I must return home, for I am also expecting guests this evening. Would it be acceptable to you if I came to call tomorrow? Perhaps our tour may include a bit more real estate, perhaps down to Bridgetown. We could look in on the construction of the new church—and the new fort as well."

"That would be lovely, Lady Picker—I mean, Lady Jenny—I mean, Jenny. I would like that very much."

"We could stop and call on Mr. Foxton, for his home is not far off the road to the harbor. Perhaps he would appreciate a short visit, owing to your special relationship," she said with a nudge in her voice.

Lady Pickering hoisted herself up into her carriage and clucked the reins, and the horse took off in a slow walk. "Until tomorrow, then, child," she called. "Rest well."

As the carriage rolled onto the dusty lane and turned away from town, Kathryne's mind was filled with an absolute jumble of names and thoughts. Her heart was beating rapidly, and she felt nearer the verge of panic than she had ever felt in her life. Being kidnapped was even less tormenting than this very moment.

*If we go to the church, we will no doubt see Vicar Petley. If we go to the fort, we will no doubt see William. If we go to Mr. Foxton's house, we will no doubt see Geoffrey. My heavens, a more perplexing and vexing situation I could have scarce imagined!*

## 6

The sun was nearing its zenith, flowing into the drawing room and over the sleeping faces of Lord Aidan Spenser, Peter Carruthers, Lord Samuel Holston, and Sir Everett Eversham, who must have stumbled into the room after Aidan had closed his eyes. Their toastings had gone on until well past the sun's rising.

Aidan Spenser had felt no obligation to match them drink for drink, but more like sip for swallow. Yet despite his earnest attempt at limiting his intake, as the party progressed he had felt increasingly unsure of his balance and knew that his words had begun to slur.

Aidan sat up, trying not to stir too loud for fear of waking those who reclined on the divan, a bench, and, for one unlucky slumberer, the hard floor. As he rose to standing, a drumbeat began in his head, and he placed both hands to his temple, trying to quell the vicious staccato pain. His stomach, at the same time, rolled slightly, and he felt what seemed to be seasickness wash over his being.

*If this be the result of such imbibing, I shall never partake of spirits again,* he whispered in his mind, for even his thoughts seemed to clang at his temples. *And moreover, how is it that others suffer through such agony on a regular, if not daily, basis? Such excruciating pain for such a fleeting pleasure,* he grimaced.

Aidan stood there, weaving slowly in the sunlight, and the slight creaks of the floorboards roused his host, Peter Carruthers, who piled himself up in a most disheveled and wrinkled fashion, put a finger to his lips, and led Aidan silently from the room. Without saying a word, the pair, each holding one hand to the side of his head—for Aidan it was his right, Carruthers used his left—and using the other hand to reach out and touch the wall, stumbled toward the kitchen, each afraid that his balance would be most endangered if he let go of the surface of a friendly, secure vertical surface.

The kitchen was quiet. The breakfast clatter had passed, and the dinner hubbub had yet to begin. Carruthers' cook, an indentured servant from County Cork in Ireland, Brian Flaherty, took one look at the two men and merely shook his head in both amusement and disdain.

"I be takin' it that ye prefer old Brian to be speakin' with the tiniest of voices this fine mornin'," he whispered.

Both men nodded weakly.

"And that ye come to old Brian for ye be thinkin' that a lad from the land of Erin might be knowin' a wee proper remedy for what ails ye."

Both men nodded, though Aidan would later say the man's thick burr was so tortured that he might have been saying anything at all. Indeed Aidan merely nodded to mimic the actions of his host.

Brian Flaherty laughed softly and set about to gathering some herbs and liquids, mixing, mashing, and stirring them into a vile, dark, thick concoction that he poured, with a great flourish, into two tankards in front of the men. As he served it, he expertly cracked a single egg into each vessel, not bothering to stir the resulting mixture.

"It be the only remedy that will be savin' ye poor heads from burstin', gentlemen. Now drink it up in one swallow, for there be no second chances at a complete recovery," Brian said with a wide smirk on his face.

Both men closed their eyes, tilted the tankards back, and began to swallow. Aidan finished first, and he dropped the tankard to the table, his eyes red, his breath coming in fast spurts, a cough in his throat.

Carruthers did not finish, placed his tankard down most carefully on the table, then dashed out of the room and toward the outdoors. Aidan heard the vague and liquid sounds of Carruthers being noisily ill.

Surprisingly, the drink seemed to refresh Aidan rather quickly. Within a few short moments, the pounding in his head stopped, his vision cleared slightly, and he no longer felt as if a live fish lived in his stomach.

"Thank you most kindly, Mr. Flaherty. Your libation seems to have had a positive effect on me," Aidan said, his voice soft.

Flaherty bowed slightly at the waist, making a small show of his acknowledgement of Aidan's gratitude.

"Do you think that perhaps I may have some bread and . . . something else that might be easy to eat? I feel that if I eat, I may indeed survive this day," Aidan said ruefully.

"By all means, sir. How about a small portion of bread with a wee bit of fried eggs to go with it?"

Aidan nodded. "That would be most appreciated." After the meal, Aidan felt his color and his strength slowly return.

"May I be asking you a most important question, Governor?" Carruthers whispered in an almost collusive tone, as if worried about those who might seek to overhear. "I understand your position regarding we planters having to employ English ships to haul our sugar back to market. But Aidan, if we do that, our share of the profits shrinks to a pittance. The English merchants charge twice the shipping rate— nearly bordering on the usurious—and they would be applying every tax that now exists on our cargo. All the planters on this island agree on this. However, if we employ Dutch merchant ships, there will be more for us when it comes time to sell—perhaps as much as a full quarter's increase. And those Dutch are so blasted accommodating that it be hard for a planter to say no to them."

Carruthers paused and looked about the darkened kitchen. "Now I'm sure it comes as no surprise that I understand—from the loose tongues of several libertines—that Radcliffe would have allowed for the wholesale bypassing of the English traders and taxes. And I have also heard that many of the planters have already begun to make such arrangements."

Carruthers leaned closer. "My question, Governor, is will you take up active arms to prevent such actions? Will you monitor such shipments from our island and risk the wrath of many powerful planters?"

Lord Aidan sat back, trying to hide his outrage and shock. "Are you proposing that I allow—or worse yet, condone and facilitate—an outright breaking of English law, the law that I am sworn to uphold? If that be your question, then of course, as a Christian man and duly appointed representative of His Majesty, the answer is an emphatic no. I will not, nor cannot, turn my back on my king and his law."

A dark quiet had settled about the room. There was the sound of distant footfalls, but not close enough to have overheard, Aidan surmised.

"But, Governor," Carruthers pleaded, "surely there will be a time or two that even the good governor must blink or rest his eyes from eternal vigilance." Carruthers' face reddened, and his voice grew loud and animated. "Even you must agree to that. I mean, my stars, Aidan—no governor can keep his eyes open both day and night."

Aidan was set to protest as Carruthers banged his hand on the table as an exclamation. But his aim was not quite perfect, owing to his consumption of drink the night prior, and his thumb caught the edge of his plate, still littered with eggs, grease, and crumbs. It flipped and tossed its contents, striking Carruthers's hair, face, and neck with a deluge of breakfast remnants.

For a moment, Carruthers was shocked into stunned silence, then began to laugh heartily.

For all Aidan's repose and decorum, the sight was indeed comic, and his robust, distinctive laugh soon joined his friend's, their amusement echoing along the silent halls of the ground floor.

Outside of the room, well out of sight but not out of range of hearing, crouched two men, Bickley White and Davis Wallace. The two planters, newer arrivals to the island, both had sugarcane crops that would be ready for shipping in six short months. They had awakened no more than a quarter hour prior and were drawn to the darkened basement rooms by the powerful smells emanating from the kitchen. As the pair approached the kitchen from the wrong end of the hall, having lost their way and battling through a rummy fog, they heard Carruthers outline his initial question concerning the English and Dutch shipping. They hushed each other broadly and thought it wise to use stealth, drawing closer in silence, to ascertain the governor's true response.

After they heard the governor laugh in joy at Carruthers's remark about turning a blind eye to certain planters and their shipping requirements, they slipped further back in the shadows. In a moment they slithered out a rear door into the blazing afternoon heat.

"It would be better had Radcliffe bested that man," White hissed, "for at least Radcliffe played no favorites. His brother seems to favor the noble born, like Carruthers."

"Aye, that be the truth," Wallace added, a menace in his voice, "for if Carruthers can ship with the Dutch, then I shall do no less. It appears most truthful that our Governor Spenser plays most loose with his morality and honesty."

"And be sure not to mention this to others," White whispered back, "for I want to be one of the few who use the Dutch. If we all join in, we'll have the English navy at our heels, no doubt."

## 7

Kathryne watched as the dust of Lady Pickering's carriage settled.

She heard the door squeak, as if someone was being so very tentative in opening, to avoid disturbing someone. Without turning about, Kathryne said, "Yes, Hattie, what is it?"

A voice from behind sparked alive, and the door swung open. "Lady Kat'ryne, you be havin' eyes from behind? How you be knowin' it be me?"

Kathryne turned and replied, "I have my ways, Hattie."

For the first time, Kathryne looked closely at the face of the slave and stared into her dark, wide eyes. *I can see she is near as puzzled as me. She has never been a chambermaid, and I have never had to command a . . . slave. But we both must do what is expected of us. . . .*

Kathryne smiled a wide, honest, genuine smile. Hattie smiled back, unsure of what response she might offer, what work might be given, or what orders might be barked.

"Hattie, I believe I would like you to help me sort through the trunks that Lady Pickering brought—to evaluate each gown for its style and fit. I will need to do so sooner rather than later. Perhaps you will know what is appropriate on this island and what is not."

Hattie kept nodding and smiling in return.

"Shall we go to my bedchamber and begin that task, Hattie? You could offer me the greatest support."

"Well, Lady Kat'ryne, I don' rightly know all dat you says, but if you needs help, I be wit' ye to help. Dat much I knows."

Upon their return to her bedchamber, Kathryne asked Hattie to open all the windows, for under the hot sun the room quickly warmed to an uncomfortable temperature.

"But, Lady Kat'ryne," Hattie protested, "Lord Spenser say dat de wind is full of bad airs and we are to be shuttin' every window we got."

Kathryne placed her hands on her hips and stared at her. "Well, Hattie, my father will not be living in this room, will he now?" she asked with playful conspiracy.

"He won' be, dat be a fact, Lady Kat'ryne," Hattie agreed.

"And if I want the windows open, then they should be—what?" Kathryne asked.

Hattie screwed up her face, deep in thought. "I believes dey should be . . . open?"

Kathryne clapped her hands together. "Yes, that's right. They should be open."

And with that they went about to each of the six windows, unlatching and lifting sashes, spreading the temporary curtains to one side or the other, letting the wind carry some of the heat from the room. The windows faced west and south, and the sea could be seen from them, glistening as a jewel in the distance.

As she raised the last window and set its fastener in place to hold it open, Kathryne happened to see the manufacturer's mark on one of the thick mullions. She at once recognized the name and realized that it was this very window that she had arranged shipment for—shipment on William's ship—so many months ago. She ran her hand over the etched letters, cut into the hard wood, and stared out, to where Will was, no doubt, then to where the vicar was, and then in the direction of where Geoffrey Foxton was as well.

"Hattie," Kathryne said, trying to bring her mind to the business at hand, "would you mind opening those trunks and sorting the gowns. Those that look like evening wear—the fancy ones, with trims and lace—place those on the bed. Plain gowns, like the one I am wearing now, you may place on the pegs along that wall."

"Yes, Lady Kat'ryne. I can do dat," she said as she began to carefully unpack the first trunk.

Kathryne stayed by the window, the warm wind wisping through the room, pushing her hair back from her face, teasing her nose with a scent of the sea, a scent mixed with an intoxicating hint of jasmine.

*I will not think of William now. How I wish that life was simpler. I wish that noble birth meant less than it does. My heart has been captured by that man, and I will not disavow my feelings. But I know that I must consider more than just one person's feelings about this matter.*

"Lady Kat'ryne, be dis a gown for evenin', or would ye be wearin' it about durin' de day?" Hattie asked, holding up a dark silk gown trimmed in velvet. "It be thin enough, but it has dese heavy cloth patches on it and all."

Kathryne looked over, turned her head to the side, and replied, "I believe I would wear that at nighttime, Hattie. You may place that on the bed."

*But what of the future?* she thought, her face a pensive mask. *If I am to bear children . . .* That thought jumped hard against her soul. *Do I not have to consider their best interests at heart as well, perhaps consider them even more highly than I do my own heart and desire?*

"And dis one here, my lady?"

Kathryne looked over at an orange-and-brown-colored gown, with slits of yellow silk displayed on the sleeves.

"That one, Hattie, I will never wear—day or night." Kathryne smiled.

*Poor William.* Her throat closed, near tight, and she knew tears were close to her eyes. *No, I will not cry. Geoffrey Foxton is a well-bred and decent man who has great potential. He is a man of fine Christian standards. What could I hope for with William Hawkes. . . .*

She did not want to allow her mind to consider this so soon upon her return. Kathryne had battled these thoughts since the *Serendipity* bumped against the pier in Barbados.

*What hope could there be, except being the wife of a common man and living a most common life. . . .* Tears began to form, and her chest tightened. *A common life that would be filled with honest love and service to God.* Kathryne braced herself on the window frame, staring at the sea through her salty tears.

*No! I will not allow that to happen. I must be strong . . . I must obey my father . . . I must allow God to set my path . . . I must. . . .*

Her tears fell freely as she thought about that night on the beach of William's secret island, looking at the stars.

"What about dis one, Lady Kat'ryne?"

Kathryne turned to see Hattie holding up a fur-trimmed dark russet evening gown against her more than ample frame. She looked as if she were hugging a tall, thin jungle creature to herself.

Through her tears, Kathryne started to giggle, trying to hold back the laughter through her sobs.

Hattie smiled with her, then looked most confused, and doubly so as

Kathryne ran to her and embraced her, the russet gown pressed between them.

Hattie found herself saying in comfort, without knowing what troubled her mistress, "Der, der, my lady . . . you see, dis dress not be dat ugly. It not be dat bad."

And Kathryne's tears continued to fall, through both her laughter and her pain.

━━━━━

William bid Calvin good-bye, promising that they would talk again, and set off at a slow pace toward the fort. As he turned the corner, he thought he saw Geoffrey Foxton striding toward the Goose, with a thin leer set on his face.

*It is indeed a small island, no doubt,* he thought, *and he has as much right to it as do I. But I will never stoop to spying on him. Let him be about his own business, but 'tis truly an early hour for a visit to an alehouse. It is too late for breakfast and too early for a midday meal. What other reason would a man have to visit an alehouse at this time of day?*

Will ignored the strong desire to judge and focused on his task at hand. The fort—at least the foundation of the fort—that had been constructed was situated at a slight distance south of the pier area, on a narrow spit of land that closed about the harbor like a mouth. The land was higher there, and rocky, and the finished fortification would have a commanding view of the entrance to the heart of Barbados and Bridgetown. Much of the west wall, stretching near to the water's edge at high tide, was completed. A short wall had been built facing north, too, and the beginning of a tower could be seen, but that was as far as the building had gone under Radcliffe's supervision.

Taking Kathryne's words to be true concerning the position of captain of the harbor defenses being unfilled, William desired to know what sort of task would lie in store for the new man holding that job. *What better way to determine the task remaining,* he thought as he walked toward the empty fortifications, *than to take stock of what's been left and what lies ahead.*

The wounds to his shoulder gently pained through his being. The powder that Luke had provided to the open slash had prevented it from worsening, but Will realized that the pain from the sword cut would echo in his bones for several weeks.

*I will keep this reconnoiter brief,* he thought, *and then return to the ship to speak with the crew. I am sure they are most anxious concerning my future plans, as well they should be.*

From the foundations and stakes in the ground, Will determined that the fort would not be a huge fortification, perhaps seventy-five paces square. From the completed west wall, he realized that it would not be a tall bastion, such as existed back home in England, hulking along the coastline, warding off enemies.

Will climbed to a parapet at the northwest corner of the fortifications. His progress was slow due to his shoulder, and he awkwardly made his way, often off balance, up a rickety rough construction ladder to the narrow ledge that ran its length. From there he gazed across the harbor. A dozen ships gently bobbed in the quiet, blue-green waters, lying peacefully at anchor, sails wrapped tight.

*From this spot, with a single cannon,* Will thought, as he imagined sight lines and arcs over an imaginary gun barrel, *a single squad with good aim could keep an armada at bay. Anyone who attacks this island will not do so from the sea, at least not here, for the rocks are too rough to land marines, and they would be hard pressed to attack along the narrow area of land where this fort lies. A single squad with muskets would make short work of any unprotected attack. No one could sail in without coming under heavy fire for a long and slow sail into the wind. The man who selected this site selected well.*

Will walked carefully along the narrow wooden ledge to the far south end. From there he saw the coast recede in the distance, dotted with boulders and rocks, and the waters beyond the shoreline, marked with the gradually darkening greens of reefs and submerged rocky ledges.

*And to be sure, no one could be landing a large vessel there. Ten cannon and fifty men, ammunition and sufficient powder, and I could make this harbor—this entire island—impregnable from any raider party, save perhaps the combined armadas of all of England's enemies.*

Will pushed his blond hair back from his eyes. *I will seek out the barber today as well,* he mused.

*And I shall seek out the governor in haste as well, for to defend this island would be a simple task, and one that might leave time enough for other activities.* . . . He stared out again across the water to the west, then returned his gaze to the gentle hills that led away from the harbor. . . . *Such as courting the governor's daughter. I know I have much to learn of the ways of a civilized gentleman. I am certain that if I held the position of captain of the harbor defenses, that should give me enough standing to enter into Kathryne's world.*

He stood there for a long moment, the gentle breeze pouring over his face and chest. He smelled the sea, of course, and a more subtle scent from the island's interior. He sniffed at it, his face showing a puzzled look. *Was that faint aroma lilacs?* He shook his head. *The nearest lilacs must be four thousand miles away, back in England.*

The sun felt warm and comforting, and its gentleness seemed to help the ache in his shoulder. He looked up at the sun, calculating that it was nearing noon, but he felt neither hunger nor thirst. He turned and awkwardly hoisted himself to the top wide stone of the wall and straddled it so he could see the harbor, the ships, the sea, and the hills of the island in one view.

He looked to his side, back to the shore, to the point at which was formed the spit of land on which the fort was located. An outcropping of rocks lay behind it, and the land then flattened for a half-dozen acres. The field was filled with tall sea grass and short palmetto trees.

Will squinted at it, trying to imagine it differently.

*I could easily clear that land. It would support a fine spacious cottage, with room for a garden and a small stable, perhaps enough room for a chapel as well. I could build the cottage of island stone, perhaps—the better to withstand any violent winds and rain. A pleasant cottage would fit that site well. A short stroll to the markets in town, a walk of only a moment to the fort, access to the sea for a longboat or small skiff that could be docked at the water's edge there by those rocks. It would be the most perfect site for a home for Kathryne and myself. And children—of course children.*

Will knew well that most sailors were superstitious to their core, and that the fact that he dared dream of such a desirable culmination, they would say, gave the sea gods of chance full rein to deny the dream's fruition. But Will took no stock in their superstitions and could not let the dream of Kathryne and himself together slip from his thoughts this morning.

He saw the walls of his cottage, painted white, with a thick slate roof, and vines climbing the sides of the house, a small tongue of smoke slipping away from the chimney as beautiful Kathryne tended to the evening meal as he returned home from the fort.

*It could happen that way,* he assured himself. *It truly could. For I know for a certainty that she has pledged her love and affection for me in such a way that she cannot undo. She herself has said that if God ordains a result, then that result shall occur—regardless of the plans of men to the contrary. Well, I believe God would not have allowed me a glimpse of this vision if it were not to be so.*

He looked out on the field, as the sea grasses waved in the gentle wind, washing away his vision with their tranquil swaying.

He looked out to sea, the vastness stretching away from him, and closed his eyes.

*Almighty God, I thank thee for thy protection and guidance and the fact that thou hast deemed me, a wretched sinner, worthy of thy grace. I humbly ask that the dream thou hast presented to me in Kathryne Spenser be allowed to become a reality. I will ask for little else, Father, if this is in line with thy will for my life.*

William opened his eyes, surprised that there were tears in them.

# CHAPTER

# 8

The sun arched to the west, nearing midafternoon, and the winds ceased. The island seemed to still and hush. Will spent most of that midday sitting silently on the wall of the fort, staring at the sea with eyes all but unfocused. After his prayer, he forced himself to put Kathryne out of his mind and consider a new topic—how to most correctly approach the governor of the island with the supplication that he be placed in charge of the harbor defenses.

*What better way to stop a pirate,* he thought, *than to employ the services of a pirate as guard! I am well versed in the ways of such men, which would enable me to better protect this island from their attacks.*

His eyes scanned the horizon of the azure water before him. Seagulls floated on a gentle current of wind. *What if the governor asks why he should believe that such a leopard has changed its spots?* he asked himself. *I shall tell him it was through his daughter's gentle reproach and guidance that I abandoned my evil ways and accepted God's amazing gift of eternal life. Since doing that, I could no more live the life of a pirate than I could fly in the sky as a bird.*

That line of reasoning would be most persuasive on such a noble-born man as Lord Spenser, Will thought. *And I am sure my time spent as a naval officer shall serve me in good stead as well.*

As Will made his way back to the deck of the *Serendipity,* some of the men stood and gathered about him as he made his way up the gang-plank. Their chatter had quieted, and they watched him with expectation on their faces. Will was no longer their official captain and leader, yet virtually all looked to him for guidance and direction. The crew knew little else but the way of the sea, and sailors were accustomed to taking orders and carrying them out without question.

The governor offered clemency for all, following their brave and unexpected rescue of himself and his daughter from Radcliffe's evil clutches. No longer considered pirates and outlaws by the Crown, the sailors were free to take the prize money they had accumulated and seek other employment—legal or otherwise.

Will had been a most generous captain, providing his crew double the expected rates of division of plunder. And while a privateer, Will had been most fortunate in his choice of targets—some very large caches of gold and silver had been seized from England's enemies. Even though each plunder taken was shared with the Crown, a great amount was left for the crew.

Each ordinary sailor had received in the past eighteen months more than a hundred pounds of gold and silver as his share. If a man so chose, he could purchase a small cottage back home in England, perhaps a few acres of fertile land, some livestock, and still have half the sum remaining to ease the worries that farming entailed. Some enterprising crewmen might purchase a small concern, perhaps a livery or blacksmith shop, or invest their capital with other businessmen.

Will called out for the rest of the crew to gather about him. He stood on the quarterdeck stairs and waited for the men to assemble.

"Men, we have been granted a great honor. Our lawlessness of the past has been forgiven, and we face a clear future as free men. The course of action I intend on taking is to endeavor to stay a free and honest man. I am honor bound by the oath that I swore that I shall turn my back on the ways of piracy.

"You are aware of the amount of gold held as your share of the *Reprisal*'s plunder. That gold is held here on Barbados by my barrister. I will see to it that you are given your share as you ask. It is, for most, a large sum of money. I will insist that you use it wisely. For some so inclined, a farm and a home may be your future. For others, perhaps a shop or fishing vessel. Whatever your choice, use this wisely, and do not let the lures of wine and women steal your dreams.

"I know that many of you have families back in England. There are ships in this harbor now who would be well served to hire you on as sailors and will begin the return voyage to our homeland within the full moon.

"I will not be returning to the sea, for my future is here on this island. You may come to me at your leisure for your funds. I will offer whatever advice and counsel I can."

Will's voice began to quiver. A most unexpected wave of tender and sad emotions cascaded over him. "I want to thank you all for what you have done for me. You are the bravest and most able crew a captain ever set to sea with. For your efforts and bravery, I salute you."

William snapped a crisp salute to the crew, some sniffing loudly, some surreptitiously dabbing at their eyes with their sleeves.

John Delacroix, Will's second-in-command, had stood to the side. He now jumped to the rail and shouted, "For Captain William Hawkes, the best captain on any of the seven seas. Hip hip, hurrah! Hip hip, hurrah! Hip hip, hurrah!"

The crew joined in the cheers, and Will stepped down from the helm station.

From the gangplank came another voice. Several heads turned in its direction. An older man, portly and sweating profusely in the humid evening, stood at the top of the gangplank dressed in silks and wools, a great feathered hat resting like a great seabird on his head. He was shouting out for their attention.

"Sailors!" he cried. "Sailors of Captain Hawkes' vessel!"

The crew turned toward him, curious.

"Sailors, please listen to me. To honor your great victory over the evil Radcliffe and to honor your bravery and valor, we, the citizens of Barbados, are inviting every one of you to a celebration. I am Lord Charles Carrington, and I am inviting you all to attend this gala, six days hence. It will be held at my plantation. It is no more than two miles' walk from this harbor. I trust that you will all join us. There will be food and drink in great abundance for all!"

An even louder cheer came rumbling up from the ship in response to such an unexpected and welcome invitation, louder by double than the cheer given for Will.

That evening, when the stars were spread out against the tropical sky like the petals in a field of iridescent flowers, Will and John Delacroix sat against the rail of the rear deck of the *Serendipity.* They had eaten a meal at the Pelican and had returned to the ship, their temporary home in Barbados, full of talk and conversation; yet the clarity of the celestial heavens above them seemed to quiet their need to converse.

"Such a sky makes a man feel small and insignificant," John said in a low voice as he puffed on his pipe.

"It did to me before," Will agreed, "but now I realize that the God who made those heavens also made the world that produced you and me, and we are among his creations as well. It is not that the skies do not overwhelm me anymore—it is that everything in God's creation now overwhelms me."

John nodded in agreement. He paused, seeking the proper wording. "Will, I am greatly pleased to see you've found a sense of peace. Without doubt, I was most worried for your well-bein'. You seemed lost and so alone, and angry at the same time. We all felt so powerless to help you."

Will put his arm on John's shoulder. "You could not have helped me. Only God could have allowed me to see the error of my thinking. And I believe, John, that we shall need to further discuss your soul as well."

John smiled. "True enough, Will. We shall. Anythin' that effects such a change in a man like yourself must be worth a great deal," he admitted.

"John," Will said, "it is most freeing to know of the love of the Almighty. And imagine, using a girl as beautiful as the Lady Kathryne to turn me about."

John puffed loudly, billows of smoke slipping into the darkness of the harbor. A few men were left on deck, quietly murmuring among themselves. The ship bobbed gently on the still water.

"Will, what of the Lady Kathryne?" John asked. "Luke said you saw her last evenin' near midnight."

Will turned and stared back into town. "I did see her, John. She returned here from the celebration, and I escorted her back to her father's home. In truth, *mansion* would be a more accurate word to describe her new home. They call it Shelworthy."

From the distance an owl shrieked, from near the fort, Will guessed.

"And then what happened, Will?" John asked.

"John, my friend, she said in response to my question if I may call upon her, and I quote, 'Why yes, Will, you may. I would look forward to that.'"

"She didn't!" John exclaimed.

"She did indeed," Will assured him, "although I feel it most proper to wait for a few days to allow her to settle in before I officially call upon her. Perhaps we shall be together at the celebration six days hence."

John stared at his friend. "Will, you are a most amazin' man. You will be the first fellow I have ever known who had the courage to court a member of the nobility. You are a braver man than I, Will—much braver—for I would have no idea of the manners or the proper conduct of those of the upper classes."

A cold thought skirted through Will. *He is right! I do not know much of their manners or ways.*

But he forced himself at that moment to stay of good cheer, for he imagined he would be seeing Kathryne soon. The thought of gazing upon her kind and beautiful face warmed his heart.

After a few moments, Will asked, in a quiet voice, "John, what will you be doing after you realize your share of the plunder from the *Reprisal?* Will you stay at sea, or go back to England? And what of our crew? What have they indicated to you?"

John stopped to fill his pipe again before replying.

"From what they have told me, most will sign on with the next ship that sails from here and take their treasure back home. Those who have families are in desperate need of that money. Some others have spoken about of the possibility of purchasin' a small tract of land on this island and raisin' sugarcane. I think it could be a most profitable operation, and these lads all have come from good farmin' families."

"And John, what of yourself?" Will asked. "What will my old friend do with his portion? 'Tis a most substantial amount."

John nodded, silhouetted against the golden disk of the moon. "Less than yours, Will, but substantial nonetheless. In truth, more than substantial. Almost more than I have a right to possess," John said. "I could take my share, purchase a cottage on the sea, and if I were frugal, would never have to lift a finger in labor again."

"So you'll be doing that then, John. Will it be here or back in England?" Will asked.

"Blimy, Will, do you not know me better than that?" John protested. "I could not merely sit and wait for the passin' of days till I departed this earth. I shall need more activity than that."

"Then it will be back to the sea for you, John?" Will asked.

"No, not that either," John replied, "for that provides too much activity. I believe it best not to be on the receivin' end of a pointed sword or musket balls. No, William, sailin' is a young man's game."

John took a step over to the starboard rail and pointed to a large building just at the water's edge. "Will, do you see that structure over there—the large one, with a second story?"

Will squinted through the dimness. By the piers, facing the water, stood a tall building, its facade gazing toward the deep water in the harbor. The sea nearly lapped at the front door.

"Yes, I do. What manner of structure is it?"

"It is now but an empty buildin'. And I have decided to purchase it."

"For what purpose?"

John smiled. "I will fashion a ship's outfittin' center in that space. I may not want to sail further, but others shall still need to. Remember the frustration we felt when we sailed into harbor with the damaged *Artemisia* and could find no skilled laborers to offer repairs? In that buildin' I can store canvas and rope, offer provisions and supplies—provide the same sort of service that our friend Thomas Delby offers in his chandlery back in Weymouth."

Will stared at John, admiring his well-thought plans.

"I have already asked the Tambor brothers to sign on as my first employees. Bryne is a most skilled shipwright, and John is . . . well, John is most enthusiastic."

William laughed. John Tambor, the younger of the two, did seem to always be at full sail with no specific destination in mind.

"John, that is a most capital idea! And one that I am sure will be most successful."

John stroked his chin. "I am unsure of how to be presentin' this to you, so I will enter in boldly. Would you be carin' to join forces with us then, Will? I am sure that the need for our services will be sufficient to support us both."

Will was surprised into silence. After a moment, he answered, "I most kindly thank you for the offer, John, but I believe I am to pursue other activities. I know that the position of captain of harbor defenses is presently unfilled. I believe I may indeed seek out that office."

John pondered a moment. "'Tis true, Will, that I could see you do well in that role. Good friend, I wish you well. If you are in the fort and I in my yard, we will have only a five-minute walk dividin' us. I will take comfort with that, my friend."

"And I as well," Will said, and the two old friends embraced in the dark.

**9**

*December 1641*
*Weymouth, England*

The *Bella Guarda*, following an uneventful voyage from the Virginia colony of Jamestown in the New World, docked near noon in the quiet waters of Weymouth Bay. Stevedores began to unload the ship—bales of top quality tobacco from the fertile lands along the Carolina coast, and cotton bales as well, bound for looms and weavers of Birmingham and Leeds. Shouts and calls echoed from the hold as the aromatic tobacco was hauled up and loaded onto carts and horse-drawn wagons.

The captain picked up his locked wooden box and made his way to the office of the harbormaster, leaving his second-in-command to oversee the rest of the unloading. He first headed toward the public house of Weymouth, passing the coach stop just outside, and entered the dark interior for a brief moment.

"Be there a postboy here?" the captain called out.

From a stool in the corner came a lad of no more than fourteen. "Yes, sir. I be on the post route. Have you a delivery for us?"

"Indeed I do. Here is a packet of letters and government correspondence that is to be taken to London. Here are two postings for here in Weymouth, and the last . . . let's see now . . . oh, yes—this one is penned by a mostly lovely young lady, and it be going to—Hadenthorne, up near Barnstaple, if I recollect what she said correctly."

"Yes, sir. Hadenthorne be near there. I have been through there on me routes, and I believe a man be headin' in that direction on the morrow."

"That be grand, then. Here's a half-shilling for the Weymouth letters, two shillings for the London letters, and a shilling for the one to Hadenthorne."

The captain placed the coins in the boy's hand. "These coins be sufficient, be they not? For the Hadenthorne letter, the young lady truly spent her last coppers on the posting cost."

"Aye, sir. A shillin' be sufficient."

The captain's duty with the mail now completed, he stepped back into the sunshine to seek out Herbert Dorling, the harbormaster.

The young postboy kept the London letters with him, for that was his destination two days hence, and placed the thin letter bound for Hadenthorne in a worn and scuffed leather pouch, which hung on a peg on the wall of the public house. It was bulging with letters.

"Me hopes Henry be sober by the morrow, now that he has a full pouch to deal with," the young boy said to no one in particular.

CHAPTER

10

*Unnamed Island,*
*Caribbean Sea*

A large rock flew through the air and struck a frigate bird squarely on the head, knocking it senseless, and it dropped from its nest. From the thick jungle below came crackling sounds as a man crashed among the dense foliage. Radcliffe quickly came upon the fallen bird and wrenched its neck, killing it quickly and efficiently. The nest was high, but he was hungry and climbed up the spindly palm to retrieve two large eggs.

"Supper and breakfast combined," Radcliffe said with satisfaction as he began to pluck the feathers from the bird and then slit its gut, depositing its entrails on the dirt at his feet.

Within minutes he was back at the beach. The longboat, the most treasured debris Radcliffe retrieved following the battle between the *Serendipity* and the *Reprisal,* was resting on the sand, securely tied to a palm tree near the water's edge. A sheet of canvas was spread over it, providing protection from the hot sun. The ale cask was yet half full, and Radcliffe had gathered another half-cask of rainwater, having set up a second canvas sheet to collect it as it fell. There was a small frame of green twigs he had built near the fire pit, now sagging under the weight of smoked fish, bird, and turtle flesh. He was stockpiling supplies for his upcoming journey back to civilization.

A small compass was part of the longboat's supplies, much to Radcliffe's great relief. Without the compass he would no doubt perish, eventually, on this deserted isle. But with it he had means to escape. Radcliffe knew he was several days' sail south and east of the Bahamas. With luck, at high tide tomorrow he would sail off this uncharted island and make his way to where he thought the Bahamas lay. He had friends there—business associates, in reality—who owed him favors. Radcliffe saw no reason why he could not venture back to England to retrieve his small treasure that he had hidden in Broadwinds and secreted among several notorious barristers—enough, he thought, to be able to start over again in grand style.

"Or if the winds favor another direction, I could sail to Florida and St. Augustine. I am sure that my Spanish friend, Captain Diego San Martel, will provide for me handsomely if I confide to him what I know of the weaknesses of my brother's little island."

He stroked his stubbled chin. "Perhaps I should aim for Florida first, even if it is a longer journey."

Radcliffe stood up, the fabric of his clothes hanging about his ankles. For protection, he had been forced to use Kathryne's clothing and had employed a number of her gowns. He picked up the hem of the dress and walked to the fire, adding a log of driftwood.

He walked to a quiet tide pool to check his fish trap and saw his reflection in the quiet water of the afternoon. He saw how the red silk fabric followed his thin frame to the ground. He looked at himself for the longest moment.

"How I wish I had a looking glass," Radcliffe said aloud to himself. "The surf never holds my image long enough to allow me a full inspection."

And with that, he picked up a leg from the fallen frigate bird, now fully roasted by the fire, and began to gnaw at the pink flesh, the juices running down his chin, now covered with thin black whiskers.

# CHAPTER

## II

*Barbados*

The sun had barely begun its ascent over the eastern hills of the island when a loud voice called from the pier, "Captain Hawkes! I say, is there a Captain William Hawkes on board?"

Will scrambled awake and made his way out of the small cabin he had been sharing with John Delacroix and Luke. He charged up the steps and encountered a portly gentleman standing on the gangplank, making it sway most precariously. The man was dressed in an odd assortment of colors—a bright blue overcoat, deep purple breeches, a patterned doublet of scarlet, greens, and lavenders. He was carrying a large felt hat, decorated with bright green plumage. It looked as if a small piece of a flowering garden had arrived dockside.

The stranger, nearing half a century in age if a day, Will surmised, looked up and squinted. "You be the Captain Hawkes, my good man?" he called.

Will was usually most circumspect in situations of direct inquiry and would insist that the questioner be identified first before any answer. But the little man seemed so outrageous as to be rendered innocuous. Will could do little but smile.

"I am the man you seek," Will replied, pushing his hair back from his eyes.

"And I am Conrad Paley," the man on the pier stated, with a most elegant formality.

Will stared blankly back.

"Lord Conrad Paley," he repeated, a little louder, as if the words were spoken too soft and left unheard when first voiced.

Will's visage changed little, except perhaps to grow more puzzled.

After a moment, he finally spoke, his tone questioning. "I am sure that I should take pleasure in your greeting, Lord Paley, but the name means little to me. Have we met prior?" Will was most certain that they had not crossed paths.

"Perhaps not, young man, but you should be aware of my name." He paused, letting the silence build. "My good man, it is I—Conrad Paley—who own the vessel on which you are now standing."

In a rush, the name connected in Will's memory. The vessel had been *borrowed* from another plantation owner by Radcliffe and his cohorts, he recalled.

"I am most pleased to make your acquaintance," Will stammered. "I know that I and what remains of my crew indeed have no right to lie about your ship here in harbor. But these men, fine men all, had no other lodging. Please pardon our impudence. I will instruct them that they must gather up their belongings and depart at once."

Paley placed his hands on his hips, looking every bit exasperated. "My dear fellow," Paley soothed. "I have not come all this way to evict you. I have come to meet you and bid you welcome to this place. I was supervising the construction of a sugar mill on the north coast of this island when I heard of your return. This morning was my first opportunity to call."

"And we are not being asked to leave?" Will asked.

"Good heavens, why would I do that? Your presence on this ship does not lessen its value," Lord Paley countered.

He looked about at the splintered rail, the torn and broken topsail on the mainmast, the ripped and shattered decking—all damaged during the furious battle.

"I believe that if there has been a reduction of this vessel's value, that lessening was suffered some days ago," Paley continued. "A few men on board will do nothing to worsen her state. All this broken and torn wood and canvas can be remedied. Do not fret for this ship. Besides, I will bill the Crown for every penny of it, as the damage occurred under charter to the government. I will suffer no financial loss over this incident."

"But then . . . ," Will said, unsure of what to say next, unsure of what Paley may want.

"Captain Hawkes, please remain on board as long as you like. I will not need the services of this vessel for two months. That is when my sugar crop will be ready to export. I trust that all repairs will be made to this ship by that date. The true reason I have come this morning is to ask if your crew might be interested in making needed renovations and signing on as her crew. Much of my former crew and officers are gone or are in chains."

At that moment, John Delacroix came up from belowdecks, rubbing at his eyes in the crisp morning air, running a hand through his hair, which was still quite tousled from sleep.

"Lord Paley," Will said, "I will not speak as to manning this vessel, for I have decided to retire from the sea. But I do have a solution for your other needs."

William turned to John. "Mr. Delacroix, I would like for you to meet Lord Conrad Paley, the owner of this fine vessel. Lord Paley, this is my former second-in-command and current proprietor of this island's finest shipwright's yard and repair facility, located on the north pier of this harbor. I am sure the two of you will need to discuss proper terms of effecting needed repairs."

"The finest shipyard, Mr. Delacroix?" Paley asked, puzzled. "Until today I would have sworn that Barbados had no such ship-repair facility. And yet today yours is the finest?"

John smiled as he extended his hand. "Captain Hawkes is correct. We at Delacroix Chandlery and Shipyard are, as yet, without peer . . . or competition," John said with a smile. "Shall we meet over breakfast and discuss the necessary work—and our terms?"

Paley seemed first to shrug, then he nodded and smiled. "A most wise plan, Mr. Delacroix," he said and turned and walked over the gangway to the pier.

John leaned to William and whispered, "Might I convince you to come along, Will? I believe I may need your skills at oratory. I do not think as clearly as you at such an early hour as this."

Will draped an arm over his shoulder. "I would be honored to represent your interests, John—for a small commission of course," he said, laughing, as the two of them followed the gaily clad shipowner, his hat's feathers dancing over his head as they headed straight for the inviting dim coolness of the Goose.

After only a few minutes of negotiation, John and Lord Paley came to an agreement as to the cost of repair to the *Serendipity*. Lord Paley downed the last of his ale and rose to leave, his feathered hat sweeping off more crumbs from the table as he stood and took it in his hand.

He looked back at the two men.

"You are coming to the celebration, are you not? I had heard that Lord Carrington had offered an invitation to the entire crew."

"Yes," Will replied. "It was a great kindness to include us. The crew, as one might expect, is regarding this event with great anticipation."

Paley took a few steps to leave, then turned back. "Gentlemen, would you indulge me for one brief moment?"

John and Will exchanged uncertain glances. Then Will nodded, bidding Lord Paley continue.

"I realize that it is not of my right to do so, but I am an old man, and old men are allowed to have their eccentricities. Mine is for honest speech. I trust that I will not offend you, but I would offer one timely suggestion."

Both Will and John leaned forward, set to listen to a portion of wise counsel.

"I would burn those rags you're now wearing."

Will looked at John, and John looked at Will, both of their faces lined with surprise. Will turned back to Lord Paley, his face a question mark. "Burn this good attire? But why, good sir? Perhaps we are not the most stylish, but these are far from rags," Will said in their defense.

Paley stood back, stroking his chin. "If the truth be told, they are indeed rags. Not slave rags, but rags to a gentleman nonetheless. I beg your pardons, but I am not one to soften the truth. Please—you are sailors, and being suited for the sea is of a different nature than the attire that will be accepted in polite, civilized society and mannered company. If you want to be taken seriously as merchantmen—or even as a candidate for captain of the harbor defenses, Mr. Hawkes, for I have already heard of your intentions—it would be best to start afresh. And that must include a new wardrobe."

John, still examining his outfit, a plain doublet over a plain shirt and breeches, began to protest. His garment was worn and had been mended in a place or two, but it was not the tatters of a barbarian. And perhaps it was only slightly soiled at the neck and sleeves.

"Are not these the clothes of an honest workin' man?" John asked.

"Perhaps," Paley answered as he stared back, "but working men you are no longer. You seek entry into the merchant class, do you not? That is one large step above where you now consider yourself."

The trio was silent a moment.

"I would not deign to order you to reoutfit yourselves, gentlemen, but I would heartily suggest it. Those of you who have the means of purchasing new attire should do so. At the very least, employ your best clothing for such an affair. I would not want any man at any social gathering to be embarrassed by his choice of apparel. The noblemen on this island and the planters and the like put a great stock in fancy frills and feather, as you can see from my outfit. Perhaps you will not avail yourselves to this level of finery, but a new jacket and breeches would no doubt accelerate your acceptance."

Both John and Will turned to stare at each other, as if, for the first time, regarding the true state of their simple and frayed wardrobes. Almost as if on cue, they nodded together as if agreeing with Paley's words.

"There is a wonderful tailor at the end of James Street by the name of Johansen. Mention my name, and he will have new coats and the rest of it made up well in advance of the gala. But I would counsel that you must avail yourselves of his services this morning."

Paley nodded again, obviously pleased with his advice. "Till the celebration, then, gentlemen. I hope that you shall have a good day."

He left the Goose, the door swinging wide, letting the brilliant sunshine stream in in a torrent.

"Well," said Will as he edged to the door, "perhaps we should make a stop this morning. . . ."

He began to walk, with a quicker step, soon matched by his friend John. And in another moment, the two men were laughing, running at full speed up James Street in a race to see who might arrive first to be properly outfitted, so as to easily and comfortably participate in all that island society might offer.

CHAPTER

12

The music was loud and gay and carried in a swell across the greening fields of sugarcane and tobacco waving gently in the warm breeze. The Carrington estate was aglow with torches and candles shimmering in the dusk. The night air was punctuated with lilting and often raucous laughter generated by dozens of early guests, and it rippled across the fields. An octet of instrumentalists, made up of slaves and indentured servants, was performing on the front porch of the plantation residence, providing a joyful welcome for guests as they arrived. The musicians, with nowhere near the polish of proper English-trained musicians, had just finished a more lively rendition of an old alehouse favorite.

In England such frivolous themes and tempos would not be allowed. But all those in attendance at this affair knew that this was not England—not by a wide gulf. Barbados, some four thousand miles distant from the social prohibitions and anxieties of England, lay well beyond the imaginary line that ran north to south through the center of the Atlantic Ocean. It divided the civilized, well-tempered society to the east and north to England and the hot-blooded, tropical, and new society of the Antilles. It was a line drawn between the conventions of the Old World and the limitless possibilities of the New World.

The Americas had a fair share of Puritans, preachers, and reformers. But such men had seldom sailed through the Caribbean. John Williams and his Puritans had settled in Rhode Island, and of course there were the Puritans of Plymouth Rock—but in the Antilles there was but sugar and slaves and rum. Each was equally important to the islands' economies, all vying to be the most valued commodity. That heady mixture all but left the Puritan sensibilities in a whirl.

Men and women lived closer to the edge of propriety on these isolated bits of land so far from the conventions of established society. Ideas discussed and actions performed in these new colonies would often be a direct mockery of the staid and straitlaced constraints that were deemed normal and expected in their English homeland.

For the small group of pioneering, entrepreneurial adventurers who made up the colony on Barbados, all keenly felt the great distance from England and even greater distance from the religious, political, and social turmoil that now marred its landscape.

Following the defeat of the army of Charles I by the Scots at Newburn, a massive breakdown of public confidence in the accepted structure of politics was occurring. Religious zealots marched lockstep through London, with tight grimaces on their faces while London plummeted toward anarchy. After Bishop Laud's impeachment and imprisonment in December 1640, all of society was in turmoil. The king was guilty of questionable acts of policy as well; he had levied money without parliamentary consent and sponsored an ecclesiastical revolution, threatening the very nature of the English Church. His too-little, too-late attempts at peaceful reform gave birth to serious opposition, especially from fiery Puritan orators like John Pym. Pym took great delight in claiming the royal government was in consort with the antichrist and the devil. Pym and his supporters accused the king of conspiring to erect in England a despot who would return the land to Rome and Catholic domination.

These matters, coupled with financial shakiness, caused vast hordes of unemployed citizens of London to take to the streets. Violent riots ensued during that hot summer. And with the lack of a strong man of the cloth heading the Church of England, the pulpits of the churches were now free. Clergymen could pick and choose what observances they liked, restrained only by the wills of their congregations.

John Pym urged Parliament to accept his Ten Propositions. He called for King Charles to replace every current minister with one of the Parliament's choosing. The king petulantly refused. In a deliberate act of defiance, twelve of his bishops were impeached by the House of Commons, found guilty of high treason. The House of Lords whisked them to the Tower. The king could only watch, desperate, as his powers shrank. He took the offensive, accelerating his plans for a military coup d'état. The public responded in an outcry decisively against him.

The king and queen retreated in a blind hurry to Hampton Court, fearing for their own lives. The king secretly hoped to raise support in the provinces—land that was free from the intrigues of London. But he found scant support. Civil war seemed as likely as ever.

The news of these events reached the island of Barbados in a sketchy and disjointed fashion, being brought sporadically by letter and by crewmen of incoming ships. The reaction of islanders was generally that of disbelief, for the distance from their homeland brought an element of unreality to the stories they received. So while concerned, they were unaffected, and for the most part chose to remain neutral in their stance on Parliament versus the king and proceed with their lives and their mission of transforming that wild isle into a civilized plantation society.

For the noble elite and the commoners of Barbados, having Governor Aidan Spenser return safely, with his beautiful daughter Kathryne in tow, was by far a more important event and cause for the grandest celebration in the island's history. What added a zesty spice to the stew was the fact that Kathryne was the first holding noble lineage to arrive with matrimony her unspoken, yet understood, goal.

The welcoming gala, only six short days in the planning, seemed to consume the efforts of the entire population of the island.

From a distance the Carrington house seemed to glimmer and float over the fields, bathed in the golden fires of torch and candle. Cattails and reeds, bound together and soaked in pitch, were staked at arm's-length intervals along the wide drive that led to the plantation home. The flames burned slowly, providing a thick, smoky illumination. The moon was near full, golden and heavy, and what scenes the torches did not illuminate were bathed in its translucent glow. Horses with riders and carriages were winding their way along the rutted and dusty roads that meandered throughout the island. A warm rain had fallen for a dozen minutes that afternoon, tempering the dust.

The Carringtons lived nearly three miles from town, at the far edge of the cultivated properties. Beyond this plantation was jungle and primeval forests. Yet only a matter of time stood between the jungle and the more polite and civilized fields of cane and tobacco.

Will and John were on foot, walking to the celebration, both quiet, their speech muted by their new fine doublets, shirts, and breeches. Will had gone so far as to purchase a new pair of black leather boots for the evening, knowing that his scuffed and nicked ship boots were too worn for such an important social evening.

Behind the two men and a few paces to the rear, like a group of puppies following closely their mother's lead, were the members of Will's crew who had remained on the *Serendipity* and accepted the governor's offer of a full pardon. A few of the sailors had splurged and purchased new shirts or scarves for the affair. Others gamely cleaned and sewed older garments, making them look as presentable as possible. It would be the first time most of them had ever set foot inside such a grand dwelling, and Will had felt ripples of their anticipation and excitement building over the last six days.

And now, wearing Mr. Johansen's new creations, Will and John approached the grand estate of the Carringtons. From the opulence of the plantation, it was most obvious that the Carringtons were of great wealth.

"'Tis a grand house, is it not?" one crewman spoke, his voice low.

"Never been this near such royal folk," added another, his nervousness most obvious.

"I understand that Lady Kathryne will be there," John Tambor whispered. "I most would enjoy seein' her again."

"Just don't you be upsettin' her with your crude behavin'," his older brother, Bryne, scolded, as a reminder to all the crew.

"Crude behavin'! Who you be to call my behavin' ill-mannered! Ain't like you got any fancier ways than me!" John answered loudly and pushed at his brother's shoulder.

"Mind who you be pushin', you big lout!" Bryne answered back, even more forcibly, and returned the shove with a near punch to John's shoulder.

John was about to rear back and leap on his older brother, but a second before the younger Tambor launched himself in the air, Will circled around and grabbed him about the arms, as John Delacroix contained Bryne.

Will shouted, louder than the both of them combined, "I will have none of this tonight! You will both behave like civilized men and resist the urge to butt heads at the drop of a hat! You call yourselves Christian men, do you not?"

Both Bryne and John nodded, their eyes flashing.

"Well, I am certain Christian men forsake combat of this type. That be a true fact!"

Both Bryne and John stood still fuming, their eyes now downcast.

"Now shake hands and apologize to each other," Will ordered. "Do so now or I shall see that you are not allowed to attend this evening's gala. I will see to it that Lady Kathryne will ignore both you brutes."

With that, they looked up and cautiously extended hands, and in a moment all was well.

When they were within earshot of the music, Will stopped and motioned that he wanted the men to gather about him.

"Men, we are being graced with a rare honor. To be asked, as guests, to attend such a grand and glorious event as this at such a noble estate is a privilege. I want each of you to promise me that you will comport yourself in a civil manner," Will instructed. "I want you to promise that you will limit your intake of libations to a minimum. I want you to eat what food that's offered in a polite and civilized manner. Forget how you eat on board for one evening. No feeding at the trough, if you please. Eat as you saw Lady Kathryne eat while we were at our island base. She paused to talk and never opened her mouth while there was food still in it."

John Tambor was most perplexed. "But how will I be takin' a drink of ale to wash it down if I can't be openin' my mouth whilst chewin'?"

"I am sure the food of the nobility will not have to be washed down with anything. I am sure it is finer than you are used to," Will explained.

"Gentlemen, you are the bravest and best sailors I have ever been with aboard a ship. I want you to continue to make me proud by behaving in a manner most unlike a sailor. Pretend that your vicar is standing beside you, watching every move you make. Measure your words and actions this evening against a man of the cloth's sensibilities," Will stated firmly.

He stopped to survey their faces. Their excitement was little dimmed by Will's admonitions.

"Will you do this, men? Will you behave yourselves and do me proud?"

There was silence all around. Finally Bryne Tambor, who often acted as the elder statesman for the crew, spoke up in his soft yet rumbling voice. "We will most certainly try, Captain Will. If any man makes a fool of himself, it will be I and John Delacroix that will toss the offender out without warnin'. I put you all on that alert."

Will stared at each man, his eyes piercing. "Be those orders understood by all?"

His request was met by a low murmur and muttering, but all eventually said, "Aye."

As the group set off once more, John Tambor was heard to mutter, "It not be much of a celebration is all I say. No one can be drunk, no one can be fightin', no one can be havin' much fun, if you be askin' me."

Bryne muttered back, "We not be askin' you, now are we? Just behave like you promised."

■ ▪ ■ ▪ ■

A grand carriage rumbled down from the northwest road, the direction of the governor's mansion.

*Is that the governor's carriage?* Will wondered, his face flushed at the thought of reuniting with Kathryne.

Indeed a man and woman could be seen descending from the carriage, but from where Will stood, their faces could not be made out.

*I wish I knew what was to happen here tonight,* Will thought, as a cloud of unsettled feelings swept across his heart like a cold squall in a rough November sea. *I am sure that we shall not be as familiar as we were when we spoke last, for this will be a large gathering, and time for private conversations may be dear. But I am certain that she will provide to me some sort of sign, some manner of encouragement. Perhaps she will invite me out for a breath of air on a porch and ask me of my progress.*

A grimace set on Will's face. *What if she expects to converse with me during a dance of some sort? She may think I have that skill. I am sure other gentlemen would indeed know such steps and machinations. I cannot dance. I am sure I will be made a fool of in front of all. Why have I not considered this problem prior to this moment?*

As Will's spirits sank lower and lower in a sudden and most unplanned self-pity, a horse galloped up behind the group. The horse whinnied up to a stop, then walked even with Will and John.

Mounted on the handsome Arabian was Geoffrey Foxton. Foxton and Will locked eyes for a brief moment. Will's face communicated dismay at his rival's presence. Foxton appeared first surprised, then annoyed, at the presence of Will. Foxton's horse matched the walk and cadence of the men as if trained his whole life to precisely mimic their pace.

He leaned down from his saddle, the bits of gold embroidery along the sleeves and cuffs of his elegant and rich doublet sparkling in the torchlight.

"Mr. Hawkes," Geoffrey called out, "how surprised I am to see you. I would have thought your 'doctor' would not allow you to attend such festivities with such a serious wound. I trust that you have healed sufficiently so as to have this evening be no threat to your health."

Will hesitated, not knowing how to answer. He knew he should be civil and polite, but in his heart he wanted to snipe at this unworthy challenger for Kathryne's affections.

Finally Will looked up and smiled. "Thank you for your kind concern, sir," he said evenly. "I seem to heal quickly. Perhaps God is indeed watching over me."

Foxton sat up straighter in the saddle and reined the horse away from the crew and Will. "Well, Mr. Hawkes," he said, as if now dismissing a lesser man. "I am glad for your healthy state. Now, if you will excuse me, I will ride ahead. This horse does not take kindly to a slow pace. And in that trait, he is most like his master."

Foxton smiled as he dug his spurs into the horse's sides. The beast whinnied again and took off at a fast canter toward the house, now no more than a quarter mile distant.

From the crowd of sailors Will heard one of the crew say, with a most astonished tone, "That man smelled just as Lady Kathryne smelled, of lavender and lilac. If I hadn't been here meself, I would scarce have believed me nose."

■ ■ ■ ■ ■

At the same time, a rough and battered wagon was slowly reaching the crest of the hill behind Will and his men by perhaps a quarter mile. An ancient swaybacked mare was tethered to an even older rig and was plodding, with great deliberateness, along the road, resisting every effort the driver made to encourage its speed.

"It will do no good, Vicar Petley, to ask the beast to travel faster, for she'll simply refuse. Her steps are as paced as a slow heartbeat, and I have never had her increase her steps above that pace," explained a red-faced Vicar Coates.

Vicar Petley, his face streaked with rivulets of sweat even in the coolness of the evening, slapped the frayed reins against the horse's haunches every few steps in an attempt to increase her speed.

"I would simply appreciate arriving at this celebration before it is over, Vicar Coates," Vicar Petley grouched. "This is my official debut as St. Michael's new vicar, and I would appreciate being prompt. If you had mentioned the fact that the church has in its possession a single wagon such as this is, and a single horse—which back in England would have been dispatched to the knacker's yard several years prior— why, then I might have arranged for better transportation, or at the very least, to have left at an earlier time."

The longer Vicar Petley talked and sputtered, the redder his face became.

Vicar Coates merely smiled a curious half-smile. "Vicar Petley," he replied, "you will find that these celebrations are not punctual affairs. And no doubt this one will continue until well into the next day. A half-hour difference in arrival will cause no one any undue concern."

Petley fumed in silence for another moment or two, switching at the horse several times and producing absolutely no discernible effect.

"Well, that may be, Vicar Coates, for you have been here longer than my very brief stay. But I have been sent to help guide and modulate this island, to bring it closer in step with the morals and practices of our home in England. Arriving punctually is the first step in that process, and I greatly desire to be practicing the dictums that I will be preaching."

Vicar Petley took a large kerchief from his pocket and mopped at the perspiration dripping from his brow, stinging his eyes with its saltiness.

"Perhaps it will be less hot at the plantation when we arrive."

Vicar Coates remained silent, a smile wide on his face. He knew that nothing could be further from reality.

## 13

Kathryne descended from the elegant governor's carriage, holding the hem of her gown in her left hand, her right being held by her father. She smiled at Lord Aidan.

*It is such a wonderful feeling to gaze upon my dear Papa again,* she thought. *When I think of what might have happened. . . .*

A cold shudder slipped past her heart, but for only a fleeting moment. Her memory of that terror was dissipating faster than she expected, as if the coldness of that day was melting in the hot tropical air.

Kathryne stood at the foot of the steps leading into the grand house. She was dressed in an elaborate yellow gown, one of the evening gowns given to her by Lady Pickering. The dress, made of a gossamery fabric, was near translucent if viewed in a single fold, yet when the fabric was gathered and multiplied, the end result simply shimmered and glistened in the candlelight. The gown, shirred sharply about her waist and the bodice—now let out to accommodate Kathryne's figure—was more daring than she had ever worn in England. The edges of the gown, along the sleeves, hems, and bodice, were done in a lace as thin and delicate as a spider's web. Around her neck Kathryne wore a single strand of white pearls with a small locket resting on her chest.

She had applied only the mildest of cosmetics. She knew, within hours of being on the island, that whatever artificial colorings might be effective in England would be near useless in such a hot climate. Rouges, coverings, and creams would simply melt away. Unless she was willing to have the makeup done in a thick waxlike procedure, which produced a deathly pallor, she determined that a natural look would be best suited for Barbados.

She did apply various scents and powders, however. Poor Hattie was assisting in that process, and the dust caused her to stop and sneeze for a quarter hour without ceasing. Kathryne had then promised the watery-eyed girl that such toiletries would be employed on a most selective, and very occasional, basis.

Kathryne stood bathed in the light of the torches and candles, the flickering illumination reflecting off her ivory skin and her deep green eyes. All eyes seemed to stop and find rest on her form. It could be argued, with great truth, that Kathryne was the most exquisite woman on the entire island. Her dark hair, in curls from the humidity, rested lightly against her fair shoulders. Her hair set off her remarkable skin, which glowed almost as though lit from within. Even the octet of musicians wheezed to an unsettling stop when she stepped out into view. After a dozen or so heartbeats, the fiddle and harpsichord wheezed back into sound.

Off to the distance she saw a golden mare canter toward the house. *That is, without a doubt, Mr. Foxton,* she thought, an odd rise in her heartbeat accompanying the thought, *for no one else would ride with that style.*

Geoffrey, true to his word, had not visited Kathryne, allowing her to rest her first six days on Barbados. But he had sent a half-dozen notes during that time, asking if he might provide any service she desired and inquiring about her health and well-being.

*A most thoughtful and caring man,* she thought.

And just behind the golden mare, a large group of men followed on foot, with two men at the lead.

*That would be the sailors of the* Reprisal, Kathryne thought. *And at their lead would be John Delacroix and William. . . .*

At just the thought of completing his name in her mind, an even more curious and fulfilling rush of emotions swept over her body like a hot shower. It was curious what she noticed, what filled her eyes, and what stirred through her.

*My knees,* her thoughts trembled, *seem not willing to hold me upright.* Her eyes welled with involuntary tears.

She turned to her father for just a glance, for she was sure that the beating of her heart, now in a wild gallop, was noticeable to all, even above the music and the laughter about her.

Without thinking, and acting just on feeling alone, her hand raised, first to the bare skin just above her heart. She felt her heart pound, hard and swift beneath her touch. She raised her hand lightly to her lips, and in an instant, the memories of Will's lips against hers washed over her being like a great sea wave. She closed her eyes for a long moment.

"Kathryne," a voice interrupted, "Kathryne, are you felling ill? You look like you have viewed an apparition."

It was Lord Aidan who spoke, and Kathryne opened her eyes and allowed the tingling to ebb from her, its power over her slowly weakening.

"No, dear Papa. It was nothing. Just a moment's tremor as I recalled . . . the events of the past several days. I am feeling most fit, indeed."

And as she said those words, she looked further into the distance and viewed a rickety horse cart being pulled by a very old horse and attended to by two men, dressed all in black.

*It is the vicar,* she suddenly realized. *I had all but forgotten his presence on this island.*

*This portends to be a most vexing evening indeed,* Kathryne thought; and then, in an effort to quiet her racing mind, she closed her eyes for a moment and prayed. *Lord, lead me into the paths thou hast set out for me, for I have lost the map and will depend on thy Spirit as a compass for my life. I am unable to plot my course. Please guide me tonight.*

And as she finished by saying a quick amen under her breath, she opened her eyes to a golden mare sidling up to the porch. Atop the magnificent animal was perched, casual and grinning, a confident Mr. Geoffrey Foxton, beaming back at her. His eyes focused a degree lower than Kathryne thought proper, but soon met with hers, finding intimate rest there.

Will watched as Foxton lifted up and dismounted lithely, grandly taking the hand of the woman in the yellow dress and gently placing it to his lips as he bowed deeply.

*It most assuredly is Kathryne he is greeting,* Will fumed as he picked up his pace, striding with longer steps towards the plantation house, *for he would greet no other woman with such obvious enthusiasm.*

In a moment Will was a dozen paces in front of his crew, and John Delacroix turned to whisper that they best hurry if they wanted to arrive together.

Will heard the sound of a horse loudly neighing and the aggravated cry of someone trying to pull it back to heed. He glanced sideways, not breaking his stride, and caught a glimpse of an old mare pulling a wobbly cart toward a small stream. In the rear backboard lay a vicar, near tumbling off, clinging to the seat between his splayed legs. In the driver's seat was Vicar Petley, pulling and slapping the reins and looking like he was about to curse at the horse's disobedience in veering from the road to take a drink. He was perched at one far side, near to falling, as the cart bounced and swayed along the uneven ground, pitching both riders back and forth.

Bryne noticed their troubles as well.

"Captain Will! Should I be offerin' to help the good vicar? Appears that his horse has bested his efforts at tamin'."

Will slowed for a moment and realized that the two hapless clergymen would be most fortunate if they could even get the mare back to the road, let alone themselves and the cart.

He nodded his head slowly. "If you are pleased to do so, go ahead, and offer assistance quickly. I do not want to delay our entrance to the celebration."

Bryne and his brother, John, bounded through the high grass of the open field and within a moment, after allowing the horse to drink its full, led it, the cart, and two overheated men of the cloth back to the dusty road.

Will had slowed a little, just enough to allow the Tambor brothers to provide the service to the vicars and return to the group so all could enter as one. When he returned his eyes to the house, Kathryne was no longer on the porch, and neither was Geoffrey Foxton.

As Will and John stepped onto the elegant wide staircase that led up to the grand house, the band began to play *Glorius Rex,* the unofficial anthem of the court of Charles I. Other guests quickly emptied from the grand salon to watch the sailors' arrival. At the top of the stairs stood Lord Carrington, regal in a velvet doublet and breeches of deep bloodred scarlet. His shoes glistened, and his shirt was of the finest silk Will had ever seen.

"Captain William Hawkes and crew!" he called out. "Welcome to my home."

And at that, the rest of the crowd began to applaud, smiling and nodding.

Lord Carrington held his arms up to quiet them. "It is because of your bravery and sacrifice that our Governor Spenser has been returned to us, and that his lovely daughter, the Lady Kathryne, is again safe, and that the evil plotting of Radcliffe has been prevented. It is with gratitude that we welcome you this evening."

Will scanned the crowd curving about the steps and down to the drive, looking for Kathryne, but did not see her wonderful face. Lord

Aidan was at the top step with a slight smile. He also recognized Peter Carruthers, William Hillard, George Reading, Conrad Paley, and a few other planters with whom he'd had dealings.

"We are grateful for your gift to the island of Barbados—the rescue of a fair, honest governor, and thus a civil government. I am not one for long speeches, so I will end here and allow others to speak longer after we have had a chance to partake of the food and entertainment of the evening. I will simply close my remarks by welcoming you again to my home."

And with that, he walked the few steps to Will, extended his hand and, taking Will's, pumped it enthusiastically to the cheers and the clapping of the crowd.

"Come in, Mr. Hawkes," he said, pulling Will closer and shouting in his ear over the noise. "Come in and allow me to introduce you to some important planters on our small isle."

And in a soft whisper, he added, "These are the men on whose fortunes hang the fortunes of Barbados. It be most wise that you acquaint yourself with them."

Will was swallowed up by the assembled crowd, leaving only a small wake for John and the rest of the crew to follow him inside.

Will spent the better portion of two hours being led about by Lord Carrington, unable to seek a convenient means of exit, not knowing what might constitute a graceful parting. Carrington had latched on to Will's arm and with a death grip held on as they spoke to planter after planter after planter. Will watched from a distance as a few of his crew stationed themselves at the food tables, a few by the ale barrels, and a few by the group of Irish indentured serving girls who were attending to the guests.

As Will was introduced once more as the savior of Barbados, he turned to hear a great commotion and nervous laughter from across the room. In the hubbub of voices and guffaws, Will noticed John Delacroix being grasped much too firmly and obviously in a most friendly way by Lady Carrington, their hostess of the evening. She was a short woman, with white hair piled above her head in an amazing series of twists and turns, Will thought. The heat, now more intense than before from the effect of so many people in such a closed space, was in evidence on her, as the colors and shadings on her face began to look a bit indistinct.

Her laugh was coarse as she pulled John into the center of the room.

The Tambor brothers and several crewmen were near to his side, all grinning broadly from the ale as well as the attention, Will surmised.

"Now, Mr. Delacroix, I will have none of your shy reticence. You are our guest, and as such I implore you to humor your hostess. It is apparent that we will get no true account of the pirate attack on the *Serendipity* from our Mr. Hawkes. He has no flair for the dramatic, but I am sure you must."

Her voice was loud and shrill, perhaps to be better heard over the general noise.

"But, Lady Carrington, I am not a storyteller. I am a sailor," John cried out, smiling. "I could never mount a story that would do justice to such events."

"Good lady, Mr. Delacroix is bein' most modest," Bryne called out from behind. "When we was in ports, it was he who held us all near spellbound, tellin' tall tales and the like. He be a truly fine one to tell such a story."

John held up his palm. "But Lady Carrington, this tale would pale if told by but a single voice." His eyes were animated as the crowd grew quieter. "I will share none of the story unless I have the able assistance of my friends and fellow sailors."

Lady Carrington visibly brightened. "Then you must enlist your fellows to help," she cried in a gay voice, edging toward a wanton tone. "All were with you as this most heroic event unfolded, were they not?"

John nodded as he looked over the faces of his men, all glistening with a thin layer of sweat, their smiles broad and leering.

"Lady Carrington, they were indeed in attendance. Without them, I would not be here as well."

Lord Carrington detached himself from Will and walked over to John. "Then you simply must recount the story for us, Mr. Delacroix," he implored. "Tell it but just this once, and we will all have our fill of such dashing derring-do. It will be easiest in the long run to heed our requests now."

John hung his head in smiling submission. "Very well," he said, "I will tell the tale. And for our actors this night, the good crew will assume those roles."

Lady Carrington clapped her hands together at her breast. "Yes! Yes! That would be a most stimulating display! Imagine! Acting out a glorious sea battle in our home! Simply grand! Just like the grand masques back home in England."

The crowds encircled their host and hostess and the impromptu acting troupe. John looked over to Will, who had remained at a distance, and from his withering and scolding stare, John realized that his friend would draw no closer, even under the point of arms.

John gathered up the crew. They were laughing and playfully jostling each other like bear cubs tumbling together in the spring.

"I will narrate the action," John said loudly. "Bryne, you may play Captain Will, John may play Radcliffe Spenser, and the rest of you will split evenly between our crew on the *Reprisal* and those of Radcliffe on the *Serendipity.*"

He pointed out who should be on which ship, and the players gathered to each side, whispering loudly as to what role they might play.

Lady Carrington rushed to John, pressing against his side. "May I play the part of the Lady Spenser? Do I move about much? Will I be placed in any danger in our drama?" She gushed at John, her voice trilling like an excited schoolgirl.

At that instant, John caught a glimpse of Kathryne, a row or two behind the front, watching the action with a look that ranged between bewilderment and sadness and contained more than a hint of fear as well. Not yet a fortnight had passed between the reality and this gay melodrama that was about to be reenacted.

John looked away, then nodded to Lady Carrington and told her where to stand. "This chair will be the mast of the *Serendipity,*" he explained, "and to that mast was Lady Kathryne enchained."

Lady Carrington's eyes opened wide. "In chains! How wonderfully exciting," she purred, her face glowing in the flickering candlelight.

Part of the crew, who had been given silver cutlery to use as weapons, and led by Bryne, who had been given a large serving spoon to serve as his cutlass, walked a dozen paces away and huddled closer together to mime sailors crowded on board a small ship. Their audience was hooting and offering shouts of encouragement and advice as to how best to portray their roles.

The remaining crew, banded together around John Tambor, who was playing the evil Radcliffe, did their best to represent his nefarious henchmen and were grimacing and hulking about, hunched over in wicked slouches as their giggling hostess, Lady Carrington, pretended to struggle against imaginary chains.

John stood up tall and began to speak. "If it please your guests, Lady Carrington, may we allow this drama to begin? Good ladies and gentlemen, I will endeavor to help illuminate the events as they occurred."

He reached up and wiped at the sweat on his forehead with his sleeve.

"It began as we lay at anchor all durin' the night, waitin' for the ship bearin' the good Governor Spenser to arrive."

He continued with his narrative, and the crowd hushed and leaned forward as a single unit, forming a tight circle around the impromptu acting troupe.

John spoke of the transfer of gold for their captive and how they saw Kathryne roughly seized and chained to the mast, along with her father. As he spoke of the *Reprisal*'s turning against the wind rather than sailing away, his crew began to shuffle as one unit toward John Tambor and their hostess, chained to her chair.

Speaking in booming tones, he imitated the roar of the cannons, as their shells whipped through the canvas, mere feet above Kathryne's head. He described the chaotic scene as the ships collided in a wrenching screech of wood and iron. With that, the *Reprisal*'s actors shuffling ever closer, pretended to leap from one ship to another and raised their spoons and cutlery in a furious mock combat.

John paused to illustrate a single battle here, with himself and an enemy, and then to another side, when Bryne Tambor tossed an opponent into the sea.

"But then," John's voice cut through the evening like an explosion, "then it was our Captain Will, bravely slashin' his way through the evil crew like the angel of death! As is expected of any captain worthy of his rank, Captain Will would be at the very apex of any and all battles—and this day was no exception."

With that, Bryne leaped from his small crew toward the others and, with his silver cutlery, slowly and with as much drama as he could add, imitated the thrusts and parries of swordplay. In the span of a moment or two, Bryne, acting as Captain Will, had cut a wide swath through the counterfeit pirates, the vanquished writhing on the floor before the wide eyes of a rapt audience.

As the drama unfolded, Will felt the blood rush to his face. It was not a flush of embarrassment, but the sort of flush when one fully confronts the enormity of a rash action. As the full impact of his untold sins played out before his eyes, he caught a small glimpse into the abyss of depravity he had entered as a pirate. The truth of that gulf now welled up before him, and Will felt his blood pound hot and heavy in his body, his heart aching over what might have been.

He looked down, trying to prevent tears of guilt from filling his eyes, and then looked back up again to see the face of Kathryne from across the room. Her face bore no guilt or shame, as did Will's, but was the face of terror, reflecting the horrors of her ordeal. As Will's face was tainted with guilty blood, hers seemed to be devoid of its substance, and she paled, white and ghostly.

John continued his narration, building energy and drama into the scene. Bryne and his brother, John, imitating the final confrontation of Will and Radcliffe, were circling each other, their spoon swords clashing, their eyes locked, Lady Carrington feigning terror at the sight.

It was a scene most worthy of the Globe Theatre in London, and the audience as rapt as an audience has ever become. This play to them was not merely an exercise in theatrics or an elaborate masquerade. Rather, it was a true re-creation performed by actual participants. It was more real than any story might become. This play was as true to them as any real life occurrences might have been.

"And at that moment," John cried out, cutting through the hush as cleanly as a knife blade through tender flesh, "the mast, towerin' above them like a giant tree, now weakened by a cannon shot, began to creak and shriek. The topsail rail snapped like a musket soundin' in the air and began to sweep down, archin' in a wide rush."

Bryne was kneeling, as Will had been, spent and at the mercy of an evil Radcliffe, who was about to deliver a deathblow.

"And at the moment, as Radcliffe raised his blade, the rail swept down with a heavenly vengeance and swept him into the angry seas, where the denizens and sharks have feasted on his bones," John cried, his voice a mix of terror and triumph.

John Tambor leapt backward, falling to the floor, clutching at his heart, his spoon clattering on the wooden floor, then skittered away, coming to rest at the feet of the now-terrified Kathryne.

The crowd broke into wild applause as Bryne released the fair Lady Carrington, who rushed into his arms. Bryne's face immediately reddened, and he looked more terrified than he had ever been in any sea battle prior.

Will looked at Kathryne, only to see her turn and run. She rushed from the room into the cooler evening air of the garden at the rear of the house.

## 14

The party-goers crowded about the actors, congratulating them on a fine performance. Will, now free from his host's attention, headed to the garden doors, running a gauntlet of well-wishers offering plaudits over his bravery.

He shut the door behind him as he stepped into the garden. The noises nearly vanished in the thick tropical night, the lush garden plantings acting as a barrier between the loud coarse sounds of the revelry inside and the calming darkness of the island. He could hear echoes of the crowd's laughter, now even at a higher pitch, and of the musicians playing a spry number.

He looked about, the garden lit by a few flickering torches, most nearly spent. *Has Kathryne run further into the night?* Will wondered with alarm as he rapidly walked through the elaborate plantings, marked with benches, small hideaways, and intimate corners.

Off to the his right, he saw a flicker of glistening fabric. "Lady Spenser?" Will called out, in a soft and gentle voice. "Lady Spenser? Are you there? It is William Hawkes."

As if a spirit materializing, Kathryne appeared from behind a high wall of shrubs and stood, arms dropped at her sides, facing William.

"Yes, Mr. Hawkes?"

She stood before him, unmoving, as if a gentle deer caught in the eyes of a hungry wolf, not knowing if it should run to the left or right, paralyzed by a greater fear.

Will stopped as well, perhaps a half-dozen paces from her, and their eyes met, briefly, before William lowered his, still feeling the shame from the realization of his part in her fractured and tortured journey to this island.

"Lady Spenser," he stammered, his eyes slightly averted from hers, "I saw that as my crew acted out the drama you became most visibly upset. For that, I am truly sorry. Had I been aware of such an effect on your senses, I would have stepped in their midst and prevented them from continuing. I should have said that such entertainment is most unseemly. To make light of such a tragedy . . . I should have shouted that . . ."

"Mr. Hawkes," Kathryne said, her voice much louder and with a shriller edge than Kathryne had desired, "the fault is not yours." She raised her hand to her throat and let it gently lie there. "Our hosts insisted, and you did not participate. I think it would have been most difficult for Mr. Delacroix and the rest to not have done as they were bid."

"But I am injured if what transpired has caused you discomfort," Will said in a further apology. "As if what I have done has not caused enough grief to be born in your life."

Kathryne held up her hand, bidding him to cease. "Mr. Hawkes, you must not continue. Yes, such theater merely reminds me of that day, but its effect will be most assuredly fleeting."

The two stood there in the night, with an occasional laugh or shout faintly filling the silence. The music, now a more soothing waltz, gently flowed about them.

"Lady Spenser . . . ," Will stammered, unable to find the words to proceed.

*How am I to speak of my feelings for this woman? I am a common-born man. How am I to ask further if I may call upon her? How much of a fool was I when I asked if I may see her again that first night on this isle? How befuddled was she with pain and fatigue and sorrow to have agreed with my foolish request?*

"Lady Spenser . . . ," he tried again.

"What is it, Mr. Hawkes?" Kathryne asked, her voice even and calm.

*It is not a time to renew our intimacy—even a coarse lout as myself can view that as truth. She is frightened by the reality of who I was, and I am certain she cannot ascertain the quality of the man I yearn to become.*

She took a step toward him and raised her hand as if to offer it to him, then almost immediately seemed to think better of that invitation to renew a touching relationship, and her hand, barely raised, dropped surely and quickly back to her side.

Will saw her truncated gesture, and in an instant, recognized its true import. *I will not ask of her what she cannot tonight grant,* Will decided.

"Mr. Hawkes?" Kathryne asked, her voice smaller now.

"Lady Spenser, I desire, on this evening, to make a vow unto you."

Will saw her stiffen and lean away from him.

*Yes, I was right,* he thought. *Tonight is not a time for making a request of her to honor her vows of love spoken on the island. She cannot honor them now.*

"Lady Spenser, I make a vow to you this evening. . . . I will vow on my personal honor that I will . . ."

Kathryne audibly gasped, her hand again went to her throat.

". . . never again raise my hand or take arms in an offensive manner against any man. I will promise you that my arm or my blade shall never be raised in anger or in attack of another human as long as I shall draw breath."

Kathryne relaxed and breathed again. On her face were the first signs of relief and comfort that Will had seen visit her countenance.

"But Mr. Hawkes," she said, her voice barely above the whisper of the breeze, "you are mistaken."

It was Will's turn to look frightened. *Mistaken? What could she mean by that?*

"Mr. Hawkes, it is not to me that any man should make a vow—or a covenant. I am but a childish girl."

*You are not childish,* Will wanted to shout. *A child does not capture a man—body and soul—as you have captured me.*

"Your vow is misplaced, Mr. Hawkes. For assurance that a vow will remain unbroken, it must be made to the one who has never broken a vow or a promise. And that one is the everlasting God. Make your vow to God, Mr. Hawkes, and I will be privileged to honor it by being a witness. That is how such things are done."

Will's breath returned to his chest. "Then that will be my vow before the Almighty, to never take up arms again in an act of aggression. I vow that, with you as my witness, before God."

Will dropped to his knees before Kathryne, and that gesture so touched her heart that a tear was in her eye almost as quickly as his knee met the soft earth of the island.

"I renounce the evil of my past," Will prayed aloud, "and the evil of my soul that permitted it to occur."

At that moment a breath of cool sea air poured across the garden from the east, and the music and the laughter were pushed away. At the corner of Will's hearing, not as a voice, nor echo, there came . . . it was like a voice, Will thought, but not like a voice. It was an expression that he felt in his being rather than a sound that filled his ears. He felt it at his fingertips, and it filled him with a clarion call, sharp and clear, the words near visible as if written by the stars across the dark sky: *William. You are my child. You are forgiven.*

And as those simple words were felt, the voice, the call simply slipped away, leaving all around him in stillness. Will cast his eyes to the heavens, his body aglow from the experience.

*The Almighty has spoken to me,* he thought, in a most calm manner. *Those words were from the Most Holy God. I am forgiven!*

He dropped his eyes from the heavens to meet Kathryne's eyes. They were wide and bright.

In a most small voice, as a child speaks in a hushed cathedral, he asked Kathryne, "Did you hear those words as well, Lady Spenser?"

To Kathryne, the words were more distant, like the echo of an echo of an echo, yet they were there, reverberating from the man kneeling before her. Both Kathryne and Will had shared the same perception at that same moment. Kathryne could only nod mutely in agreement.

Suddenly the wide doors of the plantation house were swung open, and the music, laughter, and boisterous sounds washed over the stillness in the garden for a moment, like a huge wave of the ocean crashing against a serene and protected cove.

Will looked up and slowly rose from his knees. He felt empowered, emboldened. "Lady Spenser, I know that we are of two different worlds. I know that the gulf between your nobility and my common origins is as wide as the sea."

Kathryne hesitated, for perhaps a moment too long. A quick response would have comforted Will. Her delay in response caused his heart to tighten in pain. "Mr. Hawkes, your origin is of no consequence to me. I have told you that in the past and in all truth, and I repeat those words this evening."

*She is repeating those words, but they seem much less heartfelt than when she spoke them before,* Will thought. *But no matter, for I must press on or forever hold my tongue.*

"The gulf is there nonetheless, Lady Spenser," Will said. "But perhaps on this island, society may have a different view of what may be proper."

Kathryne nodded. "That may indeed be true, Mr. Hawkes. We are many miles from England, after all."

"And that because of such a distance, perhaps it might be different in this locale than it would be in England." Will's words were hushed.

"Yes, Mr. Hawkes, go on," Kathryne said in reply.

"I have shared more with you, Lady Spenser, than I have shared with any other woman," he said, and reddened slightly from the thought of their kiss—glad that the darkness hid his state. "And I am aware that while our worlds were very different, and still are different—perhaps . . . well, perhaps life on this island may bring those worlds closer together."

Kathryne, again in the voice of a schoolmistress, said, "Why, that might indeed be possible, Mr. Hawkes."

"And perhaps, Lady Spenser, your most kindhearted invitation . . . your most considerate offer to allow me, a poor commoner, to call upon your home and yourself . . . well, perhaps that was not just a figment of my own overwrought imagination. Perhaps there will be a method so as to allow such a thing to take place. I . . . may I ask if . . . that would be proper—to call upon you at some day in the future? Any day of your choosing?"

*I must press forward, for if I stop now, I may never have a second chance.*

"If you need to ponder such a brazen request further, I will most surely understand," he added.

Kathryne stood, mute and immobile again, her brows arched, her thoughts tossed in complication. "Mr. Hawkes, I . . . "

Will thought he heard an edge of fear in her voice.

And from the darkness behind Kathryne came the loud rustle of twigs snapping, and then Geoffrey Foxton slipped from the darkness to a few steps behind Kathryne.

"My lady, there you are," he said in a voice too loud for the stillness. "I thought for a moment you had slipped back to the harbor to sail back to England. No one would have blamed you, following that most outrageous display of melodrama."

Kathryne turned toward him, keeping her eyes on Will for as long as she could. "N-No, Mr. Foxton. I would not think of doing such a thing."

"But you left so suddenly. No one seemed to know where you had gone," Geoffrey said as he looked past her shoulder at William standing a half-dozen paces beyond. "I was most concerned over your safety . . . and virtue as well."

Kathryne said firmly, "Mr. Hawkes and I were speaking of the drama as well. You had no reason for concern, I assure you. Mr. Hawkes is a most Christian man."

Geoffrey tilted his head slightly. "That is comforting to hear, my dear Kathryne, and I too am a Christian man. But a combination of the planters' punch, the moonlight, and a beautiful woman such as yourself . . . well, even the most pious man may prove weak in his resolve. And we are all well aware of Mr. Hawkes' history. Such a history is most difficult for any of us to forget."

The last sentence was said with no attempt to hide its implied threat.

Will stepped one pace forward, his face tight and coiled. "History is of the past, and that is all. If Lady Spenser were to be put in peril by anyone, Mr. Foxton, they would have need to deal with me first," Will said coldly, nearly forgetting for a heartbeat his vow made only moments before.

"I am glad for that, Mr. Hawkes. Most comforted, indeed." He extended his hand to Kathryne, his fingers spread slightly. "Lady Spenser, if you will, our hosts have asked if the two of us might return to partake in a minuet with them. They are most anxious to have you return to the festivities."

Kathryne turned back to Will, her eyes pleading understanding.

*What would a noble gentleman do?* Will asked himself. He gulped once and then spoke. "Lady Spenser, please rejoin the celebration. I will remain here for a moment longer to enjoy the coolness of the evening," Will said with as much polish and enthusiasm as he could muster, realizing that the truth in his words was most transparent.

"Thank you, Mr. Hawkes. I am sure that we will speak on this again," Kathryne added, her voice thin and even.

Will stopped in the darkness and watched the pair go, Kathryne's arm tucked into Mr. Foxton's, as they climbed the few steps and reentered the plantation house. As the doors opened, the laughter and the music flowed out again. Then the garden, as well as the island, fell silent as they were closed once more.

*Almighty God, is this yet another test? Am I to pursue her despite such barriers?*

He shook his head slowly, then lifted his eyes to stare at the moon. In its now brilliant light, the North Star was all but invisible.

## 15

*Unnamed Island,
Caribbean Sea*

"The more I ponder my current travel plans, one fact is inescapable—Florida makes more sense than any other destination," Radcliffe said with a loud voice, even though he was the only human within hundreds of leagues. He sat near the edge of the water, unrippled and cloak calm in the night stillness. His fire, several long steps from the shore, crackled and popped, sending small showers of red sparks circling up into the night sky.

Radcliffe knew he would need to sail north and west to make landfall along the Florida coast. As he traveled, he would pass other islands—Hispaniola, the Bahamas, and other small links in the chain that made up the islands of the Caribbean Sea.

Not one of those landfalls held much promise for Radcliffe. By now, word of his attempted plot to do in his brother and niece would have spread, and all settlements in sympathy with England would have placed a price on his head. *Like a common criminal,* Radcliffe thought. *Imagine being brought back to that witch Kathryne and my foolish brother in chains!*

Even the most remote possibility of that occurring brought bile to his throat and a twist to his thin lips.

"I will not risk myself being made a fool of," Radcliffe said aloud, over the buzz of the crickets. "Unless I am forced otherwise, I will sail to St. Augustine and to my friends there. As the moon begins to fill again, I will start my voyage."

## Weymouth, England

Henry Eames rode his gray cob-footed horse with great care. Eames was a large man who struggled in the best of times to mount any horse, even unconcerned with grace or style as he was. After a night at the alehouse, when deep into his cups, as he often found himself, such a feat was nigh to impossible without the help of a nearby wall on which to perch.

It had been three days since he had taken his full pouch of posted letters from the public house in Weymouth, and he wound his way, from town to town and alehouse to alehouse, heading northwest to Barnstaple and the coast of Dorset and Cornwall in the west of England.

He traveled only the main routes, and then only in daylight hours, for a single rider alone on deserted roads was tempting prey for highwaymen and brigands.

Eames burped so loud his horse picked up its head and cocked its ears backwards.

"Excusin' me, little horsey," Eames slurred. "No harms bein' done to your dainty ears, now is there?"

The beast shuffled its head and snuffled loudly, almost as in answer. As the wobbly rider and horse continued in a rhythmic *clip-clop,* a rise in the green and dappled hills appeared. Eames stood a bit taller in the saddle and craned about to peer over the hedgerow brushing his shoulder, seeking to locate a glimpse of Hadenthorne.

"If it be Hadenthorne," Eames said brightly, "then it must be the Coat of Arms. And I am most partial to their rum flips."

He burped again, and the horse clipped a step or two faster as if in response.

Nestled in Eames's worn leather bag was a rare item—a letter to be delivered to Hadenthorne. In the past year, Eames had stopped in the small Taw Valley town only three times, and two of those times were simply to slake his thirst at the village alehouse and gossip among its patrons.

But this time an actual letter was to be delivered. It would be a special day for someone in Hadenthorne, Eames surmised.

## Barbados

Kathryne returned from her welcoming gala as the dawn first colored the hills to the west of Shelworthy. She descended from the carriage and stood on the top step of the porch watching the sun slip up into the sky, a moment at a time, and she felt its first warming rays on her face.

*It will be such a wondrous feeling to sleep this day,* Kathryne thought, *for as the playwright stated, it is sleep alone that can knit up the raveled edge of care.*

She had searched for Mr. Hawkes the rest of the evening, looking for his face as she danced about with a dozen partners, each less adept at such practiced steps than the one before—or perhaps it was simply a combination of the late hour and the consumption of ale and brandy that affected their feet and timing.

She had danced with Geoffrey several times, and the last she had seen of him that night, as the noise began to crescendo throughout the house, was at the arm of Lady Wycliffe as the two waltzed in a darkened corner of the grand ballroom. After that, Mr. Foxton disappeared into the shadows.

She had stood by an immense table laden with heaps of roast fowl, seafoods of all description, and a grand silver platter mounded with roasted boucan strips surrounded by delicious-looking exotic fruits and vegetables. Kathryne had slipped one small morsel from the mound, careful not to make the rest tumble to the table, and nibbled at the crisp meat. It was then that Vicar Petley had sidled up beside her and had placed his hand upon her bare forearm, all the while smiling widely at her with an unfocused intensity.

"Vicar Petley, I saw you arrive, and it did my heart well to know that you have recovered from your ordeal," she had said with her best, most sincere tone as she had slipped her arm from his grasp.

"My dear Lady Spenser, I thank you for your concern. I am sure my condition was most precarious as I suffered, struggling to regain my health," he had said.

"Kathryne, I know you have not called upon me before this moment so as to not complicate matters between your father and that Geoffrey Foxton and yourself. I recognized that this would be a delicate matter, and one in which I would be most willing to wait upon."

Kathryne had not answered, but had merely screwed her face into a question.

Giles had reached over again and had taken her forearm in his hand, leaving a thin streak of grease from his food upon her skin.

*Would it look so rude if I paused to wipe at that?* she had thought as she felt her flesh tremble.

"Kathryne, I will grant you time in order to sort out the proper response to all of this. I am not a complete fool. I am aware that Mr. Foxton is your suggested suitor—suggested by your father."

Kathryne had remained blank.

Giles had leaned toward Kathryne, not loosening his gentle, but firm grip on her arm. The music started again, and the voices and laughter made polite conversation difficuLieutenant He was within a few hand widths from her ear, his voice warm against her.

"Kathryne, I understand. You must wait for the proper moment to tell your father of us. I do not wish to see him upset—especially so soon returned to his island."

Kathryne had said nothing and was most beleaguered as to knowing what to answer, since it appeared to her that no question had been asked and that she had merely entered into the middle of a conversation that the vicar was having, she having missed the first and most important elements.

He had then placed his hand on hers and whispered loudly, "You will know when it is time to tell your father of us, Kathryne, and then you will call upon me when you do, for we will need to make plans. The parsonage so desperately needs a skilled feminine hand as yours to bring it up to our noble standards."

And with that, he had slipped from her side and greeted Sir Chester Evesham as he strolled across the center of the room.

▪ ▪ ▪ ▪ ▪

In the month that followed that evening, Kathryne spent only a few moments at rest and alone in the quiet, for as the stillness overtook her thoughts, so did the intrusions of her choices. And for once Kathryne decried having too many choices to be decided among. Each clamored and shouted for her attention. Mr. Foxton was most insistent. His notes arrived at Shelworthy almost daily, presented to her on the silver platter held stiffly by the new doorman, a tall ebony-colored slave, Boaz, who spoke passable English, heavily accented by the French tongue. The vicar had sent a half-dozen notes, all cautiously worded and laced with hidden and double meanings, she thought. And Will sent a single note, pleasant and impersonal. It was a most puzzling time for Kathryne, and she would merely glance at each, then place it back on the tray as it was held before her. She would look back into Boaz's face and softly say, "No reply," to each note as it came.

Rather than dwell on that deep sea of decision that would eventually need to be crossed, she busied herself. The first weeks were spent in organizing Shelworthy as a home befitting her father and his position. It was patently obvious that no woman had been consulted on any of the decisions as to the interior furnishing of the home. Radcliffe had been the one making the decisions, and while he had fine taste, he had no understanding of how a house must function for family life and entertaining. Some rooms, such as the women's parlor, were oddly formed and at too great a distance from the formal drawing rooms. All the bedchambers lacked proper chests and washbasins. The kitchen was only barely furnished with the proper utensils and supplies. Rooms on the main floor had been painted, and to Kathryne's critical eye several were in dire need of a repainting, for the colors chosen seemed to have been the choices of the painters rather than the proprietors. The green color in her father's study was not nearly deep enough and seemed too feminine; it called out to be richer, more masculine. The red pigments in the study carried too much pink and needed deepening as well. And the green in the dining chamber was too pungent a tint for comfortable dining, and Kathryne sought out a lighter shade for relief.

A draper had been found to produce window coverings, and while completing the work for the entire house would take several months, at least Kathryne now had finished draperies and bedcovers for her bedchamber as well as that of her father.

To be truthful, she had proven a most adept household manager, for within that first month the house had become a greatly more comfortable and efficient operation. Laundry was being done on a proper schedule. Each room of the home was receiving a regular and thorough cleaning. Food was being stored properly and prepared more in the style that Kathryne and her father found acceptable, and running water had been brought into the kitchen and scullery.

Her father, two weeks after the welcoming party, in the cool of an evening, once broached the subject of Kathryne's future.

"Kathryne, I will try to be most delicate about this matter. I believe I have allowed emotions and sensibilities to have settled after our ordeal at sea. I believe it is time to speak of such matters with you, Daughter, for I would like to see you settled and content. And it is a matter of considerable importance to Mr. Foxton, who has shown admirable restraint."

Kathryne tensed at the mere mention of such arrangements, and a panicked look swept across her face. "But, Papa, the wounds are still fresh. Even my wrists still bear vivid bruises," she said, holding them out for his inspection. "I think that perhaps this discussion is too near such a disturbing event."

Aidan sighed loudly, clearly showing his impatience. "Kathryne, you are a woman now. And as such, and being a Spenser, I believe you must face your obligations with the proper degree of politeness and decorum." He pointed at her as he spoke, much as he had when scolding her as a small child.

"My future is to be hinged on being polite to a man I barely know? I must be charming when being offered as so much dowry?"

Aidan's look softened. "Kathryne, I did not mean my remarks in those terms exactly. It was just that I . . ."

Kathryne's eyes filled with tears, and she put her hand to her mouth and ran from the room, her father hearing her footsteps sound up the stairs to her bedchamber.

*I will never truly understand women,* Aidan thought as he heard her door slam, *for I would consider marriage to such a man as Geoffrey Foxton to be a pleasant thing.*

And upstairs, on her bed, her eyes still tearing, Kathryne wondered to herself, *Why am I so upset over this? Mr. Foxton does appear to be a most respectable gentleman—and most handsome as well. I should be most grateful that such an appropriate man is on this island.*

And yet there was a thought that curled at the corner of Kathryne's awareness, a thought that she had unwittingly prevented from surfacing. That thought was of a man, standing at the edge of the sea, pointing at the moon and the stars, his golden hair lifted by the soft night breeze.

# *January 1642*

William awoke with a start. He reached with his right hand to the thick scar snaking along his left shoulder and hesitated for a breath. He then placed a finger with a feather touch upon it.

*There is no pain,* he thought as he rotated his arm and shoulder.

Every day for the past month, the dull ache that had been there, glowing beneath the scarred flesh, had burned a little less bright. And today, as he blinked in the early morning light, there was no pain to be felt at all.

*Curious,* he thought, *that such things slip away with no notice. At first it was all I could dwell on, whether I would have mobility or face a lifetime with such a lameness.*

Will leaned back and stretched, breathing in great gulps of morning air.

The ship was empty save for him. He had spent much of these last weeks in the business of closing up his sailing ventures. The first day after the welcoming celebration at the Carrington plantation, Will had returned to the ship in a dark and befouled mood, yet within him there lay a resolute determination to make a clean start on life.

*If Kathryne has chosen to exclude me from her life, then I will need get on with mine—and attend to the things that need attending to,* he thought that first morning.

And as his soul tightened, he told himself, trying to convince himself of the thought's truth, *It is for the best, I am sure. In time my heart will recover.*

He had spent nearly a week settling up the shares with the rest of the crew. John's initial assessment had been correct: the largest number of men took their gold and signed up on ships heading back to England, to share their wealth with their families, long in suffering due to the deplorable wages of most sailing men.

A handful of sailors, all from farming backgrounds, pooled their resources and purchased a tract of land on the northwestern coast of Barbados. Their land was a distance from port—nearly seven miles—and inexpensive because of it. Yet their acreage was sizable, and if sugarcane grew as fruitfully there as it did elsewhere on the island, that group would prosper admirably.

The Tambor brothers and John Delacroix established themselves most nicely in their ship repair and chandlery. The *Serendipity* was only one of four repair projects that John had taken on, and they hired on three more of Will's old crew—one as a joiner, and two as rough carpenters. The sounds of sawing and hammering were the sounds to which Will had awakened for the past several weeks.

Will had spent as much time distributing the shares as he did advising the recipients as to its best usage. Owing to his wise and studied business acumen, most crewmen solicited his counsel and recommendations. He had accompanied the men who purchased the land and acreage to examine the location and to help ascertain its fertility and ground waters. He had been with them as they negotiated the price for its purchase. He acted as their barrister when the contracts needed to be drafted. He read to them the codicils and amendments to the legal documents. He had also assisted the two former crewmen who purchased fishing vessels, offering his input as to their fair purchase. He participated in loan discussions for two men who together had needed to obtain a mortgage on another vessel. He also spent a fair amount of time trying his best to speak sense into the handful of men who had seemed to take up permanent residence at the island's alehouses. The newest such drinking place, called the Reprisal's Share, had been started by two more of Will's former crew.

It was of great sadness to Will that of the half-dozen men who had so chosen a rum-tainted lifestyle, only one of them responded to Will as he shared with them the message of change through God's love and power. Will had spent several afternoons talking, cajoling, nearly pleading with each of these men to turn from their fascination with rum and ale, for it was clearly a path leading to destruction.

It was as Will spoke of being forgiven, of having heard the Almighty's voice offering total assurance of his own complete forgiveness of all his sins, that Rinton Lawsoner dropped his tankard and caught his head in his hands and began to weep, copious and unashamed, like a newborn babe.

"Ain't no one offered such a thing to a wretch such as meself," Rinton sobbed between gasps of air. He looked at Will, his eyes full of tears. "You be sayin' this square, Captain? This forgiveness notion not be only for the high and mighty, but for a poor misbegotten sot such as me?"

"Indeed it is, Rinton," Will said, "for my sins are no less evil than yours, nor anyone else's misdeeds. God forgives us all if we acknowledge him and accept the gift of the blood of Christ, his Son."

It was his hurried transformation that most surprised and pleased Will. That day, his eyes still wet from his tears, Rinton gathered up his coins from the stained table of the Goose and soberly signed on a bulky square-rigged fluyt that was headed to the Bahamas and back to England within the week. Rinton spent his last days on Barbados, sober and alert, and promised Will that his ways had been reformed.

"'Tis your doin', Captain Hawkes," Rinton said on the day of his departure. "No other man ever shared with me that truth. My changed life be credited to your good efforts, sir." Will had encouraged him to secure a Bible as his first act when setting down upon English soil.

*And now,* Will thought as he stared out over the placid harbor, *it has come time to set my efforts about my life as well.*

His hand went to the small locket about his neck, nestled there again as a comfort and anchor to his thoughts and emotions. When troubles welled up, a simple touch and a short prayer smoothed the wrinkles in his day.

William had spent little time these past four weeks thinking of Kathryne, yet every waking moment he struggled without being fully aware of the battle in his soul to keep her image from flooding into his thoughts. His last glimpse of her had been that night of the party, as she strolled back toward the house arm in arm with Geoffrey Foxton.

He had spent another long hour in the dark and still garden that night, thinking of what could be and what might have been. Sure that he didn't want to see Kathryne dancing and laughing with Foxton, he had walked away from the plantation house and toward the harbor alone, shadowed only by the silver moon.

It was apparent that no one had noticed his absence at the party for the rest of the evening, for as his crew had arrived back at the *Serendipity* the next day, stumbling and cursing the light, no one had inquired as to his turning up missing.

"You were gone?" John Delacroix had mumbled as he fell into his berth. "After our little play, everything seemed to have increased in speed—eatin', drinkin', talkin'—and more drinkin'. How some of those planters stay upright is beyond comprehension. I thought it be the sailor who could best hold his libations. But now I see it be the planters who put them all to shame."

Will had sent Kathryne a short note, saying he was glad that she was well and that he wished her the best and would most assuredly encounter her in the near future as this island was not large enough to hide from anyone for very long.

He had received no reply, though none was truly expected, for it was merely a polite and social note—not one requesting an answer.

Will had anticipated seeking out the governor a day or two later, to inquire as to the position of captain of harbor defenses, but he was told by the Lord Aidan's new assistant, Daniel Bancroft, that no change would take place for at least one month. Until the current captain of harbor defenses, Ellis Harlan, was tried and either convicted and shipped back to England, or acquitted and allowed to keep his position, no one would be considered for that post.

So Will had busied himself for the past four weeks by settling his affairs of finance while keeping the affairs of his wounded heart hidden and silent.

## 17

The harbor and the hills surrounding Bridgetown filled with fog—a dense, thick, enveloping fog. Not a single ship left nor entered the harbor that day, for every sailor knew that it was unwise to treat the blinding whiteness with anything other than the utmost respect and caution.

Even the laborers constructing the steeple at St. Michael's had stopped their work, fearing their vision too greatly impaired.

"But this work needs to be continued," Vicar Petley sputtered, exasperated at the slow progress of the church. "To lose one day here and another day there for other small excuses is simply untenable. This church needs to be finished!"

Golding Idris, the master builder in charge of the twenty-man crew, wiped his hands, wet from mixing grout, across his dark and stained doublet.

"My good Vicar, I knows that this church needs to be completed, but if any of these good laborers falls from the heights 'cause he can't see the ground, well then, you will be no further along than you be now," he explained in a calm tone.

"You mean to tell me that no further work will be done today because of fog?" the vicar said, incredulous.

Stroking his chin, leaving small gray streaks in his stubbled whiskers, Golding nodded. "We had planned to work up there," he said, pointing to the unfinished steeple, "but now this bad blow of weather prevents that from happenin'. I believe it most prudent to wait till it clears."

As he was speaking, several of the men had packed up their tools and had begun to slip quietly away, toward the Delacroix Chandlery and

Shipyard, where they had been commissioned to add an enclosed shed at the rear of the building to be used as living quarters.

Vicar Petley took a few steps after them, peering and leaning into the fog, attempting to discern their destination. His face was screwed into a tight mask of indignation when he turned back.

"Your men are leaving here because the fog is too thick for work to be carried out, yet they seem to be heading to that pirate's shipyard to work there. I do not understand how they may see there, but not see at this location."

Golding, using both hands to punctuate his words, said in a rapid delivery, "If we works here, the fog be dangerous for the heights and all. If we work there, it be safe, for we be usin' no ladders. To remain at this site, logic calls out that the steeple be our goal, for we cannot work in advance of its completion. It must first be the steeple, then the rest of the roofin'. Be most improbable to happen the other direction. So if we stay, we cannot work. If we go, we can. Does not that make perfect sense to you, good Vicar?"

Vicar Petley felt his face redden in anger. He was near to responding, allowing his true feelings to show, venting his frustrations, but knew that a vicar kept all emotions, especially anger, in tight rein. Instead of shouting, he narrowed his eyes and waved the man off with a long, dramatic, sweeping slap at the open air with his palm. He walked away muttering, as Golding smiled and picked up his carpenter's box, tucked it under his arm, and began to walk through the fog to Delacroix's.

The vicar stormed back into the parsonage, slamming the door so soundly that the glass seemed near to shattering. Mrs. Kreble jumped as he rushed in. She had been a nervous woman to begin with, and life with Vicar Petley had only amplified the boundary of her nervousness.

"Where is Vicar Coates?" he shouted.

Mrs. Kreble cowered and cringed back. "He took the wagon to be visitin' at the Carruthers, I believe. Said to me that no supper was needed for him and he may not be returnin' till the morrow."

"Blessed saints alive," Giles muttered under his breath. "This island and this assignment will be the death of me yet."

He glared at Mrs. Kreble, who seemed to shrink a bit under his stare. "Are there horses for hire in this town?" he asked.

Mrs. Kreble simply shook her head no.

"Any carriages to let? Any four-in-hands? Any hackneys?"

Again the housekeeper indicated no.

"There was this horse that the blacksmithy once hired out," she remarked after a moment.

"And . . . ?"

"But the poor thing was lost to last year's chills."

"The blacksmith?"

"No, the horse."

Vicar Petley narrowed his eyes and set his face in a tight scowl. "Blast it all," he muttered. He looked down at his boots, a new pair he had purchased a week prior, the only pair left on the entire island, apparently. And no cobbler had yet set up shop in Bridgetown. The vicar's previous pair of boots, mottled and moldy, were the only pair that he had left from his voyage to this island following his abduction with Kathryne and subsequent rescue. All but a satchel of vestments, heavy and hand-tailored in London, had been lost to the hungry sea.

*I will not sacrifice these boots on our muddy roads,* he thought to himself, *for good footwear is too dear for such trekking.*

"Does Vicar Coates have an extra pair of boots, Mrs. Kreble?" he asked.

Her eyes opened wider. "I . . . I . . . do not believe he has, Vicar Petley," she stammered.

He stared back without a blink. "But if he had, they would be stored in his room, would they not?"

Mrs. Kreble took a step to place herself between the steps to the second-floor sleeping quarters and the vicar. "I . . . I . . . do not think they would," she said.

The vicar brushed past her and bounded up the steps two at a time before she had a chance to protest.

From halfway up the steps, she called after him. "Vicar Coates will be most upset if you be takin' his boots, good sir. I do not think he would like that occurrin'."

Vicar Petley appeared at the top of the steps wearing a tall set of black leather boots, near to his knees. He turned an ankle and lifted his heel. "Most striking boots," he said, "and the fit is perfect."

He walked past Mrs. Kreble and, as he closed the door behind him, called out, "If anyone should ask, I will be on a visit to our noble governor at his home. I will not return for supper, for I am sure the food at Shelworthy is a sight more palatable than here."

It was a walk of nearly two miles north to Shelworthy, along a rutted trail that paralleled the shore several hundred yards inland. The fog seemed to creep into every crevice, wetting surfaces with a thin skin of dew. The roads, never far from muddy, forced the vicar to muck from one side to the other, seeking the driest route. To walk off to either side was often impossible, as they were marked with slick wet grass, moss-covered rocks, and sharp, flinty coral—a most inviting place to slip and fall. In a few minutes, Vicar Coates's boots were muddied and soiled past midcalf.

As he marched along the road, heading for an unplanned and unexpected call upon the governor, and of course, on Kathryne, Vicar Petley ruminated on his first month of service as the head vicar of Barbados.

It was true that his thoughts had remained addled for the first few days after his arrival. It was not until the governor's welcoming party that he felt truly fit and whole, despite a number of bruises remaining. His talk with Kathryne had gone well, he thought, and it gave them both the luxury of waiting. He knew that Geoffrey Foxton was the intended match, but that Lord Aidan would have had no way of knowing that another member of nobility—and a man of the cloth, no less—would be interested in seeking his daughter's hand.

*There is no comparison between us,* Giles comforted himself, smiling a hidden smile. *We are both of noble lineage, but I am a vicar, and he is just a farmer—a grass-comber, as I heard the sailors call planters.*

After the celebration, the vicar jumped into the ongoing construction of St. Michael's Church, designed to be the largest English church in the New World. He preferred to call it a cathedral. The foundations had been built, the framing was nearly complete, and the steeple at the far northern end of the nave had been started. Waiting in a massive crate on the muddy ground was a grand polished bell lying in wait for the steeple to be completed. *Such a sound it will make,* the vicar thought, *when it first calls men to worship on this heathen-tainted island!*

Managing such a building project was a complex task for any man, and Giles thought himself as fortunate to have studied architecture and drafting as part of his education. While not a skilled draftsman or planner, nonetheless he was adept in making certain that the craftsmen were accomplishing the details that such an edifice required.

Complications abounded during the weeks after Giles assumed leadership of the undertaking. Most had to do with two major distractions. One was that the supply of skilled tradesmen was short, and Giles had to put up with the temperamental foreman, who indeed had his pick of projects to labor upon. And more important was the chronic shortage of building materials, such as nails, quality hardwoods, slate, mortar, finishing hardware, and the like. When a shipment arrived in the harbor, it was not unusual for planters with construction underway to row out to the ships before they set anchor in the harbor and bid exorbitant amounts of gold for entire cargoes. These unscrupulous men were not averse to letting the cathedral construction suffer a shortage as long as the building of their massive homes stayed on schedule.

Giles had sent Kathryne several notes over these weeks, none of an intimate nature, of course. *One never knows whose eyes may happen upon such correspondence,* the vicar thought, recalling the time in London, at the chancellery, when he had come upon the archbishop holding up sealed envelopes to the sun, trying to gauge their contents.

Giles was not upset, but puzzled, in an inquisitive way, as to the reason that Kathryne had returned no notes to him during this time. *Perhaps she considers such an action as too forward for a gentlewoman such as herself to engage in,* he told himself.

The fog was thicker and heavier the further north Giles walked. At one point along the way, he heard slaves musically chanting as they worked a field by the road, the fog so thick as to render them formless, save their strong, rhythmic voices drifting along the muddy road.

By the time Giles arrived at the gate to Shelworthy, he was bathed in sweat and wiped at his face with a large kerchief. The day was not yet hot, but the closeness of the air fell about him like a humid blanket. His dark vestments were stained even darker along the middle of his back and under his arms.

He walked up the roadway, the crushed oyster shell crackling with a liquid crunch under his borrowed boots, now muddy to his knees. He lifted the brass, shell-shaped door knocker and heard it sound loudly through the house. The door opened a slight crack, and Giles saw a single eye peer through the small opening. There was no welcome, no greeting, and the door did not open further.

Giles, perturbed, forced himself to remain composed. "Is the Lady Kathryne Spenser in residence? May I inquire if she is taking visitors this day? I am Vicar Petley, and wish to, perhaps, to have a tête-à-tête with her."

The door neither opened further nor closed, nor did the person behind the door make any attempt to fetch Lady Spenser.

"Well?" the vicar asked, his impatience rising.

"You wants Lady Kat'ryne?" the person behind the door asked in a nervous tone.

"But of course," he sputtered. "What do you think I said?"

From beyond the door, Giles heard a lilting, cheerful, most feminine voice—unmistakably Kathryne's—call out, "Hattie, has someone knocked at the door? What are you doing there? Where is the door-man?"

The eye disappeared for a moment.

"Der be a man here for you, bein' all in black with muddy boots," he heard her call back. "And I don't knows where be Boaz."

"Well, Hattie, do open the door," Kathryne said. "It is most rude to let a guest stand outside."

With that, Hattie swung the door open wide and stood back to one side. The vicar took one step inside as Kathryne stepped out from the hall. They both stopped where they stood, Kathryne's hand jumping to her mouth, a smile warming the vicar's face.

"Kathryne."

"Vicar Petley."

*Vicar Petley? Not Giles?* he fumed to himself, his concern quickly rising. *Why not Giles—unless she chooses not to be familiar in front of a slave. Ah, that must be it. Good, good, keep such intimacies from the prying ears of the staff. That would be most proper.*

Kathryne lowered her hand quickly, then walked toward him, extending it to him. "Vicar Petley, how wonderful of you to call, and so unexpectedly as well. What a most pleasant . . . surprise."

"Kathryne, you look most robust. I am assuming that you have suitably recovered from your ordeals?"

She hesitated a moment, then replied, "Why, yes, thank you. I am feeling most fit."

"And you have settled in at your new home?"

"Yes, I have. It is a slow transformation into a home, but progress is made day by day."

They both stood there, a few feet apart, and the quiet between query and reply was deafening, virtually filling the house and the two of them with an absolute silent roar.

At that moment, Lord Aidan walked from his study. "Ah, Vicar Petley," Aidan called out in a cheery voice. "How wonderful for you to drop in on us. Are you well?"

Aidan walked up and, with a vigorous grip that was not returned with like power, shook the vicar's hand in a warm and enthusiastic greeting.

"Thank you, Governor, for inquiring as to my constitution. I have recovered in time following our harrowing adventures. I am glad to be able to venture forth and to begin to call on those who are in St. Michael's parish."

"Splendid indeed," Aidan said. "You will be joining us for our midday meal, then, will you not? It would be a privilege to share our table with you, good Vicar."

Giles noticed a fleeting but distraught glance from Kathryne to her father. It was obvious that the governor had not noticed, as he clapped the vicar on the back and insisted that he be given a short tour of their new residence.

"Well, Vicar, as you will see, some of our rooms have yet to be finished—but what with a shortage of skilled hands on this island, I think it is a complaint that is echoed by more noblemen than merely myself," Aidan explained as they walked into his study, still lacking in chair rail and crown molding at the ceiling.

"To be true, Governor, it is a problem that perplexes me as well. As you know how anxious I am to have the cathedral finished. Even today the laborers, because of the fog, claimed working on the steeple to be dangerous and left the site at morning, only to go to work at the new chandlery yard."

They spoke of trivial affairs as Aidan led the vicar around the house, ending the tour in the dining chamber. During the long, elaborate midday meal, Giles and Kathryne's father spoke at great length, with Kathryne only a quiet bystander. The two men commiserated with each other over the frustrations of completing building endeavors on Barbados. Lord Aidan reassured Giles that he would use all the power and influence available to him because of his office and ensure the prompt completion of St. Michael's.

"After all, I would like such a royal edifice to be completed by spring. It would be a most inviting place for a wedding to occur," Aidan explained.

Giles looked at Kathryne, and Kathryne looked in a panic at her father and then back to Giles. The vicar was about to make his desires known to the governor, but before he could get the words out, Kathryne's voice filled the silence.

"Father, would you excuse the vicar and myself for a spell? It would be so pleasant if he and I could spend a quiet moment together—not speaking of troubling matters like buildings and shortages." Her words came in a fast stream, and her face grew flushed.

Aidan looked up, surprised, then smiled. "Of course, Daughter. I have forgotten for a brief moment how much you and the vicar have endured together. By all means, I will take my leave, for I do have much correspondence to attend to. Good day to you, Vicar."

As he walked away from the table, he added, "Vicar—may we have the pleasure of your company at our evening meal? Lord and Lady Wycliffe will be in attendance, as well as Mr. Leon Codrington. Please say you will stay until then."

The vicar smiled and nodded. "I would be delighted, Governor. Most delighted."

Kathryne settled onto a small bench on the porch, and the vicar selected a pewlike bench with a tall backrest and winged sides, adjacent to her. The fog had thinned some, but the stand of palms at the edge of the drive was still lost in whiteness. The sounds of the day were muted in the softness, and a silence descended on the two for several long minutes as they sat, still and hushed.

The vicar coughed, and Kathryne looked up at him, her eyes wide.

"Kathryne . . . ."

She heard no question and did not speak.

"Kathryne, it is true, as your father stated, we have shared together a most dramatic episode in our lives—more drama and tragedy than most people would dare experience." He looked out to the whiteness. "Kathryne . . ."

She held her response.

". . . I am sure that St. Michael's and the new parsonage will be complete by spring. The exterior structures shall be in place in a matter of weeks, and the interiors will soon follow. Kathryne, I am not a man who has the sensibilities to know the needs of such a residence. I . . . I would like you to assist me in selecting the proper colors and furnishings and such. I see evidence of your skill in every room of this wonderful house. Would it be too much an imposition if I were to ask for your assistance?"

Kathryne kept her jaw from dropping. This was not the request that she thought would be voiced. "But of course," she quickly replied. "I would be most delighted."

"And, Kathryne, there is something else as well."

Her smile froze.

"When St. Michael's is completed, I would like to propose something that I know you hold as precious as do I."

*This is the question that I most fear,* Kathryne thought.

"I would like to begin a school for the children of this island. I realize that there are few children as of this date, but with more settlers, more will come. And they will need a proper school. Would you agree to assist me in this planning as well?"

Again, she kept her jaw together and her face a plain mask. *This is most surprising,* Kathryne thought, relieved. *Most unlike the man I knew on the island of our captivity. Such a pleasant change in his demeanor and attitude. . . .*

"Of course, Vicar. I would be so honored to continue to be able to help teach."

And then he leaned forward. "Kathryne, there is one more thing."

*One more request?* she thought, panicked again. *Is this the question I most fear?*

"There comes a time in every man's life when thoughts must be focused on the future and what is best for a comfortable and pleasurable existence."

She remained silent.

"You and I have been through much together, Kathryne, and I think it only proper that I ask your father for the right to call upon you as a potential suitor. I desired to inquire of you first before I made that request of the governor."

He leaned back, all but hidden in the bench. "Kathryne," he said as he swung his arm out to punctuate his question, "shall I ask your father for that permission?"

Just as he swung his hand out, Hattie appeared, carrying out a silver tray with petit fours and a full pitcher of sweet island punch. His hand struck the maid's thigh, and she shrieked, thinking it was some animal that ran into her leg, and nearly tumbled to the ground as the tiny cakes and the pitcher and most of its contents splashed across the vicar.

As the vicar leaped up, swiping at the sugary liquid that drenched his chest and face, the Wycliffe's carriage trudged up the muddy trail and turned onto the drive leading to Shelworthy.

"Vicar, we must get this cleaned off of you at once!" Kathryne called. "Hattie, please fetch a towel and a basin of water quickly."

Then turning to the vicar, hiding all traces of the smile that was determined to creep onto her face, she said, in as calm a voice as she could manage, "We will need to speak of this matter at a later date, Vicar Petley. I am sure we will not have the privacy needed this evening."

As she dabbed at his vestments, she whispered a quick prayer of thanksgiving for what may have been God's kind—and humorous—intervention in her predicament.

CHAPTER

18

*February 1642*

The heat rippled off the dusty road in undulating waves. The afternoon grew hotter and hotter, and even the birds in the dense foliage that lined the road were still and quiet. The sun seemed to hang in the sky like a giant's fire, wrapping its hot fingers around all that moved about that day.

Will walked slowly, sweat dripping into his eyes. He had taken off his doublet and carried it, along with his formal captain's coat, as the heat worsened. He stopped at least twice and walked to the shore, splashing the warm turquoise water onto his face. It cooled him, but in a moment the heat seemed to intensify even more.

*I must be a fool to take this walk today,* he said to himself, *but I have procrastinated long enough.*

When he had started out, his boots had been clean and his coat and doublet laundered. His hair had been trimmed shorter and was secured at the back of his neck with an attractive tie he had purchased from Mr. Johansen's shop. In the distance, Will saw Shelworthy shimmering through the heat. By the time he reached the main gate, his shoes were dust covered, sweat had darkened his shirt, and his hair hung in wet strands on his face. He pushed his hair back into place and flagged his doublet and coat in the air a bit, trying to dry them as well. But he soon realized that the air was too heavy with moisture to allow any cloth to dry.

His boots crunched on the oyster-shell drive. The sound brought his heart up short, for it was only weeks prior that he had walked Kathryne up this short drive, on the night they had first returned to Barbados.

*And she said I may call upon her,* he thought, his heart paining at the memory. *Well, it followed such tumultuous events that I do not fault her for not knowing her own heart.*

His steps sounded loud in the hot stillness. *And I do not blame her, but myself, for not realizing the lunacy of my supposing that a person of my low standing could think establishing a social relationship with a member of the nobility such as Kathryne was possible.*

This thought was the same one that he had held in his mind for the past long weeks, repeating it over and over again, so as to lead his soul to believe its truth. It had nearly worked.

He stopped a dozen paces from the house, scanning the windows to see if Kathryne was visible at any of them. As his eyes jumped from one opening to the next, his heart lurched at each stop as well.

Desperately wanting to gaze once more upon her face, he also desperately wanted to avoid the pain that such a sight would bring, for he knew that he could never again gaze into her eyes, never have her hand in his, never feel the gentle pace of her heart against his.

He stood, still and silent, and blinked his eyes. And with all the strength he could muster, he reached into his heart and turned a part of it off, for he realized that it could never be again.

He looked about and gathered up his courage, allowing his heart to slow. He reached up and lifted the heavy brass door knocker forged in the shape of a large shell, and let it fall against the door. It echoed loudly from inside, and William felt transported, back to the time when he and Vicar Mayhew had petitioned Lord Robert Davis for his first naval posting.

*That was more than a lifetime ago,* he thought, *yet here I am again, petitioning the nobility. And once again they hold my future in their hands.*

The door swung open, and a tall black man peered down at William. "*Oui?* What is it that you seek?" he said in stilted English.

"I am William Hawkes, and I have an appointment with Lord Aidan. I am certain that he expects my call." *And I am sure that Kathryne, alerted to my coming, will not be seen this day.* A series of notes had traveled back and forth between the two men, requesting the meeting and agreeing upon a time.

"*Oui,* please if you will, to follow me."

After a short walk down a hall hung with ornately framed oil paintings, Will entered a large room. Its paneling was thick with dark green paint, and heavy, bloodred damask curtains hung at the windows. The governor sat behind a massive wooden desk. As Will had suspected, it was hotter than the outside, for the windows allowed the sun to stream in, but were closed to whatever breezes might be offered by the sea.

Lord Aidan, dressed in a simple yet elegant weskit, stood at Will's arrival. He extended a hand to William, revealing that his shirt literally clung to him from the heat and sweat.

"Mr. Hawkes, I am so pleased that you have called," Aidan soothed as he came around the desk. "I have been anticipating your visit for several weeks now."

Will nodded and sat in the chair that Aidan indicated. "I, too, Governor, have looked forward to this meeting," Will said, trying to match Aidan's polite tones and inflections.

Aidan slid a second chair toward Will and sat, facing him closely.

"I understand, Mr. Hawkes, that you seek out an appointment from myself," said Aidan as he folded his hands in his lap.

*Should I fold my hands as well?* Will thought in a panic.

"Yes, Governor Spenser, that is correct," Will said, and then folded his hands as he had seen Aidan do. "I knew that you would make no changes until the trial. And now that Ellis Harlan has been found guilty of conspiring with Radcliffe to commit treason, that appointment as captain of the island defenses must now be open. I have come to ask, humbly, if I might be considered for that same posting, now vacant."

Lord Aidan looked down at his hands for a long moment, then back to William. "Mr. Hawkes, you have been granted a pardon by this office, but I am reminded that you have once been a lawbreaker—of the most serious sort, I might add." Aidan brought his hands up to his face, as if praying, then dropped them back to his lap. "Why, good sir, should such a position of trust and authority be extended to a person like yourself?" he asked.

William had anticipated such a question and had prepared a studied response.

"It is true, Lord Aidan, that I once was such a person, a highwayman of the seas. But that has changed. My heart has changed. My soul has changed. It was the Almighty who changed it. I could no more conceive of such acts today than I might determine to fly in the skies as a bird."

William looked at Aidan, hard and without hint of cowering. "I am a new person, Lord Aidan. I have made a vow, a vow to . . ." Will stopped short, knowing that to mention Kathryne's name now would be ill timed. "I have made a vow to God that I will honor him in all that I do, sir, and I will do all that is necessary to keep that vow."

Lord Aidan remained silent for a moment, as if in thought. "And your qualifications?"

Will outlined his training in the English navy, his studies of architecture and building, his skill at commanding men, his business acumen, and his desire to make Barbados his home—and as such, a securely protected, well-guarded place.

"Mr. Hawkes," Lord Aidan said, as if in summation in the House of Lords, "I am sure that it comes as no surprise to you that I have taken the liberty to speak with several people of your character over the past weeks. I have interrogated planters you have had dealings with and officers aboard your vessel. I must tell you, good sir, that to a man all have extolled your abilities and changed character. I take their word in good stead."

He paused again, and silence filled the room. Will heard laughter from somewhere below, perhaps the kitchen, and wondered if Kathryne might be down there, out of sight and awaiting his departure.

"Mr. Hawkes, I am casting a most unorthodox nomination this day, for I am offering you the appointment as captain of the defenses of the island of Barbados. I am trusting in you, Mr. Hawkes, and trusting that God has indeed changed your soul, for this is not a position to be taken lightly. Be informed that this post administers only the island's defense. The harbormaster duties have been granted to Barnum Griffith, an innocent who had been appointed to the position just as my brother Radcliffe began to plot his treasonous acts."

Will felt a stream of relief immerse his being. *At least something in my life is settled.*

"Lord Aidan, please rest well, for I know that God has done his work in me, yet I admit that I have much to learn of his Word as well as the intricacies of defense."

The two men conversed for another quarter hour about matters pertaining to the construction of the fort, the garrison of Royal Marines, and necessary supplies.

Then Lord Aidan remained silent for a moment, and Will waited for him to speak.

"Mr. Hawkes, I am not sure how these words shall be most properly phrased, for I have little experience in what I am about to bring up."

Aidan looked, Will noted, very uncomfortable. "Lord Aidan, please be most free. I am at your command."

"This is a most personal matter, Mr. Hawkes," Lord Aidan said, his voice hushed. "But I feel that I must broach this subject now. Mr. Hawkes, I love my daughter more than any person or possession in this world. I want you to be aware of that."

William, with a most puzzled look upon his face, merely nodded.

"And a father's responsibility, his charge, is to see that his child receives all that is her due in the world."

William nodded again.

"Mr. Hawkes, I will be blunt, as sometimes a father must be. I know that you and Kathryne have shared . . . have shared some . . . kindness in the past—kindness to each other while she was your captive, I must remind you. I am aware that Kathryne helped you to acknowledge the need for the almighty God and that she feels a certain sense of gratitude over the fact that you so courageously risked your own life and fought to save her life, as well as my own."

William gulped. "Yes, sir. Those facts are most plain to me."

"Mr. Hawkes, I simply wish to state to you . . . to remind you that Kathryne is a woman of noble birth and as such, she is a woman destined to continue her noble lineage."

In a smaller voice Will answered, "Yes, sir."

"And while I rejoice over the change in your heart and soul, I must, in all honesty, remind you of the fact that you are a . . . you are a pardoned criminal. I know that God can change a man's heart, and I am sure he has changed yours, Mr. Hawkes. But the fact remains that you were once a brigand of the seas."

William resisted the urge to hang his head and merely nodded.

"It is not proper to say that Kathryne somehow deserves the privileges that will accrue to her, but, Mr. Hawkes, you must admit to me now that . . . that she . . . she simply cannot know you on a social level."

Will felt his heart scuttled as Lord Aidan spoke. He had known that these words would some day be spoken, and he expected to hear them. But yet—yet there was that tiny sliver of hope in that hidden part of his heart that grimly clung to the possibility that Kathryne, a headstrong woman, would see such matters in a different fashion. He hoped and prayed that her will would be strong and that she would request—even demand—a more fair hearing of Will's intentions.

*Perhaps she has done so,* Will thought in her defense, *and perhaps such actions were simply overruled by a stern father.*

It was quite apparent that such an outcome, an outcome that included the names William and Kathryne in the same phrase, was merely a fool's dream, a trifling of a misdirected man who dared to aspire beyond his position.

Will pulled himself upright in the chair and, in an unflinching voice, said, "Lord Aidan, again I must tell you to rest with my assurances. I have realized that fact as well. I am not such a dreamer that I cannot

see the reality of life and social conventions. I am gladdened that
Kathryne is back in her world, and I in mine. I will do nothing that
impedes her happiness."

Aidan looked away, then stood up, signifying that their talk was at
an end. "Mr. Hawkes, I am gratified to hear such a response," he said
with finality. "I look forward to receiving from you a report on the
status of the defense matters we have discussed. After all, Mr. Hawkes,
who better to foil a pirate than a pirate?"

Lord Aidan extended his hand. "Until then, Mr. Hawkes, I bid you
farewell."

And with those words of blessing, William walked out of the stifling
heat of the governor's office and strode into the seething tropical
afternoon, his soul now chilled to its core.

## 19

Moments after Will was dismissed by Lord Aidan, Geoffrey Foxton slowly rode up to Shelworthy. Geoffrey arrived in a shimmer, looking crisp and fresh, though his horse was slick from the heat.

He dismounted and tethered the mount in the shade of the house. He patted its neck and pulled his hand back, wet from the animal's sweat. As he climbed the stairs, he shook it off in the air and finally wiped his palm across the thigh of his britches, leaving a thin watery streak across the tan fabric.

Geoffrey grabbed the shell knocker and banged it against the door firmly, a sense of purpose guiding his hand. He had the look of a man setting out after a goal, a man on a mission.

Lord Aidan greeted him warmly. "Geoffrey, how pleased I am that you have called upon Shelworthy," Aidan said. "I have not seen you since our welcoming gala, and that was more than a month past."

The two men sat in the same chairs and in the same positions as had William and the governor only moments before.

"I have heard that the second sugar press has taken a great deal of your attention, so your absence has not caused me alarm. But it shall if such an absence continues," Aidan added.

Geoffrey wrinkled his brow, confused.

"But, Governor, I have written several dozen notes to Kathryne requesting a dinner engagement, attendance at a small gathering of noblemen, or even an afternoon conversation—but to this date, she has said no to all my requests. As a matter of truth, she has only answered my notes when a direct question has been posed."

Geoffrey saw Lord Aidan's face blanch, the words obviously taking him by surprise.

"Therefore, Lord Aidan, I have come to you seeking an audience to determine what it is that I have done wrong. I thought, perchance, I may have offended the Spenser family in some way, and that these refusals of my invitations were in retaliation for a perceived affront on my part."

Aidan's mouth moved, but no words had yet to be spoken.

"I know that Kathryne has suffered much at the hands of that pirate Hawkes, and that if time were needed to heal such wounds I would be most willing to allow time to pass." Geoffrey leaned forward, his face only a short distance from the governor's. "But, kind sir, I am most puzzled by this. Am I to continue to assume that you still seek a combining of our two names, or has Kathryne, or you, decided to the contrary?"

Aidan held his hands apart, his palms upturned. "My dear Geoffrey, this has all taken me most by surprise. I had no idea that Kathryne has rebuffed so many efforts of yours. I would bring her down to explain such actions, but she has chosen to spend today with Lady Pickering."

Geoffrey stood and walked to the window. "Lord Aidan, forgive me, for I did not mean to surprise you. I had assumed that you had full knowledge of Kathryne's sensibilities, and that her responses had been in accordance with your wishes. I most humbly ask your forgiveness, for I seek not to disrupt the harmony in the Spenser house."

Geoffrey had turned to face Aidan, the sun streaming about him, framing him in a golden silhouette. Aidan then arose as well, balancing the perceived power of a standing man.

"No, Geoffrey, it is I who should be asking forgiveness. For my daughter to have snubbed your attentions such as she has is most uncivilized. I will speak firmly with her when she returns, and I will set this matter straight."

Geoffrey realized that his tack was veering in a most dangerous direction. To have such a spirited woman as Kathryne forced to be civil to a suitor was a most vexing situation. *True,* he considered, *we would then be together, but I think that our relationship would be most cruelly strained and tense. No, this will not fit in my plans at all.*

"Good sir," Geoffrey said as he walked up closer to Aidan, "I beseech you not to reprimand the poor girl. I am sure that she would obey your wishes, but her obedience would stand upon the heels of resentment and anger. That is no method of beginning a life together."

Aidan looked perplexed and sat back down. Absently he picked up a solid glass paperweight from Venice and looked at the prism formed in the sunlight.

After a moment of silence, he looked up. "Geoffrey, it is true that my daughter has been at sixes and sevens these past weeks, as indeed have I, though her period of captivity has scarred her all the more. Only time will allow the wounds to heal."

Geoffrey nodded in agreement.

"But I also admit that I scarce understand the workings of the feminine mind," Aidan said as he dropped his hands to his sides in an expression of frustration. "I am sure it comes as no surprise to you that Kathryne possesses a keen intellect and has perhaps the most skilled sense of judgment when it comes to business dealings, save a shrewd trader or two in London."

Geoffrey nodded again. "I humbly agree. I have encountered few women that could be her equal in her mental abilities or appearance."

Aidan stood and walked behind his desk, stirring and straightening his stack of papers. "But the vexation occurs when we talk of other things, Mr. Foxton. She has finished the last details of this house with great skill and has trained the household servants, as well as the slaves, in how to operate and maintain a proper order as expected by a member of the noble class."

"Most admirable, Lord Aidan," Geoffrey assented, "and I envy you the domestic skills she has brought to Shelworthy."

"And as we speak of other things," Aidan continued, "such as the relationship between her and yourself for a single example, she holds her wrists out so I can view her all-but-faint bruises and cries that the wounds have not yet healed. And then she runs from the room in tears."

"Those scoundrels," Geoffrey all but spat.

Aidan sat back at his desk in a clump, his palms held out and up. "I do not know what direction to take to steer her soul and heart back to what is best for the Spenser and Foxton families."

Geoffrey walked over and perched on the corner of the large walnut desk, on the corner that had begun to warp ever so slightly on the humid island.

"Lord Aidan, be not troubled, for I know how perplexing the feminine mind can be. I have," Geoffrey said with a straight face, "garnered a smattering of experience in matters such as this. For until we met and discussed the future commingling of the Spenser and Foxton lines, I have 'sat at several tables,' as they say. I believe I may have a worthy solution to our current quandaries."

Aidan looked up, squinting into the sunlight that now poured directly into his face. "And good sir, what might your plan be? I am truly at a loss to determine a proper path."

"Lord Aidan, the quandary is this: Kathryne does not perceive herself to be *ready* for such a relationship to begin. Perhaps she is still in . . . well, how do I say this without disrespect . . . perhaps, she is still *enamored* in some small way with that vile pirate Hawkes."

Aidan brightened somewhat. "I believe that may be a partial answer. But what can be done?"

"I have heard say that absence makes the heart grow fonder. Well, I believe that is a false statement. When one is absent, the other turns one's attentions to what is at hand. She will not be receiving that brigand into this home, will she?"

Aidan shook his head vigorously to indicate the negative.

"And I am certain that a man of your nobility and reputation would have no social dealings with such a ruffian."

Aidan nodded. "That is true, though I have offered him the appointment of captain of the harbor defenses. After all, who better to stop a pirate than another pirate, I say. But I could not conceive of a time when he would be welcomed in this house as a social equal."

Geoffrey stroked his chin, and a smile began to spread about his face. "I had hoped as much, Governor."

"But what of your plan for Kathryne? Do I simply order her to obey? For despite her recent behaviors, she is an obedient daughter. I am most certain she will follow my decision if I insist."

Geoffrey held up an open palm signifying no. "'Tis exactly what should not be done, Lord Aidan, if you forgive me for saying so with such bluntness."

Lord Aidan smiled. "'Tis a rare man who will be blunt with a governor. I appreciate that quality. It shows bravery, courageousness."

"Then I shall be a brave man, Lord Aidan, for I know you value the truth," Geoffrey said, his smile still wide. "And as for my plan—though I would never deign to call it a plan in front of the dear Kathryne, for it smacks of devious plotting—my plan is to simply allow us to spend time together."

"And how will that be accomplished?" Aidan asked. "I had thought that a dozen of your proposals had already been rejected."

"True enough," Geoffrey agreed, "but perhaps each encounter posed was of too much of an intimate nature. Dinners and small gatherings have a reputation for entwining people in a closeness that may be threatening, especially to a woman who has undergone such an ordeal as Kathryne."

Getting up, Geoffrey walked to the window again, smoothing his doublet by tugging at its bottom. "Lord Aidan, my home, much less grand than yours, is nearly bare and devoid of ornamentation. I have seen the skill that Kathryne possesses in such matters. What Ridge House needs is the touch of a feminine hand, and I propose to you that I invite dear Kathryne to undertake that task of decoration and to supervise the project. This will accomplish two things: We will spend time together in a way that no one can deem intimate, and the house, when finished, will reflect Kathryne's heart and will become inviting and attractive to her in the process. Ridge House will be of her design, and I will simply charm her into forgetting her past."

Aidan was nodding while he straightened the papers on his desk into a neat stack. "Admirable plan, Geoffrey. I do believe that will do what we desire." Aidan looked serious for a moment. "And how long do you anticipate this process to take?"

Geoffrey smiled again. "No more than a few short months, good sir. And, Lord Aidan, what would assist in this process is if you were to bid Kathryne that she is now permitted to make her own decisions concerning our proposed union. Of course, I would assume that you will also endeavor to foster a beneficial attitude in her, and in general speak in glowing terms of how you might react to such an eventual outcome."

"A most judicious plan, Mr. Foxton. And I believe it will be most agreeable to Kathryne as well. For while she would obey, I am not that stern a taskmaster. In this manner she will be allowed to reach my favored conclusion on her own without my interference."

"Exactly," Geoffrey affirmed broadly.

"Well, then, I assume that this matter is settled," Aidan said, standing. "Please, if you would, Mr. Foxton, allow a day or two to pass, then proceed to inquire if Kathryne would assist you in the furnishing of your home. By freeing her from a sense of obligation about the matter of marriage, I believe the path will be clearer for you, as it were."

"My humblest of thanks for your wise counsel, Governor."

With that, Geoffrey left Shelworthy that afternoon, whistling a bright tune.

*I wonder what I should say exactly in my note inviting Kathryne's assistance?* he thought. He looked up at the golden sun, now hanging heavy in the western skies. *And I wonder what might be happening at the Goose? I can go there for refreshment and pen my letter to Kathryne. And perhaps Eileen may be free as well.*

10 February

*My dear Kathryne,*

How I long to see you again. I trust that your labors to finish the interior decoration of Shelworthy go well and that you are nearing completion. I understand that your abilities rival those of the best decorators in England. Lady Pickering spoke of the estate's charm and sophistication. I look forward to attending the first gala that will be held there.

I must apologize, dear Kathryne, for I have been so preoccupied with my own building efforts that I have been prevented from paying you and your father a visit for these many weeks. The second sugar press is nearly complete—according to the Dutch merchants that are erecting the apparatus, that is. Work is tedious and painstaking, and I have been required to add my assistance to hasten its completion.

Indeed, I write this letter from a crude shelter near the press, a thin layer of palm fronds separating myself from the elements.

I have been assured (again!) that completion is but a few days in the future. And with that, I will be in attendance at the first harvesting of my fields to the east and their pressing for sugar and molasses. Such a process is greatly complex, and I will not confuse you with such overwhelming details. I know a beautiful woman as yourself has more pleasant matters to consider, such as the appointing of a fine house and the tending to details of home and hearth. There is no success to be gained by boring you with this arcane subject.

My true reason for this posting, dear Kathryne, is to present a great need on my part. I would hesitate pressing you for such a favor, but it was at the urging of Lady Pickering that I pen these lines.

I admit my failings, Kathryne. I admit that I now require a remedy that I believe only you can offer.

If it not be too much of an inconvenience, I would greatly appreciate if you could attend me at Ridge House, my most modest domicile, and assist me in the decoration plans for the dwelling's interiors. As a man, I find that such details are most puzzling and even overwhelming. Would it be possible to attend me at some future date that you find agreeable and accompany me there—with a proper chaperone, of course—and offer me advice and counsel concerning such a matter?

I would be most grateful if you would concur.

*I remain your most faithful,*
*Geoffrey Foxton*

As he slipped the quill back into the inkwell, he looked out over the harbor at Bridgetown. From where he sat, in a cozy second-floor bedchamber of the Goose, Geoffrey congratulated himself on a most perceptive and, hopefully, convincing letter. This room, small as it was, was much more convenient to his requirements than his empty bedchamber at Ridge House. And to be sure, his time at the sugar mill was even more limited. Being so close to the jungle and slaves was disquieting, and Geoffrey thought it unseemly to spend more effort there than required. The Dutch advisors had matters well in hand.

*It is time to get on with this matter of capturing Kathryne,* he thought. *I am not one to spend unnecessary precious time waiting for any woman to come to me.*

He slid the quill back out of the inkwell and began to write again.

P.S. Kathryne, it seems only proper and fitting that you have a voice in the matters of colors and furnishings since, if God be willing, and your heart be so moved, we shall share those spaces. I have chosen not to show aggression in such a pursuit, knowing that a delicate woman as yourself would need time to recuperate from your ordeal. I believe that the pleasant task of assisting me in matters of my home would do you most well to hasten your recovery. And of course, hasten the time that we can begin our shared life together.

Yours,
G. F.

With that he whistled, and in a moment a soft tap sounded at the door.

"Mr. Foxton?"

"Come in," he called back, without shifting his view, and held the sealed envelope loosely in his left hand.

Eileen walked in and took the letter from his hand.

"Shall I see that this is taken to Shelworthy this morning?" she asked, her voice soft and sultry in the warm air.

Geoffrey turned back and smiled. "No, there is no urgency with the posting, sweet Eileen. A messenger can be sent later in the day." He smiled, tilting his head slightly to one side. "No urgency at all."

## 20

After his meeting with Geoffrey Foxton, the governor had raised all the windows in the office nearly six inches, despite the medical warnings to the contrary. A thin breeze had cleared the room of its stuffiness, and the temperature was noticeably more bearable than a few moments prior. It had been at Kathryne's insistence that he began opening windows. And now, after only several days' practice, he was quite gladdened that he had taken her advice.

Lord Aidan had just gotten back to the business of the day when he looked up in surprise to see that Vicar Petley had been escorted to his office by Boaz. He smiled and gestured the vicar in.

"Vicar Petley," he said. "How delightful that you should call on such a beastly hot day."

The vicar strode into the room, extended his hand, and sat down wearily on one of the chairs in front of the desk. The governor did not move about the desk to join him, for where he sat a most pleasant breeze was tempting at his back and neck, relieving much of his discomfort.

"I trust that St. Michael's is nearing completion?" Aidan asked, curious as to the nature of the vicar's visit.

The vicar looked exasperated and snorted. "Delays, delays. It is either the fog that stops the work, or the rain, or lack of materials, or the right materials delivered to someone else on the island. And when that happens, the entire crew simply chases out after the supplies and, I would hazard to guess, uses most of them on another project."

Aidan nodded, feeling that no comment was needed.

"But, in spite of all that, we are coming closer and closer. The roof is near complete, and despite what appears to be a thousand small undone elements, Mr. Idris assures me that the final nail will be hammered in a mere three months' time if all goes well, four if the weather conspires against him, and six months if I add my standard deviation for the timing of a builder."

Giles smiled as he said this, his attempt at levity making no impact on Lord Aidan, who sat staring straight ahead. Aidan shook his head slightly and focused his eyes again.

"Well, 'tis a good thing, that . . . that all goes well."

"Lord Aidan, I have come to you directly, for I have a request of you that involves your daughter, Kathryne."

Aidan raised his eyebrows.

"As you most surely know, Kathryne assisted me as I taught in the free school in Dorchester before I was assigned to this island, before she and I were so horribly detained by that ghastly evil pirate Hawkes."

"Yes," Aidan said, nodding. "Kathryne wrote to me of such an endeavor. She seemed to take great pleasure in the activity."

"I believe that to be true, Lord Aidan," the vicar said. "As the church here nears completion, we are also nearing the completion of several rooms to be used for instruction—instruction in the catechisms as well as the rudiments of reading and writing."

Aidan looked interested. "That is most encouraging, Vicar Petley. As this island develops, more settlers will come, and more children will follow. It is wise that we do not neglect the education of those who qualify."

"Indeed, Governor. Kathryne has agreed to assist me in planning for such a school. She is a most clever woman, and I would be most grateful if you allowed her to do so, seeing how it is unusual for a woman to be placed in a position of such responsibility."

"Well, I see no reason why Kathryne could not offer such assistance," Aidan said.

The vicar clapped his hands together in a noiseless joining. "Splendid," he said. He looked directly at Lord Aidan, then leaned closer. Aidan noticed the thick smell of damp wool about the vicar's rich vestment, which was buttoned to his throat, his white collar showing wet and stained about his neck.

"Lord Aidan, I have one more matter to discuss with you." He looked about the room. "Is Kathryne nearby, may I ask?"

"No, Vicar, not today, for she is visiting with Lady Pickering."

The vicar looked relieved. "It is a most delicate subject, and I admit that I have not the skill in such social graces as a more gregarious man might enjoy."

Lord Aidan leaned back, catching more of the breeze across his face.

"As I taught at the free school, and Kathryne assisted, the two of us shared pleasant moments together, Governor. Perhaps she had written to you about such times?"

Lord Aidan searched his memory. She wrote of the school, but scarce mentioned the vicar by name.

"If not, it is of no matter, Governor," the vicar said, "for I could understand her reluctance. And I also understand her reluctance since arriving on this island to speak about such things."

Lord Aidan had a most puzzled look on his face. *What is this fellow speaking about?* he asked himself. *I am sure that Kathryne has not mentioned Vicar Petley in any context—or has she?*

"Allow me to be precise about this matter, Governor. Kathryne and I began to enjoy our shared times together—so much so that a more . . . intimate understanding developed."

Lord Aidan felt a shock at those words. *A member of the clergy would not have taken liberties with my innocent Kathryne.*

The vicar must have noticed the change in the governor's countenance, for he quickly and firmly added, "It was the most platonic of relationships, I assure you, Governor. On that I would swear upon the Scriptures. For a man of the cloth to offer to do so entails a vow of the utmost seriousness."

Aidan relaxed a breath.

"But Kathryne and I shared a great many things, and I believe that her heart was . . . softened toward me. I have heard that Geoffrey Foxton has been suggested as a suitor for Kathryne. I would never deign to usurp your rights in that regard. If this were England, my father, the earl of Ipswich, would have spoken to you directly. But alas he cannot, and I must take this matter into my own hands."

Aidan was not quite sure where this was all leading, and he waited for the vicar to reach his point.

"Lord Aidan, I, being a member of nobility, as is Mr. Foxton, and owing to the previous relationship that has developed between your daughter and myself . . . well, good sir, I am humbly asking if I might be considered as a suitor for your daughter as well. My prospects are most sound. Following this assignment, no doubt I shall be eagerly received at any open church in London—or in all of England, the truth be told. I trust I am not speaking too brazenly, but if you were to consider a liaison between Kathryne and myself, I can assure you that she would be most well treated and would be offered a splendid future, considering her deep spiritual commitment to our Lord. She would be such an asset to a man in my position."

The vicar stopped and leaned back, and then leaned forward again and added, "Governor, I am not seeking a rapid reply, for I know that this is a most unusual request—coming from the intended suitor directly—but I saw no other way to make my plans known. I beg forgiveness if you consider me too bold, but I am sure that you are a man who respects courage. I would be satisfied this day to merely know that my request is being considered."

Aidan grasped for words. "Do you . . . does Kathryne . . . will you . . . is my daughter aware of this request? Have you spoken to her?" Lord Aidan asked.

The vicar leaned even further forward. "By all means, Governor. Kathryne and I spoke of this on the night of your welcoming gala. In no uncertain words I told her that I would seek your permission to continue the relationship we began in England."

*By the heavens!* Lord Aidan thought in a bolt of understanding. *Perhaps this is the reason for Kathryne's curious reluctance to walk further on the path with Mr. Foxton!*

Aidan leaned further back, further away from the cloying aroma of wool emanating from the vicar. *If true, I will now admit that I shall never, ever understand the workings of the feminine mind. And how shall I address this new wrinkle? I cannot afford to upset the church just yet, and I need their assistance in governing this island as well. I must play the politician and seek a delay in deciding—without having it seem like that is my goal.*

"My good Vicar, I will admit that your request has taken me by surprise. Kathryne can be most coy when it comes to matters of the heart. And as a father, I perhaps do not hear the more subtle nuances that a mother would perceive and take to heart more quickly."

"That is most insightful of you, Lord Aidan," the vicar agreed.

"Will you hold a confidence, good Vicar?" Aidan inquired, taking a deep breath, and leaning forward, closer to Giles.

"Why, of course," he said, his hand spread against his chest. "After all, I am a man of the cloth."

"I have been concerned about Kathryne these past weeks. Her horrible detainment, as you so aptly called it, was most troubling to her. I do not think she has yet recovered." He leaned back and away and gulped in fresh air again. "I will consider your request. I once met your father in London and was most keenly impressed with his bearing."

*He was a man of large appetites,* Aidan recalled, *with a florid face and a harsh, braying laugh.*

"But I must treat my daughter more delicately at the moment than I know to be normal, for I do not want to cause her more concern and alarm. I will wait until the time is proper to discuss this . . . matter of your request with Kathryne."

Giles leaned forward, looking as if he was about to miss a hackney to St. Paul's. "But, Governor—"

Lord Aidan held his palms up, stopping the question. "My consideration of Mr. Foxton is on deferral as well, for Kathryne is in too delicate a mood to continue with such matters as a potential marriage. No decisions will be made for at least as long as her mood persists—perhaps as long as several months. And of course, we will need to stay in communication concerning this matter, as long as our words remain in closest confidence. Is that agreeable to you, Vicar Petley?" he asked as he rose from his chair.

Giles nodded somewhat glumly. "Thank you, Governor," he responded quietly.

"I shall ring for Boaz, then, to see you out."

## 21

Will stopped at a narrow outcropping of jagged gray rock that jutted into the blue of the Caribbean Sea. The sun was slipping toward the west, and the calm waters reflected its gold in a thousand prisms, each sparkling and winking as the heated breeze fell from the shore and across the deserted beach.

He carefully made his way along the rock and sat near the end, his feet inches from the water. The heat of the day was spent, and as the sun lowered and the air began to cool, the evening was most pleasant.

Will watched as a pair of brown pelicans swooped along the water's surface, reaching down for their dinner, cutting through the golden fluid reflections like a knife.

*I want to pray,* Will thought, *but I am not certain how, exactly. But I must speak of this to someone or I shall burst.*

He folded his hands together, and as he performed that small action, a vision of Vicar Mayhew flashed into his awareness—a vision of the vicar on his knees by his bed, his hands firmly clasped together, tight and red in effort, eyes closed, murmuring softly and then sometimes not so softly his evening prayers.

*I shall not kneel here,* Will thought, *for my knees would not take kindly to the rough surface. Yet I am sure that God can hear regardless of my position.*

*Dearest Father in heaven,* Will began, *I thank thee for thy exceedingly wondrous blessing, for allowing a person such as I to come before thee on thy heavenly throne. I thank thee for all the other blessings that I can count as my own.*

He opened his eyes and simply stared out into the vast, calm sea spread out before him, the sun now dipping into the western horizon.

*This is better,* he thought, *for I can see what I am thankful for.*

He paused a moment, then began again, eyes open.

*I am unskilled in the ways of prayer, but I must confess my anger. When thou allowed Kathryne Spenser to show me the proper path to thee, my gratitude knew no bounds. Since thou hast brought her into my life, I must admit to thee that I thought she could stay in my life. I am angry, Lord, for it seems that I have lost so many people I have held close to my heart. I am angry for seeming to lose yet one more. But, Lord, perhaps this was not what thou hast willed for me. I know that thy ways are, to us, unknown and unknowable. Hast thou allowed her to touch my heart only to bring me back to thee? Was my dream of somehow . . .*

Will looked up at the blackening sky to the north, trying to find the proper wording for his desire. *Was my dream of spending my life with her an invention of my own and not authored by thee?*

As he sat and prayed, his heart seemed to quiet, his anger ebbed as the tide, his soul felt free this evening, and unfettered by the passion he had harbored.

*Lord, I am thankful for thy gifts. I am thankful for my life, for I know that I have been within a sword's blade of losing it many times. If my life is to be lived without Kathryne, allow that dream in me to fade without pain. If my days on this earth must be spent without her beauty and grace at my side, allow me to know it unquestionably and without regret. If thou should have another path for me, allow that path to be shown to me clearly.*

William blinked his eyes shut for a moment. When he lifted them, he saw in the distant waters a small caravel heading in on the light evening winds toward the safety of the harbor.

*Lord, if I am to seek a home, is that the direction that I should sail? Back to the harbor and away from Kathryne?*

Just then, a small echoed boom was heard. It was the cannon the fort sounded when allowing a strange ship to enter the calm waters. To him, that small clap of rolling thunder always meant peace and safety.

*Is that the answer, Lord? That I seek the harbor and seek its safety?*

Will looked up and saw a single brown pelican this time, perhaps one of the pair he had seen earlier, perhaps a lone male out on his own, winging its way south, back to its nesting grounds south of Bridgetown. He looked up at the moon, now slipping into the sky left dark by the sun's departure.

*My father the gamekeeper taught me that thy will was always revealed in thy creation. I will take these all as signs, Lord. I will return to Bridgetown, and I will seek to begin my life there as thou will direct me. I thank thee, Lord. I thank thee with all my heart. Amen.*

Will stood, brushed off the seat of his breeches, and began to walk with a purposeful stride to the ship. As he walked he began to dream of his small cottage by the sea, the kind he would build.

## The Straits of Florida

As the sun was setting that evening, a small boat bumped against the white sands of the Florida coast. A thin man, burnt red by the sun, jumped from the craft and pulled it up onshore. He smiled into the darkness in a wide, leering way, and began to laugh.

In the boat were a trunk, two casks filled with water, and ale enough for a two-week journey, and smoked meat and fish to last even longer.

"Well, this must be the Florida coast," Radcliffe exhaled aloud in a proud huff. "I have made the crossing with provisions to spare."

He pulled the boat up further onto the sand and tied it off on a thick root of a mangrove tree.

"Tonight I will sleep here," he said as he looked about for driftwood to build a fire. "And tomorrow, if the winds are clean, I will aim north to my future."

# CHAPTER

# 22

*Hadenthorne, Devon*
*England*

After his second tankard of flip at the Coat of Arms, postrider Henry Eames shuffled through his bag and extracted the letter bound for the village where he sat. As he drew it out of the leather bag, the woman who stood behind the bar gasped in surprise.

"Who be gettin' a letter, Henry?" Inez Ockleman almost cried. "Be not me, 'tis it?"

Her son had traveled to the New World nearly a year ago, and a letter from him most likely meant that he had come to tragedy.

"No. This one be addressed to . . ."

Henry peered at the writing, curved and delicate, and squinted at the lines, his mouth moving in relationship to the letters. "This one be addressed to . . ." His face was a mask of concentration. "Be addressed to one William Hawkes."

Inez cackled, then began to cough. "He hasn't been here for years. Moved on to the New World, is what they says."

Henry squinted on. "It be in the care of . . ."

Inez gulped, coughed again, then leaned closer, though she had no knowledge of reading.

". . . the vicar of St. . . ." He looked up at the barmaid, her hand laid out flat on top of the bar. "What be the name of your church here?" he asked.

"It be called St. Jerome's."

"Then this letter be in care of the vicar of St. Jerome's," Henry said with proud relief. "That be if William Hawkes not be here."

"Hawkes not be here," Inez stated with firmness. "But which vicar does it say? We had a couple of 'em in the past months."

Henry picked the parcel up again and squinted. "Doesn't say. Just says here 'the vicar' and that be all." Henry looked up, a bit puzzled as well, then brightened. "I would say that the vicar can read it and tell who it might be for."

Inez peered again at the writing. "Does it also say who be writin' the letter?"

Henry looked one last time. "Be from a Missy . . . something . . . Hol . . . Hol—e—der."

"Missy Holender!" Inez cried. "We best be fetchin' Mrs. Cavendish. It be certain to be troublin' news. And her so ill and all."

That afternoon, Henry and the barmaid, with a few other villagers in tow, had gathered about in the garden of the parsonage as Henry delivered his posting. Mrs. Cavendish had been alerted of its arrival, but she was too weak to travel the short distance to the parsonage.

Vicar James Chadwick took the letter and carefully slipped his thumb under the wax that sealed the parchment. Bits of the red wax tumbled against his expansive chest, and he brushed them away with a wave.

It had only been six months that Chadwick had been in Hadenthorne, replacing Vicar Sheedy, who was a most unpopular vicar. Chadwick felt at home in the village, he said, and most parishioners seemed to agree with his genial ways and manners. Most villagers had hoped he would have a tenure at least as long as Vicar Mayhew had enjoyed.

He opened the letter and stood with his back to the sun to better make out the faint lines inside. Quickly scanning its contents, he looked from the page to the expectant faces of the small crowd that had gathered to hear the news. Their faces were etched with sadness—an emotion most familiar to them, for they were so often the recipients of tidings that brought sorrow.

Chadwick looked up. "Where is this William Hawkes? Do any of you know?"

One of the men from the back called out, "I hear he be in the West Indies."

Another said, "I heard tell it be the island of Barbados."

A few more voices murmured their agreement.

"If one were to take that letter to a Captain Waring in Weymouth, he could send it on, for the two of them been dealin' together in shippin' and the sort."

"Aye, that be the truth."

"Captain Waring would know the whereabouts of William Hawkes."

Chadwick scanned the faces. "I must see Mrs. Cavendish, for the letter is from her daughter-in-law, Missy."

As he walked to the Cavendish home, the crowd followed him, a step or two behind, speaking in hushed tones.

"Why be she writin' to William?"

"Be her husband dead now, too?"

"Perchance she believes that William be back in Hadenthorne now."

"Maybe she be in Barbados lookin' for him."

No one mentioned Missy's family, for her mother and father had perished nearly a year prior from the pox, and her two young brothers had been sent to live with a cousin of Mr. Holender in East Anglia. What monies had been left in their estate, after the Holender farm had been sold off, had been entrusted to the cousin for the care of the two Holender boys.

The vicar knelt by the bedside of Mrs. Cavendish. Two of her sons remained with her and now stood motionless behind the vicar.

"Mrs. Cavendish?" the vicar called out in a low soothing voice. "Mrs. Cavendish?"

A few of the crowd murmured from beyond the bedchamber.

"Her time be so small. Why be he givin' her grievous news now?"

"Why not spare her heart any further pain?"

The vicar stroked her hand. Since he had been in Hadenthorne, Mrs. Cavendish had been ill. She had grown weaker and weaker over the months, yet stubbornly clung to the glow of life. Vicar Chadwick liked the old lady, for she still struggled to rise when he visited and cook something for him, opening a bottle of her best cider to make her small home inviting. He had been told her history by others and had heard small bits and pieces about William Hawkes and Vicar Thomas Mayhew and her relationship to them both.

"Mrs. Cavendish, can you hear me, dear?" Chadwick called out.

She opened her eyes and focused on the vicar's kind face.

"I have a letter from Missy."

"Missy?" she repeated in a faint voice.

"Your son's wife," Inez called out in a louder voice from over the vicar's shoulder. He turned about and glared at her.

"I know who she be," Mrs. Cavendish croaked as she strained to lift her head. "Why she be writin' now? Is it me son Dugald? Has he come to harm in the New World?"

The effort of three sentences in succession almost proved too much, and her head fell back hard into her pillow.

"No," the vicar said, in a most convincing tone. "She writes that all is well and that Dugald is a fine man and that their land is most productive."

Mrs. Cavendish narrowed her eyes sharply.

"That not be a reason to post a letter, Vicar. There be more than that."

Vicar Chadwick stroked her hand again, trying to soothe her. "True enough. She writes . . . for she is expecting a child. And by the date of this post, I would daresay that you be a grandmother by now."

Her eyes lit up, and a calm, yet excited murmur spun through the crowd. "Be that true? I be a grandmother? Indeed 'tis good to hear."

Mrs. Cavendish lay back down, sinking a little further into her bedding. Her grayed hair was spread about her like an aging halo. "That be most wonderful news . . . a grandchild. A wee grandchild." And she drifted off to sleep in a heartbeat more.

The vicar rose and walked through the crowd, who parted for him like water on a ship's bow.

As he reached the path back to the parsonage, Constable Markham tapped at his shoulder.

"Be that the truth of the letter, Vicar? Does seem like much ado before a birth was accomplished."

Vicar Chadwick turned and faced the man. "What would you say to a woman who is dying, Constable? The truth, or a gentle falsehood that provides a balm for her pain?"

The constable looked about and shrugged.

"I have chosen to allow her to think pleasant things as she prepares to meet her God. There is nothing more than that."

He turned away and after only a few steps, stopped and called back.

"And if any man should ask, good sir, no words of such were ever spoken between you and me concerning this letter."

The constable nodded.

The vicar sat at his desk in the house-place of the parsonage of St. Jerome's, the letter spread out before him. He added a line to the front of the letter: Please forward to Captain Waring, Weymouth. Under that bold address, he added: Please see that Mr. William Hawkes receives this letter promptly. And then he signed his name.

Before resealing the letter, he read it one last time.

*My dearest William,*

I am so sorry that I did not wait for you—but I was told by all that you were never to return to Hadenthorne. I am praying that this letter finds you quickly, for I am in the most desperate of straits and I cannot return to my father in such a sorry state of failure.

Dugald is gone. He said that life in this primitive colony of Virginia is too hard and that he must seek his fortune without ties to a wife. I believe he has grown tired of me, for he had changed into a person I did not know as we left the shores of England. I am left alone here, William, in this small drafty hut with no way to support myself. This New World is cold, filled with nothing but loneliness and despair.

If this letter does not find you soon, I will be forced to sell myself as an indentured servant—or worse—if I cannot locate other arrangements.

Can you find it in your heart to forgive a foolish girl?

I pray that I will receive your reply.

*Love,*
*Missy*

# CHAPTER

## 23

*15 March 1642*
*Barbados*

*Dear Lady Emily,*
How my heart yearns to be near you! You could have no understanding of how I miss your wise counsel and sage advice. I can scarce believe how sorely I miss you.

Indulge me as I try to recapitulate what has occurred in the past several months.

You are aware from my previous letter all that transpired in my captivity and rescue. That correspondence also included the complex tale of the gala in celebration of our returning to Barbados—the celebration where all three men nearly intersected with each other. It has caused my heart no end of confusion.

How I wish you were here. I have become dear friends with Lady Pickering, of the Pickerings of Bath. Perhaps you know the family? Her daughter, near to my age, perished in a fever only months prior to my arrival on this island. Jenny, as she asks to be called, has been most gracious, taking me under her wing and showering me with as much attention as a mother might.

She advises that Mr. Foxton is the only suitor who is proper for my considerations. Vicar Petley will remain poor, says she, and of course we have not discussed Mr. Hawkes, for I know her sensibilities would be shaken if I were even to mention his name.

But I have raced ahead, and I need explain what has transpired these last weeks. I trust my letters do not bore you, dear friend, but placing word to paper acts to settle my divergent thoughts into one crystal-clear stream—faster flowing perhaps, but fordable.

Even Papa seems to have tempered his rhetoric concerning the

PASSAGES OF GOLD                                      125

question of my courtship and marriage. He made a little speech
stating that due to my ordeal I would be allowed the luxury of time
in these matters, and he has spoken little else about the subject since
then. Even the attentions of Mr. Foxton seem to have cooled, yet I
see him more often now than I would a suitor. He is so taxed for
time, what with his presence being needed as it is at his sugar mill, as
you know, and he has an entire house to furnish and decorate, and
an entire staff of servants (and some slaves as well) to be trained in
proper household duties as befits an English gentleman. I have spent
countless afternoons helping coordinate all those functions, working
with painters, plasterers, and joiners as I seek to help Mr. Foxton
transform his house from an attractive shell into a domicile worthy
of his residence.

To be honest, I am quite enjoying the process. It is most gratifying
to see an empty room be filled with color and texture and pattern
and warmth. (Although warmth is one item that we often have an
abundance of on this tropical island!) And I must also admit that I
am finding the new, relaxed Mr. Foxton to be quite charming. He
laughs easily, has a wicked sense of humor (which sometimes verges
on the ribald, which he has agreed to temper in my presence), and a
pleasant and agreeable nature, which is most refreshing.

My original assessment of him as a ladies' man has been most
unfair and has proven false. He has attempted no liberties with me
and is always the most gracious and gentlemanly. I have begun to
look forward to the time spent helping him in his endeavor to make
his home a pleasant and inviting place.

So, you must be asking, dear Emily, "What is the problem with
that?"

The problem lies not with dear Mr. Foxton, but with a second,
and then a third, player in this drama that my life seems to have
become.

You remember Vicar Giles Petley, of course. We spoke of him at
length at Broadwinds. He is doing remarkable work overseeing the
immense building project of St. Michael's Church. Nowhere near as
grand as the most humble church in London, St. Michael's
nevertheless will be the first and most beautiful church in all the
Antilles. Giles insists on calling it a cathedral. I look forward to the
dedication ceremonies a few months in the future.

I had assumed that Giles, according to his own words, would seek
my father's permission to court me as a suitor. I do not believe he has
spoken to Papa, or if he has, neither man has spoken of it to me.

I seem to be in demand as an advisor on matters domestic on this island—an inferior version of Inigo Jones, the master designer, as it were, for now Giles has sought my assistance on furnishings and colors of the new church and parsonage. In addition, he and I have spent long days conferring on the tasks needed to furnish and equip the new school when the church is complete.

Even though the man struggles in this beastly heat (for he refuses to give up on his thick black wool vestments) he has grown greatly in his role as administrator. I have heard his plans and dreams for St. Michael's, and I am impressed each time he expounds on the subject. He is still most fussy and precise, and the heat seems to have exacerbated those qualities. Perhaps that is the reason for his changing personality. What I admired in his character in the cooler climes of England seems to be magnified and intensified in the tropical sun—and most often to his detriment, I am afraid to say. Yet . . . he is most thorough and careful—traits that he had demonstrated in England and which serve him in good stead on this island as he oversees the construction of St. Michael's. It is true that he does have a vision for the church—and that is for it to be a large and growing body. I cannot help but admire him for that, at the very least. And yet (and this I find most puzzling) if he seeks to be my suitor, he has been discreet to the point of invisibility. Perhaps he is biding his time until the church is done, or perhaps Mr. Foxton offers too intimidating of a competitor. Whatever the reason, I find men to be such a puzzlement.

I have admitted this to no other person, my dear confidante, and I do so now only to help sort out such a tangled mix of ideas and fears and dreams.

The man's face I continue to see in my dreams is that of William Hawkes. I see his smile in the sun and hear his gentle laugh on the breeze as I walk along the shore on mild afternoons. I sense his thoughts in the clouds as they slip along in our blue, blue skies. And his eyes—his eyes haunt my dreams and every waking moment.

But Emily, other than a short, almost formal note of two months ago and a stilted and abbreviated conversation at our welcoming gala, I have had no contact with the man. And this was after such an intensity of emotions shared on his island hideaway.

I do not understand his reluctance to at least speak to me. It is almost as if Papa has forbidden him to communicate with me. But Papa assures me he has issued no such prohibition.

I wonder as I lie in bed at night what he has done during the course of a day and what he dreams of as he sleeps.

Lady Emily, are these normal feelings for a woman such as I—to have her heart held by a man who offers no share in her life? Can I ever hope to find happiness with a man such as Mr. Foxton, or even Vicar Petley, when such a man as William Hawkes is hidden in the shadows, beckoning me? Have you known of this to have happened? Please, if you would, provide me counsel on such things.

Dear Emily, I must stop here. Papa will be most upset with the amount of parchment I have borrowed from his desk. I trust that this will find you well. I am told that a Dutch merchantman will sail tomorrow. With good winds, this will reach you by mid-May.

*As always, your friend,*
*K.*

The clouds hung low over the eastern edge of Barbados that afternoon, and a thin mist filled the air with a warm, wet embrace. Will stood by the thin strip of land that led to the half-completed fort. He had spent several days reviewing the plans and making notes and corrections on the draftings that would allow a more efficient construction to take place. He narrowed his eyes to slits and imagined the fortifications as complete, and with a tall tower at one end, offering a full, unobstructed view of all the sea approaches to the harbor.

*It will be at least six months until I can see it complete,* he thought, *for materials are short and workers even more dear. But with a small crew of a half-dozen men—if I can secure them, perhaps I can continue its progress.*

He turned about and began to walk toward the level stretch of ground by the promontory that he had first seen and admired more than three months ago. A carriage rattled down the narrow lane that led south from the harbor. That single road led past Needham's Point and past Oistin's Bay, stopping only as it reached South Point, overlooking the South Point reefs. The carriage rumbled to a dusty stop a few paces from where Will stood. The door opened, and first to exit was the long feathery plumed hat of Sir Isaac Howell, followed by the frail, spindly man underneath it.

"Mr. Hawkes," Sir Isaac said in a velvety soft voice, "how good to see you once again."

William extended his hand and grasped Howell's limp, bony hand in his. "I am so grateful that you agreed to my proposal, sir," William said.

"You had no compulsion to personally come to conclude this transaction. It would be of no problem for me to have come to you, good sir," he added, deferent to the man's obvious status and delicate bearing.

"Nonsense, Mr. Hawkes," Sir Isaac coughed. "I have always attempted to transact all my financial dealings face-to-face. I can learn a great deal of the nature of a man by watching his eyes. You should try it."

Will looked at him, his blue eyes wide. "And what do you see in my eyes, Sir Isaac?" Will asked him, in a polite manner.

Howell wizened up his face and peered back up at Will. After a moment, he broke the contact. "I see a man with a mission, who doesn't know what that mission is."

Will arched his eyebrows in surprise. "For true?"

Howell reached forward and took Will's forearm in his bony grip. "I do not tell falsehoods, Mr. Hawkes. I never have, and I shall not begin with you."

He turned back and motioned to the carriage. A second man—Howell's assistant—then exited, a nondescript little man dressed in drab colors, carrying a small wooden traveling desk, an escritoire.

"Now then, Mr. Hawkes, this is the land we have discussed. From that tree by the promontory, to the shore, down to that rock outcropping and back to the crest of that small knob consists of . . ." He turned to his assistant and snapped, "How many acres is this again?"

"Thirty acres total, sir," came the nervous reply.

"Yes, of course, thirty acres in all." He pointed to a single page of parchment on Howell's small portable desk. "And that is the purchase price we agreed upon?"

William peered forward and squinted at the small writing. "Yes, that indeed is the price. And this is a draft by my financial holders on the island that will transfer the funds to you at the first available occasion."

Howell nodded, a thin smile on his even thinner lips. "Excellent, then. What is needed is only your signature on this contract, Mr. Hawkes."

William took the quill, balanced the contract on the escritoire held by Howell's groomsman, and signed his name with a flourish.

*That ties me to this land forever, then,* Will thought. *If only my father and mother could see me now, the first man in the Hawkes lineage to actually purchase a grounding of soil on which to live.*

He looked about at the expanse, filled now with tall sea oats, pangola grass, palmettos, and mangrove trees. *I thank thee, dear Lord, for this rare privilege,* he prayed.

Howell peered at William as his manservant shuffled the documents into the escritoire. "This the first land under your name?" he asked.

"Indeed, Sir Isaac. In truth, the first land ever owned by a member of the Hawkes family."

Howell was attempting to return to the carriage, assisted by his servant, when he stopped midstep and turned back to William.

"This land shall be for your dwelling?"

"That is how I have considered it."

"It will be good land for such purpose, Mr. Hawkes. Good land for that."

As the carriage started up with a jump, Howell leaned from the window and called out, "Be sure, Mr. Hawkes, that suitable people live together in that dwelling. It will make all the difference."

William nodded deeply and gave a brief wave as the carriage drove off, heading back towards Bridgetown.

He looked about at the four corners of his land and imagined a plotter's line dissecting it into quarters. *The house will be situated there,* he thought, *and the gardens will be just there.*

He imagined placements as he walked about and soon stood in the very middle of the square. Slowly he looked east, then north, then to the south and west. Without thought or pretense, he knelt there, all but hidden by a tall cluster of sea oats. As the breeze hushed through its blades with a faint sweeping call, Will lowered his head and allowed his eyes to close as well.

*If it be thy will, O Lord, let this land be filled with love.*

And as he prayed, the small spot in his heart that had held a clear image of Kathryne, standing by him at the edge of the sea, her deep green eyes staring out into the infinite blueness of sky and water, began to fade into a white mist.

As the image softened and disappeared, a thin band about his heart tightened once, then stopped, a curious reminder of what once was and would not be again.

# CHAPTER

## 24

*April 1642*

John Delacroix struggled with the makeshift ladder, the rungs spaced wide and the bars rickety, but he managed to haul himself up and onto the thin parapet that ringed the interior wall of the fort by the harbor. Will was a step or two behind him. They both stood there, slightly gasping from the climb, staring at the results of Will's work. The fort, a mere sketch of a structure on a parchment scroll a few months prior, was now beginning to take the form of a proper English defensive fortification.

Will had been successful in finding a small crew to continue construction. Three of the men were English sailors who had grown tired of the sea. Improbably, six were black men who came to the island on a small raft of thick timbers held together with lashings of rope and vine. With Luke aiding the translation, Will gathered that they had come from an island off the South American coast. They had been abandoned there by a Spanish ship that had been tormented by a deadly fever, laying waste nearly half the crew. The black men had borne the blame for causing the illness and had simply been cast off the ship as if they were so much debris. Their number had been twice as large, but half had perished as they attempted to sail back home to Africa, an impossible journey even for a well-equipped vessel and a childish attempt by innocents on a raft with a sail made from scraps of canvas and bark.

As if in gratitude for a place to sleep and food to eat, and for a scattering of small coins, the ragtag crew worked with an impassioned intensity on the walls of the fort. Their first task was to select heavy sea stones. Each one would be lifted from the shore, carried by a thick canvas sling to the site, and then hammered and chiseled to an angled shape. Then, the entire crew would come about the rock, and with every hand tucked beneath an edge or cleft, they would chant and lift, carrying the massive piece to the walls.

Three of the walls had been built to a height of eight feet, and a narrow parapet of wood had been added to them. A second level was planned with ledges for musketeers. The cannons would be positioned in gunsights in the lower wall. The fourth wall, facing north, would be the largest and thickest. Its foundation, reaching near the shore, had been completed for some time, the work finished under Radcliffe's supervision. Will found it an easy task to simply layer a narrower foundation on top of what was existing. That wall faced the sea and would be required to withstand a fusillade of cannonballs from any ship or armada that sought to storm the island.

Will positioned his gun locations carefully. The west-facing wall bristled with emplacements. A full dozen openings had been built, and a fat eighteen-pound cannon would rest in each bay, offering an iron wall of cannon shot as a master defense. The remaining walls were smaller, at least at the start, for no military man worth his salt could imagine an overland attack on the island.

"An attack on Bridgetown would arrive from the sea," Will had said, explaining his revised plans to the governor as he inspected the site, "and will be quickly and soundly repulsed by what we have built as our defense."

Governor Spenser was most satisfied with the progress and commended Will for his initiative.

Now, several weeks later, John was admiring Will's handiwork as well.

"William, I would have said it a fool's folly to accomplish as much as you have in such a brief period. This fortress has arisen like a dream. One moment the site was but a bare bluff," John said, "and a moment later, a fort appears."

Will nodded. "I appreciate your kind words. Progress has been swift. And I have the Spanish to thank for it, for if those black men had not washed up on our shore, the sailors and I would have accomplished but a tenth as much."

Will unrolled the large parchment with the detailed plans and indicated at which location would be constructed the barracks and stable and armory and the rest of the dwellings and structures a fort required.

The two men sat at the top wall, straddling the thick rock-and-stone rampart, looking out to the cobalt sea. After a moment or two of silence, the loudest sound being the *chink-chink* of hammer and chisel against stone, John coughed and cleared his throat.

"Will, have I mentioned to you that Mr. Foxton paid a visit to my chandlery two days past concerning shipping?"

Will shook his head no. "Why would you be telling me about Mr. Foxton's shipping concerns, John?" he asked. "What he ships or purchases is no business of mine."

With his fingers John smoothed the rock on which he sat. "Will, I do not know how to phrase what I need say, and I . . . and you are right. It be none of your concern, truly. But I thought that . . . well, that is to say . . ." John stared down at his hands.

"My friend, we have shared much in our travels. You have protected my flanks with your life on more than one occasion. I see no reason why Mr. Foxton and his shipping request would now tie your tongue. Please, John. Speak freely, if you will."

John found a small flinty pebble in the mortar between the rocks of the wall and was endeavoring to extract it. Without looking up, he began to speak. "Will, Mr. Foxton placed a request with a joinery firm in Weymouth to have a rather elaborate full bed frame—headboard, footboard, and rails—built to his specifications."

"And what is unusual in that request?" Will asked evenly.

"Mr. Foxton be claimin' it be his weddin' bed—for he and Lady Spenser."

When John looked up, Will's stony gaze was averted, directed out to sea.

"I did not know if I should say a word of this, Will. But I knew that you and Lady Kathryne had shared somethin' the rest of us could but dream of. And now with that philanderer Mr. Foxton statin' that she be his intended—well, Will, I knew that I had to say somethin' of this latest occurrence to you."

The sound of the breeze and the rhythmic chink of the hammers replaced their conversation. A gull swooped low and cawed, then dove toward the water.

"Will, did I speak in error? Should I have remained silent?" John asked, sensing a darkness about his friend.

Will turned back and stared at his friend for a heartbeat, his blue eyes piercing deep. Then a faint smile came to his face, looking forced and thin, and he slapped playfully at John's leg with the parchment scroll. "How long would you say the completion of such a request would consume in time—until the actual . . . item of furniture would be returned to this place?"

John scratched his head a moment. "Be the best part of five months, I would venture," he said. "Perhaps nearer a full half-year if I understand the workin' of joiners."

John looked about, then whispered in a loud voice. "Now that I am a tradesman, I understand the value of havin' more than a single job at one time, which indeed always adds to the time allotted for each individual order."

Will's smile began to look more natural. "John, my friend. Six months is a long time. Many things may happen."

Will looked back out to sea for a long moment. John watched Will's face without staring and thought he saw his eyes fill with the hint of sadness.

"John, as much as a man can desire a woman, that is as much as I desire Lady Spenser. But now that God is in my life and in control of my steps, I must allow his all-wise hand to guide me. I will ask you to keep this in your confidence, John. Governor Aidan has stated to me that such a partnership between myself and his daughter was but a foolish dream. I did not dispute his remarks."

John looked hard at Will. "But, Will, she said you could see her again. You yourself repeated those words to me."

"Indeed I did, good friend. But perhaps she spoke as a child."

"A child? I would not describe Lady Kathryne as a child."

Will placed his hand on John's shoulder. "I am at peace, John. I have placed this matter into God's hands. I have asked that my life and my land be filled with love. If that be his will, God will cause it to happen. And I am as sure of that as I am sure of the dawning."

John returned his smile, but not near so enthusiastically. "William, we will need speak of this faith in God at length, for I do not understand its workin's. But with regard to Kathryne, if I were you, I would fight for what I want. That is how it is done."

One of the workmen called up, interrupting their talk. "Cap'n Will!" he cried. "We needs you."

Will rolled up the parchment, stood, and edged back toward the ladder. "We will speak again, John. And I believe God will answer my prayer—in one manner or another."

# CHAPTER

## 25

*May 1642*

Vicar Petley fussed about the dark recesses of St. Michael's, carefully examining the work that had just been completed. He had bent to scrutinize the last pew when the massive door in the narthex squealed and banged open, letting in a blast of hot sunlight.

Giles blinked a few times from the brightness, holding his hand to his eyes to shield them from the sun. The door swung shut, and Giles made out a figure standing in the haze of the darkened interior.

"Who is it?" the vicar called out.

"William Hawkes," came the muffled and soft reply.

"What is it you want? Why would you be stepping foot in the house of God, you pagan?"

William took a step forward, and a thin shaft of light from a small demilune window lit his face. "Vicar, I do not mean to cause you any concern. I have but one request of you."

Giles snorted in derision. "A pirate with a request. How novel. How unlike you to ask for what you want. I thought you were most accustomed to merely taking by force anything you desired."

William seemed to lower his head. The movement, however slight, hinted at guilt and shame.

"Vicar, I know my presence brings you alarm and concern. I cannot blame you for that. Indeed, I acknowledge that you have every right to fear me."

Giles laughed, trying his best to have it sound scornful and brave at the same time. "Me? Afraid of you? Do not flatter yourself, pirate. When a captive, I was but one against a hundred of your ilk. You think any man could stand brave against such odds?"

William did not speak for a moment. Giles was silently congratulating himself on besting the man and was marveling at his newfound confidence. *Giles,* he thought, *this island temperament agrees with you. It has emboldened you greatly.*

"Vicar, I am truly sorry for my actions against you. I have asked our Lord to forgive me. I have come to ask you to do the same."

The vicar snorted. "Forgive?" The vicar leaned forward without moving his feet. "God may have forgiven you, but he was not the object of your brutalization as I have been."

Just before the vicar crossed his arms over his chest, he touched at the spot on his temple that had borne a large purple bruise.

"No, pirate, forgiveness is not that easy."

"Vicar Petley," Will began, "I shall not trouble you again. I know that my visiting this church will cause you consternation, and I would be unwelcome by others. If my presence would cause such discomfort, I will seek to worship elsewhere."

The vicar laughed again. "A pirate seeking to worship? How noble."

"Despite what you may think, that is the reality of my new life."

An awkward silence fell across the church.

"Vicar, I spoke of a request," Will said at length.

The vicar snapped back to attention. "You did, but I shall not grant you it, regardless of its nature."

William, his hands loose at his sides, his blond hair reflecting the sun from the small half-moon window above, spread his palms open in a small gesture of supplication. "I need only a copy of the Scriptures, Vicar. I am told this parish has near a dozen such copies."

The vicar let his jaw drop open. "And you think I will supply you with such a precious item? You, pirate, are suffering from delusions of the highest order."

William let his palms fall. "I am offering you fifty English pounds for a single copy."

After several moments' hesitation, the vicar replied in a hushed voice, "What did you say, pirate? You offer how many pounds for a single copy?"

William spoke slowly, his voice cold as marble. "Fifty pounds, Vicar. For a book that you did not purchase. Fifty pounds for a book that you will not miss. Fifty pounds for a book that I require." William let his voice trail off into silence and then added, "Fifty pounds could buy a great deal of Bibles, Vicar, or fill a room with pews."

The vicar flinched, then uncrossed his arms and took one step closer to William. His feet hesitated as he moved, and the new leather of his boots squealed against the wooden floor.

"Fifty pounds, pirate?"

"In gold coin."

Will extracted a small leather pouch from his pocket, held it up, and hefted it once. The coins jangled with a dull echo from within. Will's eyes narrowed. "I could easily dispatch a request to England for a copy, but I wish to have it now. I do not wish to wait upon shipping that could consume upwards of a quarter of a year. I am in need of the Scriptures now."

The vicar was about to laugh, but something stopped him.

"And to whom will you read this Bible? Those black men at the fort, perchance?"

Will lowered his head and softly said, "Yes."

A chill ran into the center of the vicar's chest. He put his hand there as if seeking its origin. After the longest of pauses, the vicar spoke. His words were subdued and cool. "You may have your Bible, pirate. I will send it to your fort this afternoon."

Will stepped forward, handed the vicar the leather pouch, and then stepped back into the shadows. In a moment the heavy door swung open, and Will stepped back into the torrent of sunshine. The door swung closed again, and the vicar was left in the dusty dimness. He placed the pouch into a pocket of his vestment and stared at the closed door for a dozen heartbeats. Then he slowly shook his head and turned toward the parsonage. It was nearing the time of Kathryne's visit.

In the hall that led from the sanctuary to the parsonage, one would need to look quickly to see Kathryne Spenser run, in a flash of lace and linen, from the darkened church. She had arrived early and had made her way through the construction from the parsonage entrance in search of the vicar. She had come upon him as Will entered the building as well. She had stood there, hidden in the shadows, as the two men had talked.

Her heart was pounding. It was not only the words Will spoke, but the simple sound of his voice that seemed to bore directly into the core of her heart.

And now, as she ran back to the parsonage, her dress flowing and flapping behind her, she wiped at her tears with the fine lace on her sleeve.

## 26

Geoffrey rapped at the door to the governor's office. His knock was muted from the soft leather glove he still wore from his ride. They were new gloves that matched the color of his leather breeches and doublet, almost as if they were cut from the same hide. He was unwilling to take them off just yet.

"Come in," Lord Aidan called from inside.

"Good morning, Governor Spenser," Geoffrey said with cheer. "And how are you this fine day?"

Lord Aidan looked up from his desk and replaced his quill in the inkwell. He looked as if he had been awake since before dawn and had yet to stop and partake of breakfast. He folded his hands on his desk and sighed loudly.

"Mr. Foxton, if the Crown were ever to fully explain the true demands of an appointment as governor of a small island such as Barbados, I daresay there would be no man in all of England that would rise to the task."

Geoffrey sat in a chair before the desk. "From your harried and strained countenance, I would assume that you speak the truth."

Aidan reached up and smoothed back the hair about his ears. "Simply the weight of the detail required for a single report on parish boundaries takes up a full dozen pages of documents," he said as he lifted a thick sheaf of parchment.

"Lord Aidan, I think it is time for you to add an assistant to your staff. One that can do the detail work that may free your time to truly govern, not merely draft reports and correspondence."

Aidan slumped in his chair. "But I have tried that. The last man had no skill at organization. We spent more hours of more days simply searching our rooms for misplaced documents."

Aidan let out a long, loud sigh. "And making a bad situation intolerable was that he left a month ago to seek his fortune on that new settlement on Jamaica. Now I am forced to make do on my own."

Geoffrey stood and paced to the window, now open a full quarter, and felt the morning breeze.

"Perhaps I may present you with a solution to your predicament, Governor, if I could be so bold," Geoffrey offered.

Rummaging through a stack of tax warrants and freight dockets, Aidan looked up, his eyes wide. "A solution? That would be news of happy import," he said.

Walking back to the desk, Geoffrey looked about the room, cluttered with parchments, maps, stacks of papers, and an assortment of books and ledgers in various piles.

"Lord Aidan, I have in my employ one Caldor Bane, a recent arrival to this place. He is indentured to me, with a promise of a place to sleep, clothing, food, and five acres of land in seven years. I sought him out to manage and oversee my second mill."

Geoffrey leaned in close, his hands—still gloved—spread out at the edge of the desk. "The poor fellow is a complete waste to me as a supervisor, for his demeanor and manner are too . . . mild, too gentle to produce results with unruly darkies and crude Dutchmen."

"But then," Lord Aidan interrupted as he continued to shuffle his papers about the desk, "why would he prove of worth to me?"

"It seems that Mr. Bane has a first-rate faculty for numbers, accounts, and minutiae of that sort. It appears that he once served as chief clerk for the Lord Mayor of Leominster."

Aidan paused, his eyes flitting from one stack of unfiled documents to another. He stood up, his hands folded behind him, and walked to the window. "You are sure the man can be trusted? That I will have no cause for concern?"

"Yes, sir. I would warrant that to you with my entire being."

"And that he is competent and knows how to compose letters and to cipher all manner of transactions?"

"I daresay he does better in both than I do myself. Indeed, he is the most organized and methodical being I have yet to meet."

Aidan put his hand to his chin, nodding in agreement. "Well, I do have little to lose."

"Excellent, sir. I know you shall not suffer disappointment over your decision. I shall have him report by morning of the morrow, if that time suits."

Aidan glanced about the room at the dozen and more piles of papers. "It will suit me most well," Aidan said heartily. "And Mr. Foxton— please accept my thanks."

Geoffrey waved off the compliment with his still-gloved hand. "Good sir, I ask that you think nothing of my deed. It is the least I may do to offer my support of your position."

Aidan smiled, paused, and added, "Mr. Foxton, there is, of course, another item of great import that we have not discussed."

Geoffrey arched his eyebrows in a question.

"That subject is Kathryne," Aidan stated. "May I inquire about the progress she has made on your residence, and the progress you may have made with her?"

Geoffrey smiled, then withdrew it quickly. After all, it was Kathryne's father whom he was standing before.

"Kathryne has done wondrous things for my humble home. In the briefest period Ridge House has begun to look like a proper Englishman's abode."

Aidan narrowed his eyes. "And Kathryne? Has she softened?"

"I do believe that her heart is warming to me as well. She has agreed to share an evening meal with me a few days hence. But Lord Aidan, for such a precious gift as your daughter I am most willing to wait until her heart has turned of its own volition—and I believe that she has started on that journey."

Aidan smiled and extended his hand, and the two men shook with a friendly vigor.

On his way out of Shelworthy, Geoffrey found it hard to contain his smile.

*I must be sure to brief Mr. Bane on his role,* Geoffrey thought, proud of himself. *For the matter of a few pounds in Caldor's skinny pocket, I shall have my own personal ear at the governor's side!*

He slipped up gracefully onto his horse and reined her back to the narrow road that led to the governor's estate. *And who may know how valuable that conduit of information may become in time?*

<hr />

It was dusk, and William walked about the fort, noting the progress the day had brought. Walls were indeed climbing, straight and thick. The foundation of the barracks had been laid in heavy stone; heavy timbers were fashioned for the gate; and ramparts were stacked in piles, waiting to be cut. If Will narrowed his eyes, squinting just so, erasing the mounds of debris and stone chippings, he could begin to envision how the completed structure would appear. It was a strong and sturdy facade, and the narrow gun slits harbored the teeth of a sleeping beast.

At the far corner of the fort, nestled against the southern wall, were two rough shelters. In the larger one were the six black men, sitting around a meager fire, roasting a dozen small fish. The smaller shelter held the three English sailors, who sat in the fading light, one of them smoking a pipe, waiting for their kettle of turnips and cassava roots to boil into a thick soup.

On most nights Will slept alone under the stars on a small smooth patch of grass in the middle of his land next to the fort. As was his usual custom, when evening came, he took his meal at one of the taverns in town, returning later to his canvas bedroll and his solitude. On most evenings, Luke would amble over, in the near dark as dusk fell, carrying a roll of canvas. He seldom spoke, knowing that Will desired no words to pass between them. He would lie and sleep a half-dozen paces away, and was often gone before the sun first arose. It was the rare evening that brought rain, and when that occurred, Will slipped over to John Delacroix's chandlery and slept on stacks of fresh canvas. Their musty scent was a comforting aroma that recalled his time at sea and seemed to bring about a dreamless sleep.

But this evening Will had not yet eaten. He did not feel any hunger, but a sense of restless anticipation gnawed at his stomach. Vicar Petley was true to his word, and the Bible had been delivered to Will that day. He now held the Scriptures in his hands.

He looked over to the men, speaking in low, quiet tones, their voices tired from the day's labor. In a moment he stood before them, then sat on a flat rock midway between the two sheds. Every eye turned to him. His presence was unexpected and unusual.

Will cleared his throat. "Would any of you like to listen as I read from the Holy Scriptures?"

The English sailors were surprised. Bible reading generally occurred on the Sabbath, and most men looked forward to that time. Hearing the Word read aloud was not a privilege that any of them took lightly. The black men did not know enough English to truly understand Will's question.

One of the sailors, Percy Culver, spoke first. "Captain Will, if you care to read, we will all be most happy to listen. To be honest, sir, it will truly be better than to listen to one more of our stories. I believe we have told all of them more times than we like to admit."

"And there not be any we be believin' anyhow," laughed Malther Townes.

"What about the darkies? They won't be knowin' any of the words you use, Captain. Be like tossin' pearls before swine, eh?" said Samuel Perkins.

Will smiled and then looked over to the faces of the black men who all seemed to lean forward to him in curious anticipation.

"That may be, Mr. Perkins. But their knowledge of our spoken language must begin to be refined at some point, and I think it wise to begin with God's Word rather than mine. And Luke can help when the words need to be further translated." Luke smiled and nodded.

Will coughed again, turned slightly to catch the light from the fire, and began to read. "In the beginning, God created the heavens and the earth. . . ."

As the words sounded out and slipped into the darkness of the tropical night, Will looked over and saw the dark faces of six curious men, thousands of miles from their birthplace, poor, without hope, listening with rapt attention to a white man read words that they could not yet understand, telling the story of the God who offered them freedom and abundant life.

*Powerful Lord,* Will prayed in a short heartbeat, *please reveal thyself to these men. If thou would will it, use me, your most humble servant, to show them the way.*

# CHAPTER

# 27

A scamp of a breeze flitted about the narrow road as Kathryne pulled at the reins of the horse she was riding. Kathryne breathed in deep the scents of the island, filling her lungs with the most intoxicating perfume of sea and flower that followed the breeze about her. She was on her way to dinner at Mr. Foxton's, no more than half an hour's ride from Shelworthy.

She looked up into the clear sky, the blue so deep that it almost hurt the eyes as they tried to comprehend its depth and intensity. And the birds along the way—brightly plumed popinjays and parrots—cawed and squawked and danced to a rhythm so unlike those heard in England that Kathryne often looked about with a surprised smile on her face.

*How dreamlike this all is,* she thought, *and how I am growing to love my senses being filled with the sensations of this island.*

She came to a flat section of the road, and the path then narrowed to a thin route with the jungle on one side and the gentle sea on the other. Kathryne dismounted and led the horse along, walking with slow, languid steps.

Her thoughts slipped back to her visit with Vicar Petley three days ago.

*What a shock it was to see Mr. Hawkes, and what curious things his mere voice did to my heart. Those tears were most unexpected. It must have been a reaction to the trauma that we experienced together, and no more.*

Kathryne had spent the first few hours with the vicar in a near daze, pushing away that image of William, bathed in the oddly illuminating shaft of sunlight from the demilune window, outlining his chiseled jaw, his golden hair, his penetrating eyes, framing his broad shoulders and large powerful hands. She had struggled to remove it from her mind, and in time was able to concentrate, somewhat, again.

*But his words—willing to pay a small fortune for a Bible to read to such wretched men—so tore at my heart,* she thought, and then pushed that thought away as well, for its implications so vexed her.

Before the sun had neared the horizon that day, Kathryne had sought her leave to return home before dark. Giles had been most insistent that they speak of their future together. He had stated that he knew of her confusion over such matters following her abduction and return, but the weeks were becoming months.

"I will need an answer from you soon, Kathryne, for even a man of the cloth has his limits," he had urged as he took her hand in his and his eyes scanned her face. "I will allow you a few more weeks, perhaps, but then I simply will insist that we arrive at a decision on the timetable for our future."

He had nodded at this and looked for a moment like he expected his pronouncement to be sealed with a kiss. A very stern look from her had seemed to cool his ardor, and they had bidden each other good-bye in a friendly but less intimate manner.

And as she thought of such an experience, the face of Geoffrey Foxton slipped into her thoughts, and she stopped on the path, looking out to sea, and took a deep, cleansing breath of ocean air, then remounted her horse and not so gently nicked at his sides, pushing him to a brisk canter.

She arrived at Geoffrey's house at midafternoon, several hours before dinner was to be served. She was greeted warmly by Seth, Geoffrey's groom.

"Mr. Foxton not be here, Lady Kathryne. He said he be back shortly."

Seth took the reins of her horse and helped her dismount. She smoothed her linen skirt and tugged at the bodice of her dress, which was one of the many that Lady Pickering had supplied to her.

"Lady Kathryne, would you be carin' for a drink?" Seth asked as he led the horse around to the stable.

Kathryne thought for a moment, then nodded. "Perhaps some cider would be nice. I am quite parched."

She selected a bench on the front porch and sat and looked out at the wide band of blue sea, the water almost within a stone's throw of where she sat.

In a moment, a parlormaid came out with a full goblet of a deep red liquid. "De cider gone bad, me lady. Here be some good wine dat Massa be savin' for special 'casions. And dis be one special 'casion," she chirped in her singsong manner.

Kathryne sipped at the wine, taking more than she would have preferred, for indeed she was thirsty after the ride. She had considered asking for water, but quickly thought better of it, for she knew that many illnesses and bad humors bred in well water not fresh from a spring. She knew that Geoffrey had no such spring on his land but had a shallow well behind the house.

She sipped again and sat peacefully as the sun dipped lower and lower, and the water reflected its changing colors, from a thick turquoise to a rich amethyst. Such hue changes were common to the island, the sun illuminating different underwater formations as its angle changed, and Kathryne never tired of the sight.

She had taken the last sip in her glass when she noticed a cloud of dust from the road to the south, and in a moment Geoffrey climbed the steps, a bit dusty from the ride and issuing a great profusion of apologies.

He explained that he had problems with the Dutch advisors passing on the proper procedures to his new foreman of the sugar mill, and this had detained him.

"Communication is never easy when one party speaks Dutch and the other barely speaks English at all," Geoffrey laughed. His new foreman was from the Hebrides off the coast of Scotland, and his burr was so thick that he was doomed to repeat his words two and three times until the listener caught their true meaning.

"Please, dear Kathryne. You must forgive me."

And, of course, she did so as she laughed politely. "I have enjoyed myself immensely, Geoffrey. I have watched as the sun set, and I have enjoyed a healthy serving of your 'good wine.' I must admit that it was far more than I usually consume. I fear that, until our meal, I will be lightheaded and a wee bit giddy."

She giggled as she spoke, and her hand slipped up to her mouth, harder and faster than she thought it would, and it appeared that her hand surprised her face by arriving in such haste, which caused her to giggle even more.

"Dear Kathryne, I will see to it that dinner is prompt this eve. A full stomach oft mutes the effects of a wee drop of wine."

Geoffrey excused himself to change into more suitable evening attire and to wash the dust of the day from his face and hands. As he entered the house, he first raced to the kitchen.

"Whatever you have made for our dinner," he called to the cook, "needs more salt—and lots of it."

The woman looked at him blankly.

"More salt! Do you understand?"

She nodded after a moment.

"And we are out of the 'good wine' and only have one bottle of claret left, and the rest are bottles of rum and port. Is that understood?"

The cook looked puzzled. "But, Mr. Foxton, your wine cellar is full, with a hundred bottles or more."

Geoffrey glared at the woman, and she seemed to shrink under his narrow eyes. "No wine left save one bottle of claret, and then it is rum and port we are served."

The cook stood still.

"Do you understand?" Geoffrey asked again.

The cook stammered, "Yes, sir—one bottle of claret, then the rum and port."

And without saying another word, he sped off to his bedchamber, peeling off his doublet as he bounded up the steps.

At dinner, carefully lit with just the right amount of candlelight, the claret was gone midway through the second course, and the servants brought three bottles of more potent, thicker port.

Geoffrey beamed as Kathryne laughed at his retelling of the confusion of the day, trying his best to imitate the rolling burr of the Scotsman and the chopped, harsh tones of his Dutch advisors.

As the cheese was served Geoffrey offered several toasts to the evening, how dazzling Kathryne appeared in the candles' glow, how wonderful the night had become with her laughter, how alive the house seemed with her in attendance. Kathryne's hand had become less steady throughout the long meal, and she simply did not see as the servants rolled their eyes when, in quick succession, she spilled two goblets of port onto the starched linen table covering. Each mishap was followed by a ringing of Kathryne's musical laughter and Geoffrey's assurance that all was proceeding well. In a twinkling, the spilled wine was replaced by a new goblet, filled to its capacity. Kathryne herself seemed surprised at her thirst, for she had never sipped so much liquid at any meal before.

The final platters were cleared from the table, and Geoffrey, who had kept his consumption more even, rose, walked to Kathryne, and knelt beside her, taking her hand in his.

"That was a most delightful meal, Kathryne," Geoffrey said, edging in closer. "I believe it was the company that made it so appetizing."

Kathryne smiled and mumbled a thank-you.

Geoffrey moved his face even closer, within inches of Kathryne's lips. He felt her breath on his neck, hot and thick with spirits. He lifted her chin and tilted his face to her, and in a moment, their lips met.

He felt her arms drape over his shoulders, and as his heart leaped and began to beat wildly, he felt them tighten around him for a heartbeat; and then, unexpectedly, they relaxed. They slipped ever so slightly at first and then fell to her sides.

He broke their embrace by the smallest of inches, and as their lips parted, Kathryne smiled at him for a moment, her eyes fluttering once, like an injured butterfly, and then they closed. Then she slumped in her chair, her head falling limply to her chest.

*Things were going so well, too,* he thought with anger. *And she was becoming so receptive.*

He carried her to the third bedchamber—the one most distant from his own—and instructed two of his chambermaids to ready her for sleep. He then sent a speedy runner to the governor's house, with instructions to say that Kathryne had partaken of a food that did not agree with her and that she would rest at Geoffrey's until the morrow, under the most watchful eye of the housekeeper.

Later, in the dark, Geoffrey stood at the front steps of Ridge House, looking out at the sea, his appetite far from satisfied. *Curse my poor timing and my miscalculation of her sensitivity to spirits!*

## 28

Kathryne arrived home near midday, looking pallid and wan, her head pounding like the angry surf following a storm. Aidan took a single look at her face and immediately sent his daughter to her bedchamber with instructions to the cook to immediately produce a thick broth coupled with a pot of herb tea to be brought with haste to her room.

Kathryne had not the strength to argue, for the ride back was the most taxing she had ever taken. Every hoofbeat, every roll of the horse's flanks navigating over the deep ruts caused her to grasp the saddle harder and focus her eyes on a distant horizon to avoid becoming more ill. Geoffrey had been sweet and attentive that morning, and his apologies to her had had no end. He had claimed it was all his fault for her condition, running out of cider as he had.

"I should have sent for more, knowing how sensitive your delicate workings must be to such stronger libations, my sweet Kathryne," he had soothed as he held her hand.

"Nonsense," she had countered. "I am simply a foolish girl who did not realize the fruits of my actions. I knew full well I am not accustomed to such drink. I should have declined any further consumption."

She had rolled her tongue in her mouth. "But I had such a powerful thirst," she had said, then added, in a soft whisper, "If you were to inquire of me, I would say your cook uses altogether too much salt in her preparation. Half as much would be sufficient."

Geoffrey had shown no sign of surprise, but had nodded in agreement. "I will be sure to inform her of such a distinction."

He had practically demanded that Kathryne take his carriage back to Shelworthy, but she had been similarly adamant in saying no.

"The fresh air will clear my head, for I know I could not take such jarring as a carriage provides."

Geoffrey had reluctantly allowed her to leave, helping her mount her horse. Taking the reins, she had looked down at Geoffrey in the bright sun.

*He is a most handsome man,* she had thought.

"Geoffrey," she had said in a low voice that he had had to strain to hear, "I am not sure how to phrase this, so I shall just ask. Would I be a horrible person if I asked you not to speak of last night to others? I feel so dreadfully foolish and so dreadfully sinful for allowing myself to get into such a ticklish situation. I have prayed this morning that God forgive my lapse, and I wish to speak of it no more."

Geoffrey had looked up, his face an innocent mask. "Kathryne, I am most confused. Did anything go awry last evening, other than a bite of tainted food? I observed nothing worth repeating. Nothing at all, indeed."

She had bent over a few degrees—not many, for she felt her stomach rumble as she left a perpendicular plane—and had touched at his cheek with her gloved hand.

"Thank you, sweet and kind Geoffrey. Thank you for being such a gentleman."

She had straightened and nicked the horse with the reins, and he had lurched forward, Kathryne trying her best to smile through her intense discomfort.

*I am praying, Lord, that thou will forgive me for such a horrible sin as drunkenness.*

And now, nestled in her bed at Shelworthy, with a cooling breeze sweeping through the room and a wet cooling cloth on her head, she began to feel a small distance closer to normal.

Hattie had tiptoed about the room, gathering up clothing, speaking in low tones, and just as she was about to leave, her face brightened, and she near shouted.

"Almos' forgot, Lady Kat'ryne!" she cried, and Kathryne winced and recoiled even further into her bed. "You gots a postin' this day," she added, softer now, and handed Kathryne a vellum parcel from the pocket of her apron.

Propping herself more upright she examined the address. It was a letter from Lady Emily. She eagerly tore at the seal and spread out the thick sheets on her upturned knees.

*Dearest Kathryne,*

How I miss you and your sweet and tender voice. London seems empty without you and I find myself adrift.

The writing of the account of my travels about the countryside goes well, but there is such turmoil here, what with the impending confrontation between Parliament and the king. It seems that Charles and his entourage have now moved from Hampton Court to Windsor, but his position continues to deteriorate. Queen Henrietta Maria left for the Continent in February in search of assistance, but it seems that neither Louis XIII nor the Prince of Orange, still embroiled in their own war, is in any position to help. By contrast, Parliament's authority has not been in the least bit diminished, and John Pym has been most convincing in both Houses, which appear to be overtaken with the irresistible momentum of revolution. I am wishing to take leave of the city to find some peace and quiet in the more bucolic counties, but I hear tell that there is rioting in the northern and western shires as well. I shall go to Dorset shortly. I am in no danger, I assure you, but the whole economy and social order seem to be at a point of breaking down, and I can only pray that God will see fit to intervene in these affairs and bring reason to those to whom our governance has been entrusted.

I feel so lost, not knowing of your life—the post is so inadequate for maintaining a friendship such as ours. I understand that Barbados is a beautiful, intoxicating place—

As Kathryne read the word *intoxicating,* she winced.

—and that you are settling in well to the routines of island existence, whatever they may be. How I envy you—to be warm all year round, with no need for fires and furs.

Am I to understand that your heart is leading you down dark and unknown paths? Such a statement is not unusual when it comes to matters of the heart, for indeed it is the most unfathomable organ of the human frame. Poets and balladeers would have no words to pen if it were otherwise.

Kathryne, offering advice in such matters is truly a risk-filled proposition. If a confidante such as myself were to advise in one direction, and that love soon turns sour, then who shall receive the blame? And if one were to advise in another direction while your heart secretly yearns for the other, on what logic does a decision rest?

And even if I advise to listen to the gentle murmurs of your heart, that, sadly, is not always a reliable standard. Is one's heart swayed easily by appearance or money? Does one's heart listen too closely to the musings of others?

And Kathryne, most important of all is God's plan for your life. How is that determined? May I suggest several likely paths: prayer, the wise advice of God-fearing friends, more prayer, a critical examination of any suitor's most beneficial character traits as well as their least, even more prayer, and lastly, additional prayer. Unless your decision is bathed in supplication to our Lord, the decision cannot be of him.

Forgive me if I have written too forcibly of such intimate matters. But I know you have no mother to provide such uncluttered talk, and I feel led to do so now.

I must put down my pen, for the hour grows late and the light is dimmed. I think of you always, and you are in my prayers. Perhaps someday we shall hold each other again, and this distance and separation will seem as a dream of brief duration.

*Fondly,*
*Emily*

Lord Aidan sat with hands folded upon his desk, looking back at Sir Rutley Hubbard, recently returned from London and Amsterdam. Sir Hubbard kept glancing nervously at the windows, open nearly six inches to the morning breeze from the ocean. His hand, clutching a lace handkerchief, fluttered to his face as the breeze flowed through the room.

Aidan no doubt recognized his guest's slight discomfort, but was luxuriating in his newfound freedom to allow air to freely circulate through the room.

"So, Sir Hubbard, what news have you returned with of London and the court?"

Sir Hubbard looked about again, making sure that none of his words were to be overheard by a casual or deliberate eavesdropping servant. He leaned forward and lowered his voice.

"There has been seditious talk heard emanating from several well-placed courtiers," Sir Hubbard whispered. "I have heard that Lord Cromwell and his Roundheads have actually spoken of a coup d'état and would seek to see the king deposed from his throne."

Aidan smiled at the term *Roundheads,* an obvious statement of the grooming practices of Lord Cromwell and his followers, who shaved the top of their skulls bare and let only a fringe of hair grow about the ears. But could such an odd group truly hope to overthrow the king of England? The idea was near preposterous.

"But, good sir," Aidan replied, "do these rabble-rousers truly think that the public would support such a horrific concept as Parliament, without a king, leading the greatest country in the world? I venture to say that Cromwell thinks too highly of his own abilities."

"Parliament has begun to mobilize an army of ten thousand men to occupy London, with the earl of Essex as lord general. There is talk of Parliament raising taxes to pay for the troops. Charles is raising his troops to reoccupy London. It is said he relies on the generosity of the earl of Worcester and other noblemen to pay their wages. Now Newcastle has been seized, and the Royalists have captured a handy port. I am sure that you have already heard that Northumberland and Durham have been secured as well."

Sir Hubbard looked about again, peering out the windows from his seat, sensing strongly that their conversation was being monitored.

Aidan noticed his discomfort and reassured him. "Sir Hubbard," he said, "there is no need for concern of a spy in this house. My daughter is away this morning, my assistant has not yet arrived, and the rest of the servants would have no inkling of the true import of your words."

"One may never be too careful, Governor. But do not take this threat lightly, for more well-placed men than I have taken sides on this matter. Many of the upper classes are taking the side of the king. Yet many will side with Cromwell. Even Sir John Hotham of Yorkshire is casting his lot against the monarchy and has refused the king entrance to the town of Hull. Many families are divided, with members on both sides."

"Hotham?" Aidan said, shocked. The man he had known would never have consented to even consider such a rash action had there not been widespread support from many noblemen for such a drastic response.

*Then indeed,* Aidan thought, *events have taken a curious and malevolent turn. I must be cautious as to how these sentiments and alliances are played out on this island. A spark set in the wrong flax will torch the entire island.*

Aidan drew his hand to his chin and stroked it, deep in thought. After a moment he spoke. "I thank you for speaking so plainly of such political maneuvers," he said. "But in truth, I must tell you that I will endeavor to place the politics of England well outside the realm of our island politics. We have no need to take sides in this matter, being at such a distance from home. I will seek to keep either faction from becoming preeminent."

"And what of the sugar tariffs, Lord Governor?" Sir Hubbard asked. "There has been talk as well from the admiralty circles that the Royal Navy will fall under the control of Parliament with the earl of Warwick as commander. I am sure that he will seek to force all shipping to be done with English ships. How else will he collect the necessary taxes to raise an army?"

Aidan was confused. "But why would anyone at the court or at the admiralty think such an action is warranted?" Aidan asked. "All the planters on this island know of the regulations of the Crown and the taxes to be paid. I am assured that all such requirements are being met."

Sir Hubbard raised his eyebrows in surprise. "Is that indeed the truth, Governor? While in Amsterdam, I heard scuttlebutt from the docks that more sugar was being tasted by the Dutch than was being used to sweeten English tables."

Aidan stood, almost in anger, and his chair squealed along the wooden floor. "Perhaps a few barrels have been slipped past my harbormaster, but no more than a few, I am sure. What you have heard was a deliberate attempt at deception by some foolish men."

Aidan near stomped to the western window and looked out to the sea. From his vantage point, the sails of ships in the distant waters were small tassels of white, sweeping along the azure coast.

"I shall post my word as an Englishman before God that in the future, if there be any such smuggling discovered—any at all being done by any planter on this island—it shall be met with the harshest possible penalty. It matters not if the man be highly connected or not. He will suffer the consequences of flouting the laws of England. You may report my words directly to all to whom you speak, Sir Hubbard. The position of governor will not be undermined by the pursuit of the almighty pound. I will use the Royal Marines as guards and sentries if needed. I am sure that I may trust them to be my honest eyes, and I shall scatter them about the hidden coves of this island."

He spun about to face his guest directly. "Do you understand that, Sir Hubbard? Have I made my point most clear? Smuggling will not be tolerated as long as I am governor."

Sir Hubbard nodded. "I understand, sir. In truth, I was expecting to hear a shallow promise to 'look into' the matter. But I can see that you are most sincere in your desire to uphold the laws. I am most impressed and shall pass your words and sentiments along to the proper parties."

In the dim hallway, just by Aidan's inner office, Caldor Bane stood, still as a statue, unwilling even to bend for fear of causing the floor to creak under his shifting weight. He had his ear pressed to the gap of the double doors, listening with hawklike intensity.

*Won't Mr. Foxton be pleased,* he thought, *and wouldn't the governor be surprised if he knew.*

Caldor smiled, and as the governor's guests bid their farewells he scurried along the back passageway to appear at the front door, bowing to the plantation men as they departed, making sure his smile did not betray his secrets.

# CHAPTER

# 29

## June 1642

It was early afternoon on a gently warm day when William stopped at St. Michael's to ask Vicar Coates about a portion of the book of Romans that had puzzled him. Did God truly choose and ordain from the beginning of time those who are to come to faith in him? And did we indeed have free choice in such a matter? Will knew that Vicar Coates was well studied in Greek and Latin and perhaps could provide a more complete explanation of that troublesome set of verses.

Will left the vicar's side after nearly an hour of discussion, not truly having been satisfied at the conclusion. He thanked him for his patient efforts, although he knew that the answer was much too convoluted and obtuse for the laborers who listened to Will's Bible readings at the fort.

Will picked his way through the darkened church on his way back to the fort. The windows had been covered with thick canvas to protect them as the painters and plasterers finished their work on the exterior. He could hear their muffled talk as they worked on scaffolding near the roof. He stopped for a moment near the altar, a handsome piece of joinery work, done in a rich, dark mahogany. He passed his hands along its polished and waxed front and looked out at the empty space before him.

*Does man need to find God inside this building?* he wondered to himself. He thought about the small group of roughened sailors and ex-slaves who had been gathering about him as he spoke of God and read from the Scriptures.

*Such men are hungry for the truth,* he thought, *but would be reticent to step inside such an intimidating structure as this.*

Slowly, he walked down the center aisle, his boot heels resonating in the empty darkness. At the end of the aisle he looked up and almost cried out in surprise. There standing before him was Kathryne, whose face showed bewilderment equal to, if not greater than, his. She had one hand to her throat. Neither spoke for the longest moment, but both stood, silent and still, staring at each other.

Kathryne wore a plain long linen gown, modest in its cut, yet flowing in graceful curves about her. Her long dark hair, even more curled in the humid tropical air, was pulled tight at the back and secured with an elegant satin bow, which flowed about her shoulders. Her eyes, in the dimness, seemed to be lit from behind, their deep green color shining through.

It was Will who first broke the silence.

"Lady Spenser," he said in a more formal tone than he had ever addressed her in the past. "You have taken me by surprise. I thought no one here. I apologize if I startled you."

Kathryne was holding a large book in her hands. Bits of fabric swatches hung from the closed pages.

"Mr. Hawkes, the apology should be mine. I should not have come by way of the darkened sanctuary, but I had no thought to find anyone inside."

William felt his heart beating faster than a mild surprise warranted. "I was on my way out, Lady Spenser. I merely had a question to pose to Vicar Coates concerning a portion of the Scriptures that is troubling my crew of laborers."

Kathryne tilted her head and the smallest of smiles creased her lips. "Your crew?" she asked, "Troubled by Scripture? I am afraid that I do not grasp such a connection, Mr. Hawkes."

Will felt his face redden so very slightly. *It is that voice,* his thoughts raced, *that purely magical voice that does this to me.*

"At evening tide, I have begun reading the Scriptures to the men who work on the fort. Some sailors from Mr. Delacroix's chandlery have joined us as well. Most are rough and simple men who would not feel welcome in such a place as this," he said as he gestured with a wave of his hand. "And while I am well acquainted with the Bible, there are parts that I do not understand myself. I came to Vicar Coates to ask for his wisdom concerning the meaning of a section of the book of Romans."

Kathryne took a small step towards him, her eyes fixed on him.

William almost stepped back in response, yet he forced himself to be still. *I can barely stand to be this close to her,* his thoughts cried out. *How can she not know what agony I am enduring?*

"Mr. Hawkes," she said, in a lilting, almost lyrical voice, "I am most in awe of what you are doing. To be using your talents to present the truth of our Lord to those who would otherwise remain ignorant of it . . . well, that is a most wonderful, generous, and kind thing you are doing."

Will was anxious to avoid reddening at her compliment, so he quickly responded with a question. "And, Lady Spenser, what brings you to St. Michael's? Are you here to see Vicar Petley?"

"I am offering my limited skill at textile and color selections for the church interiors. The island does not yet have a skilled architect to handle such things." She paused, then almost whispered, "Most men have no idea of what color is correct in what location. I hope that I can ensure that St. Michael's is properly appointed."

Will almost sighed in relief. Their conversation stopped, and the silence returned, filling the room with a huge void. After several moments, Will broke the silence again.

"Well, Lady Spenser, I will not keep you from your appointments. And I must return to the fort. After all, that is what the Crown pays me for."

He turned and walked toward the door. "It was most pleasant to have seen you again, Lady Spenser," he said as he placed his hand on the black iron door latch.

Before he could open the door, she called out, a bit louder than she had planned, "Will I not see you at the dedication of this church, Mr. Hawkes? I understand it should occur within a fortnight or so."

Will looked back at her, a lonely smile on his face. "No, Lady Spenser, I think not. My appearance would do nothing but upset Vicar Petley. And with good reason, I must add. For that cause alone I will not be in attendance then—if ever."

Kathryne looked hurt, near anguished. "But, Mr. Hawkes, this is a house of God. All are welcome."

"All *should* be welcome," William corrected. "Yet the whole world belongs to the Almighty, Lady Spenser. I believe I can worship him in any location."

"But, Mr. Hawkes, . . ." Her voice trailed off.

"Please, Lady Spenser," he said, trying his best to offer comfort. "This is an insignificant matter of a single man. Please be assured that I can, and I do, worship God in other ways and in other places. Do not be distressed. I know that my decision is for the benefit of all concerned."

Just before he slipped out into the bright sunlight, Kathryne called out to him again. "Perhaps one day soon I may visit you at the fort while you read from the Word."

"Thank you for your interest. I appreciate your kindness."

And with that he was gone, and Kathryne was left alone, all alone in the silent dim interior of the church.

Will walked away, scarce seeing what was to his left or right, the echo of Kathryne's voice gently reverberating in his ears, the image of her breathtaking form still pressed before his eyes.

On the ride back to Shelworthy that afternoon, Kathryne paid scant attention to the sea, or the umbrella trees, or the hummingbirds that darted among the foliage, stopping to feed now and again on tender bougainvillea blossoms entwined with the vines that circled the road.

*Why did such a short conversation cause so much consternation in my soul?* she thought to herself. *'Tis true that Mr. Hawkes appears to be accomplishing a wonderful work, almost a missionary among the lost of this small island. And he seems so confident about such an endeavor. If only Geoffrey were as spiritually aware as Mr. Hawkes. Such a quality would make him easier for my heart to embrace.*

As the road veered inland toward Shelworthy, Kathryne dismounted and tethered the mare to a tamarind tree. She picked up her skirt and walked toward the sea. A cliff of rocks and boulders edged into the calm surf and azure water at this point. Kathryne climbed to the top of a smooth flat rock and sat staring out to the west. The sun, a short hour from setting, tinted the western sky with purples and golds and reds, as if the Master Painter were breathing color into the heavens and the water.

*Lady Pickering would say I am most foolish. Mr. Foxton is rich, she would say—or at least well on his way to becoming rich—and that a more handsome man cannot be found in all the Antilles. And I must admit to the truth of her stance. Geoffrey is a most attractive gentleman and most patient with my foolish reluctance to reach a decision concerning our future.*

*I am becoming a woman, and I must make mature decisions. Honestly evaluating the truth of a matter is what Lady Emily taught me. Mr. Foxton is of the right standing and will provide most generously if I am ever to be blessed with children. And I admire his skill at business*

*matters. He is most liberal with his laughter and most kind to compli-*
*ment me on my opinions.*

Kathryne stared out at the ocean and tossed a pebble into a quiet
pool at the base of her rocky perch. From its small splash, the ripples
widened across the surface.

*I need to view this matter in the most practical of terms. I must think*
*of my future and my family, not merely consider my heart.*

She looked down at the pool, its surface calm again. A tear had
formed at her eye, and she reached up with the back of her hand and
brusquely wiped it away.

"God may not always provide us with what we want," she spoke,
"but he will always provide what we need. Of that I am sure."

She looked up at the moon, slipping into view over her shoulder in
the darkening eastern sky.

*Oh, God—is not that the truth?* she prayed as another tear followed.
*Please, God, let my heart accept what my thoughts have known for*
*many months.*

Holding her hands together, she bowed her head. *And please,*
*please—I beseech you, Father—allow me to forget Mr. Hawkes.*

## 30

Dangling more than fifty feet from the ground, William rested on the top of the wall of the fort, up as far as he could climb. He stared out to the western horizon as the reds turned to purple, then black. The moon was but a slight crescent in the eastern sky. Without a sound, Luke appeared on the narrow parapet behind Will. The ledge was only a foot wide, yet Luke, who had the sinewy graces of a jungle cat, seemed most natural on such a precarious perch.

"Massa Will?" Luke called out.

Startled, Will jumped and then swung both his hands to the wall to steady his position.

"Luke!" he called out, almost angry. "You are too quiet in such situations."

Luke looked up, puzzled.

"You are like a spirit that materializes out of nothing. My heart scarce can take the shock. Do be more pronounced with your arrivals," Will scolded.

Luke screwed up his face. "You want Luke to always be makin' noise?"

Seeing Luke's obvious confusion, Will smiled. "Not all the time, Luke. Just when you sneak about on your cat's feet."

Luke still seemed puzzled, but Will continued.

"Luke, why are you up here in the dark? Are you in need of something?"

"Massa Will," Luke said as he elbowed his way past him and then swung up to the wall and sat facing him. "Massa Will be sad. His eyes be sad."

Luke kept nodding as he spoke and peered into Will's eyes. "You see Lady Spenser this day, be that right?"

No longer amazed at Luke's ability to read volumes into the smallest detail of a person's demeanor, Will merely shrugged and nodded.

"Dat make Massa sad? Luke saw Massa and Lady kiss on dat island. Why she make Massa sad now?"

*How do I tell him that she has returned to her proper world?* Will wondered. *How do I tell Luke that she could never consider me as an acceptable suitor, that our backgrounds are just too diverse and that the gulf between them can never be bridged. And that we would never be allowed—not by society nor family—to be together.*

Luke leaned over and pointed a bony finger at Will's face. "Massa Will best not be sayin' such a thing not happen. If God say it to be—it be."

"Luke, I know that God can move mountains. I know that he can do anything. But I know that he wants what is best for Lady Spenser as well. And what is best for Lady Spenser will not be found with me."

He reached over and put a hand on Luke's shoulder. "Luke, I am not unhappy. Truly, I am not. I am pleased that Lady Spenser has made the right decision."

Luke pushed Will's hand away, a gesture so near to anger that Will was dumbfounded.

"Don't be sayin' what be best for de lady. Only God know what be best for her. You got to do what God says. He says not to lie. Massa tell de lady how Massa feel. Dat's what God be wantin'."

And with that, he swung his long legs over the wall, perched on the thin ledge, and slipped back into the darkness.

Will did not call after him, for he knew Luke was right. He wanted to tell Kathryne how he felt, yet he was sure that by now she had made a decision that eliminated him from her life. And he knew that it was the right decision. How could a commoner such as himself expect a noble-born beauty as Kathryne to lower herself to be with him? It just was not done. What happened on the secret island was months in the past and had only occurred because she was his captive. If it had not been for the fact that she had been taken as his prisoner, she never would have entered his world.

It was enough to remember those glorious nights under a blanket of stars, and enough to thank her for leading him back to the path to God. Yes, the memories were sufficient, and the gratitude he felt was enough.

In time, he knew, the wound would heal. In time, he would be able to say her name without that sharp tug at his soul. In time, he may be able to gaze upon her face without his heart melting. In time, he rationalized, all wounds will heal and all paths will be made known.

## The Virginia Colonies

Jamestown's harbor was crowded with lines of slaves, dozens in each line, bound tightly together with clanking chains and thick, black leg irons. The black men's expressions were totally lacking in emotion, having spent what terror and anguish they possessed in their souls on the voyage from Africa.

Buyers had gathered along the docks to inspect the fresh human merchandise. Some of this cargo would be bound for plantations in the American colonies, some bound for resale in the Caribbean islands or perhaps even in the French or Spanish colonies along the coast of South America.

The humidity was thick, and the smells of the slave ships wafted over the still waters, covering the area with a sickly scent of pain. The rickety wharf echoed with the auctioneers' calls and the shouted bids of slave buyers.

Missy Cavendish edged her way along the far side of the street along the piers, on a narrow, muddy road mixed to a thick quagmire by the planters' and slavers' heavy wagons. She was wearing the only present-able dress she still owned, and carried another more tattered one tightly bound in a thin blanket tucked under her arm. The rest of her posses-sions, what she had come with to the New World, had been sold, bit by bit over the past months, for food. She was at the last of her coins and at the end of what she could sell. She sought work, but at the places she inquired was told that no help was needed. At the alehouse at the end of the dock, the man behind the bar leered at her, eyeing her form with great, salivating slowness, and whispered that she may find work there, and pleasure with it as well. She reddened at his lustful smirking and turned quickly from the room, running back into the street.

*It was not to be like this,* she cried to herself. *This was to be a glorious new world filled with endless possibilities.*

She had wept more these past months than she had ever wept in her life, and now her emotions were ragged and torn, yet no tears would come. She felt empty and alone and so terribly desperate.

Remembering a tale William Hawkes had once told her of Irish men and women coming to the docks to sell themselves as indentured servants, she sought what was perhaps her only means of escape. They

seek out a sea captain, Will had said, for captains know who might be
seeking the services of such desperate people.

At the far end of the docks, far away from the slave auction, Missy
gulped and walked toward a ship tied to the strong pilings of the pier.
As she approached the gangway, several sailors noticed her and began
to hoot and shout. No lady visited a seagoing ship, save the kind that
might be offering much more than Missy was prepared to sell.

Ignoring their calls, she stepped up to the edge of the planking and
called out, "Is the ship's captain on board?"

Two men, both well dressed in expensive velvets and feathered hats,
looked down at her from the quarterdeck.

"Yes!" the taller one called, "I am the captain. What is it that you
seek? If you be a lady of easy virtue, this is not the ship for you."

"Captain, my name is Missy Cavendish. I have been abandoned by
my husband in this strange land," she called out in bold tones.

"But what is that to us?" the other man called back.

"I have come to ask if you might know of a planter or merchant who
seeks to purchase an indentured servant. I am healthy and would
provide an able hand to any task."

The shorter man stretched up and whispered into the captain's ear.
Then each whispered back and forth several times.

Finally the taller one called out. "You assure us that you are a woman
of good moral standing?"

Missy was confused at the reason for the question, but answered
quickly, "Yes, sir. Only because of great duress am I here. For in truth,
my husband abandoned me."

"And you have no family nor resources?"

"No family save my husband in this land. No money save a few small
coins. I could not purchase my way back to England, nor would I suffer
the shame of returning home in such a state."

Again the two men whispered to each other.

"I believe we may be able to offer you assistance," the shorter man
said. "A most dear friend of ours is seeking house servants for his estate.
I know he would be most agreeable to place you in such an indentured
position. Please come aboard, for we will be sailing on the morning
tide."

Carefully walking up the bowing gangway, Missy stepped onto the
deck of the vessel. The taller man seemed to glide over to her, stopped
a few feet from her, and leaned toward her, squinting as he stared.

The shorter man remained on the quarterdeck. "I trust, Missy

Cavendish," he called out with near glee, "that you will find the island of Barbados to be as absolutely enchanting as we have."

"Yes, most enchanting indeed," his partner exclaimed. "And in a few weeks, you will be at your new home. How splendid for you—and for your new master."

Missy looked from one to the other and tried to smile in response to their obvious happiness, but such an emotion would not come. At least not until she felt the sea move under the ship and the Jamestown harbor disappear in the distance.

## St. Augustine, Florida

In an elegant upstairs room of the massive stone fort that hulked over the entrance to the Spanish-controlled Florida harbor, two gentlemen were about to partake of a large platter of boiled shellfish. Both raised their golden tankards, filled with a thick, bloodred port, in a toast.

"May we be blessed with a successful mission," Diego San Martel uttered, his English thickly accented.

"And may we both gain the treasure that we seek," said his dining partner, a thin, sunburnt Radcliffe Spenser. He gulped hungrily, the potent liquid near burning his throat as he swallowed.

*And praise be that I will have the chance to seek revenge,* Radcliffe thought, and a thin-lipped smile crossed his face.

CHAPTER

31

*Barbados*

Cooling winds were rare that season in the Lesser Antilles, yet this Sabbath dawning cast Barbados in a hue of wet slate, the sky so low that one was tempted to reach up and stir the clouds with an outstretched hand. The gray wind was out of the northwest, a rare point of origin, and with it came thick, chilled rains. The winds continued to nip at the island, and many a person grown so accustomed to the hot tropic breezes off the trades sought out a shawl or stomacher for warmth and protection.

Will woke early, before the dawn, as was his custom, and walked along the shore, thinking of his plans for the day. He carried a woolen blanket with him and draped it about his shoulders. The wind whipped at its edges, and they snapped loudly. The waves, seldom severe on this side of the island, rolled in loudly on this colorless morn. Will felt the spray on his face as he made his way along the rocks below the fort.

He felt the cold lap of the sea at his ankles as he walked, barefoot, in the sand. It was a Sabbath morning, a time that Will treasured. There was no work to be done on the fort that day, and the men would not gather by the western wall for Will's "sermon" until near noon.

*Sermon,* he thought and then smiled. *If the good Vicar Mayhew could only see me now, reading the Scriptures to others and attempting to interpret their truth to them. God indeed must have a keen sense of the absurd.*

Will nearly laughed at the image.

*How puzzled Thomas would be that I, who had turned so far away from God, might now be drawing so close to him, and that a person who had no use for all his stories and illustrations may now be racking my memories for just such illustrations as those he used.*

Will stopped and faced the wind curling about the rocks, slipping up from the water's edge with a kiss of salt, rushing past his ears, and blotting out the world around him. He closed his eyes.

*Dear Lord, I thank thee for leading me to this place. I thank thee for the privilege to spread thy truth to others.* He opened his eyes and squinted into the stiffening breeze. *And I pray that Kathryne will find the happiness that she deserves.*

And as he prayed that last thought, realizing that now he only called her by her Christian name in his prayers, he felt that familiar hitch in his heart, and his hand, without a conscious move, slipped up to his chest and touched the locket that lay upon it.

Will completed his usual circuit—walking briskly along the fort walls, down to the seashore, past the whistling caves now filled with the waters of the high tide and a thick carpet of seaweed, around the narrow promontory on which the fort lay, and back to the front gates. The nearly hidden sun had colored the sky a few shades brighter. Will returned to the fort, shook off his blanket, and slipped in behind the thick main door.

Will looked at the work remaining. Perhaps no more than a month of construction was left. Cannons had to be positioned and set into their pits. Two dozen of the deadly instruments sat in a lethal row in the fort's center, each resting under a canvas shroud. The ramparts had been completed, an interior walkway around the interior circumference of the fort, so men could quickly run from one spot to another without risking their safety. Cut into the top of the wall were thin slits for the musketeers to fire through. From the sea it looked like the bottom jaw of a great beast, with its teeth bared, snarling back in fierce defense. The barracks and the scullery were only partially roofed, but would comfortably house a full squadron of marines, gunners, and other workers. The kitchen would be sufficient to feed a consignment of twice the number that Will anticipated, for it was wise to plan in excess of one's true needs.

Later that day the skies brightened, the winds dropped to a gentle current, and the clouds thinned, allowing a weak sun to warm the air. Will looked out at the small crowd that had gathered, now lying, sitting, and standing beneath the wide porch on the western side of the fort. The porch had been fitted there, made of thin saplings lashed together as a framework, then covered with a thick matting of palm leaves and canvas. In the usually hot tropical sun, its shade was a welcome relief, but this day, most were wearing thicker clothing than usual. In attendance today was Will's entire crew of laborers, masons, joiners, and carpenters from the fort and a full dozen black men, who sat together, off to one side, by themselves. Luke had joined them, as was his custom, and helped when he could with the translation of words and phrases. Will knew that Luke's knowledge of English was not yet perfect, but he trusted God that the proper words would be used to help guide this small "congregation." In addition to all these men, near two dozen in all, several ladies from the Goose were in attendance.

One of the women had slipped up to Will as he took an afternoon meal at the alehouse one quiet day.

"Mr. Hawkes," she had said in a most bashful voice, much softer and more demure than her normal alehouse braying, "I have heard that you be preachin' the Word at that fort on the Sabbath. Be that the truth?"

Will had been surprised that such news was of importance to this woman, but he had kept his face blank and had nodded. "I do my best, ma'am. I read a bit and talk a bit about it as best as I am able."

"And I am told that the blackamoors sit there as well."

Will had nodded again. "I have instituted no restriction on who may listen to my humble words and thoughts. It would not be proper nor pleasing to the Almighty if I thought I was better than those men."

The woman, whose face was always brightly adorned with colors and who had lavishly applied her scented water, had looked up at Will, her eyes wide with what looked like hope.

"That is also the particulars that I have heard," she had said with firmness.

*Is her name Maggie? Or is it Mary?* He had searched his memory.

"Mary," he had opened, taking a chance on her name. He had seen to his relief that her eyes brightened, knowing he had picked the right name. "May I ask why you inquire?"

She had looked down at the nicked table and traced a lazy circle in the crumbs from Will's meal. After a long moment, she had looked up at him with more than a hint of wetness pooled at the bottom of her eyes.

"Would it be proper if I . . . and perhaps another friend . . . would . . . attend those . . . times you speak, Mr. Hawkes?"

Will had sat back, having no expectation of such a question being asked by her, and having no answer quick to his lips.

"We would understand if you say it be unwise, Mr. Hawkes, us bein' the type of women we are and all. But sometimes we get the urge to hear somethin' better in life than what we listen to here. And I know for a fact that we could never show our faces at St. Michael's, even though we be more than a tad acquainted with some of those parishioners."

This time Will had been perhaps a moment too slow in answering such a request, trying to find the right words. A shadow had fallen across Mary's face, and she had begun to slide from the bench where she sat and return to the bar.

"No, Mary, please," Will had said and had placed his strong hand on her bare forearm, preventing her departure. "I did not hesitate in order to say no. Your question was . . . unexpected, is all."

She had looked up at him with a tense look, almost as if expecting a blow of sorts to fall upon her frame.

"Please, Mary, by all the truth I may utter, I assure you that you would be most welcome to attend on the Sabbath. I hesitated only because I had never considered that you would be interested in . . . would want to come and hear of the . . . would be concerned for things such as . . ."

Mary had smiled and had placed her other hand atop his on her arm. She had spread out her fingers slightly, encompassing his fingers in hers. "It be fine, Mr. Hawkes. There be no need for more explainin' to be done. I reckoned that my request would be most unusual."

"Mary—you have succeeded in flustering me most deeply. But also know that you are indeed welcome. In truth, if I do not see you in attendance on Sunday next, I will be keenly disappointed."

"Then I will seek not to disappoint you," she had said as she smiled widely.

Will now looked out on this Sunday afternoon at the small crowd and saw Mary, her face most assuredly unpainted this day, as well as two of her coworkers. The three women sat off to another side by themselves on a thick canvas spread.

Will stood in front of the small crowd on a flat sea boulder nearly three feet square. He read in a loud voice from the book of Nehemiah, the language rich and textured. Some of the men nodded as he read; some seemed puzzled by the wording; some had their eyes closed in a form of personal reverence.

Will had studied through the first chapters of the Old Testament book and found it fascinating that Nehemiah had confronted his critics when they opposed his rebuilding of the walls about Jerusalem. It was not just prayer that he used, but he had posted guards and had set up a warning system of trumpeters and sentries to ensure the safety of his followers and workers. Will tried to explain that all will encounter opposition in doing work for God, and one must not let the disfavor found by their critics stop their work.

After speaking and reading for perhaps half of an hour, Will stopped, having no more words to share. He looked about and smiled. "May I close this day with a prayer for you all?"

Luke stood up from the side and called out in his singsong voice, "Be singin' a God song today, Massa Will?"

Will smiled again. He had no voice for such matters and was indeed most self-conscious about it. "I will let someone else lead such a hymn, for I fear that I would scare all of you away if I attempted to lead."

It was then that Mary stood up. "If I may, Mr. Hawkes?"

Will swept his arm in a wide circle, giving her the floor.

In a clear, crystal voice, Mary began. . . .

> *"To Father, Son, and Holy Ghost,*
> *The God whom heaven and earth adore,*
> *From earth and from the angel host*
> *Be praise and glory evermore."*

She sang the verse of the hymn alone once, with the rest of the group joining her in a thin blending as she sang it again.

When the voices stopped, Will began to pray.

"Our Lord and heavenly Father, I thank thee for thy most gracious bounty and that thou hast brought these people here on this morning. Thank thee for the gift of life. Thank thee that we have been provided with sustenance. We ask that thou watch over thy poor servants as we work this week and that thou lead each of us down the right paths. We ask that thou would forgive us our sins, knowing that it matters not how scarlet we are, but the gift of thy Son will make our hearts as white as snow if we accept that gift of salvation. Amen."

He looked up and saw Mary's face stained with tears, and at the same time saw Luke mouthing the word *snow,* for he had never heard that word, nor had any concept of what it might be.

*I will explain it to him later,* Will thought to himself with a small, hidden smile.

The Tambor brothers came up to Will afterward and shook his hand, as they had done so hundreds of times as they exited their church on Sunday mornings back home in England. It was times as these that Will felt almost as a vicar himself, but when he did, the image was so curious and odd to his spirit that he just as soon dismissed it. He recalled the disappointment in Vicar Thomas Mayhew's eyes when, as a young man, Will had told him that he would not spend his life in the work of the church, but would seek his fortune in the English navy. Will now hoped that, wherever he was, somehow his dear friend knew in his spirit of Will's unexpected, humble attempt at doing God's work.

CHAPTER

32

Geoffrey Foxton stood outside on the porch on that same gray Sabbath day and surveyed the greening fields of sugarcane, planted as a thick carpet all about his house. He had left little acreage to flowers and ornamental shrubs and the like, save for the garden at the rear of the house.

*The cane looks rich,* he thought to himself, pleased and happy.

His second mill had been completed on time, and he had secured two of the Dutch builders to stay on and manage the operation. If the early results were true, Geoffrey would have in a few scant months enough processed sugar, molasses, and rum to send three ships back to England, their cargo holds filled with the sweet gold. At current prices in Amsterdam, even a fiscal conservative would agree that Mr. Foxton would be well on his way to amassing a secure place in the financial history of Barbados.

He sat on the top step, his feet bare, his boots and stockings left in a pile near the front door. He would ring for the servants in due time, when it was nearer the time to depart for St. Michael's. He sat there and looked out at the sugarcane and smiled. He had in his right hand a tankard full of a thick, sweet mixture of rum and pineapple pressings, topped with a dusting of cinnamon. It had fast become his favorite libation. Thinking back to the week just transpired, Geoffrey smiled and placed the tankard to his lips, downing a full half-dozen swallows. The liquid burned pleasantly as it traveled through him, and the warmth felt fine on this less-than-tropical morning.

Midweek, he had called upon the governor, having sent a card and a messenger the day prior to Lord Aidan. Caldor Bane presented such notices to the governor, and as he had peered at the fine, curled writing on the small note card, he saw that Mr. Foxton had added on the bottom lip of the card a small check mark. It was his prearranged signal that he wished to see Caldor afterward, in private.

Geoffrey had arrived at the appointed time, dressed in leather breeches and doublet, this selection dyed to a rich hazel tint, and a loose silk shirt tied at the neck with a gold drawstring. On the ride to Shelworthy, he had loosened it, and the shirt fell half open as he rode. He had made little attempt at pulling it closed, his meeting with the governor notwithstanding. For he had hoped that he might cross paths with Kathryne that morning as well, and he wanted to be ready for such an impromptu meeting.

He had been formally announced by Mr. Bane, and Geoffrey had winked at his cohort as he walked into the governor's office and took a seat opposite Aidan's large and cluttered desk.

"Mr. Bane must be of great help to you, sir, for the piles of paperwork seem to have been reduced in weight and volume," Geoffrey had laughed.

"Indeed, Mr. Foxton, he has been a godsend, for without him I would be near to drowning in all this," Aidan had said, indicating the stacks of parchment and open books and ledgers spread about the room. "At least now I have been able to keep the office navigable on most days."

"Then that is reward enough, Lord Aidan, to know that I have helped in some small manner to lessen the heavy load you carry."

"It is always pleasant to have you visit. It seems that it is the only time I receive news of my dear Kathryne, for I scarce have conversation with her. She is either at your home offering training and advice, or at St. Michael's assisting with plans for the new school, or out riding with Lady Pickering. I trust that all goes well between the two of you and that progress is being made?"

Geoffrey had reached to his neck and had tucked several strands of loose hair back into the ribbon that held his mane of hair in a neat tail.

"Indeed, sir, and I thank you for asking."

He had related to Aidan that Kathryne was most involved in the final selections of colors and fabrics of his home and had even managed to supervise the installation of the joinery work in the library and dining areas of the house.

"The staff has ne'er been more efficient, nor the house appeared more beautiful, than under Kathryne's keen eye and ability," Geoffrey had stated.

"And has she softened her stance toward you and the possibility of marriage?" Aidan had asked in a small voice.

Geoffrey had placed his hand to his mouth, as if deeply pondering. "I will attempt to answer such a query with as much honesty as I am able to, good sir. I believe we are most near to an agreement. When we are together, she is most charming and delightful, yet I am sure that you are most aware of such attributes in your daughter. We speak of many things—religion and families and the need for man to serve God in everything that he does. We are in most common accord on such matters. I believe that until perhaps only weeks ago, the lack of understanding of the commonality of our dreams was the true barrier to her allowing herself to let go and follow the will of her father."

When he had spoken these words, he saw Caldor Bane, standing in the far corner by the door at Aidan's back, roll his eyes heavenward. Caldor had overheard an intimate conversation between Kathryne and her father as she spoke, in great, teary length, of her fears that Geoffrey was not as God-fearing a man as she might think was purposeful to her life. And Caldor had taken the liberty of telling Geoffrey of the details of such a conversation. Only days later, Geoffrey, sitting alone with Kathryne in his small garden at the rear of the house, had spoken eloquently and at great length of the very same matters. He had seen in her face that Kathryne felt the walls of resistance begin to tumble down. It had taken many months, but Geoffrey finally appeared to be that man to Kathryne—or at least was growing into that mold.

"'Tis a most comforting thing to hear, Mr. Foxton," Aidan had replied, "for indeed, such worries plagued her. I am heartened to hear that you have finally shared with her the truth of your own heart and that your spiritual quests are in agreement."

"Indeed, good sir, and it has been such a rare privilege to become better acquainted with Kathryne. It took me too many months to know that she was the person with whom I could share such intimacies."

The two men had spent the next hour speaking of plantings and sailings and gossip.

At noon Geoffrey had taken his leave, and as he had fetched his horse from the stables, Caldor had noiselessly slid up next him.

"I see that my information on Lady Spenser has proved to be of some value to you," Caldor had snickered in his dark manner.

Geoffrey had turned angry in a heartbeat, for such familiarity was beyond Caldor's station to either observe or make comment on. "It has been of sufficient help and no more, and you have received more than substantial payment for such information."

Caldor had stepped back, feigning insuLieutenant "Oh, good sir, do not take offense," he sneered. "I am but a poor servant who has no thought as to the usefulness of such news."

Geoffrey had stopped walking and had stared hard at Caldor.

"I do not seek much, Mr. Foxton, but merely to be treated with the respect that you think you yourself deserve," Caldor had stated.

Geoffrey had looked away. "I have erred. You have been most helpful."

Foxton had made motions of checking the cinches and stays on his saddle. "You have heard, no doubt, about the governor claiming to be more . . . aggressive concerning matters of shipping and the sugar taxes?"

"Indeed, good sir, I am well acquainted with the governor's policies on such matters, as well as the plans for their enforcement."

Geoffrey had looked about and had slipped his hand into a front pocket of his breeches. "Mr. Bane, this is strictly a supposition on my part—a theory, if you will—but if a lawless man sought to . . . circumvent such detection, where would that man find most liberal leeway in anchoring a ship and loading from shore? Would Stroud Bay be too far north for such activity?"

Caldor had looked down his nose and sniffed loudly.

Geoffrey had then taken a two-pound gold coin from his pocket, flipping it repeatedly into the air in a most casual manner.

"I would venture that if such a lawless man were to exist on such a law-abiding island, Six Man Bay just north of Speightstown would be far enough removed from the prying eyes of whatever troops Governor Spenser might command," Caldor had whispered.

*Six Man Bay?* Geoffrey had thought. *That is but half the distance I would have thought cautious and secure.*

Geoffrey had smiled. "I shall make sure such *lawless* men are so apprised," he replied. And with that he had tossed the coin one last time, and without waiting for it to fall nor watching its descent, had lifted his foot into the stirrup and hoisted himself to the saddle.

"Until a week passes, Mr. Bane."

"A week then, Mr. Foxton."

■■□□■□

Lord Aidan was in a most expansive mood as he rode back from church. He lingered on his ride home, stopping the horse at several vistas along the way—places where one could either stare at the vast turquoise sea or watch it as it rolled gently against the rocks and sand.

It was at one such stop that he dismounted, tethered his horse to a low shrub, and walked until the pliant earth began to give way to the white sand. He stood there and looked north for a long moment, then reached in and removed a letter from a pocket of his tasteful blue doublet.

He unfolded it and gazed at the slow, feminine strokes of pen against paper. The writing was small and most deliberate. He stared at the single page of linen paper, almost rose in color. He made no attempt to focus his eyes on the words just yet, but allowed the blurred lines to simply exist before him. Then after a long moment, he gave his head a small shake, focused his eyes, and read the letter, dated a month prior, for the dozenth time.

*My dearest Aidan,*
How much I miss you. When I was in London and you in Hadenthorne and we saw not a whit of each other for years, I felt no loss as dire as I feel now. But then dear Kathryne entered my life as a student, and I was able to share much of your life through her.

How delicious those days were, and how I most miss them now that the flavor is only a subtle memory on my tongue.

I write to you, my second letter of this day—the first being a missive to your daughter offering my humble advice and counsel in matters of her heart. I am sure that you are more wise in this than I, for I am so far away and so greatly removed from the realities of your world. I advised Kathryne to pray, seek God's will, and to follow what he will place in her heart. I trust that this meets with your approval.

London is dreary these days, with Lord Cromwell exhorting his followers to be of dour faces and stern dispositions. I know that as Christians we must not lower ourselves into the sin of the world about us, but does that mean we are to ignore the beauty in the world—in nature, in painting, in music, in art? Did God not give us these things for our enjoyment? I see a world robbed of such things as a pale and mirthless place, yet I believe that we must dedicate ourselves fully to our Lord. I find myself most confused.

I have finished my small book on travels about England and have secured a firm that is willing to print several thousand copies. A most exciting happening, yet curiously flat with no one to share that joy with—at least no one that I hold as dear as the Spensers.

When my dearest friend, your lovely wife, Beatrice, passed away, I thought my heart would break, even more than when my husband left this veil of tears. But I was most grievously wrong. What is more painful is living in a world that has not laughter and the closeness of good friends such as Kathryne and yourself.

I think of you often, dear Aidan, and wonder to myself how you must be getting on in such a far and foreign place as Barbados. I hear talk at Court that the king remains most pleased with your leadership, but I am sure that comes as no surprise to your ears. You were always so able at all you set your mind to do.

I sit in my chamber by the light of a single candle on this gray evening and I think of you—your laughter and your smile, your warmth and gentle ways—and that helps to bring lightness into the room.

My dear Aidan, such an odd letter to write, but you are on my mind most every day. Would it be too bold of me to admit that I look forward to seeing you again? I hope not, for I am going to my bed this evening with those words on my lips.

> Yours,
> Emily

And as Aidan read those last lines again, he felt his face redden slightly. He looked to the sea, scanning along the coast of the island, from where all ships from England arrived. He felt a certain longing when he thought of being near to Emily once again.

*Is it wrong to think such thoughts?* Aidan wondered. *For after all, I am a man of advancing years. . . .*

He walked back to his horse, mounted him, and turned him towards Shelworthy.

*No, I do not believe it is wrong,* he thought, *for I have not felt this buoyant in years.*

# 33

It was during an amazingly elaborate dessert at the Pickerings' latest dinner party that the subject of Kathryne's future was broached, and Lady Pickering led the way.

"Kathryne, we have spent this entire evening in conversation, and yet you have scarce mentioned the good Mr. Foxton. To me, it seems like a most curious omission. I am to understand that you have spent a great deal of time with him these past few weeks. Has nothing worthy of note occurred during such visits?"

Lady Pickering could be the sweetest and most pleasant of women, Kathryne acknowledged, but when she desired information, she possessed the grim-faced and single-minded determination of a hound in pursuit of a hapless fox.

Kathryne blushed, as she seemed to be blushing in great abundance in recent days, most oft caused by discussing this very subject.

"Things of worth have occurred," Kathryne stated, and then looked to her father to help extricate her from such a personal conversation.

Yet he merely sat there, looking as if he was interested in her answer as well. She narrowed her eyes, hoping that he might sense her reluctance, but the subtle gesture must have eluded his note.

Lady Pickering leaned forward and placed an elbow on the table, then cupped her hand in her open palm. "Then by all means, dear, please inform us as to your activities."

Kathryne pursed her mouth, looking as if she might bolt from the table.

"Kathryne, my dear," her father injected, "perhaps I understand your reluctance."

*Finally!* she thought with relief. *He has taken my hint.*

"I understand . . . to a point close at hand," he added. "I think it may be the appropriate time that we discuss these things. After all, you have been on this island for several months now."

Aidan followed his hostess's lead and leaned forward as well.

"It seems that everyone I speak to, with few exceptions, continues to ask when a date between you and the charming Mr. Foxton might be set for nuptials—especially seeing that St. Michael's is so near completion."

Kathryne sat back, with her hand nesting at her throat.

"But, Father, are not such matters best left spoken of in a more private setting?" she said, trying her best not to sound as if she did not want to include Lady Pickering in the discussion, which quite clearly she did not.

"The Pickerings are the souls of discretion," Aidan said, nodding to his host and hostess, and they both returned his nod with a sidelong smile of sorts. "The fact that you and Mr. Foxton are destined to be man and wife at some point in the near future is no secret to any of those seated at this table. I can hold no rational thought as to why we must be forbidden to speak of such things."

Kathryne closed her eyes for a moment, then sighed loud and long and opened them, taking a moment to look deeply into the three faces staring back at her with such intent and deliberateness.

"Very well then," she replied. "I can see that I shall have little, if any, peace unless I bare all my intimate details to you."

Lady Pickering looked as if she might blush. "Dear child, we do not want to know *all* such details. After all, we are all upstandingly Christian here and do not want to be informed of such goings-on as might cause us to think less of our Mr. Foxton."

Kathryne glowered for a brief moment, then her face softened to a smile, as did Lady Pickering's.

"Very well then. I will speak of this if you all make promise that we will cease including it in tonight's conversations? Will you all agree?"

All nodded, smiling.

"Mr. Foxton and I have had many pleasant times together as I assisted him with the interior details of his home. However, in the last few weeks, I have learned a great deal about the man. He has chosen to be open with me and has shared many intimate feelings with me that he had kept, up to date, hidden and private, such as his feelings of God and service and children and family. It was as if that side of the man was blank until he confided with me. I am trusting God that he would

not bring into my life a man who did not share my dreams in such
spiritual matters. And to my delight, Geoffrey has spoken of the very
same spiritual issues that I consider to be paramount in life with such
heartfelt eloquence that I found my heart swaying toward him. It was
truly a wondrous thing to have happened."

She looked about the table and saw both her father and Lady
Pickering near beaming with delight. Lord Pickering was uninterested,
having dozed off some moments prior as was often his custom.

"My heart was so unsure—that is, until this past week and our more
lengthy conversations. In truth, it has been the first time that I have
considered Mr. Foxton as a potential husband. And for such leading, I
am grateful to God."

Lady Pickering clapped loudly, startling her husband awake. He
sputtered a few times and closed his eyes again.

"That is most extraordinary news, dear Kathryne," she said as she
swept about the table and embraced the younger girl in a tight grasp.
"I am so happy that you have come to this decision."

Aidan stood up as well and placed his arms about them both.

Kathryne felt it most overstated, since neither Geoffrey nor herself
had set any dates, nor had he formally made a request of marriage to
her. Their enthusiasm was heartfelt, she knew, but premature.

*My dear Kathryne,*

How I dislike such a time between correspondence. Months pass
between letters, and the world continues to change with such
rapidity that I am afraid my most wise counsel becomes outdated
and so much fodder by the time it reaches your eyes.

In your last letter, you wrote of your continued confusion over the
choice of too many suitors. (Such a predicament to be suffered by my
innocent Kathryne!) I wish I could meet all these men and offer an
unbiased estimation of their character to you, but alas, that is not
practical, I am afraid.

How then to advise my favorite student in matters of the heart?

Continue to pray without ceasing, as we are commanded by
Scripture. If you are most earnest in such matters, God will direct
your paths, but you have to trust him to do so. You cannot rely on
your own understanding of such things, for that is when our human
frailties will most certainly disappoint us. We are strongest when
most weak and humble before him, for it is only then that his power
can be displayed in us.

You write as though the vicar is no longer a serious contender for the position of suitor. I will admit something to you now that you must never declare to any other living person—and had he been your first choice, I would have taken this thought with me to the grave. I confess that I have not thought highly of the man, having met him that once in London. I felt that he was too taken with himself and the fact that he was a man of the cloth. You can and shall do better for your life, my dear Kathryne. (And unfortunately I am also acquainted with his father, and a more pompous, overbearing boor has yet to make my acquaintance.) How terrible and gossipy you must think me, but I would never repeat these words under pain of death.

This William Hawkes sounds like a most complex and interesting man, but as you wrote, he is not due a reasonable consideration for the status of his birth. It is unfortunate that we are bound by such restrictions, but that is a truth that we must face.

And what you write of Geoffrey Foxton is most admirable—a wealthy man, or at least soon to be so. Considerate, handsome (a most enviable, yet unnecessary attribute), gentle, thoughtful, and chivalrous—a man who leaves little to be desired, from what you write.

Yet there seems to be a hesitation. Is it his spiritual life? Is it his views of religion? That indeed is a most serious obstacle to overcome.

I suggest that you pray that his true soul be revealed to you somehow and in some fashion. You will know when it happens, and I am most certain that your father, and your heavenly Father, will lead you in the proper path.

I shall wait by my door for the postboy every day until you reply.

How I yearn to be with you and share your life with you. Perhaps someday we shall see each other again.

> *Yours,*
> *Emily*

As Kathryne lay in bed reading and rereading those lines—the ones that spoke of Geoffrey revealing his soul and hopes to her—she felt as if she had received most wise and sage advice. In fact, her heart was most unsettled until he had spoken the words she had longed to hear. And now she could rest easy that the path, and her destination, led to Mr. Foxton, for he had expressed himself to be the man whom Kathryne had dreamed about for these many years. It was her foolish heart that hesitated and was confused by a rogue pirate. Understandable all, she thought, that her steps were most tentative. She could now begin to walk forward with great assurance.

Her father was happy. Lady Pickering, who was fooled by no one, saw the marriage as a most wonderful thing. Even Lady Emily, who had not even met Mr. Foxton, seemed to speak from four thousand miles away and confirm this direction. How could all these wise people be in error?

"Why, they simply could not be wrong," Kathryne said aloud to herself. Her voice seemed to distress Willy, the pet Williamson thrush she had brought with her to this island, and who had endured with her all the great adventures. He jumped from perch to perch in the large cage that had been built for him.

She looked up at the bird and realized that for the last several days he had refused to sing. He cocked his small brown head and focused his black eyes on her, seemed to ready his body for song, and then after a long moment, jumped back and turned from her.

Kathryne dawdled over her midweek breakfast, though she had appointments to keep at St. Michael's. Aidan walked past and came into the dining chamber, surprised that his daughter remained at table, eyes somewhat unfocused, sitting before a cup of cold tea and a plate full of broken biscuit ends.

"Kathryne?" he called. "I had believed you had long since departed."

He pulled a chair next to her, dropped a sheaf of papers on the table, and took her hand in his. "What troubles you, my child? To have you in this state is most unusual."

Kathryne smiled at him and shook her head indicating nothing was amiss. "Thank you for asking, Papa, but there is nothing with which you may offer assistance. Ever since our discussion at the Pickerings last week, I knew what I faced today, and I have dreaded it since then."

"Discussion at the Pickerings? Which part of our discussion caused you such distress?"

Aidan looked at his daughter's eyes, placing his hand gently beneath her chin, holding her head up. Suddenly he arched his brows in awareness.

"Ah . . . your decision in favor of Mr. Foxton as your intended, is it not?"

Kathryne nodded.

"And with that decision, there is another man who must be informed of such, is that not correct?"

Kathryne nodded again.

"It is not an easy task, Daughter."

She nodded again.

"Is there something I might do to ease your troubles? Perhaps I shall accompany you and explain that the decision is truly a father's right and that I have insisted that you follow my determination in this matter?"

Kathryne placed her hand over his.

"Papa, a more considerate father I could not have been given had I wished for such. But no, this is a call I must make on my own, for it truly is my decision, and I shall not seek to place the onus on others. I must tell Vicar Petley that he cannot consider himself a suitor for my hand. It is not proper that I allow two men to place themselves in competition. I must tell him the truth of the matter and allow him to seek his future elsewhere."

Aidan patted her hand. "A man is not a man until he experiences the pain of the heart. Perhaps this is the first such true distress that the vicar will have felt. The hurt he experiences will make him a vicar more understanding of the pain of others."

Kathryne looked up. "Is that the truth, Papa? Will some good come of this?"

Aidan leaned over and embraced his daughter. "Let us pray that I speak the truth," he said, "for once I myself was told as much by others."

"Is that so, Papa?"

"Indeed," he replied, "for as I courted your mother, there came a time in which I thought I had lost her affections by paying attention to another lady-in-waiting at court."

"Papa!" Kathryne called out, aghast. "Mama never spoke of this. Were you truly such a cad?"

"It was merely a case of mistaken intentions that gossip inflamed. But for a long fortnight I believed that I had lost your mother's affections. Friends tried to be a balm to my hurt by offering their platitudes. I am afraid they did little to ease that pain."

"And that is how the vicar shall respond?"

"Perhaps, Kathryne. I know if I were to lose a person such as you, I would be most miserable."

"And there is nothing I may say that lessens the blow?"

Aidan shook his head. "I am afraid that there is not, my poppet. Merely purpose in your heart to be completely honest. Do not fabricate falsehoods to try to soften the blow, for that is a most sure method of making the pain worse in the long run."

"Oh, Papa. Being a woman can be most unpleasant at times."

Later that day Kathryne rode to town, the longest ride she had ever taken, and after she and the vicar finished speaking of what books and materials must be ordered for the new school, she took him by the hand and led him into the stillness of the garden behind the parsonage. They sat on two separate benches facing each other.

"Vicar Petley, I must speak clearly now, and I beg you to listen, for I have most distressing news to share with you."

The vicar smiled sweetly and brushed at some merrywhigs flapping about his face. He did not expose his disappointment at her not calling him Giles as she had in the past.

"Kathryne, that is nonsense. There is nothing you might say that could cause me distress."

"But, good Vicar, there is indeed," she replied, her lower lip beginning the slightest tremble.

Kathryne stated her decision, and a half-dozen moments later, the vicar jumped up and bellowed, "Geoffrey Foxton! The man is a rogue and a bounder if I am any judge of character! You do yourself a supreme disservice by assenting to consider him your intended!"

Kathryne had resolved not to be swayed by anger, pain, or even logic, for her mind was firmly made up. To admit that the decision needed revisiting would then allow the renewal of the consideration of a certain Mr. Hawkes as well. And Kathryne was not allowing that possibility.

"Most unbelievable, Kathryne, that you should follow this path," he muttered as he turned away from her.

"I am truly grieved that I caused you such pain, Giles. It was never my intent," she explained through her tiny sobs. "Will you ever find it in your heart to grant me your forgiveness?"

The vicar spun about on his heels, the polish of his boots shining from beneath his long cassock that flowed about his ankles like drapes in a wind.

"Forgive?"

He placed a hand to his chest, to finger the large crucifix that hung there on a thin leather strap. His voice was not cold, and was not warm nor expansive either, but a tight, controlled tone.

"You forget that I am in the business of offering forgiveness and peace—or at least showing others the way. It would not do well for a true man of the cloth to refuse to forgive when asked."

He stared down at Kathryne, his eyes slits in the afternoon sun.

"Of course, Kathryne, I forgive what you have done to me and how grievously you have wounded my heart with your actions. Of course I forgive you for selecting comfort and security above love and honor."

She began to rise from where she sat and was about to offer a rebuttal, but he raised his palm toward her face.

"It is no matter, Kathryne. I will get over this hurt, as I am sure you will as well. And in the future, when we meet, we will say nothing of this day, as it never will have happened in our memories."

Kathryne caught the words she had formed before they left her throat and merely sat back down, lowered her eyes, and dropped her head in an act of contrition that she hoped would appease the angry man standing before her.

# CHAPTER

# 35

*27 July 1642—*
*St. Michael's Dedication Day*

The whole of the island had gathered in the square before St. Michael's—plantation owners, wealthy merchants, traders, their wives and children, and the clergy of Barbados as well as several from neighboring islands. All stood, swaying slightly in the hot stillness, waiting for the last speech to be delivered before entering the new church on this its dedication day.

From the podium where Governor Spenser stood at the front of the crowd, the assemblage appeared to be large and heavily feathered. Both men and women had selected their finest apparel for the day, each outfit including a plumed hat with ostrich, osprey, crane, parrot, peacock, and toucan feathers all bobbing in the wind.

Aidan kept his remarks brief and spoke for no more than a half hour. He welcomed all to the celebration marking the island's entrance into proper English society. "Now that we have a fitting place of worship, which is the true heart of any location or city, in truth we will face a more godly future." His remarks included thanks to Vicar Petley for his skill and acumen in overseeing the finishing of this marvelous structure ahead of schedule and under budget. Aidan would have sworn that Giles visibly expanded in size as he made those remarks.

In less than two hours the oak doors swung open, and the crowd surged forward and filled the cool, darkened interior. In moments, the first official church service on the island of Barbados began with Vicar Petley striding confidently to his perch in the pulpit to the left of the altar.

In his homily, which ran a few sentences longer than one hour, the vicar covered a wide array of Scriptures and theology.

Midway through, as he looked out on the bobbing feathery head-wear of the crowd, he thought it distracting and wondered if he could insist that all parishioners, both men and women, remove their hats upon entering the church. And as he considered this prospect, he lost his place in his message and, rather than shortchange his audience, started again at the top of the page, repeating three-quarters of a sheet of notes and remarks.

Following the dedication, the crowd slipped out into the square and the garden, partaking of such libations as the church provided—only weak wine, watery ale, and a few plates of sweetmeats—all of which were gone by the time the servants managed to penetrate the crowd only the first few people deep.

Geoffrey had Kathryne off to himself in a quiet corner of the garden, hidden by some large palms and shaded by fronds. He carried two large tankards of good claret wine with him. Kathryne took one and merely sipped it, not wanting a repeat of her previous experience with the heady drink.

"A most gratifying occasion," Geoffrey said, "and I am most comforted to know that this church is finally buiLieutenant To provide this island a focus for its faith has been a most dire need for years."

Kathryne looked at Geoffrey and smiled at his words.

"And now we have a place to worship, which is what the heart of man searches for—a place where he can enter into the practice of faith with others," he added.

She smiled, her eyes bright.

Geoffrey almost winced, for he had just repeated her very words of a few days prior almost verbatim, as reported to him by an attentive Caldor Bane. Geoffrey usually had the presence of mind to rephrase such sentiments into his own words, but these slipped out without thought. He breathed a sigh of relief, for the smile stayed on her face without change or flicker.

From where Kathryne stood, she needed only turn her eyes a quarter to the south and her vision would be filled with the looming presence of the fort, now all but complete. An English flag flapped noiselessly on the far corner of the northern wall. Kathryne laughed at a clever remark of Geoffrey's, who had the uncanny ability to mimic those around him with great accuracy. Geoffrey looked about, making sure he would not be overheard, then repeated a very convoluted phrasing, borrowed from Vicar Petley's message, in the vicar's higher-pitched presentation voice. Kathryne's eyes widened as she listened, and she quickly put a hand to her mouth to hide her laughter. As she regained composure, she playfully pushed against Geoffrey's shoulder, chiding him for being such a jester in such solemn surroundings. Then she began to giggle again, her face reddening from the effort to keep her mirth still.

As she laughed, her eyes caught a glimpse of a flash from the fort, as if the sun had caught a mirror placed on the upper ramparts of the north wall. Her laughter slipped into a broad smile, then she slowly turned back and faced Geoffrey again, who was now in the process of presenting a wicked mimicking of Vicar Coates's slower, more hesitant style of speech.

From across the bay, Will sat in the uppermost rampart, nestled in a niche carved from thick stone. Propped on his bended knees was a new telescope, the most powerful he had yet used. It was focused due north on the celebrants who spilled out around the new church. With a slow and deliberate sweep, he examined face after face. The thick, heavy glass instrument made it seem as if each person was merely standing across the dusty road rather than across the bay.

It was after many moments that he saw the ultimate target of his methodical observation—Kathryne—as she stood off to one side of the crowd. She was laughing; he could see her eyes sparkle and dance in the sun. While her laughter was mute and silent in the distance, every note of it sounded in his heart. He knew the music that her laughter was, and how his heart yearned to dance to those lyric rhythms. He saw her hand flash to her mouth, holding that laughter pent up and still. He saw her playfully reach out and touch the shoulder of the person she was with, and then laugh again.

Will's heart nearly stopped when he recognized her companion to be Geoffrey Foxton. He knew that Kathryne must now be nearing a formal announcement, marking the intentions of her future, but now, seeing them happy together before him caused his heart to ache and tighten.

He watched for only a moment more, until Geoffrey held out his hand, silent in the distance, and she placed hers into his and then turned and walked back to the crowd, disappearing into the grand sea of plumage.

Will heard from behind him a deliberate scraping, and knew that Luke was only a few steps from him. Without turning, Will called out softly, "What is it you seek, Luke?"

Soundless, Luke appeared behind Will and stared out across the bay.

"Massa be watchin' church?"

Will smiled. "I am simply using my new telescope, Luke, attempting to see how it functions, is all."

Luke narrowed his eyes. "Lady be at church, yes?"

"She might have been. I am not aware for certain."

"Massa not be lyin' to Luke. Dat be sin, and God don' want Massa Will to sin."

Sighing, Will admitted that Kathryne was there.

"She be der wit' dat man?"

"She is," Will said with little emotion, yet it hurt when he repeated it.

"And Massa never tol' her 'bout his heart?"

Will placed the heavy telescope in his lap and stared back hard at Luke. "And why would I do that, Luke? To make me miserable and her angry? She has to follow her path, and it does not lead to me. I know that. She knows that. The whole island knows that."

Luke stared back, just as hard. "Luke don' know dat. Luke know dat God don' be stoppin' love once he started it. An' Massa not tol' lady what in his heart. And dat be wrong. Dat be most wrong. Dat why you sad, Massa. Dat be why."

Without further words, Luke spun about and nearly sprinted away along the parapet to the steps that led down to the ground. The lithe black man continued to run, his long legs loping along like a speedy deer, and he disappeared out of the gate in the direction of the harbor.

Geoffrey looked around cautiously and lowered his voice. The two men with him leaned in closer, their feathered hats forming a small, colorful tent above them.

"Six Man Bay," Geoffrey whispered. "There will be five Dutch ships anchored there at the full of the moon. That is less than a fortnight from now."

"And how are we to be assured that the governor's troops, or at least his spies, will not be there waiting to seize our entire cargo?" whispered Wallace Davis, his tone edgy and brittle.

"And why do you include us in these plans, Foxton? What do you have to gain?" rasped Bickley White.

"Gentlemen," Geoffrey oozed, "I am assured of the safety of this plan by a source that is truly beyond reproach. And for my troubles in arranging such shipments," Geoffrey added, "to escape London's absurdly high usurious taxes, all I ask is a thin slice of the sale of your goods."

"Thin slice?" echoed Davis.

"Think of me and St. Michael's in the same breath," Geoffrey stated, "for all we ask is a mere tithe of such resources."

"Ten percent?" exclaimed White, a little louder than comfortable, and he glanced about him to see if anyone had noted his outburst. None had, the general talk becoming louder and more animated with each tankard drunk.

"It is a trifling—such a little cost, my dear man, since sugar sold in Amsterdam returns near double the profit than when one follows the rules and sells in London," Geoffrey declared.

He examined each man's face, slowly, deliberately. In a moment, he was most satisfied.

"Good fellows, I will consider this to be a firm arrangement, then?"

Looking most reluctant, both men nodded, and Geoffrey extended a hand to both of them as a sign of their agreement.

■ ■ ■ ■

Halfway across the western skies, the crowds began to depart from the church and head off to smaller gatherings, celebrating the dedication. The parties would begin at sundown and last through the following midday meal.

Aidan had returned to Shelworthy an hour earlier to supervise final preparations, since he was hosting the official celebration. But Kathryne and Geoffrey had stayed at the church and now decided to head for home. Kathryne mounted her horse, preferring that form of transport to a bone-jarring carriage ride. Geoffrey was a horse-length behind her as they wound their way to the harbor proper and then sought the coast road on their way back to Shelworthy.

As she passed the Goose, she noticed several of the establishment's women loitering about the windows, watching as the island's elite rode or walked past their place of business. Kathryne's horse had passed, then Geoffrey rode by. As he did, from the corner of Kathryne's eye she noticed a woman wave excitedly from the upstairs window. While her sight was somewhat obscured by her position, she thought she saw Geoffrey's shoulder and hand move, as if he wanted to respond with a wave, yet caught the movement before it progressed too far. She turned about, a forced smile on her face.

Geoffrey looked up, as innocent as a young boy, and smiled to return hers. He called out, "Kathryne—is anything wrong?"

Kathryne shook her head no and turned again to face the front.

A few moments later a second, even more curious event occurred. As they turned the corner on High Street, Kathryne was most startled to see Luke standing alone beneath a tall palm that stood sentinel at that spot. As she passed, with Geoffrey only a few feet to her rear, Luke seemed to be deep in prayer. As she came alongside him, only a pole length from him, he opened his eyes. Kathryne was about to wave and speak a friendly greeting, but the intensity of his stare stopped her from responding at all. Something passed from the black ex-slave healer to Kathryne that she felt in her soul rather than in her thoughts. It brought her mute, and she remained silent for the rest of her trip back to Shelworthy, puzzling over what had transpired.

CHAPTER

**36**

*August 1642*

A ship neared the Bridgetown harbor, tacking hard into the gentle leeward winds, an occurrence of no great import except to one man.

Will, awake with the dawn, saw the sails in the thin light and headed to the harbor to meet the ship. It was carrying cargo he needed. He clucked at the two horses hitched to his rough wagon as they pulled it toward town.

The *Lady Rose Ann* slipped in next to the pier, and Will caught one of the mooring lines and in a moment had it tied and snug against the piling.

The captain, Grent Foster, called out, "A good sailing, Mr. Hawkes. Almost as speedy as your best."

Will smiled. "You do your best to flatter me, Captain."

For the next two hours Will and Foster spoke of the trials of the voyage from England, the vessel running into a fortnight of high swells and fierce rain and wind. It sounded as if it had been a dicey crossing, and the crew looked most relieved to be in calm waters next to firm, dry earth.

Barrels of salt cod were lifted out of the hold and rolled to the end of the pier, standing like obedient soldiers, waiting for orders. Following the salt cod was salted beef, then barrels of flour and rye and crates of axes, plows, and machetes.

Finally, as the afternoon approached, Will's iron rings were brought up, one huge crate at a time.

"Ballast be ballast," Captain Foster laughed, "and this was freight-paying ballast to be true. It be the kind I like best."

The crew, with Will's help, unloaded all two dozen crates. The wagon held only three crates, and Will sent it off to the fort, staying with the rest of his cargo. He sat up on the high stack of heavy crates, and in the far western side of the harbor, noticed a second set of sails that day.

Will turned to Foster and called out, pointing to the west, "Who might that ship be? Have you passed her in the days prior to today?"

Foster turned and squinted at the small two-masted fluyt. "We have not, Will, but she looks like a coaster. I would not venture a ship that small out where the sea gets angry."

Will looked hard and added, "She might be a fishing vessel."

"Could be," Foster agreed.

He then slapped at his forehead. "Ye gads, how could I have forgotten? I have a posting addressed to you in my cabin. Captain Waring in Weymouth made me swear on a stack of the Scriptures that I would not sink or lose my way here."

"Captain Waring?" Will called out to Foster, who scrambled back on board, heading toward his cabin. "Why has he written to me? Is he well?"

Foster stopped just before ducking down the hatch. "Captain Waring is fine, Will. This letter has been forwarded by him. It comes from your home in Hadenthorne, I believe."

"Hadenthorne?" Will replied, nearly stunned.

As he spoke that word, he imagined that it would be informing him of the death of Mrs. Cavendish perhaps, or that they had received word of the vicar, or that some other calamitous event had occurred.

In a moment, Foster was back on the pier and passed a thick envelope to Will. As Will looked down at the first return address—the posting from the Virginia colony and the feminine hand that penned the words Missy (Holender) Cavendish, his heart seemed to freeze a full beat, then leaped into his throat.

He slipped his finger under the thick seals, noting the tortured path this post took to reach him. As he opened the letter, the incoming small fluyt slipped to the other side of the pier where he stood and was quickly tied off. Will paid no attention to it, for the import of what he now held in his hand was so great.

He held the letter up to his face, gaining better vision of the thin lines in the penetrating sun. He read the few lines that indicated Missy's great misfortune, her pain pouring from that page, drenching Will in a torrent of regret and near agony. He looked at the date, months prior to this day's date.

*What has become of her?* Will's thoughts cried out.

He read and reread the brief letter, calling, imploring him to rescue the woman he had first loved.

It was a long moment until Foster, who had stood by Will as he read, said in a gentle voice, "William, what is it? Is the news bad?"

Will did not move.

"Mr. Hawkes," Foster called out louder. "What has happened?"

Will lowered the letter, his eyes going soft and hazy.

From just beyond his shoulder, and just behind him, he heard a most feminine sound call out, a voice that spoke of apparitions and spirits.

"Will? William Hawkes?"

Will spun about and there, just off the small fluyt to his right, stood a pale and barefooted Missy Cavendish.

Will could not find words in his soul, could not find the power of speech, could not locate the source in his being that commanded movement of limb.

A dozen, then two dozen heartbeats sounded. Will moved his lips, hoping that sound would come.

"Missy?" he questioned in a croaked whisper.

With that single word, the young woman who stood before him simply crumbled to the ground. She fell, noiseless, without a whimper or sound, her golden curls fanned out like a halo about her head on the rough wooden planking, mere feet above the beckoning turquoise waters of the warm Caribbean Sea.

## 37

Will leaped to Missy's side and placed both his strong hands on her face, turning it toward him, cradling her delicate features as a new father cradles his child.

"Missy! Missy!" he called out in the gentlest firm voice he could muster, yet her eyes remained closed. To Will, it seemed as if she had stopping taking breath as well.

*Oh, God, she cannot be taken again! This will not be my fate!* his brain screamed. *It will not be!* Will turned his face skyward, a glistening hint of tears already forming at the corners of his eyes.

"I will not lose her!" Will shouted, angry, looking up at the heavens. "Do you hear that! I will not lose her! Not again."

Captain Foster looked to the skies as well, seeking in amazement whom Will might be addressing. The two officers of the small schooner scuttled up to Will, nervous and confused.

"Is she alive?" one screeched.

"What have you done to her?" the other demanded.

Will, at the verge of panic, slipped his arms beneath her and, as a child might lift a limp doll, scooped Missy up into his arms, cradling her tightly to his chest, her head nestled in the crook of his arm. His eyes wide with fear, Will began to run down the dock in long strides—leaping past crates and stevedores, lines and rigging, canvas sails in stacks, longboats upturned for repair—and in a few heartbeats made the street. He began to shout, "Luke! Luke!" as he ran to the fort.

Will began to pray that the black man could set things right.

He was running faster now, people's faces a blur as he passed. The two officers began to follow him, but soon were lost in the crowds of the harbor.

Down the busy main street lined with fishmongers, peddlers, and sailors, Will ran, faster and faster, Missy's long blonde curls flowing over his arms. Her right arm was tight against Will's chest, her left hung limp, and with every footfall, it rose and fell, keeping rhythm to his steps.

*She weighs nothing,* Will thought as he ran. *I wonder when she last ate.* He knew what tragedies occurred to those who lacked enough food—the slightest injury, the slightest fever, the slightest shock, and their hearts would simply stop beating.

*Not this time!* Will's thoughts roared.

"Luke! Luke!" he continued to shout as he reached the narrow path that led to the fort. *Oh, God, let him be there.*

"Luke! Luke!" he continued to shout, louder and closer to hysteria.

When Will was a dozen steps from the gate, it swung open and Luke was running out with a blanket, his bag of herbs and potions, and a thick rectangle canvas. Luke stopped by a flat area and threw the canvas down, covering thick pangola grass and soft earth in the warm shade of the front wall.

"Here, Massa. Put her here," Luke called out.

William would have run to his cottage, but realized in a flash that it possessed no furniture other than a rough table and bench. Will still slept on a mat laid on the stone floor. He might have run to the captain's quarters in the fort, but it still lacked a roof, and its interior was a jumble of debris and stone chippings.

Will knelt and laid Missy out as tenderly as a bridegroom places his bride on their wedding bed, her hair a golden pillow for her head. She lay there, limp and unresponsive, pale as the dawning's clouds.

Will knelt back, and Luke leaned forward, placing his ear close to Missy's face. A group of laborers had come to the gate and stood in a wide semicircle about the two men with Missy between them. They were speaking in low voices, twos and threes putting heads close together, pointing to the ship, then gesturing to the woman.

Luke stood back up.

"De lady be breathin'. Her heart still beats," Luke said, with scant little of his usual assured tone. "But it be little sound. It be heart sound of little bird."

He poured some water into a small crockery cup, sprinkled three types of ground herbs into it, and swirled it around. He thought for a moment, then added a fourth element—a foul-smelling ocher powder.

"Be most powerful medicine I make, Massa."

Luke knelt down and slipped his knuckly hand under Missy's head, tilting it forward. He placed the cup to her mouth, once full and red, now thin and bluish. Slowly, with great care, Luke wedged the cup's edge between her pliant lips, then tilted it upward, allowing the pungent drink to ebb into her mouth, a few drops at a time.

Will searched her face for a sign of vitality, watched to see if any of the drink was swallowed, but saw signs of neither. She remained as limp as a deer struck with the hunter's musket shot.

After a hundred heartbeats Will thought he heard the slightest of coughs, more nearly a faint groan. He leaned forward, the shade of his body eclipsing her face. Another slight groan seemed to emanate from deep within her. It was not unlike the sound a man makes as his spirit leaves his body.

Will closed his eyes and prayed harder. He had heard that sound too often in the past, and its faint rumbling terror chilled his heart. In the densest, most fierce sea battle, a man could lie on a bloody deck, breathing near his last, and that sound would be heard above all others. Men would turn to locate that hiss, that moan of a soul's departure, either praying for safety or offering thanks that it was not their soul that sought to leave this desperate tempest of life.

Will closed his eyes tight. *No, God,* he prayed. *Please, not this time. Let this poor child live. Do not take her from me. She does not deserve to be a sacrifice.*

Missy's eyes fluttered slightly, like a butterfly trying its wings after a morning thunderstorm. The movement was tentative, cautious, and hesitant. The blue that Will saw there as her eyes trembled open was the most beautiful color he might ever imagine—the very color of the sky in heaven, he would say later.

Luke looked over to Will and then nodded his head. Will slipped closer and placed one hand at Missy's head, taking Luke's place. With his other hand, he touched at her cheek, tracing an intimate line from her eye to her chin.

"Missy?" he asked in a child's voice. "Is it really you?"

"William," she finally whispered, her lips only inches from his ear. "God has honored me and answered my prayers."

Will felt her warm tears pool against his hand.

"God has answered both our prayers, dear Missy," he whispered back. "He has answered both our prayers."

Missy closed her eyes again and sleep found her in an instant. Will rose as quietly as he could. Luke remained there, resting on his haunches, as a watchdog. He would not leave her side, and Will knew he need not ask.

Will gathered up his crew and sent them running in several directions. Three he sent to the chandlery with instructions that regardless of the project John Delacroix and his men had before them, they were to drop all and within the day produce a sturdy bed and frame. They would need make the mattress of cotton ticking and stuffing.

"Nothing fancy, but I will not have her sleep on the cold, hard ground," Will instructed them.

Others he sent to the tailor with specific instructions for bed coverings and at least two gowns for Missy, in whatever style he thought would be appropriate.

"I know nothing of a woman's sensibilities, but whatever he produces, it *will* be done by sunset. I will tolerate no excuses."

The entire crew of black men was sent to the cottage, only recently completed. "Wash and lime every surface inside," he called out. "And the floor needs to be swept and washed down as well. Do you understand? Your work will need to be completed by sundown at the latest hour."

Will called over a carpenter named Rowell, the most educated of the group working on the fort.

"Will you attend me on a more delicate mission?" Will asked in a quiet voice as he draped his arm about him.

Rowell nodded, unsure of the nature of the task being presented to him.

"Go to Miss Eileen at the Goose and ask if she might spare whatever it is ladies use to . . . bathe and such. It appears that Mrs. Cavendish has spent many months without such a luxury, and I would anticipate that access to such feminine things may help her recover."

Rowell arched his eyebrows high. "You want me to visit Miss Eileen and inquire of her about such womanly intimacies?" He looked about, scanning others for the hint of a volunteer, his face now reddening. "Is there not someone else that you might send on such an errand? I feel most unsuited. Truly I do. I am but a carpenter, not some gentlemanly fop with experience in these matters."

Will placed both hands on Rowell's shoulders and squeezed, perhaps a little harder than need be. Will saw the man's eyes tighten as he did so.

"Nonsense, Rowell. I am sure that she will be most willing to offer assistance. Of course, I will pay a premium if need be."

Rowell rolled his eyes. "I think Miss Eileen is accustomed to assessing a premium price on most of what she dispenses," he said, resigning himself to his fate.

The two men remaining were sent to gather food for an evening meal.

"No turnips and potatoes, mind you. I want a fresh cut of beef, with fresh fish and a full share of the freshest vegetables available. And add to that a half-dozen bottles of good wine and a small barrel of proper ale as well."

Through the increasing warmth of the morning, Missy alternated between sleeping and waking. When her eyes fluttered open, she would call for Will, and he seldom left her side for more than a moment or two.

"It be the potion, Massa," explained Luke. "Lady sleep den not sleep. By night, she be better."

The sun was nearing the western sea, and the sky was an explosion of golds and reds with ribbons of purple. Thin bands of clouds poured to the west as well and framed the colors in shifting bands of white, then gray, then black.

Will watched as six men came at a trot from town, each holding on to a separate part of a large bed frame and mattress. A sturdy-looking piece, the bed was built of honey-gold Carolina pine and was waxed to a bright shine with linseed oil and nut wax. The two headposts each featured a simply carved pineapple, the symbol of hospitality. At the right corner was John Delacroix, his face coated with sweat and sawdust.

As the bed neared Will's cottage, John called out, "Your request has made one Dutch merchant angry at his unfilled order, Will, but I could no more deny you a favor than I would deny myself."

Soon the bed was nestled in the bedchamber of the cottage. As John left, Will stopped to shake his hand in gratitude.

"When you have a free day, John, I will require a smaller bed of a similar design to be constructed for myself."

John stopped abruptly and stared at his old friend. "But I thought . . . I mean the . . . the bed be large enough for two. I had thought . . ."

Will noticed a slight reddening to John's cheeks beneath the layers of wood shavings.

"Missy is an old friend from the town where I grew up, John. I will have no man cast aspersions on her character. She has been on this island just this one day, and is still in a most delicate condition."

John held up his hand, almost as an apology. "William, I merely thought . . . well, after what your men have said about your behavior and actions this day and all. . . ."

"It is of no matter, John. I understand what they have assumed. It will not be, for to be so would damage my Christian witness. Luke will provide what chaperone is needed here. None can doubt the innocence of the arrangement with him present. Perhaps someday the relationship may be different, John, but all in good time."

## 38

"A woman, you say," sniffed Vicar Petley as news of Missy Cavendish and her collapse was brought to him by an eager tradesman working on the parsonage.

"Indeed, Vicar," the carpenter said. "She be the most beautiful servin' wench that I've seen for many months." He wiped his hands on his greasy and tattered apron. "And they say she took one look at Mr. Hawkes and collapsed like a spilt load of bricks."

Vicar Petley turned his head to the side. "Indeed?"

He walked over to the southern window and peered out. From that position he could see the whole of the harbor and the hulking mass of the fort further south, across the blue waters. It was too great a distance to see individual faces, nor make out a gentleman from a servant, but Giles squinted nonetheless.

"And Mr. Hawkes took her to his cottage, you say?"

The carpenter coughed and wiped at his mouth with his forearm. "Carried her like a husband carries a bride, Vicar." He smirked. "Beggin' your pardon for such frankness."

Giles placed his face close enough to the window to fog it with his breath. He stroked his chin with his thin fingers.

"Our good and noble Mr. Hawkes may not be all that he seems," Giles whispered to himself. "Most men are not."

After a moment, he spun on his heels and went to seek out a messenger. "I believe this is news that Lady Spenser will find most interesting," he muttered as he descended the staircase in search of parchment and pen.

Geoffrey sat in the back room of the Goose as Will's man Rowell came in asking for Miss Eileen. He sidled up to the interior doorway and listened as Rowell breathlessly, and in a most nervous manner, asked Eileen for her assistance.

*She must have smiled her bewitching smile at the man as she replied,* Geoffrey thought, *for his answer was stammered and stuttered.*

In a few moments Rowell had laid out William's request for his new houseguest, and Eileen answered, laughing in her clear, dulcet way.

"Of course I will assist Mr. Hawkes with his needs."

Geoffrey had stood with his ear to the door, trying to understand some of the muffled conversation.

In a few moments Eileen gathered a sackful of powders, lotions, and even a few colorings, along with a comb and a small looking glass that she possessed as extra items for her boudoir.

Geoffrey pushed his ear tighter to the wood.

"Tell Mr. Hawkes that he now owes me a favor," Eileen laughed as she handed Rowell a full leather pouch of scented and delicate feminine requirements. "Do not forget—I will demand payment of Mr. Hawkes in the future."

And with that the outer door opened and closed, and Geoffrey hastily retreated to the inner bedchamber.

*Our noble Mr. Hawkes may not be quite as noble and virtuous as he claims,* Geoffrey mused, and he smoothed his hair back into position. *But then, who among us is?*

Missy remained on the thick canvas spread, a thin sheet covering her in the comforting warmth of the afternoon. Luke remained with her, watching her breathe rhythmically until the sun had begun to set and night began to fall.

Will lit some small torches and hung them in a nearby tree.

"She is a most beautiful woman, Will. Your description of her pales in light of the reality of her features."

"Indeed, that is the truth, John."

The cooking fire in the cottage had been lit for several hours, and a full English dinner, worthy of nobility, was nearing completion there. Will's men had purchased four proper chairs for the dining table and proper crockery plates and tankards. In addition to the bed linens, the tailor had finished not two, but three gowns of varying styles, using as a pattern the ragged and worn extra dress Missy had brought. He was hesitant to even touch the wretched garment and immediately threw it out after measurements were taken.

Just before the sun dipped finally into the west, Missy sat up and asked for water. Luke was there in a moment, a cool ladle of sweet springwater held to her lips. Will was at her side a moment later.

"Do you feel able to walk the short distance to my cottage, Missy? I could easily carry you there, if your recovery is not to that point," Will asked, kneeling.

Missy smiled, and reached out to touch Will's face with her fingers. "It was not a dream. I thought it might be, but it is not."

Will placed his hand over hers on his face. "Missy, it is not a dream, yet it is."

She nodded, knowing well what he meant. "I believe such a short walk may do me well."

Will helped her to her feet and took her arm to steady her.

"It is like a paradise here, is it not?" she said as she looked at the purple evening skies, the sea hissing intimately against the sand, the palms waving gently in the cooling breeze, with hints of frangipani and persimmon on the air.

"True, Missy, it is now," Will added, and he pulled her closer to him.

She suddenly stiffened and stopped, her hand to her throat. "But what of my contract, Will? I have sold my term as a servant to come here—for a full three years—to a Sir Felton," she said in a panicked voice. "He will be expecting me." Missy turned back to face the harbor and town. "Do you know of this man, Will?"

Will took both her hands in his, and his eyes found hers.

"Missy, you must not think of that now. I will send word to Sir Felton. I do not anticipate that you will need be concerned about this matter, now or ever."

Missy's eyes showed concern and surprise. "But, William, I have signed a contract. It cannot be ignored. I must—"

Will placed a finger tenderly to her lips and hushed her to quiet.

"It is not a concern of yours, Missy, not any longer." He cocked his head at her. "Now, let us make our way to the cottage. Perhaps you may be able to share supper with me?"

"You live here, Will?" Missy asked as she beheld his cottage.

Will nodded.

It was not an expansive home, but well built of polished stone from the shore. It had three large windows facing the sea and the west. The large front door was built of thick oak planking and fit snugly into a curved archway. Slabs of flat, smooth rock formed a path to that door, ready to line a proper garden. The roof was a thick thatch of palm fronds woven into a tight, waterproof surface.

On the ground floor were three main rooms—a large living space at the center of the cottage, dominated by a huge fireplace on the east wall; an adequately sized dining space with a fireplace in the corner; and a snug kitchen with a cooking fireplace, with rails and nooks for heating, and a long oak scullery table. Beyond that was the home's bedchamber, where the large bed, completed only hours before, had been placed. The cottage stood two stories tall, with an unfinished loft upstairs, where additional bedchambers would someday be.

Will reached the door and opened it, allowing Missy to enter first. The smells of dinner—roasting meats, spiced fish, and pungent ale— filled the air with an intoxicating blend of scents. Missy breathed in deeply, appearing near to swooning again. Will reached out, instinctively, to steady her, taking firm hold of her arm, keeping her upright.

She turned to him, smiled, and placed her small hand over his.

"I am fine, Will. It is simply that I have not had the pleasure of such delicious scents for what seems like years."

A loud growl came from her stomach. She giggled, and her hand covered her mouth.

"Missy," Will said, "dinner will be ready in a moment. I have taken the liberty to . . . acquire a few . . . things that I thought you might need. You will find them in the bedchamber, along with a washing crockery and towels and the like."

He gestured toward the door. "I assure you that you will not be disturbed," he added.

Missy arched her eyebrows at Will's caution and slipped behind the door and pulled it closed. After a moment, Will heard a squeal from behind the door and ran to it. He listened at the door for a moment, then heard water pouring from a pitcher into a basin, then the rustle of clothing and delicate splashes.

He blushed, red and deep, and turned back to the kitchen to supervise the final touches on the evening's meal. Two of his men had spent the afternoon preparing it, complete with biscuits, cottager pudding, vegetable stew, roasted shank of beef, grilled fish, stewed cabbage, grilled pineapple, cheeses, wines, and a large spiced flannel cake with lemon sauce. A vast assembly of dishes and pots was gathered in the middle of the large table, each steaming in the faint light of the evening.

Candles had been set on spikes in the wall and on the table, the room bathed in a flickering glow.

After perhaps a half hour Missy appeared at the doorway between the great room and the kitchen. Will, busy carving the beef shank, looked up and saw the two men in the kitchen stare over his shoulder, their mouths virtually agape. He turned to see Missy standing before him.

She had selected the blue gown made that day by the tailor. It fit her form fairly well, but the neckline traveled farther south than Will would have thought proper.

Missy followed Will's eyes to that spot and giggled, and with a calculated move, tugged the material up to a level of Christian modesty. Her golden hair was combed and pulled back to her neck with a thin white ribbon. Her lips, no longer pale, had been colored slightly with one of Eileen's cosmetics, and powder was lightly dusted on her face.

Will stood still as a cat readying to pounce on an unsuspecting bird, and slowly lowered the knife and fork to the platter.

"William," Missy whispered, "this is like the entrance to a dream. You have saved me."

She put her hand to her hips, gathered the fabric of her gown between her fingers, and pulled it away from her, looking back at Will's eyes.

"You have saved me, and clothed me in the finest gown I have ever possessed. You have saved me and provided shelter. . . ."

Her voice dipped to a whisper, nearing silence, as tears filled her eyes and she ran into his arms. "Will, . . . you have answered my prayers."

He held her as she sobbed, her face against his chest, her hot breath warming his heart. He stood there, holding her, for the longest of moments as his cooks silently padded about, putting the final touches on the meal, then slipping out the front door. Will looked out the window as they left and saw Luke sitting on a large boulder in front of the house. Their eyes met for a moment, and Luke smiled a curious half-smile.

*I don' know who dis lady be, God,* Luke prayed as he watched William and Missy embrace in the kitchen of the cottage. *Luke don' think dat lady be de lady dat Massa's heart be wit. But den Luke hear dat lady be marryin' a man on dis island who grows de cane and be ownin' slaves.*

*God, Luke be most confused. Is dis lady here de lady for Massa? Be God changin' what he wants for Massa? God best be tellin' Luke, for*

*I be most confused. But days been long since Massa been smilin' like dis.*

Luke sat there in the darkening evening as a thin mist filled the air like a silent prayer. He wiped at his face with his long fingers, wiped the cooling, cleaning moisture from his face, and stared at the couple, sitting before him together, sharing a meal.

*Luke be most confused, God. Best be helpin' me know what's to be prayin' 'bout.*

Will decided that Missy needed to eat more than he, so during dinner he took the lion's share of the conversation. He explained what had transpired in his life since the two were last together so many years ago in Hadenthorne. Will spoke of his disappointment upon finding Missy married and gone to the New World, but added quickly, after seeing the pain on her face, that he knew she alone could not be held accountable, for she had been pressured by her parents and Mrs. Cavendish. Even the clerical weight of Vicar Mayhew had been placed against her desires.

"I would have thought it most difficult, if not impossible, to have waited for such a foolish man as myself to settle his confusion, Missy. I bear no ill feelings about such events."

As he spoke of this, she had for the first time that evening stopped eating and watched Will's face as he spoke. Her eyes spoke of the pain she had felt in such a decision, their delicate and deep blue seeming to fade to a lifeless, cold slate gray as he spoke the words.

Will summed up his years at sea and his gradual descent from privateer to pirate. He spoke at some length of the final climactic episodes that brought him both to this island and to the knowledge of God in his life. He barely mentioned Kathryne Spenser in his narrative. He most certainly avoided the retelling of their adventures on his island and her role in opening his eyes to the face of God. *It will serve no purpose this evening to alert Missy of the existence of Kathryne—at least not this early after her arrival,* Will thought.

At the end of their meal, Will stood, extended his hand to Missy, and invited her to sit by the fire in the living room. The weather had turned damp and chilled that evening.

She walked into the room and with the innocence of a child spun about on her heels, her gown flaring about her ankles and knees, her arms extended like a child's top. She collapsed on a bench placed near the fire, and it rocked back a moment, then righted again.

"I feel as a princess," Missy cried out. "For the first time in months

I have eaten my fill at the table, and I am clothed in such a fine garment."

She held her hand out to Will, who was adding a log to the fire. He took it and sat down near her.

"You will not vanish like a sprite in the dawning, shall you, Will? And will I awake to find all this gone?" she asked as her eyes took in the warmth of the room.

*How do I answer this?* Will thought in a rush. *Is she asking for a guaranty of the future? How do I offer such assurance?*

"Will? Shall you and your cottage be gone in the morning?" she asked, her voice warm and inviting.

"Missy, this is all most real and true. I shall be here in the dawn. It is where I live. I have nowhere else to journey to."

She smiled at him and pulled his arm about her shoulder like a shawl. She tugged again at the bodice of her dress, for during the evening it continued to slip, as if it had a mind of its own.

Missy giggled again. "What lady has lent you this gown has a more womanly frame than I." Missy blushed.

Will stammered a reply. "But the tailor used your own tattered gown as a pattern. Has he sewn the sizing in error?"

Missy sat upright and spun to face Will directly. She had her hand at her throat. "Will, you mean that this is . . . my own dress? It is not attire that needs returning?"

"Of course not. The tailor has sewn the three dresses for your keeping—the one you now wear and the two others in the bedchamber—and used your other as a template. I assume that he was simply too rushed."

Missy lowered her head and touched at the sleeve with her hand.

"My own . . ." She looked up. "To keep? For certain and not a jest?"

"But of course yours to keep."

Missy leaned forward and held Will about the shoulders and pulled him closer. She felt smaller to him, and more delicate, than his memories of their days in Hadenthorne.

She pulled back, her eyes wet again with tears. "Will, that other dress was done up years ago back home . . . when . . . when food was plentiful. I fear that I have lost much weight since then."

Will placed his hands on her shoulders, and she reached and tugged the fabric nearer her throat.

"Missy, you will never need worry about a meal again. I swear to you of that," Will promised, not truly understanding what he was offering, but knowing that he would never see her go hungry again.

"And tomorrow, may I visit the tailor?" she asked, her eyes open and innocent. "I cannot spend all my time protecting my modesty like this," she added, smiling as she tugged again.

Will nodded and embraced her again, holding her close, offering the protection of his arms.

With her head resting on his chest, her breath became slower and rhythmic, and her eyes closed gently in sleep. Will waited a moment, then gently lifted her from the bench and carried her into the bedchamber. He arranged her on the new bed, placing a thin blanket over her.

He looked at her face haloed by her golden hair. He bent at the waist and with the most delicate of touches, placed his lips against her smooth forehead and kissed her there. She seemed to smile in her slumbers at the touch of his lips.

Silently, he slipped out of the room, latching the door behind him.

He opened the front door of his cottage and stepped into the gentle mist. There sat Luke, wet as a sheepdog in an April rain on the highlands, staring out to sea.

"What are you looking for?" Will whispered.

Luke did not flinch, for his ears must have been waiting for William in the dark. "Luke be waiting for God to speak, Massa Will."

It was near silent, the ocean muted in the darkness.

"Has he said anything yet, Luke? Has he answered your questions?" Will asked as he sat down on the damp rock next to the black man.

Without moving his eyes from the dark horizon, Luke replied, "God not spoke yet, Massa, but Luke sure he answer. He answer when he be ready."

# 39

Before the first rooster crowed, Will returned to the docks to speak with the officers of the schooner that had transported Missy to Barbados. He hastily scratched a note to Sir Felton. In it, he wrote:

*Kind Sir:*

It is my understanding that you have contracted Missy Holender as servant to you, indentured for a period of three years for the amount of twenty-five pounds to be paid upon completion of said contract.

As a friend of Miss Holender's family for many years, in good conscience I will not allow her to serve in this capacity. I am offering you a doubling of that rate—a full fifty pounds—to assign her contract to me.

*Truly yours,*
*William Hawkes, Captain of Harbor Defenses*

◾◾◻◾◾

"An indentured servant, you say, Caldor?" Aidan asked as he popped the final bite of a honeyed biscuit into his mouth.

"Indeed, sir," Caldor responded, avoiding the obvious glance of Kathryne's eyes as she sat next to her father at the table. Caldor Bane had been informed of the entire story of Mr. Hawkes and his most recent "purchase"—at least as much as had yet transpired—early this morning by a breathless Mr. Foxton. Geoffrey had arrived at the first flinty light of dawn, walking his panting horse the last stretch to Shelworthy to avoid alerting anyone still sleeping in the governor's residence.

"And he paid twice her contract price to obtain the woman?" Aidan asked, trying to clarify the story.

"And would have paid more, I understand," Caldor said with a slight hiss to his voice. "It is said the woman is most beautiful," he added.

"And he purchased gowns, and a bed as well?" Sir Aidan asked. "In the space of a single day?"

"A bed sufficient for the comfort and pleasure of two." Caldor smirked. "As well as several powders and lotions of a feminine nature," he added, his eyes darting to Kathryne.

She sat there, quiet, hoping that her racing heartbeats would remain unheard and that her face would remain calm and not flushed.

"Well, a most curious event, then," Aidan stated with finality. "If Mr. Hawkes seeks to find a woman in that manner, then I am afraid I may have misjudged his commitment to our Lord and moral, upright Christian principles."

And with that pronouncement, Aidan returned to the matter at hand, completing his morning meal.

Kathryne, her face suddenly white, looked down at her plate, as yet untouched. She pecked at her breakfast, not tasting anything, not truly hearing her father's words as he expressed further disdain for the temporariness of the high moral stance of certain people. After he rose and excused himself to attend to the matters of government, she sat there for a moment or two, fighting back the urge to cry out. Her heart seemed to climb into her throat, and she felt it pounding there, angry and hurt.

She slid her chair back with a loud squeal and first walked, then ran up the stairs leading to her bedchamber throwing herself onto the bed in a heap, the tears coming hot and fast.

*Why is Mr. Hawkes doing this to me?* she wailed, her heart grown empty and cold.

Willy, alone in his cage, hopped from perch to perch, as if agitated at her display of emotions. He chirped loudly, but without song.

Kathryne looked up, her world gone hazy and vague through the saltiness of her tears. A bewildering mosaic of memories clamored for her attention. In one instant, alone on the open seas, she was kidnapped by a pirate, and a moment later, she was at the top of a bejeweled waterfall in the arms of that very pirate, his potent blue eyes on hers. And then, heart to heart, his lips fell upon hers, and she responded to his tenderness. An instant later, it was Geoffrey Foxton's face that she saw, with his wide and inviting smile.

She blinked her eyes, then squeezed them shut, trying to clear the maze of sights that flew before her.

She opened them again, tears flowing freely down her cheeks, splashing noiselessly on her clenched fists. *Why is that man attempting to break my heart in such a wretched and ignoble fashion?*

Her eyes narrowed to slits; she noticed a thin, elegant note card propped on the pillow of her bed. The scrolled and flowered script bespoke of being written by Vicar Petley. On the front, in bolder lines, were the words *MOST CONFIDENTIAL. To be opened by Lady Kathryne Spenser alone.*

She slipped her trembling finger under the seal, the scarlet wax breaking in a dozen fragments, tumbling into her lap. She left them there as she pulled the note from the envelope.

*My dearest Lady Spenser,*

Not wanting to be the harbinger of evil news, yet not wanting you to be shocked at hearing such perfidious news from another, less compassionate source than myself, I must inform you of a most unfortunate incident that has been related to me. It appears as though the good Mr. Hawkes has purchased a harlot from a disreputable merchant sailor (a sea captain reported to be a sodomite, of all things). I have heard that he has purchased from a woman at the alehouse named the Goose all manner of seductive cosmetics and the like. I can scarce believe it myself—Mr. Hawkes' high-handed "preaching" on Sundays notwithstanding. It appears that such men are truly seeking only one thing.

I am most sorrowful to have to tell you this, but owing to your recent history with the brigand, I thought it wise to inform you myself rather than to have you hear about such things from a local gossiper.

*In proper Christian service,*
*Vicar Giles Petley*

As her eyes finished following the last elaborate curl on the signature, she buried her face in her hands. The sobs poured over her as a waterfall pours itself in a wet, shattered crescendo onto the rocks on the precipice below.

◾◾◾◾◾

After completing his business at the docks, Will walked to the surf near his cottage and stared out to the rolling waves. Dawning always brought quiet and a peaceful stillness. He stripped down to the barest of attire and began to wade into the warm waters. As the liquid lapped at his waist, he plunged in, deeper in the surf, and began to stroke further from shore.

Anyone who partook of such activities was considered a true eccentric, willing to risk the ill humors that plagued sea waters and the open air. Will considered such thoughts themselves as ill humors.

With a strong stroke, learned as a boy in the gentle, muddy waters of the river Taw in Hadenthorne, he pulled himself near the ridge of coral protecting the shoreline. There the sea remained calm all the day, and Will spun about, lying on his back in the buoyant salt waters, and floated, his face toward the sun, the sea filling his ears with its gentle splashing, beckoning him to remain.

He floated there, with small movements of his hands and feet, caressed at the surface between the air and the pull of the cold deep below him.

*This must be how a bird of the air feels as it wings its way home,* Will thought, as he watched the clouds slip past overhead.

After many moments, he slipped his feet below him and paddled there, staring back to shore. To his left was the fort, looming above the edge of the sea, threatening all that came near with its bristly defense, its sharp cannon teeth ready to devour all who might dare to snap in attack. To Will's right was his cottage, its three windows winking out to sea. Around it grew pangola grass, and short palmetto trees waved their heads in the morning breeze. The fire must have been lit for the morning meal, for a thin streak of smoke curled from the stone fireplace in the kitchen.

It was a strange, liquid place to pray, but Will stopped there, on those mornings that called him into the sea, and shut his eyes and spoke to his Creator as he floated.

*Almighty God,* Will prayed, *I am most confused. Missy, a woman whom I once loved—at least I had thought that there was love between us—is now sleeping under my roof. My heart rejoices at providing her shelter and comfort and freedom from despair.*

*But, dear Lord, is this the woman thou has brought to me instead of Kathryne? I have prayed that my home and land be filled with love. Is Missy the woman who will do that? Hast thou brought her here to answer my prayers?*

*I thank thee for providing her safety to this place. But, Lord, I am confused. Please, God, provide a light to my path that I may know the proper steps to take.*

*In thy most holy name, Amen.*

Will sat on the shore in the weak morning light for half an hour, feeling the salt dry on his skin. He would wash with springwater later.

Protected from being seen by a large sand bluff, Will waited until he was dry and slipped into his clothing—a simple pair of breeches, loose and unfitted at the calf, a simple linen shirt, and his one concession to his position—an embroidered doublet, done with gold braiding about the buttonholes and hem.

He shook his head, and his hair flew quickly into a wild tangle. Attempting to pull it back into a mane, he tied what he could with a single strand of leather lacing he kept in his pocket for such occasions.

By the time he reached the stone walk of the cottage, he was greeted with the scents of whatever beef was left from last night's repast being cooked on a hot fire. Luke had turned the corner from the rear of the house, his arms full of split wood that was stacked there.

"Mornin', Massa Will. Be a good day, true?" Luke asked, cheerful.

Will nodded. "Is Miss . . . Missy . . ." Will stopped there, a puzzled look on his face.

*Miss Missy is a most curious salutation. Perhaps I shall simply call her Miss Holender, or Missy, to closer acquaintances.*

"Is Miss Holender awake yet, Luke?" Will asked.

Luke nodded. "She be cookin' at de fire. Dat what dis wood be for."

Will entered his home, a small sliver of apprehension settling on his spirit. Luke was only a step behind him as he did so.

"William," Missy called out, her face expressing both great cheer and a strong current of affection. "I was near troubled that the sea had swept you away. Your man Luke here tried to inform me of your habits. Bathing in the sea, Will?" For a brief moment, Missy's face darkened. "Do not they say that the sea is the source for all sort of maladies and illnesses? You are not placing yourself at risk with this, are you, William?"

Will smiled, both at her concern and the thought of Luke and her in conversation about such activities.

"I have done so for these many months I have lived upon this island, and I have seldom felt more full of good spirits and health than I do now, Missy. I believe that the doctors and those who heed those warnings are in grievous error about such matters."

Missy pursed her lips, and in a moment, she smiled, staring at Will. "I must admit, William, that you indeed look in the finest mettle. Perhaps the sea waters are a tonic, then."

She turned back to the fire and with a long fork poked at several strips of meat held on an iron frame and roasting by the small blaze in the fire alcove.

"I have near forgotten what it is to prepare a proper English breakfast, Will," she said as she moved a few heavy pots about on the cooking hooks. "I do so hope that all this meets with your approval."

Without a warning she placed the fork on a small shelf, turned to Will, and ran full stride into his arms. She began to sob softly at first, then with deeper cries coming from her very heart.

Will glanced at Luke, who looked every bit as puzzled by her behavior as was Will. He embraced her as a father would embrace a daughter and stroked her hair, murmuring soft and tender words to her. He motioned to Luke to attend to the meats and pots at the fire and led Missy back to the great room, to the large pewlike bench there and helped her sit down.

"What is it, Missy?" Will asked, more than a bit bewildered.

"It is my parents, Will," she sobbed into his chest. "Why did they not add a note to my letter before it was forwarded to you? It arrived in Hadenthorne. They would have written a line to you, for the village vicar would have known them. What has happened to them?"

She began to wail louder, and Will held her closer to him, hoping to engulf her with as much security and peace as he could offer.

*I am most sure that her parents, and most likely her entire family in Hadenthorne, are dead. There is no other explanation of why they would not have written to me as well.*

"Missy, do not be fearful," Will whispered in tenderness. "I am sure that they have merely chosen to write at a later time. Perhaps the reason their letter is late is that it sailed with a later ship."

Missy sniffed. "No, Will. I am certain that a grave misfortune has beset them. Silence means that they are gone. And I will never see them again!"

She began to sob anew. Her plaintive cries lessened in a few moments, and she sat back up and wiped at her tears with her hand. She again tugged at her gown, pulling it back closer to her throat.

"William, I feel at sixes and sevens this day. I have gone from servant, to princess, to orphan at a most bewildering speed. I trust that you think no less of me for my weaknesses."

She placed her hand on his chest, just above his locket, and pressed in a most delicate manner against his body. He covered her small hand with his larger, more callused hand.

"Missy, I could never think that of you." He was staring deep into her blue eyes, now the color of the sea following an afternoon rain as the sun strikes the waters from the west. "You were the first woman who ever held my heart in her hands. I could never think lesser of you."

She looked up at him. "Is that truly said, William? That I was the first woman in such regard?"

"Indeed," he replied, feeling the smallest tug at his heart—not a painful tug, but as a dream that began to diminish, perhaps to be replaced with another.

Missy sat back up and looked to the kitchen. Luke was standing by the fire with a long spoon in his hand, stirring a steaming pot. She wiped again at her face, clearing away the trails of the tears that still lingered.

"William, it is time that I tell you of my travels, as you have shared yours last evening. But let us partake of our breakfast meal as we do so. It appears that my appetite has not yet been slaked."

Will helped sit Missy at the table and sat opposite her. Luke slid in on a small bench at the other side, and Will saw a fleeting look of surprise on Missy's face as she, most likely, sat nearer to a black man than she had ever in her life.

*I will speak of Luke to her later,* Will thought, *but for now I will let her speak.*

In between bites of meat and porridge and a thick, spicy kedgeree of rice and fish, Missy told her story.

It was at the urgings of Missy's parents, Mrs. Cavendish, and Vicar Mayhew that she at long last gave up on the possibility of Will's reappearance in Hadenthorne. Eventually the pain in her heart diminished, and Dugald Cavendish, the most clever Cavendish son, began to show her attentions. His boots were filled with the urges to escape the narrow hedgerows and tight confines of England. Missy and he were married, and within two months, Dugald had made arrangements for passage on a ship bound for the Virginia colonies. Missy would be an obedient wife, she said, and follow her husband where he willed, for that is what the Scriptures commanded.

They landed in Jamestown harbor, the same harbor in which Missy would later sell her life as a servant. Dugald was a deft and shrewd talker and within a few weeks had managed to obtain an option on a dozen acres of land that lay thirty miles south of the city on the marshy and desolate region south of the James River by a small settlement called Wakefield.

With only a smattering of tools, Dugald sought to clear the land of the thick thorns and saw grass that clung to the rich soil. The weather was hot, and the air was a thick humid shroud. By the time autumn approached, Dugald had completed his work on the site and constructed a tiny, clinker-built shelter. But they had precious few supplies that first winter. They gathered nuts and roots, fish from the small streams, and traded what meager supplies they had for flour and meal.

Season followed season, and they battled the land and the rain and the winds and began to grow barley, malt, and corn. The land looked black and fertile, yet yielded little. They scarce saw other settlers in their isolation—perhaps only on an occasional walk to the village some ten miles distant. Dugald spoke less and less as the months went on. During the last month he and Missy had shared the same roof, he had spoken perhaps a dozen words in total.

And, with tears clouding her eyes, Missy spoke of their last morning.

She awoke alone, with darkly overcast skies overhead. She tended to the fire and waited for Dugald to return. The sky brightened only briefly that day, and night was soon upon her. She was near frantic with worry. The next day she walked, almost at a run, to the small shanties that made up Wakefield. Dugald had indeed been there the previous day, she was told. He had not said much, other than to sell his thin wedding ring for a few coins. The man who bought Dugald's ring claimed that he had headed west, a thin smile on his face. He explained that Dugald stated his wife had left him and he was on his way to seek his fortune elsewhere.

Missy's voice was hoarse, a mixture of sadness and pain.

She was left adrift, as a ship in a storm that has lost both rudder and sail. She survived for several months by selling off what possessions they had owned, eating through their meager provisions, hunting and gathering what she could. She realized all too soon that it was but a matter of time until she had nothing left and would starve to death, alone in the marshy wilderness.

She was too ashamed to return home, for she and Dugald had left assuring all that they would find immediate success across the sea. And to be true, she had no resources sufficient to purchase passage. In that darkness, she had considered turning to other means to earn money. Women were not plentiful in the new lands, and many a man would pay handsomely for the comfort only a woman could provide. But even as such ideas entered her mind, she shuddered and vowed that it would be best if she were to starve before she would turn to such a life. It was at that point, as her spirits ebbed to their lowest, that she penned the short letter to Will, begging for help, and walked the lonely miles to the Jamestown harbor, handing over her desperate missive—and the only coins she had left—to a kind sea captain.

"I knew it would never reach you in time to allow you to intercede on my behalf, but knowing that it may eventually be in your kind hands gave me the most warm sense of comfort and hope," Missy said, her voice small and calm. "It was then I realized that my life was hopeless and I was broken. I gave all that I had to the Almighty and prayed that he lead me. And, William, that is what happened."

She returned to the small hovel and waited until she was at the true end of her resources. What was left of her possessions could be carried in one hand, and Missy bundled up her courage and stored away her pride, and again walked the three days to the Jamestown harbor, there to seek out her future. And now, in the matter of a few short weeks, she found herself here, sitting at a table laden with delicious provisions, wearing a new gown, facing a man who had once loved her.

She bowed her head at the end of the tale, and the room grew quiet.

Luke sat up straight. "Missy pray to same God we pray to, Massa Will?" he asked brightly.

"She does indeed," Will replied.

"Den maybe dis be de lady I be prayin' 'bout?" Luke asked. "Maybe she be de one, Massa."

Will noted the strange tone of uncertainty in Luke's voice. He looked at Missy's face, drawn and thin, yet filled with the glow that heralded beauty's quick return. Will looked at Luke, his face marked with the expectation of answered prayers.

Will shut his eyes briefly and prayed a quick prayer. *If this is indeed the woman, dear Lord, please make it known to my heart as well.*

And as he opened his eyes, his heart felt curiously calm.

# CHAPTER

**40**

Geoffrey rode his horse to the wide sandy curve of Six Man Bay, just north of the tiny village of Speightstown. He had urgent business that Sunday, but it was not at the mill as he had told Kathryne and Aidan as he made his excuses for not attending church. His appointment was further north up the eastern coast of the island. He emerged from the shadows of the palms and jumped from his horse, peering out to the western waters, and far in the distance made out three sails, just at the horizon.

Only a few yards from where he stood were more than two hundred barrels of thick molasses. Two hundred additional barrels were due that afternoon. Two-thirds of the sweet cargo was Geoffrey's, the other third was pressings from the plantations of Wallace Davis and Bickley White. Three of Geoffrey's men, with a new brace of pistols tucked into their belts, stood guard over the precious sugars.

That evening, as the sun settled low to the west, the three Dutch ships would tack toward shore and anchor in the shallow bay, as close as they could to the sand. The tide would be rising throughout that night, so they would be poled closer and closer to shore as the moon rose in the darkening sky. A half-dozen longboats would paddle between sand and ship, carrying up to ten barrels a trip, to be winched aboard and then stored belowdecks.

If the weather remained calm, the ships would be fully loaded by dawning and the high tide. After a simple transfer of documents, the vessels would swing back into the warm waters on their way to Amsterdam and the sugar markets there.

Geoffrey smiled wickedly, and while he waited and watched he began to calculate his profits.

# CHAPTER

# 41

## 21 August 1642

*Dearest Emily,*

This is the first letter that I have begun with a salutation that avoided your true title of Lady. Up till this date, I felt as a child, a mere innocent in your presence, whether it be via a letter such as this or when I had such luxury of being in your physical presence.

While my life was not free from pain and sorrow—such as the untimely passing of Mama—it was free from most of the devilment and vexations that seem to occur in others' lives and never in my own. Now it seems that blissful situation has changed. My ordered and neat world seems to have been turned upside down, and I am most often at a loss to decipher what to make of such vexations.

I am penning you these words with the most deep hope that you will be able to offer me your wisest counsel and advice. I pray that you will respond in the shortest possible time.

Through an odd and most convoluted manner, a woman (possessing great natural beauty, I am told) arrived upon this island a fortnight ago. She sailed to these shores, having offered herself as an indentured servant to one of the island's more successful planters. Yet that was not to be her fate, for she was met on the docks the very moment she arrived by Mr. Hawkes, who had been there on some business. Upon seeing him, the woman simply fainted dead away, only to be scooped up by William and taken to his cottage, where, I am told, she now recovers. She has been attended to by Luke, the black healer of whom I spoke before. I have come to understand that this woman is the very same woman who William was once enamored with back in his home village of Hadenthorne in Devon. Yet in his absence, she married another and set sail for the New

World, only to be abandoned. That is what brought her to this island. And William has now paid to secure her contract, and has established her in residence under his own roof—without benefit of marriage! (I am not suggesting that the two have done anything immoral, but the face of such actions seems most improper.)

Dearest Emily, I have reviewed my writing to this point and my very tone accuses me of what I have feared. I am acting as one who has been rejected by a suitor for another. But my heart feels so wounded and scarred, and by a man who has no claim to it.

What does all this mean? I am endeavoring to forget Mr. Hawkes and be happy with Mr. Foxton, who is a most pleasant man. And then William complicates it all by acting in such a flippant manner toward me by finding another woman to harbor in his home. Are all men as this? Do all their species think so little of womenfolk that they care not how cruelly they behave? Am I being foolish by thinking that he should care about my feelings?

It was Mr. Hawkes, after all, who swore on the light of the North Star that his love for me would be pure and everlasting. And now he has sullied that vow by having that woman share the fruits of his labors with him. I have been told that he has even spared no expense and purchased three lovely gowns for her to wear, as well as costly lotions, powders, and colors for her to use. And I must ask (and forgive me if I am verging on the scandalous): How does this woman intend to repay his kindness? Mr. Hawkes is a trusting soul and can most easily be taken advantage of by such a woman. Is not such behavior improper? Am I not justified in my indignation?

Please, Emily—write back words that will settle this problem in my heart. I know that you are wise, and I will have such counsel in you.

Hurry your reply to me.

*Your friend,*
*Kathryne Spenser*

## 21 August 1642

*My dear friend Emily,*

It was with such great surprise that I read your recent parcel addressed to me. I have taken great pleasure in reading and rereading your most kind words to me. I have waited until I have had a day free from obligations in which to offer you a response.

(I beg you to forgive if this language appears stilted or contrived in some manner. It has been decades since I last put pen to paper with the recipient of such a letter being a lady—especially one as lovely as yourself.)

I offer hearty congratulations on the completion of your recent tome and securing rights to publishing. I expect you to send a copy to me when it is done (and of course I will purchase it; I do not expect to receive it gratis).

I have heard also of Cromwell's growing influence on the affairs of state. Some say he sees himself as a new king, sans the royal lineage. I pray that it is not the case, for we need a strong monarchy if England is to prosper throughout the world. Shifting allegiances and powers are a sure way to invite marauding nations to see England as weak in resolve.

You say the king and his court find pleasure in my abilities— that indeed is most pleasing news. I have heard as much through official correspondence, but I daresay what is written and deemed official often does not match what is said and issued as unofficial. I am enjoying my tasks here on Barbados and in the Antilles.

Your words have said that I am on your mind most often. Emily, I must admit upon reading that, I felt myself curiously stirred. I trust that I have not misread your words, for I too have thought of you most often. Kathryne speaks of you nearly on a daily basis, as to what you would say to this or that matter, and how you must be getting on alone in dreary London. When your name is spoken, I, too, picture your physical presence. It would be a most heartwarming reunion to see you again and to speak at length with you. Perhaps in a year or two I may return to London on governmental business. If that is to transpire, will it be within the bounds of what is seen as proprietary to call upon you? I would greatly enjoy spending an evening of dinner and conversation with you.

I too remember the days of the past when you and I and Beatrice were young and foolish. I am gladdened to realize that in the mirror one shows the passage of time, but in our minds and in our thoughts we remain eternally youthful.

*Until we write again, I remain faithfully, your friend,*
*Aidan Spenser*

# 1 September 1642

The *Kindred Spirit* entered the warmer waters south of the Azores and had turned west. Lady Emily stood as near the bowsprit as she could get without being sprayed by the rising swell against hull as it cut through the pearl gray waters, now edging to the early green hues of spring.

Emily rested against the railing, and her smile was as broad as it had been in years. Every groan of the rope against yardarm, every noisy snap of the canvas filled with winds, every tumbled splash of wave to hull was a joyous melody to her ears. Her cabin was most Spartan and small, but she would have slept in much tighter quarters, or even on the open deck beneath a thin blanket, if necessary, for the thrill of riding the waves west.

Four weeks ago Emily had settled all ongoing accounts in London, placed her funds with a trusted solicitor, arranged to have a caretaker and his family live at her residence, packed up three large trunks full of clothing and books, and secured passage on a large English galleon bound for the Canaries and on to the Antilles, with its first stop in Bridgetown.

*In a few short weeks I will see the two people in the world I am most fond of,* Emily thought.

She turned such memories over in her mind, smoothing and shaping them like well-rounded stones are smoothed in a fast-moving riverbed. At first it was Kathryne she was most anxious to see, but now Emily was not as sure of the relative importance of she to her father.

*I will be overjoyed to see them both equally as much,* she declared to herself, though not yet truly believing her statement, as the sea spray misted her light red hair.

## 42

Will awoke at first light and noiselessly climbed down from the loft of his cottage. He and Luke had been sharing the large empty space since Missy had arrived on the island. Will would not sleep in the cottage without a proper chaperone, and Luke would not allow William to sleep under the stars as he himself had become accustomed to. A compromise was reached as Luke slept by the wide-open window just under the eaves. Will slept on a thick canvas mat just to the other side. That way they could both enjoy the light of the stars and the moon on their faces, and Will could feel secure that no tongues could wag concerning the virtue of his houseguest.

In the early dawn Will ran his fingers through his tangled hair, grabbed at his shirt and doublet, climbed down the ladder and, like a cat, slipped outside and headed to the sea. At the edge of the sandy bluff, he turned and faced his small home by the sea.

*I like having her there,* he thought, *for it is a most pleasing emotion to have a smiling face wait at the door for my return.*

Their first, and truly only, argument of those first few weeks had transpired between Missy and himself when she had discovered that he had purchased her contract from Sir Felton. She had vowed that he was not to mortgage his future to save hers. Indeed, she had packed up her few belongings and began to walk to town in an effort to seek out Sir Felton and reverse Will's purchase of her contract. Will had caught her by the arm, halfway to her destination, and demanded that she return with him.

*She has no way of knowing that fifty pounds is but inconsequential to my resources,* Will had thought at the time.

In truth, Will's total worth stood nearer a hundred thousand pounds and was increasing every month due to several shrewd investments procured both by Captain Waring and Will's solicitor in Weymouth. Indeed, Will could have bought and sold dozens of the nobility who owned land upon the island, for many of them existed from the generosity of the king's land grants, the Dutch lending banks, or extended credit from other noble relatives.

Missy had demanded one concession, and Will had begrudgingly acquiesced to that demand. Missy insisted, in an attempt to repay Will for his kindness, that while she remained under his roof she would cook and clean and sew and take all the necessary domestic duties under her wing.

Will slipped behind the bluff and into the warm waters, stroking again through the surf. With Missy under his roof, there were fewer and fewer times available to him when privacy and solitude was guaranteed. Alone in the sea was one of those times, and Will treasured it greatly.

*I like having her there,* he thought, *for I have never enjoyed such a clean, well-scrubbed house, nor have I eaten as well as I have these past few weeks.*

He stroked to the calm water and floated, staring out to sea, toward the angry swell off the far reef.

*Neither of us have mentioned the future. It is as if we are both reluctant to say what is on our hearts. Does Missy truly love me? Do I truly love her? And is that love—the love that poets and romantics speak of—called a necessity by the Almighty for two people to live as man and wife? Can we both not grow together in love, or does it need to exist first and we simply nourish its life?*

Will spun about and floated on his back again, staring at the gray clouds slipping past, low and dark in the sky. Slowly he began the swim back to shore.

Luke was awake and had stoked the embers of the fire, adding a few small logs for the morning's meal. His features seemed pursed tight, and his smile, once easy and free, had been absent for the past several weeks. If one were to ask, Luke would simply shrug and in his singsong voice admit to no ill feelings.

But Will could tell that it was God who puzzled Luke. Since Luke had come to believe in God, his prayers and questions were answered quickly and with a most definite response. Indeed, it was Missy's presence that so greatly troubled Luke. He had prayed for love to be brought into Will's life, yet Missy's was not the woman's face that Luke saw in his dreams and prayers.

It was only the night before that Luke had whispered loudly to Will, as they readied for sleep, "Massa Will know a lady wit' light red hair?"

Will thought for a moment, then answered. "The only woman that comes to mind is Miss Eileen."

Luke tightened up his eyes. "No. A lady dat be more old. Luke see a face wit' . . ." Luke struggled to find a word, and pointed to the wrinkles and lines on his face by his eyes. "A lady wit' dese on her skin," he explained.

"Wrinkles? A lady with red hair with wrinkles?" Will asked softly, as not to disturb Missy.

"Dat be what I see," Luke confirmed.

Will held up his palms in regret. "I am most sorrowful, Luke. I have not made the acquaintance of such a lady."

Luke snuggled down on his mat, his arm tucked under his head as a pillow.

"Der be such a lady, Massa Will. God show me dat lady. She be here. Luke don' worry. She be here."

■ ■ ■ ■ ■

"John, welcome!" William called as John Delacroix made his way from the dusty road to the stone walk.

John smiled broadly and waved. He spotted Missy, framed by the large window in the kitchen, and waved a greeting to her as well. She responded with a dazzling smile as she lifted back a few tendrils of her golden hair from her face, tucking it with a soft gesture behind her ear. Her eyes met his for a long moment, and even from the distance of the walk, John felt the warmth of her gaze slip into his very being. And yet here was William standing before him, his arms crossed over his chest, a smile waiting there for an old friend.

*What I am thinking is not right,* John scolded himself, *for Missy is not a woman whom I would even deign to consider in that way.*

John extended his hand to Will, who took it with his familiar enthusiasm and power.

"John, I am so happy that you have allowed the chandlery to function for an evening without your presence. It has been too many days since we shared a table together, my old friend."

"Indeed, Will. Both our responsibilities now seem to conspire to keep us apart. We should have made a pact never to seek success, for it does consume too much of our time."

Will laughed. "It does seem as if only the rich and the poor, who are removed from the contest, have time enough for such relationships," Will said as he reached around John's shoulder and hugged him close. John nudged at Will's side and snickered. "What brings your laughter, John?"

John nodded, smiling. "It appears that your . . . friend? servant? . . . It appears that Missy's talent in the kitchen agrees with you, Will. You have added a slight layer of substance about your middle."

Will stepped apart from him and looked down.

In a whisper, he added, "You may be speaking the truth, John, for I have never had three full meals every day cooked by someone with as much skill as Missy. A most pleasant change, I must say."

The evening was indeed most delicious, and Missy was both enchanted and dismayed at their stories of the treacheries they experienced together on the high seas.

Perhaps what transpired that night was merely a nudge of John's imagination. The first time he sat with them at a meal, Missy's eyes never left Will, and she seemed to anticipate his every want and need. But at this dinner, it was he, the guest, who was offered the choicest cut of meat, not William. Missy seemed to laugh loudest at John's remarks, and her laughter was not as free and open in response to Will's speech. And as he took his leave, later in the evening, long after the moon had spread its faded light across the dark heavens, Missy embraced him when offering her good-bye and held him for what John thought was most certainly several heartbeats too long.

He walked back to his small living space at the chandlery with his thoughts in a most curious muddle. Missy was indeed the most comely and handsome woman he had ever met, and one of the most charming as well.

*Yet Missy is with Will, and is his intended wife . . . is she not?* John puzzled as his footsteps echoed along the lonely and quiet piers along the water's edge.

*And what is a friend's role in such matters as these?* John asked himself, not expecting to receive an answer from the darkness that eddied about him.

## 43

"Lord Aidan, what a great surprise!" called an ashen-faced Sir Thomas Tenby as he stepped, sweating and stained, from the hot and sticky sugar mill. The mill, a ramshackle affair, was a small stone building nestled in the denser foliage at the edge of the vast field of cane. The palms and palmettos nearby were tacky from the bubbling vats of cane juice. Tiny flies swarmed in thick clouds above the mill, seeming to suck the sweetness from the heavy air. Caldor Bane, looking most uncomfortable perched upon a horse, arrived a moment after the governor, his riding skills most rudimentary in comparison.

Tenby mopped at his forehead with a yellowed handkerchief snatched from his pocket. His weskit was streaked and matted with juices and dark splotches of sugar pressings. Around him were a dozen slaves, hauling bundles of the rough cane to the large maws of the mill. The stone cylinders, powered by oxen, or slaves when the oxen refused to turn anymore, ground together and forced the sweet residue out of the crushed cane. The slaves, their ankles cut and torn from the sharp cane stubble, their shoulders raw from the heavy bundles, had an unfocused, lost look in their eyes, as if their spirits had retreated deep inside, far away from their horrific reality.

Aidan looked down from his mount and was tempted to cover his mouth with his lace handkerchief, to prevent the cloying sweetness from fouling his breath. To the uninitiated, such an aroma often came near to overwhelming.

"Sir Thomas, I had understood that your harvest was approaching completion and I, as governor, am keenly interested in the progress of the yield per acre of our fertile lands. It does me well to know the true worth of such land when relaying to the king the true value of his holding as well as what value he may place on land grants in the future."

Tenby nodded, the sweat forming a thick sheen on his forehead, almost as rapidly as he might wipe it off. His toil had colored his complete attire a full shade darker, due to his sweat.

"True, Governor. Such truth is needed."

He wiped again, this time with his bare hand on his sweet slippery forehead. *What in blazes is he doing here? Why would the governor consider my yield as important?*

As if reading his thoughts, anticipating what his question might be, Aidan reined back on his horse and stated in a loud voice, "I have been in conversation with Mr. White and Mr. Davis, and I was most saddened to hear of how sparse their yields were. As governor, I feel a pressing obligation to ensure the successful operation of all plantations on Barbados and am willing to offer what assistance as I may, good sir."

Tenby snapped his fingers, and within a moment a slave appeared with a tankard of cool springwater. He drank some, then splashed much of the rest on his face and neck, using his soiled handkerchief to mop up the excess from his features. His hair, damp and wet, stood out like spikes from his head.

"Your kindness and concern are most unexpected," Tenby said, trying to hide the obvious distrust in his voice. "But I assure you that we have such matters well in hand."

Aidan nodded, then added, almost as an afterthought, "How well *is* your yield this season, Sir Thomas? What sort of barrels per acre will you expect?"

*Why have I been cursed with his interference, unless it is because of that blasted Davis and White. I am sure that to avoid his attentions to them, they have sent him here. Blazes!*

He looked at the barrels stacked about, in a casual disarray, and the half-dozen carts arranged in a line, waiting to be loaded with the sweet treasure.

*Can I fabricate a small yield?* he wondered, then saw Caldor Bane as he totaled up the number of barrels waiting in the field, nodding slightly as he counted each one.

*Blast it all!* Sir Thomas grimaced and then snorted, loud enough for Governor Spenser to say, "God bless you," then answered through clenched teeth. "Nearly eight."

Caldor turned to the governor, looked about for a brief moment, then nodded with the slightest of movements.

Aidan nodded as well, making no attempt to cloak his action. "Eight barrels—a most impressive performance. I am sure that such a cargo shall bring a great reward for the lucky English captain to sail it back to London," Aidan stated calmly.

Sir Thomas narrowed his eyes to a slit. "I am sure it shall," he grumbled. "I am sure it shall."

Aidan bid him farewell and both men rode off, their horses making muffled clumping noises in the soft, black dirt as they trotted off.

Just under his breath, Sir Thomas cursed again, a vile curse involving certain men's parentage.

"Just wait, Messrs. White and Davis! Your turn shall come soon enough!"

With that he spun around to face a ragged line of black men, staring out at him. "What in blazes are you doing? If you stand still again I will call for the whip. This land shall never yield eight barrels per acre unless you move. Now move!"

## St. Augustine, Florida

With a deep, formal bow, Radcliffe Spenser rose, excused himself in practiced Spanish, and left the table of Captain Diego San Martel. Captain San Martel had just been honored by the governor of St. Augustine for his daring exploits and his return to his home port, laden with gold from Dutch, French, and English merchants hapless enough to stray under the range of his mighty guns.

Radcliffe considered the man to be swinish, boastful, and not the least cultured, yet he was willing to endure the unpleasant afternoon to curry his favor. Radcliffe needed a skilled and ruthless sailor to bring his bold plan to success. It would be many months until the small flotilla of new vessels, now under construction, would be ready to sail. Someone needed to recruit sailors and officers, train them, and execute the plan. San Martel had a reputation of cunning and cruelty, and Radcliffe knew that, among all the privateers sailing out of St. Augustine, San Martel was the most qualified. Eventually Radcliffe would be required to make good on his promises of great wealth, ripe for the picking, that lay in wait for the Spanish on the quiet island of Barbados. And if payment would be required, Radcliffe needed to find the right man for the job.

*I can endure the most boorish of gentlemen,* Radcliffe thought to himself as his steps carried him past the thick fort walls, *if it assures me eventual success.*

San Martel maintained his small quarters, luxuriously furnished, in a suite of rooms in a wing of the massive defensive fortifications overlooking the harbor. The looming stoneworks held barracks, a hospital, an armory, shipyards, and a prison. It was the prison that kept growing with each new decree of the governor and with each new ship falling prey to the Spanish raiders.

It was the shank of the evening, nearing midnight, and a few torches lit the way as Radcliffe walked with slow paces. It seemed as though some unfortunate wretch tumbled from the jagged and confused tangle of walls on a nightly turn. One was lucky to survive such events with only a broken bone or two. Radcliffe slowed, having no desire to delay his grand plan because of carelessness.

With a hand to the moss-covered wall, he felt and stepped his way, using the outside wall of the prison to guide his progress. It was a dank place, even in the most stifling sun, for the Spanish governor had little concern for the niceties of life, claiming that it was simply squandered on the men inside the walls. With few exceptions, all would die soon anyhow.

As Radcliffe turned the corner to the brighter courtyard that faced the main gate, he heard a man's voice speaking in low tones from within the walls. Normally he would have thought little of it, but this voice was speaking Spanish with a most curious accent. *English,* he recognized as he leaned toward the tiny barred window.

*An Englishman in this jail? It may be worth knowing who the unfortunate soul is, just in case I may have need of his talents,* Radcliffe thought, never one to overlook an opportunity, an edge, no matter how small the edge was.

"You there!" Radcliffe called out. "The man who speaks with the English accent! Come to this window!"

For a moment all was silent, then a polite whispering stirred the stillness, then the sound of slow footsteps traversing the dark gloom of the large cell. The steps marked the man as having many months of experience navigating the space in the light as well as the dark.

"Who asks for the English speaker?" the voice called out.

The tone and the accent marked a man of some education, perhaps from the south of England.

"Be no matter of yours, you filthy prisoner. Just be sure that I could have your head on a spit by the dawn," Radcliffe shrilled out, with a venomous edge to his voice.

The voice from within did not flinch nor cower. "A simple courtesy is all I asked," the voice said.

"And again I say—who are you?" Radcliffe demanded.

"I am Vicar Thomas Mayhew of Hadenthorne in the county of Devon. I have been held here since the ship I sailed upon was seized by Captain San Martel."

Radcliffe's entire body began to quiver, as a lion quivers before leaping on an unsuspecting fawn.

"And whose ship was this upon which you sailed?" Radcliffe asked, desperate to keep his voice from betraying his emotions.

"It was captained by William Hawkes," the voice answered.

And in the darkness, Radcliffe fell to his knees, a sweet smile upon his lips. As he pulled himself upright again, his sky filled with stars and a yellow moon, as if showering him with celestial gifts.

Pausing until his breath became normal and steady again, Radcliffe added with a whispery sneer, "Well, Vicar, perhaps I shall return on the morrow, for I am English as well, and we may have matters to discuss."

Radcliffe then slipped into the pitch-black courtyard, his steps echoing gaily in the night.

CHAPTER

44

The *Kindred Spirit* sat in the waters north of Barbados, unwilling to sail closer to the shores, cradled in the swaddling band of darkness. The crescent moon marked the eastern sky like a smudge of Dover chalk. At first dawning, men clamored up rigging and set sail to wind, and the ship creaked and hissed, chopping the light swell into foam and ripples at the bow.

Lady Emily had slept but a moment, perhaps two, the entire evening. Now, as that chalky moon disappeared in the warmth of the new sun, Emily's heart began to beat faster, and she felt a most dizzying excitement in her bones. The ship ducked into a swell, and the spray spilled over the rail and misted the air about her as she stood at the rear quarterdeck. The drops of seawater caught in the long lashes of her closed lids and spangled the arc her light red hair, pulled back and plaited at her neck.

As the sun warmed and neared its zenith, the sailors began to furl sail until only the rear mizzenmast had canvas to find the breeze. Slipping into the calmer waters, the ship's English flag was raised high on the mainmast. From the main tower of the fort, three pennants were raised, signaling that the ship was welcome to enter the harbor waters.

A smile never left Emily's face as she viewed the greened island, the white sand framing the shore. Her nose was filled with the warm air, fragrant with exotic scents. The scene numbed her eyes with its painter's palette of brilliant colors, especially after so many weeks of only sea and sky.

Within minutes the *Kindred Spirit* was nestled snug against the creaking pier. Emily's three trunks were unloaded, and with the captain's kind assistance, a driver and cart were located.

By the time the sun neared its late afternoon position, Emily was seated in an open hackney, her trunks piled and roped down behind her, on her way to Shelworthy.

At every turn Emily grew more spellbound. She was made near mute by the lush jungle that edged the road, by the calls and the colors of jungle birds as they flapped about, by the thick waves of sugarcane, by the bands of sweating black men and women slaves as their machetes spangled in the sun, chopping through the thickness with a hypnotic rhythm that she could scarce have imagined only weeks prior. She heard a song as she passed one field, slave voices coupled with the sweep of burnished blade, marking the time. Emily felt as if she had an ear to the very heartbeat of the island, and it thumped loudly and hotly in her ears with an exotic pulse.

She dabbed with a lace handkerchief at a thin bead of sweat that formed at her upper lip and forehead. *Such a sound would never have been heard in London. In all my life, I have never felt such a mixture of all my senses, and all at such a fever pitch.*

With a wide, jangling circle, the hackney turned onto the drive of Shelworthy. On her left was the sea, sparkling in the afternoon, the sun a hotness suspended in the sky, and to her right was the lush, darkening jungle of green, filled with beckoning calls and intoxicating fragrances.

She scarcely saw Shelworthy, her vision carried away to the more exotic environment about the residence.

The hackney stopped, and the driver jumped out and extended his hand to her, offering assistance. She alighted, her boots crunching on the hard-packed shells, the sound loud in the still afternoon.

She stepped up to the front door as the driver made loose the ropes holding her trunks. She lifted the shell door knocker and let it fall twice, the sound echoing inside. In a brief moment, a large-framed black woman opened the door. She was smiling, her eyes wide in a gentle question.

"Yes'm? Be ye seekin' the govern'r?" she asked, her accent as thick and exotic as the heat.

"Please tell him . . ." Emily said, and stopped, hearing a rustle of dress against steps.

"Hattie? Who might it be at the door? Is it a visitor for Papa?"

Hattie turned to face the staircase, then back to the woman at the door. Her face was that of an innocent child asking a question that has no answer.

In three more footsteps, Kathryne reached the entry. She had the hem of her gown in her hands and had been watching her steps, having tripped all too often on the stairs, her feet entangled in the cloth.

"Hattie?" she asked, then peered around her maid's right side.

It was at that moment that Emily leaned to the left, and the teacher's eyes locked with those of her former student.

Kathryne, for a moment, showed no surprise on her features. Then as a sudden cloud skitters across the face of the sun, her face widened, her eyes opened wide, the color slipping from her skin. With a sudden shock of awareness, Kathryne's hand jumped to her throat, and she crumpled to the floor like a wet sheet falling from a clothesline.

"Hattie, who is it?" called out a masculine voice from the far room on the left, the room that bore the seal of the governor's office. Aidan was alone, for Caldor was in Bridgetown seeing to the posting of deeds and land claims.

Watching Kathryne slump to the floor, Emily was, in an instant, kneeling by her side, cradling her head in her hand, fanning at her face with her closed fingers. Hattie had pressed against the wall, her palms flat against it, her eyes squeezed shut, as if preparing for the vicious blow of a hurricane.

"You there," Emily barked. "Hattie, is it? Fetch us some cold water and a soft towel—hurry!"

Hattie opened her eyes to a mere squint, and seeing her mistress still in a state of collapse caused her to squeeze them tight again.

"Hattie!" Emily called out again, as calm and soft as she could, sensing that Hattie was not well-suited to handle the stress of this situation. "Hattie, listen to me. Kathryne has merely fainted. She needs cool water and a soft towel. She will be fine as she awakes."

In a long sight more than a twinkling, Hattie lumbered off in a rumple toward the kitchen, her footsteps reverberating in the warm quiet of the morning.

"Hattie!" the male voice called out again, this time the pitch rising, on an obvious path to an irksome crescendo. "Hattie! Who is it? Where is Lady Kathryne? Why will no one answer my calls? Where is Boaz? Is this entire house to be collapsing about me this afternoon?"

Hattie spun back around the corner where Kathryne lay, narrowly missing Emily's shoulder as she slid by, her bare feet callused and slick on the polished floor. A second set of footsteps was intermingled with

Hattie's, coming from the other wing. In a heartbeat the steps closed in nearer, and Aidan spun from the hallway at the same moment Hattie slid to Kathryne.

Hattie squealed in childlike terror, holding the large pitcher of cold water in front of her as a shield. The pitcher was sideways for a moment, its liquid contents splashing forward in a torrent, a torrent aimed at the chest of Lord Aidan Spenser, governor of Barbados and all the Lesser Antilles.

The water struck Aidan full force, and the maelstrom splashed on his chest and over Hattie, the rest falling as a heavy rain on Emily and Kathryne, still prone on the entry floor. Aidan reacted instinctively, flailing his hands in front of him. Hattie's feet failed on their attempt to gain purchase, and she slid with a resounding, thumping crash onto the floor, only to be stopped when wedged against the open front door. Through the cold waterfall against his chest, Aidan felt the heavy pitcher bounce off his right arm, and he flung out his left to catch it before it fell. Catch it he did, but he slipped as well during the attempt and harrumphed down with the aching sound of bone to hardwood. His face was dripping wet, and his doublet thoroughly drenched. His daughter's chambermaid was prone by his feet, his daughter was lying, pale and white at the foot of the steps, and water was spread everywhere in great puddles. Aidan blinked his eyes through the water, and a lady with elegantly plaited hair raised her head to him, for the first time revealing her face to his confounded vision.

His heart beat near a dozen times before she spoke.

"Aidan, I trust I have not come at an improper time?" Emily asked in the most civil, proper, and polished of voices. "I do so apologize for not sending a messenger with a calling card before I came."

And with that utterance, that small vestige of English civility, Emily began to smile at first, then giggle, hiding her laughter behind her free hand, the fainted Kathryne, cradled in her other hand, almost forgotten.

Aidan simply sat there, his face a blank mask of astonishment. After the longest of moments, he turned from his knees, sat full on the soggy floor, and began to laugh as well.

By the purpling dusk of that day, the spilt water had been dried, wet clothing had been exchanged for dry, and Aidan, Kathryne, and Lady Emily were seated in the formal drawing room of Shelworthy, each with an elegant goblet filled with a ruby-colored Madeira wine.

"Emily," Aidan said with a smile, "I daresay that I shall never be able to recall this evening without a smile overtaking my face in a pleasant hurry."

"Aidan, if I had spent more than a moment thinking of the consequences of what was to happen the moment after I arrived at your doorstep, perhaps it would have been more the drama than the farce." Her voice was sweet and calm.

Kathryne, once revived from her faint, was in a most silent and agitated state. For the past many months she had thought that having Lady Emily at her side would do wonders to settle the nagging questions that still ragged Kathryne's heart, questions of the appropriateness of Geoffrey Foxton as a suitor, her heart's continued pull toward Mr. Hawkes, and her inability to settle the issue on her own. But now that her confidante and advisor was here, sitting one chair distant from her, in a quiet room in the governor's mansion on Barbados, nothing seemed settled at all. It was as if Emily were a looking glass, and her presence merely reflected—and in some ways magnified—Kathryne's problems. Kathryne looked over to Emily, whose smiling face was turned at first to her father, then turned back to Kathryne, who tried to return her smile. But all she could see in her toothsome grin was a mocking reflection of the childish and immature dilemmas of her heart. Lady Emily's calm was a clasping, tearing barb to Kathryne's maturity.

And in a thunderclap of discernment, Kathryne realized, watching her father's eyes, that Emily had come to this island as much for her father's company as for hers.

Emily laughed again, and Aidan seemed to grow more comfortable with each passing moment. Kathryne looked from her father to Emily and then back again. Neither of them watched her, or seemed to notice that her heart was becoming most troubled.

Kathryne pursed her lips, furrowed her eyebrows, and stood suddenly. "Papa, Lady Emily," she said with chilled formality, "I am finding myself simply at the end of my tether. I do ask your indulgence, for I shall take my leave now."

Aidan straightened up in the chair. Emily turned and looked up at Kathryne.

"There is no need to rise," Kathryne said in a clipped tone. She walked to the door and turned back. "It has been a most exhausting day. Lady Emily, I am overjoyed that you have joined us here. I am most eager to show you the treasures of our island."

She gave a token curtsy to them both, then with a quick step, ran up the stairs and shut the door to her darkened bedchamber behind her.

It was an hour, perhaps more, since Kathryne had retired. Emily arose in the stillness and with quiet steps, walked to Aidan and placed her hand upon his shoulder. It would have been a more intimate gesture had Aidan still been awake.

"Aidan," she whispered close to his ear. "Aidan, I believe it is time to retire."

Aidan snorted and sat upright, blinking his eyes and peering into the darkness.

"Aidan, you had just begun to sleep, and I knew that a proper bed offers more comfort than this chair might."

He drew his hands across his face, rubbing at his eyes. "It *has* been a most full day, Emily. My heart had only recently returned to a steady beat."

Aidan stood, blinking his eyes. They walked, side by side, silent, down the quiet hall, marked only by the illuminations of a few flickering candles, then softly padded up the long curved staircase to the first floor. At the top, Aidan took Emily's right hand and stepped back one step.

"I am so joyful that you are here, Emily. I have no words that truly can express my emotions."

He spoke in a quiet voice, and looked as if more words were forming, yet he remained silent.

Emily waited, then replied softly, "I, too, am gladdened that the risk was taken. These are most powerful feelings."

She watched his eyes as she spoke, and in the dim light she saw the joy, but a slight tint of apprehension was added to them.

She had more to say, but it was her first night, and there would be time enough on a hundred morrows to speak.

"Until the morning, then," Aidan said. He moved ever so slightly toward her, stopping at a full arm's length.

"Yes." Emily smiled back. "Until tomorrow then."

And the pair, without turning back to watch the other, silently walked to their bedchambers at opposite ends of the home. The door latches sounded in unison as the hall became empty and still again, leaving only a wash of great expectancy lingering in the air.

*October 1642*

Will paced nervously back and forth in the great room in his cottage, his hands fussing with the buttons on his new scarlet doublet made of the finest velvet Will had ever felt.

Missy sat in the far corner, slowly shaking her head and smiling. "Will, ye have no need to be nervous, to be sure. It is only a simple dedication ceremony. I'm sure that it will be over and done before any of us realized it has begun."

She arose, walked to him, almost gliding across the floor. It had been weeks since she had arrived, thin, drawn, and lost. While on Barbados, living in Will's cottage, preparing his meals, cleaning, working the new garden outside the small home, her lost poundage had returned. Her frame had begun to assume its former dimensions, the curves and swells becoming most pronounced. The sun had lit her wan features as well, and despite the fact that a proper Englishwoman sought to maintain an ivory, almost colorless skin, Missy looked healthy with a slight dash of sun on her cheeks. When she walked into town and along the piers to procure provisions, it was the rare head that did not turn to follow her gently swaying steps.

Will turned toward her and smiled. She patted at the lapels of his doublet and straightened the collar of his fine linen shirt, brushing away a few loose threads and a crumb or two from breakfast. She reached up and fussed with the knot in his cravat, a long blue silk scarf tied about his neck.

"William Hawkes, you are the most handsome captain of the harbor defenses I have ever seen." Missy smiled.

For a moment, Will looked befuddled, as if unaware that Missy had noticed his looks. Then, he smiled in return.

"And perchance how many captains of the harbor defenses have you made acquaintance with, my good Missy?"

She put her finger to her chin and looked deep in thought. "Well, counting you, the total is . . . one," she said, laughing, and brushed his doublet a final time.

Will looked out the front door of the cottage and saw, along the road from town to the fort, the first carriages rolling toward him. It was time for him to leave and greet the dignitaries as they arrived for the dedication.

He placed both his hands on Missy's shoulders, and she gazed up into his eyes.

"You will join us there when the music begins to play, will you not?" he asked.

She nodded. "I have not come halfway round the world to miss my own Mr. Hawkes in his hour of recognition."

He smiled back at her. *She does seem so pleased at the success I have made. It is so warming to have a person to share life's joys,* he thought, pleased, verging on content.

Impulsively, he bent toward her and placed his lips on hers for a long moment. They indeed were as soft as he remembered from their days together in Hadenthorne.

He began to pull away, but Missy placed her hands on his face and held him close for a moment or two longer, then allowed him to stand upright.

They stared at each other with no words exchanged, then Will turned, and on a silent step began to walk to the fort as the first carriage rounded the crest of the hill from town.

Will walked to the gate, opened wide to greet all the special guests for the dedication ceremonies at the fort. The crew of six ex-slaves had each been outfitted with tan breeches and a simple copy of Will's scarlet doublet, made in a felt material and without the gold braiding, of course. Two of the largest of the crew, thick and muscled, stood at each side of the gate, with a tall gleaming poleax in his hands. Just below the polished axhead, a covey of fluttering red, blue, and white silk banners was tied. The rest of the blacks attended to the carriages and horses, tethering them in the wide expanse of pangola grass to the south of the fort.

Inside, the squadron of Royal Marines stood watch at their posts, all wearing their finest dress attire, buttons burnished and side arms polished to a fierce gleam. A team stood at one of the cannons, ready to explain the operation of the firing sequence to anyone who might ask. Others stood watch from the ramparts, arms held stiffly at their sides.

The fort itself perched at the end of the promontory overlooking the harbor and the sea approach to it. The structure was nearly seventy-five yards wide and was near to square as possible. The walls that faced the sea were of two levels, the bottom holding the cannon pits and their firing openings, and the top level a wide rampart with toothed positions from which men would fire muskets. The other two sides, facing inland, were of a single level, with a rampart along those walls as well, in order to defend against a land-based attack.

In the center of the fort was a large parade ground, open and flat. On one side was a long, low, thatched-roof barracks, able to house fifty men with comfort. A common scullery was at one end.

On the other side was the captain's quarters, a small square dwelling of two stories. In the shade of the walls were smaller, simpler sheds housing the armory, the infirmary, and stores.

For the dedication day, a small platform had been built, and gay bunting hung from the rails. A simple lectern stood at one end. In the shade of the barracks, a quartet of musicians began to tune their instruments. Two violinists, a cellist, and a servant who played a brass horn had been assembled to provide music for the day.

Will stood by the gate for more than an hour, receiving all who had come for the ceremony. By midafternoon, the crowd inside the walls had swelled to nearly two hundred noble ladies and gentlemen. Lord Aidan, owing to his function of governor, was inside the walls of the fort, taking great pains to speak to every man and woman present. If he was nervous about presenting the dedication speech that day, he hid it well.

All eyes turned to Aidan, and the crowd stepped in closer to hear him. He was wearing his most formal blue doublet with long tails outlined all in gold edging over a frilled shirt. He had chosen not to wear a plumed hat, as was the custom. Instead, he had tied his shortish hair with a red ribbon at his neck.

Aidan stood stiffly at the lectern and raised his hand to quiet the murmuring of the crowd. "Good ladies and noblemen," he began, his voice strong, stirring. "We are gathered here this day to dedicate this wonderful fort, to be known hereafter as Fort Charles, in honor of England's sovereign ruler, King Charles."

The crowd broke into a modest wave of applause and polite hurrahs. No one wanted to go on record as offering their enthusiastic support of either the king or Cromwell—at least in not such a public venue. Yet despite their less-than-ardent support, most would agree the naming of the fort after the sitting monarch was a most expeditious choice by Governor Spenser, who, after all, ruled at the behest of the king himself.

For nearly an hour, Aidan spoke and Will stood, swaying and uncomfortable, behind him. He had kept his eyes lowered for the first few minutes, then raised them to scan the crowd.

It was then that he first saw her, his eyes not having visited her face for more weeks than he dared consider. Kathryne stood with an older woman at her side and remained at the rear edge of the assembled group. Mr. Foxton was not at her side, as Will had imagined he would be.

Will's heart seemed to stop for a moment as she filled his vision.

He could bear to gaze only for a moment. Their eyes did not meet, and he looked back down at his feet, for his heart told him that this was all the torment it had wanted to shoulder that day.

*This is not how I am to feel,* Will scolded himself, *for I know that she is the intended of another. This is a finished matter, and my heart has no bearing on how I must conduct myself.*

Aidan continued to read, hesitantly and slowly.

*Yet why does my heart hurt so? It is as if the image of Kathryne has danced upon it, and its rhythms now reflect her delicate steps.*

He bit at his lower lip. *I will not allow this to happen.*

Will glanced up again and saw Kathryne facing the woman he presumed was Lady Emily Bancroft, whom he had heard had come from England for a visit. Will saw Kathryne laugh, her eyes alive and dancing in the sun, her head thrown back a moment, her tender throat bared to the light.

*I will not allow this to happen.* And he bit his lip harder and felt a small drop of warm blood pool there.

Aidan continued to speak on, and William kept his eyes averted until the governor began to offer his concluding observations.

At the end of Lord Aidan's remarks, the crowd responded with polite applause, the men and women turning to each other and nodding their approval.

Aidan held his hand aloft to procure quiet, and in a few moments the crowd had stilled. A small number of the noblemen had taken this occasion to edge toward the barrels of ale and rum.

"Good gentlemen and gentle ladies, I would like your continued attention," Aidan called out, his voice at once calmer now that his speaking was finished.

"I would like to call up to the fore the gentleman who has shouldered the responsibility of completing our splendid Fort Charles in such good time," Aidan called out and turned to motion toward William, who stood to his rear by several steps.

"Hear! Hear!" shouted out several of the crowd.

William blanched and held his palms out in defense, shaking his head no. As the governor reached his side, William whispered loudly, "Governor Spenser, I cannot speak to this group. I have given no thought to remarks that might be suitable. I would make a mockery of this day."

From the corner of his eye, Will saw Vicar Petley, his red face a mask of controlled anger, standing off to the side. He was scheduled to conclude the official dedication with a prayer and a short homily. His eyes were wide, his teeth clenched.

"Nonsense, my lad," Aidan said as he put his arm about Will's shoulder and pulled him to the front of the platform. "I have heard of your teachings to your little church group at this fort. You have skill enough as an orator to match this humble occasion."

By then, they were both at the lectern.

Aidan looked out, his arm still about a nervous Will's shoulder. "Good gentleman and ladies, may I present to you Captain William Hawkes."

The crowd responded with a polite wash of claps.

William grasped both sides of the rough lectern and stared out at the crowd. His eyes first stopped at Missy in the far right corner. She was beaming as he took to the stand. Beside her, close at her side, was John Delacroix. He was smiling as well. At the far left corner of the crowd, in the shade of the wall facing the harbor, stood Kathryne and Lady Emily. It appeared as though the older woman was having a day of great enjoyment, but Kathryne, Will noticed as he stepped to the front of the podium, looked as pained as his own heart felt. Her eyes were darting about the crowd, and for the long moment that William looked out, they never once settled on his person.

He blinked several times and looked up into the sky for a moment. *Almighty God,* he prayed, *grant me peace.*

His eyes opened, and he began. "Most noble men and ladies, I stand before you, most apprehensive. For this task of speaking brings more fear to my heart than would I experience in facing the bloody cutlass of a Spanish pirate.

"I have been given a great honor. That honor is to defend this island.

With these fortifications, these bulwarks now complete, I can offer you the security of such defense."

Will coughed and looked down for a moment. "You know who I am. I have been a man who has sinned in a mighty way against the almighty God. But I have now been saved by his grace."

He looked to Kathryne, whose face was hidden by the shade.

"It is true . . . I have held a blade and a pistol in my hand, and men have died in terror before me. I have seen men breathe their last as they lay on a bloody deck defending their treasure. Cold steel has been plunged into their flesh, and their lives have ended in the defense of gold and silver."

He coughed again and felt sweat forming at his forehead. "I have learned that gold and silver are not what is to be treasured. It is life, and above all, it is truly life only if knowing the Almighty. All men should have the chance to know that truth."

Will stopped for a moment and wiped at his lips.

"It is now your lives that are my treasure. I will make this vow to you—every one of you who stands before me now. With my life, with my very breath, I will defend your lives—for now each and every one of you present here today are my treasure."

He looked about and saw Missy, a tear on her face, and then Kathryne, still hidden in the shadows.

"That is my vow to you. I will offer my life in your defense."

He blinked several times, and when he realized he had no words left to say, simply mumbled, "Thank you." He slipped away from the podium, stepped from the platform, and stood by himself in the governor's shadow.

It was several moments until the applause started, at first cautious, then growing more robust. Several "hurrahs" were shouted as well, and a "bravo" too.

The noble-born crowd was applauding what they felt was their birthright—the sacrifice of more common men to defend their rights. Will's remarks, though simple and short, were most stirring. The applause lasted many long moments, giving Lady Carruthers, whom Will had noticed was most entranced by his speech, a chance to edge her way closer to him.

Vicar Petley stood at the podium, arms raised in an effort to calm the applause. For the longest time the noise refused to cease. When it did, he began his brief remarks.

When he called out his final "Amen," the crowd cheered again, loudly, though for a mere few moments, for the breeze had shifted, and the aroma of the food and drink simply poured over the crowd as they listened. Whether it was a cheer for the vicar's words or for the fact that he finished in such short time was never discussed by any of the polite society.

The music piped up again only moments after the vicar was finished speaking. Missy, dragging John by the hand, weaved her way through the crowd, seeking the straightest line to William's side.

"Most marvelous words, William," John cried over the growing murmur of the party. "Most stirring indeed," he said as he pumped Will's hand.

Missy beamed at him and embraced him in a warm and lingering hug. "I am so proud of you, William," she whispered loudly his ear. "I believe I have always known that you would accomplish great things."

A servant in a stiff black coat came up to the three with a silver tray laden with glasses filled to the brim with red wine. Missy took one, never having held such an elegant piece of finely etched crystal. William saw her eyes widen at the experience. It seemed that this entire day, as well as her entire stay on this island, had been a mix of new experiences for Missy, who seemed only the slightest bit intimidated by the swirl of cultured nobility about her.

Others of the crowd were sweeping around them. The nobles sought to express their congratulations to William for finishing the fort and for his words of sacrifice. Noblewomen sought to thank him and to stand close to a man who had been a pirate and now was redeemed to offer himself in their service. Lady Carruthers in particular stood by Will with her arm in his, pulling him tight to herself.

## 47

Nearly one hour had passed, and the noise grew louder with each passing swallow. William hoped that he had met and spoken to everyone he needed to, for he wanted to slip out and run to the quiet of his cottage.

Will had managed to escape from Lady Carruthers by guaranteeing a private tour of the fort at a future date. She had replied to his offer with a wink and a coarse giggle, much to Will's consternation. John and Missy had drifted to the edges of the gathering, and Will slipped among the celebrants until he was next to them again.

"Finally," he whispered theatrically, "I have escaped."

As he stepped to his left, he stopped, as still as a stone, for blocking his path were Lady Emily and Kathryne Spenser. He looked at them for an instant, then his eyes darted to Missy and John.

*What do I say?* his thoughts cried.

Missy stepped beside William, with John at her side.

Amidst the clattering of the celebration, amidst the joviality that the wines had loosened, there seemed to be a cloud of silence that blanketed this small tableau.

It was Kathryne who first spoke, after what seemed too many moments. "Captain Hawkes. I was most impressed by your words."

*Her voice is like music,* William thought, then immediately winced to himself.

"Thank you, Lady Spenser," Will replied, and silence returned for a moment.

Kathryne spoke again. "Mr. Hawkes, this is Lady Emily Bancroft of

London. I believe I may have mentioned her to you. She has just arrived on Barbados, sending a great wave of surprise through Shelworthy."

William bowed at the waist, as he had seen other noblemen do upon meeting such a lady. "Welcome, Lady Bancroft. I trust that your visit has been pleasant."

Emily nodded and said with a smile, "I have been enchanted by every day, Mr. Hawkes. You are kind to ask. To speak the truth, my most serious question is why I have not sailed to this place at an earlier date."

From the corner of his eye, he saw Missy lower her head for a moment, as if unsure of what to do next.

*What do I do now?* Will wondered, near panic.

It was Kathryne who spoke again. "Mr. Delacroix, how pleasant to see you again. From all that I hear, your ship's chandlery is thriving. I am most pleased for you."

John reddened from her gracious words. "Thank you, Lady Kathryne," he stammered. "It is kind of you to say so."

John looked at Kathryne, then at Will, who seemed frozen, then to Missy, then to Emily.

"And you must be Missy Cavendish," Kathryne said with a curious, edgy voice, extending her hand. "I have heard of your arrival. I do hope that you are getting along well."

Missy seemed to blush, curtsied, and took Kathryne's hand. "Thank you, Lady Spenser," she said in a small voice. "Thank you for your concern. Indeed, I am most fortunate to have friends such as Mr. Delacroix and Mr. Hawkes. Without exaggeration, I would have perished without their aid."

Kathryne smiled, and Will's heart leapt in his chest, beating wildly.

"Indeed," Kathryne replied, "now both of us have had the distinction of having our lives spared by their intervention. A most select group we belong to, do we not, Miss Holender?"

Facing the enemies' guns was a mere trifle in comparison to the terror William now felt. *I have spoken of none of this to Missy,* his thoughts roared, *and now how will I explain such a sordid past?*

Missy giggled. "Indeed we do."

Will turned to her with a most dumbfounded look on his face. *What is she saying?*

Missy looked at Will, then to Kathryne, then back to Will. "John has spoken of the incident to me, William. Such matters are not the realm of private affairs, I am afraid. And if he had not told me of it, there were a dozen others in town who offered their version of Lady Kathryne's rescue," Missy said in the most calm and even voice that she could muster.

For the longest moment, no one spoke. The silence was deepening.

From the corner of William's eye, he saw a corporal of the Royal Marines scrambling along the farthest parapet, running at top speed to the signal cannon, mounted to the most westerly portion of the wall. The corporal carried a burning torch in his hand. He slapped the torch to the cannon's flash pan, and with a roar the signal cannon bellowed, an orange flame circling its mouth in a fiery halo. A dozen tankards and nearly another dozen delicate glasses were dropped to the ground when the cannon thundered, splashing their potent redness among the crowd. Women shrieked as the cannon's roar echoed and rumbled across the harbor. Soldiers began to run to the parapets with muskets unlimbered.

The corporal with the torch turned to the crowd and bellowed to William, "There be a ship sailing for port, Cap'n. And she be on fire!"

William scrambled up the nearest ladder for a better view. Indeed, just beyond the breakers and the white surf, a battered merchant ship, a Dutch galleon, Will determined, was floundering in the waters. By her stern, from the captain's quarters from the look of it, poured out a thick, angry smudge of smoke, trailing behind her as she struggled in the swell. Her mainmast was gone, a splintered finger all that remained. Her foremast and mizzenmast were solid, but their canvas was pierced by dozens of holes, marking heavy cannon fire.

Will called for his telescope and whisked it to his eye.

A dozen men lay on deck, perhaps dead or injured. Gaping holes were torn in the rail, and the deck was splintered in more places than not. A sailor held on to the whip stand, controlling the rudder. It splayed back and forth with quick jerks, the rudder catching on the heavy surf, or perhaps the top ridges of the coral reef below. Entry into the harbor was never easy, even on a calm day with all hands on deck and a full complement of sails. Scarred as she was, the ship lumbered on, closing toward the shore.

Will turned from the wall and bellowed out, at once showing the authority of captain of the harbor defenses.

"Fetch Luke and send him to the harbor. Marines! Stand guard at your guns, for her pursuer may still be in the hunt. Call the blacka-moors to stand to their defenses."

He grabbed the outside edge of the ladder and slid down to the ground with a graceful fluidity.

"Missy!" he called out, seeing that John was sprinting toward the harbor. "You must stay within this fort for safety. Do not return to the cottage unless I send word."

John had cleared the front gate at a full run. To have a burning ship slide into harbor was a great danger, made more grave if she carried munitions and exploded as she burned. The entire fleet of small boats would be in peril as well, as would be the entire harbor area, the piers, and the town. A fire would spread hungrily through the wooden buildings.

Will raced to the harbor and leaped into a longboat manned by six blackamoors. John sat in the aft with the Tambors. They all began to pull hard on the oars. Within moments, they had passed the first deep reef, canting at steep angles, cutting through the turbulent surf in the small boat.

John shouted above the ocean's roar, "Who do you think might have blasted her?"

Will shouted back, "John, we were the only crew that was brave or foolish enough to have operated east of this island. Whoever is raising cannon out there must be cocksure of his abilities to sail away with no fear of an English vessel in pursuit."

In a few more moments the longboat sidled up next to the burning galleon. Indeed she was a Dutch ship, the *Ver Plant*, out of Amsterdam. Rigging had spilled over the sides, offering a slippery ladder up to the deck. Bryne tied off the longboat and began to climb up, followed by Will and John.

Will and John stormed down the captain's ladder to what remained of his stateroom. Several cotton bales and thick pads of hammocks were strewn in the rubble. A cannon shot, or several cannon shots, had torn most of the stern gallery away, leaving only shards of glass and splintered wood as a flimsy skeleton. The bales and hammocks were smoldering, spewing forth a thick greasy smoke that choked and burned. Will grabbed at one end of a bale and John the other, and they pitched it through the gulf that was once a window, into the sea. Several more bales were tossed into the water with a hiss, and within moments, the cabin was cleared of burning debris. Will looked about, nodded, then ran back up to the quarterdeck.

"She's safe to sail into harbor now, John," he called as he made his way to the whip stand. The rudder was being manned by a young sailor no more than sixteen years old. His shoulder was splayed open by a thick gash from a long sword, and his thick weskit was pocked with a hive of angry, bloody splinters.

"Stand down, sailor," Will said. "You have done well to take her this far. I know these waters better than most, and I will guide her in."

The young sailor appeared as if he were about to speak, perhaps offer thanks or express gratitude, but before a word could be spoken, he slumped to the deck, falling first to his knees, then to his side with a soft thump.

"Cut down the sails. She'll take too much speed if we don't."

Machetes flashed in the afternoon sun, and the foresail crumbled to the deck like a sheet on a fine bed, billowing out as it rumbled down. The vessel, heavy in the water from a hole blasted at the waterline, sidled in slowly to the calmer waters of the harbor.

Will had one chance to catch it next to an open dock, and with a practiced hand, he slid the vessel alongside an empty pier. Ropes appeared, catching the timbers and pulling it to a stop.

As soon as the ship stopped, he knelt to the young sailor, still lying at his feet. He slipped his hand under the lad's head and knew he held a lifeless body. The lad's eyes had remained open and had gone glassy and opaque. Will reached down and gently pushed his eyelids closed.

The hapless Dutch sailors had been carrying a sugar mill, food stores, and a full hold of plows, machetes, and muskets. Their captain, Willem Vollker, a man Will had met several times in Weymouth and Amsterdam, had been tacking north and south, looking for Barbados, when out of the east there came a huge Spanish pirate ship. The Dutch crew attempted to outsail their pursuer, but within half a day they came under range of the Spanish guns. Within less time than it takes to have a proper breakfast, the Dutch ship was crippled, most of her crew lying on deck, her captain blasted nearly in two by a cannonball.

The pirates boarded her, removed all valuable cargo, then sailed off, suffering not a single casualty. The few Dutch sailors left had no recourse other than to attempt to limp into Bridgetown. It was that or die a slow death as the vessel began to take on seawater.

"What was the name of the ship that attacked?" Will asked one of the sailors.

"It was the *Frontera Nueva,* captained by San Martel."

Will stiffened at the words and turned slowly to John.

It was the pirate who had kidnapped, and most likely executed, Vicar Mayhew. The blood in Will's veins turned as chilled as springwater at the sound of the name. Just below his breath, Will muttered a curse. "If any man deserves to face death," Will whispered, "it is he."

■ ☐ ■ ☐ ■

Geoffrey Foxton had excused himself from the dedication of the fort, claiming that urgent matters at his sugar mills called him away. It was a useful ruse that few could find fault with, for there was seemingly an endless supply of crises with the cantankerous equipment. In truth, Geoffrey wondered how his Dutch supervisors managed to produce any sugar at all, what with the amount of grumbling and hysteria that usually accompanied a pressing season. But after every fortnight, additional barrels were filled, and Geoffrey tallied his rewards.

At the hour when Aidan began his speech, Geoffrey was on the windswept cliffs at Cuckold Point. As of yet, this northeastern part of the island was less than sparsely inhabited. A few sheepherders had put up shanties along the coast, and a few farmers had small plots farther inland, but no town or village had developed. The waves crashed a hundred yards below him on a jumble of jagged rocks and sharp coral fingers. The winds were a constant rush, and as he stood there, scanning the eastern horizon, he was buffeted and pummeled by the gusts.

Just to the south of Cuckold Point was the Landlock, a small protected bay. If the tide was out, the ship he awaited would lie off the coast there. If the tide were in, the ship would slip farther south to Gay's Cove, a shallower and even more secluded anchorage.

It was noon, and Geoffrey had spent the morning with telescope in hand, watching for the first hint of a sail. He desperately wanted the meeting to take place today, having no desire to spend an entire night out in the wind and the cold. He had provisions packed, of course, but would prefer to be on his way back to Bridgetown by dusk.

It was then that a sail had appeared off to the northeast. The tide was in, and Gay's Cove would be used. Geoffrey rode along the rocky palisade looming over the rocky beach. Gay's Cove was less than an hour's ride south, and horse and rider did not need to hurry.

By the time Geoffrey had stumbled down the narrow, twisted path from the cliff top to the beach, the ship had just begun to anchor, no more than a half-mile off the shore. He watched as two longboats were lowered into the sea and rowed to the beach. Within moments they hissed upon a fissure in the pink sand, and Geoffrey arose from the rock on which he waited.

"Mr. Foxton," boomed the voice from a tall, swarthy man who debarked. His craggy face seemed devoid of all humor and joy. "How pleasant to see you again."

He had a thrusting, leonine seriousness about his being.

Geoffrey bowed at the waist in his best formal fashion, then stepped forward, his hand extended. The man, standing at the edge of the surf, the seawater lapping around his ankles, did not raise his hand in greeting. After a moment, Geoffrey lowered his, as if nothing was out of the ordinary.

"Captain San Martel. It is good to see you as well. Too many years have passed since we have had this pleasure," Geoffrey said, keeping his tone formal.

"Indeed," sniffed San Martel, who motioned to a man on the second longboat. "I am afraid that my presence in these waters is not as secretive as I had assumed in my last posting."

Geoffrey blanched and spun about, his eyes wide with fear, scanning the bluffs that loomed over his head.

"No, Mr. Foxton, no one has followed you here to this forsaken beach."

San Martel chuckled, turned to his men, and in rapid Spanish, barked out orders. "Do not flatter yourself, Mr. Foxton," the Spanish captain said. "It was I who announced my coming. In the calm waters out there," he said, pointing back to the east, "a hapless Dutch merchant ship wandered into our path. It was too tempting a target to ignore."

Geoffrey looked aghast. "You attacked a ship in these waters? Why? I understood that all aggressive activities were to cease—at least for the season."

With an astonished look, San Martel gestured to his men and ship with a sweep of his arm. "You think that a pirate follows a season—like your foolish gentry and their inane chasing of the foxes? No, Mr. Foxton. When there is prey, one hunts. But perhaps we should conclude our business, for the tide will be out within the hour."

Geoffrey extracted a large parcel from his valise. "These are the documents, maps, and drawing that were requested."

"Excellent. Well done," San Martel said as he passed the parcel to a lieutenant standing behind him.

"You should be informed that the fort overlooking the harbor has just been completed. In truth, today is the day of its dedication," Geoffrey stated.

Laughing in great guffaws, San Martel said, "Then perhaps I should have selected this day to begin my plan. Such a fitting test of their defenses would be most illuminating."

Darkening, Geoffrey replied, "I would not take this fort's captain lightly. He seems to have a great deal of skill concerning these matters."

"A captain by the name of William Hawkes, am I correct?"

Surprised, Geoffrey nodded. "How did you know?"

"No matter," San Martel sneered. "But I do not fear this man. And even less so now."

"The fortifications appear to be most formidable."

With a wave of his hand, San Martel seemed to dismiss the subject. "Have you walked the beach by the fort as I requested?"

Geoffrey nodded.

"Are the entrances still in place?"

Geoffrey nodded again.

San Martel smiled back, and as he bared his yellowed teeth, a chill settled in about Geoffrey's heart. The Spanish pirate slipped a fat, clinking pouch from his doublet.

"Then here is your second payment, Mr. Foxton. I trust that the first payment has produced handsome returns for you?"

Geoffrey looked down at his feet, near buried in the loose sand, then nodded.

San Martel had met Geoffrey Foxton many years prior, in a small public house in London, as San Martel was in service with the Spanish ambassador to the royal court. A curious friendship of sorts had developed, and it was Spanish monies that had provided Mr. Foxton the opportunity to purchase his first tract of land on Barbados. The Foxton fortunes had been close to dissipated by Geoffrey's father on a series of untimely investments and unscrupulous women. The money that San Martel supplied was named as a loan—a loan that had never required repayment until now—and then only in information, not gold.

"I trust, Mr. Foxton, that your parcel includes an accurate summary of the politics of this island? And its readiness to defend itself?"

Geoffrey nodded again.

"Then our meeting is done. I will send word when we shall meet next."

With that, San Martel turned, stepped back into his boat, and never once looked back to shore.

Geoffrey stood there for a long moment, then sighed deeply, feeling the weight of the leather pouch in his hand. He turned back to the island and began to climb the tortured path to the bluff above him.

CHAPTER

**48**

"Boaz, have you ever attended the . . . well, the church service held at the fort? I understand that there are dark men such as yourself who attend."

Lady Emily was standing on the porch of Shelworthy, waiting for a groomsman to bring her horse from the stables.

"Lady Em'ly?" he asked, apparently most unaccustomed to being asked questions of a personal nature.

"I asked, have you ever attended the service at the fort. I understand that there are dark men and ladies who do so."

"Oh," Boaz said stiffly.

"Have you?" she asked again.

Boaz looked fretful for a moment, as if unaware of how to comply with the request, then shrugged and nodded. "I been der many Sabbaths," Boaz said softly.

"And who does the preaching?"

"Be Mr. Hawkes. Boaz don' understand all he say, but it be powerful words, Lady Em'ly."

The groomsman appeared at the side of the house, leading a chestnut mare to the front. Boaz looked most relieved.

"Can anyone attend such a service, Boaz?"

He screwed his face up in a tight squeeze, then replied, "I 'spects so, for nobody say I can't be der."

Lady Emily turned from the saddle and smiled at him, a most sweet smile. "Thank you, Boaz."

Lady Emily was glad to step into the fresh cooling air of the morning. The service at St. Michael's had just concluded, and Emily took Kathryne by the arm and began to stroll down the street to the harbor.

How Kathryne could have felt an attraction to Vicar Petley was beyond Emily's comprehension. How a soul could have remained alert through his homily, not to mention awake, was near the end of her comprehension as well.

*He seems a decent enough young man, but where is his joy?* Emily had wondered as he spoke. *It is not enough to simply have faith. There needs to be evidence of the joy of the Lord in one's life. Of that I am sure.*

But that was not the prevailing opinion of many of the Puritan reformers in England. Back home, Lady Emily knew, all manner of changes in church and state government continued to be enacted. Fearing the return of Catholicism and with the encouragement of Puritan reformers among Parliament, both Houses had voted to abolish episcopacy, terminating the bishops, and agreed to reform the English church "according to the word of God."

The Puritan Oliver Cromwell was the rising star of the "New Model Army," displaying a precocious brilliance as cavalry general. His soldiers, nicknamed Roundheads because of their close-cropped hair and round helmets, were well equipped, well disciplined, and effective. King Charles's well-dressed, long-haired Cavaliers, lightly armored and poorly disciplined, stood little chance against them. In his attempt to reoccupy London, halted by Cromwell's forces at Turnham Green, the Cavaliers failed and were forced to retreat in a panic to their headquarters at Oxford.

But King Charles had declared war on the Parliamentarians. The civil war had begun.

Lady Emily knew that, as in any war, people had to choose sides. She had friends who supported the king—great landowners, people in the north and west of the country—who believed Parliament had gone too far in challenging the power of the king. She also was close to many whose allegiance lay with Parliament—most of whom lived in London and in other large towns and seaports, who hated the king's taxes and were in favor of the reforms in the church. She was a praying woman, and rather than choosing sides herself, she asked God to accomplish his will and bring something good out of the current turmoil.

Emily also prayed fervently for Kathryne, for she felt as a mother to the young woman who at the moment, she thought, stood in need of an intercessor to pray for her future. This day, after much contemplation, meditation on the Scriptures, and more prayer, Emily had decided on a bold course of action.

Aidan was in Speightstown that day, ostensibly to offer assistance to

Sir Thomas Tenby on his sugar harvest, but in reality to ensure that the bulk of it be accurately recorded and shipped on English vessels. A great torrent of sugar was leaking from the island like grain from a slit canvas bag. Aidan's resources were stretched to the limit to prevent such midnight shipping.

Emily had instructed Boaz, who had driven them to the church that morning, to take the Spenser carriage immediately to the fort. In that manner, he could attend a church service of his own, and Kathryne and Emily could enjoy the walk from St. Michael's to the fort.

"Lady Emily, where are we going?" Kathryne asked as they crossed the river at Bridge Street, a rickety plank-and-post affair that creaked and swayed with every step. The crossing was unnerving, yet short of fording the river upstream, this was their only choice.

Emily hushed her former student. "It is a most pleasant day for a walk. I wanted time with you alone this morning. I have been most derelict in my duties and obligations to you—my most favorite student and dearest friend."

Kathryne smiled for the first time in what seemed as weeks and patted Emily's hand on her arm. "Dearest friend, such a condition was not caused by you. It is my own petulant behavior that has kept me silent."

They walked along for several moments, then Kathryne spoke again. "I had so long imagined that your presence and your insight would simply solve all my problems. But when you arrived, I found that I had no one to look to for solutions save myself. The answers are not to be found in others, but in one's own heart."

Emily nodded. "But when we look only to our own ability, Kathryne, we do ourselves a disservice, for has not our Lord promised to lead and guide us when we ask?"

Kathryne lowered her head and did not reply for a long moment.

"I have asked, Emily," Kathryne nearly whispered. "I have prayed about these matters, but have received no solid answer that I would deem as coming from the heavens."

They turned a corner by the harbor. It was often still and torrid, but this day was filled with a cooling breeze slipping down from the highlands in the northeast.

"Where indeed are we walking, Emily?" Kathryne asked again. "We are heading away from Shelworthy, not toward it."

"I know, dear, but I allowed Boaz to bring the carriage to the fort in order to attend the service. I am sure that it is not often that a man such as he is allowed the freedom to attend such a gathering."

Kathryne pulled up short and stopped. "The fort? But Mr. Hawkes

will be there. I do not believe I can face him again." Kathryne sounded
as if in an emotional panic.

"Nonsense, dear," Emily said, "for there is no fear that should not
be faced." She added at a whisper, "And we may stand in the shadows.
Mr. Hawkes will most certainly not know of our attendance."

The older woman took Kathryne by the arm and tugged, insisting
that she follow.

"In addition, I would most like to hear the man speak. I understand
that his lucidity puts the good Vicar Petley to shame," Emily said,
mischief etching her words.

Giggling in spite of her fears, Kathryne covered her smile.

In a few moments, the two ladies, the most elegantly dressed members of the motley crowd in attendance at the fort that day, edged into
the shadows.

A large group of men and a few women sat to the left of William, who
stood on a small rise, perhaps a foot above the average level of the
ground. Most of his blackamoors were in attendance that morning, as
well as Luke and a handful of free black men, and a few domestic slaves
who had been permitted this one luxury.

On Will's other side, with a clear line separating the two groups, sat
a most curious mix—the workers of John's ship chandlery, a smattering
of white indentured servants, a few landowners who had but a few
acres to till, and several ladies from the Goose, as well as a few visiting
sailors. Missy sat there as well, Kathryne noticed, on a thick canvas
spread next to John Delacroix.

Will stood, dressed in a somber dark blue doublet, holding a heavy
copy of the Scriptures in his right hand. It lay open, and he leaned over
and began to read, his strong, sober voice filling the confines of the fort.

"These words were written by St. Paul to a small church, perhaps no
larger than this group assembled here today. This church was near the
sea, and the scent of salt marked their air, just as the air is marked here.
He wrote: 'Not that I speak in respect of want: for I have learned, in
whatsoever state I am, therewith to be content. I know both how to be
abased, and I know how to abound: every where and in all things I am
instructed both to be full and to be hungry, both to abound and to suffer
need. I can do all things through Christ which strengtheneth me.'"

Will stopped reading and looked up at the crowd. He knew most of
these words made only slight sense to some who listened, and to others
made no sense whatsoever. He closed the book and held it in the crook
of his right arm.

"Do you know the meaning in what St. Paul wrote?"

William waited a moment, knowing that no answer would be forth-coming, nor was an answer expected.

"St. Paul wrote these words to say that because of Jesus Christ, he was happy with what he had, with however much he had, or however little he had. He was happy. He was content. He could smile when he was hungry or when he had eaten. St. Paul wrote this Scripture to tell us that if we are poor, Christ allows us to be content. If we are rich, Christ allows us to be content. You black men have little, yet if you know the person of Christ, then you will be content, and even joyful, for your reward is not here in this world."

Will stopped, then addressed his next comment to Luke, who sat in front. "Do these men understand, Luke? Do they know what I say?"

Luke rubbed his bony hand over his face and head, ending at the base of his neck. "Massa, it be hard thing to know—this man bein' happy with nothin'. It be hard to say dat havin' an empty belly is as happy as havin' a full belly be. But if God be sayin' dat it happens, it happens. Dese men, dey understand de words. Dey know dat heaven be a most better place dan dis island. Dat is what we be waitin' for—and we know it be better in heaven dan here. And de only way to gets to heaven is wit' Jesus. All dese men know dat to be de truth."

William smiled and nodded.

"St. Paul wants us to be content with loss as well as plenty. For each of us will have dreams denied, and each of us will have prayers unanswered. St. Paul tells us that we must be content regardless of what is about us, for it is Christ that gives us contentment, not the simple urges of our heart. The Almighty will provide for us what we require. 'Tis not what we think we need that supplies us with happiness, for true joy comes from what God gives us."

As Will spoke these words, he looked at Missy with a smile.

Will's smile to Missy was unmistakable to Kathryne.

*Here is a man who knows more of the spirit of faith and of God's truth than any man of the cloth I have ever known, and he is saying that he is satisfied with what God has given him—and that is Missy Cavendish not me.*

The tears filled her eyes, and she turned and ran as fast as she could away from this man, away from this place, and away from the pain.

## 49

"Aidan, I had no preconception that his words would cause as much pain in her heart as they appear to have done."

Emily was explaining her observations to the governor as they ate alone in the large dining chamber of Shelworthy. Upon their return from the fort and hearing Mr. Hawkes teach from the Scriptures, Kathryne had sought refuge in her bedchamber and had not ventured forth for more than two full days. She had even answered her father's angry knocking upon her door with an angry, "Go away!"

Emily continued, "I merely considered that it was indeed a closed case and that she would have appreciated seeing his ministry to that group of poor unfortunates at the fort."

Aidan shook his head slowly. "Since arriving on this island she has gone from a young woman with an imperturbable air about her to a woman who is always at the verge of tears or anger."

Aidan put down his fork and slid his plate away. "I take no pleasure in my daughter's pain, but I am at considerable consternation in knowing how best to deal with such a situation. I had once thought that the . . . arrangement that was understood between her and Mr. Foxton was progressing in a splendid fashion. But I see that my judgment was most grievously in error."

Emily had that morning decided that the Spensers were wonderful traders and politicians, yet when it came to matters of the heart, they were like lost children in a dark and threatening forest.

She had decided that to deal with Aidan and to deal with Kathryne would take boldness, and she now took a bold step. She reached out and placed her hand over his and cupped his strong fingers in hers.

Aidan's eyes seemed to open wider at this move, for up until this moment he and Emily had behaved in a most proper fashion, as old friends must behave, with a sense of civility and decorum. Aidan had wished for more perhaps, but was too much the gentleman to pursue a closer involvement with such an old family friend.

"Aidan," Emily whispered, "you are a man with a man's sensibilities. It has become apparent that Kathryne is most miserable."

Aidan stared down at his hand in hers. After a long moment, he managed to stammer, "Whatever do you mean?"

"Aidan, Kathryne does not love Mr. Foxton. I do not think she ever has."

His eyes never left Emily's hand on his. "Has she told you of this?" he asked. "It is her obligation to obey her father in matters of matrimony. Love has little to do with this."

Emily tilted her head slightly and smiled. She squeezed his hand. "Aidan, you are a dear man, but I am afraid that such thinking may not be best suited to such a settlement as Barbados. Such an arrangement would make most sense back in England, for she would have had a greater opportunity to have grown accustomed to a potential suitor. But this island is like a hothouse, and affairs seem to be accelerated in the heat. I do not think such a fatherly right offers the same benefits here as it does four thousand miles distant in England."

She squeezed his hand again and barely slid her fingers up against the back of his palm. Emily was not certain, but she thought she noticed Aidan's face flush slightly.

"And, Aidan . . . ?"

He gulped and nodded.

"How would you have felt if your father had told you some thirty years prior that love has nothing to do with marriage?"

He gulped again. She squeezed his hand again and rose from the table, trailing her nail upon his hand until well past the wrist and only leaving his skin when the cuff of his doublet prevented her from a further distance.

"I believe you should speak to your daughter about this."

■ ■ ■ ■ ■

As Aidan and Emily spoke that day, another man and woman on the island were seeking to set things to right, to let their lives and actions speak the truth, to be as honest as their hearts demanded.

This day Missy had left the cottage at midmorning and spent a quiet hour in the cool darkness of St. Michael's in a pew near the rear of the church. Missy did not consider herself a proper Christian woman. She felt haunted by the legacy of her failed marriage, as of yet still valid in the eyes of the church. She knew that many saw her as a kept woman.

Yet for all William's amazing generosity, an unsettled feeling bubbled in her heart. She owed him everything—even her very life, if she could believe Luke's account of his intervention that day of her arrival. Will had spent a king's ransom on her contract, for she had heard soon enough that he had doubled the original amount. It was more gold than her father could earn in ten years, and Will had paid it without request of repayment or favors. He provided a roof and clothing and food. There was so much that she could hardly grasp the enormity of his sacrifice.

Yet after all this, she wondered, through her silent tears at night—after all of this, why did her heart not respond to his presence as it did once in England those years hence? She prayed to God for her feelings to change, to return. But God was most silent, it seemed, and her prayers remained unanswered—perhaps even unheard.

It was then that she had decided that perhaps it was because she was not in God's house and had to seek out a time at St. Michael's, the only proper English church within a thousand miles of her heart.

Sitting in that silent, hushed room, with only the calls of the gulls for music, she knelt in prayer.

*Dearest Almighty, I beg of thee, change my heart if it be thy will. I am most confused and fearful, for William has not said as much, but I think that he expects us to become as man and wife. To do so would be a worse crime, dear God—the crime of selling myself, for my heart is now turned toward another.*

Missy shuddered as she prayed those words, for she had never admitted that fact, even to herself, let alone to almighty God, who had the power to strike her down for her unrepentant sins.

*Dearest Almighty, I beg thy forgiveness for such brazen words, but I know that the words are true from my heart. Please, God—present me direction as to how thy will shall be done, for I am most lost and scared.*

Missy bowed her head and her tears began to fall, and in a moment her body was racked with sobs so strong that she scarcely could catch a breath between them. She cried without ceasing for many moments until the tears gradually stopped, the sniffles ceased. She raised her head and opened her reddened eyes, and at that moment a cloud slipped from before the face of the sun, and a brilliant afternoon sunbeam splashed and splayed against the tall stained-glass window at the front of the church, the beam striking her full in her face, filling her eyes.

It was the image of St. John that filled her eyes with such brilliance. The last remnants of her tears had remained, and through the prism of them, it looked as if the saint was smiling at her.

A new tear formed, for she took this as the sign she had asked for. She rose, gripping tightly to the pew in front of her, and she silently mouthed the words, *Thank you, Lord.*

And she turned, picked up the hem of her dress, slipped out the front door, and began to run toward the ship chandlery and John Delacroix.

CHAPTER

**50**

The tapping at the door was so slight that, at first, Kathryne imagined a mouse had snuck into her room, nestled under the bed, and was gently patting at the fringe that hung at the edges of the bed's coverlet. A muffled voice from the outside said, "Kathryne, it is your father. I need to speak with you. May I come in?"

As the sun had settled in the western skies that day and the purple night edged its way along the island, Kathryne had begun to realize that she could not spend the rest of her life inside her room. It was time, she knew, to let go her anger and hurt. It was hard work, Kathryne realized, to hold the bitter rage inside.

She closed her eyes tight for a moment, wiped her hands across her cheeks, then called out, in a voice that was neither happy nor sad, "Please, Papa, come in."

The door swung open, and Aidan backed into the room. He turned about, and Kathryne saw that he was carrying a silver serving tray laden with tea, biscuits, meats, candied fruits, and a flagon of wine.

Aidan smiled at his daughter. "I knew that you would be hungry, and speaking one's heart over food seems an easier task."

"Papa," she said, rising and taking the tray from his hands, "you are the kindest father in all of the world, and I have done nothing since arriving on this island other than to dishonor your wishes."

She put the tray on her dressing table and embraced her father in a great, long hug. Neither spoke for many moments, just holding each other, reveling in the sensation that seemed so rare in recent months. Kathryne slipped out of her father's arms and reached over for a plateful of sweet biscuits. The aroma was most intoxicating, and Kathryne's stomach growled in response.

Aidan sat down on the bench by the window overlooking the sea. He looked out at the blackening waters, dark as the most midnight hour of the darkest night, rolling to the shore. The whitecapped waves roared in the distance.

He sat there in silence, the sound of the surf mixed with the small sounds of Kathryne as she nibbled upon the foods that Aidan had brought. He turned to his daughter.

"Kathryne," he said softly, "has coming to this island brought you happiness? I want an honest answer, without tears if it can be done."

She swallowed a large mouthful of sweet biscuit followed with a gulp of the weak wine. She felt such a warming comfort at this sustenance, such a sense of well-being, that it seemed incongruous to follow the pleasantness of that with an unpleasant lie from her lips.

"Papa, if you ask for the truth, I am honor-bound to supply you with honesty in return."

She looked up, her eyes dry, perhaps for the first time in weeks. "Papa, I will no longer lie to you, for you deserve a daughter who is not malicious and duplicitous such as I. I am not happy, but that is a concern not of yours, but of mine."

Aidan was about to speak, but Kathryne raised her hand and placed a finger on his lips. "Papa, it is my turn to speak, and I must speak my heart now."

With his face a mask of concern, he nodded.

"I desire to be an obedient daughter. My happiness is derived from obeying my father and should be nothing more and nothing less. You have been so gracious and loving, and I have done nothing but offer you heartache and grief.

"You have decided that Mr. Foxton will make the most suitable mate for me, and I will trust in your judgment. I will offer no more defense. Please, Papa, please make what announcements and arrangements are necessary so I may fulfill your wishes. That will be what returns me to happiness and contentment. I see now that disobedience has brought me pain and sadness. All I need to do is to obey, as the Scriptures call for, and I will be at peace."

She gulped, and her hand edged a tear from her eye. It was a small tear. "I will obey you, Papa, and I promise I will make you proud of me as your daughter."

Aidan's eyes turned moist, and he wiped away a tear. "Dearest

Kathryne," he said, his voice near a croak, "it is I who must offer heartfelt apologies, not you, for I have wronged you."

Kathryne looked up, puzzled and confused.

"It is a father's responsibility, a privilege in truth—to suggest, to aid, to counsel," Aidan said, his voice firming. "But if a father's decision brings about his child's heartache, then has he made a decision that honors the Almighty?"

Kathryne's eyes grew wide.

"Mr. Foxton is a fine man, and I would think that a pairing with him would offer great potential. But Kathryne, do you not see? That is how a father thinks. If your mother were still alive . . ." He looked into the distance for a moment. "If your mother were alive, she would have tempered a decision that offers great potential with her womanly intuition. She would have steered me back to considering your heart as well.

"I have not done that, my dearest Daughter, and that action has caused my soul to rend. If a marriage with Mr. Foxton offers no peace, then I shall not be an obstinate father and insist on such a course of events. I am sorry for my failure to see your pain. And this island offers too much of God's beauty to permit a heart to be broken." He placed his arm tenderly about her shoulder and whispered, "Will you forgive your father for being inconsiderate of your heart?"

She tilted her head and looked at his pained face for a moment, then pulled him close and tight. In a moment, and only for a moment, they were both engulfed in tears.

After a quiet minute, Aidan sat back and smiled at his daughter. Her face was now etched with tears, but these tears were of amazement and gratitude.

"Kathryne, it was Lady Emily who opened this door of realization. Without her I might have thought it locked and the key lost."

Kathryne smiled. "Then I shall need offer her my thanks."

Aidan reached over and pulled from the serving platter a cold leg of fowl and took a large bite from it, chewing it with great relish. After swallowing, he looked over at Kathryne. Her face was alive with promise, with hope, for the first time in months.

"Perhaps, Daughter, it might be time to speak of this William Hawkes."

■ ■ ■ ■ ■

Will walked out of his cottage into the hushed night. He looked over his right shoulder and found the moon in his eyes, yellow and full in the east. It was as if every step he took, every sound he heard, found his ears for the first time—the soft crunch of his boots against the sandy gravel road, the faraway calls of sea birds as they roosted in the trees by the edge of the salt marsh, the gentle rush of the wind as it rustled through the tall sea grass, and the tiny shimmering clacks their delicate shafts made as they rattled against each other.

*It is odd what one notices at times such as this,* he thought, strangely dispassionate.

Stopping at the bluff overlooking the glassy sea, he turned back to face his cottage, the darkened fort, and the sparkling torchlights of the town beyond. Through the bay window of the main room, he could see the pleasing form of Missy perched at the edge of the seat by the fire. Luke was sitting on the floor a few feet away, quiet and faithful as a sheepdog.

It had been a quiet evening—a simple dinner of bread and fish. Conversation had been sparse, only a dozen or two words had been exchanged between the two, and if Will had been asked, he would have said Missy's thoughts were a hundred miles distant. Such quiet had been the expected state for the past several weeks. Missy seemed preoccupied with deep, entangling thoughts that kept her words brief and at the edge of being perfunctory. Her eyes, at first most joyful, had taken on a darting, distracted look, and her laughter seemed forced.

After their meal, William had excused himself and walked from the house. On these warm and enfolding nights, the sea called to him. He sat with his feet hanging over the edge of the bluff, facing the dark waters, his hands behind in the grass, bracing himself upright as he looked out to the blackness of the western sky.

*Dear God, I come to you confused. When Missy reappeared in my life, my heart leaped for joy, for I had considered her an answer to my prayer that this house be filled with love. But what was once in my heart for Missy has vanished. Is my love for her simply hidden, or has it disappeared for all time? I am not a man who understands well the feminine heart, but it seems that she has longings elsewhere than with me. I seek to follow your will, dear God, but where is the path I should take? Is Missy here for me? Or has she come to point me in another direction? Dear God, show me the way, illuminate thy will. Am I to be with Missy, or am I . . .*

He closed his eyes and breathed in deep the clean air off the sea, filling his lungs with its pungent scent, the scent of faraway places, the scent of departure filling his senses.

*. . . or am I to be elsewhere? Am I to stay at this beautiful place, or*

*is there someplace else that I need be? Have I been disobedient in making this island my home? Am I to seek a harsher place in which to witness and to serve you? Dearest God, I seek thy face and thy guidance, for I am unaware of the proper direction for my steps. Please direct me.*

Will sat up straight and pulled his doublet around him, then lay back, a hummock of tall grass as a pillow. He looked to the sky, to the stars that marked the celestial boundary of the heavens. A cloud, a small scattering of cover, slipped across the darkness, low and sparse.

He closed his eyes and waited for God to reveal himself. He waited and prayed for the God of all creation to light the path before him that he might know what steps to take.

## 51

The next day, Emily arose before the dawn. She slipped out of Shelworthy, still silent with sleep, and gently roused Jeb, the groom, to help her saddle a mount. Within moments of the sun first entering the sky on the eastern horizon, slicing through a thick shelf of clouds, Emily turned onto the road winding south along the sea, leading to the harbor, riding at a fast canter. The clouds thickened, and the wind came in great, humid gusts.

Bridgetown remained at sleep. Emily passed only a handful of people on her ride, mostly fishermen on their way to the water and slaves on their way to the fields.

She arrived at the fort as the roosters in their pens began to crow. She tied her horse at the edge of the path to Will's cottage. Looking down at her boots, she closed her eyes and tried to prepare some well-suited words. Kathryne would have been horrified if she had known of her friend's errand that day, but Emily knew in her heart that it was time for action.

She stood silent for a long time, and yet no words seemed to form the correct sequences in her mind.

*Dear Father in heaven,* she prayed, *I beseech thee to guide what words I use.*

Opening her eyes, she saw a man at the edge of the bluff. He pulled himself up and began striding through the tall grass. His hair was wet and in tangles from the sea. It was William, she was sure. Emily realized from the first time she met him that she would never forget such a handsome profile.

She wanted to wave, to step boldly toward him, but realized that such an action was too brazen, even for her.

As Will walked home, he saw a tall woman with radiant red hair standing still as a statue by the front door. Her horse gently nuzzled the grass at the end of the walk. A puzzled look came over his face as he approached the cottage.

"Lady Emily. What brings you here on such an unsettled morning?" he inquired, bowing slightly as was expected.

"Mr. Hawkes, to be true, I am both as sure of my reasons as I am unsure. But I know that I am called to be here this day. It is not something that I can fully explain. May I have a word with you now? I know this is most regrettably early in the morning to receive a visitor, particularly one that you have not truly been acquainted with, but I feel that time is of the essence."

As she rattled out her greeting, she saw a black man turn the far corner of the house, his arms laden with a full split of wood for the breakfast fire. She noticed his eyes grow wide upon seeing her with Will. With a dry, clattery tumble, he let the wood fall from his arms, and he extended a finger toward her.

"Massa Will! Dat be de lady in my dream! She be de lady dat God tell me 'bout."

■ ■ ■ ■ ■

Kathryne arose early that day as well, feeling more rested and peaceful than she had since arriving on the tropical island. For the first time since stepping on Barbados she faced a morning in which the presence of Geoffrey Foxton did not loom above her like a thundercloud. She had berated herself so often these past months for feeling ill will toward the man, for perhaps no good reason other than the gentle stirrings inside her. And yet her quiet prayers to God had been answered. She had turned over to him control of her life by willing to be obedient to her father, and she was rewarded with the freedom to truly listen to her heart.

Gently tapping at Emily's door, she eased it open a tiny crack and whispered Emily's name. It had been much too late last evening to impose upon her, and there was now so much that she wanted to share with her dear friend. She slipped into the room and found it empty. Kathryne padded downstairs and found Hattie in the midst of breakfast preparations, flour dusting her dark skin.

"Have you seen Lady Emily?" she asked.

"No ma'am. She be gone by de time I be up."

"Gone?" Kathryne asked, surprised. "To where?"

"Don' know fer certain. Jeb say she ask 'bout de fort and if sunrise be too early."

"The fort? Lady Emily was going to the fort? Did she say that she was seeing Mr. Hawkes?" Kathryne's voice was edging louder and shriller as she spoke.

"Miss Kat'ryne, I don' know. Jeb don' say nothin' bout dat."

Kathryne turned and ran from the kitchen, calling out loudly as she bounded toward the steps, "Have Jeb saddle my horse for me. Now!"

■■■■■

Holding a thin sheet of paper in her trembling hands, Missy stumbled over the words once more, making certain of their meaning. The envelope had been delivered to her only that morning.

*Missy (Holender) Cavendish,*

I am penning this letter on a most sad occasion. I have been informed by trappers visiting out to the west that your husband, Dugald, passed on. They were unaware as to the causes of his demise, but assured me that his burial befitted a Christian man. Perhaps there is property in his name that now becomes yours. You have our sympathies.

*Tavis Talvern*

It was written by the man who so many months earlier had purchased Missy's wedding ring. The letter traveled the same route that she had followed, even sailing on the very same ship.

Missy read it one last time. She bowed her head, knowing that what had died in her heart so long ago was now final and closed. She could not smile at this news, but she took it as a sign that pointed to a happier future.

She knew that she must act on her heart and follow its strong push.

That same dawning, as Will swam in the morning surf, Missy had silently gathered up her few belongings from her bedchamber. She took only a dress to wear that day and had left behind the rest of the items Will had purchased for her.

*If I am to leave, I will not take advantage of Will's generosity,* she thought.

She left each dress carefully folded upon the bed and placed the powder, comb, and mirror next to them. Next to them, she placed the thin sheet of paper sealed with a drop of candle wax. In her unpracticed hand, Missy had penned the following words.

*Dearest William,*

   I am leaving this house and am going to John. That is where my heart is. Do not hate me. Do not hate John, for we take no joy in hurting you. I will repay you for all you have spent on my behalf as soon as I have such money. I am most eternally grateful to you for all you have done for me. I will always love you for your kindness.

                           *May God bless you for saving my life.*
                           *Missy*

   With a quiet pull, she closed the door of the room. As she did, a breeze from the window lifted the paper from the bed, and it breezed beneath a chest of drawers, all but hidden from view. With careful and soft step, she slipped out into the dew-filled morning. Stopping at the end of the path, she looked one more time at the cottage, then began to walk at a brisk pace towards town and St. Michael's Church.

Kathryne near leapt upon the horse just as Jeb had finished snugging the saddle tight. With the snap of her switch, the horse bolted, and Kathryne clung to the saddle horn, her dark curls flowing after her as the tail following a comet in the sky.

   *Why on earth would she have gone to William?* Kathryne wondered. *She cannot be sharing with him what Papa and I spoke of last night, for that is not hers to share. What if she tells William, and he laughs in response?*

   She dug her spurs in deep against the flanks of the horse.

   *I must prevent her from presenting such news in an inopportune manner, for if William is to be with Missy, I will not interfere.*

   She switched at the horse again, spurring it on, faster and faster, a great cloud of dust rising behind them.

The singsong notes of Luke's prayers swayed gently in the air and matched the sound of the surf in the distance. The breeze had begun to hurry, and dark clouds were slipping across the sky from the north.

   Lady Emily turned to the ex-slave mumbling his odd words in the faint light of dawn, and she smiled. She had no idea of what he was saying or why, yet she understood the import of Luke's words.

Emily then faced Will and placed her gloved hand on his forearm, a gesture that spoke of intimacy and truth. "Mr. Hawkes, I am most brazen to have come to you today as I have, without escort, without sending a proper note announcing my intentions, but sometimes the bother of all that formality simply prevents free discourse, do you not think?"

Will nodded, not truly understanding what he had just affirmed.

"Kathryne is not aware of my visit, Mr. Hawkes, and I am not certain that either of us should inform her of such. She would be most scandalized, I am sure."

Will nodded again. Overcoming his initial shock, he realized that, as host, he should invite her in. "Lady Emily, please forgive my crude manners. Will you come inside? I can offer you tea, or coffee, or ale, if you prefer, and breakfast as well. For certain, the earliness of the hour has precluded your partaking of breakfast."

Will gestured to the door with his outstretched arm. As he did so, he realized with a cold clump to his heart that Missy would be inside. *How do I explain her to Lady Emily?*

Relief washed over him as Lady Emily declined his invitation with a shake of her head.

"Mr. Hawkes, I may only stay a few moments. I have but one thought to pass to you, and then I will be gone."

She bowed her head for a moment and closed her eyes. If Will had to guess, he would have said that a prayer was uttered as well.

"Mr. Hawkes," she chirped brightly, "I am not a woman given to hysterical urges or wild intuitions. But at the dedication I saw your eyes as they met Kathryne's. I saw what transpired behind them. There is no denying the power that was in that single glance. Forgive my boldness, Mr. Hawkes, but I am learning too late in this life that one must sometimes act with courage. Our lives are much too brief to squander over waiting until fear leaves our hearts."

She swallowed and took a deep breath. "That day, I also saw the young woman who has lived in this house with you—Missy, is it not?"

William nodded with a nervous glance to the cottage.

"I know you have done a wondrous and compassionate work, rescuing her from servitude. But, Mr. Hawkes, what I saw in your eyes as you looked at her was not love, but simple care and concern. Your eyes do not lie. I know how passion manifests itself between a man and a woman, and what was between Missy and yourself was not passion."

Will did not attempt to speak.

"Mr. Hawkes, I beseech you to forgive my audacity. It is not that I desire to be the ruination of any relationship, but I cannot be silent in the face of such a mistake. I will not sit idly by."

Will was still attempting to formulate a response, but he could find no specific sentence to utter.

"Search your heart, Mr. Hawkes. Admit honestly what is there. Do not live the rest of your life based on what you perceive is an obligation to the past. That will serve no one well."

Will opened his mouth, as if to speak.

Lady Emily, however, spoke first. "You do not need to respond to me, Mr. Hawkes. You must respond to your own heart. That is where you hold the truth. Follow your heart."

She reached over and smoothed an errant strand of Will's blond hair from his face. He shivered at the gesture, his soul crying out, for it reminded him of his mother's tender care. Without thinking, he touched at the locket resting over his heart.

"All will be well, Mr. Hawkes," she whispered, then leaned forward, arched up, and kissed his cheek, almost drawn to the action without thought, and whispered again in his ear, "Follow your heart."

She turned, walked to her horse, lifted herself up, and rode back toward Bridgetown.

Luke squatted there by the cottage door and continued to talk to God. Will edged past him and into the quiet cottage.

The black man rocked back and forth in prayer, giving thanks in his native language for the gift that God had given him. He knew not of Lady Emily nor her friendships. All he knew is that he had seen her face in his dreams. She was the lady that would make all hurts dissolve.

It came to pass as he had predicted to Will when the dream first occurred. And now that the lady with red hair had come, Luke felt peace wash over him, the peace that he knew came only from the Almighty.

A heartbeat later, Will leaped out of the front door. "Luke! Where is Missy?"

Luke rocked two more times, craned his neck up at Will, then stood, his knees cracking and creaking. "She gone," he said with a soft smile on his face.

Will ran his hands through his hair, looking most vexed. "I have discovered as much," he said.

Luke smiled, unaware of Will's concern. "Den why ask Luke 'bout her?"

Will glowered at him. "Where did she go, Luke? When did she leave? Why was I not told?"

"Din' ask, Massa Will. Missy gone to town. She gone by sun's light."

"Luke," Will asked, exasperated, "did she not explain her leaving? Where has she gone?"

Luke said nothing and shrugged his shoulders.

"Did she go to market for bread or fish? Perhaps she simply went to purchase supplies?"

"Massa Will, she don' go to buy fish dis day. She not be buyin' at de market dis day."

"You make no sense, Luke. Where did she go?"

"She go in de dark. She don' see me, so she don' tell me." Luke stared into Will's eyes. "I don' stop her 'cause in de dream she not be here. God say not to stop Missy."

Luke got up and walked to the fort, where he often had his breakfast meal with the blackamoors.

Will stood by the cottage door, alone. He looked about, at Luke's back, at the graying sky, at the empty cottage.

*Where has Missy gone? And why? I've got to find her!*

Will began to walk, then run, to town.

# CHAPTER

## 52

Kathryne's horse galloped to town, its sides heaving in and out, its breath coming in great gasps. Kathryne bent to the horse's neck and patted at its slick coat.

She dismounted and led him by the reins along the narrower streets of Bridgetown. As she turned a corner, she saw a young golden-haired woman bounding toward her in obvious joy. When this woman noticed Kathryne in the street she pulled up and stopped still.

"Mrs. Cavendish, is it not?" Kathryne said, almost curtly. "It is pleasant to see you again."

Missy curtsied, out of habit, and replied, "Good morning, Lady Spenser." She tried to hide her smile, but could not.

Both women stood silent, each examining the other. After several moments of odd silence, Kathryne buckled up her courage and spoke.

"Mrs. Cavendish, will you be walking back to Mr. Hawkes and the fort? Perhaps I may accompany you?"

Missy smiled a curious smile. Kathryne, without truly being aware of the reason, was suddenly filled with great, immense, overwhelming relief. From the innermost core of her being, where a woman's intuition and reason joined, Kathryne at that moment knew that Missy was not returning to Will.

Missy, her smile never fading, but growing in confidence, replied, her voice small but sure, "I will not, Lady Spenser. I am on my way to the chandlery," she said, "and to John Delacroix."

Her words trembled in the gathering breeze, then wisped away toward the sea. Kathryne was almost at a loss for response. For both women, hours of conversation had been truncated into these few sentences, an entire day of talk distilled into these few crystalline moments.

"Well then, I wish you the best, Mrs. Cavendish. May God go before your steps."

Missy smiled, lighting up the street with her glowing countenance. "And you too, Lady Spenser. God bless you too."

■ ■ ■ ■

Will turned the corner past the Goose and faced the buffeting winds as his eyes scanned the streets for a sign of Missy. Dust, carried along in the breeze, stung at his eyes, and he held his hand up to shield them. *A good storm is rising,* he thought.

Another gust pushed him along, and he ducked into a narrow, dark alley that wound along the dock, sheltered between two rows of buildings and out of wind.

*Where would she have gone?*

He turned again, taking another path in the malodorous confines of the narrow alley that led to the docks and the chandlery.

*Perhaps John will know of her whereabouts.*

Soon he arrived at a narrow arch separating the dark alley from the larger street in front. Will stepped carefully, avoiding a dark trickle of putrid water edging to the sea.

It was then that he saw her.

At first, he told himself that it was not Missy running along the far edge of the harbor's wooden planking. But the flowing, honey-colored hair belonged to no other woman on this island. Will was a heartbeat away from stepping into the pale light of the street when John Delacroix emerged from the chandlery. Always an early riser, Will knew, he would have been sitting in the front window, watching the boats bob and drift in the harbor.

The pair now stood a mere arm's length apart. The two, John and Missy, spoke to each other, their lips moving, their words washed away by the wind.

Then, as if they had practiced before, they met in an energetic embrace. John lifted Missy from her feet and swung her about in a whirl of happiness and laughter.

Will heard none of their happy sounds, but the sight grabbed at his heart.

The spin stopped as John set her down and met her lips with his. It was most apparent that Missy did nothing to resist his advance.

William bowed his head, his heart strangely at ease, and slipped back into the shadows of the empty street.

The thin, nearly transparent curtains fluttered in the wind, their bottoms pulled at first through the open window, then as if the wind had taken a breath, blown back into the room with a snap.

Geoffrey had just pulled his boots back on and sat down on the bed. Eileen had risen earlier, having had to answer the persistent tapping of a customer.

*Why anyone would come to the Goose for food at this hour shows a great paucity of taste,* Geoffrey thought.

Eileen stepped back into the room. *I prefer other enticements they have on their bill of fare,* he thought as he looked at her.

"It was our noble Mr. Hawkes searching for Missy Cavendish," she said as she sat on the edge of the bed and began to comb her hair. "Perhaps they have had a lovers' spat."

Geoffrey laughed again, a laugh that was tinted with dark tones.

"Does the weather bode ill for this day?" he asked.

Eileen nodded. "A strong squall, from the darkness of the clouds."

"Blast it all!" Geoffrey barked. "I have three Dutchmen at Six Man Bay waiting to load. I can't load if the sea is high, and if I miss this tide, they'll be waiting another week."

Eileen did not turn, but simply shrugged. "No man stops the rain, Mr. Foxton."

In a moment, Geoffrey leapt up and ran to the steps and then out the rear door.

Aidan rose early that morning. The wind had loosened a shutter, and it had awakened him with a start, banging loudly against the window and frame.

Silent, he walked down to the dining chamber and rang for a cup of morning coffee.

He sipped the thick hot drink and reviewed the last day's activities in his mind. Foremost in his mind was the tender trailing of Emily's most beautifully delicate finger on his skin. In his mind he could see it as it journeyed from his palm to the back of his hand and gradually slid and scratched along his skin to his wrist and above.

He looked down at his hand, feeling her slightest presence against him. Yet for all its delicate pressure, it echoed as if a cannon had been fired in his soul. *How sweet her tender touch felt,* he thought, and took another long sip of his coffee, feeling its warmth as it filled his mouth and throat, its glow warming his being.

He picked up his cup and walked toward the front door. He reached the entry as the front door swung open, filling the great hall with the bluster of the storm. As if blown in by the torrent of wind, Emily flowed in, her long riding cape spiraling and entwining about her, her red hair filled with the wind, her face streaked by the rain that was just now beginning to fall. Her eyes were full of light, alive.

The door swung open wider now, slapping against the wall, and the rain and wind twisted and coiled about Emily and Aidan as they stood, facing each other, silent.

Their eyes met, locked in a visual embrace.

As if the sea could resist the pull of the moon and refuse to allow the tide to turn, so they tried to resist the yearnings deep within.

But the sea could hold still for only so many moments.

Aidan blinked once, let the cup in his hand tumble in a jangling crash to the floor, and took the first step toward Emily.

CHAPTER

53

The sky had just begun to open, the warm rain splattering down in heavy drops, producing wide circles of moisture in the dust of the street. Will slipped down the narrow street and made his way to the sand and the shore. From here, he could walk along at the edge of the sea until he reached his home.

It was not as if his world had collapsed as he saw Missy and John embrace. In truth, his heart felt suddenly unfettered, unconstrained, as if the last months suddenly made sense. Missy's laugh had filled the cottage, but lately only when John had come to dine with them. *Her eyes did seem to sparkle and dance,* Will recalled in a sudden burst of awareness, *but only in John's company, not mine.* It was not as if she had gone cold and cruel with William, but as a torch outshines a candle, so did her brightness with John overshadow her affinity to William.

As Will walked along the sand, the winds whipped along the shore, forcing the spray of the waves back to the sea in great gusts. The scud of clouds became thicker, denser, more ominous. From the north, a band of blackness pecked at the horizon and began to roll toward the island of Barbados.

▬ ▭ ▬ ▭ ▬

Kathryne's horse, Porter, arrived at Will's cottage in a clatter of hooves. Kathryne was reacting, not thinking; she was doing, not considering; she was being, not devising.

She jumped down from the horse and with purposeful strides marched to the door of the cottage. In her mind, there was no thought to what she might say, no plan for what she might ask, no vision for what might transpire.

Throughout her young life Kathryne had not been one who acted without prayer, but as she galloped from Shelworthy to Bridgetown that windy morning, she realized that it had been many weeks since she had truly communed with God.

It was true that she had prayed about the wisdom of obeying her father in the matter of Mr. Foxton, almost demanding her will, not God's, be done. But it had been so very long since she merely spoke what was on her heart to the Creator, as a child would speak to a father. She had lost the intimate closeness to her Lord that she once knew, she realized. *Perhaps that is why I have been so miserable of late and have found no peace in these circumstances.*

As the horse had galloped along, the pain of this loss was sharp against her heart, yet she seemed to have lost the language needed to pray. It was then that she gave up, admitted that she was lost, and let the Holy Spirit in her take her jumbled thoughts to the almighty God. She had taken humble pride in her ability to formulate most pleasing and thorough prayers in the past, but as she rode that day, all that pride slipped off her being like so much chaff in the wind. She simply allowed what was in her soul to express itself to her heavenly Father. She knew that he would understand, and with each mile closer to the harbor, as she submitted her life to his will, Kathryne felt more and more at peace, allowing him to handle the outcome of this day.

She knew the proper words would come when she met William.

A thunderclap sounded, and a sharp, crackling needle of lightning crashed into the sea a dozen leagues to the west.

She knocked at the cottage door, not harshly yet not gently. She blinked her eyes twice, licked her lips, and squared her shoulders.

The door swung open, and Luke stood in the open doorway, his face a wide grin. "Lady Kat'ryne. You be here now. Dat good. Luke know. You come in now. You wait for Massa."

Kathryne smiled and stepped through the door.

They waited in the dim, cool cottage, the storm intensifying with every heartbeat that passed.

*Why am I doing this?* Kathryne wondered. *It is as if a dam has burst, and I am swept along, unable to stop my forward movement. But yet, as I tumble forward, my heart is the most calm it has been since I left England. Does this mean that God is finally revealing himself in this? Does a calm heart mean God's approval? Does an open door mean that it is God's plan?*

Luke sat across from Kathryne, who primly sat at the edge of the bench by the flickering light of the fireplace. He stared and smiled. Neither of them said a word for many moments, yet for Kathryne, it was not a nervous time, but a time of serenity. Then Luke spoke.

"Dat lady wid red hair be here dis mornin', Lady Kat'ryne. God said she be here in my dream, and she here. Now you be here. Dat what God tole me, and now you here. Dat be most good."

Kathryne nodded, glad that Luke's words confirmed that this was indeed God's will.

"Massa Will be here soon. He be by de fort. You wait. He be here soon."

After fifteen minutes of tortured waiting, Kathryne saw Luke stand up, pointing to the west.

Kathryne stood up and spun about, following Luke's pointed finger. She saw Will turn the corner on the south side of the fort, along the rocky rise that then dipped to the sea.

She could not stay inside to wait. Her heart would not allow it, and she ran to the door, flinging it open with a bang. The wind and rain formed a garland about her frame, coiling tightly around her. She wrapped her riding cape about her shoulders, pulled the hood over her head, and ran out into the storm, toward William.

Will stepped cautiously among the rocks and coral fingers along the shore. Wet from the rain, the rocks, slick with moss and seaweed, became dangerous. He looked over at his cottage and saw nothing. He looked down at his feet, locating safe footholds, finding a stable place to stand.

He looked back up, and the form of a woman appeared. She was running toward him, wrapped in a dark hooded cape, her face hidden. The wind slipped down and lifted the hood from her face, pulling it back, freeing her dark hair into the tempest of the wind and rain.

His heart skipped a beat.

It was Kathryne.

Without even looking down, Will leaped from smooth rock to jagged boulder to sharp coral, each step met with safe purchase. In a moment, he was at the bluff overlooking the sea.

They both stopped a dozen paces from each other, the wind wailing and the rains splattering about them.

For many moments the two simply stood and stared, their eyes filling with the sight of the other. The wind had lifted Kathryne's long dark curls, playing them out in a dark halo. Her cape was flowing out from her, her gown snapping about her ankles, its fabric now dampened by the rain. Her green eyes were the color of the sea before a storm—deep, dancing with reflections. Will stood, face to the wind, his blond hair wet and blowing behind him.

He took a small step toward her, and she did likewise.

Each step was followed with another, and in a dozen heartbeats a mere hand's width separated them.

It was William who first spoke.

"Kathryne, I do not have the words to tell you of my heart. . . ."

She reached up and placed her open palm against his cheek as he spoke and merely closed her eyes, feeling his words with her hand.

"You have the words, William," she said, almost at a whisper.

He placed his hand over hers.

"My heart does not beat in my chest without yours to match its rhythm. There is no sun or stars without you. Even the North Star had faded to darkness knowing that you were to be with another man."

She reached up and placed a finger tenderly on his lips, silencing him for a moment. "William, I know. For me as well, the world had become a dark and joyless place."

William knew he had to ask the question directly. "And what of Geoffrey Foxton?"

Kathryne smiled, an expression that carried both pain and pleasure. "My father has allowed me to follow my heart, William—my heart alone and not his arrangement."

She looked down. When she lifted her face back to William, her eyes were full of tears. "My heart led only to you, William. There was no other destination."

William could wait no longer. He bent tenderly to her and placed his lips upon hers for just a moment, tasting the salt of her tears as well.

He stepped back and, without taking his eyes off her face, took her hands in his. He stared into her eyes, feeling as if he were swimming in her soul.

"Kathryne Spenser, I have loved you since I first saw you, and I will love you until I breathe my last upon this earth and my eyes are forever closed. You hold my heart in your hands, Kathryne. Until this moment the sun has not shined, but now the sky is filled with gold. I have been reborn."

Kathryne leaned to William's ear and whispered, "I love you, William Hawkes."

She pulled William to her and embraced him in the fiercest hug her arms would avail. It was done with such force that he felt the breath near leave him for a moment.

They stopped, silent, then Will again leaned over and placed his lips upon hers. And as they did, the earth and the skies seemed to disappear, and all that remained was their two hearts, now beating side by side in a matched rhythm.

From the cottage, out of the wind and rain, an overjoyed Luke stood and watched Will and Kathryne come together.

"Dat be what God tole me would happen," he called out softly to himself. "God is great."

CHAPTER

**54**

That evening, in the drawing room of Shelworthy, William and Lord Aidan Spenser sat facing each other in two formal chairs, placed at right angles to the warming fire. A glass of rich, expensive port had been poured for each. Both men had taken tiny sips, and Will waited, stiff, uncomfortable, for the governor of Barbados and all the islands of the Lesser Antilles to speak.

"Well, Mr. Hawkes . . . A nasty spell of troublesome weather this day, was it not?"

Will nodded.

Aidan sat up straight and folded his hands in his lap, as if striking a most contemplative pose. After a moment, he nodded to himself, then spoke.

"I have given much thought to your request to court my daughter—to present yourself as a suitor. Sudden as it was, I have had some opportunity to ponder the implications of such an arrangement."

"Thank you, sir. I do admit that such a matter, while sudden in its appearance, was many months in its development."

"Indeed. But, William, you must understand my predicament. I will speak bluntly this eve, for such a request calls for honest speech in return."

Aidan cleared his throat. "You are not born of nobility. That is a simple truth, and one that vexes me greatly. But I have begun to realize that perhaps this island has caused us all to relax the confinements of the past. I will not speak of it now, but a man such as yourself—once a pirate—will need to learn the cultured and mannered ways of a respectable Englishman to feel comfortable in the world that Kathryne knows."

William nodded. "I understand that there are matters, such as civility at the table, social graces, and the like, in which I would need instruction."

Aidan looked relieved. "And you agree that you will undertake such an education?" he asked.

"Sir, I would do nothing to bring dishonor to Kathryne. I will attempt to be the most polished former pirate that ever existed." Will smiled gently.

"A most wise course, Mr. Hawkes. I am sure Lady Emily can be of assistance to you in that regard."

Aidan paused a moment, then continued. "I would imagine, that you would . . . well . . . if presented the opportunity, shall I say . . . that you could support Kathryne in a manner that, quite frankly, she is accustomed to."

Will nodded.

"And I am aware that as master of the harbor defenses, the Crown pays you fifty pounds per year. It is a good sum, but I daresay they will not increase it simply because you are courting a member of the noble class."

"No, sir. I did not expect the Crown to do so."

Aidan took another sip of port.

"Kathryne will come into her money in due time—the majority of it not until I have departed, and that may be years away."

"Yes, sir. I am aware of that. It is my hope that that date be many years distant."

"Fifty pounds is not a royal sum, William."

Aidan seemed genuinely puzzled by this situation—that his daughter, raised in luxury, would willingly step away from it to be with a man of such common means.

"Lord Aidan, Kathryne and I have never before discussed my resources. Hence I do not know what she might expect me to possess. That said, I must conclude that she could be content—if the future I envision shall come to pass—with those fifty pounds and my cottage by the sea."

Aidan nodded. "I suppose that your observations be correct, William—but fifty pounds?"

"Sir, I do have other assets . . . investments of my sea shares."

Aidan arched his eyebrows. "Indeed? Which investments specifically? I hope that such a request is not prying, but you must understand that I am duly concerned for Kathryne's welfare."

Will took a sip of port and began to tick off, using his fingers as counters as he spoke. "I have part ownership of several dockyards in Weymouth—those used by the English fleet in that port—perhaps two dozen in all. In my name are one thousand acres of grazing and farming land in Dorset, purchased months ago from Lord Archibald, who suffered greatly from gambling losses, I am told. There are near ten thousand sheep upon that land. Between Captain Waring and myself, there exists a shared purchase of an armaments foundry, used extensively by the English fleet. Last year they produced some two thousand cannon and three thousand muskets. In joint tenancy, we have a full tithe of shares in the East India Company, expected to return a doubling of investment this year. In addition, we have a joint hold on some two thousand acres of wheat land near Dover."

Will furrowed his brow, trying to think if he had overlooked a holding. "My solicitor in Weymouth has letters of credit in my name, backed by gold of course, for nearly twenty-five thousand pounds. And my solicitor here on Barbados is holding perhaps another ten thousand pounds."

Silence flooded back into the room. Aidan thought for a moment, making sure his jaw was still closed.

"And the cottage and land on this island as well," Will said with finality.

A natural mathematician, Aidan had been adding the sums and placing arbitrary, yet low, estimates on each holding. With a sudden start, Aidan stiffened. It was clearly obvious that the young man sitting before him was perhaps a few thousand pounds from having accumulated as much wealth as did he.

A most vexing emotion stirred within him. After a moment, he managed to regain his composure.

"Well, William, I do believe that you have sufficient means. But to look at your lodging and attire, one would never assume such vast holdings."

"I am from common stock, as you say, Lord Aidan. I have simple tastes."

Aidan gulped and then stood, extending his hand to William, who rose and took it.

"William, as Kathryne's father, I allow you such privilege to present yourself as a suitor to my daughter. I trust that God will always reign over your behaviors."

For a moment Will was speechless, thinking that the questioning would be more intense. It was his turn to stammer.

"Thank you, good sir. God has blessed me richly. Meeting Kathryne was a most undeserved and exceedingly great blessing. I will do my utmost to bring honor to her, to you, and to God."

Emily and Kathryne had been kneeling in the adjacent room, their ears to the door, trying to hide their giggles, acting as schoolgirls on a prank. Neither could hear completely as Will described his riches, but both could discern, as clear as a roar of thunder, Aidan's official sanction of their proposed union. In the dark, Emily and Kathryne leapt up, embracing each other in a torrent of silent laughter and tears.

*St. Augustine, Florida*

The storm that swept through the waters of the Antilles was but the first of several that formed their gray clouds above the flatlands of the Florida peninsula. It was an unusual direction for clouds to take, but it had been a year of odd weather. A second set of hot and humid thunderstorms crashed above the thick walls of Fort Augustine. For the prisoners held captive inside, it was a momentary relief from their discomfort. But when the clouds passed, the cool grayness was replaced by the angry tropical sun and thick humidity. The captives stewed behind the hot walls, waiting for a breath of coolness—a breath that seldom came.

Radcliffe Spenser had insisted that the vicar be given a better cell and improved rations, but to Radcliffe's great surprise, both amenities had been turned down. It appeared as though the vicar would not leave his newfound flock and chose to remain, sweating in the bleak, black hovels filled with fetid, vile air.

This day, when the vicar was brought to the almost-pleasant white-washed interrogation cell, Radcliffe sat, sipping at a goblet of wine, his feet propped up on the table before him.

"Ah, good Vicar. And how is your flock today?" he asked as the clergyman sat in a tall, straight-backed chair of uncomfortable design.

Vicar Mayhew, thinner now by a dozen pounds, and chalky white, attempted to smile, gracious and open. Yet there remained in his eyes a hesitation, and Radcliffe knew it.

"They are well, as well as can be expected in their state. Yet even in the darkness, light does shine and the heart of a man does grow."

Radcliffe chuckled again and swallowed half the wine in a single gulp. "Well, Vicar Mayhew, I understand that you have refused my offer of food and a new cell. A most unfortunate choice."

The vicar sat with his hands folded and did not speak.

"I cannot offer better views to the entire population of prisoners here. That much is certain. But I can offer them better food. Thanks to your stubbornness, rations will be doubled with tomorrow's dawn. I will not have you looking drawn and weak. If you will not eat what others do not have, I will simply feed all of you more. It is most amazing what our hosts here will do for me—all because of such lovely and such rewarding information I possess. It is good for you, Vicar, that I know of English forts and fleets and gold. The Spanish covet what I know. 'Increase the swill to the prisoners,' I ask, and the deed is done. They will do most anything to use what I have stored away in my head. And what is stored there has served you well."

The vicar nodded and whispered a quiet thank-you.

Radcliffe rose and walked away, turning only as he reached the door.

"And I have managed to get you a copy of your beloved Scriptures that you have been babbling on about. I trust that you will honor me by repaying my kindness at some point in the future."

For a moment the vicar was stunned to silence. The look on his face told Radcliffe what the vicar's next words confirmed.

"Thank you, Mr. Spenser. I will indeed repay your kindness. I would offer my very life if need be to have the Bible in my hands again."

*That won't be necessary,* Radcliffe thought. *At least not yet.*

CHAPTER

**56**

*Barbados*

For the three days following the storm that battered Barbados with its wind-driven ferocity, William walked about dazed. His smile was most open, broad, and frequent, and he took to wandering off during the day—at odd times, and for hours. The men would search about the fort, calling aloud for him, needing a question answered concerning a particular measurement or fitting or finish. But as they called out, over and over, no trace of William could be discerned.

The first day Luke had found William sitting on a smooth boulder watching the tide slip in, gently trapping him in the hushed surf. The second day Luke spotted him standing on that same rock, simply staring out at the harbor. When Luke arrived at his side and greeted him, William turned slowly, looking surprised at the voice. His face was becoming creased by a permanent grin. The third day, Luke scanned the horizon, called out for Will along the entire length of the beach, then loped to town.

Luke returned, near sunset, alone.

"I don' find Massa Will no place. He be loony wit' dat lady."

William arrived back at the cottage near dark, his clothing wet, his hair damp and tousled, and missing his shoes. Yet he was smiling.

Luke shook his head, stirred the cooking fire, and began to heat their dinner, a thick stew of smoked pig and turnips. When the stew was served, William sat there, as if dreaming with eyes open, sliding the food about the plate in front of him, sipping at his ale, yet not truly drinking it at all.

After perhaps an hour of pretending to refresh himself, Will cocked his head to the side and spoke the first complete sentence Luke had heard leave his lips in three days.

"Luke, do you think that you might find some sort of hamper in which to carry food?"

Luke narrowed his eyes. "Ham-per? Luke don' know dat word."

"Like a basket. To carry food for a picnic," Will explained.

"Pic-nic? Luke don' know dat word neither."

"For a quiet tryst . . . outdoors."

"Massa Will," Luke sputtered, "Luke don' know dem words. Luke not help if he don' know de words."

William looked over at Luke, his chin on his hand, his elbow on the table, and just smiled in response.

■ ■ ■ ■ ■

Will and Kathryne arrived at Needham's Point, a short ride south of the fort. The land there rose to a sharp bluff overlooking the sea and the town and provided a most pleasant viewing spot. It was a perfect day for dining *alfresco,* as the Italians would say, William recalled. The sky was clear, the breeze was moderate, the air warm, the food consisting of the best that could be procured on the island.

Will spread a thick blanket on the coarse pangola grass and then placed a finer woven spread atop that. He placed the hamper at the corner of the spread, and for the following blissful hours as the sun edged from overhead to its low afternoon position in the west, the couple nibbled and drank, talked and laughed, watched the sun dance on the waters below them, and fed cawing gulls crusts of their bread.

In all of William's life, in all the experiences he had lived through, in all the emotions that had washed through his being, he knew for a truth most certain, that his heart had never been as full and happy as it was this day.

Looking at Kathryne, watching her lips move as she spoke, watching the graceful arc of her hand as it fluttered in the warm air illustrating her words, was like watching a gilded butterfly dance from golden flower to golden flower. Will was enraptured by simply existing this close to the woman who held his heart. By merely extending his arm, he could take her delicate hand in his, he could touch her sweet and graceful arm, he could place his fingertips on her most beautiful face, he could tangle his fingers through her silken hair.

*Has the sea always had these luscious shades of blue and green?* he thought as he watched her take a dainty nibble on a ripe plum. *Have the gulls sounded this sweet before? Has food always been this rich and potently satisfying in the past?*

Shadows began to deepen and the sea began to darken, and Will knew that the afternoon was near an end, yet he wished it would last for an eternity longer.

Kathryne had been still and silent for many moments, and he had been content simply to sit beside her, watching the western horizon slip into its purple and scarlet evening robes.

"William," Kathryne asked, her voice even and dreamlike, "how do you see the future?"

He sat straighter and furrowed his brow. He had not thought beyond the present for hours, and to do so now was jarring.

She turned to him, now facing him directly. "I do not mean the future with you and me, but—"

"I do not see a future without you present, Kathryne. Perhaps these words are spoken too early—but without you I have no future."

Kathryne lowered her eyes and perhaps blushed a bit.

"Thank you, William, but what prompted my question is separate from that reality. In these past months I have struggled so with knowing God's will for my life. I ask my soul how that obedience manifests itself in my actions. How do I please God with my life? I know you believe, William, but how will God use you? How will you know what his plan is for you? How, then, will you know that you are pleasing him with your life?"

Will turned and sat cross-legged facing Kathryne. He set his mouth to a stern visage and looked down at his hands while he pondered. "Kathryne, you ask no simple question, and as such, can be given no simple answer."

She reached over and placed her hands over both of his, as if to reassure him. "I intend no pressure, William, on your response. Indeed, such a response is most personal—between the almighty God and a man's soul. But I so yearn to understand how I am to inhabit this world."

He looked down at her hands on his, and for a moment all his thoughts vanished, as a covey of quail might explode with a fluttered whir into the air, flushed from their hiding place by dog or hunter. It took several moments, but he recomposed his thoughts and replied.

"Kathryne, you are aware that I owe you a debt to never be repaid—that of pointing me to the path to the Almighty. I know we have spoken of this before, and I will not belabor that thought, but my gratitude is there.

"How do I know what God intends for my life? A man can do no wrong by living his life in accordance with the Scriptures. I have tried to do as such. But what of where I am to live and what I am to bring to the Savior? God has placed me here, in this place, for what I believe is a mission that no man of faith has undertaken."

Kathryne leaned forward. "And that is what, William?"

"You know that I, in my own feeble manner, attempt to present the truth of the Scriptures to that small group of men, ladies, and blackamoors that gathers in the fort on Sundays?"

"I am, William. Your message is often more direct than those one hears at St. Michael's. Or so they all say."

It was William's turn to blush. "Who has said those words has no gift for discernment," Will stammered. "But those few souls have nowhere else to turn in order to hear the truth of God's love. If I were not here, those souls may be lost."

Silence slipped around them for a moment. The surf growled in a friendly manner from below as the tide rolled in.

"And that, William, is that is what God has as his plan for you? To be, as Paul, a missionary to the lost?"

"Kathryne, if I could say for certain that it is God's plan that I do this forever, I would be elevating myself to the position of knowing as much as does the Almighty. But at this time, on this island, I am called to do what I may do—and I believe the Almighty is blessing that work."

As he said those words, he put his hand over hers and squeezed it gently. She responded with a smile so bright that Will felt as if the sun had stopped its travel west and had risen in the east once again.

## 57

"How does this infernal mechanism work?" Vicar Petley sputtered to no one, fuming and distracted. Vicar Coates had ruined his perfectly fine day by announcing that he had seen William Hawkes and Kathryne Spenser walking toward Needham's Point that noon, with what looked to be a basket of provisions.

Giles had blanched white. *Kathryne and that pirate? Alone together? That is most ludicrous.*

"Surely you are mistaken. Perhaps it was Mr. Foxton?" Giles responded.

The short Vicar Coates shook his head in reply. "No, it was not. I am sure of who I saw—and it was indeed the two I mentioned."

Within the hour, Giles had purchased a telescope from the chandlery and made his way up the new but rickety ladder in the church tower, carrying the heavy glass instrument in his left hand. He was determined to prove Vicar Coates to be mistaken.

For more than a dozen minutes he fussed with the device's length and aiming techniques. Resting his arm on the railing, he swung the telescope about to the south and first found the path that led away from town. He followed it with the glass and, after a few jerks and starts, found his eyes targeted on the tip of Needham's Point, the objects there so close they appeared no more than a stone's throw from his high perch.

Indeed, there were two figures on a blanket there—and one was Kathryne Spenser. No one could mistake her exotic mane of flowing, curled dark hair and most alluring silhouette.

*But who might the man be? He is too lean to be Mr. Foxton.*

Finally the man turned and faced north, full into the scope of Vicar Petley's glass, who nearly dropped the telescope from the bell tower, grasping it only at the last moment before it tumbled into space.

*It is that infernal pirate! Blast and blast it again! How in blazes did this occur?*

As he made his way down the tower, his mood grew blacker and more ominous. *How I will enjoy uprooting that evil sprout from his makeshift pulpit. Mr. Hawkes, you will have met your match in me.*

Giles would have laughed his high-pitched cackle there in the dark confines of the bell tower, save for a sudden calamity brought on by his new boots. The bottoms were slick from newness, and his right foot missed its purchase on the bottom rung of the ladder. He slipped off his footing, tumbling the last three feet to the ground, end first, splitting his new breeches. Stunned, he sat there in the dusty dimness, rubbing his haunches at the spot that was sure to produce an evil, purple bruise.

■□■□■

That Sunday a new facet of Vicar Petley emerged—that of a fiery commentator, decrying the evidences of a crumbling social order. A headlong destruction was being brought about by the subtle, perfidious downward slide of morals and the godless easing of divine restrictions, he claimed.

He bellowed at the congregation that day and walked about the pulpit, depending less on his written notes than he had ever done before. He was inspired, he knew. Only a few moments into his message, the sweat began to form rivulets on his forehead.

He thundered, "Can a righteous man allow the good women of this island to be sullied, to be debased by associating with heathen criminals who have only one true thought in their fevered bodies?"

He slammed his fist down on the pulpit, causing a small cascade of dust in the sunlight.

"Does 'living beyond the line' mean that such wantonness goes unnoticed?"

He pounded on the pulpit again, and Vicar Coates, sitting in the special vicars' pew at the front, noticed a small crack form at the side of the pulpit's wooden frame, running from base to top along a seam. He thought for a long moment whether to rise and alert Vicar Petley. He decided that it would be a worse offense to stand against Giles's torrent of words, so he remained seated, his hands folded demurely in his lap.

"Do you think that the Almighty turns a blind eye to the casual, and dare I say, near promiscuous mingling of upright and moral souls with the debased and the wicked?" Giles continued. As his voice neared its crescendo, it thinned and edged towards a shriek. "Do you think the Almighty is a blind God?" he shouted, staring directly at Kathryne, whose face showed no acknowledgement nor shame. "Are we not supposed to be free from the temptations of this world? Does not that mean we are to be separate? Does not that mean we stand for a higher level of purity?"

The vicar's nostrils were flaring, and those in the front pews could hear his breath whistle as he inhaled.

"Do you think God has closed his eyes?" he shouted one last time, and struck the pulpit with a flat echoing slap of his palm.

This last emphatic gesture caused the joinery to fail, and the left side of the pulpit simply fell away with a wooden crash. The remaining bits of the pulpit teetered a moment and then fell the other direction in a dry, splintered counterpoint to the first.

The congregation fell into a long moment of stunned silence, and then a hushed giggle slowly crept through the church interior, spreading like a fire from person to person. Vicar Coates sat silent, his hand over his mouth, his body shaking in rhythmic vibrations as he struggled to prevent his laughter from erupting.

Even as inspired as the vicar was, he could not ignore this catastrophe. He struggled to finish his remarks, feeling naked without a pulpit to shelter him.

*The first thing tomorrow,* he thought as soon as he concluded his duties, *I shall have a few choice words for that inept construction crew!*

After the service, as Kathryne waited for Lady Emily, who was speaking to an acquaintance from London, Geoffrey approached her. He was clearly agitated, his demeanor edgy and nervous.

"Kathryne," he blurted out, "was the vicar speaking of you this day? He looked straight at your face as he spoke! Have you lowered yourself to meet that murderous pirate again?"

She glowered back at him and did not respond, though her jaw was set and tight, its muscles pulled taut, revealing a thick, tense line in her cheek. Kathryne knew she would need inform Geoffrey of her decision, but had begged her father to allow her to pick the proper timing. It appeared that this was the appointed hour.

"By your face," Geoffrey snarled, "I can see you are the woman he spoke of. I had thought better of you than this, Kathryne. To debase yourself in such a common manner, with such a common man. And you do disservice to me as well. Do you think I revel in being played the cuckolded fool?"

Kathryne's eyes seemed ablaze, but she held her tongue in check, biting down on it, to prevent her response from finding voice. A thousand thoughts raced through her mind, but she could sound none of them.

Geoffrey eyed her with a sidelong, angry stare. "Tell me, is this what you call proper? Civilized? God-honoring?"

He waited for her to defend herself and claim it all untrue. But she stood, still and silent, and neither admitted nor denied his words.

"Very well, Kathryne," he sniffed. "If you choose to be obstinate . . ."

With that she squared her shoulders, clenched her hands into loose fists, and looked as if she would pull her arm back and lash out at Geoffrey.

"Then I will take my leave of you now. I will allow you this flirtation with this crude, evil pirate, but I will not allow it for long. And after that, you will behave. But be warned, Kathryne. I am not a man who may be toyed with. Do not dismiss me with such ease."

He pulled at the reins of his horse, placed his foot in the stirrup of the saddle, and lifted himself up.

"A fortnight, Kathryne, and no longer will I wait for you to regain your senses."

■ ▢ ■ ▢ ■

Late that afternoon, Geoffrey pulled all the shutters tight and sat in his darkened study, a full tankard of rum before him, tossing thoughts of Kathryne about in his mind. It was no matter that he often dallied with others since Kathryne had arrived on Barbados. That excused none of her behavior. A sliver of his heart began to hurt, for he had seldom, if ever, suffered the rejection of his affections. Women simply did not turn away from what he offered. Kathryne was the first woman who had the audacity to say no, and to say no often. And now this almost complete rejection.

He took a long swallow of rum and felt the liquid burn as it edged down his throat, hot and thick. In a flash, Kathryne's uncle came to his thoughts. He had often spoken of his niece in the most unflattering terms—terms that now seemed to echo and fill Geoffrey's thoughts as well.

He closed his eyes for a moment, as if clearing a most unpleasant memory. When he opened his eyes, he had a tight set to his jaw. He pushed the tankard, now nearly empty, to the far point on his desk. He reached behind him and retrieved a silver inkwell and quill and a thick, golden sheet of paper. He dipped the quill into the bloodred ink and began to write, the scratches of quill to paper filling the room with the hushed sound.

*My dear Radcliffe,*

How I miss your company. Barbados seems most dull without your brand of pleasure.

If I am to believe San Martel, you are well. I trust that such information as I have discovered will be of use.

And the following is information that may be of amusement and benefit to you as well.

As he dipped the quill into the ink again, he began to taste, in the far depths of his soul, the first sweet pressings of the intoxicating libation called revenge.

## 58

Bryne Tambor shook his head in mock disgust as John Delacroix wandered off in the middle of the day to purchase flowers in the market by the harbor.

"A man in love serves no useful purpose," he spat. "Just makes 'im crazy and moon sick."

John Tambor smiled as he gave his brother a playful shove.

"You be forgettin' what love is like, for there be no maiden with eyes so bad as to think you attractive," he teased.

Bryne shoved back, laughing. "That be most untrue. But I be sayin' yer chances improve when the lights dim and the moon is darkened."

John had set not only to do what was moral and right with Missy, but what was moral and right with William as well. The day after Missy first arrived, John walked to the fort. It was the longest, hardest walk he had ever undertaken in his life. He had feared that in choosing Missy, he had lost William as his closest friend.

John, nervous and stammering, had laid out to Will the brief story of their growing respect and their eventual discovery of their deep love for one another. To John's surprise, William enveloped him a great, fierce hug, offering congratulations and praise. It was then that Will shared his news about Kathryne and his amazement at the intricate workings of an all-knowing God.

"You do not mind then, William, if Missy and I plan to be wed? I would so like to have your blessings on this union."

Beaming, Will answered, "There is no event that would bring me greater joy, old friend, than to see you happy."

John looked most relieved.

"But there is one element that you need to remedy, John."

"You only need ask, Will. There be nothing that I would refuse you."

"Then I need to ask if you be settled with the Almighty."

John shrugged, his face sheepish.

"Let us go for a walk, over by the sea, where we may speak alone," Will suggested, as he draped his arm about his old friend.

They sat together at the edge of the small sandy bluff, just south of the fort. The sun was at its peak, and the winds had calmed to a whisper. As he looked to the sea, Will saw two small fishing vessels plying their way back to port, their holds filled with a day's catch in the rich waters of Needham's Bay.

"John, you know that all this," he said, waving his arm to encompass all of the view before them, "all of this was given the breath of life by the Creator of heaven and earth."

John nodded. "William, I do not struggle with that, for I can see no other origin of so varied a world. I acknowledge his creation. It is his interest in me that I most struggle with. You have so often said that he is interested in my worthless life—but I find that truth most baffling."

"It is truth, John."

John looked away, staring out to the empty horizon. "William, does your past trouble you?" he asked in a soft voice. "Do the things we have done in the name of the Crown and in search of gold—do those memories shadow your pleasant thoughts?"

Will gulped. In truth, his past did often bring disturbing remembrances, but through the grace of God they were simply reminders of his sinful nature and not a crushing burden of guiLieutenant

"Yes, John, at times I have struggled with who I was."

Picking up a handful of small pebbles, John began to flick them toward the surf and said, "In the darkness of midnight, I lie awake, my body wet with sweat. In my dreams I see a flashing saber slicing through the flesh of a man standing before me. The blade cuts a gaping wound, and a great flow of blood erupts, staining my hands. I stand there as his life ends—at my hand, William. I watch as his eyes turn cold and dull."

The sun, up till then hidden behind the clouds, now swept over them, a great shaft of light pouring down on the bluff where they sat. It was still, save the constant low rumble of the surf.

"I ask myself how many men that dream enfolds, for I cannot count all their faces. I remember the first man to die—and the last to die at my hand—but if God sees all, he has watched my every angry thrust. He has seen each time my blade had pricked a man's heart."

He wiped at the dust and sand on his palms as the clouds edged out the warmth of the sun. "It is too much for even your God to forgive, William. I am too much of a sinful man."

Will let John's words drift off into silence.

"Do you know the story of Christ's death, John?"

"I have heard you speak of it. A most moving story—that such a man would be willing to die for those he did not know."

Will turned to John and put his hand on his friend's shoulder. "Do you know who died next to Christ that day?"

"Thieves, were they not?"

"St. Luke calls them malefactors. They may have robbed others. They may have killed men as well."

"Not well-respected men, you say," John replied.

"Indeed not, John. But what we were—at our worst days on the sea—we were no better or worse than those two thieves. Have you heard what one of those thieves asked of Christ?"

John shook his head.

"One thief must have been like me—arrogant to the end—and said that if this man who called himself the Christ was indeed who he said he was then he should have been able to save both himself and the thieves from their death."

"William, if I had hung there that day, I may have asked the same."

"But the other thief shouted back, 'Dost not thou fear God, seeing thou art in the same condemnation? And we indeed justly; for we receive the due reward of our deeds: but this man hath done nothing amiss.'"

John's brow was furrowed as he struggled to understand.

"But that second thief," Will continued, "knew he was hanging on a cross next to the holy Son of God. He must have whispered when he said to Christ, 'Lord, remember me when thou comest into thy kingdom.'"

John looked puzzled.

"That thief acknowledged Christ as God, as a man who could offer eternal life to him. Christ knew that the thief's soul was ready and that he was giving it to God with that question."

John swallowed hard. "I am near to that point, William. But I am still a sinner."

Will pulled John closer to him, whispering in his ear. "Then Jesus said to him, 'Verily I say unto thee, Today shalt thou be with me in paradise.'"

"By simply acknowledging Christ as God?" John asked.

"By simply acknowledging that Christ died on that cross to bear our sin, John. If you accept that truth and then turn from your sin and live as Christ commanded, eternity shall be yours."

"It is that simple?"

Will nodded.

"What of my past sins?"

"Christ forgives them. To him you have no past."

"What of my evil nature?"

"The Almighty fills you with his Spirit."

John's words were but a whisper, a raspy, edgy prayer of sorts. "I am afraid, William, for I know not the proper words."

William nodded. "Words are not important—your heart is," he replied, then paused. "Do you take God and Christ as the truth? Do you believe that Christ has died for you, John?"

A long moment of silence followed—a chasm of soundlessness.

"William, I cannot take that step," John whispered, his voice edgy and thin. "I simply cannot."

"But John, if you take the truth to your heart, then you can be indeed a new creation, for God will claim you as his son."

Will looked at John and saw the flood of pain and hurt behind his eyes and yearned to take it from him, to release him from its grip.

"Will, I understand what you say, but this day will not be the day that I can say those words with you."

William leaned closer. "But who is to say if there will be a tomorrow, John? Can you say you will have this chance again?"

John shook his head. "But Will, I cannot lie either. This will not be such a day. If almighty God wants me in his family, he'll have to keep us both breathing for a little while longer."

John's words were etched in hurt, but they were as firm and decisive as Will had ever heard. He knew it would be no use to continue. The Holy Spirit nudged at Will's soul, beckoning restraint. He would wait until God's timing was right.

Without a word, Will embraced John in a fierce hug for a long moment.

Will then whispered in his ear, "Then I will pray for that end, my friend. I will pray that your burden of pain be relieved. I will pray that you will be able to take his gift."

In the smallest of voices, John replied, "Thank you, my friend. Thank you."

## 59

The fire snapped and popped in the darkness. Its warmth was unnecessary, but it spoke of intimacy and nestled time, and a fire reminded Aidan of home in England. That evening, as they had dined at Shelworthy, solid black clouds poured in from the south, and lightning flashes began to light up the darkness. Rain pelted at the house, splashing at the windows with a heavy liquid splattering.

Two large chairs had been drawn up near the fire. A brass grate surrounded the firebox, and to either side stood solid shelves of walnut, filled with porcelain vases and figures that Aidan carefully had shipped from Broadwinds, his estate back in Dorset.

Emily sat in the chair opposite him, sipping at a sherry. Aidan sighed, feeling most blessed and satisfied with his life.

"It is most pleasant to have an evening at home, without the obligation of parties or politics to draw me away," Aidan remarked.

Emily looked up and nodded.

"Has Kathryne spoken to you of Mr. Hawkes?" he asked her. "From her smiles and laughter, I can only assume that she sees a brighter future."

"She has not shared many details, Aidan, nor have I felt obliged to pry. But I do agree with your assessment as to her happiness."

He leaned forward in his chair. "Emily, I have not spoken to you of such matters before—yet I feel the need since I am unable to ascertain a woman's perspective on this. If such a relationship is carried out to its logical conclusion—that is, a union of the two—what would be the consequences, as you deem them, of such a situation? In terms of commerce and politics and all, that is."

Emily scowled back at him with a mock frown, then smiled. "Oh, Aidan, you have such a streak of romance in you."

"Perhaps I spoke too analytically, then?" He was sheepish in his tone.

"Quite."

"But what are your thoughts, Emily? Am I the only one here who is somewhat troubled by this pairing? After all, regardless of what he owns and how civilized he becomes, Mr. Hawkes is not noble born. I suppose I am old-fashioned for thinking that such a thing matters?"

"Aidan, I understand your concerns. But this is not England. It is a new world. I think William represents that new world. And Kathryne seems genuinely happy in his presence."

"But what of his birth? I know I have allowed Kathryne to choose her husband, but I am afraid I did not consider the cold reality of such a situation."

Taking a final sip of sherry, Emily folded her hands in her lap. The wind continued to whistle against the grand house, and thunder rumbled deep, like a giant beast.

"William will never be, by birth, nobility. But he is a man who understands life in its fullest sense. He understands more of the Scripture and its import than most men of the cloth I have ever heard. What he teaches at the fort to those poor unfortunates is worthy of being copied and presented in a book of sermons. He is a kind man, and gentle, and more noble than most noblemen I have met."

"But what of the days to come? How will Kathryne face a future of not being entitled?"

"Aidan, do you not trust our Lord? Do you not trust him to guide both he and Kathryne along the right path? I do. I believe our Lord has his hand on their lives."

Aidan furrowed his brow. "And you can trust in that? For certain?"

Aidan, as he had with Beatrice, his departed wife, often leaned on those with greater faith than his, drawing strength from their faith.

"I can trust it—for certain."

As if a celestial exclamation point, a peal of thunder roared above their heads, and the night was filled with the whiteness of lightning.

Emily leaped up, her hand at her heart, fear in her face. She ran to Aidan and near threw herself on his lap, huddling against him for protection. He was shocked, and for the briefest of moments, was unsure of what to do. But then, as if a memory had moved his arms, he encircled her and held her close, quieting her fears.

CHAPTER

**60**

On a gray Tuesday afternoon, Kathryne appeared at the fort, her horse Porter in tow.

The crew, now finishing their work on the infirmary, simply stopped, their tools in midair, most of their jaws slightly opened, their eyes wide.

Kathryne stood there, her hands folded in front of her, wearing a delicate blue dress the color of a thin summer sky.

She smiled back at the group, unsure of who might be in charge. She did not see William and simply stood there, quietly waiting. Luke popped up from a far side of a nearly completed wall.

"Miss Kat. Dat be you."

He loped over toward her, and she relaxed.

"Hello, Luke, how are you this day?"

"Luke be fine. Luke always be fine. You look for Massa Will?"

She nodded. "Yes, Luke. Is he here?"

Luke craned his neck up, extending his tall, lanky body even taller, swiveling his neck about like a great bird.

"Massa Will!" he screeched as loudly as he could. Kathryne cowered in surprise. She had thought he would simply fetch him.

"Massa Will!" he screeched again. "Where you be?"

Kathryne smiled, trying not to laugh at Luke's loud cries.

In a moment, Will emerged from a cannon pit, wiping at the dust on his weskit. As soon as he saw it was Kathryne, he redoubled his efforts to remove the morning's dirt, and ran his hand through his hair. He waved as he trotted over.

Luke stood there grinning. "Massa Will. Miss Kat be here."

William smiled. "Thank you, Luke, for announcing her in such a refined manner."

"Luke don' know dat word," he said.

"No matter, Luke." He turned to Kathryne. "Will you join me for the midday meal in my house? It is near that hour."

"I would be delighted."

The trio made the short walk to Will's cottage. Kathryne smiled as she entered the home, pleased at its cleanliness and orderliness. Many bachelors, she had heard, had no concern about a tidy household.

Lying quietly on the cool stone by the hearth was a great, golden-haired and good-natured dog, who had adopted Will a week prior. His tail thumped happily when he saw Luke and Will enter. He shuffled to his feet and sniffed at Kathryne's feet. He looked up at her clear green eyes, then grinned as only dogs can do and sat at her side, his tail wagging again.

Luke busied himself preparing a thick soup while William escorted Kathryne on a tour of the small home. She smiled and kept her hands folded in front of her as Will pointed out the bedchamber, loft, the main room, cellars, and gardens.

Kathryne smiled, nodded, and uttered pleasant remarks of delight as she carefully examined each room and feature. Her expression was easy to interpret. She noticed its cozy spaces, but was enchanted by the pleasant feelings they contained.

Resting open on a small table of lashed bamboo was a copy of the Scriptures. She ran her finger along the pages, delighted to find it open and used.

She turned to William and said, "Indeed, this is a most pleasing home, William. I am so impressed with what you have made."

Surprise reflected from Will's face. "Indeed? You consider this a suitable dwelling?"

She reached out and placed her hand on his forearm, still covered with a fine haze of wood shavings, and squeezed it slightly. "This home has the Scriptures, William. And it has you. If I were to design a more perfect place, I would be lost without those two elements."

"But as home for a family—it would need expansion. Perhaps a separate dining chamber and rooms for servants and additional bed-chambers and a library," he said in a haste, wanting to assure Kathryne that such things could be done.

She nodded again. "Perhaps so, but it would not be necessary upon first examination."

Luke poked his head into the room where they stood. "It be soup," he called.

William asked a blessing for the meal, something that, Kathryne noted, Geoffrey Foxton seldom did without prompting.

"Kathryne, what is the most important element to be included in a home? As a man, perhaps I have overlooked an important detail that needs improvement."

She looked about from her seat, peering through the kitchen, into the great room, out the window.

"William, I see nothing in this house that I would change." She looked down a moment and spoke without raising her eyes. "You already have what it takes to make a house complete. You have an open copy of the Scriptures. If you allow our Lord to guide those who live inside the walls, then the house will be filled with love and faith. That is the most important element in constructing a dwelling—to invite the Lord to live there with you."

When she looked up, she first looked at Luke, who was wiping something from his eyes. Then she looked to Will, who appeared to be afflicted with the same malady.

## 2 November 1642

*My dear Mrs. Cole,*

How I miss you!

I scarce can decide where to begin. So much has transpired on this tropical island. I thought that life would be simpler here—yet I am finding that, if possible, it has become more intense, more vivid, and more passionate than England ever was.

I have written of Lady Emily's arrival. I do believe she and Papa are becoming the *closest of friends*. (But as an obedient daughter I shall say no more on this subject. Yet if you were here beside me at this moment, I would wink and nudge at your side to convey my meaning.)

I have written of Papa's decision to allow matters of my heart to be my decision. This island is indeed small, and many tongues wagged on for days, chiding him in private as well as public for his rash and, some say, foolish decision. But none of them know how such a cloud of despair was lifted from my heart when Papa said those words to me. I thought Geoffrey Foxton a most decent man, but lately I have been troubled by remarks I have heard (from both the vicar and Lady Emily) as to various reports that disparage his conduct and character. I have no guaranty that such observations are correct, but as you have said, that if smoke exists, then is there not cause to suspect fire as well?

You know I am not a theologian, but I believe that our Lord does demonstrate his will for our lives by providing in us a sense of peace—of calm. It is now that my soul and heart knows that peace—and I point to Mr. William Hawkes as the source of much of it.

He is a most godly man, and a man that knows—and practices—the tenets of the Scriptures. He teaches the Word to a diverse group of people at the harbor fort every Sunday. He is most generous with those in need. He has a wide breadth of knowledge in all manner of subjects, with a most humble manner about his intellectual capacities. He is most gracious with his praise of others. His laugh comes freely. He provides pleasant company. And he has been the most perfect gentleman these past few months.

I can scarce imagine the future if it did not include him.

He has built, overlooking the sea, the most romantic and cozy cottage I could imagine, with a lovely bedchamber that is filled with the sound of the crashing surf. Of course, if it were ever to be a proper home, it would need additional rooms for children and servants.

Mrs. Cole, I simply must close now. My heart cries out for your companionship—as well as the delectable scent of your kitchen. How much I miss them both.

May God protect you and give you happiness. I send my love.

*Yours,*
*Kathryne*

## 61

Vicar Coates stood before the small group, a most nervous cleric. He had performed only one marriage before, and that had been three years prior in London, with only the bride and groom standing before him. This day there were nearly two dozen people in attendance, and such a crowd caused his nerves to tighten.

The Lady Spenser came to him, as if sensing his charged nature, and whispered a few kind words of encouragement in his ear. He was unsure if it was her words or simply her soft hand as it rested on his arm as she spoke that his heart responded to.

He cleared his voice, and the low chatter ceased.

John Delacroix, in a new doublet and breeches made especially for this day, stood at the vicar's left. His demeanor was calm, but his eyes darted about the dim interior of the church. Missy Holender Cavendish stood beside him, clad in a shimmering white gown that Kathryne had lent to her for the occasion. The sunlight seemed to intensify its whiteness as it struck the fabric, and she appeared as if in a halo of purity. She carried a potent bouquet of hibiscus in her hands, and her smile had yet to leave her face.

Vicar Coates coughed again and then began.

In no more than half an hour he solemnly pronounced that the union "which the Almighty has sanctioned and ordained, be everlasting, and curses upon the person who attempts to sunder its loving ties."

After embracing, John and Missy turned to face their friends, who were clapping hands and offering words of congratulation.

William, who stood to the side of John and served as his witness, was the first to congratulate him. Will and John clasped in an enthusiastic hug, punctuated with great slaps upon the back. Will broke free and chastely embraced Missy as well, placing a most avuncular kiss upon her cheek.

"I pray that you have found abounding happiness in John," he whispered in her ear, "and that the Almighty will bless your union."

Missy stood back from him and could only smile, so great were her emotions that day.

A great banquet had been prepared at the chandlery, and all the guests, including workmen and many of the townspeople, had gathered to celebrate. Casks of rum and brandy were tapped, and the air was filled with the music of violins and concertinas. Four burly servants even brought over a full-scale harpsichord from Shelworthy.

Afternoon ebbed into a warm, fragrant dusk, then night slipped its darkening cover over the harbor. Dozens of torches were lit, and their flickering, wavering light filled that corner of the harbor with a gentle glow.

It was perhaps two hours till the midnight bell when William took Kathryne by the hand. She had been in dozens of animated conversations that eve, the first being with Missy. They had been off to one side of the gathering, blushing, whispering to each other. Their conversation ended with a great gale of laughter, a few more hushed comments, and both women, turning scarlet as they giggled in each other's arms, their eyes darting in a laugh toward Will and then John. And after those glances, even more laughter came from the pair of confidantes.

When asked, Kathryne simply refused to inform William as to the matters that caused both women such embarrassment and hilarity.

Several hours later, as the wedding party built to a crescendo, Will took Kathryne's hand and led her away from the celebration. The bubbled voices, the music, the laughter, all diminished into the distance as they walked along the harbor docks, away from the chandlery and toward the fort.

In the space of no more than a dozen moments, after leaving the lights and the joviality of the wedding feast, they entered a hushed world of moonlight and the soft rushings of the surf against the white sand beach. They walked hand in hand along the pier and then onto the beach. There they parted, and Will walked closer to the water than did Kathryne, peering out in the blackness of the western sky, punctuated by a heaven full of stars.

Kathryne stopped and looked out to sea, then back toward the harbor and town. From the distance she heard the call of a small island owl, its hoots soon answered by another.

William watched as the edge of the surf rolled toward his feet, then ebbed away. He turned around and, almost as if gazing upon her for the first time, saw Kathryne illuminated in the silvery softness of the moon, bathed in its gentle light. Her hair was flowing, curls cascading to her shoulders. Her eyes possessed an inner glow about them, and her smile was near as bright as the stars.

Will caught his breath, closed his eyes for a moment, and as he listened to the sea, he heard the words *"Go to her now"* whispered just over the waves.

*Was that God?* he thought. *Was that a word from the Almighty?*

He looked up at Kathryne, and her eyes were on him. He felt a calmness spread through him, a peace that washed over his soul. Since being held in his mother's arms, he had not felt such a strength of that emotion.

*It must be,* he concluded, *for such peace can only be authored by him.*

Unaware that he had done so, he tapped at the locket on his chest, touching at that little bit of gold next to his heart, feeling its reassuring presence. He closed his eyes a moment, then walked to Kathryne, his steps cushioned and silent on the sand. He stopped before her and took both her hands in his.

She smiled, a curious sidelong smile. "William, what is it? You appear as if you are set to undertake a great mission."

He nodded, gulped once, took a deep breath, and then spoke, his voice strong, but near wavering.

"Kathryne, I have imagined this day might come for . . . for all my life, if I am to be truthful. Your presence has always been in my dreams, but until our paths crossed, I did not know your face."

He looked down at his feet. He could hear from across the harbor the strains of a harpsichord and violin locked in a swirling mix of notes and sounds, lightly etched with laughter.

"I am most certain that the words that I will speak are words of a man who lacks refinement and polish, but I can only speak from my heart."

In a velvet voice, Kathryne replied, "If your heart speaks the truth, then I want to listen with mine, William."

"Kathryne, . . ." A look that could have passed for pain set upon his face.

"William, speak to me. Speak of your heart."

"Kathryne, . . . what language shall I borrow to tell you of my love? For the words I know are but as shallow as a summer pool, and I have need of an ocean to speak what truth I feel.

"Kathryne, I know now, as I think I knew the moment I first set my eyes upon you—back in Hadenthorne as a child, and in Weymouth for that one brief instant—that I would desire to wake every morning gazing into them. My heart has not changed. The desire has only grown stronger.

"I know that I am not of noble lineage, but my heart and soul demand that I not consider that shortcoming. Kathryne, I believe that I could offer a happy future to you. Your father knows of my circumstances, and he has granted me the right to court you."

Kathryne squeezed his hand. "William, think not of my father this moment. Tell me of your heart."

The look of pain on Will's face was supplanted by one that came close to fear.

"Kathryne, without you my life would be empty. You have become my sun and moon. You have become the beating of my heart. I offer you my being, whole and true—for without you it is of no use to me. I love you, Kathryne. I love you more than I understand. I love you more than the next breath I take, more than the sight of the ocean at dawn, more than the sum of every memory I possess. Without you, I cease to exist."

With that, Will knelt before her. "Kathryne Spenser, I humbly ask that you consider my proposal of marriage. Know for certain that the love I pledge for you this night will never change, save grow deeper and stronger over the years."

Silence filled the beach. The owl hooted again. From over Will's right shoulder, Kathryne saw the sweep of a falling star as it streaked through the velvet darkness.

"William, . . ."

He looked up at Kathryne and saw the faint tears in her eyes.

"William, . . . please rise, so I may speak to you."

He stood, apprehensive and nervous.

She slipped her right hand from his and touched her fingertips to his cheek. She sniffed softly, and a lone tear rolled down her face.

"I have rehearsed the words to say on such an occasion—and now that the occasion is here, they have simply evaporated."

"Then speak what is on your heart, Kathryne," Will whispered.

"There is only one word on my heart, William Hawkes," she said. "And that single word is *yes.*"

A gust of wind puffed along the beach, and Will thought he had misheard. "Yes? You said yes?"

"Yes, William. Yes! Yes, I want my eyes to open each morning and see your face for the rest of my days. Yes, I want to be able to hold you when I am frightened. Yes, I want to live with you in your cottage by the sea. Yes, I want to bear your children. Yes, I want to marry you."

"Yes? You said yes?"

William's world was a twirl of emotions, twisting about him like a squall on the ocean.

"Yes, William. I want to be your wife. Yes."

He dropped her hand and scooped her up in a vigorous embrace, then twirled her about, her feet swinging freely.

He stopped, placing her feet gently to the sand again.

"Yes," he repeated. "You said yes."

Through her tears and smiles, she nodded and placed her hands on his face. She pulled his face to hers and gently, near reverently, placed their lips together in a kiss that simply encompassed the stars and the moon and the world.

After a very long moment, they parted, and their laughter was borne over the gentling waves by a tender breeze into the warm night.

## 62

From the floor above, Kathryne sat by her open window. She was waiting for her father to speak to her about his discussion with William. William had set an appointment with Lord Aidan to formally ask for Kathryne's hand in marriage, but it was not proper for her to be in attendance at such a meeting.

She sat by that window quietly, with a copy of the Scriptures in her lap, trying to read as the two men met. She accomplished little in the way of actual reading, yet had prayed through every moment. She had beseeched God that his will be done, and while she knew her own heart's desire as to the outcome, she knew what actually would transpire was in the hands of her Lord.

Then on that afternoon breeze she heard her father's voice slip up from the porch below as he gave William his answer. He had sanctioned the marriage! For Kathryne, it was as if the sun finally dawned after decades of waiting just beyond the horizon. Tears did not come, only a sense of complete peace.

And as she heard the front door of Shelworthy open and close, she began to rehearse how she would respond to her father. His footfalls creaked outside her room, and she tried to hold her face blank as he approached her bedchamber.

When he solemnly tapped at the door, to Kathryne it sounded as if the angels had come calling, and her soul began to soar.

## 15 November 1642

*Dear Mrs. Cole,*

It seems like a lifetime since I last wrote—and that a lifetime of events have occurred in that same period.

I have struggled knowing where to begin, and finding no easy solution I shall simply wade into the middle of that fast-flowing river and begin.

(Perhaps I may warn you that I suggest that you sit as you read the next few lines.)

I am to be wed, Mrs. Cole. Is not that the most amazing news you have heard? The gawky little girl who you scolded when she 'borrowed' food from your kitchen will soon be a bride and a wife. In less than five months, I will become the wife of Mr. William Hawkes.

I have written enough of him to you that I am sure you know him as well as you might. Dear Papa was so torn when faced with this hard decision, but I know in his heart that he feels God's provision in all this. (And it has helped that he has found out that Mr. Hawkes has a fair degree of wealth accumulated on his own. I will never lack for comfort, is how Papa phrased it, with Mr. Hawkes's resources.)

However, a great many tongues have begun to wag on this small island. Lady Pickering asked if I was simply trying to make a radical statement with such a rash act. Geoffrey Foxton was most noble, I think, when I informed him, but he has not offered many words to me about it. He offered only congratulations through pursed lips, shook my hand, and then quickly left my presence. I hear, though, that he was most irate and spent many days speaking ill of Mr. Hawkes and threatening him in a veiled manner. I am sure that in time he will recover and find a woman who is suited to his needs. Vicar Petley was even more livid upon hearing the news. He made a trip to see me and attempted to argue me out of such a choice. He was near to calling it the work of the devil and said the hot tropical airs had affected all our sensibilities. Yet, I remain unconcerned, for the people whom I trust most—Lady Emily, Papa, and others here who love me—have fully endorsed such a path. If they know of William's heart and his character, they approve. Those who do not, gossip most cruelly, for they have little else to do here than tell tales and inflame stories. As I pray, Mrs. Cole, our Lord fills my heart with peace, giving me calmness in the face of such criticism.

These are but minor sticking points to an otherwise wondrously joyful time. The lace and silks for my wedding gown (which you helped me pack) are still in perfect order for the seamstress who will sew for me. How I wish Mrs. Willoughby were here, but, alas, we have but her pattern to follow. I have ordered china and silverware, linens, and household goods that I will need to provide a comfortable home to Mr. Hawkes.

   William has already begun to plan additions to his simple cottage.
His position on the island requires a more substantial residence, and
he has solicited my advice in such planning. His humility and
generosity are just two of the reasons I find him so deserving of my
love. I have insisted on separate quarters for servants, and several
bedchambers will be added in case the Lord blesses us with children.
It will not be a grand residence such as Broadwinds, or even
Shelworthy, but it will be filled with love, and that is enough. And as
the years pass, and as we have the ability, we may add to its living
spaces.

   Lady Emily and I are most busy preparing for the wedding. As
governor, Papa must present invitations to nearly everyone of any
consequence who lives here, plus all manner of officials from other
islands as well as any nobility who would be friend enough, and
willing, to make the voyage from England to here. I am sure, despite
my desire to have a simple and meaningful ceremony, it will become
the social event of the year in the Antilles.

   How I wish that you could be in attendance, Mrs. Cole. You have
been the dearest person to me after the death of my mother, and I
would so rejoice to see your loving face again. Yet I know how deep
your roots run in English soil. I will write again and again and tell
you all that occurs as the date draws near. And indeed, as I promised
to you before I left England, I will commission a wedding portrait
that you may hang in Broadwinds's great hall.

   All other news pales so in comparison that none becomes worthy
of penning. We are all well and express our love to you. Papa asks if
you may instruct Mr. Dobbins, the caretaker, if he would address in
his correspondence the state of the stables and horses remaining at
Broadwinds. I believe Papa wishes to ship several of the younger
horses to this island as breeding stock.

   I will close, and I remain

*Yours,*
*Kathryne*

## 63

"So many preparations, my poppet," Aidan said as he looked over the pile of correspondence that lay neatly stacked before Kathryne. "I trust that such intricate plans are not overwhelming to you."

Aidan looked hot and dusty, having come from a ride to the north of the island, ostensibly to observe the plantings of three of William's former crewmen. But he had taken a telescope with him and had stopped at a dozen vantage points along the coast, observing if vessels lay at anchor in the secluded coves and bays. This trip he had found none. Either no such activity was occurring, or someone had passed on word to those engaged in smuggling, and they had purposefully cleared the northeast shore of all activity.

Kathryne looked up and pushed away a stray wisp of hair from her face. As the day of the wedding drew closer, Kathryne grew slightly more harried, yet at the same time began to radiate a sense of joyful anticipation.

Aidan had seen the same emotion many years earlier, perhaps better described as an attitude of joy amidst the hustle and bustle, as it was exhibited in his dear wife prior to their own wedding.

*The acorn falls not far from the tree,* he thought as he walked to the window seat and perched at the edge, unwilling to let his dusty riding breeches dirty the fine cushions.

Kathryne slipped from her chair and ran to him, embracing him in a fierce, unexpected hug, taking no concern that he was covered with road dust. He put his arms about her and gently stroked her hair, doing what he had done when Kathryne was a mere slip of a girl, resting in his lap at the end of the day. It was the time of his most pleasant memories, when the light was but a sliver of its daytime illumination—a sky that looked as if what remained in it was but the bones of the sun. He realized with sadness that his little poppet—the greatest treasure of his life—was soon to be given away by him to another man forever.

After many long moments, Aidan gently cleared his throat.

"Kathryne, if a devoted father asked of his daughter a foolish question, would that obedient daughter guarantee to respond in absolute truth?"

Kathryne leaned back, a thin streak of road dust visible on her cheek. "Of course, Papa. But you do not have to ask for honesty, for I have tried always to be as truthful with you as my heart allows."

"Then may I ask of your heart's condition now?"

A puzzled look set in her eyes.

"I am requesting that you be honest and truthful with me this hour. . . ."

He stopped speaking for a moment, for Kathryne's eyes mirrored the eyes of the young girl that Aidan had taken in his arms nearly three decades prior. As Kathryne aged, she became more and more the image of her mother, and Aidan continually caught himself seeing Beatrice in Kathryne's reflection.

". . . And tell me of your heart. Is this wedding with Mr. Hawkes a true fulfillment of the desires of your heart and soul? I seek to hear that you harbor no speculation as to this path you have chosen being the proper one for you."

The silence that followed was interrupted by Aidan, asking his earnest questions. "Does this man make you happy? Are you certain, with no doubt, that he is the one whom God has selected for you?"

Kathryne turned and took her father's hand in hers.

"I know, Papa, that you seek to see me follow God and to fill my soul with his truth." She paused, thinking of the best words to tell him of her thoughts. "And, Papa, this is the path that I am to follow. . . . I had this as a dream—without being able to put a face upon it—for my entire life. To lead a simple life, to be devoted to a man and raise a family, and to be devoted to serving God. Papa, William is that man. He is the man who has been in my dreams. His heart breaks to bring the truth of God to others, and my heart will break if I cannot share my life with him. It is not simply that I desire him, Papa. *I must do this*. It is the only path that will bring peace and happiness to me."

"You have no fears, Daughter?"

"I have fears that I will trip on my gown as we walk down the aisle. I have fears that my tears will prevent me from speaking my vows that day. I have fears that the heat will cause us all to melt in our wedding attire," Kathryne exhaled in a rush. "But I have no fears as to this man William Hawkes. It is he God has chosen for me. I know that as certain as I know the sun will rise in the morning and set at night. It is a truth that cannot be denied."

Aidan took her hand and squeezed it. "Then my heart rests easy and rejoices for you, dearest Daughter. And I am sure your mother smiles at you from heaven."

As he spoke of her mother, tears welled up in an instant in her eyes. In the smallest of voices, Kathryne asked, "Do you think that is the truth, Papa? Does she smile on this as well?"

Aidan hugged her close. "She could do no other. For her, to see your smile was a greater happiness than life itself. And to see you do God's will—why, that was simply an indescribable joy to her."

He stroked her hair. "Indeed, my poppet, your mother will rejoice with us that day. I am as sure of that as I am of the sun rising and setting."

"I love you, Papa."

"I love you, Kathryne."

Will stood off in a corner of John's chandlery, staring out the wide doors and moving a small pile of wood chips with the toe of his boot. His hands were clasped behind his back as if he had all the time in the world. John and the Tambor brothers hulked over a capstan assembly recently removed from a Dutch cargo ship.

Bryne nudged at John, nodding his head toward Will. "Do you think he be sick with love, or do you think he just be 'fraid of what be comin' at him?" Bryne whispered.

John looked up and smiled. "If my particulars be any judge, well, then, our good captain be a little of both."

With a puzzled look, John Delacroix turned back to the Tambor brothers. "Did William announce that he was here?"

Both brothers shook their heads.

"Has he said anything to anyone since he arrived?"

Again they motioned no.

"Do you think I should have a word or two with the poor fellow?"

Both Tambors grinned and nodded enthusiastically.

John walked over to William, wiping at the wood shavings clinging to his shirt. Before John had a chance to speak, and without turning his head to acknowledge his presence, William softly questioned, "John, do you believe in fate?"

John blinked a few times, thought for a moment, then answered. "If you mean that we all are to become someone at a specific place and time—then it be true that I believe in fate."

Without moving a muscle, Will made a second query. "Does a man ever truly know what his fate is?"

John had not anticipated being quizzed—concerning such weighty subjects at least—and was unprepared with clever answers. "All I can say is that I never knew what my fate would be."

Will turned to face him. "Did you ever imagine that you would be settled on this island, settled with a woman, settled with a business of ships' repairs?"

Running his fingers through his hair, John replied, "Never in me wildest dreams of fancy did I think what has occurred would indeed come to pass. Having Missy as a bride . . . having this place—why, I would have said a man be possessed if he had claimed this as my future."

Will squinted. "And all of this would have been a dream a few short months ago?"

"Indeed, Will, it would have been," John replied. "To even think that a woman as fine and beautiful as Missy would stoop to allow me to court her, much less marry her—why, that would be unthinkable enough. And the rest of it—the chandlery, my home—the rest turns it all into a dream."

"Do you ever feel that it all was meant for some other person and that in time you will awake and find it all disappeared like a vapor?"

John was set to answer the affirmative when he realized the question Will was truly asking. He stepped toward Will and put his arm about his friend's shoulder.

"Will, men like us," he whispered confidentially, "have been told so long that we be worth nothin' in the eyes of culture and society. Will, that ain't true. Since you be tellin' me about the Bible and all, you need to remember yourself what the Bible says about us all bein' the same in the eyes of God."

Both men stood silent for a moment.

John continued. "The first day as Missy's husband, I woke up thinkin' it all might vanish. The second day as well. But by the time the twentieth day came, and then the thirtieth and the fiftieth—well, it began to be real to me then."

Will turned and asked, "That be the truth? It seems like it be normal now?"

"It does, Will. You have to let it happen. And seein' as how you're makin' a bigger leap than I—well, maybe it will take a fortnight or two longer for you. But, Will, as you've been tellin' to me—you let God do the plannin' and you do the livin'."

Will merely picked at the dinner of grilled fish and yellow squash Luke had prepared, leaving the majority of it for Beauregard. Luke fussed, claiming that he didn't enjoy cooking if it was meant only to be fed to the dog. William nodded as Luke scolded, but he offered no defense. The dog, a breed with long golden hair, sat quietly by the table, his large tail thumping loudly against the floor, as Luke set Will's unfinished plate before him.

When Luke grew silent, Will stood and walked into the darkness. He sat on the short stone wall overlooking the black and restless sea. The surf was loud that night, a cooling breeze pushing the waves from the southeast. It was nearing the midnight bell when Luke came out into the darkness and climbed on the same stone wall, a few feet from William.

"Massa Will be troubled?"

Several moments passed until Will answered. "No, Luke, I am not troubled exactly."

"Massa Will be troubled to be married to Miss Kat?"

Will sighed deeply. "No, to be with Kathryne is a dream made real."

Luke scowled in the darkness for a moment, his eyes narrowed, his brow furrowed deeply. He spoke, finally, with a softness that was most unlike his usual tone.

"Massa Will, . . . I knows you father be dead. Be you troubled . . . be you troubled not knowin' what it take a man to be a husband?"

Will turned to Luke, their faces dimly lit by the thin fire in the cottage and the sliver of the moon through the clouds. Luke had an earnest, helpful look about him.

"In my village it be de father who tell son 'bout dese things. My father tell me. Massa Will want me to tell him?"

For a long moment, William looked absolutely puzzled and confused. Then, as quickly as a torch's flame fills a room with light, Will became aware. And after another moment he hoped that his blushing would not be noticed by Luke.

William took a deep breath and replied, "No, Luke, I thank you for your kindness. Indeed, a father would do as your father did in the past, but having lived onboard ship, there is little mystery to me about certain aspects of life."

William smiled. For a long moment, Luke smiled as well, trying to understand what Will was saying. Then his smile was replaced by a harsh look, and without warning, Luke reached out from where he sat and swung his palm at William, soundly thwacking him on the head.

Will was shocked and mouthed a silent ouch.

"Luke! What was that?"

Luke crossed his arms over his chest. "Massa Will be no more smart than mule," Luke chided. "Luke don' talk of dat. Men know *dat* from when they start to be a man. That not what father tell son."

"Then what did you want to tell me—if not *that?*"

"Any man can do what a husband do. Dat easy. It be most pleasin'. But dat don' make a husband. A husband treats de wife nice—you say nice things, you say nice things to all others 'bout de wife. It be sayin' dat in the Bible. Massa tell Luke 'bout dat. You be mean—you get mean wife. You be nice—you get nice wife."

Luke reached down and thumped at his chest with the hard edge of his index finger. "Wife be in here, Massa Will. Dat where Massa keep her."

Luke leaned forward, staring at Will from just inches away. "Massa Will understand?"

Will nodded.

Luke continued to stare for many moments. "Massa Will believe Miss Kat too pretty for him?"

Will nodded and added, "I think her too pretty, too smart, too . . . too everything for a man like me."

Luke reached back and almost appeared to be ready to swing at Will again, but this time his palm stopped short and he patted at Will's cheek.

"You be right, Massa Will. Miss Kat be too good for you."

Will stopped still, thinking he had misheard Luke.

"She be too good, but all women be too good for men. Luke be puzzled why any woman say she love man. Dats why you be good man to Miss Kat—so she can love you. You be good to her."

Will reached up and placed his hand over Luke's, grasping it tightly in his hand. In the quietest of voices, Will whispered, "Thank you, Luke. Thank you for everything."

*8 March 1643*
*The Wedding Day*

Will wiggled, uncomfortable and unsure in his new clothing. His entire outfit was newly sewn for this occasion—a rich blue doublet with gold trim, new tan breeches, new black leather boots, and a new crisp white linen shirt with lace trim and mother-of-pearl buttons. He stood in the main room of the cottage, fussing with the fit of the doublet, pulling at it and waving his arms to expand its breadth and room. It had taken William at least a full hour to ready himself—more than he normally would spend in an entire week. He washed fully. He shaved carefully, wanting to avoid any nicks or scrapes. He carefully combed his hair and tied it back with a thin white ribbon at the back of his neck.

Luke had busied himself, as Will prepared for his wedding day, by finishing cleaning the cottage. Days earlier he had moved his herbs and potions and his few possessions into a large room in the fort. Now the cottage looked as clean and tidy as it had ever appeared, Luke and several of the blackamoors having spent many hours dusting and whitewashing and bringing in fresh flowers.

Will stepped out into the warm sunshine and took one last look about the property—viewing his island home for the last time as a single man.

Kathryne stood in the middle of her bedchamber, with Lady Emily in a lovely yellow gown holding a long white veil. Hattie hovered behind the bride, holding a pair of delicate white silk gloves between her thumb and forefinger, as if she feared her callused hand would soil them.

Kneeling before Kathryne was the island's seamstress, who was making last-minute adjustments to the wedding gown and train. Hems that seemed just right a few weeks earlier somehow had lengthened, and the trims that had been double-sewn now popped and snapped at the slightest touch.

The silk gown had elaborate lace layered over the top of its voluminous skirt and was brought up in places with clusters of pearls and delicate bows. The deeply cut and tightly fitting bodice was trimmed in lace and sewn with thousands of pearls and dainty bows as well. Lace, pearls, and bows also trimmed the narrow slashed sleeves and the long, full train. The reflection in the tall looking glass before the bride was a vision of femininity and purity.

Kathryne's face looked full of both panic and peace. All preparations that could have been made had been. She tried to avoid thinking of all the things that might go horribly wrong and tried to focus on the wonderful thing that was about to happen—becoming the wife of the man of her dreams, William Hawkes.

She looked out the window and smiled. The weather had cooperated, and the day, while warm, was tempered by a consistently pleasant breeze from the north. The clouds were high, promising only shade and no rain—at least that is what William had taught her about reading the signs of nature. *Even if all else goes wrong,* she thought, *it will at least have been a beautiful day for it to happen.*

■ ■ ■ ■ ■

By midafternoon, when the bridal carriage carrying Kathryne and Emily arrived in Bridgetown, the church was nearly filled to its capacity by every nobleman on the island, as well as by visiting nobility and governmental officials from neighboring islands and also a few that had arrived from England a fortnight ago.

A gasped hush spread through the congregation, who swiveled as one to glimpse Kathryne as she made her entrance on her father's arm. Her dress was the white of the crest of a wave on the ocean, and its layers and veils cascaded to the floor like a beautiful poem repeated in moonlight. Her hair had been curled and tied up so it rolled in wonderfully tight twists and flowed about her face and shoulders. Upon her face, marked only by the barest use of colorings, was a most beatific smile. It was as if the creation of a master painter had come to life on this earth and deigned to walk among the peasants.

Will, standing at the altar to the opposite side of the vicars, had nervously adjusted and readjusted his wedding doublet perhaps a hundred times in the last half hour. But at the moment when the sanctuary door opened and his eyes met Kathryne's, he ceased fidgeting and stood enraptured. Tears of joy escaped from his blue eyes as he beheld his bride.

Despite Vicar Petley's obvious displeasure for one brief moment, even he rose above his emotions, and all in attendance would later claim that they had never beheld such a wondrous and magnificent marriage ceremony, one that brought such meaning and import to the occasion. In truth, it was the beauty of the bride and the obvious devotion expressed in the groom's eyes and in his words, that marked their union as a most loving liaison.

When the ceremony ended, the couple ducked under a floral archway as wedding guests threw flower petals. The elated crowd ebbed and flowed about Aidan, Emily, William, and Kathryne. Congratulations were expressed and tears flowed in those precious moments, and Emily reached out and took Aidan's hand in hers and squeezed it ever so gently.

The first crimsons and golds of evening were filling the western sky as William and Kathryne climbed into the royal governor's carriage and departed from the lavish celebration in their honor. Before stepping inside the carriage, Kathryne stopped and embraced in turn her father and then Emily, whispering "I love you" in each's ear.

Aidan and Emily joined hands again as the bridal carriage clattered away, taking the short drive to William's cottage by the sea.

By the time William helped Kathryne step down from the carriage, the sky had begun to streak with deeper purples, as if the angels were painting an appropriate backdrop to the day.

Will stopped at the door, Kathryne's hand held tightly in his. Neither had said much on the short ride, both overcome with the immensity of their emotions. Off to the right side of the cottage, Will noticed as he glanced over, was a trio of men with violins. Luke was behind them, nodding furiously, pointing to the couple. It was the musicians cue apparently, for they began to play a soft melody—one of Kathryne's favorite classics, Will recognized—colored with the unique flavor of the tropical night.

Luke leaned closer to Will and Kathryne. "Dey be gone soon. Play dis many songs," he said as he held up his hand with all five fingers extended. "Den you be alone, Massa Will, Miss Kat."

Will smiled, opened the door, and turned to Kathryne.

Above the door Will had added a small hand-carved plaque, which read: "As for me and my house, we will serve the Lord."

Kathryne pointed up at the words and smiled. "Oh, William," she said softly, "I am so happy."

Will took her hand, pulled her close, and picked her up in his arms. "As am I, Kathryne."

Will carried her across the threshold and to the middle of the main room. They both stared in wonder. The room was filled with candles, their golden flickering illumination warding off the dark. Every other conceivable surface was filled with flowers—mounds of orchids and great bouquets of hibiscus and bougainvillea. The scent wafted in and out, borne on the warm evening breeze. And outside, the violinists began their third selection.

Soon the music ceased, and the cottage was bathed in the music of the island—the wind, the sea, the jungle. The breeze strengthened slightly as the dark spread across the waves, and the surf began its pleasant roar against the shore. Moonlight streamed in soft shafts through the windows.

Will gently lowered Kathryne from his arms and embraced her gently, as if afraid that he would bruise her if his true desire were known. She looked up at him, and their eyes met. Barely a dozen words had been spoken by them since they had confirmed their vows as husband and wife—yet neither wanted for communication. It was as if their hearts were speaking an honest language of their own, and their love for each other simply overflowed.

Will bent down and placed his two fingers under her chin, tilting her head to his. Slowly, as slowly as a feather falls from the sky to the earth, did he lean towards her, their lips growing ever closer. And when they met, it was as velvet meeting silk. All that existed for Will was Kathryne, and all that existed for Kathryne was Will.

For Will, after that night, he could never pass a hibiscus flower without a secret smile creasing his lips. For Kathryne, she could never sit by the crashing waves of the sea without near becoming overwhelmed by the powerful waves of emotion and feeling that welled up from deep within her.

And that night, off in the tropical distance, the call of a Williamson thrush, after a wait of so many years, was answered by the call of another, in clear, trilling notes that hung in the darkness like the sound of an angelic choir.

*St. Augustine, Florida*

Radcliffe had heard via Geoffrey Foxton that Kathryne was to be wed, and he spent a week in a black, vile temper.

Even though the ships being readied for his venture were only six months from completion, he felt no joy.

"It will be another half-year until the crews are sufficiently trained," Radcliffe complained to San Martel. "Is there not any way that such a process can be hurried? What if the king sends more ships, more men?"

San Martel sneered back at Radcliffe. "We will be ready, regardless. Our sources will keep us abreast of the situation. If need be, we sail before the crews are fully trained."

"I know. But the longer we wait the greater the possibility of our being discovered."

"That should not be your greatest concern," San Martel said. "Our governor is growing most impatient with your Vicar Mayhew."

"He is not my Vicar Mayhew," Radcliffe snarled back. "Remember that his life is a most wonderful indemnity for our plan."

"So you have said. But the governor finds your vicar to be most upsetting. He has now begun to try to convert Papists as well to his Puritan ways. I have threatened the man with the rack unless he desists," said San Martel, sipping at his glass. "Yet he continues, my friend. It is becoming harder to protect him."

Radcliffe sipped his port. "He does not fear death and does not desire for riches. Such attributes make him very hard to control."

"Well, my friend, indemnity or not, his life hangs by a thread."

Silence filled the room. Often, when the guards and inquisitors were at work, men's screams from deep within the prison could be heard in the Spanish captain's quarters. But no such sound was now heard.

Suddenly, San Martel turned his head and nodded to himself. "Radcliffe, I think I may have a plan that secures your vicar for our use and yet removes him from his role as a Puritan troublemaker."

Radcliffe smiled for the first time in days. "And what might that be?"

San Martel drained his glass. "How do you feel about sending him on a short sailing voyage—just a few days to the south of here?"

## 15 March 1643
## Guajiro

A longboat set out from San Martel's flagship, and eight sailors grabbed onto the oars and began to stroke with measured beats. The small craft cut through the choppy surf toward the shore of a small island.

Vicar Thomas Mayhew and two young black men—half Carib and half Spanish—sat perched upon the middle seat. Each was shackled, hand and foot, to a length of chain that ran along the far side of the seat.

The vicar squinted into the afternoon sun, his face a colorless mask, wan and sickly pale. It had been months since he had felt the sun on his skin. It had been even longer since he had taken in a breath of sea air. Its salty edginess brought a great grin to his lips.

He closed his eyes and breathed deeply, thanking God for such a wondrous experience. After so many months in dim captivity, such openness was a libation for his soul. He opened his eyes and turned to the officer on board the boat, calling out to him in Spanish.

"What island are we traveling to, good sir?"

Eduardo Diego, a slight young man from Toledo, Spain, grunted back, "It is called Guajiro. But, Vicar, do not get your hopes raised. There will be no ships calling on you. There will be no escape."

A wave sloshed over the bow of the vessel, and saltwater sluiced along the floorboards, swiping at ankles.

"That is, unless your God permits you to swim to heaven." Diego guffawed, and several of the sailors began to laugh with him.

The vicar smiled.

Soon the longboat bumped along the rocky shoreline, a thick snake of black rock and coral fringed by a wisp of sand at the water's edge. The sailors jumped from the ship and pulled it tight to the shore with ropes at the boat's fore and aft.

Diego bent to the vicar and unlocked his chains, as he did also for the two black men. He gestured with his head toward the island. He gathered two large bags of stores and tossed them out onto the shore. The two black men picked up one bundle each, shouldering them with ease.

"Vicar, these two will take you back to the village. It is but an hour's walk from this spot. They have been given instructions that you are to be kept alive. If they allow you to die, their village will be set to the torch."

The vicar looked aghast, as if he had misunderstood the officer's language. "But, good sir, these poor men cannot control my fate. If God is to take me, it will be beyond their ability to prevent it."

"Then they will be praying to the wrong God, Vicar," Diego laughed. "You will be kept here until San Martel comes to retrieve you. I would recommend you do your best to remain breathing—or the lives of every villager will be sacrificed."

The vicar nodded. He knew he was being sent here because of his activities within the jail. He knew that the priests had spoken against his actions of witnessing to others of the power of God. What harm could he do on this island?

"You take care to stay alive," Diego called out as the longboat slipped from the shore. "Captain San Martel would be most agitated to find you dead."

With a grunt, the vicar's companions started to walk into the jungle, one calling out an odd native word.

*It must be the word for home,* the vicar said to himself and repeated the word again, feeling a great comfort as he formed the sound in his mouth. He tapped at his black jacket and felt the reassuring weight of the Holy Scriptures resting in its wide interior pocket.

*Perhaps this is the mission field I have prayed about for so long,* he thought as he stepped into the darkening green of the tropical forest, hurrying his steps to match those of the two who went before him.

*September 1643*
*Barbados*

It was a most grand morning in Bridgetown. The sun was bright, but had not yet warmed the air to an unpleasant temperature. A cooling breeze, in from the ocean—often a rarity in the harbor town—had freshened and swept the narrow streets of the stuffiness of the past weeks.

Kathryne Hawkes, after finishing a relaxed breakfast with her husband, set off for the markets at the harbor.

To her, it was such a great pleasure to be occupied in such simple pursuits. Growing up the daughter of a nobleman, she never needed to be engaged in any of that type of activity. But now she did it willingly, feeling a sense of accomplishment as she carried breads, fish, and all manner of food back to the cottage. Her time in the kitchen of Mrs. Cole served her well, for she often lent a helping hand in the actual cooking of it as well. Some of her attempts had been met with less than sterling results. William would have never claimed that any of her meals tasted less than wonderful and would bravely smile and eat every last morsel on his plate, even when Kathryne knew that he keenly disfavored a sauce or seasoning that she had attempted. He would nod and smile and insist it was all quite delicious—and she loved him all the more for his noble attempts at complimenting all that she did.

Kathryne stopped halfway to the harbor and wandered down a few steps from the dusty road to sit on a smooth rock overlooking the sea. The crashing of the waves enthralled her. It was a sound that she would never tire of. She looked back to the cottage and then to the fort. Will was inside the fort somewhere, seeing to its proper running. It was a complex position, and everyone said that William accomplished his tasks with great skill. The crew of the small garrison adored him as captain, all showing great deference to his leadership. Kathryne felt so proud of him when his men bowed as he entered the fort. His was not leadership by fear but by example. He would never assign a man a task that he himself had not done in the past or would be unwilling to do again in the future.

As a husband, Kathryne thought, William deserved the same accolades. He was gentle and kind, full of laughter and grace, always complimenting her on whatever she tried. She had been teaching a handful of children at the church several days a week, and he had been most supportive of her tasks and shared in her joy of that work.

She and William seemed to have lived the last six months in a dream, every day bringing new pleasures and joys, every evening bringing them closer as husband and wife.

Kathryne's smile had scarcely left her face in the months since the wedding. And now the small servants' wing of the cottage—three small rooms, a storehouse, and a summer kitchen—was nearing completion.

Though she thoroughly enjoyed cooking and all the other domestic duties, it would be ever so helpful to have the aid of a cook and a house servant. Just that morning, as she and William prayed together, she offered a silent prayer that the right servants be brought to her, for it was most critical that a house be run in a harmonious fashion. Both she and William had agreed that their home would not employ slaves, regardless of the cost. That choice would make staffing their needs more difficult, but that was indeed their prayer and their passion.

As she stood and continued her walk to the harbor, she noticed several ships jockeying for position in the waters. Two vessels sailing under the English flag and a Dutch trader were new to the island. She paid it little mind, since she had not been expecting any new deliveries of household goods, and correspondence would make its way to the cottage in due time. In the past she had run to meet ships, but only succeeded in frustrating herself, for sea captains did not enjoy handling the fussiness of personal correspondence before their better-paying cargo was unloaded.

So she walked past the noisy harbor piers, filled with sailors and merchants. She walked past, serene, smiling, and quite unaware.

A voice called out, almost shrill, yet demanding in a most familiar manner. "Kathryne Spenser! What are you doin' with those fish!"

Kathryne hesitated, but then continued walking. Her name was no longer Spenser but Hawkes. It had been an adjustment at first, but now it felt as natural as breathing. And everyone on the island knew of her marriage and would not be calling her by her maiden name.

"Kathryne, I say! Stop! What on earth are you doin' with those fish and that bread, little missy?"

This time, Kathryne indeed stopped and looked about. *Might there be another Kathryne that is being hailed?* she thought.

She scanned the faces that jostled about on the pier, then to the shore and the shops.

In a moment, her eyes set upon Mrs. Cole, standing no more than a dozen feet from her. Kathryne nodded calmly, then proceeded to turn away and took one more step toward the fort.

"Kathryne!"

Kathryne finally realized who it was, and her eyes widened in shock. The basket tumbled from her hands to the ground with a soft, fishy thump.

She turned slowly, her face blanched. In the softest of voices, she called out in a bewildered whisper, "Mrs. Cole?"

Mrs. Cole stepped forward. "Be you not thinkin' to offer me a hug, dear child?"

Kathryne literally leaped the distance to the older woman and wrapped her arms about her in a great embrace. After many moments she released her and looked, her eyes still marked with befuddlement, assuring herself that it was Mrs. Cole before her, then hugged her tight again.

It was no more than a moment or two later that Mrs. Cole struggled to be released. "Child, let me look upon you again. I had scarce thought this day would ever arrive."

Kathryne's mouth moved, but no words were heard.

"I am sure you be surprised, child. I grew weary of cookin' for just three people at Broadwinds. Your letters made it clear—you'll not be returnin' to England while my eyes are open." The older woman, her face lined and creased, smiled broadly.

"And I knew that I had to be in attendance when you bear your first child." She placed her hand just over Kathryne's stomach. "'Tis six months since you've become a wife, and I knew that it might be close."

Kathryne still said nothing, her voice struck mute. *But there is no child yet!* her heart cried silently.

"Child, I know this be sudden and all, but I had the resources in which to make the voyage, and I am certain that someone on this island needs a cook. There was no ties that held me to Broadwinds anymore. My heart was with the Spensers."

She looked at Kathryne and then took her by the shoulders. "You are not sad that I've come?" she asked. "Are you, child?"

Kathryne began to weep with joy and embraced her old friend again.

After several moments, Mrs. Cole pulled back. She looked at Kathryne with a stern eye. "Kathryne, I believe you best pick up your fish before the gulls take to it."

Kathryne obeyed, glad to have something normal to do.

"And child, be there a house that you know of that needs a cook such as me?"

*She really did come all this way for the love of our family,* Kathryne thought. Then she reminded herself of her prayer of that morning. *Thank you, dear Lord,* she quickly offered, smiling, as she picked up the large red fish, dusting off the side that had landed on the street.

## October 1643

Mrs. Cole stood, still as a statue, in the kitchen of the cottage. She was pointing to a far wall, and her other hand covered her mouth.

Kathryne turned in near horror and spun about to see what beast or villain must have entered the house. She saw nothing and turned back to Mrs. Cole, who pointed with her finger at the wall. Kathryne looked again, then smiled, realizing what she was aiming at.

Kathryne rose from the breakfast table. Will was still asleep, and she would not call him for this matter. She walked to the wall and, with a deft snatch of the hand, grabbed a three-inch-long green lizard between her thumb and forefinger.

Mrs. Cole retreated, sinking further into the firebox alcove.

"Mrs. Cole, if you plan on living on this island," Kathryne said, forcing herself not to use the creature to taunt her new cook, "you must become accustomed to our little friends."

Mrs. Cole shuddered as Kathryne deposited the small reptile out the window, and it scurried away into the grass.

"They cannot bite you, nor can they eat you," Kathryne explained.

"Child, neither can a mouse, but I do not prefer to have them livin' inside with me."

In truth, over the past month Mrs. Cole had become accustomed to the ways, the foods, the manners of the people, the weather, and the new customs of the island—all save the lizards. She had been the Hawkes' first official servant to grace their cottage, and William could not have been happier that she had traveled so far for a servant's position. The foods she prepared were remarkably improved over Luke's efforts—and over his wife's efforts as well. Kathryne seemed happier and more at ease having such domestic burdens relieved. And Mrs. Cole seemed delighted that her work was appreciated. Even Luke seemed happy the times that William invited him to dine with them, although Mrs. Cole found the prospect of a black man—any black man—most unsettling.

This morning, Kathryne had awakened early, after she and Will had returned near midnight from a dinner at Shelworthy. She was wide awake, for she had been bursting with such glorious news that she had to share with someone.

"Child, you look odd this morning," Mrs. Cole said as she set down a full service of tea before her, with a heaping plate of biscuits and honey. She stepped back and cocked her head to one side. "You have news?"

Kathryne nodded enthusiastically.

"Be the news big?" Mrs. Cole asked, enjoying the suspense.

"Indeed," Kathryne responded with a smile.

"Be it news that I be prayin' about?"

Kathryne was set to answer, but stopped. "I . . . I do not think so, Mrs. Cole. But I am now at a loss to think of what that might be?"

Mrs. Cole looked slightly crestfallen. "Kathryne, dear, I had hoped you might be tellin' me a child is on the way, but I daresay you not be tellin' me that this mornin'."

Kathryne paused a moment, sipped at her tea, then shook her head no. "I know your heart's set on that, Mrs. Cole, but that is not the news today."

Silence filled the room.

After a long moment, Mrs. Cole said softly, "Be you tryin', child?"

It did not take much for Kathryne to blush, and the little girl in her was most visible when she sat with Mrs. Cole in her kitchen. Kathryne reddened to scarlet and answered in a hushed voice, "Mrs. Cole, that is *not* the problem."

Mrs. Cole arched her eyebrows.

Kathryne tensed up her face back at her. "It *isn't*," she added, more firmly.

"As you say, child," Mrs. Cole replied with finality. "So then, what be the news? You be up early for a reason."

Kathryne took another sip of tea and a big bite of a biscuit slathered with honey that tasted of England. Through her chewing, Kathryne responded.

"Oh yes," she mumbled, "it's Papa and Lady Emily."

Mrs. Cole, holding a large pot of springwater, stepped forward.

Kathryne swallowed with an effort, swigged more tea, then added, "They are to be wed in six months' time."

With that, Mrs. Cole let loose the pot, and it crashed to the floor with a bang, splashing the water on both happy women.

8 March 1644

It was one of the rare evenings on Barbados when the wind was slight yet comforting, when the air was warm yet not hot, when the air was neither dry nor humid.

A circle of torches had been set out upon the porch of Will and Kathryne's cottage, gracing the area with its soft flickering glow. The moon was fat and full that night and would provide near enough illumination for virtually any activity, but the torches added a golden, warm glow missing from the silver moonlight. A table and two chairs had been set outside, lit by two racks of tall, elegant, white taper candles.

Mrs. Cole had insisted that she make all the preparations for this special evening—the night that marked the one-year anniversary of the marriage of William and Kathryne. Mrs. Cole had wanted all to be perfect—the food, the table setting, the weather. Even though a devoted Christian, she still found some solace in many customs of the past. She had heard her mother say—and her mother's mother, for that matter—that if a bride was not with child by the day of her first anniversary, then the marriage was doomed to be barren. While not fully believing such a tale, she nevertheless wanted to hedge her bets and help speed along the course of nature.

*There is nothing like fine food and a restful dinner to engage the heart,* she thought.

And now that evening had begun to settle, the special supper had begun. Mrs. Cole had employed the services of two blackamoors that evening to help take serving trays to and from the kitchen. Despite her initial misgivings about having men of such black skin near her, she had warmed to them and was amazed at their willingness to work long and hard with nary a complaint nor comment. She continually struggled with their thick, almost impenetrable accents, but with signs and pointing, coupled with a patient heart, Mrs. Cole managed to convey what she meant, and they usually accomplished what she required.

The moon had deepened in color by the time the desserts were brought out to the table. Will tried his best to look freshly hungry as a great tray filled with flannel cakes, figgy-dowdy pudding, and delicate pastries was laid on the table.

"Now, I know you might be a bit full from the dinner," she said as Will tried to prevent a groan from escaping his lips, "so we'll just leave these tasty bites here for you to nibble and peck upon. And there is a small decanter of port here as well."

*I haven't fed them too much, have I?* she wondered as she slipped away. *Will they be asleep too soon?*

After Mrs. Cole said good night, Will focused all his attention on his wife.

"A year ago, God blessed me with the most beautiful wife, and my life has been filled with such happiness that I can scarce describe the fullness of my heart or the gladness of my thoughts," Will said softly.

Kathryne lowered her eyes and blushed, for Will had not made a habit of such talk before, and the reality of his emotions stirred her.

He reached across the table and took her hand in his.

"I could not imagine life without you, Kathryne, for without your smile and laughter my world would be bleak and cold. Thank you for this year—and for giving my heart reason to beat."

She blushed further, yet felt his words bathe her soul in their warmth.

Will kept hold of Kathryne's hand, caressing it as if it were a great treasure.

"Kathryne, dearest, look at me," he said, his voice low and throaty.

She looked up into his face. She had wakened to it for a year and never tired of the view, his deep blue eyes filled with love, his lips always ready for a smile.

"It is true, dearest, what I have said. I cannot imagine life without you. You have made my life so very rich and full and showered me with a love that I claim I do not deserve, yet clamor for. Dear Kathryne, I am so glad that you are my wife."

She had not shed many tears this past year, but now they came. They welled up in her green eyes and slipped down her full, red cheeks, leaving small trails of wetness.

"William, it is the same for me. This year has been the most precious and most fulfilling one of my existence. You have loved me so honestly and truly—and I have never felt as protected and at peace than when I am in your arms. I, too, dear William, am glad that you are my husband."

Will rose from his chair. He still held Kathryne's hand and bid her rise, which she did. In a sweep, he embraced her in his arms and held her tight, his lips finding hers like the practiced moves of a dancer upon the stage—fluid, passionate.

Will leaned back and placed his right hand under her chin. He was smiling, as was she.

"I suppose that we need no more hints than Mrs. Cole has provided, do we, dear wife?"

She giggled, averted her eyes downward, and felt her skin blush again, the redness now spreading down her throat. In the faintest of whispers, just heard above the surf and the breeze, she replied, "I think not, dearest husband. I think not."

Will stepped back and extended his arm to his wife.

He turned his head to gaze out to sea and the harbor, part of his nightly routine of checking to see if all was well before retiring.

And in that single moment he stopped and stiffened, pivoting back to fully face the harbor.

He dropped Kathryne's hand, ran to the short wall near the table, and leapt up on it, leaning as far into the darkness as he could without toppling forward. Under his breath he muttered, "Who are they?"

Off in the distance, just at the edge of the rolling surf, where the whitecapped waves could still be seen in the bright moonlight, Will saw a sail, then another, then another—a string of them—deadly pickets in the dark. Kathryne quickly recognized that these ships, now counting a half-dozen that she could see, were not expected.

"Will," she cried out. "What is it? Whose ships are those?"

Will ran to the end of the stone wall anchored by a taller, shoulder-high column of stone and climbed atop. He turned to her, his face ashen. "They are not friends, Kathryne. Friends do not come calling at nightfall like a thief. I believe them to be pirates, bent on attack."

He leapt down from his perch and within a second was beside his wife. "Kathryne, I have always trusted that you were a woman of deep courage."

She nodded, her eyes still reflecting confusion.

"And that you were a woman who would remain calm in times of great crisis or danger."

She nodded again.

"Then I must ask you to be brave this night."

Her voice began to quiver as she replied, going against her head's command and responding to the fear in her heart, "What is it you desire of me, Will? Pray, tell me."

Will spun back and looked at the ships, making slow, yet steady progress against the slight wind coming from the east, and said, "I have only a single moment to instruct you. You must listen well."

She nodded, this time feeling tears well up in her eyes.

"Gather up Mrs. Cole. Take blankets with you and hide yourself in the cellar below the kitchen. Take the dog and the two pistols I have hung by the door—they are both loaded. Bolt the door behind you, and do not venture out until it is I who calls for you. Do you understand that?"

Kathryne was too frightened even to nod.

"Do you understand!" Will shouted, breaking through her panic.

She nodded, her eyes wide and saucerlike.

Will bent to her, kissed her tenderly on the mouth, and whispered in her ear, "I love you, Kathryne. Always. Pray for me—and for this island as well."

He was about to pull away when she grabbed him by the shoulders and held on in a fierce embrace.

"You will be back, William," she whispered, commanding him to return. "I will allow no other ending."

He bent to her, looked into her eyes, and replied, his voice dead calm and serious, "There is no force on earth that could keep me from you."

He kissed her again, broke from her embrace, and ran into the cottage. In less than a heartbeat, it seemed, he returned, buckling his sword and scabbard and tucking a single pistol into his beLieutenant He glanced one last time toward Kathryne, then began running, arms and legs pumping furiously, to the fort.

Kathryne peered at the ships on the shadowy horizon, now numbering nine, perhaps ten. Her gaze swept over to the harbor, to the assembly of English ships lying peacefully at anchor.

Will had not spoken of the cargo they carried, but Kathryne knew. After all, it was a small island, and its citizens loved to share the little news they possessed. The vessels made up a treasure fleet, on their way back to London, full of gold collected—or looted—from Indian cities, deep inland from the Venezuelan coast. A dozen ships formed the small convoy and were scheduled to depart on the next full tide—five days hence. The combined gold loaded in their cargo bays was a king's ransom by any man's count—rumored to be valued at more than 250,000 pounds.

Kathryne bowed her head, but her thoughts were silent.

*How does one pray this night?* she wondered, her mind in a twisting whirl. *Dearest God, let your will be done.*

She turned and ran, her gown rustling in a wake behind her strides, while shouting, "Mrs. Cole! Mrs. Cole!"

As she opened her mouth, the first cannon roared, belching fire and death, illuminating the massive seawall of the fort in its angry light.

## 69

Will reached the fort and began to call out orders, bellowing loudly so that all marines and blackamoors could hear.

The first signal cannon had been fired by the officer of the watch, who looked out in terror as the unknown armada suddenly appeared, like a ghost, upon the rolling pale of the moonlit sea.

If it were a friendly sailing, a lead ship would have approached the harbor with its national flag posted high on the mainmast. But there was no lead ship in this convoy. If it were a friendly sailing, it would never enter a harbor at nightfall. The risks of sailing after sunset increased greatly, and no wise merchant sailor would risk a harbor landing, even with a full moon. These ships, making their deliberate headway toward Bridgetown, seemed unconcerned as to the possible dangers of hidden shoals or reefs. They all kept to the safe, deep water, almost as if they had an intimate knowledge of the waters of the bay.

"Good men, stand to your positions!" William cried out, and within moments, two dozen men assembled before him in varying stages of readiness and dress.

He chose not to wait for a full formation, knowing that some men would be in town or away from their barracks.

"Cannon crew, to your positions and begin loading!" he barked. "Marines, to the walls with muskets and lances! Powder boys, begin your assembly! All take side weapons with you!"

He knew that this was a pirate convoy—most likely of Spanish origin—intent on scavenging the gold from the English treasure fleet.

Will stood in the middle courtyard of the fort, his hands resting on his hips, watching as his men followed through on their practiced routines, sighting cannons, setting to ammunitions, laying in powder and shot.

Sergeant Lewis Cathold, senior officer of the squad of Royal Marines, ran up to Will, breathless. Fumbling with his doublet and scabbard, he looked panicked. "Who be these ships, Captain Hawkes? Will they be attacking? What be they after?"

Will turned to him. "I believe they are pirates, Sergeant. Most likely Spanish, owing to the cut of their sails."

He saw that at each word he spoke, the sergeant blanched one shade lighter. He reached over and placed his hand on Cathold's shoulder in an effort to calm him.

"Sergeant, they have not come all this way—by night no less—to pay a social call upon us. Indeed, they mean to take what belongs to us—by whatever means at their disposal."

Will smiled. "We are most well suited for repelling their advances, Sergeant. I think our guests will be most surprised by the teeth of our defense."

As Will readied the fort's defenses, five longboats, painted a dull gray, each manned by two dozen sailors dressed in gray, were nearing the beach just to the west of the fort. From each side, a half-dozen oars pulled in unison, and the small sturdy vessels slipped unseen through the water. In less than a moment they would be sluicing upon the sand, just below the fort's seawall.

In the rear of the last longboat in the procession huddled a thin, angry man, his hand tightly coiled about a long, sharp cutlass, the blade honed to the cutting edge of a razor.

Radcliffe Spenser looked up at the fort growing larger and larger before his eyes and was unable to control his glee as an evil laugh bubbled up from his heart.

"In a few moments, I will have my revenge on your entire island, Lady Kathryne, my dear niece. Indeed, we will see who laughs last and to whom shall come the Spenser fortune."

"Mrs. Cole! Mrs. Cole!" Kathryne shouted as she grabbed her husband's pistols.

"Bo! Come here, Bo!" she called to the dog.

In a moment Mrs. Cole ran into the kitchen from her quarters, a nightcap perched on her head and a long robe flapping about her legs.

"What is it, my child?" she cried. She stopped dead as her eyes widened on the two black and deadly pistols Kathryne carried. "What in heaven's name has occurred? What has Will done? I heard a shot."

Kathryne smiled in spite of the terror of the moment. She ran to the older woman's side, as she tucked a pistol into the belt of her gown. She grabbed Mrs. Cole's hand and placed her face almost next to hers. Speaking as calmly as she could muster, she said, "Will is fine and has done nothing. But a pirate fleet is about to attack the harbor. We must protect ourselves. Will issued a most firm command. I am to take these weapons, blankets, you, and Beauregard into the cellar and bar the door behind us."

Mrs. Cole showed no sign of comprehending her words, nor the slightest hint that she would be able to move in the near future.

"Mrs. Cole!" Kathryne shouted.

The cook simply stood there, her hands fussing, trying to make a knot in the belt of her robe.

*A pirate attack is not of her world,* Kathryne imagined, *for such things would never occur at Broadwinds.*

"Mrs. Cole!" Kathryne called out.

In a flat, unemotional tone, she responded by whispering the words, "Blankets . . . blankets."

Kathryne turned her about. "Yes, Mrs. Cole. Blankets. Gather up several and return to me here immediately."

Gathering blankets must have seemed to be a normal response to a pirate attack, for Mrs. Cole simply scurried off and in a moment returned with her arms full of them.

Suddenly Kathryne was not sure why Will instructed her to gather blankets. *Was it for comfort,* she thought, *or perhaps camouflage?*

She took Mrs. Cole by the hand and led her to the large cellar, the door and stairs tucked in a corner of the floor in the cottage's kitchen. The dog followed them obediently.

"Good, Bo. Good dog," she comforted.

Kathryne heard another booming cannon roar and felt a cold shudder crawl about in her bones.

She bent down, lifted the heavy door by the iron ring, and swung it open with a dusty bang. She grabbed a tinderbox full of candles and flint and steel with lighting moss and escorted Mrs. Cole down the eight steep steps. She returned to the kitchen, grabbed a bucket of water, and brought it down with them as well. She took one candle, lit it from the still-burning firebox, and descended into the cellar, the single flame illuminating the cool storeroom with a flickering light.

The damp room was no more wide than the height of three men, and only as high as a short man. It was filled with small barrels of squash, beets, carrots, peas, pickles, flour, lard, wine, ale, cider, and its raftered ceiling was crowded with drying strips of ham and beef.

Kathryne set the candle on the bottom step, slid several barrels around, and in a moment had a short wall of foodstuffs between the steps and the far wall. There she spread out the blankets and pulled Mrs. Cole to the dark corner and sat her down, her back against the farthest corner. She settled Beauregard next to her. Carefully she pulled the hammers back on both pistols until they cocked with a loud snap. She needed both hands to accomplish the task and then laid the two pistols just at the edge of the blanket with their black muzzles facing away from them. She retrieved the candle and blew it out.

Mrs. Cole gasped as the room was plunged into blackness.

Kathryne first felt for the position of the pistols and then leaned back and felt for Mrs. Cole's hand. She picked it up and squeezed.

"All will be well, Mrs. Cole. The pirates will be driven off in moments. Once they see how strong the fort is, they will quickly retreat."

Mrs. Cole said nothing, but Kathryne thought she heard a sob being stifled. The dog whimpered softly in the dimness.

"William will allow no ill fortune to befall us, Mrs. Cole. He promised that he will return."

Kathryne heard another sob, and she squeezed the hand again. "Perhaps it would be wise if we prayed?"

As if waking from a sleep, Mrs. Cole said, "Yes, Kathryne. That would be most appropriate."

Kathryne began to recite out loud, "Our Father, which art in heaven—"

Another cannon roared, then another, and another. A fourth explosion was heard, this one louder and more intense than a cannon.

*Was that a scream?* Kathryne wondered.

"Hallowed be thy name . . ."

A rattle of musket fire erupted, a furious *pop-pop-pop*. Beauregard whimpered again. Kathryne stroked his fur gently.

"Thy kingdom come . . ."

She heard another scream, most certainly the scream of a man in pain.

"Thy will be done . . ."

A roaring boom echoed throughout the cottage.

"On earth as it is in heaven. Forgive us this day our trespasses . . ."

The rattle of musket fire grew louder, from behind the cottage this time, perhaps toward the harbor.

"As we forgive those who trespass against us . . ."

Several cannons roared, almost in unison, and the clatter of musket fire echoed about.

"And deliver us from evil, for thine is the kingdom forever and ever . . ."

A man screamed, this time from just behind the walls of the cottage.

"Amen."

A crashing roar from no more than a stone's throw away vibrated through the entire structure of the cottage, followed by human screams of pain slicing through the night.

CHAPTER

**70**

As Kathryne was gathering up Mrs. Cole, Will was ensuring that all the fort's defenders were at their proper posts. A few stragglers who had been spending the night in Bridgetown came running through the still-open gates.

Will positioned himself in the center of the fort and called out orders and commands. The cannons all had shot and powder, and all but two crews were at full strength.

Will walked to the westernmost cannon slit and peered through the narrow opening. He had to bend from where he stood, for the cannon pit was lower than the courtyard.

*That's odd,* Will thought. *It appears that those ships are no closer to the harbor than when I first viewed them.*

"Sergeant Cathold!" Will cried out as he clamored into the deep cannon pit and elbowed his way through the six-man crew to the opening. "Fetch me a telescope at once."

He extended the brass tubes and focused the instrument. The entire armada was simply tacking slowly to the north, then switching tacks and sliding to the south—as if content to ride back and forth in the face of a slight wind and to make no substantial forward progress.

*Why in heavens would they sail in our faces like that?*

He turned to the cannon crew. "Have they sailed closer than their position at present?"

"No, sir. They be hanging just beyond our range, Captain Hawkes."

He turned back to see the vessels again change tacks to the south.

*Perhaps they need time to prepare their guns. But they have had an entire voyage to make such preparations,* he thought. *There is no logic to their actions.*

Suddenly Will's face changed from puzzlement to terror. He ran to the gun slit and peered down to the surf and beach below. Most of the view was hidden by the fort itself, for the cannons had no provision to aim or discharge at an angle below horizontal. Will pushed his head through the slit, only the width of man's shoulders, and looked down. As he did so, a musket volley, then another and then a third sounded from below. Like angry wasps they whizzed past Will's head and crashed, with a whine, one after another, into the stone arch above him. Stone fragments scattered about, and Will felt them stinging against his back. He ducked back in, like a fox who had just been spotted by the hounds.

One of the cannon crew was slumped against the weapon, a red stain spilling from his back, the victim of a ricocheted musket ball.

"Musketeers!" Will bellowed as he ran from the pit and began to scramble up the far steps to the top rampart. "Musketeers to the ramparts!"

A few men reached the heights before he did and began to fire. From the sands below, musket fire ensued with a hissing fierceness, and in a heartbeat, three men who had been positioned in the teeth of the ramparts slumped backwards, their muskets clattering from their dead or dying hands.

As Will ran to the top rampart, he bellowed, "All cannons fire! Set double charges for your next volley. The ships must be damaged!"

Will grabbed a musket from a fallen marine, a red stain spreading across the man's chest like the tide, and leaned over the wall. A musket ball whizzed past Will's ear, only inches from his head. He ducked back, then edged out, the musket against his shoulder. He could see a half-dozen longboats beached against the sand. Perhaps a score of Spanish musketeers hunched behind them, aiming at the fort's top defenses. He watched as three of them fired upward, and one of the marines pinwheeled away from the wall, clutching at his head, then toppled backwards to the stony ground with a hollow thump. He lay still. Will moved up and fired back, and one of the enemy attackers spun around, clutching at his shoulder.

Will ducked back to reload, and thought, *Why are they attacking there? There is no way to mount the walls.*

Will stood back and fired, and another of the invaders spun about and fell in the sand.

*And where are the rest of them?*

In an instant flash of awareness, Will knew, and he began to sprint from the wall, calling his marines to follow him down.

*They have hidden in the rocks. And what would happen if a single powder charge was exploded in those confines?*

A dozen of the marines heard his call over the musket fire, loud and mingled with the roar of the cannons, and began to leave their posts on the ramparts.

The cannons had fired their first volleys and reloaded with double shot. A double charge of powder extended the range of the cannons just enough to reach the pirate ships. But with the use of extra powder, the barrels grew hotter when fired, and the risk of explosion increased.

Will was sprinting across the open courtyard, with a handful of marines at his heels. *I may be fortunate and get there in time,* he thought to himself. *I just may be fortunate enough. Perhaps we can thwart their plans.*

As he reached the gate, he heard a dull roar that crescendoed into a maelstrom of an explosion and rolled along under Will's feet like an earthquake.

Will looked back to the northwest corner of the fort—the corner closest to the sea and farthest out over the seawall. The sight that met his eyes was the strangest and most terrifying he could imagine. The explosion lifted up the entire corner of the fort, like a child lifting the corner of a sand castle with a spade, and redeposited it down again. The walls began to crumble and topple in on themselves, just as gold and red flames blasted through the crevasses and licked at the crumbling fortifications.

Will stood dumbfounded as the entire northwest corner of the fort nearly collapsed into the sea in a great heaving mass of rubble. Will knew what the invaders had so skillfully accomplished.

While all eyes were on targets beyond their reach, the longboats had rowed in, carrying kegs of powder. It was a simple matter to load a half-ton of explosive black powder into a deep crevasse in the rocks under the fort.

The explosion had sheared through the brittle rocks, undermined the foundation of the fort, and sent it in a small avalanche falling to the water below. With those few cannons out, the invaders would have a simpler time sailing into the harbor. Will remained still, struck immobile by the explosion, as did many of his fellow defenders.

*At least there can be no armed attack on the fort,* Will thought. *We will still be able to shell the ships as they enter the harbor. Even if anyone else lands, the debris will prevent any invader from entering this fort.*

But a squeal of metal against stone dashed Will's most carefully constructed plans. Will spun around to the left, then right, and knew that he was doomed.

Before he had taken over the construction of the fort, now more than a year prior, much of the foundation had been completed, including a most sophisticated drainage system—with large metal grates at the southwest, the northwest, and the northeast corners of the fort—lying at the courtyard level. The first few heavy rains had proven to Will that the system was more than sufficient, and he had taken great satisfaction that even in a deluge, the water was quickly drained from the fort to cascading spouts by the sea.

Since the drainage system was adequate, Will hadn't inspected it closely. Now he realized that it was designed to allow men in as well as to let water out.

As Will stood visualizing the routing of the drainage tunnels, the grate to the southwest squealed from its anchoring, and, like rabbits, a handful of men carrying axes and muskets leapt into the darkness. Then another dozen men leapt out of the northeast grate. They quickly shouldered their muskets and fired at the marines caught in the open. Others, all in gray, followed them, carrying torches and small casks. They ran to the closest cannon pit, set torch to fuse, and tossed the cask into the pit. In a second, the pit exploded in a billowing ball of flame, and the screams of men burning in agony were soon drowned out by another explosion in the next pit over, only a few feet distant.

Will screamed, raised his musket, and fired at a man holding a cask with a lit fuse. The cask tumbled from the man's hands as he fell, and in a heartbeat he was enveloped by a rolling ball of fire.

On the west wall, three cannons lay destroyed, most of their crews dead or dying. A few had escaped and had picked up swords or clubs and were fighting back—not to defend the fort, but merely to stay alive in the conflagration.

Will pulled his sword free and rushed to the northeast wall, which faced the harbor. If the pirates could be beaten off, and if a single cannon could be saved, then there was the slimmest of hopes that perhaps, with God's provision, the invaders could be halted—or at least slowed.

Will had run only three steps when a musket barked, and he felt a burning sizzle in his calf. He looked down and saw his breeches torn in a neat hole, outlined in crimson. He stumbled and fell to his knees, grasping at the wound. Touching the flesh, wet with blood, sent another wave of pain up his leg, yet he detected no broken bones. Using his scabbard as a cane, he hoisted himself back up to his feet and continued to limp toward the northeast wall.

Two cannons on that wall continued to fire, protected by a ring of marines and blackamoors, all firing at the invaders. Will tripped again and began to drag himself closer to that wall, turning in time to see the fort barracks explode in flames.

A burning timber, tossed from that explosion, landed square against Will's right shoulder. He pushed it to the side, his shoulder crying out in pain.

*I hope that Luke was not in the barracks,* Will thought, *for his skills will be sorely needed if any of us survive this night.*

Will turned on his back and looked behind him. More than three dozen gray-clad men had positioned themselves along the southwest wall, whose cannons had all been destroyed. The Spaniards were repeatedly loading and firing into Will's men clustered at the northeast wall. Perhaps half of the original fifty men had gone down, killed or wounded in the first minutes of this battle. Will leaned up on his elbows, hoping the pirates' attack had faltered.

He called out to his men, "Are their ships sailing forward?"

In between the musket fire, one man called back, "Aye, sir, and headed straight for the harbor."

"Do you have powder left?" Will called out.

A few moments passed until Will heard a voice reply, "Enough for a half-dozen volleys, sir. No more than that."

*That is not enough to stop them,* Will realized, and he turned and began to crawl toward the powder house, set near the center of the fort.

Two blackamoors realized what Will was attempting and rose, running to offer assistance. Before they had gotten within ten yards of him, both had fallen in a fierce volley of musket shots. The air above Will's head was a whir of angry shots, humming no more than a hand's width above him. Will was a realist at times such as this. If he made it to the powder house, he could only carry a half-dozen charges with him—if that many. He tilted his head back toward his few men that still survived. His two cannons stood little chance against a dozen Spanish ships, he knew. If the invaders concentrated their fire on the fort, it could be reduced to rubble in an hour's time.

He looked toward the enemy. He knew that, as pirates, they had little to hope for but victory. It was win or die for most of them, making them ideal soldiers and combatants. They asked for no quarter and gave none.

A wave of hopelessness began to wash over Will, and he lay back down. He stared up at the stars, hidden now behind a thick pall of smoke, and began to pray. He knew not what to ask for, so in a few short words he prayed for the souls of the men who had died that night, asking that they might find peace with God.

Meanwhile, a half-dozen gray-clad men rose, after a withering volley of muskets, and ran to the closed gate of the fort. In a moment, they swung it open and began to run to the harbor.

Will leaned up, craned his neck, and looked out. That was when he felt his heart contract and tighten in his chest.

His cottage was in flames.

While Will lay prone and bleeding, a half-dozen longboats had been beached to the south of the harbor, apart from those that had attacked the fort. They had been assigned to set fire to the town and create as much panic and diversion as possible, while the main force aboard the ships tended to their plunder. Their route led them from the beach, past the cottage that Will had built, over the small rise, and then down the gentle slope into Bridgetown, its wooden buildings ripe for the flames, its citizens ill equipped and most unprepared for defense.

Each of the seventy men in the longboats carried a long, lit torch, an ax, a dagger, and a belt full of small torches, soaked in tar and pitch. Climbing up from the first rise from the sea, over the sand and long saw grasses, the leader stopped and stared at the cottage. According to Radcliffe, the meadow where it stood was supposed to be empty, but it had been many months since he had seen the local geography.

"Quickly, men, take a look and then set her afire!" he called out.

A handful of men kicked through the front door of the cottage, even though it had been unlocked, and ran from room to room. One man grabbed up a handful of Kathryne's silver, another picked up her jewelry case, filled with brooches and rings, some from her mother, grandparents, and other ancestors. Another grabbed Will's telescope, one tossed books about, looking for more gold hidden behind walls or secret panels. The candelabra from the table outside was snatched and bagged, as well as a silver pitcher. Three men entered the kitchen on a run, grabbed handfuls of meat and bread, and pulled a heavy wooden larder over from the east wall, thinking it held a safe behind it. There was no safe there, but the larder fell square and flat against the cellar door, locking in both Kathryne and Mrs. Cole.

"Time enough on this peasant cottage," the leader called out in a garlicky rasp. "On to the town!"

Three men at the rear stopped long enough to light two torches each and toss them at the cottage. They landed on the thatched roof over the kitchen, the great room, and the bedchamber of the small cottage. Soon flames were beginning to lick their way through the thatching, and sparks began to fall on the furnishings below.

Mrs. Cole cowered in the dark corner. Kathryne had draped one arm protectively over the older woman, and the other firmly held the loaded pistol, pointing it in front of her in the dark. The dog whimpered and growled between them, the hair on its neck bristled and stiff.

They had heard the voices, speaking a low guttural Spanish, and none of their words were clear. She heard the crashing from upstairs, and the sounds the attackers made as they pawed through her precious possessions. She clenched her teeth tightly, trying her best not to call out in anger, and Mrs. Cole stroked Beauregard's back to keep him from making more noise.

When the larder fell to the floor, both women jumped, Kathryne almost pulling the trigger from reflex.

Then in a moment, all grew quiet.

She said a prayer of thanksgiving and leaned back in relief. And in a few more moments, Kathryne sniffed deeply.

She smelled smoke.

She grabbed for the candles and tinder, but in the dark, her hands could not locate them.

"Where are they?" she cried out through clenched teeth, the tinder-box only inches from her palm.

"Dear Jesus," she prayed, as fervent as any prayer she ever offered, "please help me."

On her hands and knees she moved forward, her palms slowly searching the darkness before her. She found the first step, climbed to the top, and pushed against the door.

It did not move.

She pushed again, setting herself at a better angle. It felt as solid as the earth, and only the wooden step under her bowed beneath her efforts. One last time she pushed, but the door moved not a whit.

Smoke was filling the air, and Kathryne coughed.

*Dearest God, please let me see my husband one more time,* she prayed.

She backed down the steps and bent to her knees again. "Mrs. Cole," she called out. "Are you all right?"

She heard a cough. "Yes, child. I am."

The dog barked in response.

As she crawled toward the corner, her hand grazed the water bucket. She reached out for the handle and carefully lifted it, pulling it forward. The smoke was filling the air, coming closer to the ground with every moment. Kathryne could hear the crackle and roar of the flames that she knew were devouring their home.

Her eyes were tearing, and not only from the smoke, for she felt much of her soul being consumed as well.

She sat down next to Mrs. Cole, the water bucket at her feet.

"Will we die here, child?" she asked Kathryne, her voice innocent and unafraid.

"No, we will not," Kathryne said after a moment. "We will not die down here. Have faith, Mrs. Cole. That's what you always taught me. Quickly, under these blankets." When they and Beauregard were covered, Kathryne lifted the bucket and poured it out over them, wetting the blankets as fully as she could.

"It is now up to God to protect us," Kathryne said firmly in the wet and woolly darkness. "He has in the past, and I see no reason why that should stop this night."

Mrs. Cole was shivering, and Kathryne put her arm about her.

"Do not worry, Mrs. Cole. He will not abandon us," she whispered, just over the roar of the flames. "He will not abandon us."

The roof of the cottage was half ablaze when Will first looked up from the fort.

"Kathryne!" he screamed, and began to lift himself up, again using his scabbard as a cane. In a moment he was on his feet, ignoring the growling, angry pain in his calf, and began running toward his home, running toward Kathryne.

"Oh, God," he cried out, "protect her. In the name of Jesus, protect my love."

The fire had begun in the common room of the Goose when a torch flew through an open window. Miss Eileen had heard the first cannon fire and looked out of her window to see the fort engulfed in explosions and flames. Within the space of a few moments, a band of men, shouting and cursing in several languages, entered the town and began to throw torches as if they were bestowing flowers on the establishments lining the narrow streets. By the time Eileen was clothed, much of the Goose was already consumed, the flames hungry for the dry wood and barrels of spirits in the public room. She skirted down the second-floor hallway, pounding on doors, throwing them open when they were unlocked, making sure that all were alerted to the flames. Men and women in varying stages of dress ran before her as she called out, running toward their homes or the safety of the water in the harbor.

■ ■ ■ ■ ■

John Delacroix had refused to awaken at first, claiming that the roars Missy heard were no more than distant thunder. But she refused to be dissuaded and ran down from their rooms behind the chandlery to the front walk. It was there that she first saw the ships looming closer to the harbor, then the cannon fire from the fort, then the explosions and roars of flame.

She ran back, screaming John's name. In an instant, he arose, grabbed his sword, unused for so long, and ran to the street, hobbling into his boots.

■ ■ ■ ■ ■

Will, eager to reach the cottage and oblivious to the musket shots zipping past him, was nearly past the powder house when a thin figure leapt from the shadows and knocked him to the ground, striking him on the head with the brass hilt of a cutlass. Will rolled to his side and looked up, his eyes fogged from the blow.

Hovering above him was a leering Radcliffe Spenser, with a red scarf draped about his neck and a thick gold earring hanging from his right ear. Radcliffe stood protected from the musket fire from Will's men.

"Ah, Captain Hawkes. How pleasant to see you again. I was so overjoyed to know that you had left the front door to the fort open for our visit."

Will lifted his sword and began to rise. Radcliffe kicked out fiercely, and his boot caught Will just below the ribs. By the time Will stopped coughing, Radcliffe had his cutlass nestled under Will's chin, its blade leaving a small bloody trail on Will's throat.

"I think not, Captain Hawkes. Do not rise just yet."

Radcliffe looked about him, his face bathed in the glow of a dozen fires.

"Such a splendid evening, is it not, Captain Hawkes? I had so feared that my plan would come to naught and that you had stopped up my little tunnels."

When the seawall exploded in a shower of rocks and mortar, Radcliffe had beamed like a child at a birthday celebration—for it was his contention that the fort was vulnerable to such subterfuge. Now, almost casually—as if taking a sip of wine—he kicked William again, his heavy boots finding Will's ribs.

"But then a fine gentleman like you—in the sewers? I thought not and simply planned accordingly."

Once more Radcliffe kicked, and Will curled into a ball on his side.

"I have two things to tell you, Captain Hawkes. It is most fortuitous that we have met this night."

And again he kicked out, hard and fast against the small of Will's back. He slipped his sword into its scabbard, pulled a dagger from his belt, and bent down to the gasping William. He grabbed him roughly by the hair and pulled his face up to his, holding his dagger at Will's cheek.

"First of all, happy anniversary, Captain Hawkes," he oozed, waiting for the surprised look on Will's face.

Will stared ahead, only hate showing in his eyes.

"I thought you might be surprised that I knew of your marriage to my whorish niece. Oh well, 'tis no matter. But this date worked out so well—the treasure fleet in harbor and all—and I am sure your attentions were elsewhere this evening, were they not?"

With that, he scratched a thin cut along Will's cheek, the blood forming in tiny drops along the line.

"And the other thing, Captain Hawkes. I would suggest that you do nothing heroic following our little visit—for I know how fond you are of such things. Do not attempt to bring us to justice."

Will's mouth was set tight, and he showed no response.

Radcliffe was almost giddy as he spoke next. "I know you would prefer to, Captain Hawkes. But perhaps I shall dissuade you."

He bent to Will's face and whispered through clenched teeth. "I have a friend of yours, Captain Hawkes. A good friend of yours. I vow that if you attempt to follow me, I will take the greatest pleasure in slipping a knife into his heart."

Will attempted to move, but Radcliffe responded with an elbow across Will's nose, sounding loud and wet as it struck him.

Radcliffe leaned back and rustled in his gray doublet, extracting a small letter. "A page from your poor Vicar Mayhew's Bible, Captain Hawkes."

Will's eyes, for the first time, showed surprise.

"Ah," Radcliffe purred, "finally a response from our brave captain. How gratifying."

He let the page drop on Will's chest. The page held a section of Psalms, including the forty-sixth chapter, where the verse "Be still, and know that I am God" was underlined.

"He sends his greetings. He is well, God is in his heaven, blah, blah, blah."

Radcliffe bent close, again grabbing William by the hair. "Remember, Mr. Hawkes. If you follow us, the good vicar's heart will be cut out and placed squarely on your head."

He leaned back. "Understood?" he asked gaily.

Will did not respond.

Radcliffe rose and kicked Will again, with all the effort he could muster.

"Understood?" he screamed, the veins in his neck protruding like cording. "Understood, Captain?"

Will nodded weakly as he attempted to pull himself to his feet.

"Good man," Radcliffe said. Before turning to leave, he kicked out one last time. "Good man," he said.

As Radcliffe kicked Will that last time, a flare shot into the air and exploded with a boom over the harbor.

"Ah, our signal of success," Radcliffe remarked, as calmly as if sitting down to afternoon tea. He whistled over at his men, pointed to the glow of the exploded rocket, then waved his hand in the direction of town.

Radcliffe then poked his head around the corner of the building, toward the last few defenders. The two remaining cannons had long since run out of powder, and their crews, decimated by three-quarters or more, had been cut apart. A handful of marines may have been left alive, but they had ceased to be a threat to the invader's ships.

Radcliffe smiled again and broke into a quick trot, heading toward town.

John stood on the walk in front of the chandlery, his mouth agape in bewilderment. The harbor was full of ships and longboats pushing through the smoke and mist. Men were screaming in the dark, and the sound of muskets echoed about the wharf and water. The town seemed to be ablaze, the fire's dull orange glow illuminating the night.

In a moment, John was flanked by Bryne and John Tambor, Bryne carrying a heavy wooden ax, and John a tall sharpened pole with an iron tip. Both were clad only in nightshirts.

"We bein' attacked, Mr. John?" Bryne called out over the pop of muskets.

"They be after the gold," his brother replied.

John Delacroix stood there, immobile, not knowing what to do first. He and two men were not sufficient to defend the harbor.

*Why isn't the fort firing?* John wondered.

He craned his neck to see over the sails of a Spanish pinnace that had just crashed into one of the English ships, its crew of cutthroats screaming as they launched themselves at the English sailors.

He knew why. The fort was ablaze itself, the forward point a mass of rubble and smoke.

John heard a thumping coming from one of three piers he had constructed to serve his customers, allowing their vessels to anchor there while work was completed.

He motioned with his head to the Tambors, who nodded, and the three of them padded quickly to the farthest pier.

At the end of the pier, by a Dutch fluyt in for repairs to the mizzenmast, were four shadowy figures chopping away at the stern and rudder assembly, just within reach of the wooden deck.

"Ahoy there," John called out, unafraid. "Stop what you are doing!"

The figure wielding the ax stopped for only a moment, spoke a few words in Spanish, then swung again. As he chopped, his three companions made their way toward John and the Tambors. After only a step, John pulled out his blade.

"We best prepare for a fight, good friends!" he called out as he launched himself at his attackers.

Within the span of a brief moment, two of the three attackers lay on the deck, bleeding and cursing. The other, John had clubbed with the hilt of his blade against his head and sent tumbling into the water.

But the price of victory was high. John Tambor lay on the pier, his head cradled in his brother's arms, an enemy blade having pierced his chest. Bryne was mumbling through his tears, calling for his brother to awaken from his sleep.

"I knows you be only restin', Brother. But you canna rest now. You canna," Bryne cried. He was smoothing back his brother's hair, his tears flowing freely.

John had no time to offer his sympathy just yet. He advanced through the dim shadows toward the figure wielding the ax.

John knew that fighting a skilled opponent who carried such a weapon was dangerous business. A single, well-placed blow from an ax was usually fatal. John sidled along the dark pier, his blade wavering in small circles in front of him. The man with the ax, still in darkness, held it firmly in two hands, ready to sweep out.

John feinted once to the right, then backed away quickly.

His opponent was no swordsman, for he took the feint, swung mightily with the ax, and sliced through only empty air. John dove at the man, clubbing him about his shoulders and head with the hilt of the blade, knocking him down to the deck. In a flash, John straddled the man, who continued to struggle. John rapped him again on the head, not to kill but to alert him that further resistance was futile.

He reached down and grabbed at the dark scarf wrapped about the man's mouth and nose and yanked it from his face.

John leaned back in astonishment. "Mr. Foxton?" he cried.

By the time Radcliffe reached the harbor, seven of the twelve English ships had been set ablaze. Four of the remaining five had been thoroughly looted of treasure and their ballast cocks opened to allow seawater to pour into the holds. Burning was more destructive, but often it was just the masts, canvas, and rigging that burned at first. A ship with damage such as that may be refitted in a matter of weeks, too close for most pirates' schedules. A ship lying at the bottom of the harbor, however, was another matter. Seldom, if ever, could they be raised, and to salvage cannons or muskets from such wrecks was a most dangerous activity.

One English ship, the *Water Sprite,* a small oceangoing pinnace, had been anchored a bit further away from the main fleet. Its captain soon realized the extent of the attack and the vast numbers of his opposition. He instructed every crewman to stand down and hide themselves belowdecks. He cut the anchor ropes holding the ship still and let the vessel drift away from the harbor on the high tide. Several pirate ships had sailed adjacent to him, but when they saw his decks quiet and empty, they all ignored the ship, thinking that it had already been looted and stripped clean of sailors and treasure.

<hr>

After watching Radcliffe's departure, Will managed to lift himself from the ground, blood forming at the corners of his mouth, his leg screaming in pain, his shoulder stiffening. All he could see was his cottage, the fires burning softer now, the stone walls stark as bones in the moonlight.

He grimaced and began to run, as fast as his tortured muscles could carry him, calling out in a hoarse voice, "Kathryne, Kathryne!"

He reached the porch where, only a short time before, he and Kathryne had sat down for their romantic anniversary supper. The table had been overturned; knives, food, and chairs were strewn about the area; and the remnants of a dozen broken plates littered the porch with their sparkling and sharp edges.

He ran through the front door, the main post of the ceiling still afire, his books still smoldering on the floor.

"Kathryne!" Will screamed.

*Perhaps she and Mrs. Cole escaped before the fire was set,* Will tried to tell himself, yet was not comforted, for he knew what most pirates would do upon finding a woman as beautiful as Kathryne.

He staggered into the kitchen to the cellar where he had told her to hide.

The larder was still over the cellar entrance, and the flames had consumed its back but had not consumed the entire framework.

"Kathryne!" he bellowed again.

Thinking that he heard a cough—or a dog's bark—in response, he bent to the charred woodwork and pushed with his shoulder. It squealed, and a hot ember burned through his ragged doublet, blistering the skin on his left shoulder. He felt it sear into his flesh, but would not stop, could not stop.

He puffed and gasped and pushed harder and harder, and the larder slid away to the side. The cellar door was near intact, with only a board or two charred at the edge.

"Kathryne!" he screamed and reached down to the iron handle and yanked it up. It had been heated in the fire, and it too burned Will's hand, yet he did not stop. With a crash sending up sparks and cinders, Will flipped the door back and away, calling out, "Kathryne! Kathryne!"

He clearly heard a cough this time and jumped onto the stairs. Having been weakened by the flames and heat, they gave way with a crash, and he tumbled into the darkness.

"Kathryne," he called again, weaker this time, as he struggled to his feet.

And from the darkness of the far corner he saw the muzzle of a pistol aimed directly at his heart. The menacing weapon wavered in the air.

After a long silence, the loudest sounds being the crackling of the dying fire, a small voice cried out, "William?"

His eyes adjusted to the dark, and he now saw Kathryne standing before him, her face streaked with soot and ash, her clothes black with smoke.

She dove into his open arms, crying and calling out his name, followed by Beauregard, who jumped about Will's legs in circles.

Will looked behind Kathryne and saw Mrs. Cole slowly struggle to rise to her feet and then methodically, with an expressionless face, fold the charred blanket and drape it over her arm.

■□■□■

Aidan and Emily had just finished dinner, alone in the dining chamber at Shelworthy. Aidan excused himself and walked to the front porch to take a breath of fresh air. He sat down on the front steps in a most informal manner. He looked to the sky for lightning bolts as he heard the thunderous rumble from the direction of town.

"Seems like a lot of thunder for this evening, and the skies looked clear before dinner," he muttered to himself.

He peered out from the porch and stared upward, looking for clouds, but he saw the heavens filled with the usual sparkling of stars and the full moon.

"Curious."

As he sat there, he glanced from time to time toward the harbor. He squinted, thinking that the colors of the evening had changed.

*I cannot be getting this old and feeble,* he thought, *for my eyes seem to be playing tricks on me.*

"Emily," he called out, "would you step outside for a moment?"

In an instant, the door swung open, and Emily, smiling and radiant, walked out. Since the announcement of their engagement, she had adamantly insisted that she take up residence with the Pickerings until the nuptials, lest anyone claim their relationship was tinted with even the slightest hue of scandal.

This night was the one evening of the week that she permitted a private dinner with Aidan.

"Yes, dearest. What is it that you want?"

Aidan stood on the first step and pointed toward the harbor. "Do you see something odd from town?"

She peered into the darkness. "What sort of odd?" she asked.

"A color, I imagine. . . . Sort of an odd tint to the sky?"

Emily squinted into the distance. "Well, indeed, I do now. A slight orange glow?"

Aidan nodded, then took a sniff to the air. It was then that he realized that age or oddness had nothing to do with this color, and he immediately shouted out for Caldor Bane to have the horses brought about quickly.

"Bridgetown is on fire," he declared, his voice masking his fear.

*God, please watch over my family this night,* he prayed.

■ ■ ■ ■ ■

By the time Aidan arrived at a full gallop, much of the waterfront was orange with flames. Caldor was only a hoofbeat behind him.

"Good sir," he called out, "I shall ride to the chandlery—for it appears that it has been spared. Perhaps I can help there with a watering team."

"By all means, Caldor, do so," Aidan shouted. "I shall attend to the defense of the church."

As Caldor rode off, his mind was racing. *The chandlery should have been in flames by now. That was Foxton's job.*

He spurred his horse again, harder, for it was resisting running toward the flames.

Under his breath Caldor muttered, "If Foxton has failed, I will kill him this night."

He spurred again. "That is, unless some other fortunate soul has beaten me to the pleasure."

Will gently escorted Kathryne and Mrs. Cole through the smoldering ruin of the cottage. Virtually no possession had escaped the flames. Perhaps a book or two might have remained unscorched, perhaps a plate or knife may have avoided being broken or melted by the flame. He brought both women to the wall near where they had dined that evening. Their two chairs had been spared. Will righted them both, slid them close together, and bid both women be seated. The dog was at Will's heels, growling as it sniffed the smoke-filled air.

Kathryne extended one hand to Mrs. Cole, who grabbed at it as if it were a lifeline. Will took her other hand, gently, as if fearful that she had been injured during her ordeal.

Will leaned against the wall and closed his eyes for a moment, hoping and praying that this had all been but a frightening dream, and that he would wake and the cottage would be restored and his greatest challenge would be to taste a bit of every dessert Mrs. Cole prepared. He opened his eyes, and all that remained of what once existed was cinder and smoke, ashes and ruin.

He looked into Kathryne's face, near blank with fatigue and shock.

*Yet what was most precious to me was spared,* he thought, *and for that I am eternally grateful to the Almighty.*

Geoffrey's arms had been roughly tied, tethered to a stout pole in the chandlery's workroom. His hair was matted with blood from the battle with John, and a wide gash reddened his side. The cut was long, but not deep.

John Delacroix had restrained Bryne from simply slicing the man in two with his own ax, yet he felt much of the same anger. If anyone deserved to suffer for the losses of this evening, it should be the traitorous Foxton. But such an action was not for John to decide. He would simply hold Foxton as a prisoner until the fires and the panic had subsided. Other men, not he, would decide on his fate.

But questions swirled through John's mind as he lashed Geoffrey's wrists together with thin strips of sailor's leather. John paused a moment, long enough to ask a simple question.

"Why, Mr. Foxton? Why did you do such terrible things? Why align yourself with such evil pirates?"

Foxton laughed, as if pretending this was all a simple game of quoits back in London. "You would not understand, you simple carpenter," he coughed, a gurgle forming in his lungs.

In a burst of anger that John did not fully understand nor anticipate, he grabbed Foxton by the doublet, and as he pulled him toward him, the threads shrieked as it tore across the back and neck. John noticed that the tearing seemed to have pained Geoffrey more than his wounds.

"You have caused the death of one of my closest friends," John hissed, "and God knows how many more be on your head." He threw him back against the pole.

"You want an answer?" Foxton coughed. "Then ask your noble Lady Kathryne. She is the one who caused me first to stumble. Toying with my affections as she did. Promising more than she could deliver. She is nothing more than an expensive trollop. Miss Eileen is much preferred—and more versed in pleasure—than the likes of her, if you . . ."

The back of John's hand cracked across Geoffrey's jaw, knocking his head back before it fell forward.

"You'll not be speaking ill of Kathryne. It be your heart that be evil. She is too pure for the likes of you."

Geoffrey lifted his head and coughed again, rolling his tongue inside his mouth, searching for the broken skin and blood.

"God alive, I hate this island," he spat out. "I hate the sugarcane and the disgusting slaves with their horrid smells. I hate the sugar mills and the putrid sweetness that covers a man when he nears them. I hate the heat and the sweat and the coarse drink in this abysmal place."

John stood an arm's length away. "Then why didn't you just leave?"

Geoffrey laughed, his head bobbing back and forth with a dismal gaiety. "And how would I then live? I am now in debt to more than one banker. It will be another year until I realize even one pound of profit from this blasted sugar—and what I do earn will simply go into the purse of my creditors."

He coughed again and tried to wipe his mouth on his shoulder. "No, you simple carpenter, you would not understand. I cannot live with less than I do now. I cannot be relegated to some stinking hovel behind a shipyard."

As the captive nobleman said that, he sneered at John, indicating it was his hovel he was referring to.

"I am Geoffrey Foxton," he crowed and drew himself up to his full height, holding his head erect.

There was silence for a moment.

"If it had not been for you, I would have slipped out with Radcliffe and San Martel, and in three days I would have been sitting in the shade on the pleasant island of Guajiro. I would have received my fair share of this entire undertaking—a guaranteed twenty-five thousand pounds in gold."

John shook his head sadly. "You sold us like Judas, Mr. Foxton. You betrayed your friends. You turned on all of us. You are no better than a mad dog in the street."

Geoffrey looked up at John, simple disgust and hate so evident on his face.

"As if such sentiment matters to a peasant such as yourself! You'll see. Once I am back in England, all this will be explained away, and I shall be free. And you shall still be sweating away on this horrid, stinking island."

The front door crashed open, and Bryne Tambor burst through, his eyes wild and furious. In his hand was a pistol, cocked, his finger curled about the trigger.

"You be the scoundrel that caused the death of me brother!" he screamed.

With a deliberate slowness, Bryne lifted the pistol and fired directly at Foxton's chest. The musket ball missed John by an inch and slammed into the nobleman, knocking him back against the pole, his legs splaying out beneath him, his head folding tight to his bloody chest. In an instant he lay slumped on the floor, a faint gurgling sound following his prideful boast.

## 73

The winds were still that next morning, and smoke from active fires rose in a direct line to the sky. The waves were hushed, reaching only with small, quiet fingers along the rocks. Even the dawning sun seemed hesitant to show its light on the confusion and horror that was Bridge-town.

Will stood on the narrow stretch of land that led from the island to the fort. From that slight apex of the narrow isthmus he could see the town, the church, the fort, his cottage, and the empty sea—all within a slight turn of his head. A thick pallor of smoke filled the air, its acrid taste bitter on the tongue. The light was just sufficient to paint a bleak rendering of the results of the battle of the night before.

He first looked to the north side of the harbor, toward the church, the chandlery, and the courthouse. The structures there had suffered only minor damage, for the winds blowing in from the north kept the fires at bay. None of the pirate invaders had gone to that distance in their plundering and looting—save for the thwarted attack on the chandlery led by Geoffrey Foxton. The rest of the Spanish pirates and brigands had concentrated their efforts on the English ships in harbor and the waterfront establishments.

The harbor was filled with sunken vessels and burned-out hulks, some still barely afloat in the greasy black waters. Of the dozen and more ships that had lain at anchor just one day prior, all but three were either destroyed or damaged beyond quick repair. Two of the large English galleons lay beached, lying on their sides like great gasping sea creatures, huge holes torn in their hulls by explosions of black powder.

Their masts rocked back and forth as the tide lifted and settled the vessels with each wave.

One English naval vessel, the *Resolve*, had been spared, as well as the last vessel in the chandlery docks—the small Dutch fluyt that John Tambor had died protecting. And a small pinnace, anchored further away from the main fleet and set adrift by her captain during the attack up the mouth of the harbor, had been saved as well.

The harbor front was like a dead man's grin. Great toothy black gaps existed. For every structure that escaped harm, it seemed that two lay in smoldering, charred ruin. The Goose was rubble, as well as two other public houses, and fully every business and shop on High Street was gone—devoured by the hungry flames. Some of the piers had burned, leaving only jagged posts near the waterline.

Will looked at his fort and saw only a hulking ruin. The northwest corner, following the explosion, had slipped into the sea, forming a great pile of debris. The pirates' flames had consumed every freestanding structure behind the fort's walls, save the powder house. Miraculously, the embers and sparks from a hundred other fires had left it unharmed.

In the distance, Will could see dozens of citizens milling about in the ashes, not fully comprehending their lot, not truly knowing where they might take rest. A few carried armfuls of sooty possessions about, trying to protect the few things they had managed to save.

Will blinked a few times, clearing his eyes, blaming his tears on the smoke. But he knew that at least three dozen men under his command lay still in that fort that morning, waiting only to be taken to their final rest.

And he wept.

He at last turned to the cottage—his and Kathryne's. The stone walls outlining its form remained standing. The roof was gone, but a few charred timbers held fast to the roof joints. The windows were shattered, and the interior had been consumed by the great fire.

In the lee of the kitchen wall, in the darkness of night, Luke and Will had constructed a small linhay, with canvas stretched between cut green saplings, as a sleeping tent for Kathryne and Mrs. Cole.

Both women had been nearly in shock when Will found them huddled in the cellar, spared from the flames and the looting but covered in ash and soot. Both had washed the black from their faces and hands, and within minutes of lying back on rough canvas mats had fallen soundly asleep. Bo had lain at their feet, his head on his paws, watching the harbor for the entire black night.

*This morning will be more difficult for them than even last evening's terror was,* Will thought, *for there is so much death and destruction that must be confronted.*

Luke was off tending to the injured and dying, and all was quiet.

Will had intended to kneel this morning and to thank God for sparing both him and Kathryne. But as he tried to bend to his knee, his wounded leg thundered in pain. And his sides, bruised purple from Radcliffe's boots, were no less painful.

*I imagine that God will hear the prayers of a standing man,* Will thought, *and I know I need to offer thanks.*

*Dearest Lord, almighty Creator of heaven and earth,* he prayed, *I come to you this morning confused yet thankful. I am grateful beyond any words I could use that Kathryne was spared, as was her father, and Emily, and Mrs. Cole, and so many others. But, Lord, so many have perished. So much destruction has occurred that I would deign it near impossible to make a fresh start.*

*Is this all part of your plan, Lord? What am I to make of this? Do I give thanks, as Paul did, for all things? How do I thank you for this? Where is my peace found? Lord, give me strength to deal with this day. I ask this in your most precious name. Amen.*

Will hobbled back to the cottage. It would soon be brighter, and he would need to climb into what remained of the cellar to find foodstuffs for breakfast.

■ ■ ■ ■

Kathryne had lain awake for hours, her eyes opening well before the first hints of the false dawn came creeping over the eastern hills. She lay quiet, blinking her eyes, which still smarted from the great billows of smoke that had poured into that small cellar.

She dared not move just yet, not willing to disturb Mrs. Cole, whose rhythmic breathing next to her was a great reassurance.

She lifted her head up so very slightly and saw William standing alone in the morning's dimness.

*Thank you, my God, for sparing his life,* she prayed. *I do not know how I might have continued if he had been taken into your arms last eve. I thank you for my life as well, and Mrs. Cole, and Papa, and Emily. I scarce know how to pray in the face of what has happened.*

*Lord, provide in me the strength and peace that I need to make this day a blessing unto you—in some manner and in some way.*

*I ask this in your name, dearest Lord. Amen.*

Miss Eileen stood by the rubble that had been her home and place of business these past eighteen months and which now was no more than cinders. She kicked through the ashes, her toes catching a tankard, then a plate, then a twisted and blackened knife.

She folded her arms across her chest and stared out to sea, hoping that winds would soon drive the stench of the dead and the burning buildings from the town. Her gown was charred at the hem, her face was streaked with soot and black, and her hair hung in wild tendrils about her face.

*How could this have happened? Why did the fort not fire upon the fleet? Where were the marines in all this?*

She kicked out at the jagged edge of a platter, and the brittle plate shattered in a dozen shards about her feet.

*And is it true that Radcliffe Spenser led the charge? Can I believe that Governor Spenser had no knowledge of such an event? From what the sailors had told me, there was a fortune in gold in our harbor . . . until last night.*

Feeling the first liquid touchings of a tear crease her cheek, Eileen quickly smoothed her palm across her face. If a looking glass had escaped the flames, she would have seen the small angled streaks of white that the tears left as she pulled them away in her hand.

Sniffing, Eileen held her head up, turning to face the aureole of the sun as it crossed the first ridge of hills of the island of Barbados.

Hours before sunrise, John Delacroix had cut the cords holding Geoffrey Foxton to the pole and had dragged his body to one side of the large workroom. From a rear storeroom he had gathered up an armful of canvas and had laid it over him, tucking the ends under the stiffening form.

"I will tend to him when the sun is fuller and warm," John had spoken to himself as he left, not wanting to be in an empty room with the body.

John had seen many men die, even at his own hand on some occasions. Standing beside dying men, he had held their hands as they slipped from this world to the next. And though the experience was not novel, a cold shudder passed over his spine on every such happening. And the past night he had watched four men slip that mortal coil—

Foxton, two unnamed Spanish pirates, and his dear friend John Tambor.

Bryne, after firing upon Mr. Foxton, had crumpled to the ground, tears splashing his face like an angry autumn rain. The pair had gathered up Bryne's brother and, with great tenderness, had laid him in the protective well of a longboat and covered him with canvas. Bryne had made a small pillow for his head, tucking it in beneath him as a father putting a son to sleep.

"Bryne, we will do the rest properly on the morrow," John had said. "But it be best now if we offer what help we can to our friends across the way."

And now, hours later, as the dirty and bone-weary pair walked back to the chandlery, the same thought raced through their tired minds: *How could this thing have happened?*

Aidan sat on the edge of a pier that had been spared by the flames. His left arm was burned from wrist to elbow, with white blisters pocking the reddened skin. He had been injured when a timber slipped from a roof and struck his arm as he hauled water in buckets from the sea.

Though the arm throbbed with pain, Aidan paid scant attention to it. *There will be time enough to visit Luke this day,* he thought. *Let him tend to the seriously injured first.*

He stared out to sea, across the blackened hulks and hulls lying in the harbor waters, and his thoughts refused to focus. *How could this have come to pass? William assured us all that the fort was invincible. Is it true that Radcliffe led part of the mob that attacked us? How could he have survived being lost at sea so long ago? How could he have been allied with the Spanish?*

Aidan looked down at his boots, caked with thick black muck. *And how will I explain to London that Radcliffe—a man sharing the name of Spenser—made off with the king's gold and jewels? After the tale travels four thousand miles east, who will believe that the Spenser in the governor's chair had nothing to do with such a loss?*

He closed his eyes and allowed a pained, brittle sob to escape his lips.

Lady Emily had spent the night pacing back and forth along Shelworthy's long porch. She had watched the orange glow from the harbor brighten and had shut her eyes in prayer and pain as the faint echoes of explosions rolled up along the first rise from the sea.

Several slaves and servants had come and gone during the long night, searching for more buckets and blankets.

It was as dawn neared and the smoke began to drift out to Shelworthy on a light morning breeze that Emily sat down for the first time in hours.

The door creaked, and Hattie stepped out into the cool dimness. "Lady Emily," she whispered. "You be wantin' breakfast?"

Nodding, almost unable to form words, Emily forced herself to stand.

Hattie spoke again and lowered her head in a slight, but unmistakable gesture of shame. "Lady Emily?" she whispered. "Be it true what Jeb said—dat it be Massa's brother dat done dis attackin'?"

Emily nodded again as she made her way into the house. "Hattie, that is what Jeb reported. I cannot tell you if it is indeed the truth."

"Be it den true what de slaves be sayin'—dat Massa Aidan done know about dis before? Dat he be sharing de gold with dat brother?"

Emily stopped and pulled herself up tall, facing Hattie, a shocked look on her face.

"Hattie!" she cried. "How can you say such a horrid thing? That is simply a lie—and anyone who thinks such a horrid thing is wrong. It is evil to repeat such a dreadful falsehood."

Hattie stepped back, and her head bobbed even lower, as a dog slinks back from a beating. "I be sorry, Lady Emily," Hattie replied, her voice cracking. "I don' believe dat at all. I just repeatin' what de slaves done said."

Emily scowled back, angry and frustrated.

"I don' be believing such a thing a-tall," Hattie insisted.

Emily did not answer.

"I don' be believin' any of it," Hattie insisted. She added after a long moment, "But dey be folks dat do."

━ ▪ ▪ ▪ ▪ ━

"Once a pirate, always a pirate."

"Now that he's married to the likes of that woman, he be needin' a sight more gold to keep her happy."

"Dinna he be claimin' that no man could be sailin' into the harbor without fallin' under his fine and polished cannons? Where be the guns last night?"

"I heard the three of them claim that Radcliffe be swept away to a watery grave. I daresay someone be tellin' us lies."

"And then they shot Mr. Foxton in cold blood—while he be tied to a post, I hear say. I would wager that he be one who tried to stop them traitors, and they done him in for it."

"I heard say that Foxton came upon the Spanish splittin' the gold with that Delacroix fellow, and he tried to stop 'em. And now he be dead and gone—as well as all our gold."

The Heather Downs was fairly full with customers, despite the previous night's catastrophe. That day's early-morning patrons were small acreage landholders, craftsmen, fishermen, and sailors—none of whom seemed to have been affected by the attack. In fact, the few public houses that remained undamaged did a very brisk business that morning, even though their food and drink were all lightly tainted with the smell of smoke.

John Delacroix decided to have breakfast at the Heather Downs after his long and tiring night. When he entered the public house, heads turned, elbows nudged sides, and the talk grew softer. Yet John had heard some of their remarks and accusations as he made his way in. He walked briskly to end of the bar, then turned to face the dozen men who sat there.

With his face glowering and angry, he barked out, "Who here be accusing me of doing wrong?"

There was silence, and several men bowed their heads to avoid his glare, staring instead into their tankards.

"Who here be accusing Captain Hawkes of doing wrong?"

Again, silence met his question.

"Any man here desire to confront me on my actions?"

Silence filled the room, tension drawing mouths tight.

"As I expected," John muttered, turning away, his appetite fading with each moment.

As the door behind him slammed, each of his silent accusers turned to assure themselves of his departure. It was only a moment later that a small hostile voice was heard muttering at the end of the bar.

"It be fine and well of Mr. Delacroix to be so theatrical. But to be true, his denyin' don't be changin' the facts."

And a curious, affirming mutter spread through the room, like brackish water leaking from a rotten cistern.

■ □ ■ □ ■

Luke had spent most of the night tending to the injured and the dying. Nearly a dozen times in the span of a few hours Luke had reached into his deep leather pouch and extracted a handful of thick leaves.

"Chew on dese to help wit de pain," he had said many times. Then, standing by the injured, he would pray for a moment, knowing that others needed him and that these souls had no hope of seeing the dawn.

As the sun rose, Luke stood by the fort's gate and stretched, the bones in his back cracking loudly. He had tended to all that needed him there and was about to head back to town, knowing that the governor, for one, still required his skill.

He saw William and waved to him, then walked to him with his long strides. "Massa Will be after dem men?"

William looked out to sea. "The pirates?"

Luke nodded.

"Luke, I made a promise not to raise my hand to attack another soul. I made that promise to God," Will said, his face a blank mask. "And to Kathryne."

Grabbing at his shoulder, Luke replied, his words snapped and urgent, "Massa Will, dat promise be before. God be understandin'."

Will brought his hand up over Luke's. "But a promise is a promise. And a promise to God is sacred."

Luke stepped back. "Don' know dat word."

Luke looked down at the ground, his face tight, as if he were thinking a most difficult thought. "Massa Will, God see all dis," he said, sweeping his hand to his side, taking in all the harbor and town. "God see all dis, and he see Massa Will. God understand if Massa Will need change his mind."

And without waiting for William to say another word, he turned and loped toward the harbor.

CHAPTER

74

By midafternoon of that day, William, limping and wincing, had gathered up a few of their possessions that were not consumed by the flames, and he, Kathryne, Mrs. Cole, and Bo set out on a borrowed wagon and mule and headed to Shelworthy. Will would not allow Kathryne to stay in the rubble of their cottage, and her father's home had a half-dozen empty bedchambers.

As they rode past the sidelong stares of many of the townspeople, Will looked straight ahead, his hands firm on the reins.

It was near the afternoon bell that John Delacroix and Bryne Tambor met with Will and Aidan in the governor's office.

Before anyone else spoke, Aidan asked, "Have you seen Caldor Bane? I assumed he had returned to Shelworthy, but no one here has seen him since last eve."

"I have not seen him," Will said, "and I have not heard his name mentioned as one who had been killed."

"Caldor Bane . . . ," John said, almost to himself. "He be a tall, bony fellow, with a face like a hawk?"

Aidan nodded.

"His hair all long and wild about his head?"

Aidan nodded.

Without pausing to consider the import of his words, John said, "Last night, perhaps an hour or more after Mr. Foxton's death, I thought I saw a man like that. He stole one of my shore boats and paddled out to sea. By then I was too tired to give chase."

They both turned to John, amazement and shock in their faces.

Noting their response, John quickly added, "I am not for certain that it be him—'twas dark and I had more important things on me mind at the time."

Aidan dropped his head into his hands and groaned. "I would have considered such horrible accusations as lunacy a day prior. But now— and may God forgive my thought—now I cannot remain certain."

⬛ ⬛ ⬛ ⬛ ⬛

"What vow?!" John exclaimed, his face angry and red, the veins in his throat tightening like cords.

"A vow, William?" Aidan asked, more polite than John, but in clipped tones.

"You canna be speakin' the truth, Cap'n Will. You canna be sayin' that such men be allowed to slip away with no chance of punishment," cried Bryne Tambor. "These be the devils who took me brother's life, Cap'n Will. Does not that move you to seek revenge?"

Will walked to the window, stared out at the smoke still hovering over the harbor, and then turned back, silhouetted by the strong afternoon sun haloing about him.

"I made a promise to God that never again would I raise my hand in offense against another human soul," he said with slow, deliberate care. "I do not see how I am to hold to my faith if I treat a vow made to God with such disdain."

John took a step toward him. "But did you not take up arms last eve? Did you not use blade and musket against the pirates?"

Will nodded. "Indeed, John, I did. But it was to defend this island, not to raise arms against others."

John's brows were arched in surprise. "And that be a difference, Will? Force of arms be force of arms—no matter who be attackin' or defendin'."

Will shook his head. "That cannot be how God sees my vow."

Aidan sat quietly, his hands folded across the leather blotter on his desk. He reached up and slid his quill pen an inch to one side, centering it along his silver inkwell, a gift from the king on the event of Aidan taking the office of governor of Barbados.

"Will," he asked, his voice moderate and even, "you say you love my daughter."

Will cocked his head an inch to the right, reacting in surprise to the question.

"More than life itself, sir. I hope that my care for her is evident."

Aidan smoothed his palms against the desk and slid them apart. "And you will allow the men who sought to end her life to sail away unchallenged? You will allow those men—who had they found her would have done unspeakable things to her—you will allow them to simply vanish into the sea?"

"But, sir," Will responded, his voice quaking, "I do so love your daughter. But to do as you ask—why, it would require me to turn my back on a promise made to God and to Kathryne. How can I do such a thing to the very God who gave me life?"

"But, William, do you not think that God understands the enormity of last eve's destruction? Do you not think that God gives his servants the right of free will and the power to make their own decisions? Do you think the Almighty desires blind, uncritical loyalty, subjects who do no reasoning on their own?"

Silence filled the room.

"I think not, William. I think not," Aidan stated, answering his own question.

Will's heart was aching. He did love his wife and did respect and honor her father. But this was not a matter of love or respect or honor. To William it was a most simple decision. He, on his knees and before God and his beloved, had made a solemn vow that he would not lift his hand in anger to attack another human being. He would defend his loved ones, his possessions, this island—but to defend what was owned and to attack another to regain lost gold were two matters, most separate and distinct.

"But, sir, to take up arms against those who attacked us names me the same as them. I cannot do so. I have made a vow. I can no more think of shattering that promise than I can think of not breathing nor loving your daughter. To do so would sully all that I hold dear and precious and make me no more honorable than a wild dog in the street."

Will's arms were loose at his sides, his shoulders bent. "I can do no more, sir. I simply cannot do as you ask."

Aidan sighed deeply. John turned away to stare out the window at the sea. Bryne looked crestfallen.

After a moment, Aidan spoke. "Then, John, Bryne, together we must gather what forces we have and seek pursuit of our invaders."

Aidan looked over at Will's downcast face.

"William, you must excuse us now, for we have much to plan."

# CHAPTER

# 75

Miss Eileen stood by the water's edge and looked back over her shoulder, first at the rubble that had once been her home, place of business, and future as well. Then her eyes gazed at the fort, its jagged openings bared to the evening sky. Her life felt as if it were all ashes and smoke. She had only but a few small coins saved for such an event as this. It had been her practice to spend what she had on the pleasures life had to offer.

*Where is my future now?* she wondered.

She had washed the smoke from her face, combed her hair back, and tied it with a ribbon. She looked down at herself and saw that her gown was sooty and ripped in several places.

She looked about and saw no one near. Kneeling, she unlaced her boots and slipped them off, placing them neatly, side by side, in the warm sand. She walked to the edge of the sea, hesitated for a moment, then stepped in, the waves riding above her ankles and calves, her gown floating about her in a watery circle. She stepped again, feeling the water higher, to her knees. She had been on the island for more than two years and had never once stepped into the ocean.

*It is odd that I wait until this day to experience such a thing,* she thought. *It is a most pleasant feeling.*

She stopped now, the water at her waist, the waves gently lifting her as they swelled about her form. Both her arms were extended to keep her balance. The tide was coming in, and she took one more step forward, to the west and the deepness beyond. A large wave broke over the coral reef, and its white jeweled top rolled in at her. It knocked her back, her feet losing their grip on the sandy bottom. The curled head of the wave crested over her face, and she saw a thousand jeweled prisms of light reflected in the setting sun.

She made no sounds as she flailed her arms. She was not trying to make her way back to shore; she was just trying to stay in the deep waters until they claimed her and took her home.

It was in those few moments that her thoughts became most lucid. Her head was turned to the fort—she could see the wide grassy area where Will had held the Sunday gatherings and spoken of the Bible and of God. It was on those quiet mornings that she had felt most at peace, a feeling rare and delicate, she recalled.

Then another wave washed over her and spun her about to face the west again and the vastness of the ocean's expanse.

*Dear God,* she called out in her thoughts, *this is my first prayer. Protect me and keep me.*

As she formed those words in her thoughts, a lone figure cleared the low grasses that grew along the shore and stepped upon the sand. It was William, who had left Shelworthy an hour before.

He stopped at the edge of the water and sighed, breathing in the sea air, deep into his lungs. From within him, a voice, a feeling, called out to his senses with the clarity of a bell. *Will! Look to the west!*

He looked out to the sea, and the sunlight haloed about the head and shoulders of a woman, lost and curled among the waves. She was wrapped in the arms of the sea, her long, dark hair lashed about her face by the waters. She raised her arms, not in defense, not in protection, but seemingly to embrace the liquid that filled the space around her form.

Will's eyes darted to the pair of shoes now resting at the very edge of the rising tide.

Will kicked off his own boots to dive deep into the oncoming waves and began to stroke out into the deep.

■ ▪ ■ ▪ ■

Aidan picked up his quill from his desk and twirled it between his thumb and forefinger, its feather swishing in the still air. He coughed and then spoke.

"Mr. Delacroix, I must trust your judgment on matters of sail and cannons and the like, for I have no skill regarding such elements."

Glumly, John nodded.

"You say that only three ships be ready for sail in harbor?"

John nodded again. "There may be a fourth, but it be a small ship to be going hunting like that."

"You say that only one of those ships is of the English navy?"

"True, sir."

"And the best we could manage is to mount three ships, perhaps four dozen cannon, against an armada of a dozen ships and a hundred such cannon?"

"That be true as well, sir. Until we began discussin' such matters, I had not realized the most dismal choices that we are now left with."

Aidan sighed again and replaced the quill with a studied precision.

"Then all is lost, Mr. Delacroix?" Aidan asked, his voice growing small. "There truly is no manner of bringing these brigands to justice?"

John looked down at his lap and shook his head. "If there be a way, it is beyond my powers to discover it."

Aidan sighed again, this time the sound being closer to a sob. Slowly, and with a great deliberateness, he lowered his head and cradled it in his arms.

Ignoring the piercing pain in his leg and shoulder, Will reached the woman in a few moments. If he was surprised that she was Eileen, he did not let it slow his efforts. He reached about her waist and pulled her to him, turning her face from his. Her features were calm, like a baby near sleep, and she pushed at his arms with the tender but ineffective insistence of a small child.

He wrapped his left arm about her and turned and kicked at the water, pulling hard with his right arm. The waves were high, and the water boiled and swirled about them. Will struggled to keep his head above the sea, and as he stroked, the current pulled at them urgently. He thought Eileen was still breathing, and redoubled his efforts to the shore. Within a few long moments he was pulling her to shallow water. She coughed deeply several times, gagging at the seawater, and then lay back, her arms at her sides, her breath coming in great gasps. Will sat beside her in the sand, as the edge of the water eddied and flowed about them.

He paused a few moments to regain his normal breath, the loudest sound being the hissing of the waves at their feet. He looked down at Eileen, prostrate before him, her eyes closed shut.

He spoke softly. "Eileen, what were you doing?"

She coughed again, then blinked. Propping herself up on her elbows, she looked first to the sea, then at William's face. She reached out and touched her fingers to his cheek, as lightly as a butterfly on a flower.

"God answered my prayer, Mr. Hawkes."

"Your prayer? I don't understand. You were praying and fell into the water?"

Eileen smiled. "No, William. I was preparing to end my days on this earth. It was not a chance happening."

Will sat back, the waves washing over his legs, his face a mask of surprise.

"You need not look so shocked, William. Look at the town—to where my home used to stand. All that I had is lost. Is not that enough reason?"

"But to take measure to end your life. . . ."

She sat up and draped the wet gown about her ankles, pushing her wet hair back from her face.

"I have not led a sinless life, Mr. Hawkes. You, as well as any man on this island, should know that. I have nothing left. This seemed the easier road to take."

She reached over and placed her hand upon his, covered with seawater and sand.

"But at the end, I called out to God, William. It was the first time I had called to him." Her eyes took on a faraway look as she gazed out to the whitecapped waves. "I called on him to protect me and keep me."

She turned back to Will. "And the moment after I prayed those words, it was your arms about me that I felt. I thought it was God's arms at first, but he sent you. He sent you to protect me."

Will looked at her face and deep into her eyes.

She said, "Without you, I would be dead. I feel reborn, William. I feel clean for the first time in my life. Thank you."

She leaned forward and embraced him, and began to weep.

CHAPTER

**76**

Will stood in the wreckage that was once the cottage he and Kathryne had shared.

All aspects of life on Barbados had changed. People nervously glanced out to sea as if expecting another invasion, another threat borne on the waves. A hue of death colored the air as well. Nearly four dozen fresh graves had been dug or started in the graveyard just beyond town, and Vicars Petley and Coates and the church were scheduled solid with funeral services for the next three days.

Will sat on the short stone wall of his cottage and stared first at the fort, then toward town, then around his own home. He had no idea of where to start. He knew that rebuilding must occur, but he could not locate the best starting point.

And he, too, looked to the sea several times every hour. He, too, expected to see sails at the horizon, cresting toward them, ready to plunder what little remained of value.

His sleep had been troubled. His dreams were a confusing and anxious stew of faces and cannon fire and waves sweeping over the innocents. He awakened several times, blinking in the darkness, sweating and panting.

Now that dawn was at hand, he sat, still and quiet.

From the north, he heard the approach of a horse, plodding with careful steps in the dim light of morning. He could see it was Kathryne, astride Porter, making her slow way up the path from town.

"Kathryne, you should not have come here. You require rest and should be in bed regaining your strength," he called out.

Kathryne smiled back at her husband. She knew how protective he was of her and was comforted by the concern.

Porter slowed and stopped a dozen yards from the house. Kathryne patted at the horse's neck as she slipped from the saddle, lowering the reins to the ground.

She extended her hand to Will, who was now at her side, and as their hands met, she squeezed his tight, happy to be near him again.

"I know, sweet William. But my sleep was troubled this morning, and I arose early. I knew you would be here. I knew that I needed to be at your side."

Hand in hand they walked to what remained of their front door, once freshly painted blue—the color of robins' eggs. Kathryne peered in at the charred remains.

Will let go of her hand and stepped into the darkened cottage, his footfalls hushed in the ashes. He took small steps, sliding his feet forward, stopping halfway across the large room. Kathryne watched from the doorway as he bent at the waist and picked up a blackened and charred device.

"It is my sextant, Kathryne," he called out, a note of excitement in his voice. "They either discarded it as worthless or overlooked it in the darkness."

He returned to the doorway, wiping the ash-covered instrument on the sleeve of his doublet. "I believe its components are undamaged. I believe that it will still serve to be useful."

He raised the sextant to the sun, looking for further damage. Kathryne tried to force a smile, then turned away from him and walked to the wall and sat down, looking out to sea. Her face bore neither joy nor sadness, but there was a pensive air about her.

"Kathryne?" Will asked as he sat beside her, laying the blackened sextant down between them with a brassy clink on the wall. "What is the matter? I must tell you that I believe that coming here will be too hard on your sensitivities—to see your home destroyed and me picking through the rubble like a scavenger. You should not have come this day. You should remain at Shelworthy until I can effect repairs."

Kathryne did not speak, but lowered her head and closed her eyes.

"Kathryne?" Will asked again when she did not respond. He placed his hand over hers, leaving soot-dark streaks on her white skin. "Kathryne, what troubles you?"

Will peered at Kathryne's down-turned features. He did not see the tears that he had expected.

She looked up, her eyes wide. Her lips were pursed tight, almost as if she had kept them so to prevent them from trembling.

He put his arm about Kathryne's shoulders and pulled her near to him, as if holding her close to his heart would cause the horrid scene before them to disappear.

He felt her breath catch in her chest, and though it felt as if she fought the onset, her shoulders heaved as the tears began.

Will kept silent and held her close as she began to weep, her tears hot against his chest, her breath as choppy as the waves in the sea. He reached up and stroked her hair, his arm aching as he smoothed the wild curls against her neck and shoulder, lifting wisps of hair from her face, tucking them behind her ears.

After many long moments, her tears grew slighter. Will did not relax his embrace, providing what comfort and protection he could.

"Kathryne," he insisted, his voice a small degree more insistent, "you will see. We can rebuild here. I can rebuild this cottage. We can replace what was lost. It will be as it was."

Kathryne pushed back from her husband, more emphatically than Will thought appropriate, and stood away from him.

"William Hawkes, our lives will never be the same—and you are aware of that as well as anyone on this island."

"But, Kathryne," he protested, "what was lost is only stone and mortar—only paper and cloth. It can all be restored."

It was then that as William sat still, his eyes closed, he heard a voice—or perhaps it was a simple urging in his heart. *Hold her.*

Obeying the impulse, he embraced her, trying to envelop her with tenderness and love. He closed his eyes for several moments as she cried in his arms. Suddenly, he knew she was not weeping for the loss of the possessions that were consumed in the flames—for their wealth combined could replace them all a hundredfold. He knew that she was not weeping simply for the loss of the cottage—for their assets would allow them to rebuild a grand manse on any location they desired.

No, these tears, William realized, were shed in grief over the lives that had been lost—as well as the peace and security that had, until now, surrounded Kathryne and her loved ones. Will realized that he saw fear in her face. Her eyes, luminous and deep, darted about like frightened sparrows that morning, looking to the town, the harbor, the sea, the fort, in rapid, frantic jumps. Will remembered—he had seen that same look in the eyes of his sailors after the first battle he fought on the seas. The ocean, once friendly and safe, now bristled with danger and evil, unseen, unnoticed. It was as if the jaws of Satan himself reared up and grabbed the unsuspecting, devouring their happiness and their very breath of life with cackling gusto.

Will knew that the fear caused by the pirate attack cut a ragged and deep crease in Kathryne's heart—her home had been violated, and she had come within a hairsbreadth of being consumed herself. Her father's reputation and the honor of the Spenser name had been tainted and sullied by Radcliffe. The evil that loomed over her had appeared from nowhere, ravaged the innocent, and now destroyed her peace. Her ease, her comfort lay broken and crushed, covered with the ashes and rubble of their dreams.

He held her as close as he could, wishing he could assume that fear in her, wishing he could have done something that would have spared her this agonizing grief. Her sobs grew hotter and tighter as the sun rose behind them.

Gently he led her back to the wall, and she sat down, her face flushed and red, wet with tears. He stroked her hair back from her face and kissed her forehead.

"Kathryne," he whispered, "our lives are in God's hands. We need to take our comfort in that knowledge."

She sniffed loudly and nodded. "I know, William, but it is so hard. It is so hard. . . ." Her voice trailed away and was lost in her tears again.

Will sat beside her and took her hand in his and held it as carefully as he would hold a baby dove. "Kathryne, we must turn to the Almighty for strength. He will protect us. I know that he is unwilling to see us suffer."

Kathryne looked up into his eyes. "Do you believe that, William?"

He squeezed her hand. "With all my heart."

She sniffed again, her eyes still moist. "William, what of my father? Will God protect my father as well?"

*And how do I answer this question?* he wondered. *Lord Aidan is in a most precarious position. How will God extricate him from being painted with the same brush that has painted his evil brother?*

Will lowered his head, trying to think of the right words. He looked up and his mouth began to move, but no words came. He stopped again and pondered, and his thoughts found no firm purchase. Finally, after a full moment, he spoke.

"God must be watching over your father. God will see that he comes to no harm. I am sure that level heads will prevail as the story of last night is told. There are reasonable men who hold sway in London, are there not?"

As Will spoke, Kathryne's face looked as if it crumpled, her eyes darkened, her lips pursed and turned down, and tears began to streak down her cheeks once more.

"I cannot bear to see him humiliated. It is so unfair. None of this evil was his doing, and yet even I have heard talk that he was with Radcliffe as his evil plot was hatched," Kathryne said.

She brushed the palm of her hand across her face, wiping tears from her cheeks. "What will happen to him?" she cried. "Will he be arrested for the loss of the gold?"

Will pursed his lips. *I am unsure of what might transpire—but to be honest, arrest is within the realm of the government's response,* he thought. He answered, "Kathryne, such things will not happen. I am sure that the events can be explained in such a manner that all will understand."

She sniffed again. "William, is it true that you have told my father that your vow prevents you from pursuing Radcliffe?"

William nodded. "We have spoken of this before, Kathryne. I see no way I can forswear that vow, of which you were a witness."

"Can John or the English navy offer any hope of providing an effective pursuit of Radcliffe? Could they bring Radcliffe to justice?"

He averted his eyes, and Kathryne began to cry again, knowing that his hesitation was as sure as stating no.

"Kathryne," he stated, trying to explain, "a most skilled captain with the few ships that remain undamaged might find it easy to locate the brigands. Their island, if what Foxton said is true, is no more than three days' sail from here. They could be found if one were to sail with the next high tide. But to recover what was lost would take the most cunning and daring man. And a great helping of luck—or divine intervention—to prove successful."

Kathryne dabbed at her tears. "And there is no man on Barbados to accomplish that?"

Will shook his head.

"Save yourself, that is," she stated, "for that is the impression your words present."

Will stood and stepped one step closer to the sea. After a long moment, he replied. "Kathryne, I am not a man to boast, and I know not if such a feat might be accomplished. Yet I do know that neither John, nor the English captain—fine men both—are men able to accomplish such a task." His hands were open at his waist, palms out. "But, dearest wife, why do you pursue such a matter?"

She glared back at him, a most unexpected response.

Will continued, "I know that Lord Aidan is in a most bedeviling predicament. I have considered his plight, and while he is not in an enviable situation, I would offer that the worst fate that may befall him is to be removed as governor of this island. Perhaps a vindictive court may remove his land grants on this soil as well."

Kathryne's face looked like it was about to crack with pain.

"But, Kathryne," he cried, "there are still the land and estate in England. There will still be reserves held in trust. There will be gold enough to leave a legacy to you. You should not be afraid of losing your inheritance."

She stood up from her seat, rushed at William, and caught him in total surprise by striking at his chest with her open palms. Her blows fell on Will's bruises, causing him great pain.

"How dare you say that!" she cried. "This has nothing to do with a desire to preserve my inheritance!" Her eyes blazed with anger.

"But, Kathryne," he sputtered, shocked and amazed at her sudden anger, "I was simply stating what appeared to be obvious—"

She slapped his chest again with her palms. "Obvious!" she shouted. "Obvious! That a daughter seeks to soothe her father's pain? That a father is concerned as how to maintain the untarnished reputation of his family's name? That a man seeks to leave his honor unblemished in the eyes of his God and his king?"

She stepped away from Will, then spun back, her eyes on fire. "You think this is a matter of gold?" she cried out. "William Hawkes, have you not listened to a word I have uttered over the past year? Have I asked you about your money? Have I spoken of the trust I will receive in a year? Have I insisted that you build the type of dwelling I am accustomed to living in? Have I insisted on a multitude of servants and maids?"

He took a step toward her, and she raised her hand to him, palm out, bidding him stop.

"Do you not hear my words as I pray to the Almighty? Have you heard me ask for riches? Have you ever heard me ask for any blessings of that kind?"

Will attempted to answer, but she barked out her own reply.

"William, if God were to take it all from me tomorrow, yet left me with his love . . ." Her voice began to crack and tremble.

". . . I would have said *your* love, William, but it appears that your thoughts are very different than mine, and you are not the man I thought you were. If God were to take all I have, yet continue to love me, then I would be rich indeed."

She stared at him, cold and angry. "This is indeed not about money, William. Until you realize that, I have no more words to speak to you."

She spun on her heels, ran to her horse, and before William could regroup from his surprise, she had leapt on the saddle and was spurring the horse toward Shelworthy.

He limped after her for a dozen yards calling out her name, pleading that she stop, asking for opportunity to explain himself, until he lost sight of her in a trail of dust.

*How can he think that my desire is to preserve the family wealth?* Kathryne thought as Porter slowed to a trot. *Does he not know anything of how my heart is set?*

She was surprised to find herself halfway to her father's home, for she had paid but scant attention to her surroundings. Porter must have taken the lead, for her eyes were filled with a mist. She reached for a kerchief and wiped them dry for what felt like the hundredth time that day, and then reached down and patted the horse's neck.

"Good horse, Porter," she cooed. "At least you seem to understand my needs. You always seem happy that I appear at your stall."

She sniffed loudly, sure that her nose was red and her eyes were bloodshot and swollen from crying.

"I wish none of this had ever happened," she called out softly to her horse, and tears began to fall again as she realized the futility of her wishes.

# 77

Lord Aidan had dismissed John Delacroix and Bryne Tambor, thanking them for their help, promising that he would send word immediately if he formulated a more logical plan in response to the pirate attack. He realized as they left that he had no options left. With one ship left in its fleet, the navy would be incapable of offering chase. The other private ships had no captains worthy of such a mission. There was no method of informing England and the naval headquarters in London before a month or more had passed, and by that time the gold would be gone, divided a hundred ways.

John Delacroix's parting words that day rang in Aidan's ears: "There be but one man able to accomplish what manner of task you seek—and that be Captain William Hawkes."

Aidan slumped in his chair behind his desk, absently twiddling a quill in his hand. He had intended to write a letter seeking help and assistance from the governor of St. Christopher, but his laughter became twisted as he realized that even sailing to that island and back would take too long.

Aidan lifted his head in response to a soft tapping at his door. "Yes," he called out.

Emily swung the door open and entered. "May I have a word with you? Perhaps this is too troubling of a time to ask such a favor?"

As she entered the room, Aidan smiled, in spite of his most pressing decisions and dire circumstances. She was dressed in the simplest gown, a swirl of greens about her, colors that so suited her complexion. Her face, showing her fatigue and concern, still radiated the joy of her heart that was so much a part of her being.

"Dearest Emily," he said, "there is no day so bleak that your presence could not improve it. Please come in, sit, talk with me."

She arranged herself on the chair and folded her hands in her lap, looking as if she was prepared to take afternoon tea.

"Aidan, much to my amazement, there seem to be no secrets on this island. Events happen, and within moments every living creature here knows of them."

Aidan nodded and smiled back at her. He was often overcome at how similar she and Kathryne were—both needed to preface their thoughts at great length before getting to the heart of the matter. Aidan had learned that he needed simply to sit quietly and wait, for to jump into the stream too early meant only confusion and miscommunication.

"And," she continued, "I would never deign to interfere in your affairs, my dear, nor the affairs of state."

He nodded again.

"And it is only recently, since we have agreed to be married, that I have thought it appropriate to even venture forth with my opinions on these matters."

Aidan nodded again, feeling that she drew close to her true desires.

"I know that you face a most unpleasant task—explaining to London what has transpired. I know that Kathryne has returned from her husband this afternoon, distraught and most upset. I know that it appears as if you have very few choices as to what may be done to rectify this distressing situation."

He nodded throughout her words, agreeing with all she said.

"May I make a suggestion, Aidan?"

"Of course, Emily."

"May we join in prayer about these matters?"

Aidan was about to speak, but he held his first words of response in check. He knew that he was not the most obedient believer. He insisted on church attendance and was a most honorable and respectable man, but he had never taken the reins of the spiritual life of his home. In fact, he often avoided speaking of spiritual matters, for knowing how little time he spent on such things, he found such conversation awkward.

But it would have proven no benefit to change the subject. He looked at Emily's tender expression and knew that her heart beat for him and that, above all, she desired him to know the peace and joy that she knew in God.

"Emily, that is the kindest offer anyone has presented me in months."

He reached over the desk, ignoring the papers and thick documents, and took her hand in his.

"Emily, I must admit I am frightened, for I see no passage through this storm. To lose this office will not concern me, for I can return to Broadwinds if I must. But to see the Spenser name so sullied and degraded—and to be forced to live in the shadow of suspicion for the rest of my days—that hurts deep in my soul."

Emily squeezed his hand. "My sweet Aidan. I would offer all I have to prevent you that pain."

"As I would for you, dear Emily. But there is no safe exit. And I have not gone to God as you have so often done, and for that my heart is troubled as well. You have been so much more faithful than I."

Emily leaned forward, her eyes bright. "But, Aidan, it is never too late to turn back to God. He calls to us day and night, and all we must do is answer."

"It is not that simple, Emily. There are amends to be made, for certain. One does not simply call upon God after all these years and expect him to listen."

Emily arched her face in surprise, pulling Aidan closer to her. "But indeed, Aidan, that is what will happen. Do not think you need do penance for past sins. He will forgive if you ask and will hear your prayers. He hears all prayers. He does, Aidan. He truly does."

Aidan shut his eyes tight. He understood her words, but could not release his heart to follow. He had relied for so long on his own strength. God would surely be at the end of his patience with him now.

"Aidan," Emily whispered, her words firm and crisp in the warm afternoon sun, "all you need do is ask. It is true what I say. God will listen."

She waited for a long moment.

"Aidan," she whispered, words etched with care, "will you pray now? Will you ask God to help you?"

There was silence.

"Aidan?" she called out again.

Aidan did not open his eyes, but began to speak. "Heavenly Father, I have not turned to you for so many years. Please forgive me. This day my soul hurts for what has happened to the people you have entrusted to my care. I am in distress, Lord. I seek no return of gold, but simply that the Spenser name be undefiled and untarnished. Can the wrongs that have occurred be made right? Can you provide us guidance and protection as we seek to do your will? That, dear God, is my prayer to you this day."

He blinked his eyes open, and Emily beamed in happiness at the wall that had just tumbled into the sea—the wall between Aidan and his Lord.

████ ██ ████

Will stood in the middle of that dusty path for many long moments, watching Kathryne disappear over the horizon. Even after she had gone from his vision, he stood, staring in her direction.

He tried to connect his thoughts, but they seemed to be lost in a maelstrom of conflicting images and emotions.

He wanted to honor his wife and provide assistance to her father, but it meant breaking his vow to one who had the most sway on his existence. How could he serve and honor God by breaking his promise? And if he did not break his promise, how could he ever serve and honor his wife?

Those thoughts swirled about as he stood there, and he struggled to lay hold of something, a thought that might provide him an anchor in such deep, troubled seas.

The anchor that God provided was Luke.

The black man had spent his morning at the fort, tending to those who needed him and then napping for a few hours in the shade of the powder house. He awoke, found a handful of cooked grains and a dried fish for his lunch. He squatted down to eat, and as he chewed he looked over at Will's cottage. He watched as Kathryne turned away from Will's arms, as she jumped upon her horse, as her thick hair flowed behind her like a stream as she rode off away from her husband. Luke chewed and watched as Will stood there, looking north along the road, not moving.

Luke quickly finished his meal, brushed the few crumbs from his doublet and loose breeches, cut at the knee and frayed, and went to Will, to where he was needed.

"Luke be watchin' Massa Will. Massa Will be needin' Luke," he stated firmly, with clear purpose, as he came up behind William.

Will started and turned, not expecting anyone, plainly appearing as if he wanted to see no one.

"Luke, I have no time for this now. I have no injuries I care for you to heal." Smiling, Will held up his arms, palms out, stopping Luke where he stood.

Luke brushed away Will's arms. "Massa Will need listen to Luke."

Will shrugged, realizing he had no choice but to hear him out.

"Massa Will not chase pirates?"

Will nodded.

"Massa Will think God be angry if he do?"

"Luke, I made a solemn vow to never attack another man in anger! Do you want me to ignore that on a whim?"

Luke growled, "Luke don' know dat word. But Massa Will be wrong. He be wrong."

"Keeping a promise is wrong?"

Luke pursed his lips, clenched his fists, and said nothing.

"Is that wrong, Luke? To keep my promise? Do you recall my promise to set you free from the chains of slavery? I kept that promise! If I had not done so, would you be here today? No. And this day you want me to break a promise made to the Almighty."

"Don' be mixin' up stories. If Luke was still bein' a slave, it be God who do it, not Massa Will. You be tellin' Luke dat a promise you made wi' God be stoppin' you from chasin' dem pirates?"

Will nodded.

"You done promise God you not be cap'n no more," Luke said, his voice going softer. "Dat be good, Massa Will. God don' like men goin' after men wi' knives and such. But goin' after dese pirates be diff'rent. You be doin' good by catchin' bad men. You not be bad man dis time."

Luke looked deep in thought as he paused. Then he brightened and continued. "Luke think you mean to promise God dat you be bad no more, dat you don' steal from inn'cent people. If you know dat you be needed to be cap'n for good reason, you'd said de promise diff'rent. Ain't dat right?"

Will's face showed his surprise. Finally he answered, "Perhaps I might have if I had known such a situation would occur."

Luke reached out and placed his hands on Will's shoulder. "God know dat promise come from your heart, Massa Will. But he know dat dis island need you now. But God know what you mean to promise. He know dat."

The two men stared into each other's eyes. Will searched Luke's eyes for comfort and healing; Luke searched Will's for courage and strength.

"Massa Will, you need to be doin' what you be good at. God make you good at bein' de cap'n on de boat. You be dat man, and God take care of de rest. He will, Massa Will. You be tellin' me bout dat all de time. God be takin' care of de things he be takin' care of, and we be takin' care of de things we be takin' care of. Dat what you been tellin' me, Massa Will, ain't it?"

Will closed his eyes. For the first time in two days, his heart regained its natural rhythm, beat at its normal pace. For the first time in two days, Will felt his soul at peace.

He looked up at Luke, whose leathery face was full of expectation and hope, full of love and concern. Will leaned forward and embraced him.

As he held Luke, he lifted his eyes to the sea, then to the harbor, and to the sea again.

As if washed in a spring deluge that cleaned the soot and dust from his eyes, Will saw what he must do.

Knowing that time was his most precious resource of the moment, William knew that he could not visit Shelworthy. The tides would be right only for a short while longer, and if he wanted to sail this week, he, and the small armada, must leave within the day.

If the truth be told, Will was not certain if he could gaze into Kathryne's eyes and tell her all of the truth. He did not think he could look into her heart and tell the words he needed to speak.

"My dearest Kathryne," he wrote, his pen moving fast across the vellum with a hasty scratch. He did not have a poet's afternoon to let his emotions be fully recorded.

The moment you read this, we will be at sea, pursuing San Martel. It is a role that only I can fill. Do not be fearful for me, for this sailing is a simple matter. If the gold is within our reach, we will recover it, and I will sail back into your arms. If not, and we are unsuccessful, your arms will still await my return.

Do not fret, dear wife, over what vexations my soul encountered with the vow I made before you so many months ago. God knows the truths in my heart—and he knows the import of a vow, uttered by a foolish man, desperate to impress a woman whom he feared he was losing.

God has used you and Luke to help me see the error of my thoughts and help me understand. It is not only Governor Spenser who needs my help, it is all of Barbados. I am not attacking, but defending England's assets, as well as the island's future, from a truly evil man. I cannot refuse to heed the call of Barbados, the land I hold so dear.

My dearest wife, pray for me. Pray for all of us. I will only think of the day when I am back at your side.

> *I remain your most loving husband,*
> *William.*

William hoped, as he sealed the letter and handed it to a messenger, that his words would all ring true. He hoped that she would believe that the voyage was merely a simple matter. He hoped that she would believe that he sailed into no great danger.

There was little time for niceties such as strategic planning and organizing before Will and his ships were to sail on the rising tide at dawn. All that could be managed in such a short period was to prepare each vessel with crew, cannon, and provisions.

John had done a masterful job at gathering up sailors and crews within the span of a single afternoon and night. Thirty-five men from the *Reprisal* still lived on Barbados, and all had volunteered without hesitation to serve again under their "Cap'n Will." John had had his pick of the English sailors, none of whom would be sailing under naval authority on this voyage, but under command of William Hawkes, most recently recommissioned as master privateer under orders of the governor of Barbados, Lord Aidan Spenser.

Within hours of combing the waterfront and public houses, John had signed on more than two hundred sailors and a full complement of junior officers, cannon masters, gunners, and marines. On this voyage, each man sailing under Will's flag would be paid a small fraction of captured treasure, if the treasure was to be found. Few men, when making their marks upon the official rosters, had questioned the division and percentages. Fewer still had questioned the odds of a successful voyage. It was enough to most that Will's distribution of shares bested the wages the English navy offered. Sailors had so few options in their lives that any chance at bettering their lot was quickly seized with little or no consideration as to its ultimate consequence.

"So if I meet me maker on this voyage," one old salt had remarked as he signed on, "it be no better nor worse than any day in which I draw breath in the king's navy."

With crews in place, the men had commandeered nearly every wagon and draft animal in Bridgetown and hauled the salvaged cannons, powder, and shot from the fort to the tiny three-ship armada.

The captains and seconds-in-command of the other two vessels—the *Water Sprite* and the *Resolve*—boarded longboats and rowed to the side of Will's ship, the *Dorset Lady*. Once on deck, the men gathered in the small officers' mess, and Will looked into their faces, wondering how many would face death on this short voyage.

The next two hours were spent charting their intended route on Will's maps. If the information that Geoffrey Foxton had voiced during his final moments was accurate, Will thought their three ships and small force might indeed have a whisker of a chance of success. Will hoped that Geoffrey had been truthful—at least this one time.

Will knew the small island of Guajiro well. Its deep and natural harbor—the only harbor capable of sheltering the pirate ships—was marked with a most distinctive feature. Its mouth was narrow and tight, formed by two great fingers of rocky outcropping coming together to almost pinch the opening of the harbor closed. Those narrow, rocky fingers were covered with a tangle of palms and vines. The mouth of the harbor was wide enough for two, perhaps three, ships to pass jointly, but no more, for jagged shards and projections of razor-sharp coral protected the shore. The channel was deep enough for the largest of the vessels, but only just so.

That was Will's trump card, he thought, for if that brief expanse of water could be guarded or protected or imperiled, the slimmest of chances for a successful undertaking existed.

Will was well acquainted with the officers of his new command, for the fraternity of sailors and captains was, in truth, quite small. Richard Nash was a brash officer, given to posturing and boasting, but yet a most competent sailor. Will had observed him once neatly squeeze his vessel through a crowded harbor, its waters boiled by the edge of a hurricane. He would be the captain of the *Water Sprite*. Austin Hough was also a fine sailor, notorious for his stern visage and punctilious manner. In all his years in the king's navy, it was rumored that the man had never smiled. He would captain the English naval vessel, the *Resolve*.

Will's plan was sketchy, brief, and bold. As Will outlined it, he recognized it was full of "possibles," "could-bes," and "if-God-wills-its." But planning time was short, and all knew that any plan would require improvisation under fire.

As the meeting ended, each officer being assigned a set of specific tasks, John Delacroix whispered to Richard Nash, "If any man can bring victory to this sailing, it be William Hawkes. His heart follows the will of God."

Nash nodded sagely.

"Will may follow God," Austin Hough added in his flat, even tone, "but I would offer additional prayers that God would follow Will."

And as he ducked through the narrow, short doorway, John saw a hint of a smile cross Hough's lips.

■ ■ ■ ■ ■

Mrs. Cole paced about in her spacious room at Shelworthy. Since the hour of the attack, she could barely keep her thoughts in order. She looked out to the waters of the Caribbean, which until a couple of days ago had brought her joy. But after having been visited by such tragedy born of the sea, her eyes saw only fear, not happiness.

She sat at the foot of the bed and folded her hands.

*Prayer will help,* she told herself. *If I pray, then peace will return.*

*Dearest Almighty, I beg for your forgiveness for my anger and my thirst for revenge. I want William to smite those brigands in your name, Lord, but I know that it is yours to seek vengeance, not mine.*

*Lord, please protect dear William. I know that he has told Kathryne that such a sailing will be a simple matter and that if the gold is not easily recovered he will sail home. I know that Kathryne believed him, Lord, and I ask you to forgive him for telling her such a falsehood.*

*Please keep him safe as he sails. She will not be able to live without him. And he will offer his life for her. Lord, bring them all home.*

*Bless us this day, Lord. Amen.*

She twisted a lace handkerchief in her hands. "He lied to her," she said softly. "He lied about the dangers, and she believed him."

She sighed and dropped her head. "May God protect us all."

*Caribbean Sea*

Luke seated himself at the prow of the ship, almost at the very tip of the forward spar, dangling his feet in the salty spray that hissed out from under the bow. The black man never ventured into the warm sea when he was on land, always walking well away from the surf when he found himself on a beach. But the allure of water as seen from the deck of a ship was another matter, and he would stay on the spar for hours, smiling and laughing as the waves tossed about him, drenching him at times in the rolling shower of seawater.

Dusk was but several moments from the horizon. An object was spotted in the water off to the starboard side. The *Dorset Lady* slipped to her right and discovered that it was an empty rum barrel—a barrel seized from an English ship in Bridgetown by the pirates.

They indeed were on the right tack.

The moon lay at an eighth, providing a sickly pale light, just barely bright enough to sail. Will ordered lanterns be set fore and aft on each ship and full sails maintained through the night. A tripling of the watch was ordered, for he wanted no mishaps to occur between the small fleet he captained.

Talk among the men was muted. So quickly had they come together that bonds and friendships were not yet close and intimate. Most likely the shortness of this sail would provide scant chance for such friendships to be set more solidly. Will knew that men fought harder, longer, and were willing to sacrifice more if they fought with their backs to an old friend. That would not occur on this voyage, and Will hoped it would not prove fatal.

John was on the foredeck as well, and as Luke saw Will approach, he sidled back along the spar of the ship and clumped to the deck in obvious enthusiasm. Despite his dislike of being in the sea, he so greatly enjoyed sailing upon it.

"'Twas a grand day for a first sailing," John remarked as he leaned against the rail.

"Sailin' be fast. Luke likes de sailin' fast," Luke said as he squatted on the deck.

Will nodded to both men.

*It has been a grand day,* Will thought. *Until I ventured back onto this ship, I had no true remembrance as to how much I loved sailing and how much I missed the wind and the ropes and the deck's roll and pitch under my feet.*

"Indeed, a good day," Will spoke after a moment. "I pray that tomorrow and the next and the next be as fruitful."

John crossed his arms across his chest in an odd gesture that spoke of a winter's chill.

"William," he finally asked, "what caused you to alter your thinkin'? When you left Shelworthy, I would have taken an oath that no force in heaven or earth would cause a modification of your resolve to keep your vow—at least not the William I knew."

"And this troubles you, John?" Will asked, his voice light. "Would you have preferred that I stayed on Barbados and sent you out in command of this venture?"

John laughed. "'Twould be a command I would refuse in a twinklin'. And no, Will, I am glad that you have done as you have." John's voice lowered and grew serious. "I seek revenge on those Spanish dogs. They killed a valued friend when they ended the life of John Tambor."

John paused, and to Will it sounded as if his friend was preventing a sob from forming in his chest. John gulped once and continued.

"William, it is because of you that I am on Barbados. It is because of you that I have by my side the most wonderful wife in all the world. And when I required a model on which to base a decision, or what manner is most proper to deal with my crew or customers—it is you whom I have used as that example. I have judged myself against the constant propriety of your actions."

Will placed a hand on John's shoulder. "Had I known, friend, I would have endeavored to conduct myself at an even higher standard, for I am sure I have presented a failed example on too numerous of occasions."

The deck rolled slightly as the evening breezes increased.

John closed his eyes for a moment, as if greatly considering his words. He lifted his hand to Will's, which was still on his shoulder, placed his over the top of his friend's hand, and squeezed.

"No, Will, that is not true. I have seen no manner of your behavior that I did not wish to follow in my own life. I watched as you dealt with your crewmen at the fort and patterned myself after that as I dealt with my men at the chandlery. I watched as you invited the blackamoors, the prostitutes, the peasants to the fort on Sunday—without reproach and with love. I have tried to be as inviting as that."

John lowered his eyes for a moment. "I watched to see how you treated Kathryne as a wife. It is much different from the examples I saw as a child, Will. You are kind and considerate and caring, never rebuking harshly, never demanding, never cruel. I try to practice those manners with Missy as well."

"John," Will said, his tone soft and tender, "I merely attempt to follow what the Scriptures have instructed. That is the best path any man may follow."

John turned away for a moment and coughed loudly, attempting to hide his emotions.

"Do you know why I had so little trouble in gathering up these sailors? Why this recruitment took only hours—rather than weeks?" John asked.

Will shook his head.

"It is because when I mentioned that you would be the captain of the voyage, the admiral of our excursion, to a man each said that is all he needed to know. If you be at the helm, they could follow without question."

It was Will's turn to feel the hot threat of expressing his emotions. He turned away for a moment to look forward, hoping the cool night air would wash the blush away from his cheeks.

"William, it is because of all of what I have said that I need your answer this night. The true meaning has just struck my heart. I feel as though I am part to blame for causing you to break a vow to God. And if that be such, I will see to it that you are set adrift back to Barbados on a longboat before the morning light—for I could not face the dawn if I caused a godly man to fall into the hands of Satan."

This time, John sniffed loudly and wiped at his nose and eyes with the long sleeve of his woolen doublet.

"Tell me, William. Have I caused you to sin?" he asked in earnest. "Did you do this—" he indicated the ships with a wide sweep of his arm—"because the governor and I begged your reconsideration? Did you do such a thing because you were afraid I would foolishly attempt it myself?"

Will turned and faced into the wind for a long moment, his hands on the rail, his body bent into the rush of cool air. He breathed in deep, filling his lungs with the cleansing air of the dark sea. He turned back to them and sat against the railing.

"There is no one on this earth that might cause me to abandon my faith in God. There is no one who could come between me and my service to him. Not you, not Kathryne, not her father, not Vicar Mayhew, not anyone."

"But, Will," John protested, "have I not caused you to break your vow to God?"

"I do not believe, John, that I really have broken my vow. For Luke has helped me see that what I spoke to God and what I meant to say were two different things. When I made my vow, I was concerned that Kathryne know that my heart had indeed changed, that I was serious in turning from my ways as a privateer and pirate. For—I must be truthful to you who have been so honest with me—I made that vow, in part, to impress the heart of a woman I loved.

"I should have said to God that I would never raise my blade in an offensive manner against any innocent person, or take vengeance out of anger. Had I thought through the logic of my promise before refusing to lead this venture, I would have seen that difference between my past activities and our current goal. San Martel and Radcliffe are hardly innocent in this matter, and I am reclaiming gold owned by the Crown and clearing the governor's name."

"But, Will," John asked, "does God not view a vow as a vow? Does he concern himself with what you now think you should have uttered?"

Luke smiled. "God done see you. He see all dat you do. It be good dat God understand."

Will nodded. "God indeed understands. He knows what is in my heart now and what was in my heart then. God seems to have placed me—William Hawkes—on this island, at this time, with my abilities and talents, for a certain reason. I don't believe he would have placed me here had he not intended for me to take action. I will be honest and admit that my heart still holds many questions. Why would God use me as an instrument of justice? Why send me and not the full English fleet? Would not that be more expeditious? Why three small ships against a whole convoy of pirates?"

John nodded, his face almost lost in the night's darkness. "Indeed the questions I have pondered as well, William."

"Why, then, do we find ourselves on this ship, sailing into the very maw of a great danger?" Will stepped towards both men. "I will speak the plain truth. Since Luke helped open my eyes, it is my heart that tells me I have done what the Lord has called me to do. My heart is at such peace that I scarce recognize its beating in my chest."

"Do not the odds against this being a successful sailing weigh against your heart, my friend?" John asked.

"When I took my leave of Kathryne—what seems to be so long ago—I knew that I would not be denied seeing her face again."

"Dat be a word from de Lord?" Luke asked, excited.

"No, Luke, I do not believe it was a message from the Almighty, but it was a message from here," Will said firmly, tapping at where his heart beat.

"Dat be de same to Luke," he stated. "God talk to de heart, yes, Massa?"

"Perhaps," Will replied. "Perhaps."

"Let us pray that Luke is correct," John added.

And as Will bent to his knees to begin to pray, his first rejoicing words—silent from the rest—were praise that it was John who called them to thank their Creator.

## Barbados

Kathryne sat on a rough wooden bench at the water's edge on the north side of the harbor, just steps away from the chandlery.

That morning she had found Will's note and had quickly roused Emily, Hattie, and a number of other servants and laborers and led them, almost as a parade, to the harbor. After seeing Will and the three ships sail off at dawn, Kathryne had led her troops to the still-smoldering ruins of the Bridgetown waterfront and had assigned specific tasks to each. Some helped clean a damaged home, some raked away the charred remnants of a building, and others helped staff a makeshift kitchen to serve food to those who had lost all they had.

After settling all those from Shelworthy in their tasks, Kathryne walked back to the chandlery and for several hours assisted Missy and others in writing letters to family back in England, informing them as to the death of a loved one. Kathryne struggled to remain unaffected and strong as men and women sat before her, in tears, relating the last few hours of the life of their wife or husband or friend. She sat at a rough desk, two wide planks spread between supports, with a full inkwell and several new quills. The makeshift desk was outdoors, in the cool shade of a large outbuilding of the chandlery.

To the grieving, Kathryne offered her prayers, her compassion, her care—making sure that she did not simply issue practiced platitudes and Scriptures in return for their pain.

It was late afternoon when Kathryne spotted a woman in a revealing light red dress edging toward the corner of the open shed where she sat. Kathryne stared without making it look obvious, for she was trying to match the woman's face with a name.

Suddenly it came to her. "Good day—Eileen, is it not? Would you like me to write a letter for you?" Kathryne indicated with her open palm for Eileen to sit at the desk.

Eileen sidled up closer. Kathryne had never truly met this woman, but she had been pointed out by others on more than one occasion. She was aware that Eileen also attended the services on Sundays at the fort, but never mingled with the rest of the attendees. Kathryne knew full well the woman's profession and made a silent vow that she would not treat her any differently than she had treated anyone else that day.

"Please sit, Eileen," Kathryne said. "Do you wish me to write to someone? I am certain it will be only a week, perhaps two, until the next ship leaves here bound for England."

Eileen smiled and shook her head. "Thank you, Mrs. Hawkes, but no. I have no need of sending a letter." She paused for a moment. "And I know how to read and write."

Kathryne stopped herself from raising her eyebrows in surprise. Women of Eileen's profession seldom, if ever, possessed that ability.

"Indeed, I did not know that, Eileen. . . . Eileen, I feel most awkward," Kathryne said, "for I do not know your last name."

"It is Palmerston, Mrs. Hawkes."

Kathryne tilted her head upon hearing that name. "Palmerston?" she replied, holding her voice pleasant and cordial. "I believe I knew a Viscount Palmerston of Taunton."

*And why did I say that?* Kathryne scolded herself. *For he and this woman could scarce be related.*

A flinty look passed over Eileen's face for a brief moment. "Indeed," she replied. She hesitated, then said, "He is my father."

Kathryne opened her mouth in shock, and then closed it.

"Then—I mean, how . . ." Kathryne let the words trail off, for no words she chose seemed appropriate.

"Mrs. Hawkes, such a story is best told at some other time. I came here this day not to reveal such a matter, but for another reason."

Struggling to slow her fleeting thoughts and regain composure, Kathryne nodded, then asked, "And what might that reason be?"

"It is about your husband, William."

And as she spoke those words, there was a moment of sheer panic and terror in Kathryne's heart. *What would William and this woman have in common that she would seek me out? Have there been things in William's life that I am unaware of?*

"Mrs. Hawkes, please. I beg you not to think what you are thinking. Will would not allow himself to be sullied by the likes of me. Oh, I tried my best on many occasions, but Will always treated me like a lady.

"I am here to tell you that your husband saved my life—and I simply knew I had to share that with someone. You were the first to come to mind."

For the next dozen minutes, Eileen sketched out, in the barest words, how she had come to the island and what had happened in the ocean that day. She told of how William had appeared when she called out to God and how he drew her back to shore, saving her from a most certain death in the warm, salty waters of the Caribbean.

"As he drew me out, Mrs. Hawkes, I felt a cleansing that I had never known could exist in my heart. It was like I was . . . unburdened. I do not understand it."

Eileen lowered her eyes. "Is it true that God forgives our sins, Mrs. Hawkes?"

"That is a truth of the ages," Kathryne said.

"And that God can forgive a woman like myself?"

"He could forgive a woman like me, Eileen. He could forgive a woman as you. Sin is sin to God, whether it be the sin of pride or greed or anger—or any sin that you may have committed. Do you remember the story of Mary Magdalene from the Scriptures? I know William has not spoken of her much—but then, men know so little of women."

Eileen managed a thin, hopeful smile through her tears.

"Mary was possessed by seven demons, and Jesus drove those demons out when he entered her life. One might think a woman like that, filled with evil, could be of no use to God. But Mary was at the foot of the cross when Jesus was crucified, and she was the first person to see the risen Christ. I tell you these words so you will understand that when Christ enters your life, the evils in your past are driven away."

Eileen spoke no louder than a whisper of a breeze. "Then I am forgiven?"

Kathryne reached out and placed her hand over Eileen's hand. "You are forgiven if you have asked for forgiveness, Eileen," she said. "Have you asked for such forgiveness?"

Eileen nodded her head, obviously overcome with emotion.

"Then you are forgiven. Jesus has forgiven you."

In a small voice, Eileen whispered back, "Is this lightness in my heart what forgiveness feels like?"

Kathryne nodded, smiling, rejoicing with her with a tear or two of her own.

Another pair of women had shuffled around the corner, weeping, each wearing the black of a widow.

Eileen stood quickly. "I shall not take up more of your time, Mrs. Hawkes. I knew I must tell you of this."

She turned, and just prior to walking away, said, "If it be possible, Mrs. Hawkes, since I cannot return to what brought me to this island, would you know of someone who needs a servant who can read and write?"

## 80

Kathryne returned home that evening, leading her ragged parade of helpers. Their walk had slowed from the eagerness of the morning, and they sniffed about, realizing that most were fouled with the smell of smoke and ash. Some smelled more of death, for Boaz and Jeb had spent their day preparing two dozen bodies for their final resting place. While everyone knew that death was but the inevitable end to life's journey, few felt comfort in dealing with anyone so soon departed. Jeb and Boaz had done much the same work in their village on the west coast of Africa and had volunteered to provide the service this day. As a result, most others kept their distance, feeling in their hearts that touching the dead changed a man, and that the spell of it might linger about a person for many days.

Kathryne was gladdened as Shelworthy came into view. She wanted to wash the dust of the day from her face. She wanted to slip on a fresh and clean gown. She wanted to speak to someone who was not about to cry or already weeping. More than anything, she wanted a thick, hot cup of coffee with a sweet cake layered in sugar and honey. For a moment, her thoughts turned to England and the kitchen at Broadwinds and Mrs. Cole's scones with clotted cream and strawberry jam.

And as the darkness embraced her parade, she felt a curious twinge from deep within her. She stopped and stood, silent and still, as the twinge grew, from a place deep inside her. Then, as quickly as it began, it was over. A very small and secret part of Kathryne knew—but the rest of her simply walked on in the darkness.

Later that evening, a cleaned and refreshed Kathryne took a light meal in the dining chamber, including the sweets she craved, with Emily providing company for her. Aidan was at the Carruthers plantation with a small group of respected estate and plantation owners to discuss what would need to be done to rebuild and repair.

"In life there is pain," Emily replied to Kathryne's stories of dealing with the words of death in a dozen letters. "There is no life that begins that does not include a certain measure of appointed days."

Kathryne nodded as she sipped at the thick coffee laced heavily with raw cane sugar.

"To be sure," she said, "we all face the same end. But when it occurs in such a manner, there are so many questions of why God has allowed such calamity to befall good people."

Emily placed her hand over Kathryne's hand in both comfort and understanding.

Kathryne sipped again at her coffee, then broke off a large segment of a butter biscuit and popped the sweet morsel into her mouth.

After a moment of silence, Kathryne lowered her eyes and spoke. "Emily, are you acquainted with the Palmerstons of Taunton?"

Emily tightened her mouth in thought at the oddly timed question, then brightened. "I believe I am. If I recall the details in an accurate manner, I was introduced to a Viscount Palmerston at a royal masque many years ago. I recall the event well, for the viscount was perhaps the only gentleman not participating in the festivities. He stood there, in ordinary court dress, as if participation would dishonor his reputation. A most dour, pinched man, as I recall.

"Why would you ask such a thing at this moment?" inquired Emily. "I do not recall hearing that a Palmerston was in residence on this island."

"But there is, Emily. There is a Palmerston."

"Indeed? A recent arrival? By all means, they should be invited to dine with the governor. The Palmerstons are most well known and, dare I say, well connected to the inner circle of the court. Shall we send an invitation this evening? I am certain Aidan will receive the idea with great enthusiasm."

Kathryne looked up, her eyes pained, her mouth tight. "I think not, Emily. There will be no invitations."

"But why?"

"Her name is Eileen Palmerston. She was the proprietor of the Goose."

A blankness fell over Emily's features. After a long moment, she replied. "Isn't that a public house and brothel in the harbor? Are you certain? A Palmerston?" Emily laid her hands hard and flat against the table. "I cannot believe such a thing. I simply cannot."

Emily blanched, as shocked as a person had ever appeared to Kathryne.

"Simply unheard of, Kathryne. A noble-born woman owning a brothel? To be associated with such an establishment would bring shame to any house."

Kathryne looked at Emily's face, lined with tension and anger.

"No, Emily, the woman did not simply own such a place. She . . . she . . . well, she was . . ."

Kathryne waited for Emily to realize the unspoken. When she saw Emily's face take on an even greater appearance of shock, Kathryne spoke again.

"Such a thing is true, Emily, for she told me so herself. Ownership as well as participation."

Emily's hand went to her throat.

Kathryne began to tell of the story that Eileen had related to her that day, holding nothing back, and ending with Eileen's acceptance of God's forgiveness and her request to find gainful, honest employment as a servant.

Emily, shocked into silence, gasped at the conclusion.

"A noble woman, a woman of easy virtue, and now a servant? How topsy-turvy has this world become? How could she have spoiled her birthright so? How could that have happened?"

Kathryne took another sip of coffee, now grown cold. She winced at the coolness, but enjoyed the taste. "Emily, I do not know now what I should do."

"Surely you are not considering her request for employment?" Emily replied, her tone edging towards outrage.

"If I were to ignore her plight, would I be condemning her to return to her previous profession? What else can she do with no funds or support?"

"But could she not return to her family in Taunton? Would not they offer comfort?"

Kathryne looked hard into Emily's eyes. "Do you truly believe that she could simply return home?"

Emily paused, and after a long consideration, replied, "No, she could not return. That is true."

"And after all, this house could indeed use a servant as literate as she. For that matter, Will and I could offer her employment as well. We will need additional help."

"Have a fallen woman in your employ? Working under the same roof as yourself and your husband? She herself told you of her desire for Will. Kathryne, please reconsider such a rash act. How would such a thing appear in the eyes of civilized society?"

Kathryne did not reply, but prayed under her breath for hearts to be softened, starting with hers and Emily's.

After a long moment of silence, Emily spoke. "Perhaps I was too hasty, Kathryne. If God has forgiven her, should not we?"

Kathryne nodded, thanking God for such a prompt reply.

"And if we are not open-armed, then who will bear others' burdens?"

Kathryne nodded again.

"And as Christians, shall we not be different from the world and their views?"

"Indeed, Emily. But I will discuss this matter with William upon his return."

And as she voiced the word *return,* a sudden fear swelled within her breast. *But what if Will does not return?*

CHAPTER

81

*Caribbean Sea*

Will gathered his small fleet in a tight anchorage just as the dawn of their third day of sailing spread its buttery warmth over the calm sea. His three ships sat still, Guajiro at the horizon. Will warned all to be alert in case the pirates were unexpectedly cautious, posting lookouts at the shore. Will was sure that the pirate fleet was there—he could see the smoke of a dozen large fires.

According to their plan, Will's sailors climbed down the sides of the *Resolve* and the *Water Sprite* into longboats. Within an hour the majority of the crews jostled aboard the *Dorset Lady*.

Will knew the island of Guajiro well. The mouth of the pirates' harbor was wide enough for only two ships to pass at a time. Two ships, with cannon crews in place, could hold off an armada seeking escape from the harbor. He ordered the *Resolve* and the *Water Sprite* to start toward the cove in two nights and to stand guard at the far edges of the cove, well out of sight of the pirates' base. On the morning of the third day they were to be ready for action.

The *Dorset Lady* set sail at midday toward the eastern side of the island—a point opposite the pirates' cove. At that point lay a small village and a shallowing reef that would serve as their anchorage.

Will knew the pirates could not be overwhelmed by his small force in a frontal assauLieutenant He had a much different plan in mind. The crew would march overland and attempt to take the pirate base by stealth, attacking from the rear. Since they were outnumbered three to one, perhaps four to one, Will's plan depended as much on luck as it did on audacity and daring.

By dusk, Will reached his goal on the far side of the island. Smoke from cooking fires near the shore indicated the presence of a small group of natives. Will prayed that the chief he knew from his sailing days was still alive and would recognize him as an old friend.

The first Englishman to set foot on the sand that evening was William, holding his palms up and out in a gesture of salutation. He called out for the chief, using as many words of the native tongue as he could recall. The beach was silent, save for the rushing of the waves about his feet. The villagers would have known of their arrival an hour prior, for a sail or ship was always cause for concern.

Will called out again. "I come to see Chief Tahonen. I am William Hawkes. I come in peace."

From beyond the fringe of palms and jungle at the edge of the beach came a chorus of shouts, calls, and whistles. William struggled to catch a word or phrase that might give indication of their intentions, but the cacophony was too varied and jumbled to be deciphered.

Then silence fell across the sand like a tree tumbling to the earth.

Will stood still, his arms raised. From his left he heard a rustle, then another from his right. *I pray that this is not the omen of an attack.*

Will knew that the entire village could have been eliminated in warfare and supplanted by another, fiercer, tribe or group.

Then from the middle of the brush fringe came a hefty rustle, snapping twigs, and laughter. Striding from the dense green was Chief Tahonen, older, fatter, and grayer. His face was decorated with bold stripes of ocher and blue, and a feather-and-shell necklace dangled from his neck. He wore the briefest of waistbands and leather patches.

In a moment, Will and Tahonen were locked in an encompassing embrace of breath-stealing proportions. The chief lifted Will from the sand and then spun him about with obvious glee, laughing and cackling in a high-pitched squeal.

An instant later a group of children descended upon William as well, laughing, shouting, grabbing at his legs, holding their palms up for treats or rewards.

After a moment the chief hushed them back and with a dramatic sweep of his arm invited Will to enter the village. Following behind him, a clutch of officers, including John Delacroix, shuffled along, their eyes darting from painted face to painted face.

With much pomp and ceremony, Will was invited to sit next to the chief on a rough, woven mat of palm fronds. Their supper had been in progress when Will's ships were spotted, and now that the visitors were found to be old friends, more food was added to the smoky fires and laid upon crackling cooking stones. Strips of fish curled and browned, and hollowed gourds filled with a yeasty-smelling porridgelike beverage passed from hand to hand. The natives slurped at the drink with clear gusto; the Englishmen sipped politely, the rancid-tasting concoction proving most potent.

"White man with blue eyes and smiles who speaks our language" was Will's tribal title, a long, vowel-laden name that Will was hard-pressed to repeat.

Will knew that to present his plans and needs too early would be an affront to these people, so for several hours, until the moon began to rise, the group simply ate, laughed, and ate some more. More than four years prior to this day, Will had spent up to a week, on several occasions, at this village. And now the chief told Will, with great enthusiasm, that Captain Hawkes was a prominent feature in many of the villagers' tales and stories.

It was nearing midnight when the chief laid back against a fallen palm tree, patting his ample belly, that Will felt the timing to be suitable.

Will first inquired if the chief knew of the presence of the other sailors in the cove across the island.

The chief spat and grimaced. Will heard him utter a mild curse, referring to them in a derogatory manner. "All but the god-man," the chief said.

"God-man?" Will asked.

"God-man with us for many moon cycles. He tell us of great God who loves us and will take us to the sky when we die—if we say we love his God."

*Missionaries—on this small island?* Will wondered.

"God-man Mayhew be his name."

"Vicar Mayhew!" Will nearly shouted, scrambling to his feet in surprise. "Is that man called Vicar Mayhew?"

The chief sat up, interested. "Small man, no hair on his head, but on his face, always talking about his God."

*It cannot be,* Will cautioned his heart, *but it must!*

"That man taken to that village by sailors two days ago."

Will breathed deeply, trying to remain calm. "We must go there, Tahonen. They have taken things that belong to us, and we have come to get them back. Will you guide us to that place?"

The chief shrugged. "No one want to go there—but if you want to go, we can show you the paths."

Will bowed his head in prayer, thanking the Lord for his provision, his protection. He petitioned the Lord to grant him yet one small miracle. *I pray that Vicar Mayhew is still drawing breath. I pray that I may see him one more time—to thank him for all that he has done in my life.*

"We will show you the path," the chief grunted, "but tomorrow, after sleep. No one want to go to visit village of ignorant people in darkness."

CHAPTER

82

*Barbados*

Kathryne rose early again, her sleep troubled by fleeting images of Will riding a sea boiled into whiteness by a storm. She had called out to him in her dream, and he had extended his arm toward her, only to be buffeted into a disappearing spray, his calls drowned out by the rising terror of the wind.

Kathryne dressed in the silence of her bedchamber, the room bathed in the gray of early dawn. She bent to slip her boots on her feet, and that simple act pulled her to her knees. It was that twinge again—that thrusting, expanding feeling inside of her.

*It is not pain,* she thought as she massaged the area with her fingers, *but more like . . . more like . . .*

And there her thoughts stopped, for she had no words in which to describe what it was that she felt.

*Well, if bending is to be a problem,* she decided, *then I shall not bend this morning.*

Instead, she sat upon the floor, drew her feet up close, and managed to lace up her boots with no more curious feelings.

Her breakfast consisted of oatmeal and plain biscuits, for the thought and smell of any other food brought a deep, roiling rumble to her stomach.

Hattie served her before the rest of the servants had risen. She removed the plate of oatmeal, only half consumed, then the black woman stopped and turned back to Kathryne, bending toward her and staring with wide eyes.

"Lady Kat'ryne be ill this day?" she asked.

"No, Hattie, I do not believe so," she lied. "I simply have eaten all I care to."

Hattie inched a step closer, bending lower, putting her face on the level of Kathryne's features. "You be different this mornin'," she declared. "Your face be . . . different."

As Kathryne rode to the harbor that morning, no one was about, save for fishermen returning from their night's work. She rode through the silent town, almost unaware of the burned and charred buildings to her right and left, then set off for the chandlery.

She knew that Eileen had sought shelter there, sleeping on a mat of torn canvas sailcloth in a small protected alcove of a rear shed.

"Eileen," Kathryne called out. "May I speak with you?"

Eileen was startled awake and clutched at the thin canvas sheeting used as a blanket. She blinked her eyes in a rush, trying to clear the sleep from them. Pulling the sheet to her neck, she dumbly nodded.

Kathryne came and stood a few paces away. There was no place to sit, and Kathryne did not feel it proper to kneel upon the ground.

"Eileen, you asked me a few days ago if I might know of a place of employment for a person such as yourself."

Eileen nodded, confused and wary, slowly gathering herself together.

"It is I who have need of your services. You said you can read and write."

Eileen nodded again.

"Our home needs to be rebuilt. I require the services of a person who can draft letters to England to procure replacement items. I need a person who can remain at that site while repairs are made. I need a person who is . . . comfortable at overseeing such construction. I was going to wait for Mr. Hawkes to return, but then I decided that having the rebuilding started would be a most pleasant surprise for him upon his return."

When Kathryne went there that morning, her soul had been filled with misgivings, but as she saw Eileen's eager face, full of hope for perhaps the first time in years, those misgivings vanished.

"Will you provide that service to me, Eileen? I am willing to pay you a full pound for your work every month."

It was generous, Kathryne thought, for many laborers provided their daily services for half that amount or less.

Eileen struggled to get to her feet, shedding the canvas sheet with a shove, tugging at her gown to assure modesty.

"Mrs. Hawkes, such an offer is indeed most gracious."

Kathryne placed her hand in a wide pocket. She extracted a gold pound coin and handed it to Eileen. "This is payment in advance. I presumed you might need to have some items replaced."

Eileen's eyes opened wide at the unexpected coin.

"And if you are able, could we meet this day at the Heather Downs for the midday meal—perhaps at the two o'clock bell?"

Eileen nodded, dumbstruck.

Kathryne was about to turn and walk away. "They do serve food there, do they not?" she asked, suddenly aware that she had never entered that establishment.

"Yes, Mrs. Hawkes, they do."

"It is not a house of . . ." Kathryne was unsure of how to ask, but she knew that she could not enter a place of vile reputation.

"No, Mrs. Hawkes," Eileen said as she lowered her eyes toward the ground. "A gentlewoman may enter unafraid."

"Then it is settled. I will meet you there anon."

As Kathryne walked away, Eileen, unaware of the proper methods and procedures of prayer, simply uttered a few simple words from her heart. *Thank you, O Lord, for caring for a sinner such as I.*

## Guajiro

Will spent much of the early morning arranging his small force at the edge of the eastern beach by Chief Tahonen's village. The longboats made dozens of trips, shuttling men and supplies to the shore. Will ordered that a small crew stay aboard the *Dorset Lady,* and as the tide rose he instructed them to sail back to the other side of the island and to wait with the other two ships. They would wait there until receiving the proper signal.

The winds were slack as Will and his men entered the thick, fetid jungle. They faced a march of ten miles—not a long distance if one were tramping about in the proper and civilized English countryside. But marching through a tropical jungle was much different. The path was narrow, and it twisted back on itself again and again as it climbed the sharp, steep ridge that ran like a spine through the center of the island. Vines swept down along the path, grabbing at faces and eyes. Swarms of stinging merrywhigs, so small they could scarcely be seen, buzzed about men's faces. The palms and foliage protected their steps from what little wind there was, but not from the heat of the sun overhead. Water was hard to find, and a thin hillside stream could almost be drunk dry by the dozens of men on the march. Stinging nettles brushed against bare legs and feet. By noon, every man was thoroughly drenched in his own sweat and stung by a hundred small insects.

Will ordered a halt in the march, and his native guides set off ahead to scout their advance. He had kept his mind clear of distractions on the trek. It was most important to stay focused. If he let his mind wander, even for a moment, that might be the very second that an enemy blade reached for the tender meat of his heart. Will struggled all that morning, but forced himself not to think of the vicar, who might be held prisoner only miles from where he now stood. Even his dreams had been bleak and barren. He attempted to keep his mind free of the image of Kathryne as well. But at that task he was also not successful. A shimmering image of her face, as he had last seen her on the dock, danced before his eyes, and he determined that it be released as quickly as it arrived. He knew that holding the picture of that scene too close to his heart might give him pause in his task. He must act without regard for what he truly held dear if he was to lead effectively.

"From this point on," Will called out to his troops, "no man may speak in a louder voice than a whisper. I do not think this way will be watched by a guard, yet they may have sent a hunting party out in search of boar."

"How much longer to march, Cap'n Hawkes?" called out one sailor. "I be accustomed to getting to places on water, not on land. Me poor feet be whimpering now. They be cryin' out, 'How much longer?'"

Will smiled. "Perhaps an hour to crest of the ridge, then a shorter time in descent. If we arrive with the sun, we will remain hidden in the jungle greenery until moonrise."

True to his word, Will's troops—sweating, tired, faces streaked with dirt—arrived at a small plateau just behind the village by late afternoon. They could smell the cooking fires and hear the loud laughter and calls of the pirates. Most of them were lazing about, sitting by crude huts, eating and drinking in celebration.

Will and his men set down their weapons and waited in silence until the sun, red and glowing, settled in the west, followed within an hour by the slight moon. A thin scattering of clouds formed at dusk and brought to the night a deeper shade of black.

Will whispered that the time had arrived. Will and two dozen volunteers rose, almost as a unit, and stripped to their breeches. Each carried a small saw and two sharp blades, each as long as a baby's arm. Six black villagers volunteered as well and led the troops down a snaked path to the water's edge, several hundred yards from the village.

Without a sound, they slipped into the blood-warm waters and began to paddle and swim to their prey—the pirates' vessels resting at anchor. Four men were assigned to each ship. They swam slowly out in the black waters, carefully making their way to the stern of each ship, trying their best to cause no splash or ripple.

The ships, indeed, were unguarded and floated empty and quiet. When each group reached the rudder assembly, with its leather hinges and rope pulleys, they began to work quickly. They sawed quietly, cutting through rope, wood, hinge, and pin. Every ship was slated to receive similar treatment. The rudder lines, leading from helm to rudder, were neatly sliced through. If Will and his men were able, the great leather-and-metal hinges holding the rudder were to be cut through as well. They sliced away at cables, cutting sections from all exposed portions, making full and quick repairs practically impossible. A dozen ships lay at anchor, and in the course of an hour they crippled every one of them. As each crew finished, they slipped silently back to shore, back to the main party to await the dawn.

Will had been asked why not leave undamaged the ship carrying the gold and simply sail her back to Barbados. He explained that there was no time to decide which ship held what gold and that it was most prudent to simply disable every ship.

As Will finished his task, paddling in the warm waters he turned to the shore, and through a break in the clouds saw the shoreline illuminated. Lying beached on the sand were two smaller pinnaces, resting nearly on their sides.

He paddled closer in the blackness, realizing that there would be no way to reach and disable those vessels without alerting a pirate on shore.

*Perhaps the tides will be slight enough to keep them there,* Will thought as he began to swim carefully back to shore. *For if not, they present a most vexing complication.*

## Barbados

Kathryne walked into the Heather Downs and blinked her eyes several times, trying to accustom her vision to the dark and malodorous atmosphere—a combination of a thousand nights of spilt ale and rum, thick smoke, and tropical sweat.

Behind the rough planking that served as a bar sat a fat, slovenly creature who appeared not to have bathed in several months. Upon seeing Kathryne enter, a woman of obvious style and breeding, he sat up straight on his stool and pulled the ends of his half-opened shirt together in an effort for greater civility.

"Ma'am," he said with a nod of greeting, "ya be wantin' sompin' from me barrels?"

His accent was so thick and textured that Kathryne fought to understand a word. She tilted her head for a moment.

"Would you be from Leominster?" she asked, straining to keep her voice calm and friendly.

"Wot?" he burped back.

"Leominster," she replied. "Does your speech indicate you are from that area?"

"By the gawds almighty," he exclaimed in a toothless smile, "'tis me home. Blimy, miss, have ya family livin' in that town?"

Kathryne almost said yes, but decided that it was too vexing to describe her connection to that spot of English geography.

"Well, I am somewhat acquainted with the area," she said. "I am to wait for someone here this afternoon. Shall I take any seat to be served?"

The barman half rose from his stool, and with a sweep of his hand indicated she could take any empty table or seat in the house.

"Perhaps I might procure a serving of coffee while I wait?"

"Ya can indeed, milady," he replied, then shouted back into the rear room, apparently the kitchen, "Coffee for the lady, ya lazy lout!"

Kathryne tried not to wince and then dusted the crumbs from a bench with her handkerchief and sat at the cleanest table and waited.

In no more than a dozen moments, Eileen stepped through the door, looking much more comfortable in the surroundings than did Kathryne. She blinked a few times, coming in from the brilliant sunshine of the morning, and walked to the table, sat down, not saying a word, then looked up at Kathryne, awaiting instructions.

The cook, a thin-faced string of a woman, delivered their plates with a flick of the wrist, the plate sailing the last inch from hand to table. The fried pork, rice, fish, and biscuits jumped in unison, some rice tumbling off to the tabletop, etched with knife cuts and nicks.

She had turned to walk away when Kathryne coughed to gain her attention.

The string lady spun about, her face tight in annoyance. "Wot?" she demanded.

Kathryne sputtered for a moment. "I . . . would desire a fork and knife, if you please."

"Zounds almighty, Miss Fancy, ain't ya," the woman muttered as she skulked away, then returned several moments later with a handful of mismatched cutlery and tossed it into the center of the table.

Kathryne looked upset, more for Eileen than for herself.

"I am certain, Mrs. Hawkes," Eileen whispered, "that this place is beneath you. I would not be upset if you chose to leave."

Kathryne waved her hand in response. "No, this will be fine. I am just surprised at the woman's surliness."

"It be a good day for her, Mrs. Hawkes." Eileen smiled. "And your request for tableware and such—well, most patrons simply use their hands to eat their food."

Kathryne was unable to hold her surprise in check. *Is tableware still that rare among the common folk?* she wondered. *William was born a common man, yet it seemed even before Emily's instruction that he was aware of such niceties.*

"This can be a most uncouth establishment," Eileen continued.

Kathryne smiled as best she could, picked up a small morsel of her biscuit, and nibbled on it. She then took another larger bite. "This is most tasty," she said finally, after consuming half the item.

"Despite its flaws and service," Eileen replied, keeping her voice quiet, "the food is the best in the harbor. Their customers put up with much in order to be well fed."

"Indeed," Kathryne said as she picked up a knife and fork and then carefully wiped each one with her handkerchief.

In a short time, both their plates were half empty. Kathryne laid down her utensils, wiped daintily at her mouth, and put her hands in her lap. She felt a sense of well-being spread within her. Her queasiness of the morning had vanished.

"Eileen," she said after a moment, "it is not for me to investigate questions of a personal nature, but I am puzzled . . . most puzzled by certain matters."

Eileen continued to eat from her plate, picking up a square of smoked fish and popping it into her mouth.

"I know I have not the right to ask of such things," Kathryne added.

Eileen swallowed. "But I am now in your hire," she replied, opening the door to further questions.

"Yet should that give me privileges of intimacy?" Kathryne inquired carefully, trying to read Eileen's expression.

"If you so choose," she replied evenly.

"What is your will, Eileen? What do you wish?"

Eileen laid her hands on the table and pursed her mouth tight. After many moments, she replied. "It has been years since I have been given the option of doing what pleased me. I truly know not how to respond."

"Surely you must have some preference?" Kathryne insisted.

Eileen shook her head, indication she had none. After a moment she looked back up. "I will grant you this, Mrs. Hawkes. Ask what questions you need, and I will answer until I choose to answer no further. At that point we will cease. Does that appear to be a fair course?"

Kathryne nodded, then appeared uncertain as to how to begin.

"How long have you been on this island?" Kathryne asked, hoping her voice was neutral and friendly.

"My time here will be two years' duration when Yuletide arrives again."

Kathryne sat there, demuring, with hands in her lap, seated like a proper English lady.

*What do I ask her next? Do I presume to need to know any of her past? How do I ask her for the circumstances of her history? How does a woman of obvious breeding find herself at this place in such a state?*

Kathryne smiled, wan and slight. *How do I continue?*

Eileen broke the quiet. "You wish to ask me of the reasons I am here, do you not?"

Kathryne fought to hold her blush from becoming noticed. "I am sure you have reasons. . . . But to be true, now that the question has been raised, it appears more and more that I have no reason to know such things."

Eileen nodded. "Perhaps you are correct in that, Mrs. Hawkes."

An uncomfortable silence filled the room, warming Kathryne's face.

"If it be of help to your soul by unburdening," Kathryne comforted, "then I shall be most glad to lend my ear to the task."

Eileen pushed her plate from before her, cupped her hands together on the table, looked down a moment, blinked several times, cleared her throat, and began to speak, her voice evoking a time long ago and miles of distance between this day and the past.

"You may ask of how I came to land on this island and become a woman of ill repute. After all, I do come from the Palmerston stock, noble folk all—save for me, the black and crippled sheep of the recent lineage."

Kathryne had to nod. "Since learning of your name, it has been a most vexing question."

"I, like yourself, Mrs. Hawkes, have come from privilege. In truth, our histories most likely share many similarities. It was an estate, a large estate, that I called my home, and I had no shortage of servants to offer care."

Kathryne nodded.

"And I, like you, lost my mother at a most early age. It was after that date that I ceased to know who and where my father was. He was most often absent, and when he was in residence on our estate he entertained a startling parade of wenches, widows, courtesans, ladies-in-waiting— a vast number, I must tell you."

"And that caused you to . . . ?" Kathryne asked, her voice trailing off as she realized she truly did not anticipate how to phrase the query.

"No, it did not, Mrs. Hawkes. I was raised to think that a proper Englishwoman had her life planned for her. Her father would select a wonderful suitor, and that would be the first step on a wondrous path."

Kathryne nodded.

"But I had the audacity to meet a boy in Taunton—the son of a stone carver—a most wonderful boy with piercing eyes the color of an oak leaf in the heat of summer. He was kind and caring, and with him laughter was always easy. I was in love, Mrs. Hawkes, and I knew the world was a wonderful place. Even at sixteen summers, I knew that I would never again scale such a mountain as this."

"And your father forbade the union?"

"Nothing so simple as that, Mrs. Hawkes. I'm afraid this is where our two histories diverge."

Eileen looked down, and Kathryne thought she noticed a tear at the corner of her eye.

"He had the boy put to death."

Kathryne gasped, and a hand flew to her throat in surprise, almost horror. "Surely this cannot be true," Kathryne insisted.

"He was accused of stealing a dozen sheep from my father and selling them. It was enough that all concerned were afraid of my father. They had the boy hanged the very day of his accusation."

"And it was your father that did this?" Kathryne gasped.

"He never claimed it to be true, but he never claimed it to be untrue."

Kathryne put her hand over Eileen's.

"And that evening I made my first gold. I was surprised that such a high price could be put on noble lineage."

Eileen sniffed and stared into the distance. "And from that day until recent days, I have seldom known an empty bed. Nor have I known peace. But I take bitter comfort in the fact that my father has not known it either. It was the only emotion that kept my heart alive."

"Eileen, I am most grieved for you," Kathryne whispered.

"But now, Mrs. Hawkes, all of that has been washed away. It is as if I have been reborn. It is as if I have only started to live this life two days ago."

Silence filled the spaces about them.

"Will that peace ever leave me?" Eileen asked, her voice as quiet as a leaf falling in a forest in autumn.

"No, Eileen," Kathryne reassured her, "it will never leave you."

## 83

It was early evening when Kathryne tapped at the door to the living quarters snuggled over the ship's chandlery.

"I am on my way back to Shelworthy, and I have stopped here to inquire if you would like to stay with us as we wait for the return of our husbands," said Kathryne when Missy opened the door. "We have several extra bedchambers, and you would not be lonely there."

Missy smiled at the invitation, but after only a short moment shook her head no.

"Thank you, Lady Kathryne. It is gracious of you to think of my comfort, but I could not leave here. There is too much in these small rooms that reminds me of John, and I would be so saddened to leave these memories behind, even for a short visit."

"But did not Will claim that they would be back in a fortnight at most?" Kathryne asked. "Will promised they would not tarry."

Missy screwed up her face. "Promised he would not tarry? But how would he be assured of that, Lady Kathryne?"

A sudden chill of fear clutched at the core of Kathryne's heart. Missy sounded as if she had foreknowledge of these matters.

"William told me before he sailed, he assured me, that this would not be a long and troublesome undertaking. If the pirates or the gold could not be found or easily recovered, then the ships would simply sail back to Bridgetown. William promised that there would be no matter that would cause his safety to be imperiled. William promised me that he would encounter no grave danger on this voyage."

An expression of sympathy and tenderness spread across Missy's face. "Kathryne," she said, dropping the formality, "I am sure William desired to prevent you from being troubled with worry."

"But William said there was no *need* to worry."

"I will speak boldly, Kathryne, for I must be honest," Missy said, her voice firm. "That is not what John spoke of to me. He said they were arming their ships for a most serious battle. Why else would they have loaded so many cannon and so much powder and shot on board? John was most anxious over the odds of their success."

Kathryne stared ahead, her only movement her blinking eyes.

"But William said there would be little danger."

Missy moved forward and placed her arm about Kathryne. "I think we should pray for their safety. For before sailing, both men left with me a statement of their last wills and testaments."

Kathryne seemed not to have heard as she stared straight ahead.

"But William promised . . . ," she said, her voice dwindling to a silent whimper.

*Did William lie to me?* Kathryne thought in a panic. *Why would he have misled me so? Why would he risk his life for this?*

And as she fought against the tears, her words spoken to William came flooding back at her. *"She made it so clear that she was concerned about having the Spenser name and reputation tarnished."*

*William, I am sorry,* her heart cried silently. *I did not intend for you to endanger your life for the sake of what others may think.*

## Guajiro

A thin shaving of white moon floated above the harbor, shedding its weak light on the still waters. The Spanish pirates celebrated loud and long into the night, their voices, shouts, and derisive laughter echoing across the water and up the jungled hillside. The cacophony culminated at two hours past the midnight mark.

Shouts and curses etched the darkness, and Will could understand most of the loudest words, their voices speaking mostly in the Spanish tongue. A boisterous exchange erupted between bunkmates who were arguing over their share of the spoils. And then, with a roar that chilled William to the bone, a musket or pistol was fired and a man screamed. The scream was followed by a second shot, and all fell silent. Only the eerie echo of the blast could be heard rumbling out to sea.

Will heard a man cry out in Spanish, *"Silencio!* There will be no more of this! Unless others would like to share this man's punishment!"

Will's men had tensed at the first shot and were ready to reach for their pistols and swords at the second volley. Will and John went around to them, whispering that they must stand down and remain still.

"It is not time yet," Will whispered through clenched teeth, holding his pistol and blade tight to his body, keeping the metal silent. "Not until the dawn, men. Not until the dawn."

In a moment, the men, still on edge, began to sit and lie on the ground. Most had one hand on their swords or pistols as they tried to return to their rest.

Will and John sidled off a few yards from the clearing, a dozen yards away from the harbor. John offered William a strip of boucan, which he took. He gnawed off a bite, chewing heartily.

John rummaged in his sack and removed a bottle of wine, which he uncorked and offered to Will, who took a long swallow and passed it back.

It was silent, save for the hum and chirp of the insects and the occasional screech of a jungle bird. Within a half hour of the musket fire, the pirate village grew silent as well, as drunk sailors began to fall into a stupor.

John looked up at the moon. "Perhaps four hours till first light?" he asked.

Will nodded. "Be time for one of us to close his eyes for a spell."

John agreed.

"You sleep, John," Will whispered. "I am certain that sleep will elude me."

John settled and laid his head in the crook of his arm and closed his eyes. In a moment, he looked up, through the darkness, at his old friend.

"Will, are you frightened?"

Will's vision was locked on the moon, and as he replied, his head remained still. "Not frightened for me, John, for I have no doubts as to my future."

"Then do you say you are frightened or not?"

"If I am to leave this mortal coil tomorrow, I will rejoice that at that instant I will be in the presence of God."

"And that you are sure of?" John whispered.

"I am as sure of that as I am sure that the sun will rise and the moon will set. That is not my fear."

"Then what?"

"It is the very thought of leaving Kathryne that makes my heart ache.

To never see her smile again, or hold her in my arms and lie with her in the moonlight."

Will stopped suddenly and inhaled, as if clearing the cry from his throat. "I know that God has my life in his hands, and I allow him to hold my soul there without complaint."

From the tree above came a screech, and both men nervously looked up into the darkness.

"Would not you regret leaving Missy, my friend?"

John did not quickly answer. After a long moment, he replied, his voice even less than a whisper.

"So much so that I nearly decided against sailing with you. It was as I bid my farewells and saw the tears in her eyes. I could only guess at the pain she hid behind her smile. Had she asked, I would have let you sail alone. But she did not ask. She kissed me once, and I turned away. It is that memory that will keep me alive tomorrow."

Will spoke of matters of faith to his old friend often, and yet there was a chasm that John was unable to cross. He had not allowed himself the freedom to lay down his arms and accept God's gift of salvation. Will realized that this night might be his last opportunity to share the truth of Christ's sacrifice with his dearest friend.

"John," Will whispered, "would you not like to speak of God and faith on such a night? Would you not desire assurance that you are a child of God? Cannot you accept this gift, even now?"

John lay back, rested his head in his folded arms, and stared into the deepening darkness.

"To do so, Will, would complicate my thoughts. I must keep such diversions from my mind—or I will be of no use to you for my own safety. Perhaps we will speak of this again when we return."

"But, John, there might not be a second chance for either of us."

John appeared to nod. "Then, Will, your God will need keep both of us alive if that be his plan for us."

"John, do not speak in such a cavalier fashion. God asks for us to decide this day. Do not harden your heart against seeking his forgiveness."

John breathed deeply. "I will speak of this tomorrow, William. Now I must gain my rest."

John then rolled to his side, his back to Will, and let his breathing slow and his muscles relax.

*Dear God*, Will prayed silently, *I ask that your will be done and that indeed I will have such a chance on the morrow.*

The first rays of the sun arrived at the cove the next morning in a most maddeningly deliberate and slow pace. Will woke his men, going between them, gently shaking them from their sleep, bidding them remain silent as they rose.

He knew that each man would require a dozen or so moments to shake the rusty slumber from his mind and to prepare for their attack.

A rustle of clothing being drawn tight was heard, along with the gentle, muted clank and rattle of sword and pike being readied, the gentle pouring of powder being funneled into pistol and musket, the silky, metallic hiss of a blade slipping through a scabbard.

Within a quarter of an hour all men were ready. They hunched down below the level of shrubs and grass and stealthily made their way to the end of the path. The jungle camouflage stopped no more than three dozen yards from the first hut of the pirate village. From that point perhaps five dozen huts and linhays were erected in a wide semicircle around the bay. Each was hastily constructed from palm leaf and stick, most leaves now browning with age.

Will wondered how many men his small group faced. Were there a hundred? Two hundred? He imagined that their only hope of success this morning was keeping their attack a complete surprise until the very moment of launch.

*Perhaps if we appear, through our hollers and shouts, to be more than what we are,* Will thought, *these pirates will react with great confusion and lay down their arms to our smaller force.*

Will stood at the head of the column of men, nodding his head each time he counted a hut or linhay.

*There might be as many as three hundred men here,* he thought, doing his best not to allow his concern to be visible on his features. *And if that be the truth, my plans are all the more precarious and troubling.*

Will mentally reviewed what he had hoped would happen with the dawning. He would give the signal to attack, and a flare would be ignited as a signal to his three ships waiting outside the harbor. They would immediately set sail to enter that calm water. His men would fan out behind him, screaming and firing their muskets into the huts, setting fire to them as well.

"Do not inflict more death than is absolutely necessary," Will cautioned his troops. "All we seek is the return of the English gold. We will hold the pirates at bay while the treasure is transferred to our ships, and then sail for home as fast as the winds allow."

His men nodded at that instruction. It was most like hunting, Will explained. A wild animal is not dangerous when unprovoked. But kick at it or wound it slightly, and it would as soon set against its provoker with teeth and fangs as run away.

"I want these pirates kept quiet, not provoked," he explained. "If angered, they are more dangerous. Killing their amigos is the most sure way of enraging them. So we do not seek death—only diversion."

Will looked back. John was a dozen men behind, and he nodded to Will that all was ready. One torch was lit from a flint and steel, and a dozen more were lit from that and passed back to the men. Will took one for himself.

"The flare!" Will whispered loudly. "Set to the flare!"

A second later a smoky whoosh was heard as the flare wobbled into the dim early morning sky, trailing a bright streak of gold sparks and flame.

"Now, men! Now!" he screamed. He stood up and began to sprint to the closest hut, screaming his best bloodcurdling scream. From behind him, his men took up the scream, and it rippled, like a snake in the jungle, from the foliage to the water's edge. Will set his torch to the first hut, and the sparks and flames soon spread up and along the back wall.

With a sleepy wail its occupants rolled and stumbled out of the hut. Will glanced back as he ran toward the far edge of the village. The occupants of the hut had indeed left without stopping to collect a single sword, musket, or pike.

*Let all our attacks be that effective,* Will hoped as he ran.

There were more huts ringing the beach than Will or John had thought. The screams and shots echoed, and it would have been impossible for all but the most inebriated celebrant to sleep through such a din. At the end of the row of huts Will saw men running, carrying a musket or sword, and sprinting for the sheltering jungle. He hefted his torch and flung it, its flaming head whooshing as it spun in the air. It hit the next to the last hut from the water's edge, and flames slowly began to creep up the brown-leafed wall.

Other pirates, awake and under attack, variously made one of three decisions. The first two favored Will. Either the pirates surrendered to the first armed man they encountered, or they took to their heels and ran from the danger. But some picked up their weapons as they ran to the edge of the jungle. With weapons, the pirates could contemplate a counterattack.

Will kicked one hut, tipping it over whole, leaving three obviously drunken men in a loose sprawl on the floor. One of Will's number arrived at Will's side, drew his sword, and shouted, "I'll keep 'em here, Cap'n Will. You kin go on after the rest of 'em."

*How gallant he is,* Will thought, bemused, *that he offers to guard others while encouraging me to press forward with the attack.*

Will called a quick thanks and sprinted off, and every step he took sent pain coursing through his body. His shoulder hurt, his calf throbbed, his ribs ached—but nothing would stop him from his mission.

Coming around one smoldering hut, Will was nearly pierced through by a Spaniard kneeling in the sand, holding an iron-tipped pike at heart's level. Will lunged to his left and fell to the sand, rolling, and pulling his long blade from his scabbard as he rolled. The Spaniard heaved the pike, and it bit into the sand a few inches from Will's neck. He jumped to his feet, his sword held out before his chest. The Spanish pirate, having thrown his only weapon, looked at Will's face, then at his blade. The brigand's face blanched, and he sprinted toward the water's edge, only to be pummeled upon the head by a thick, mahogany staff wielded by a screaming Bryne Tambor.

Sailors in a panic most often operated on instinct and would run for the protection that their vessels provided. Will had observed this in other battles and had instructed dozens of his men to position themselves near the water's edge. There, they could prevent the pirates from leaving the dangers of the shore and swimming to their ships.

Bryne was swinging his staff about his head like a whirling dervish, in great wide, sweeping circles. Every half-dozen spirals, Bryne lowered the staff's orbit a foot and let it bounce off the head or shoulders of a fleeing pirate. Most collapsed with a thump upon impact or fell to their knees clutching at the point of their injury. When the staff connected, it bounded up and wide, and Bryne simply let it ride in the wind, whooshing about like a tornado.

Will glanced over at John, who was leading a third of his men toward the far side of the line of pirate huts. In a likewise manner, John was capturing nearly two-thirds of the sleepy, surprised pirates. Yet, as from Will's attack, many were fleeing to the jungle, carrying swords or muskets.

Scanning the scene for Radcliffe's face, Will quickly dispatched two pirate defenders—one with a sharp rap of his sword's hilt to his enemy's head, the other with a shallow piercing of the pirate's calf with the tip of his blade.

*Where is Radcliffe?* Will's thoughts raced. *If I find him, I can stop the killing and injury from spreading wider. And where is the vicar?*

It was a question that Will had not dared ponder the previous night, for as the question of God vexed John Delacroix, the prospect of his being reunited with his old friend Vicar Mayhew was equally vexing. He could not allow his desire to further the risk to human life.

*If it happens, I will rejoice,* Will thought. *Yet if it does not, I will not blame God nor myself for the loss.*

Much of the village now crackled in bright, hungry flames, and men on both sides of the battle were shouting and cursing, mingled with the snap and hiss of burning palms. An occasional musket shot rang out, and the clang of metal against sharpened metal echoed through the smoke and confusion. Will spotted the three sails of his ships at the mouth of the cove and watched them for a short moment as they cleared the breakwater and entered the calmer waters.

Pockets of struggle swirled about him, and the occasional scream indicated that blood was being shed or bones broken in combat. Will stood at the water's edge, the warm sea flooding about his feet. His face was streaked with sweat and lined with soot and ash. He called out in the loudest voice he could muster that his men should cease their battles if they could, and to hold to their prisoners and secure the village.

The attack had taken no more than half of an hour, and Will gasped for breath for, like the rest of his men, he had charged in with no stopping since the attack began.

Under his orders, his men slowly ceased the fight, and large pockets of unarmed pirates were herded toward William.

Seeing John to his right, he shouted out, "Have you found Radcliffe Spenser?"

John shouted back that he hadn't.

Then Bryne called out, pulling a collapsed figure across the sand.

"Would this be 'im, Cap'n Will? I thinks I knocked the breath out of 'im a few moments back."

Will ran to Bryne and knelt down, turning the prone figure over. Though a thick coating of sand covered his face and his hair was lighter by several shades from the sun, Will knew that there was no mistaking the evil, hawklike visage of Radcliffe Spenser.

His eyes were shut, and a nasty bruise lay just above his brow, with blood seeping and caked along his right temple. Will picked up his arm and felt for the rhythmic pulses of the blood in his wrist. He looked down and watched for the rise of his chest.

"It would be him, all right," William called. "And he still has life."

He looked up at Bryne, who still had a firm fistful of Radcliffe's doublet in his hands.

"Bryne, I am instructing you to post a personal watch on this man. I do not trust him, and I want you to keep him at swordpoint until I return," Will instructed. "Do you understand? Do not let the man rise without a sharp blade slipped under his chin."

"I do indeed, Cap'n Will. He'll not draw a breath that he ain't asked me for."

"Good man," Will replied and rose and sprinted toward John Delacroix, five dozen strides distant.

"Have you seen Vicar Mayhew?" he shouted as he ran.

John shook his head no. "The good vicar ain't been spotted on my side of the village, Will. Perhaps he was injured as we attacked?"

"I think not, John. No man with us would fire upon a vicar."

Just then a loud musket roared from beyond the line of dense foliage ringing the beach, and John spun about like a child's doll tossed from a careless hand and tumbled to the sand. An angry crimson stain was spreading from between John's fingers, now tightly clamped about his shoulder.

Then another shot ran out, and a small explosion of sand marked a small crater a mere breath in front of William. He dove forward to John's side and turned him over, cradling him in his arms.

Through clenched teeth, John cried out. A pirate's musket shot had passed cleanly through his shoulder, and the blood was puddling at both sides of his torn shirt.

"'Tis only a minor wounding," he gasped. "The bleeding will cease in a moment."

Will's eyes were frantic as he looked about, cursing his decision to leave Luke on board his flagship.

"You there!" Will shouted to Horace Greenling, a sailor from Dover. "Stand over here and place your hands on both sides of this wound! The bleeding needs to be stanched."

Greenling scuttled over, looking with a nervous eye to the jungle at his left. Another shot rang out, and a man fell a dozen yards to Will's right side. Greenling dove for the sand and crawled the last few yards.

Once Greenling's hands were in place, Will stood and shouted so all could hear.

"Stand your prisoners in a line between us and the jungle. The pirates won't shoot through their own men."

Will ordered a dozen terrified Spanish pirates to their feet, and at swordpoint had them form a ragged line, ringing the prone Mr. Delacroix. In a likewise manner, Will's men maneuvered their prisoners, and in a moment a line of pirates snaked along the beach, standing as a human barricade between Will's men and the pirates that had sprinted from the attack into the jungle.

From over his shoulder, from the direction of the cove, a voice cried out. "Captain Hawkes! Which ship be the treasure ship?"

Will turned about. Two of his ships, the *Dorset Lady* and the *Water Sprite,* were now within hailing distance of the beach. Sailors stood at the rails, using long poles to maneuver them through the tangle of disabled Spanish vessels.

Will sprinted to the water, splashing it about him, shouting back, "It most likely is the *Santa Rosita* and the *Cavalier* that bear the bulk of the gold, for they ride lowest in the water," he cried, pointing to each with the tip of his sword. "Set to them first."

Just then another two shots were fired from the jungle. At the report of the first, one of the pirates was sent sprawling backwards, his chest a mass of red, his eyes cold and blank by the time he landed backwards in the sand. And as he fell, a second shot rang out. Through that newly created gap in the human wall, a second musketeer fired, his target one of Will's men. And within a heartbeat, two men lay on the sand, their lives coming to an inglorious ending on the warm sands of the pirate cove.

The line of pirates wavered, then several slumped to their knees, unwilling to be sacrificed for either side of the battle. Will screamed out.

"Make them stand! Make them stand!"

*How could any leader be so heartless and cruel as to kill his own men with such disdain?* Will's thoughts cried out.

A moment later a tall, elegantly dressed man turned to face him. A violet silk sash was about his shoulders and waist. Will stared into the black eyes of San Martel.

"You pathetic weasel," San Martel called out. "To use me and my men as a screen for your robbery. Those men in the jungle are not shooting at their friends, amigo. They are shooting at you."

He cackled as he adjusted his sash and stood up straighter in the morning sun. "My men would never harm their friends."

As Will watched in horror, a loud pair of shots rang out from the jungle, from both his right and left. An angry splash of red tore through and across San Martel's chest, ripping through the velvet and silk. San Martel lurched a step forward to the sea. He flailed his arms a bit, holding himself upright. His eyes were growing vacant, and he turned and looked over his shoulder to the source of the shots. Another musket roared and spun him about, a splatter of crimson tearing at his shoulder. A heartbeat later, his eyes narrowed in bitter hate. He lurched a step toward the sea and then, as a dead weight falls to the earth, pitched forward and landed facedown with a muted thump at the water's edge.

Another shot rang out, and one of Will's men dropped to the sand, clutching at a wound spurting blood from his thigh.

*I cannot be party to this slaughter,* Will cried silently.

He turned and saw three large trunks being hauled from the *Santa Rosita* to his ship. It would be no more than a dozen minutes until the lion's share of the gold and treasure was recovered and aboard the *Dorset Lady.*

Another pair of shots sounded, but as if in answer to his prayer, no men fell, though the entire group hunched lower in response.

*Thanks be to God that not all men have keen eyesight or steady aim,* Will thought. *It is well that the escaping pirates must not have brought powder and shot with them into the jungle, for if they had we would all be dead. And I pray that those who fled in haste carried no supplies save a handful of loaded muskets.*

"Men!" he shouted out, not wanting to test his prayers just yet. "Begin to make your way to the ships! John! Bryne! Hanley! Merchas! Stand at the ready! Have your men start their swim for the ships! Keep two men back until the last!"

Will strode back and forth along the beach, giving orders to the smaller groups who had lost their assigned leaders, shouting encouragement.

He turned and looked again at the ships. In the few moments that had passed, perhaps a dozen chests of gold had been recovered, clumping with huge loud thumps on the deck of Will's flagship, forming a small mountain of wooden containers under the mainmast.

Perhaps half of Will's men had made the short wade and swim back to the vessels. John had been carried out by three others and hauled up, hand over hand, to the deck of the *Dorset Lady*. He waved back to Will as they laid him on a pallet of canvas.

Will shouted for the rest of the men to begin to move away from the beach.

"Everyone with a musket or pistol, keep it trained on the prisoners before you. If they move, shoot at their legs."

He then shouted a warning, with more gruesome and chilling directions as to the location of their shots, in Spanish to the pirates. "You will not move until we are under sail! Do you understand?!"

A few responded with terrified nods.

Will knew that halfway back to the ship, when his men could no longer fire a musket, the wall of prisoners would flee.

*But that will give us just enough time to make our escape.*

"How many more chests?" Will shouted toward the ships.

It was a long moment until his question was answered. "It appears that we have 'em all, Cap'n Will—some three dozen chests—unless they spent some of the gold on this island."

"Stand ready to cast off!" Will shouted, scanning the shore for any of his men still left behind.

"Bryne!" he called out. "Let me assist you with Radcliffe!"

He heard no answer and swiped at the smoke that filled the air in the cove, making clear identification difficuLieutenant

"Bryne!" he called out again, a note of urgency in his voice.

"Bryne!" he shouted, running along the beach. A shot roared off, somewhere to his left. He ignored it as he ran to the spot where he had last seen his friend.

Will stopped and allowed his sword to fall to the sand. His face caved in at the pain of the sight before him.

Bryne lay, faceup, at the edge of the shore, his feet resting lightly in the water, as if cooling them off on a hot day. But the rest of the vision had gone horribly wrong. A thin handle protruded from the center of his chest, buried to the delicate hilt, at just where his heart lay. Will guessed that Radcliffe had concealed a dagger and had killed Bryne. Will staggered two steps closer and felt his anger and his terror rise, as a thick bile, into his throat.

Radcliffe had first cut the man's throat with a clean, precise slit, and then plunged the dagger into a heart that had already ceased to beat.

*It is the mark of true evil,* Will swore to himself, *and if given the chance I would risk all I had or could own to stomp such a vile person from existence. He has no right to share the same air as I do. My God, allow this killing to be stopped.*

He dropped to his knees at Bryne's side, and as gentle as a penitent lighting a candle, Will removed the stiletto blade and wiped the blood away with his hand, the warm sticky fluid staining his palm. He reached up and gently closed Bryne's eyes, which were wide open in surprise, staring up into a tropical sun.

"Dear Bryne," Will spoke in low and prayerful tones, "you were truly a good man and a loyal friend. You fought with honor. If I could have taken your place, I would have. Will you forgive me for leaving you unburied on this beach? At least you have died at the side of the sea that you so loved."

Will looked back to the ships. He chose to ignore the urgent calls that he return quickly, and he prayed out loud as he knelt in the sand. "Almighty God, Maker of all things, have mercy on the soul of Bryne Tambor. He served you as well as he could. Forgive me for causing his death. Take him to be with you this day, dear Lord. Amen."

Will bowed his head and forced his tears to stay hidden.

A scream arose from the jungle, and the pirates who had hidden themselves there rose in unison and began to rush the beach.

From Will's ship came a deafening roar as two of her cannons belched flame, fire, and shot. The metal shot passed over Will's head by no greater distance than three feet. Had he been standing, he would have met his God as well. The shell exploded at the edge of the jungle foliage, spewing a great explosion of leaf and sand. A second shot hit a dozen yards to the left, and the pirate counterattack was halted, frozen by the blast.

Will stood up, retrieved his sword, and sprinted to the water. He took a few dozen high, splashing steps, then dove into the warm sea toward his ship. He began to stroke toward safety, even as his crew began to pole their way into deeper water. Will raised his head to take a breath and saw that all was not yet safe.

At the far end of the cove, where the two beached pirate ships lay on their sides, a crew of pirates had been working. While Will and his men were busy on the beach, they had hoisted down a cannon from the badly canted decks to be set upon the shore.

Immediately they fired back at Will's ship. The shot went wide to the right and struck instead a Spanish vessel, crashing into her with a splintery, flaming roar. Flames began to sweep along the decks as fast as a brush fire in August.

Will looked back and watched in panic as the pirate cannoneers swarmed over the huge gun, making it ready for a second shot. He turned and began to stroke furiously to his waiting ship.

## 85

*Barbados*

It was nearly dusk as Kathryne made her way to the cool interior of St. Michael's. Kathryne knew that a church was not needed to assure a prayer to God is heard, but she felt comforted by the structure nonetheless.

She seated herself at the far forward bench and bent her head to pray. After the passing of the larger part of an hour, she heard the far door squeal open and looked up to see Vicar Petley enter the sanctuary, batting furiously at something that flitted about his head.

She stood and entered the aisle, and the vicar, surprised to find anyone in the church, nearly batted his hand against the side of his own face in response.

"Kathryne!" he called out, his face reddening unexpectedly. "I had no idea that anyone was in attendance. Why did you not seek me out in the parsonage if you desired prayers?"

Kathryne looked down, then replied, "I needed these moments to be alone with my thoughts, Vicar. I am most troubled about William and what I have asked him to do."

The vicar snorted. "If he dispatches all those evil pirates at once, I would be most grateful," he stated. "Perhaps I may offer prayers for your William as well?"

"Why, Vicar Petley," she responded, "that would be most gracious of you. I am sure William would appreciate your kindness."

The vicar knelt and, with Kathryne, prayed for the return of the gold, for justice to be meted out to the evil pirates, and finally for William's safe return to Barbados. It was a prayer, Kathryne thought, that was much different—more sincere and less showy—than most of his petitions.

The vicar stood and escorted Kathryne to the sanctuary door. "Good Kathryne, I know we have had our differences," he spoke, his words soft and slow. "Since leaving England I have been most out of sorts. I have been spiteful, jealous, and unforgiving—all inappropriate behaviors for a Christian, let alone a man of the cloth.

"These blasted pirates have helped to show me how petty I have been and what is truly important in this life—friends, neighbors, loved ones, and the Lord Almighty. When calamity strikes, these are the things in which one can find strength. And I discovered that there is a deficiency of people who care for me or that I care about. And much of that was the doing of my own pride and envy."

Vicar Petley paused briefly and then looked into Kathryne's eyes. "I ask now that you forgive my shortcomings. I would so like to be able to call you my friend once more."

Kathryne's jaw almost dropped at the vicar's words. She had longed for a change in the man and now was shocked to see that it had occurred. "By all means, Giles," she sincerely replied. "I would find pleasure in that as well."

The vicar set his shoulder to the massive wooden door, for the humid weather often swelled the wood to a squealing tightness. He set his feet and hefted against it with a great thrust, only to find it swing open with nary an effort. He clutched the brass door handle and nearly swung with it into the air as the door opened into the courtyard. The vicar's feet danced as if in a jig, and he lurched about, desperately seeking to maintain his footing.

The door slammed against the stop, and the vicar was sent reeling like a child's top on a polished floor. In a moment he regained his balance, and as their eyes met, Kathryne was shocked a second time that day as the vicar broke into a wide smile and then laughed.

## Caribbean Sea

The sea about William was filled with musket shot. He was stroking through the water furiously as the pirates fired at him, his ship, and his crew. Will grabbed at his ship's netting rope and hauled himself up to the deck as a musket ball splintered the wood and rail about him.

"Set sails, gentlemen," he cried out as he panted, "and please, if you will, make haste!"

The sails unfurled with a comforting thump and rustle, and they caught the slight breeze that blew sideways about the cove. It would be a short tack to the west for only a few moments, then a tack back to the east. That would place them at the mouth of the cove and then into the safety of the open seas.

By the time Will's ships had tacked eastward in the shallow, protected cove, the pirate cannon roared again. This shot was closer to the mark and struck the mizzenmast yardarm on Will's larger flagship. The damaged yardarm dangled in the air like a broken wing of a great bird, canvas flapping like feathers, torn ropes hanging limp.

Will looked up, worried. The damage might slow them some, but with luck they would still be able to sail at a good speed.

The surf rose up, choppy and rough, as the ships neared the narrow mouth to the sea. Will turned, one last time, to watch the shore, both hoping to see a black-clad vicar on the sands and hoping he would not. If that black figure was there, it would mean that he was alive—yet Will would have no method of offering rescue. He could not sacrifice more of his crew for such a venture, even if it were possible to do. Will offered a prayer for his old friend, that God watch over the vicar and keep him safe.

As Will's eye scanned the sand, he saw no such figure mixed in with the smoldering and burning village. The pirates had begun to swim to their vessels, not willing to give up their prize so easily. He could only imagine their rage when they were to discover their ships disabled and unsteerable.

The two civilian merchant ships—the *Dorset Lady* and the *Water Sprite*—slipped out into the welcoming sea as the winds began to freshen. Using a megaphone, Will shouted for the navy ship, the *Resolve,* to be brought into position. The handful of crew aboard her sailed the vessel directly into the mouth of the cove and set her sideways across the narrow channel. They dropped all anchors and scrambled belowdecks. In the darkest, most putrid bottom area of the ship were huge, round wooden plugs. Each could be removed when at drydock to drain the foul bilgewater that collected there. Now they would not be used to drain water, but to allow it in. With sledges and bars, the men set to each of the three plugs and within minutes had succeeded in opening them to the sea. Water cascaded in in an angry, spurting fountain, and the men scrambled back to the top deck. They lowered their one longboat and set out to board Will's ship.

The *Resolve* slowly began to settle in the water, the sea greedily reclaiming the vessel board by board, foot by foot. Within the time it took the longboat to reach the *Dorset Lady*, the naval ship had settled across the channel, pinned between the two shallow reefs, effectively blocking the cove.

Within the passing of a half hour, all William's men were in place on deck and ready to sail back to Bridgetown.

Will surveyed his two small ships and called out to his navigator, "Make a course for home, good sir. And may God grant us strong winds this day."

## 86

*Barbados*

As Aidan led his horse along the dusty trail to Shelworthy, his face was etched with worry and concern. He had spent the night at the Carruthers plantation, discussing the disastrous implications of the pirate attack for his small and civilized island of Barbados.

Emily stood upon the porch, waiting to greet him as he came up the long drive. A slave took the horse and led it off to the stables. Aidan slowly mounted the steps and collapsed in one of the porch chairs. Emily knelt next to him and took his hand.

"Are you fatigued, my dear?" she asked, hoping his demeanor stemmed only from physical needs, not emotional or spiritual. "Has the ride back been difficult?"

Rubbing his hands over his face for a moment, he stopped and looked deep into her eyes. "No, the ride was fine. Yet I find myself so very, very tired."

Emily saw his weariness reflected in his eyes.

"Did your meeting with the Carrutherses and the other planters cause you concern? Is that troubling you?"

He twisted his head upon his neck, the muscles tight and knotted. A few joints popped loudly in reaction.

"I can voice that the meal and my reception was cordial. There was an overabundance of food, as is typical of these planters—as well as an overindulgence in spirits. Even more so this day, for their obvious concern is over the disruption in their shipping schedules."

"But do they stand by you as governor?" Emily asked, knowing that such a question weighed heavily on his thoughts.

"They all voiced their hearty support, but hidden in their words and their demeanor was a threat. If William returns with the gold, they will stand behind me in a most unified manner—like loyal soldiers. If William does not return or returns without the gold, my loyal troops will disappear as the fog lifts with the morning sun."

"They admitted to such a self-serving stance?" Emily asked, not truly surprised at such a response from the nobility. She had seen them operate in such an underhanded manner during her years at court. Backstabbing, vile innuendoes, and Machiavellian actions were standard practice among the nobles who so graced the palace grounds.

"No one would be that foolhardy," Aidan replied with a sigh, as if resigned to his fate. "But as I listened to what was being said between their pleasant words and phrases, it became most clear to me. If the gold does not make its way back to the treasury of England, I will not be long for this posting. In fact, since it was my brother who seemingly masterminded the attack, I stand at risk of being accused of treachery and treason. Suspicion paints its victims with a wide brush, and I am most afraid that I am indelibly tainted with Radcliffe's evil."

Emily sat on the arm of the chair and stroked at Aidan's hair. "Surely this scenario is not as bleak as you portray it, Aidan. Surely there is the possibility of a more pleasant outcome."

Aidan shook his head.

"But William is a most clever and daring captain," Emily offered. "Kathryne spoke of his certainty of success—of returning with the prize."

Words seemed to catch in Aidan's throat. It was a moment until he replied. "That is not what the planters have agreed is possible. Three ships attacking an armada was like a cat bringing down a bull, they said. Not one of them stated confidence in his return. 'A noble but doomed gesture' is how Peter Carruthers described it. And others more knowledgeable in warfare and sea battles than I concurred."

"Aidan, you must have listened to only the bleakest of outlooks concerning his chances. I am sure that it will not be as they said," Emily said, trying to convince herself as well as Aidan.

"No. I heard honest and true. He may be doomed to die trying to save me and this foolish posting as governor." Aidan's words mixed with a sob. "What have I done to my son-in-law? What I have done to Kathryne?"

Emily fought her tears back and gently stroked at the back of Aidan's head, praying to God that he would protect them all.

## Caribbean Sea

The *Dorset Lady* and the *Water Sprite* sat side by side, wood squealing against wood. All sails had been furled, and a snake of men led from one deck to the other. Heavily laden sea chests, trunks, and boxes passed from hand to hand. Each box and chest was filled with gold coin, bullion, Aztec treasures, and leather bags of golden nuggets.

When Will had ordered a stop to their sailing, only moments after the pirate cove had disappeared past the horizon, all eyes turned to him, questioning his sanity.

"You be stoppin' sailin', Cap'n?" one sailor had cried. "We believes in fair play and all, but not when there be pirates on our tail."

A chorus of agreement had echoed over the water, but the order had been obeyed.

Will had held up his palms to quiet his crew.

"We have to stop to transfer the treasure from the *Dorset Lady* to the *Water Sprite*," he had explained. "This ship is slow, and the other carries herself faster in this rough chop. If I had to make a bet on which reaches Bridgetown first, my money would be on *Water Sprite*. She will carry the gold."

"But why did we not do so in the harbor, Cap'n?"

Will had smiled. "Do you believe in fair play enough to tell your enemy *all* your plans?"

Once all the treasure was transferred, Will ordered, "Carry Mr. Delacroix and the rest of the wounded to the *Water Sprite* as well."

John was struggling to his feet as Will knelt down and pushed him gently back onto his pallet. "You're not to argue with the captain, John. That would be a treasonable offense."

"But I'll not be leaving your side, Will. You must not make me leave. I have been beside you for what seems as all my life. How can you force me to leave you now? 'Tis a most unfair order."

Four men stood by the pallet, waiting for Will to rise. Will placed his hand in a most tender gesture upon John's forehead, as if a father soothing a child.

"John, you know why I must. You would do the same if you were captain."

"But that is where you are in error, Will. I would never leave you."

Will motioned that the men take the pallet.

"But, Will, what of our talk about God?" John protested, trying to gain a change of mind. "We never had the chance for that talk."

Will leaned close to John's face. "As you said, John, it gives our Lord a proper reason to keep us both alive—I still need to help you find faith in Christ."

Will squeezed his friend's good shoulder. "We'll be together again, John. I promise you that."

Will sent Luke to the *Water Sprite* as well, to care for and comfort the wounded until they reached shore.

Once everyone was aboard the proper ship, the vessels were loosed. Sails dropped and filled with rushing winds from the southeast.

"Navigators!" Will called out. "Resume the sail to Bridgetown."

He stood at the rear of the ship, against the last railing on the far quarterdeck, and turned about to watch the wake trailing out behind them as he thought of the battle.

He had lost three dozen men under his command—three dozen sons and fathers and brothers and husbands—dead on that wretched little island.

And he had left the vicar there as well.

*If only I could have found him,* Will thought.

He touched at the locket at his heart, and then his hand fell to his belt, where it brushed against the dagger that had ended the life of Bryne Tambor.

As the wind increased, whistling past Will's ears, he felt tears upon his cheeks.

## 87

"Sails behind us, Captain Will!"

At midafternoon, the shout from the crow's nest set everyone to action, their hearts beating a step faster from the implicit danger those sails presented. Will and his two small ships sailed in a part of the Caribbean not frequented often by merchants, nor even smugglers and cutthroats. The waters in these shallows could be boiled into a whitecapped frenzy by just a heavy breeze. Shoals and reefs abounded, and the unwary pilot could find his hull shattered in a moment of inattention.

Sails behind them meant only one thing: The Spanish pirates had quickly overcome the barricaded cove and now sought to take their revenge upon them.

Will shouted for his telescope. A wide-eyed sailor of no more than fifteen years of age ran to him and offered the polished glass-and-brass instrument in an air of great deference, holding it out to him at arm's length.

Will ran to the stern and braced his feet wide apart on the rolling decks. The winds had continued to increase, and the ships were being tossed about, their decks canting more and more with each roll. He leaned against the railing, hoping that he could get a glimpse of their attacker before it was too late to make adjustments to his plans.

There was a single set of sails on the horizon, perhaps no more than one, or at most two, miles distant. The pursuing vessel was not a warship or galleon, for none of those ships had such speed, even with this great sideways wind.

Will spotted the ship for a moment and then lost it as the deck rolled and pitched again. He lost his footing and struggled for balance, and in the process almost dropped the telescope into the sea. Grasping it at the last minute, he pulled it close to his chest.

"Good officers, what do you make of this?" Will called out to three junior officers standing nearby.

The officer closest to him extended his hand and asked for the telescope. He tried for several minutes to get a clear vision, yet was frustrated as Will had been. He passed the scope to the next man, who wrapped his legs between the rails and leaned backwards, away from the stern. After a long moment, during which no officer spoke, he took the glass instrument from his eye.

"She be a speedy yacht, if I be seeing clearly. Perhaps a tiny fluyt, with only two sails."

A puzzled look appeared on each man's face. Will broke the silence by asking the obvious question. "Why are they sending such a ship to pursue us? She cannot hold many cannon."

"No, sir. No more than six total."

Will scratched at his chin, and his shoulder tightened in pain. The wound in his leg was beginning to throb and pulse. He had stood too long this day and would not sit for many hours to come.

"And how many crew could it carry?" Will asked.

"Perhaps sixty men, maybe upwards of seventy-five, if they stood cheek to jowl."

The officer at the end, a Lieutenant Havers, barked out a comment. "If they be hauling men to attack us, a single grapeshot from our guns would render their mission useless. I cannot think that even a pirate would be so foolish as to sacrifice his men in such a vain effort."

Another officer, Junior Lieutenant Forbes, called out, having held the glass to his eye as they spoke, "It be a white flag they are flying from the mast. It be a white flag."

"Are they surrendering? We already have their gold," called another officer.

Will was indeed puzzled. He missed having John at his side, for he had the knack of asking the proper questions that would elicit the proper response. His skill was to spot the weak link in any argument or scenario and expose it to the light.

"Why then," Will asked, "would such a ship be following?"

The small vessel pursuing them seemed to leap through the waves and grew larger with each moment. Even with the unaided eye, the large white flag could be now seen whipping at the top end of the mainmast. The flag must have measured five yards square.

"Well, Captain Hawkes, it appears that within the hour they shall be upon us. I'm sure they'll be making their intentions known before that moment," said Lieutenant Havers, his voice calm and even. "And if it be a battle they seek, we best prepare for it."

Will stood for a moment more, staring to the north at the small ship splashing through the rough waves.

"Captain Hawkes? Shall we make ready for battle?" Havers repeated.

Will nodded. "Yes, by all means. Have the cannons set, and shot and powder distributed to all that require such."

Lieutenant Havers turned and was about to bark out those orders, when Will held up a palm, bidding him stop.

"But be assured that if any firing be done—it be done on my orders alone," he called out. "I want no more blood to be shed if it is not necessary."

"Indeed," Lieutenant Havers said and turned to set the crew in motion.

## Barbados

The sun began to arc toward the western horizon as Kathryne made her way out of Bridgetown to Shelworthy. Her day had been filled with activity and emotion.

*Eileen is a good choice to handle the details of ordering and supervising,* she thought as Porter slowly plodded northward. *And I am pleased to have spoken with Missy as well.*

Purposefully, she ignored thinking of Missy's bleak talk of the danger of Will's mission, tucking that fear into a corner of her thoughts.

*And was not Vicar Petley a changed man this day? How solicitous he was of Will's endeavor and safety. I would scarce have thought him to be the same person.*

Kathryne smiled to herself at his words and demeanor. *If God can effect such change in a man, how great is his power and how great is his love.*

It was then that a sudden lurch of the horse caused Kathryne to grab harder at the reins and lean forward, tucking closer to Porter's massive neck to avoid a spill. She found her balance, and the horse whinnied in a most plaintive manner, as if apologizing for his misstep.

Kathryne giggled in response and bent down to pat at his mane. "Do not be alarmed, good Porter, for you caused no falls this day."

Kathryne straightened back up, and as she did a sharp wincing tug spread from deep within her.

Without thinking, without conscious thought, Kathryne lowered her hand to protect that area, just above the line of her hips, with a gesture that spoke of love for a new life.

She knew at that moment what was her destiny. It felt as though a missing piece of her life was now in place, a final veil removed on what it was to be a woman.

She looked out at the waves, cut and polished by the afternoon wind and sun into a thousand prisms of diamonds and jewels. She looked to the west, praying that three sails would dot the horizon, praying that her tears would fall not in pain, but in joy.

*Caribbean Sea*

It was nearing the late afternoon watch. All of Will's officers and advisers agreed that to slow their sailing and wait for their pursuer would be foolish and an obvious breach of naval logic. Yet each league that they sailed, the gap between Will's two ships and the small ship to their stern grew ever more narrow. In no more than the passage of half an hour the small yacht would be even with them.

The vessel that carried the recaptured gold—the smaller, sleek pinnace—had to furl her foresail to keep her pace with Will's slower, more ponderous fluyt. To Will, the obvious course of action was to send the speedy ship on her way, and the faster they arrived at Bridgetown, the better for all concerned. But to do that might betray their plan to their pursuers—that she carried the gold and Will's ship did not. And to separate in this weather was most unwarranted. The winds continued to rise, and a low scud of gray green clouds swept across the southeastern horizon. The heightening and roughening surf sent whitecapped waves crashing about the ships.

Fathom by fathom, the small and speedy yacht pulled closer. From Will's vantage point at the stern, he saw a crew of no more than a dozen men manning her sails. Perhaps there could have been fifty men hidden belowdecks. However, there was but one hatch. There could be no massed swarm of attackers to overpower Will and his men. There were four cannons on deck, but each was still tied to the midship, and no one had ventured near the weapons during the last full hour. Perhaps they were loaded and could be fired, but two shots would not be sufficient to cripple, let alone sink a vessel the size of Will's.

Each passing moment brought the wind up stronger. The air blustered about the ship and felt to William that it carried the scent of ill humors, a warm, spoiling scent that spoke of storms and lightning, thunder and rain.

The velocity of the wind was a caution to the sailors as well. If a speedy yacht could catch and overtake Will's two ships, there might be a dozen more on the horizon. If his ships tangled in a battle, no matter how small or inconsequential, it would draw them from the path of the best winds, swirling them about on the roughening waters, and allow any pursuer to gain ground and perhaps take the full advantage in the span of an afternoon.

The crew had readied cannon and muskets, and each man made sure the weapon he carried—whether it was dagger, or long sword, or rapier, or cutlass—was sharpened and at hand. The men went about their duties of setting sails and tying ropes as always, but every few moments would find them swiveling their heads to assess how much distance they had lost to their pirate pursuers.

Will looked up to the skies. A thick, viscous band of clouds carried a portent of rain and storm.

From the ship behind them came a shrill whistling. A young man had sidled up along the front spar to the very farthest forward point on the vessel. The man was holding a pennant in his hands and waving it from horizon to horizon. It was a triangular pennant of gold and green, the colors that requested a fellow traveler give pause and stop. By this moment, a well-thrown stone could have been hurled between decks and found its target.

Will turned to the officers in a ragged semicircle behind him, each face lined with worry and concern. This was unlike anything they had ever encountered and therefore was cause of great consternation. Did they seek to attack? Had the pirates set their vessel, loaded with powder, only to explode in a final act of savagery? What did they seek?

"Stand down the sails," Will called out. "Allow the Spaniards to draw alongside."

Will spun about to face the Spanish captain. The man, dressed in a ragged and stained red velvet doublet, carried a small bundle tied tight with twine under his arm . Attached to this bundle was a long length of thin rope, perhaps lashing rope for the sails. The Spanish captain began to twirl the bundle over his head in an ever-widening arc, waiting for the momentum to build and the sea to bring them closer, so the package could be safely tossed from deck to deck.

And as the winds grew wilder, Will and every man on all three vessels watched, their eyes fixed to that small spinning bundle, wrapped in white silk.

## Barbados

The winds were increasing on the western shore of Barbados as well. It was not the season for storms, and the olive-colored sky seemed most unusual and unexpected to the citizens of Bridgetown as they scurried along the narrow streets to complete their marketing before the storm.

Kathryne had not noticed the winds rising until she turned toward Shelworthy. It gritted up dust and leaves about her, and she held up her hand to shield her eyes. Porter snorted and vigorously shook his head as if to clear the dust from his large, wet nose.

"We are nearly home, Porter, and you can rest easy once you're in your stable."

Porter nodded his head as he increased his steps to a canter, covering the last mile in a few short minutes.

Kathryne's mind was more awhirl than the winds about her. The hem of her dress was ruffled by the wind, and her thoughts were in a similar ruffle. Her mind could hardly find solid footing on which to light. It was as if she had not truly considered the possibility of her condition before that single moment of epiphany. The words *mother* and *child* and *birth* were no longer just words, but reality.

She stopped at the top of the drive, and the groomsman took Porter to the stable. As Kathryne opened the front door of Shelworthy, the rain began to batter the windows and doors with a staccato pacing. Kathryne turned, for a short moment, to confront the wind and rain, and her eyes blinked in the face of the storm.

Audible, but just above the wind, Kathryne called out, "Return to me, William. . . ."

She blinked again, the rain clouding her eyes, mingling with the tears that she tried to prevent.

". . . For you have a child to see born."

And she closed her eyes, her hand on the door, her head bowed, and prayed.

*Dear almighty God, allow William to return to me. Protect him from the evil one. Keep him from foolish choices and danger. Allow him to see his child born. I ask you, Lord, for this one thing. Deny, if you will, any or all the requests that I may one day present to you, if only this one single prayer be answered.*

Kathryne's tears fell against her cheeks and mixed with the warm raindrops that fell heavy against her shoulders and breast.

*I ask this, Lord, for the child you have given us, and in your most precious name. Amen.*

And with that, she opened the door and entered the protection of her father's house.

## Caribbean Sea

The white bundle whirled in the air a dozen times, the Spaniard rocking on his feet, trying to maintain his balance and accurately time his throw.

The bundle would not explode, Will knew, for there was no fuse long enough to burn the entire time it had been spun. *But then, what in the world might this be?* he wondered.

The Spaniard allowed the bundle to whirl one last time, then released the rope from his grip. It spun in a high, lazy arc toward Will's ship. The wind seemed to catch and hold it in midair, but the package buffeted through it and landed with a delicate thump on the deck of the *Dorset Lady*, only a half-dozen paces from where William stood.

All eyes had followed its course to where it now lay, and Will stepped forward and picked it up, a curiously light package in his hands. He reached to his belt and withdrew the dagger that was held there and slipped it under the thick, brown twine.

The Spanish captain shouted, in heavy and thickly accented English, "Radcliffe has your vicar in chains, Captain Hawkes!"

Will heard the word *vicar* and snapped the blade through the twine. The white silk opened as a flower before him. Sitting in the package was a small red-and-flesh-colored item, no bigger than a man's finger.

Will stared in disbelief. *It's a man's forefinger!*

It had been chopped clean at the closest knuckle to the palm. Will nearly stepped back in shock, and the severed part fell from where it lay and thumped on the deck before him, rolling until it tapped Will's scuffed boot. Will felt a chill run rampant throughout his being.

"And Radcliffe will kill him piece by piece unless he gets his gold, Captain Hawkes," screamed the Spanish captain, his voice going shrill and reedy.

"You dogs!" Will screamed back at the Spanish captain. "You brutal, vile devils! How dare you do this to an innocent man!"

The Spanish captain shrugged, as if conceding the point.

"Where is he? I want to see him!" Will shouted.

"The vicar is a prisoner on Señor Radcliffe Spenser's ship. His life is now in your hands, Captain Hawkes. We want our gold. If that is returned to us, you can have your vicar. The choice is yours to make."

Sailors and officers began to edge towards William. Lieutenant Havers knelt down and retrieved the cut finger and, holding it gingerly between thumb and forefinger, placed it back upon the white silk.

Will looked down at what was beneath it in the silk package. It was a copy of the Scriptures, torn in two, the first half of the Bible ripped asunder and discarded.

"The vicar wrote you a note, Captain Hawkes. Perhaps you should read it," the Spanish captain shouted.

In the top margin of the first chapter of Isaiah, Will read these words from the pen of Vicar Mayhew, his bold scratches obvious to all who had known him. The words were in Latin, save Will's name.

*William Hawkes—*

This statement is written freely, for no one but I speaks these words. William, do not return for me. I will meet my God with confidence. Let not these evil men triumph. Sail back to Barbados and to safety. If you value our friendship, you will do as I bid.

I love you, William, and I always will. You are a son to me. May God have mercy on our souls. Continue to seek him. My prayer is that you find your way to faith. If I could know that you are a child of God, I would pass from this life a happy man.

*Yours,*
*Thomas Mayhew*

"Well, Captain Hawkes?" cried the Spanish captain. "You have not many moments to decide. Behind this ship follow other ships, Señor Radcliffe's among them with your vicar, ready to kill you all unless you return what is rightfully ours. We want our gold."

Will's officers and crew began to speak up, calling on Will to ignore their request, to simply sail away.

"Captain Hawkes! Give us the gold, and you, the vicar, and your crew will sail away free men. You have our word on that!"

"And that be the word of a cutthroat sea dog you be expectin' us to believe," shouted Lieutenant Havers in guttural and coarse Spanish. "You think we all be daft on this vessel?"

"Let us fire our cannons into their side, Cap'n Will," begged a sailor.

"Can we send 'em all to the bottom?" asked another.

Will, his face blank and white, stared first at his crew, then at the Spanish captain, then back to his ship.

He blinked his eyes once, then closed them and held the torn Scriptures close to his heart, pinning the severed finger against his chest and locket. He knew what he must do.

## 89

*Barbados*

Kathryne pulled the door shut behind her as the rain squalled against it, making pocking sounds as it splattered against the thick wood. She raised her hands to her face and cleared the rain from her cheeks and chin, then pushed her wet hair from her forehead.

*It was so much simpler before,* she thought. *Now life seems so complex and frightening.*

From around the corner, she heard the unmistakable footsteps of Hattie slowly creaking along the floor.

"Hattie?" she called out. "Is that you?"

The footfalls ceased. "Yes, it be Hattie," came the reply. "Who dat be?"

"Hattie, you silly goose, it is Kathryne. Could you come here? I will need a dry gown and a towel."

Hattie stepped around the corner, carrying a plate full of biscuits, coffee, jams, toasts, and sweetmeats.

Kathryne suddenly remembered Cecily, her old friend from the Alexandrian, and the days when she was with child, and the voracious appetite it had created within her friend. Kathryne sniffed deeply.

"And in addition to dry clothing, I desire that tray of food as well. Please follow me to my bedchamber, for I wish to eat there," she said, turning and ascending the staircase.

"But Lady Kat'ryne. These victuals be for your papa."

Kathryne stopped midway. She stared back down at her. "And I claim them as mine, Hattie. Your assignment is to care for me, not my father." Kathryne smiled down at Hattie, that new inner glow most apparent as her wet hair curled tighter and swam about her face.

On seeing Kathryne's smile, Hattie's jaw fell open, and she nearly dropped the tray. "You gonna be a mama! Dat's what I done seen dis mornin'. You don' notice me lookin', but der be a look 'bout you. Dat's de look dat come over you. You gonna be a mama, ain't dat right, Lady Kat'ryne?"

Kathryne nodded, still smiling. She then raced down the few steps and grabbed Hattie in a fierce hug.

## Caribbean Sea

"Captain Hawkes! Your time is up! What be your answer? Do you give us what we want for the life of your old vicar? Or do you want us to kill him one bloody inch at a time?"

Will stepped forward toward the rail, yet remained silent.

Will's crew was calling out, shouting their refusal to listen to such a maniacal threat, clamoring that the Spaniards must have suffered a tropical illness to think Captain Hawkes would even entertain such a foolhardy notion.

Will looked behind the Spanish captain, to the horizon. *Could it be my imagining, or are those the sails of our pursuers—and Radcliffe?*

Lieutenant Havers stepped up to Will and placed his thin, scrawny hand on Will's shoulder, squeezing it tight to gain Will's full attention.

"Good Captain, you cannot be considering such a request. To do so would condemn every man on board this vessel to death. The pirates will kill us all as sure as I'm standing here."

Will nodded. "I agree with you, Lieutenant."

Havers almost smiled.

Then Will added, "But that is why I will return their gold to them."

Havers' narrow face pinched even tighter.

"Captain, are you daft?" he replied, incredulous. "Have you lost your reason?"

William leaned in closer to the officer. "Lieutenant, look to the north, but not so obvious that others may notice."

Havers turned slightly, his eyes quickly scanning that far horizon.

"Tell me if you see three sails upon that horizon," Will said.

The lieutenant did not voice a word, but simply nodded.

"If I do not stop this ship, we will be overtaken in time. If the Spanish catch us, each one of us will be killed. Would not you agree to that outcome?"

Again the thin, gaunt officer nodded. After a moment, he spoke, in a whispered low voice. "If those ships behind us be pirates, they'll get their gold back, and none of us will view tomorrow's sunrise."

"Havers," Will replied, "you are a brave and good officer. Yet we will lose in a battle with angry brigands who best our numbers by hundreds. I know that to be true. You know that as well."

The lieutenant looked up, his eyes lost in concern. "But what shall we do?" he asked in a small voice.

Will leaned close and whispered, "You must act as if my next commands be the only rational choice we face. You must offer your total and complete support. Will you offer that to me, good sir? It will provide these men with their only option of escape. Will you agree?"

## Barbados

Kathryne fell with a sudden tiredness upon her bed, kicking off her wet boots and stockings while grabbing at a thick biscuit laden with wild honey.

"Hattie," she explained, "you must not tell anyone else of what you know—not yet. Not until William returns home."

Hattie screwed her face up into a serious mask and nodded. "I can't tell Lady Em?"

"No, Lady Emily must not yet know."

"And not your papa?"

"Neither should he know."

Kathryne swallowed and took a long gulp of syrupy coffee.

"But ain't you bustin' to tell dis to some others?" Hattie replied, concerned. "If dat be me, I be tellin' everybody."

"But William does not yet know. I think that he should be the first—well, second—to know. Wouldn't you agree?"

## Caribbean Sea

Lieutenant Havers thought for a short moment, then nodded.

"Captain Hawkes, you are in command of this vessel. I will follow your orders."

Will stepped back, wrapped the white silk cloth about the severed finger, and tied it tight with the twine. All the while the three ships continued to bob in the rolling seas. Then he turned to his crew.

"Men of the *Dorset Lady!*" he cried out. "I . . . I . . . ."

He looked at their expectant and eager faces and struggled to find the correct wording.

"Men! Vicar Mayhew is my history and, indeed, family to me. I cannot turn my back on him. I will meet the Spanish demands and return their gold hidden in the holds below us. I have no greater wish than to see once again my dear friend and am willing to risk my life and hold the Spanish at their word," Will called out. "But I cannot ask any man to place his life at like risk."

William looked over to the Spanish captain and saw a wide grin on his face.

"I am commanding that all of you depart this vessel and board the *Water Sprite* and continue on your way to Bridgetown. There is no call for you to put your lives in jeopardy. I will remain on this vessel and exchange its gold for the vicar."

A loud murmur rippled through his crew. The fact that the *Dorset Lady*'s holds contained no gold was most obvious to all of them, yet that fact seemed not to be shown in any crewman's face. It was clear to Will as he scanned the group that they indeed understood the subterfuge. What was not so clear was if they grasped the fact that Will was offering himself as sacrifice for their escape.

Havers returned to Will's side and spoke softly. "But does not your command place your life in utmost peril?" he asked. "Once your ruse is discovered, they will kill you."

William looked at him, and their eyes met.

"Indeed that may occur, Lieutenant. But if I do not offer myself to slow the pirates' progress, I will most likely die as well—as will all of us—and the gold will not be returned to Barbados. If that occurs, my wife and father-in-law face a most bleak future. I choose to preserve their lives before I preserve mine."

Havers nodded. "'Tis a most noble sacrifice, Captain Hawkes," he replied. "Yet as you say, of the two choices available, it be the only one that contains a certain outcome."

Will nodded. "If I could choose, I would choose not to spend my last moments here this day. But it appears that regardless of my action, that event will unfold. With this plan, my wife and her family are protected."

Lieutenant Havers stepped back and saluted Will, a rare honor bestowed upon a civilian ship's captain by a naval officer.

"Draw the *Water Sprite* close sides, men! Prepare rigging and boarding timbers to make the crossing. All step lively!" Havers shouted.

The three vessels danced about on the rough waters, maneuvering about until the *Water Sprite* and the *Dorset Lady* were side by side. Ropes were made fast, and men began to jump and cross to the smaller ship. They carried nothing but their personal effects, and the Spanish ship remained near, ensuring that no gold was transferred.

As the last few men jumped from ship, a small group of five men lingered behind. Three of them were from Will's days as a privateer.

William stepped toward them and ordered them to leave.

Malcolm Trent spoke first. "Cap'n Will, I speak for these men, and I be sayin' that we will not leave you."

"But I have ordered it so, Mr. Trent," Will answered firmly.

Malcolm stepped closer and spoke in a lower, confidential voice. "Cap'n Will, we been seein' those sails for some time, too. If the *Water Sprite* is to be makin' it back to Bridgetown, we needs to be givin' 'em a bit of a chase. You cannot be doin' the sailin' alone—so we be stayin' with you."

Malcolm stepped back, then leaned in once again. "You can try us for treason or have us flogged for disobeyin' an order when we gets back to port, if you have a mind to. But this day, we not be leavin' yer side."

Each man had set his mouth in a tight, determined grin.

"'Tis a grand day to meet our Maker. How many men get to choose that day?" Malcolm added calmly. "We all agree that we won't be leavin' yer side."

Will looked at each, then replied. "Agreed then. But when we reach Bridgetown I'll be sending you all up before the magistrate."

Each man smiled briefly, nodded, then set to their tasks.

As the last crewman leaped from the *Dorset Lady* and the ropes were loosened, Will shouted over for John Delacroix.

Four men lifted his pallet close to the rail. A thin sheen of sweat covered John's ashen face.

"John!" Will called.

John raised his left hand in greeting.

"Upon your return home, look after Kathryne and make certain she is well cared for. She knows of my resources, and I know she will use them wisely."

John nodded, perhaps too weak to shout back.

"Tell her, John . . . that I truly loved her body and soul—more than any man could have loved a woman. Tell her I loved her more than I loved sailing and the sea. Tell her I loved her more than the first breath of morning. Tell her that I loved her more than I loved my life." Will's voice began to crack and tremble. "Tell her that, John!"

John nodded and cried back, in a weakened, warbly voice, "I shall, Will. I shall."

Lieutenant Havers then shouted out, "Cast off!"

The small *Water Sprite,* her decks packed with sailors—and her holds full of gold—still bobbed high upon the waters. Sailors climbed up and unfurled all her canvas in one great sweep, and she caught the wind and took off like an anxious sea beast in search of its home.

## 90

The *Water Sprite* slipped from the side of the *Dorset Lady* and caught the hot, humid southeasterly stream of wind. Within moments, Will could no longer make out individual faces upon her deck. In a few more moments, the figures themselves would be lost in a distancing blur.

Will peered at the small Spanish ship resting just off the bow of the *Dorset Lady,* then called his skeleton crew to gather about him.

"Good men," Will spoke calmly, "you know that our chances for seeing tomorrow's dawn are most small. I thank you for your bravery."

"Cap'n Will," Malcolm said, "we all know that if it were us askin', you would be doin' the same."

Will nodded in the direction of the Spanish ship.

"Malcolm, you have four cannons loaded and primed. Can you hit the mast of the pirates' yacht with one of them? I want to make this chase a bit more interesting."

Malcolm and the other four sailors looked over at the small ship, then back at Will, almost in unison.

"If the wind keeps blowin', this vessel will float into perfect position in a moment. If we be sneaky, we might be able to fire all four on the port side without them thinkin' we be goin' to. It'll take a wee bit of luck, but we can try."

"Then do so, Mr. Trent," Will said. "I will be at the helm. Fire at her mast, and then run and lower every sail you can. If we catch the wind and tack into it for a few leagues, we should be able to lure them away from the *Water Sprite.*"

"Aye, Cap'n. We'll wander over to the guns and let 'em pop on your orders."

Each man left that small circle and walked as if taking a leisurely stroll down Regent Street in London on a pleasant Sunday afternoon. Will sauntered over to the polished wooden helm and leaned against it, as if he were ignoring its presence. His men stood by the cannons or near them, not paying attention to them in the least.

The wind took the *Dorset Lady*'s stern and pivoted her about, each breath bringing her closer to a broadside approach.

Will looked over to Malcolm, who nodded.

"Gentlemen," Will shouted, trying to be heard over the wind, "at your leisure!"

Each man jumped to the cannons, and within a heartbeat, all four cannons belched fire and shot, the smoke of the gunpowder blanketing the deck like an angry fog.

None of the cannons could be aimed, for that activity would have drawn too much attention, and three of the four shots sailed harmlessly over the deck of the Spanish yacht and splashed into the sea.

But the fourth must have been blessed by a fortuitous roll of the deck. The shot impacted the pirates' mainmast at deck level, shearing it completely in two, bringing the sails and rigging tumbling to the deck in a shivering crash.

Will screamed, "Away all sails!"

Will's five men threw themselves to ropes and pinions and tore at them, releasing every square inch of canvas that the *Dorset Lady* possessed. Will grappled with the stiff helm and tugged and pulled, bringing the ship about, heading into the winds. The sails ruffled and barked as they filled, huffing against the strong winds. Will did not look back at the damaged Spanish ship, knowing it was a threat no more. If his ship could catch a steady flow of good wind, the hunted might stand the slimmest chance of eluding the hunter for a time.

"Well done, men!" William shouted as the vessel began to cant, deeply cutting into the furious swells. "Perhaps we will outfox the hounds this day and turn the chase into a true test of sailing!"

Will turned about to see the enemy's approaching convoy of ships, seeing that they had spread their ranks and had begun to widen their arcs. If the pursuit was well organized, Will reasoned, the two ships at the end of the picket line, usually the fastest of the fleet, would arc out in a very wide circle, as if to stand guard and ensure no escape at either end of the net. The two ships in the center, often slower and better armed, would follow a single straight line, aimed always at their prey.

Indeed, this was the very tack that the pirates employed. The two ships at the end of the line, most likely the two speedy pinnaces that had been beached, thus escaping sabotage at the cove, went east and west in a wide circle. If Will veered to one side or the other, they would be there first to slow his escape. Even if the *Dorset Lady* could dispatch one of the small ships or elude it, the other vessels would have the time to join the fray.

Heading into the wind, Will's progress was slow, but he desired as far easterly of a position as could be gained, for once their pursuers neared, he would spin back and take the wind at her reach, skimming along as best he could. If Will was successful, perhaps the *Dorset Lady* might gain enough time to hide in the coming darkness. That would slow the hunters and ensure a safe return of the *Water Sprite* to Bridgetown.

Will looked to the sky and realized with dismay that a full watch would pass until darkness fell, with its comforting protection.

Will kept his grip tight on the helm for near half an hour, taking a stubborn tack into the face of the wind. He, as well as the five other men, kept their eyes on the ships to their stern. The *Dorset Lady* was a sturdy craft and well built, but it was not constructed to take full advantage of the winds. It was pirates who sailed for speed, not merchants, and these brigands were no exception. Even into a fierce headwind, they gained ground with every passing moment.

Looking back one more time, Will recognized that he would soon have to try his one chance at a sprint and catch the day's wind full with her sails, heading west by southwest.

"Prepare to reverse tack!" he shouted.

Off to the far south, lightning crackled and glowed at the horizon. Great sheets of white, jagged light illuminated the lowering fists of clouds.

The five sailors ran to the foremast and mizzenmast, untied their stays, and as Will pulled the helm, they pulled the sails and retied to the other side. The mainsail huffed, then caught the wind. It filled with a lurch, and the ship jumped forward, toward the western horizon. The vessel's speed increased, and the bow rose and fell into a deep trough of waves, the spray rainbowing back along the deck, soaking each man to the skin.

As Will turned and placed the wind at his profile, so did each ship in the small pirate fleet. This brought the pursuit to a footrace among the vessels.

Every man on the *Dorset Lady* had his eyes fixed upon the northern and western horizons. If they could increase the distance that lay between them, they might elude the pirates this day. Ascertaining distance on water was a difficult matter, but to Will's best guess, his pursuers had the edge in speed. It would be perhaps no more than an hour until the ships might sail broadside. Will now knew that the conclusion was inevitable. He would not escape. He had no men to fight their way to freedom. They hadn't enough cannons to engage in a long battle. Yet every hour that they sailed with the pirates in their wake was one additional hour that the *Water Sprite* sailed closer to Bridgetown and to safety with the gold.

"Gentlemen!" Will called out. "Can you leave your posts and gather here by me? I need to speak to each of you."

Men tied off ropes, snugged rigging, set pinions secure with a heavy twist and shove, and then edged back along the rolling deck to stand before Will. Each man grabbed hold of a rail, a mast, or a line, for the deck began to tilt even further and more severely.

"Good sailors," Will began, "I am grateful for your loyal help. Your bravery shall enable the *Water Sprite* to return safely to home. The families of each one of those men aboard her, as well as the king, shall remember your sacrifice to God forever."

Malcolm shouted out, "It be nothin' that you wouldn't have done Cap'n Will. Truly it isn't."

"But while we still are able, I need to ask each one of you this day: Are you are prepared to meet your Maker? If our pirate pursuers end our lives, what will you say to God at the gates of his heaven?"

A gust of wind bucked the ship from level, and each sailor grabbed hold of his position a bit tighter.

"Do you mean will we be askin' to be let in, or will we be merely admirin' the location?" Malcolm laughed.

"Indeed, that is the question," Will answered. "My soul rails at placing your lives in peril without such a question asked and answered."

Will looked at their faces, wet from the sea, lips drawn tight, eyes mere slits from the wind.

"And what be your answers? What say you to the invitation that the Almighty gives? Will you accept God's gift and allow him to rule your lives? I know 'twill be for a few moments, but 'tis enough time to open heaven's gate for you."

Malcolm, as the leader of the group, spoke first. "I be settled on this, Cap'n. For certain I ain't the best Christian man there be, but Christian I be."

Robbie Buntles spoke out. "Aye, Cap'n Will. That be me answer, too.

I been sittin' listenin' to your Sunday talks long enough that I believe some has rubbed off on me. I believe in what you taught me. I believe that God loves me."

The bow cut deeply into the water, and a wave as deep as their ankles washed the length of the decking.

Malcolm laughed out. "The rest of ye best decide before we drown. Wouldn't want them pirate dogs to be sorely disappointed by that unfortunate happenin'."

The three remaining men stood silent. Calvin DeForr, Davis Toller, and Samuel Dogestil had lowered their heads, ever so slightly, as to avoid the probing of Will's eyes.

"The rest of you?" he shouted. "Will you not pray with me now? This most assuredly will be your last chance. You don't wish to wake up in eternal damnation and pain, do you?"

They all shook their heads.

"Then will you pray with me?" Will shouted over the winds.

They all nodded, so slightly that it was barely perceptible with all the movement on deck.

"I take that as a yes. I will pray for you, then," Will bellowed. "Each of you now, listen and pray silently with me. There is no time for the niceties such as a proper baptism and all, but the God of heaven understands."

Will looked about and saw them all bowed in prayer.

"Dear almighty God," he began, "I am but a poor sinner. I know that I cannot be good enough to gain your kingdom, nor do evil enough that you will cease loving me. I accept the gift of salvation you have provided in the death of your Son, Jesus. By his resurrection I know I shall be granted eternal life. I thank you for this, my Lord and my God. Amen."

Each man nodded, then raised his head. Will saw a smile on each face.

"Bless you," he roared out, over the waves. "Bless you all. Now, let us return to the sails. Perhaps we have a few more moments left of freedom to prepare ourselves for heaven."

Will grabbed at the helm again and turned it to the west, and the ship arced out and headed west, a little faster now than before. It would be of no use, Will knew, for their hunters used the same wind.

Looking up into the gray colorless sky, Will closed his eyes for a moment and prayed.

*Dear God, I offer myself for the greater good of those whom I love. If I can grant Kathryne and her father a secure future, then my life will have been worthwhile. Please provide your special comforting Spirit upon her to grant her peace and calm and understanding. I would no sooner part from her side than I would cease my love for you, but I must do this. Will you keep her close to you? Will you protect her with your tender care as your Word promises? I am not fearful of death, for I know my destination. Yet I will miss her smile that lights up her eyes and her wonderful laugh so greatly. I thank you for finding me and offering me the rare gift of having her—if only for such a short time. I know now that I shall be happy in heaven, for with her, I have tasted paradise here on this earth. I thank you, almighty Father. Amen.*

Will opened his eyes and felt the rain begin.

CHAPTER

## 91

*Barbados*

Hattie had left the bedchamber only moments before, taking the empty tray of food with her. She had helped Kathryne change into a dry gown and had brought water and towels for her refreshment.

The room was dim, even though it was still afternoon. Rain tapped hard against the windows of Shelworthy, and rivulets ran down in thick streaks. The shutters snapped in the rising wind.

Kathryne arose from the bed and went to the water basin and splashed the warm water against her face, cupping it carefully in her hands. Blindly, she reached out for her towel and patted the moisture from her face.

She looked up into the looking glass where she stood, her face glistening back at her eyes. *What was contained in my image that speaks of motherhood?* Kathryne wondered, looking closer at the reflection, tilting her head first to one side and then the other. *Is it an altered image of me that all can see, save myself?*

She reached into the water again and splashed about. Not reaching to dry her face, she remained standing, wet, her eyes closed, and prayed once more.

*Dearest Father God, I beg you to provide William the guidance he needs to find his way back to me. You have opened the door for William to find you. You have opened the door that William might rescue me and Papa from Uncle Radcliffe. You have opened the door that we may be wed. Please, dear Father, open yet one last door and carry William through this danger, through this storm, and home to his child. Wherever he is right now, provide him a safe haven. Provide him rescue with your powerful hand. Provide him courage and strength. I ask this humbly in Jesus' name, Amen.*

## Caribbean Sea

Will kept his hand on the helm, and the *Dorset Lady* responded by gaining speed. The winds increased and were near storm level. The sea churned and frothed, and the waves grew, threatening to swamp the pirates' smaller ships.

With only five men, the prudent action would have been for Will to order sails furled and use only those on the mizzenmast or the foremast to keep the vessel pointed into the waves, rather than let her bob sideways in the deep troughs. A vessel found parallel to a crashing wave often found herself headed for the bottom of the sea in short order.

But Will allowed himself no thoughts of safety just yet, for his one goal was to consume all the time he could manage, spreading the distance between the pirates' convoy and the English gold.

Yet through all of Will's heroic actions and the bravery of his crew—now manning sails and climbing yardarms in the biting rain and winds—they were no match for the faster and better-manned vessels that ran behind them.

Will turned one last time, and off his right shoulder sat the *Villa Terra Nova,* the fastest of his pursuers. Her bowsprit was matched at Will's stern, and her crew was readying grappling irons and pikes. They were preparing to board Will's ship.

Will felt for his sword and touched its hiLieutenant His pistol would be useless now, the powder wet and impotent. He hefted the heavy weapon from his belt and let it clatter to the deck.

His crew crouched behind the rail and netting of the *Dorset Lady,* wary of musket shot or pistol fire. Each held a long, well-used sugar machete or massive ax in his hands. Most sailors would claim that a sword was too precise a weapon. It required too much skill to wield effectively on deck. The average sailor preferred to bludgeon his opponent with quick and vicious brutality, clubbing them into submission. A sword battle was much like a ballet, and the average sailor was no such dancer.

A Spanish sailor unwound a rope, twirled it about his head, and sent the first grappling hook flying from the *Villa Terra Nova.* It landed in the churning water, several yards short of its mark. A second hurled over the waves and found purchase at the aft rail of the *Dorset Lady.*

Malcolm scuttled over, hiding as best he could behind the rail and rigging, and whacked the rope with his ax, sundering in two. A third, then a fourth, then a fifth hook landed, and Will and his crew knew that they could not prevent the pirates' boarding. Yet no one desired to allow it to happen without a fight being waged.

The sky rained hooks, ropes, and pikes, and with an agonizing squeal of wood, the *Villa Terra Nova* and the *Dorset Lady* became as one. Each vessel pitched in the sea at a different rate. The two vessels seemed as if to resist the mating, and their railings, nettings, and decks tore at each other, grinding off bits and chunks of wood with every surge of the sea.

Will turned, and there on the railing just opposite his helm station stood a baleful and threatening Radcliffe Spenser. His hair was wet from the rain, and a purple bruise snaked along his forehead. Yet his piercing eyes danced and glowed with evil joy.

Without saying a word, he pointed with his long cutlass to several of the men standing behind him. They began to make their way across slick boarding planks to Will's ship.

Will and his crew centered themselves about the helm station. Each held on to his weapon but knew that a further fight would be futile. They said nothing as they gathered and watched as a dozen Spanish pirates descended through gangways and hatches, seeking out their gold.

A half-dozen moments passed.

No one spoke.

The only sounds were the fractured crying of the ships as they tore at each other's hulls, the growing shriek of the wind, and the flutter and snap of canvas overhead.

Will shut his eyes. From below he began to hear the pirates' cursing and shouting.

Another half-dozen moments passed.

The look of triumph and victory on Radcliffe's face, at first so obvious, slowly gave way to a more coiled, angry look. His eyes stopped their dance, his glee gave way to a dark, evil glow.

"Hawkes!" Radcliffe shouted. "What have you done with my gold?"

William smiled. "Perhaps your men have been overtaken by my soldiers in the hold. Perhaps I will yet hold you prisoner, Radcliffe."

A look of terror started to spread across Radcliffe's visage. He thought perhaps that Will had indeed held men in abeyance.

"Do not toy with me, you cur," Radcliffe snarled. "I will make you suffer for every moment you make me wait for what is mine. I want my gold returned!"

A pirate, face streaked with dust and dirt, struggled through the far aft hatch, dusting at his shoulders, wiping away dark oily stains on his knees.

"It is gone, Señor Radcliffe!" he called out, holding on to the open railing.

Radcliffe, not a robust man on the best of days, turned ashen and nearly tinted green.

"What!" he shrieked. "Then you have not searched everywhere! The gold was loaded onto this ship! I saw it with my own eyes! It is here somewhere, you worthless pig! Find it!"

The sailor shrugged and ducked below again.

Radcliffe cuffed two men, standing near him, with a sharp blow to their heads, commanding that they, too, join the search. The two began to try to make their way quickly across the rain-wet boarding planks. The first man dove the last several feet and clumped to the deck in a wet tangle. The second man, older, with a greasy gray beard, inched his way across the pitching plank, his arms held out for balance.

"Move, you stupid lout! Move!" Radcliffe screamed.

The sailor turned to nod to Radcliffe. The ships rolled again, and he was pitched, headfirst, into the great wooden maw that the two vessels created. That chomping distance opened a foot, then closed about him, trapping him as a bumper between the hulls, grinding the life from him with a terrifying shriek and wail.

William shut his eyes to the sight.

The ships parted again, and his lifeless, crushed body dropped to the waves below.

Moments passed, and Radcliffe began to pace. He whipped his cutlass through the air like a riding crop, and his crew backed away from his deadly arc.

A second sailor, then a third, climbed out from the forward and rear deck hatches.

"Señor Radcliffe, it is true. We have searched in every cabin and hold. There is no gold on this ship."

Radcliffe was at the rail now, leaning forward over the deadly jaws and the sea below. He spun about.

"You are lying to me! The gold was on this ship! I saw the loading! They carried it on board! I saw it!" Radcliffe ranted on, shouting and cursing and flailing his arms about, his cutlass whizzing through the air like a wasp.

Radcliffe's jaw dropped open as he realized the deception. He lunged his sword at William, some thirty feet away.

"You filthy cheat! You transferred the gold to the other ship, did you not!" Radcliffe bellowed out, his voice piercing even through the wind and storm. A strike of lightning cracked above them, and to a man, save William and Radcliffe, all cringed and ducked where they stood.

Radcliffe looked to the south, then to the sky. He knew that the *Water Sprite* now had a lead of a full watch. Indeed, the vessel and its precious cargo may have skirted to the east of the brewing storm at this hour. Unless the ship foundered, its arrival in Barbados well ahead of any ship of the pirate fleet was assured. Radcliffe realized that William had cleverly outfoxed him, depriving him of the gold, depriving him of victory, depriving him from the very satisfaction of besting his despised brother and niece.

Radcliffe glared at William. "Seize him! Seize Hawkes, the wretched dog!" Radcliffe shrieked, trembling, as if his entire being was being rent by demons.

The sailors, their swords extended, moved cautiously, forming a large circle around the smaller circle of Will's crew, which surrounded Will.

"Do not resist!" Will shouted to his men. "This outcome is not in doubt! If you value my honor, you will allow me to surrender with dignity!"

After a long moment, Will's five crewmen slowly lowered their arms and allowed Will to walk out of their protective circle.

"I thank you, good sailors. Remember me when you speak of this. Tell Kathryne I loved her. Remember your promise to God."

Will slid his blade into his scabbard and walked to the rail. He did not turn again, but jumped to a boarding plank and with three long, sure steps made his way to the deck of the *Villa Terra Nova*.

Malcolm watched as Will was grabbed roughly by a half-dozen men and held securely.

Radcliffe bellowed out to his men, "Get back to this ship, you fools! Now!"

His men climbed, some on hands and knees, making their way carefully to the *Villa Terra Nova*.

"You dolts!" Radcliffe barked to the men on the *Dorset Lady*. "Who will be in charge of the vessel, now that your precious Mr. Hawkes is mine?"

Malcolm stepped forward. "That would be me!" he shouted back.

Radcliffe glowered at him with disgust plainly evident in his face.

"Thus tells the sad state of English sailors, no doubt," Radcliffe muttered, then grinned a jagged smile at his own witticism. He raised his voice and shouted, "So then, do you have a prayer of getting this ship back to Barbados without falling off the edge of the world? Ha!"

Even some of Radcliffe's men giggled, at least those who spoke some English.

"Aye, Mr. Spenser," Malcolm shouted, "and we'll make the trip a far sight faster than you could."

Radcliffe reached down for a pinion and angrily threw it across the rails at Malcolm. It sailed high over his head and rattled down ineffectually on the far side of the *Dorset Lady.*

"I will take great pleasure if you should arrive safely. For I have one request that you need comply with, and then I shall cast off these lines and let you sail to your freedom," he sneered.

"And what is that?" Malcolm shouted.

"Go back to Barbados and tell Kathryne Spenser—or should I refer to her as Kathryne Hawkes?—that I, Uncle Radcliffe, hold her beloved husband captive," Radcliffe bellowed, the veins in his neck bulging.

Malcolm was puzzled. "And you be tellin' us he be held for ransom, then?"

Radcliffe began to laugh and in a moment was doubled over in laughter, his face growing even redder. He stood up after a long moment, gasping for air in the wind, wiping at his eyes with a gloved hand.

"Gracious no, you stupid git," Radcliffe barked out. "I merely wish to inform Kathryne and her swinish father that I will take the greatest pleasure in killing both Hawkes and his pious friend Mayhew. Tell them that their blood will be surely on Kathryne's head. Tell her that I will strip the skin from both of them in small slices and let their flesh fester in the sun. Tell her that I will make sure that he experiences a most horrific death. Tell her . . ."

Malcolm could stand no more. He lunged at the rail, chopping and attacking the ropes that held the ships entwined. The thudding of ax on wood drowned out Radcliffe's vile monologue.

With a final liberating shriek, the ships separated and began to bob apart. Malcolm ran to the helm, called for the sails to be set, and set a course for Barbados.

He took one last look at William, surrounded by a dozen men on the deck of the *Villa Terra Nova,* and then at Radcliffe, who ran to the bow of his ship, cursing and gesturing as the *Dorset Lady* slipped from earshot.

## 92

The rain danced heavily on the deck of the Spanish ship as Radcliffe slowly made his way amidships. He held his blade loose in his right hand. With a grin, he wiped at his face and pulled his long, oily hair back from his forehead and cheeks.

"Well, Mr. Hawkes," he crowed, "perhaps this is my ultimate reward—to see your life end at my hand. Is that not a lovely thought?"

He took a step closer and lifted his blade to the level of Will's heart. "Now if I were to lunge just a step, my smiling face would be the last image your eyes would behold on this earth. Is that not a most joyous thought?"

Radcliffe let the blade lower so it aimed at Will's midsection.

"Or perhaps a wounding in your gut, which could boil and fester for days. That, too, would be most pleasant to watch."

Will could feel the breath of his captors on his face and arms, and as Radcliffe ranted on, he felt their breath increase, their grips tighten on his arms, their smirks widen into macabre grins.

*Has Radcliffe enchanted them all with his evil? Or does the civilizing veneer of men run so thin?* Will wondered, curiously dispassionate considering the danger his life was in.

A lightning flash hissed and crackled to the sea no more than a league from the *Villa Terra Nova*. Even Will shrank from the bolt, as did his captors. Radcliffe, however, seemed energized by the ghostly illumination. The flash seemed to light up his bones beneath his flesh, as if he were a specter wearing a thin sheath of skin over a rattling skeleton.

"Ah, but Mr. Hawkes, that would deprive me of my greatest triumph.

I must admit that in the midst of all this vile treachery, I forgot my trump card—the raison d'être."

He pointed at a clump of men huddled on the lee side of the mast. "Fetch him. Now!"

They scurried off through an open hatch. The seawater, sluicing over the decks, poured through after them as well. In a moment they returned holding a thin figure, clad in black tatters and bound in chains.

"You there!" Radcliffe roared. "You heathenish excuse for a holy man! Raise up your head! You have company!"

The figure arched and struggled, and one of his captors roughly grabbed at his head and tore away the black capping from his face.

Lightning clapped again, and thunder boiled from overhead, a rumbling drumroll of celestial anger. Will looked up, and his heart soared more open and free than it had ever felt. He was looking into the deep-set eyes of a battered but living Vicar Thomas Mayhew.

And unwilling to allow even one more moment to pass between them filled with uncertainty, Will shouted out, "I have searched for him, Thomas, as I promised, and God has found me. Your prayers have been answered."

Though Will's eyes welled with tears, he saw the vicar smile through his pain.

## Barbados

From the door of the bedchamber came a gentle tapping, almost in cadence with the rain. Kathryne hesitated for a moment, considering the idea of feigning sleep so she would not be required to deal with anyone. Yet the tapping continued, now a little louder.

"Yes?" she called out. "Who is there?"

The door opened slightly and Emily peeked in. "Kathryne? May I trouble you for just a moment?"

Kathryne sighed and wiped at her eyes, hoping that her tears had not left them reddened. She desired to maintain the facade that all was well with her this day. "Please, Emily. Of course you may enter."

Emily slipped in, latched the door behind her, and made her way to sit at the far edge of the bed. She placed her hand over Kathryne's and squeezed. She smiled but did not utter a word.

Kathryne looked at Emily's face, then smiled in return as she placed her hand on her stomach.

"Hattie told you of this, did she not?"

Emily nodded, trying her best to hold back her joy.

"I love her, yet she cannot hold a confidence for longer than the time it takes to descend the stairs."

In a voice both tinged with laughter and joyful tears, Emily nodded and replied, "To be true, her nature is not one for secrets."

Emily leaned forward and wrapped her arms around Kathryne and hugged her close, stroking her hair and whispering into her ear of how overjoyed her heart had become.

"I can scarce believe the small child I once held in my arms will bear a child of her own," Emily fussed as she smoothed at Kathryne's gown and sleeve. "It was only yesterday that you were born."

Kathryne wiped at her eyes again. "I do not yet comprehend the magnitude of these changes either, Emily. In an instant I became aware, and I have struggled to grasp just what it really means."

"It will come easier, my sweet Kathryne. It was much the same with your mother. I remember the awe in which I held her as she shared your upcoming arrival. How I envied her as well. Yet this day I can share with you the same. Is not our Lord magnificent?"

Kathryne nodded.

"Did William know before he left?" Emily asked.

Kathryne shook her head. She sniffed one last time and sat up straight on the bed, pulling her hair back and extending her neck in a most regal manner.

"I will tell him when he returns to me. He will be most pleased."

Beneath her smile, she prayed, *Dear God, let the truth match my words.*

## Caribbean Sea

"Mr. Hawkes!" Radcliffe bellowed. "I have decided what I shall do with you and your holy friend!"

Will turned his head and looked at Radcliffe with a smoldering anger.

"I shall let you loose, dear boy," he said, laughing, "and have sport with you."

Again a bolt of lightning crackled nearby, and the water reflected the phantasm of light across the tall chop of waves.

"I shall tire of a long, slow process," he called out gaily, as if speaking in the salon of an elegant men's club in London. "Let us finish the matter today. It will be of no slight pleasure to me that your trollop Kathryne will now think the worst. That will be revenge enough."

Radcliffe sniffed and wiped at his nose with the long, flowing sleeve of his velvet-and-leather doublet.

"You there, the man with the crossed eyes. Fetch Mr. Hawkes his sword. I wish to have a dalliance with the man."

The crew began to spread about the deck, creating a large open area for the combat, a circle of some yards on both sides of the mainmast and wheelhouse.

Will looked back to the vicar and nodded. Will knew that the end was near. Radcliffe was a highly skilled bladesman, and while Will could match his prowess in a fair fight, he had no illusions this day. Will was slowed by his wounds, and the pain in his leg and shoulder would make a mockery of any such duel. And even if Will was to assume a favorable edge in battle, a dagger or cudgel would appear from behind from one of Radcliffe's men, and Will's advantage would be for naught.

The cross-eyed sailor tossed Will's sword to Will, and he caught it by the hilt and hefted the point to his shoulder.

Radcliffe slipped out from behind the mainmast with a sleek long sword, its gleaming sides flashing in the lightning. He whipped the point through the rain, the sharpened Toledo blade hissing as it traveled.

"*En point,* Mr. Hawkes?" Radcliffe called out in a clipped proper voice. "Shall we begin?"

To Will's side, Vicar Mayhew struggled to pull himself erect, elbowing weakly at both his captors. His left hand was wrapped in a cloth of most dubious cleanliness, and the end was stained a deep burgundy, the color of dried blood. His black robe was torn and dirtied.

"William, is that truly you?" he finally cried out. "My prayers have indeed been answered!"

The rain continued to fall, warm as tears and laced with the faint taste of salt, as if being drawn from the very ocean itself by the anxious winds.

Will turned to Radcliffe, whose sword was readied, and called out, "If there is any shred of decency left in your heart, Radcliffe, you will give me a moment with this man. I ask for only a single moment."

Radcliffe stiffened and lowered his blade to his side. "You accuse me of lacking decency? You accuse me of having no heart? How dare you!" His voice was shrill and reedy.

He flicked at the air with his left hand, as if brushing away a fly. "No one claims Radcliffe Spenser to be unrefined and cruel. By all means, spend a moment of confession with your charlatan priest. Speak with him about the foulness of the weather, for all I would care."

And then he screamed, louder and blacker, "But then say your farewells, you worthless scum-laden sea dog! Say them well. For today you both die!"

Will ran to the vicar's side and embraced him, careful that he not cause further pain to his bruised frame.

"Vicar, I thought I would never see you this side of heaven! My prayers have been answered!" Will cried. "It is because of you that I am in the arms of the Lord."

The vicar coughed, then spoke, his voice hoarse and throaty. "No, William, it is my prayers that have been answered. For if what you have just stated is true, then I can close my eyes to this world with peace and joy in my heart—for I will spend eternity with you."

Radcliffe shrieked, "You have now spent one-half of your moment. Say your good-byes now!"

Will ignored the shrieking. "Good Thomas, I am married now to the most beautiful woman I have ever seen. How I wish you could meet her."

"Does she believe, William?"

"She does, Thomas, with all her heart."

"Then one day I shall meet her above, William. I have that assurance."

Will wiped at his eyes, his tears coming unashamed. "Thank you, Thomas, for never forgetting me in your prayers."

"The time is up, Mr. Hawkes," Radcliffe exclaimed. "It is now time for our deadly dance."

Will stood and picked up his sword.

As he stood, Thomas reached out with his uninjured hand and caught Will's sleeve. "William, this may sound odd being said by a man of God, but I have one last instruction for you."

He leaned toward William and whispered loudly, "Do not let that man win easily. Fight him well! Evil is not to win with a smile. Teach him a lesson in God's power."

William smiled and then he lifted the hilt of his sword and touched it to his forehead, as a sign of obedience. "I shall, Thomas. I shall."

## Barbados

Lightning flashed about the dark sky, and heavy rumbles of thunder echoed across the island, rattling the windowpanes. Kathryne tucked her feet under a thick quilt and picked up the copy of the Scriptures she kept on her night table. Beauregard jumped up onto the bed and nestled by her feet.

Another loud rumble crossed the valley. The dog whimpered softly and nuzzled deeper into the quiLieutenant Willy, her pet thrush, jumped from perch to floor and perch again in a most agitated manner. He repeated the same action during every storm, Kathryne knew, and she often wondered what he would do if he were actually out in the elements. Would he bound about in the rain, or decide that a warm, dry place was best suited?

He did not sing when so agitated. Yet this day, each jump was accompanied by a soft churled chirp, as if calling out to someone in the distance, like a beacon for someone lost.

Kathryne looked over at the little, brown, feathered creature that chirped and jumped, chirped and jumped.

"Willy," she called out. "Are you attempting to get someone's attention?"

She looked out the window, thinking that perhaps a native bird had sought solace under the eaves of the windows. But beyond the rain-streaked pane of glass there was only the gray and restless ocean.

Willy jumped again and stopped for a long moment at his highest perch. Then, cocking his head to one side and bristling his feathers, he burst into a strange call, one that Kathryne could not recall having heard before this day. The song sounded lonely, plaintive, sad. After a long moment's trill, he fluttered once to the next perch and sat upon it, as if settling in for the night.

"Willy," Kathryne called over, "I will have no more of that song—much too melancholy for a songbird such as yourself."

She petted Beauregard and opened the Scriptures. Her thoughts had still not settled and her heart was most troubled. *I need such comfort as only God's Word can provide.*

She flipped several of the thick vellum pages and began to read out loud, yet soft and almost under her breath.

"'The Lord is my shepherd; I shall not want. He maketh me to lie down in green pastures: he leadeth me beside the still waters. He restoreth my soul: he leadeth me in the paths of righteousness for his name's sake. Yea, though I walk through the valley of the shadow of death, I will fear no evil: for thou art with me; thy rod and thy staff they comfort me. Thou preparest a table before me in the presence of mine enemies: thou anointest my head with oil; my cup runneth over. Surely goodness and mercy shall follow me all the days of my life: and I will dwell in the house of the Lord for ever.'

"William, remember that *we* will dwell in that house *together*—forever. Remember that, William—forever."

She shut the book, held it to her chest, and fell across the bed, making no attempt to hold back her emotions.

## 93

*Caribbean Sea*

"Finally, Mr. Hawkes," Radcliffe oozed as the lightning crackled behind him, its long sinewy veins of ghostly light scratching across the green sky. "Shall the festivities begin?"

And just as William turned to face him, Radcliffe shouted out gleefully, "Black moves first" and lunged toward Will, his sword aimed square at his left shoulder. Even though Will ducked back, the sharply honed tip of Radcliffe's blade sliced through Will's doublet and nicked at his skin, perhaps to the depth of the thickness of a finger. A red stain appeared there in an instant, spreading its warmth about Will's shoulder.

"Such a pleasant beginning!" Radcliffe shouted over the winds as he circled the bloodied tip in a menacing circle. "Don't you agree, Mr. Hawkes?"

Will acted on instinct, thrusting back at his attacker, his blade barely catching the flesh at Radcliffe's left side, snipping a small cut in his skin. Will stepped back and held his sword out at defense point.

Radcliffe and William warily circled at each other, their blades delicately touching at the center of their circle. Every half-dozen steps, one or the other would feint or lunge. Their blades would collide together with a polite clatter, for each sought to discover the weakness of his opponent.

Radcliffe seemed to favor the high thrust, then a quick, angry slash to the deck. His first move aimed at the head, the eyes, the neck—a brutal and quick strategy. If that attack found its mark, his opponent would slump to the deck, his sword dropped, both hands clutching at the deep slice to the face or clamped upon a pulsing vein in the neck.

For Radcliffe, it was then a simple and deadly sweep of the blade to end the battle.

Will fought more upright, his blade at a right angle to the ground, deflecting and parrying until his opponent tired, often seeking his surrender before his death. It was a more cautious and less aggressive manner of battle, one that more closely suited his heart.

As dusk neared, now no more than an hour distant, the winds became more aggressive as well, sweeping up a spray of sea along the decking, wetting the crew from the sea as well as the rain from the sky. It was obvious to any who paid attention to the signs of the sky that a wretched storm was brewing and this small ship would be in the middle of the cauldron.

The sky, a translucent green at noon, had added color and depth since then. The clouds were thick and boiling above, with massive lightning bolts spiking about the open sea. Will would have wagered that such weather marked the beginning of what the natives called a *hurricane*—he being well versed in reading such signs by his journeys and travels with natives to the tropics.

As he circled the deck, jousting tentatively with Radcliffe, his eyes scanned the horizon. If Will had been at the helm of the ship, he would have lowered all sails and raced at his best speed, seeking out the shelter of a harbor or cove. At the very least he would have sought out the safety of deeper water. Shoals and reefs pocked this area of sea, and their jagged crowns, he knew, would rip the hull of any ship foolish enough to sail into the teeth of the storm.

Radcliffe swung down hard at Will, who raised his sword in defense. Their blades struck together in a small burst of sparks. Radcliffe did not retreat and slash again, but continued his attack, banging a second and a third time against Will's defense. Each blow brought Will's defense closer to his chest. Radcliffe's fourth blow succeeded, his blade finding purchase along the left side of Will's chest. A thin gash opened, a hand's width long, his doublet cut through and ragged. The damage was slight, but both Will and Radcliffe knew that the cumulative effects of such small cuts eventually weakened a man to death.

Will responded by slashing out at Radcliffe, who expertly deflected each of his parries.

*Do not let that man win easily. Fight him well! Evil is not to win with a smile. Teach him a lesson in God's power.*

Will heard the vicar's words echo in his heart, and he slashed out again in a furious attack. Blow, swing, retreat, thrust, parry, attack, retreat, attack. Not one of the blows could be carried out with a full arm's power, but several broke through Radcliffe's defenses. Two gashes on Radcliffe's left arm began to ooze red.

"You are better at attack, Mr. Spenser, than it appears you are at defense," William taunted.

Radcliffe glowered back at him. He swung his blade first at Will's legs, then spun about and slashed at Will's opposite side. Will deflected the first blow, but was taken aback with the spin. Radcliffe's blade caught him in the side, slashing deeper now, nicking the muscles.

Will grabbed at his side in an instinctive attempt to stitch up the wound. His hand was soon bathed in blood. The cut did not pulse and spurt, and for that Will was grateful. He stepped backwards a step or two and could feel the hot, rancid breath of a pirate crewman at his neck.

"Indeed, you are correct, Mr. Hawkes," Radcliffe bellowed, his eyes wide and lusting at the sight of Will's bloody injury. "Defense is for fools."

And with that, he lunged with a mighty step forward, his blade aimed at Will's midsection.

Despite his wound, Will leapt to the side with a surprising deftness. Radcliffe did not pull short his attack, and his blade continued forward and slipped into the gut of the sailor who stood just behind William, cheering the fight's progress. The sailor's face went soft as he looked down at the massive scarlet circle spreading out on his stomach. His hands fell to his sides, and his eyes grew hazy as he stared, questioning and angry, at Radcliffe. Radcliffe yanked the blade free from the man's flesh and stepped back, ready for Will's attack. The sailor pitched forward and landed, face first, upon the bloody deck.

Will held out his blade and met Radcliffe's renewed attack, flecks of blood spraying off the blade and splattering upon his face. Will knew that the longer this battle raged, the greater distance spread between Radcliffe and Will's ship carrying the English gold. Every moment fought here would help ensure a brighter future for Kathryne and every citizen of Barbados. That alone gave Will courage to continue.

Lightning spit across the sky, appearing just above the small group of ships, and the thunder rumbled like a celestial caisson rolling above their heads.

Will kept retreating along the deck from Radcliffe's frenzied attacks. He backed from the wheel stand to the mainmast, feeling its ropes against his back. He deflected another blow and stepped backwards, moving slowly to the bow of the ship. The sailors, hooting and crying out in delirium, began to crowd back and away from the deadly motions of the two men.

The clang and crash of sword were nearly wiped away by the shrill screech of the wind and the staccato rhythm of the rain. As they rode the sea at storm, the decks rolled and heaved, and Will and Radcliffe fought for life as well as for a firm foothold on the wet decking.

A bolt of lightning crashed with the power and impact of a footstep of God. The ship to their right, the *Invincible,* a squat merchantman, lit the sea for that moment, the lightning exploding her mainmast into a thousand splinters.

The fight aboard the *Villa Terra Nova* stopped, and Radcliffe, William, and every other man aboard the vessel gaped at the macabre display unfolding before their eyes.

The bolt had set the deck ablaze, despite the rain, and a cannon exploded, then another, and men and weapons rained up into the sky. The fires swept belowdeck, and soon the flames swallowed the ship whole. The fifty men aboard were either lost to the flames or quickly were claimed by the churning sea as they leaped overboard.

While the men aboard the *Villa Terra Nova* watched the disaster, they heard a great ripping shriek to their left. The stern of the *Coronado,* a smaller galleon, lifted into the air, her sails and masts collapsing into the sea. The bow of the vessel had been ripped upon the fingers of a shallow reef. Men, cannons, barrels, netting, and canvas were pitched headlong into the sea. Those sailors who might have swum were crushed by cannons or smothered and drowned by yards of wet, clinging, heavy canvas.

The crew of the *Villa Terra Nova* rushed to Radcliffe. They screamed, "Save us! Sail us away from these waters of the devil!"

Will lowered his sword to the deck and bowed his head, panting. His placed his elbow against the gash in his side and pressed to soothe away the fiery pain that throbbed there.

"It is that man who can save us!" Will heard someone shriek.

Another man echoed the cry and then another and another.

A small circle grew about William, a circled clutch of pointing fingers and wild gestures.

Will looked up and saw three faces—faces that he recognized. He had sailed with each of these men when he was a merchant sailor in these waters.

One of them bellowed to Radcliffe, "If any sailor can navigate these waters, it be William Hawkes! He has the saint's knowledge of these bedeviled waters."

The air was filled with a second shriek as the ship next to the *Villa*

*Terra Nova* passed over a submerged reef, her hull crying out in agony as the timbers began to splinter.

The eyes of the crew, a moment ago filled with bloodlust, were now filled with terror and panic. If their demand was not met, they would take matters into their own soiled hands.

Radcliffe knew the power of an uncontrolled mob. "Hawkes!" he howled. "Is that true? Can you sail us out from these waters?"

Will let his sword drop to the deck and grabbed on to the mainmast for support. He watched as his blade rolled to the rail and then fell into the hungry sea.

He wrapped his arm about his bleeding side. He looked to Radcliffe and nodded. "I have sailed these seas before. I believe I know the safe channel to deep water," Will said.

"Then you shall sail us from here!" Radcliffe commanded.

"And why should I save you or any of your miserable crew?" Will shouted back.

This time it was the *Villa Terra Nova* that lurched, a wooden rasping cry echoing up from below.

Radcliffe, sword in hand, lurched over to the vicar, still being held in the grasp of two sailors. He grabbed Thomas's arm, spun him about, and held him tight against his chest. Radcliffe slowly drew his blade up and held it tight to the vicar's neck. He drew the blade ever so quickly across the tender skin. A thin trickle of blood appeared, a cut of hairline depth.

"Because if you do not," Radcliffe cried out, his voice edged with a hint of terror, "I will gladly kill this man, and his blood will be on your head! Can you be the cause of his death with such ease?"

Will stared at Thomas, and the vicar stared back, both men's faces blank and expressionless. Both men tried to reveal their true desire— wanting Radcliffe to draw no satisfaction from their plight.

Will breathed in deeply. "Very well," he answered. "I will sail for you."

A weak cheer arose from the crew.

"But under one condition!" Will called.

"You are in no position to ask," Radcliffe hissed.

"You will set the vicar free!" Will shouted, pointing with his unin-jured right hand. "I know you will kill us both when we reach deep water. I will not have that man enter heaven in chains."

Radcliffe screwed up his face into a tight mask of bitterness, then nodded and lowered his blade. He pulled out a key and unfastened the irons from the vicar's wrists and ankles. Thomas then made his way down the pitching and rolling deck to Will's side.

## 94

The winds whipped at loose ends on the canvas sails, the rope ends snapping and cracking like a whip. The bow of the *Villa Terra Nova* pitched forward into a deep trench between the waves, and a wash of seawater poured over the foredeck in a torrent. Lightning peppered the skies.

Will grabbed the helm with his right hand, his left protecting his left side. He heard a tearing sound from behind. It was the vicar, who ripped off a thick strip of his black vestment and wound it about Will's middle, holding the wound closed.

"Set the foresail tighter and release the mizzen sail!" Will called out, and men scrambled to make the adjustments in the rigging.

Will would not send anyone up the rigging to the yardarms in this weather, for no man would stand a chance of holding on in the face of the storm's power.

"Set the mainsail to angle at the wind!"

Will looked to his right at the last remaining pirate ship in the small armada. Its captain was mimicking Will's maneuvers with sail and course.

Lightning flashed again, and Will called out, trying to be heard over the winds. "Set back! There are reefs to your starboard!"

Moments after Will spoke, the pirate ship stopped dead in her own wake, her bow catching the reef. The winds filled her sails and pushed her forward and to the side. Within a moment, the seas caught the bottom of the mainsail, and the waves pulled her to itself. The crew on deck was pitched into the dark waters and disappeared. Will began to pull on the helm, to attempt to come about.

"You'll be offering no rescue, Mr. Hawkes!" Radcliffe cried, waving his sword at him. "I am captain of this ship, not you."

Will glared and pulled the helm back to position. As he did he felt a give, a loosening of his control, as if the tiller was slipping from its placement at the rear of the vessel.

Will shoved again and felt a lurch in the helm. He nudged at it once again, and the helm splayed to the side. He lifted it back to right, and there was no tension in the mechanics. It was now disconnected from the tiller.

"Radcliffe!" Will shrieked. "Did you repair the tiller when you left?" Radcliffe looked offended.

"Did you splice the helm roping back together or simply tie the cables together?"

"Do you truly think we had time to sit and splice and mend rope? Of course they were but tied!" he bellowed.

Will held the helm in one hand and then let it drop to the deck with a dead thump. "Your repair is undone!" Will shouted. "You are doomed as well as I!"

Radcliffe ran to the helmstand and lifted the heavy lever. Indeed, there was no tension in the device. The connection between the helm and the tiller had been severed by Will's men, repaired by the pirates, and now broken again. They were at sail with no means of setting direction. The wind would take them as it desired. And that desire was pushing the vessel closer to an angry wall of surf breaking over a shallow, biting reef of white coral.

The crew that had seen the events at the helmstand now struggled with longboats, knowing that longboats might clear such dangers.

Radcliffe's face whitened, then contorted into a twisted mask of hate, as if reflecting all the evil of hell.

"This has been all your doing, Mr. Hawkes!" Radcliffe shouted. "You have been my nemesis all along! It is *you* who spoiled my plans with Kathryne and my imbecile brother! It is *you* who spoiled my dream of wealth and riches and power! It is *you* who have spoiled my fun in seeing you die a slow painful death this day! You have spoiled everything!"

As Radcliffe ranted, thin coils of spittle flew from his mouth. The veins in his neck and forehead pulsed and throbbed, as if serpents lay just beneath his skin. He flashed his sword in the rain, whipping it back and forth.

"I have been denied your blood for too long, Mr. Hawkes. I will not be denied a moment longer! I will have your severed head thrust on the point of my sword! I will let your blood wash me clean!"

A rumble began somewhere behind Will, louder, deeper, and fuller than had been heard all day. The winds shrieked as the vessel careened toward the reef; the rumble was the sound of surf crashing upon reef.

"I will have your life!"

Will stood relaxed. There was no sense now in resisting. Will had no blade, no weapon, no strength left to fight.

He bowed his head and prayed, *If now be the hour of my death, dear God, take me home into your arms. Prepare Kathryne for my death. Keep her from harm.*

Will repeated the words over and over as Radcliffe stepped closer.

"Yes, say your prayers, Mr. Hawkes," Radcliffe shouted. "Say your prayers to a God that does not exist!"

Radcliffe was now as close to Will as the length of a blade. He lifted the blade high above his head and laughed the laugh of the devil.

## Barbados

Kathryne's heart began to race, as if a terrible event was about to unfold, just beyond her vision, just beyond her hearing, just beyond her knowing.

But she felt it as sure as she felt the new life within her. She went to the window facing the sea, watching the white scars of waves crash upon the shore, listening to the thunder rattle the walls, seeing the lightning as it cut the horizon. She pressed her face to the cool, slick glass. It felt cold on her fevered forehead. She blinked as the sky flashed white and dark.

*Dear God, protect him,* she prayed, almost in a whimper. *Please protect Will.*

## Caribbean Sea

"Say your vain prayers!" Radcliffe cackled hideously.

As the blade above his head wavered for a single moment, Will looked up into the cold, vacant eyes of Radcliffe Spenser.

"God lives," Will whispered, then lowered his head and closed his eyes.

And before that polished blade moved the width of a hair, a lightning bolt streaked down in a jagged, gnarled hiss, following a path from the heavens to the tip of Radcliffe's raised sword.

The deck lit up with the light of a thousand torches. The blade arced and sizzled, and the might of the sky flowed down the blade, through Radcliffe's hand, and down his arm. His whole being pulsed with the raw energy of the elements.

With a horrendous, sizzling, snaking boom, Radcliffe was thrown from where he stood to the far side of the deck, slamming against the rail with a burning crunch. The blade was carried with him, melded into his hand as if it were forged as a part of his body. Smoke whispered about his sleeve and neck, and his doublet, though wet through, smoldered.

William looked up, dazed from the noise and the explosion. Radcliffe's eyes remained open, shocked wide and round. His lips were burnt and charred black, curling in an evil grin. His hair was scorched to the flesh on his scalp, and the nails in his boots glowed hot.

The vicar arose and struggled to Will. Sailors were rushing about, now in absolute panic and terror. Some attempted to lower longboats, some fell to their knees in prayer, some dove over the side of the ship.

The ship rolled in the water, and Radcliffe's limp body pitched against the railing, then tumbled into the sea with a glowing hiss, a puff of steam marking his entry to his watery grave.

The vicar stood at Will's side, and the two men embraced.

From the hull of the vessel came a shriek. In a moment came a louder, fuller crash as the ship ground against the shallow reef, and a wave of the warm, angry sea washed the two men from the deck.

# CHAPTER

# 95

*Barbados*

The storm hung over Barbados for two full days. No one on the island had ever seen a hurricane of such ferocity and duration. Torrents of rain whipped along the highlands, and dry streams became raging, muddy rivers overnight, etching deeper scars along the landscape.

No one dared venture out during those two days. Kathryne had come down from her bedchamber both mornings, begging to ride to the harbor to await the arrival of Will's ship. And both mornings, Aidan took her by the shoulders and escorted her back to her bedchamber.

The third day the winds calmed and the rains ceased. The sun broke through the clouds at noontide.

Kathryne could be dissuaded no longer and called for Porter. Within the hour she was at the harbor, scanning the waters for Will's ships. Her heart sank as her eyes found no familiar vessels.

She then rode to the chandlery and tapped at Missy's door.

The two kept a silent vigil, sitting on a rough bench by the front door of the chandlery. Missy busied herself with stitchwork. Kathryne simply sat, her hands folded in her lap, and waited and prayed. When day became night, she dozed there until morning, then waited and prayed some more.

On the evening of the fourth day after the storm, the sails of the *Water Sprite* crossed the horizon to the west of the harbor.

Missy and Kathryne raced from their station to the longest pier in the harbor.

Amidst great confusion and excitement, the *Water Sprite* docked, and the tale was soon told. A crew of men carried John back to the chandlery. The musket shot proved a serious wound, and despite Luke's best efforts, John remained fevered and weak.

He told Missy and Kathryne the story of their raid on the pirates, the chase, and the switched gold. But his knowledge ended when the *Water Sprite* left the *Dorset Lady*.

The storm had forced them to take a westerly course, he said, and they had sought refuge in a tiny atoll for a full day before making the last sail to Bridgetown, bringing the king's treasure safely home.

A handful of impromptu celebrations sprang up simultaneously all over the island upon the return of the English gold. All but a few bars had been recovered, and its return guaranteed Lord Aidan's continuity as governor as well as the security and the sovereignty of the island.

Aidan attempted to bring Kathryne back to Shelworthy. "Come home, my poppet, for to be with me and Emily will be a comfort to you," he implored.

"I'll not leave this harbor until William returns, Papa," she answered firmly. "How would it appear to a husband if his wife cared not enough to wait for him?"

By morning of the sixth day, the sails of the *Dorset Lady* were sighted offshore, and again the citizens stormed out to the harbor.

"At last, he has come home!" Kathryne cried. She stood, tears of joy in her eyes as the ship slowly creaked to the pier.

"Where is William?" she called out.

Malcolm did not answer, but threw ropes to the men waiting on the pier.

"Where is William?" Kathryne demanded as the ropes were made secure. "Is he belowdecks? Is he hurt? Where is he?" Her voice became more shrill with each question.

Missy had followed her out to meet the ship and stood by her side. She wrapped an arm about Kathryne's waist for support.

"You do not answer me!" Kathryne called out. "This was William's ship! Where is my husband?"

Missy tried to pull her close and calm her raging emotions. Kathryne shrugged from her grip and grabbed hold of the rail, calling out again, "Where is William?"

Malcolm climbed over the rail and clumped down to the pier. His eyes were downcast, and he could hardly bring them to view the woman before him. He rubbed his hands together, then wiped at his face before speaking.

"Lady Kathryne, Will ain't with us," he said with as much poise as he could muster. "He be taken prisoner by yer uncle."

*I will not faint,* Kathryne told herself. *I will not faint.*

"Milady, I ain't be one to likin' to be the bearer of bad news, but it appears that I must."

The sun burst from behind a cloud and filled the harbor with dazzling, pure sunshine, in direct opposition to the deadly words Kathryne now heard. The crowds about the pair were quiet and hushed.

"And it be that Radcliffe," Malcolm continued, "it be that he stated that he be plannin' to kill both Vicar Mayhew and Cap'n Hawkes."

*I will not faint,* Kathryne repeated. *I must not faint.*

"And he say that 'cause Cap'n Hawkes got the gold back for you and your father."

Malcolm looked up and saw the stark white terror in Kathryne's face. "But, milady, Will done what he done for you. Just before we parted, he told us all that he truly loved you and that he be doin' God's will. He led us all in prayers before he left the ship."

It was all Malcolm could do to continue, for he saw the tears form in Kathryne's eyes.

"Milady, he loved you more than anythin'. He loved you more than he loved his own life is how he stated it. And he be trustin' that those words would be a most powerful comfort to you."

Malcolm sniffed now and wiped at his eyes and nose with the sleeve of his shirt.

Her lip trembling, Kathryne looked down at her feet for a long moment, breathing in deeply. She touched her hand to her stomach.

She looked up into Malcolm's eyes, her eyes showing a strength that had not been there a moment prior.

"Did you see him die?" she asked, her voice soft, unwilling to sound out the terrible words.

"Milady?" Malcolm asked, unsure if he had heard the correct words.

"Did you see him die?" she asked, louder and bolder.

Malcolm looked most confused.

Kathryne stepped close to him. "Did you see William Hawkes die?" she demanded.

Malcolm took a step back and almost tumbled off the pier. "No, milady. We left before anythin' happened. We was away too soon to tell what went on."

Kathryne looked at the other four men still on the deck of the *Dorset Lady*.

"Did any of you see Captain Hawkes die?" she called out.

Missy reached for Kathryne's arm, but she brushed it back, unwilling to be deterred.

"Did you?"

All four shook their heads no.

"It be as Malcolm said, Lady Kathryne. Will said he loved you, and we shoved off. Didn't see nothin' that happened after."

Kathryne turned about, looking at the faces of the sailors and merchants and citizens. She saw Emily near the back of the crowd, her face awash with grief.

*It will not be finished this way,* Kathryne told herself.

"You have not seen him perish," Kathryne stated firmly. "It will not end this way."

"But, Lady Kathryne," Malcolm replied, hating the words he spoke, "Radcliffe said what he was going to do. I have no doubts he has done as he had planned. And then this storm and all. We was lucky to have taken our leave as we did, for another hour and we would have been lost in the shoals."

Kathryne withered him with her stare.

"All I be sayin'," he continued, "is that there be little acreage on which to plant your hopes, milady."

"I am not looking for such acreage," Kathryne replied, her voice bold. She hiked up her long skirt and stepped to the outer rail of the vessel and quickly boarded the ship.

"Take me to where William died," she commanded.

"But, milady, we can't do that," Malcolm protested.

"And why not?" she demanded.

"It not be your ship to command."

"Mr. Trent, you are mistaken. William was not a poor man. He owned this ship," Kathryne said with a grand sweep of her hand. "This vessel, the *Dorset Lady,* was named for me. And if William is gone, this vessel belongs to me, for the deed contains my signature as well as his. You will find the documents in the captain's safe, I'm sure."

"But, Lady Kathryne," Malcolm replied, "a lady cannot captain a ship."

"I am not seeking to captain it, Mr. Trent. You will be my captain—at triple wages for the journey."

Malcolm scratched his head. He was running out of complaints and reasons. "But, milady, we have only five men here, and that not be enough for a cruise—even if it be only a day's sail north of here."

Kathryne turned to the pier and stared out at the small crowd. "I need sailors—all at triple wages for the journey," she called out in a firm voice.

Three dozen men elbowed their way to the front, pushing to be selected as crew.

"There are your sailors, Captain. Take your pick."

Malcolm shrugged, then nodded. "I'll send three men for provisions. We'll sail on the afternoon tide."

Kathryne looked to the sun. The tide was an hour away. She turned to Missy.

"Explain this to my father, Missy. Emily, tell him I will not rest until I see the spot on this sea that claimed the life of my husband. I must do this, or I will die myself. Will you tell him that, both of you?"

They nodded, and Kathryne turned and walked to the foredeck and remained there until the vessel slipped out of the harbor and into the stiff, cleansing winds from the south.

As the ship turned and caught the breeze, Kathryne fingered the golden ring on her hand. She spun it once, making sure that it would slip from her hand. It would make a fitting memorial to Will if the sea would accept the gift.

## Caribbean Sea

The *Dorset Lady* anchored that night just south of the area of shoals and reefs.

"No sailor who has his wits about him," Malcolm explained, "would think to sail this way without the sun."

Kathryne refused all offers of a berth—even the captain's berth. She insisted that sitting on the foredeck was where she needed to be. One sailor, worried over a woman's delicate nature, brought a thick baize blanket to ward off the evening chill. The rest of the crew retired and went belowdecks, allowing Kathryne her privacy.

She sat in the blackness, for it was the time of the new moon and its light was gone from the sky. The waves, gentle now, lapped at the hull with hushed splashes.

Kathryne raised her face to the sky, a vast carpet of stars above her. She looked back and forth for a moment, then found the one pinpoint of light for which she searched.

"You promised me the North Star, William," she spoke, as if the man were seated next to her in the darkness. "You promised me that if my heart ever felt alone and lost, I could turn to its light and be reminded of your love. I am trying to do that now, William, but it seems so far and distant."

She stood and walked to the very tip of the foredeck, to the apex of the bow. "William, I cannot grant you the celestial bodies in the heavens, but perhaps I will give you something more special than all of that. I will give to you a child."

She sniffed, and her tears clouded the stars into an indistinct field of lights.

"I will teach our child what you would have taught him. How to be brave. How to be loving. How to love God. I am so glad that your last act on this earth was to lead others to the love of our Lord. If I could have half the faith that you possess, William, I would be so content."

Her tears splashed freely onto the deck.

"I will do my best to raise our child well, William. I will ever remind it what a noble and wonderful man you were and how much I loved you."

She sniffed again, her eyes so very wet.

"You will see our child in heaven, my darling. I promise you that. You will see it in heaven."

Her tears were dried as a fresh breeze spilled about her, a chilling breeze from the north.

"I will always love you, William. Only you. Forever."

## 96

The next morning, the crew gingerly ventured out onto the deck. Kathryne was awake, as she had been for virtually all the night. She stood at the bow, and when Malcolm came up from his cabin, she called out to him. "Take me as close as you can to that last spot, if you can. I need to be there, Captain Trent."

He nodded and called out his orders. By noon they would arrive at that location. Malcolm had been through this area several times and could tell the spot from the shapes and colors of the reef below him. He took a sextant reading and set off.

Kathryne braced herself and fingered her ring, slipping it off, then back on again, as if practicing what she must do.

At noon they reached the place Malcolm stated was near where he had last seen Will. For the past few leagues, they had sailed past timbers and barrels and great flaps of canvas, still floating near the surface. In time the sea would claim all they beheld, but for now she proudly displayed her spoils.

A few bodies drifted past as well, and Kathryne could not avert her eyes, though she knew she should. Most victims of the sea lay on their backs, their arms outstretched, their faces to the sun. It would be only a matter of time until the flesh was nibbled away by fish or gulped away by the great sea beasts that inhabited the deep waters.

"This be close, milady," Malcolm Trent called out. "I cannot be for absolute certain as to the exact spot, but this be close. The sextant calls it dead-on to that last sighting, and the reefs carry this most peculiar red only in this short parcel of the sea."

"And this is where you last saw William?"

Malcolm could only nod. The rest of the crew went about their tasks in silence.

Kathryne nodded back and then stepped to the bow and bent her head in prayer. She remained bowed for several dozen moments. Then she lifted her head, her chin high, took the ring from her finger, and tossed it into the sea. She waited for the sound of its splash but did not hear it drop, for a sea bird called out a most curious cry.

The *Dorset Lady* poled about the narrow channel and set her foresail to tack back into the southern winds. Her mainsail and mizzen sails would be lowered when the vessel cleared the shallows.

Kathryne remained at the bow, sure that her heart had broken. She knew she could never feel joy again, nor hope, nor peace—yet she knew that these all would be needed for her child.

She sat back down and wiped at her eyes, chiding herself that a good woman of Spenser stock should not waste so many hours in tears. *There now are things that must be accomplished and done,* she told herself. *A nursery will need to be planned and built, furnishings ordered, nannies selected, clothing made. So many details,* Kathryne thought as she stared to the west.

Then she noticed a movement on the horizon. *That's odd,* she thought. *That curious little bump to the west. Malcolm was most insistent that this area had no islands or atolls to offer shelter. . . . But then what must that be?*

Kathryne stood bolt straight and hesitated for a long moment, focusing her eyes on the western horizon. Then she leaped to the rail, crying out, "Turn to the west! Turn to the west! I see a ship!"

A dozen agonizing moments passed as Malcolm dodged among the reefs, banging hard against sharp coral several times. He did not possess a telescope, so no one could be sure of just what it was they saw ahead.

"It might be just large debris, milady," Malcolm cautioned. "I do not wish to see your hopes set up to be dashed again."

She chose not to respond, instead focusing her eyes on the west.

It is hard to be certain what attribute, what characteristic one recognizes first when seeing a loved one from a distance. For some it might be their height or gait. For some it might be their clothing or demeanor. For Kathryne, it was the sight of Will's hair, the color of the sun at dusk—the color of gold.

Her hand flew to her mouth first, then to her heart, in an attempt to prevent it from leaping from her chest.

"William!" she screamed, louder than any noise she had ever made before in her life. "William!"

It was but a dozen moments until the *Dorset Lady* pulled alongside the charred section of forecastle deck from the *Villa Terra Nova*. The shattered decking held five men: William, Vicar Mayhew, and three sailors. All had been wounded, and all had clung tenaciously to the small wreck for these long days, drinking sips of rainwater caught in a sail, eating raw fish caught by hand.

Will was the last to be pulled to the deck of the *Dorset Lady*. Kathryne embraced him fiercely, holding him as tight as two people might become without merging into one being. He stroked at her hair, weeping, laughing, crying, thanking God for sparing his life. Finally, she broke the embrace for a moment to kiss him passionately on his sunburnt lips, then embraced him again, weeping tears of joy.

Vicar Mayhew shuffled the rest of the crew away from them, allowing the two a private reunion.

Will held her at a distance for a moment, looking into her deep green eyes.

"Your face kept me alive, Kathryne. When I wanted to give up and return to the arms of God, it was the image of your face that kept me here."

Kathryne took his hand and brushed it with a tender, gentle kiss. Then she slowly placed his rough and callused palm against that slight rise above her stomach. She leaned close to his ear and whispered, "It is your child, William. God kept you alive so you could be here to raise a godly son or daughter."

William smiled, a smile that spread across his face like the dawning of the first day of creation. He stepped back and looked at Kathryne, their eyes locking together in impassioned anticipation.

The sails unfurled behind them with a comfortable rustle and caught the steady winds that would lead them back to their home—Barbados.

# EPILOGUE

## *Barbados*

The children hushed and giggled themselves quiet. They loved to listen to the tales told by the gentle man dressed in black. They could not understand all the words, but the tones and the faces that illustrated the tales were amusement enough.

Vicar Mayhew pulled the small Hannah close to him and looked at the face of her brother, urging them each to be hushed, and began on this day's installment.

"The chief of the natives on the Isla del Guajiro was a mighty man, round and black, full of great gusts of laughter. He wore around his throat a necklace made from the great teeth of sharks, some as big as the palm of your hand and sharp as the keenest knight's dagger. On his head he wore the feathers and plumes of parrots and seabirds, and he carried a great, knobby club to use against his enemies."

"But, sir," called out Samuel, a towheaded boy, lean and inquisitive, "what of the gold that you and Chief Tahonen discovered? You promised to tell of the gold treasure. What did the pirates do when they discovered the loss?"

The vicar smiled. *Such a memory with this child,* he thought, staring at his great blue eyes. *In him rests the fair future of this island.*

"Indeed, Samuel, I did speak of gold and hidden doubloons the last I told of this tale."

He cleared his throat and crouched lower to their faces, lit with wonder. "It was the dead of night as Chief Tahonen and I crept through the dense jungle, brushing away from our faces spiders and long, bloodred snakes that hung from the trees and branches. The great chest was left at the edge of the water and was filled with jewels and golden coins and great gold bars."

"And then you simply made off with the lot?" Samuel asked, leaning forward.

"I had no use for such treasure, and the chief just wanted bright, shiny objects for his crown. But I knew that with this gold his tribe could be freed from worry and want."

"So then you took it and fought with the pirates?" Samuel asked again, eager to progress the story.

"No, fighting is not part of this tale. The chief and I grabbed at the great, thick brass handle and dragged it through the sand into the warm waters of the cove. We knew the trunk would float for many moments, until the sea filled it and dragged it down. So we grasped it, pulling and paddling, and made our way to a far reef. There was a hidden cave there, and by the mouth of that cave was a deep hole under the sea. We took it there and let it sink to the bottom, so that only the chief and I would know of its location—to be retrieved when the pirates tired of us and left."

"And the gold is there still?" Hannah asked, her eyes ablaze.

"Indeed," the vicar replied, "for no man knows its location, save myself and the chief."

Samuel's eyes lit up. "And a man could sail there and have it for the taking?"

The vicar nodded. "That be if the man knew where he was to look."

From the room next to the children's nursery came a rustle and a click as the door snapped shut. The nanny, Jezalee, slipped into the hall, peering both ways, her eyes darting and narrowed.

Soft and hesitantly she whispered to herself. "I don't believe all dat da vicar be sayin', but he be a man of God. He should be tellin' da truth. If it be true, den there be treasure waitin' for a man to take. And if it be there, I believes I know who might be ready to do that takin'."